# The Feud

*Sunday Times* #1 bestselling author Kimberley Chambers lives in Romford and has been, at various times, a disc jockey, cab driver and a street trader. She is now a full-time writer.

Join Kimberley's legion of legendary fans
on Facebook/kimberleychambersofficial
and @kimbochambers on Twitter.

## Also by Kimberley Chambers

# Kimberley CHAMBERS

# The Feud

HarperCollins*Publishers*

HarperCollins
PUBLISHERS
Since 1817

This novel is entirely a work of fiction.
The names, characters and incidents portrayed in it are
the work of the author's imagination. Any resemblance to
actual persons, living or dead, events or localities is
entirely coincidental.

HarperCollins*Publishers* Ltd
1 London Bridge Street
London SE1 9GF

www.harpercollins.co.uk

This paperback edition 2017
3

First published in Great Britain by
Preface Publishing 2010
Published by Arrow Books 2013

A catalogue record for this book is available from the British Library

ISBN: 978-0-00-822864-4

Set in Times New Roman by Palimpsest Book Production Limited, Falkirk, Stirlingshire

Printed and bound by CPI Group (UK) Ltd, Croydon, CR0 4YY

MIX
Paper from
responsible sources
FSC
www.fsc.org
FSC™ C007454

FSC™ is a non-profit international organisation established to promote
the responsible management of the world's forests. Products carrying the
FSC label are independently certified to assure consumers that they come
from forests that are managed to meet the social, economic and
ecological needs of present and future generations,
and other controlled sources.

Find out more about HarperCollins and the environment at
**www.harpercollins.co.uk/green**

# ACKNOWLEDGEMENTS

Firstly, I would like to express my gratitude to everybody at Preface and Random House for believing in me and my books. A special mention to all the reps, who have done a wonderful job in getting my name out there.

A big thanks to Tim Bates, who is a great agent and friend and Rosie de Courcy for giving me an opportunity to make something of my life.

As always, I would be lost without my amazing typist, Sue Cox, and a special mention to Trish Scott for her help with technology.

My daddy told me I never should
Play with the gypsies in the wood

# PROLOGUE

## *Summer 1970*

As Eddie Mitchell ran his fingers along the side of the baseball bat, he could feel the beads of sweat forming along his forehead. It was one of those muggy days, where flying ants appeared. It was far too hot to be suited and booted and stuck in the back of a Transit van.

Eddie listened intently as his father repeated his instructions. 'We don't want an all-out war, so nothing too heavy, boys. This is a little warning for 'em, and if they don't get the message, then heavy'll come later.'

As the rest of the family discussed the feud, Eddie sat in silence. In his eyes, the O'Haras had taken a fucking liberty and deserved more than a little warning. For as long as Ed could remember, his dad, Harry, had run the pub protection racket in the East End. No one messed with the Mitchells, no one dared, and then, like an unwanted disease, the O'Haras appeared on the scene and tried to muscle in on their patch. Eddie was the youngest member of the family firm. His dad ran the show, along with his uncle Reg. Then there were Paulie and Ronny, his two elder brothers.

'You OK, son?'

Smiling with anticipation, Eddie nodded at his father. The O'Haras were a travelling family who had recently

1

moved to the East End from Cambridgeshire. Eddie hated travellers. In his eyes, they were uncouth, lowlife, inbred scum. In particular, he hated Jimmy O'Hara. He was the strongest of the sons, the loudest, and flash didn't even begin to describe him.

'I wanna be the one to take out Jimmy, Dad.'

Harry eyed his son proudly. Even from an early age, Eddie was the one full of promise, and Harry knew without a doubt that one day his youngest child would be head of the family business.

As the Transit van pulled up outside the pub, the Mitchells clutched their weapons.

'Right, let's do it,' Harry said as he sprang from the van.

Barging his brothers and uncle out of the way, Ed followed his father into the boozer. 'See you? You're dead, you piss-taking pikey cunt,' he screamed as he spotted Jimmy O'Hara and lunged towards him.

As the pub erupted into full-scale mayhem, Eddie was grabbed around the neck from behind.

'Do him, Jimmy, fucking do him!' he heard a voice shout.

As the knife slid down the left-hand side of his face, Eddie felt anger, not pain. With blood spewing from his face, he went for O'Hara like a rabid Rottweiler.

'You inbred pikey piece of shit!' he screamed, as he threw off the geezer behind him and repeatedly thrust the baseball bat against Jimmy O'Hara's head.

In that moment, Eddie completely lost it, and if his family hadn't dragged him away, Ed swore he would have committed murder.

Harry, Reg, Paulie and Ronny managed to clump and scare the rest of the O'Haras and, aware that Eddie's face was almost sliced in two, they quickly bundled him into the back of the Transit van.

'Let me go back. I'll kill him, I'll fucking kill him!' Eddie screamed.

'Your face is fucked. We need to get you stitched up, son,' Harry said seriously.

Ed was seething as he held the side of his face together. He was covered in claret from head to toe. The wound was so deep, it had even soaked through his suit.

Aware that his mouth was full of blood, Ed spat a mouthful onto the floor. As he turned to his father, his expression blackened.

'I'll get me own back, Dad, if it's the last thing I do. Even if the O'Haras lay off our turf, this feud ain't over. It will never be over between me and Jimmy, not now – not ever.'

# ONE

## *1971*

Joyce Smith smiled as she carefully lifted her best dinner service out of the box. She rarely used her expensive china, but today was a very special occasion and she was desperate to impress.

As Joyce entered the living room, her smile immediately turned to a frown. That lazy husband of hers was still glued to that filthy, stinking armchair of his. 'Stanley, get your arse up them stairs and get yourself ready. You haven't even washed or shaved yet and they'll be here soon.'

More interested in the 3.45 at Kempton, Stanley leaped up and down. 'Go on my son, get in there. Go on my son, you can do it!'

As his horse got pipped at the post, Stanley threw the *Sporting Life* up in the air in temper. 'Stupid, bastard nag!' he shouted.

Annoyed that her husband was ignoring her orders, Joyce picked up her broom and clumped him on the head with it. Why he betted, she'd never know. He always bloody lost. 'I won't tell you again, Stanley. Now get up them bleedin' stairs and smarten yourself up.'

Stanley knew better than to argue with his wife. She wore the trousers, and he just complied with her orders.

'Your nice blue shirt and best slacks are hanging on the wardrobe door; put them on,' Joyce ordered.

'Anyone would think the Queen Mother was coming for tea,' Stan replied, as he ran up the stairs.

Picking up the duster and polish, Joyce did her best to tidy his dirty little corner. She had a quick vac round then, to finish, sprayed a whole can of air freshener around the house. That's better, she thought as she studied her domain.

Joyce was very proud of her three-bedroomed council house. It was situated in a road off Upney Lane, but she always told people that she lived in the upper-class part of Barking. Obviously, she would have liked to have bought a private property in a better area, but on Stan's bus driver's wages, that was never going to happen.

A proper little homemaker, Joyce was always buying new ornaments and furniture to tart up her surroundings. Her neighbours all said that she had the poshest house in the street and Joyce loved the compliment. Being known as the posh woman suited her down to the ground.

Stanley mumbled and cursed to himself as he shaved and got changed. Not only was he annoyed with the jockey and nag that had just lost him money, he was also annoyed with his daughter, Jessica, for messing up his usual plans.

Apart from the one in four Saturdays when he had to work, Stanley loved these afternoons. They were like his day out of prison, when he'd escape Joycie's moaning and spend the whole day in the pub or the bookie's with his pals. Today, he wasn't allowed to go anywhere. His daughter, Jessica, was bringing this new boyfriend of hers around for tea and Joyce had insisted he stay indoors and play happy families.

Like most dads, Stanley was quite protective of his only daughter. Jessica was only seventeen and still lived at home with them. Petite and blonde, Jessica was a very pretty girl with a sunny nature. She'd had boyfriends in the past, but there'd been nothing serious until this latest one.

His son, Raymond, was forever bringing different girls home, but Stan wasn't worried about what he got up to. With Jess it was different. He knew what it was like to be a hormonal young man and he would hate anyone taking advantage of his little girl.

Stan checked his appearance in the mirror. From what Joyce had said, this new boyfriend sounded like a right Flash Harry. Call it father's intuition, Stanley just knew he wasn't going to like him very much.

Joyce stared out of the window as she plumped up the cushions. They should be here any minute and she couldn't wait to meet this Eddie. For the first time in her young life, Jessica had fallen hook, line and sinker and Joyce was ever so pleased for her. Joyce's own life had always lacked excitement and romance, and she wanted her daughter to have everything she hadn't. Sometimes she wondered why she'd even married Stan and then she remembered her mother's harsh words: 'You're twenty-two now, Joycie. Look at all your mates, every one of them married. Even that fat Doreen from across the road has found herself a husband. Young Stanley's from ever such good stock. I know all of his family, even his aunts and uncles. You don't wanna be left on the shelf, do you now?'

'But I don't think I love him, Mum,' Joyce complained.

'Well, it's up to you, Joycie. I wasn't in love with your father when I married him, but we made the most of it. Love comes later, dear. Take my advice and marry Stanley. If you say no and leave it any longer, at your age there'll be little else to choose from.'

Six months after that little chat, Joyce reluctantly agreed to marry Stanley. Jessica arrived a year later, closely followed by Raymond. Love between her and Stan had never really blossomed, but Joyce threw herself into the children and in her own way was happy with her little lot. Romeo and Juliet, she and Stan most certainly weren't, but they jogged along quite nicely, especially since he'd stopped wanting sex.

Joyce loved reading and what was lacking in her love life she found in the pages of Mills & Boon novels. Now she hoped that Jessica and her new beau would fill a void in her life and inject some much-needed romance.

Seeing her clean-shaven husband walk towards her, Joyce smiled at him. 'That's better! What a difference to see you in a nice shirt and slacks. See Stanley, you do scrub up well when you try.'

Stan tutted and flopped in his armchair. 'Scrub up well! I feel like a bleedin' pox doctor's clerk,' he moaned.

Joyce shooed him out of his chair. 'They're due in five minutes. Stand up, or you'll crease your shirt.'

Stan jumped up as though he had a firework up his arse. He wasn't the bravest man in the world and over the years he'd realised that it was easier to comply with Joycie's orders than to argue with her.

'Where's Raymond?' he asked.

Twitching the curtain, Joyce explained. 'Gone round his mate's. I told him not to come back until later. He's been a cheeky little sod lately and, as for that racket he keeps playing upstairs, I didn't want him to give a bad impression of us in front of Eddie. Quick, here they are, this is them. I'll answer the door, you go and get some beers out the shed to offer Eddie. Now, Stanley. Quick, chop-chop.'

As they approached the house, Jessica squeezed Eddie's

big hand. Clocking Ginny and Linda staring at her from the house across the road, she waved proudly. Jessica couldn't stop grinning. To say Eddie was a looker was an understatement. The expression tall, dark and handsome could have been created just for him. She was dying for her parents to meet him, especially her mum. The only worry she had was the age gap between them. Eddie was thirty but she had told her dad he was only twenty-five. Her mum knew the truth and once her dad got to know Eddie and like him, she would tell him the truth as well.

'This is it, number eleven. Now, remember what I told you about my dad. He still thinks of me as his little baby, so if he's not overly friendly, please don't take it personally.'

Eddie kissed her on the nose. 'You worry too much, Jess. I'll have a chat with your old man, just leave him to me.'

Unable to contain her excitement any longer, Joyce flung open the front door.

'Ed, this is my mum. Mum, this is Eddie,' Jessica said, beaming.

Eddie shook Joyce's hand and politely kissed her on both cheeks. 'It's a delight to meet you, Mrs Smith. Your Jessica's told me so much about you.'

Joyce giggled. 'All good, I hope?'

'Most definitely,' Eddie said, winking.

Joyce led them into the living room. 'We'll have a nice cup of tea, Jess, and let the men have a beer,' she said.

Jessica smiled as she noticed her mother had got the expensive china out. 'Where's Dad?' she asked.

Joyce offered Eddie a sandwich. 'Gone down to the shed to get some beers. Speak of the devil – here he is now.'

Eddie put his sandwich down and stood up as Stan

entered the room. 'Dad, this is Eddie who I've been telling you about,' Jessica said nervously.

At five feet eight inches tall, Stanley felt inadequate as he shook Eddie's strong hand. He thought of the jockey who had lost him the race earlier and, for some reason, felt like his twin brother.

'Would you like a piece of homemade fruit cake, Eddie?' his wife asked.

Stan flopped into his armchair and studied the object of his daughter's affection. He'd been right all along. He didn't like the look of him one little bit. Jessica had told him that Eddie was twenty-five, but the bastard looked old enough to be her dad. He was broad-shouldered, with dark hair and was wearing tailored grey trousers with a long black Crombie coat. As he turned his head, Stan noticed the massive scar that ran from the outside of his left eye to the corner of his mouth. Stan knocked back his bottle of Double Diamond and opened another. Eddie looked an out-and-out villain. He certainly wasn't the sort of chap he envisaged or wanted his beautiful daughter going out with.

As the conversation flowed, Stan could tell that Mr Fucking Charming Bollocks had Joycie eating out of his hand.

'That fruit cake was amazing, Mrs Smith. So much better than the cakes I'm used to,' the smarmy bastard said.

'You're ever so quiet, Dad. Are you OK?' Jessica asked, as she handed him and Eddie another beer.

Knowing that he was expected to join in the conversation, Stanley cleared his throat. 'Jessica said that she met you at a local party. Do you come from round here, Eddie?'

'No. My family are out of Canning Town and I live

up that way. I share a flat with me brother, Ronny. It's nothing special, we live above a pet shop along the Barking Road.'

Stanley carried on prying. 'And what do you do for a living? If you don't mind me asking?'

Eddie smiled. The old boy didn't like him, he could sense it a mile off. 'My dad owns a load of salvage yards. He's retired now, so me and my brothers run them for him.'

Stanley felt fear wash over him. Canning Town? Salvage yards? Surely he wasn't one of the Mitchell boys – please God, no.

Dreading the answer, it took Stan a while to pluck up the courage to ask the all-important question. 'Before I met Joycie, I used to live in Canning Town myself. I remember a lot of the old school. What's your father's name?'

Eddie smirked. 'Harry Mitchell. You probably know him, most people do.'

Stanley took a large gulp of his drink and started to choke. Unable to breathe properly, he fell off the chair and onto all fours.

Aware of her husband going redder and redder in the face, Joyce stood up and repeatedly thumped him on the back. Embarrassed that he'd made a show of her in front of Eddie, she tried to make a joke of it. 'He spends so much time watching them bleedin' horses on telly, he's started to behave like one now. Giddy up, giddy up,' she said, laughing.

Feeling as though he was about to have a heart attack, Stan managed to heave himself up and stand on two feet. 'Went down the wrong hole,' he gasped, as he legged it from the room.

Joyce smiled at Eddie. 'You'll have to excuse my Stanley. He's not used to having visitors, but he's a good man deep down, and once you get to know him, I'm sure you'll like him.'

Eddie grinned. He doubted that very much. 'I'm sure we'll get on like a house on fire, Mrs Smith. Now, is there any chance of having another piece of that wonderful fruit cake?'

Joyce beamed as she handed him a slice. What a charming chap, she thought.

Stanley sat in the shed and tried his best to compose himself. Canning Town had a notorious reputation for producing villainous families and they didn't come much worse than the Mitchells. Bootlegging, pub protection, illegal boxing. Rumour had it that over the years the bastards had had a finger in every pie going.

Stanley remembered Harry Mitchell as though it were yesterday. He'd been standing in a pub in East Ham having a drink with Roger Dodds, his old school pal. All of a sudden the door had burst open and the pub had fallen silent. A man in a suit and trilby hat walked towards them.

'Which one of you is Roger Dodds?' he'd asked menacingly.

Crapping himself, Stan had nodded towards his friend. Seconds later, Roger Dodds had his face slashed and his right eye taken out with a broken bottle.

The man in the trilby hat had then ordered a Scotch, downed it in one, apologised for any inconvenience and casually strolled out of the pub.

That man in the trilby was Harry Mitchell. Apparently, Dodds's father had fucked him over for a load of money and that was payback time.

Deep in thought, Stanley didn't hear the shed door creak open. It was Eddie. Stanley leaped up. 'What's going on? What do you want?' he asked nervously.

Eddie stared at him. 'Calm down, you'll give yourself

a cardiac. The girls were worried about you. They said you'd be in the shed, so I thought I'd check you were OK.'

Stan nodded. 'I'm fine now. It took me a while to catch me breath, so I came out here for a sit down.'

Desperate for some fresh air, Stanley led Eddie away from the shed. He locked the door, then was horrified as he felt a massive arm go round his shoulder.

Eddie smiled. He could almost smell the old man's fright. 'Actually, I wanted to have a quiet word with you, man to man, like.'

Stan looked at him in horror. He'd only been dating Jessica for a month; surely he wasn't going to ask his permission to marry her.

Eddie stood in front of him and looked him straight in the eye. 'The thing is, Mr Smith, I think you should know that I'm really serious about your Jessica, so I wanna get a few things straight. I'm not twenty-five like Jess told you, I'm actually thirty years old. I've also been married in the past and I've got two little boys, Gary and Ricky, who I dote on. Obviously, they don't live with me – they live with my ex-wife, Beverley. I've been straight with Jess from the start and I think it's only right I do the same with you. As I said, things are moving pretty quickly between me and your Jess, so I just wanna know that you approve of our relationship.'

Dumbstruck, Stanley stood with his mouth open and was horrified as a fly flew in and hit the back of his throat. Half choking, he spat it out and ended up on his knees for the second time that day.

Eddie helped him up. 'So, are you OK about me and Jess?' he asked again.

Stanley nodded. 'No problem, Eddie, and thanks for telling me,' he mumbled.

'There you are,' Joyce said, as Stanley returned, ashen-faced.

The polite conversation carried on for another hour or so and was only stopped by Eddie giving Jessica a secret nudge. Jessica looked at her watch and stood up. 'God, is that the time! Mum, Dad, we best be going now. Eddie is taking me to the pictures tonight. We're going to see that new film, *Love Story*. All the girls at work reckon it's brilliant. I've been dying to see it and we don't want to miss the start.'

Eddie stood up and put his arm around his young girlfriend's shoulders. 'Mrs Smith, Mr Smith, thank you so much for your hospitality. It's been a pleasure to meet you both. Don't worry, I'll take good care of your Jessica and I promise to have her home by a reasonable hour.'

Overcome by the romance of it all, Joyce stood at the door waving them off. 'No snogging in the back row,' she giggled.

'Stop it, Mum,' Jessica said embarrassed.

Joyce shut the front door and sighed a happy sigh. What an attractive, polite chap. He was like one of them Mills & Boon men, sophisticated and handsome. Thrilled for her daughter, Joyce decided to have a G&T to celebrate.

'Well, what did you think?' she asked Stanley, as she sat back down.

Stanley said nothing. He was too frightened to voice his opinions, in case Joyce told Jessica and it got back to Eddie.

Joyce kicked off her shoes and put her slippers on. 'Did you see his shoes? He's definitely worth money. Look, I know it's hard for you, Stan, but Jess isn't a little baby any more. Most of my friends were married at her age. I want her to have the best in life and that Eddie's got class stamped all over him. He's got lovely manners and he'll take good care of her, I know he will.'

Stanley cracked open another beer. He'd had the day

from hell and all he wanted to do now was watch *Ironside*. 'Do you mind if I watch the telly now? And if you're gonna keep on about it, no, I wasn't overkeen. In my opinion, Eddie's far too old for our Jess, and, no, I didn't notice his bloody shoes.'

Joyce laughed. 'I knew you had a hangup about him. I know he's a bit older than her, but you're such an old fuddy-duddy. I bet if she'd have brought Prince Charles home, you'd have found fault with him. You just won't let go of her, will you, Stan?'

For the next hour, Joyce wouldn't shut up. It was Eddie this and Eddie that.

Unusually for Stanley, he completely lost his rag. 'For Christ's sake, Joycie, I'm no man's fool. The bloke's a wrong 'un and I know it. He's thirty years old, a divorcee with two bloody kids. As for them going to the pictures, I don't believe a word of it. Jessica's probably round his flat as we speak with her knickers around her ankles. They're probably right in the middle of creating more kids for the smarmy, villainous bastard.'

Furious, Joyce stood up and hit him with the broom. 'How dare you talk about our daughter like that? She's got morals, our Jessica. What are you, some bloody pervert?'

Seething, Stanley jumped out of his chair. He rarely gave an opinion in this house and when he did he got called a bloody nonce. More than anything else in the world, he wanted to pick up Joycie's broom and smash her right over the head with it. Maybe that would make the stupid, naive woman see sense. Filled with self-loathing, Stanley ran to the serenity of his shed. Once inside, he sat on his wooden bench, put his head in his hands and cried.

His old mum had mapped out his life for him at a very

early age. 'Stanley, always remember son, it's better to be a live coward than a dead hero.'

Stanley wiped his eyes with his hanky. He feared for his Jessica. That Eddie was cold and calculating. He had those horrible dark eyes, dead man's eyes. There was sod all he could do about it though. He was far too weak a man. What the Mitchells wanted, the Mitchells got, and who was he to stop them?

# TWO

Back at Eddie's flat, Jessica fumbled with the zip of her boyfriend's trousers. Realising she still had her knickers around her ankles, she quickly stepped out of them.

Eddie threw her onto the double bed. He expertly entered her and held both of her hands down with his own. He liked it that way; it gave him total control.

'Aw, baby,' he moaned as he shot his seed and pulled himself out of her. Not wanting to be selfish, Eddie used his index finger to pleasure her.

'Oh Eddie,' Jessica cried, as she reached her climax.

Confident that she was satisfied, Eddie rolled onto his back and lit up two cigarettes. Handing one to Jess, he grinned. He'd been told in the past by birds that he had bigger fingers than most men's cocks, and he certainly knew how to use them.

'Did you enjoy that, babe?' he asked, as he studied the smoke rings he was blowing.

Jessica propped herself up on one elbow. She loved taking in his naked body and his handsome face. 'I always enjoy it, Eddie, you know I do.'

Eddie put his arm around her and kissed her gently on the forehead. 'So what do you reckon your parents thought of me?' he asked.

Jessica laid her head on his chest. 'Mum loved you. She thought you were great. Dad's more old-fashioned, but I'm sure he liked you in his own way.'

Eddie smirked at her take on things. The mother he'd had eating out of his hand, but the old man, he knew, had hated him on sight. Gently easing Jessica off him, Eddie jumped out of bed.

'I'm gonna have a quick bath and then I'll take you out for a drink.'

'OK. Save me some hot water so I can freshen up, too.'

Jessica smiled as she watched his muscly long legs and gorgeous naked buttocks walk away from her. She'd only met him four weeks ago at a mate's birthday party. Their eyes had locked and that was it, they'd been insep- arable ever since. Jessica couldn't believe her luck. Eddie was rich, handsome and an absolute bloody catch. She'd had boyfriends in the past, even had sex with a couple, but none of them compared to him. Eddie oozed charisma. He treated her like a lady, so much so that he insisted on paying for absolutely everything and picking her up every day from the shoe shop where she worked.

'No girl of mine is putting their hand in their purse or getting on buses,' he told her bluntly.

Her workmates were filled with envy. None of their boyfriends even had a car, and when Ed had first pulled up in his gold Mercedes 250C, their jaws had hit the floor.

'Jess, he's gorgeous – and look at his posh car. You are so lucky,' they'd crowed.

Jess giggled to herself. Ed had a big personality, a bulging wallet and a massive willy. No woman could want more and she was a very lucky girl indeed.

Jess thought about her mum's life. She'd hate to be married to a bus driver and live in the same council house

17

for years like her mum. Her mother didn't want that either. She was forever giving her good advice. 'Jess, with your figure and stunning looks, you can get anyone you want. Don't make the same mistakes as I did and end up with someone like your father. If a good catch comes along, take my advice and grab him with both hands.'

Jessica was aware of how attractive she was. She had long, blonde ringlets, a cute, pointed chin, an amazingly slim figure and men went crazy for her dimpled cheeks.

'The bathroom's all yours, sexy,' Ed said, walking towards her.

As Jessica walked past him, Eddie stared at her fantastic tits. When he was married to Bev, he'd played around with other birds. Meeting Jess had knocked him for six. She was a major piece of eye candy, had a terrific personality and, since they'd got together, he hadn't so much as glanced at another piece of skirt.

Eddie did up the top button of his shirt. As he secured his tie, he thought about the sex they'd had earlier. He hadn't used a rubber today, he'd forgotten to buy any and it didn't bother him at all. In Jess, Ed was sure he'd found the woman he wanted to spend the rest of his life with and the quicker he put her in the club and stuck a ring on her finger, the better.

Eddie looked up as his brother, Ronny, slammed the front door.

'Am I glad to see you.'

'What's up? Can't you spend a day without me?' Ed asked sarcastically.

Ronny walked towards him. 'Don't muck about, this is serious, Ed. The O'Haras are in the Flag. They're mob-handed and we're gonna need backup if we're gonna sort it. They looked like they were about to smash the pub up. I think they're trying to muscle in on our patch.'

Eddie's features blackened. He'd never laid eyes on any of the O'Haras since last year when his face had got slashed to fuck. He'd caved Jimmy's head in with a baseball bat that day, and the families had avoided one another ever since.

Ed had ended up with forty-seven stitches in his face, but Jimmy had come off worse. He'd spent over a month in hospital, and had to have numerous scans and tests to rule out brain damage.

The feud between the two families had been halted since then. Ed's dad, Harry, had arranged a meet with Jimmy's old man, Butch.

Harry had said, 'Look, we're all trying to earn a few bob here and no one needs all this extra aggravation. I'll do you a deal. You stick on your patch and do what you've gotta do and we'll stay on ours. If you agree to the deal, we'll let bygones be bygones. If you don't, and I find out your boys have stepped one foot in any of our boozers, I promise you there'll be a fucking bloodbath,' Harry had said.

Butch shook hands on it. 'You have my word, you'll have no more trouble from me or my lads,' he promised.

As Jessica walked towards him in a white halter-neck catsuit, Eddie kicked Ronny to urge him to keep schtum.

'You look gorgeous, darling.'

Jessica smiled. Any new clothes she bought now she kept round Eddie's. She had to look the part for her new man.

Ronny was pissed off. What was more important, family business or fucking birds?

'Where are we going?' Jessica asked excitedly.

Eddie decided to give Canning Town a wide berth. He didn't want Jess to see the other side of him. He was a lunatic when he got going and he knew if he came face to face with Jimmy O'Hara, he'd throw him straight through the pub window.

'I thought we'd go to East Ham for a change. A bloke in the Burnell Arms owes me some dough and needs a little reminder. If it's any good, we'll stay there; if it's shit, I'll take you out for a nice meal instead.'

Jessica nodded happily. As long as she was by Eddie's side, she didn't care where she went.

Eddie handed her his keys. 'Go and sit in the car, babe. I just need to have a quick chat with Ronny. It's business, you'll only be bored.'

'Bye, Ronny,' Jessica said as she left the flat. That was one of the things she loved about Eddie. She knew he was a bit dodgy and she found his little business chats and his life in general bloody exciting.

Eddie made sure she was out of earshot, then turned to his brother. 'Don't ever say too much about what we get up to in front of Jess, will yer?'

Ronny shook his head. 'Fuckin' hell, Ed. You can't put birds in front of family business. You always used to put your family first when you were married to Bev.'

Eddie stood his ground. Ronny wasn't as good-looking as him, and his bird, Sharon, was a big old heifer.

'Look, Ron, family comes first and you know it does, but there's no point in storming in the Flag tonight. We don't know where Paulie is, for a start. Listen, the O'Haras will be well pissed up by now. If you were in there, they'll definitely be expecting a visit from us. They're probably staring at the door as we speak. Our best bet is to leave it a week or two. Let them think they've got away with it, and when they're least expecting it, we'll pounce on 'em.'

Ronny shrugged. Maybe he should go and find his other brother, Paulie. He'd round up a few faces and maybe they could sort it without Eddie.

Eddie read his mind. 'Don't start organising things behind my back, Ron. I'll speak to Paulie tomorrow. We'll sit down properly, put our heads together and hatch a plan.'

Ronny nodded. He knew deep down that Eddie was talking sense, but he was still annoyed. Both he and Paulie were older than Ed, but they never got to call the shots. Even his old man put Eddie before them. It was as though they were the lackeys and Eddie was being primed as his father's successor.

Ronny let out a loud sigh. 'Look, Ed, I like Jessica and that, but is she gonna be hanging round here all the time?'

Eddie smirked. He knew Ronny was fucking jealous. 'Yes, Ron. For your information, Jessica's here for the foreseeable future.'

Eddie slammed the front door as he left the flat. When he'd split up with Bev, he couldn't be arsed buying a place of his own, so he'd moved in with Ronny. He hadn't minded sharing with him, they'd got along OK, but since he'd met Jess, he could sense things were getting a bit awkward.

He opened the car door. 'Sorry about that, darling.'

Jessica kissed him on the cheek. 'Don't worry about me. I know your business is important – you do what you have to do.'

As he drove towards East Ham, one part of Eddie's mind was focused on Jessica and the other on business. The O'Haras had taken a bloody liberty. The British Flag, better known to locals as the Flag, belonged to the

Mitchells. It was their headquarters, where they'd meet and discuss work matters. The O'Haras used the Chobham Arms in Stratford, and Eddie wouldn't dream of taking the piss in their pub. Whatever happened, they had to be taught a lesson. He'd speak to his dad tomorrow, see what he had to say.

Eddie pictured Jimmy O'Hara's ugly face. Word had it that since their little fall-out, O'Hara's finances had gone from strength to strength. Jimmy was the middle son. He was only thirty-two, and owned salvage yards out in Essex. Ed hated the cunt with a passion. Jimmy thought he ruled the world and the silly big prick even had the cheek to call himself King of the Gypsies.

'What do you think of them, Ed? Do you like them?'

Realising that he hadn't listened to a word Jessica had said, Eddie apologised. 'Sorry, babe, I had a police car up me arse and I was concentrating on that. Do I like who?'

Jessica laughed. 'T. Rex. My brother Ray is obsessed with them. He spends hours in his bedroom playing their records and he's even started wearing eyeliner like the singer, Marc Bolan. He's in a band himself, with three of his mates. Ray plays the drums and they've done a couple of gigs locally. I went to see them play one night and I was shocked – they were actually quite good.'

Eddie shrugged. He'd never had much experience with blokes who wore make-up. 'You sure your brother ain't an iron?'

Jessica couldn't stop laughing. 'You must be joking. He's a right lad and he's got a different girl on his arm every week. Raymond's one of life's go-getters. He'll make it big somehow, I just know he will.'

Eddie pulled up outside the pub. 'How old did you say he was?'

'Sixteen. He leaves school this year and my dad wants him to learn a proper trade. Raymond's having none of it, says he wants to be a rock star and he's not interested in doing nothing else.'

Eddie got out of the car and opened the passenger door for Jessica. 'Don't worry about your brother, he's bound to grow out of it. Now, what is madam drinking tonight?'

As Jessica followed Eddie into the pub, she noticed how all heads turned their way. She clocked the whispers and loved the way people fell over themselves to acknowledge and be acknowledged by her handsome man.

'I think I'll have a glass of wine,' she said happily.

'Eddie! Long time no see. Christ, you're looking well. What a lovely surprise to see you. Now, what would you and your beautiful lady like to drink?'

Eddie introduced Jessica to the guv'nor of the pub and left her chatting to him while he sorted out the money he was owed. 'Won't be a sec, babe. Just going to see a man about a dog,' he said, winking at her.

Minutes later he returned with a big grin on his face.

Jessica nudged him, 'Did you get your money?' she whispered.

'Plus interest,' Eddie said laughing.

The Burnell Arms had a band playing and Jessica was happy to stay there. Ever since she'd met Ed, she'd gone off her food, so she didn't fancy a meal. The evening flowed nicely and Jess had a wonderful time. At half-eleven, Eddie turned to her.

'I think I should be getting you home now.'

'Oh, I don't want to go yet. Can't I stay at yours tonight?' Jessica asked.

Eddie shook his head. 'I promised your mum and dad that I'd have you home at a reasonable time. I know you often stay at mine, Jess, but that's when they think you're staying at your mate's. If you stay tonight, they'll know we're at it and I don't want them to get the wrong idea about me.'

Ed thanked the guv'nor, said his goodbyes and led Jess from the pub. She only lived a short distance away and as he pulled up near her house, he noticed her look of disappointment. Pulling her towards him, he kissed her softly.

'I'd love to wake up with you tomorrow, more than anything else in the world, but we need to do things properly. I know I haven't said this to you yet, but I'm gonna say it now. I love you, Jessica Smith, and that's why I want you to go home tonight. If we're gonna have a future together, we need your parents to be on our side.'

Jessica looked at him with moo-cow eyes. 'And I love you too. Please Ed, my mum wouldn't care if I stayed round yours and she'd smooth it over with my dad,' she pleaded.

Eddie shook his head. 'It's not your mum, Jess, I know she'd be OK. Look at things from your dad's point of view. He knows I'm thirty, he knows I've been married, he knows I've got kids. If you stay out tonight, he'll be worried sick and I don't want to fuck things up for us. Trust me, I'm a man and I know how they think.'

Unable to tear herself away, Jessica kissed him passionately. Aware of him getting all excited, she put her hand on his erection.

Laughing, he grabbed her hand and moved it away. 'Don't start all that, else you'll never get home. Seriously now, come on, be a good girl. I'll pick you up tomorrow, OK?'

Jessica opened the car door. 'Pick me up lunchtime if you like.'

Eddie shook his head. 'I've got a bit of business to attend to. I'll pick you up about six.'

'I love you,' Jess said.

Eddie winked. 'Sweet dreams and I'll see you tomorrow.'

# THREE

Floating on air, Jessica let herself into the house. Thankfully, her dad was in bed, but her mum was still sitting up reading a book.

Joyce folded the page and urged Jess to sit next to her. 'I've been dying to know how your evening went. Oh, Jess, I thought he was lovely. Now, tell me everything from the start.'

Jessica's eyes shone. 'I've had such a wonderful evening, Mum. We didn't end up going to the pictures, we went to a pub in East Ham instead. Eddie's so popular, you know. Wherever we go, he has people hanging on his every word. And you'll never guess what, Mum?'

Joyce could barely contain her excitement. 'What? What's happened?'

Jessica giggled. 'He said the L word for the first time. He told me he's in love with me.'

Joyce clapped her hands. 'How did he say it? What were you talking about at the time? Did he say it in the pub?'

Jessica shook her head. 'It was right at the end of the evening. We were outside chatting in the car. I wanted to go back to his flat, but he said no. He said that he promised you and dad that he'd get me home early and then he just said it. "I love you, Jess," he said, and then he started talking about our future together.'

Joyce clasped her daughter's hands. 'That's marvellous, darling. I'm so excited. I wish I'd seen his car. Why didn't he come round in it earlier?'

'His brother Ronny wanted to borrow it. Eddie's so kind, he said yes straight away.'

Joyce smiled. 'I've never been in a Mercedes. Do you think you and him could take me out for a ride in it one day?'

'Of course. I'll ask him tomorrow,' Jess replied.

'So what happens now? Do you think he might propose?' Joyce asked.

Jessica shrugged. 'Hopefully, soon he might. I'd definitely say yes if he did.'

Joyce studied her beautiful daughter. She was no longer a little girl. She was all grown up. Joyce held both of her hands. 'Let me give you some advice, darling. True love is extremely hard to find, I should know. So if you're lucky enough to have found it, make sure you hang on to it. I mean, Eddie's thirty, isn't he? And when a man's been married, he's obviously used to a sexual relationship. Don't let him get away, Jess, you do what you've got to do to keep him happy.'

Embarrassed, Jessica stood up. She was close to her mum, but wasn't used to discussing her sex life with her. 'I'm tired now, Mum, I'm gonna go to bed. I understand what you're saying and don't worry, I won't let him get away.'

As Jessica left the room, Joyce couldn't stop smiling. She couldn't wait to tell all of her friends at her dressmaking class. None of their daughters had captured a bloke half as good as Eddie, and she couldn't wait to brag about her daughter's rich, handsome boyfriend.

\* \* \*

27

After a restless night, Eddie got up early and sorted out a meet with his father. Two o'clock at his aunt's house was the arrangement. His Auntie Joan lived locally in Whitechapel and she allowed them to hold all their urgent meetings upstairs in her house.

His Auntie Joan had all but brought him and his brothers up, and Eddie was still very close to her. His mum had died when he was five years old. Ed could just about picture her face and he remembered her giving him lots of cuddles. The only other memory he had was of her coughing continuously and spitting blood into a bucket. One day he'd gone off to school and when he returned, she was gone.

He was too young to understand what was happening at the time, but he found out years later that she had been taken to a sanatorium and had later died there. Apparently, she'd contracted tuberculosis, better known as TB, and it was that, and pneumonia, that had killed her.

. Harry, his dad, had never remarried. His house was still a shrine to the woman he had lost and he spent hours tending her grave. He visited a woman called Sylvie and sometimes took her out, but he refused to get too close. 'Your mother was the kindest, most beautiful woman in the world. No other woman will ever hold a candle to her,' he repeatedly told Eddie.

Eddie looked at his watch. His stomach was rumbling and he needed a nice cooked breakfast to start his brain functioning properly. He opened Ronny's bedroom door.

'Wakey, wakey. You getting up today, or what?'

'What's the time?' Ronny mumbled.

'Ten o'clock. I've arranged a meet with dad for two. I wanna go to the café first, then we'd best pop our heads in the Flag, see if them bastards did any damage last night, before we meet the others.'

Ronny propped himself up and squinted at Eddie through one eye. 'Sorry if I was a bit out of order last night. Jess is a top girl and I really do want you to be happy.'

Eddie smiled. 'Forget it. Now get your fucking arse in gear, I'm starving.'

A full English fry-up was followed by the trip to their local. As Eddie walked in, he was relieved to see that the pub still looked intact. John, the guv'nor, was out, so he got the lowdown off Betsy, the barmaid.

'They never touched the bar area, but the sinks in the gents were pulled off the wall. Dirty, foul-mouthed bastards they were. You should have heard the things they were saying to Kim, the pretty new barmaid. She burst into tears in the end and I had to send her home.'

Eddie ordered himself and Ronny a drink. 'Did they cause agg with any of the regulars?' he asked.

Betsy shook her head. 'All the regulars left soon after they arrived. They were so bloody loud, no one could hear themselves think.'

Eddie told Betsy to keep the change and thanked her for the information. 'Tell John I'll pop back and see him tomorrow. And if anyone comes in asking for protection money, tell him not to pay it.'

'You don't think they'll come back, do you?' Betsy asked. 'Only, I'm in here on me own till tonight.'

'I doubt it. We'll have to pay 'em a little visit, let 'em know they're not welcome.'

Betsy smiled. She loved Eddie Mitchell: he was handsome, had a real presence about him and she wished she was twenty years younger.

Eddie and Ronny left the Flag and drove straight over to Whitechapel.

* * *

Auntie Joan let them in and gave them both a big hug. 'Your father, brothers and Uncle Reg are already upstairs. You go on up and I'll bring you up some tea and sandwiches.'

Eddie got straight down to business. His dad, Uncle Reg and brothers sat quietly as the story of the O'Haras unfolded. No one said a word until he'd finished, then Ronny was the first to speak.

'They're obviously trying it on on our turf again. I bet they go round all our boozers and start demanding protection money. I think we should go in the Chobham with shooters. Can you imagine their faces if the five of us walked in armed?'

Harry Mitchell looked at Ronny as though he'd just crawled out from under a stone. 'Shut up, you idiot. The Chobham's their fucking headquarters, they'll have so many witnesses backing 'em up, we'll be nicked within an hour.'

Ronny felt his face redden. His dad had a wonderful way of putting him down and treating him like an imbecile in front of the rest of the family. He never did that to Eddie. Whenever he came out with an idea, his old man listened intently.

'All right to come in, boys?'

Harry jumped up and answered the door to Joan.

'That plate is ham and the other one's salmon. I baked you some rock cakes and there's more downstairs if you want them.'

Harry smiled as he took the trays off Joan. When his beautiful wife had been so cruelly taken from him, her sister had taken over from where she'd left off. She'd cooked, cleaned, washed, ironed and even taken care of the boys for him. Harry had never forgotten her kindness and had seen her all right over the years. When her husband, Alf, had run off with another woman, Harry had had him kneecapped and paid up her mortgage for her. Alf was now confined to a wheelchair, lived alone and was unable to walk, let alone run, the fucking arsehole.

As Harry munched away on a ham sandwich, he came to a decision. He'd leave the boys out of this one and sort it out himself. Butch O'Hara had shaken hands with him and called a truce, which had now been broken. Therefore, it should be Butch that was made to pay.

Pouring himself a cup of sugary, strong tea, Harry sipped it in almost a ladylike fashion and then wiped his mouth with a serviette.

'Right, I've come to a decision,' he said.

As always, the table fell silent as the head of the family spoke. 'I don't want yous boys involved in this one. I had a deal with Butch and it'll be him that pays.'

Paulie was the first to speak. 'You can't do it alone, Dad. His sons are always with him, you'll need back-up.'

'You're not a teenager any more,' Ronny told his father.

Harry thumped his fist on the table. 'I'm fifty-five, not fucking ninety. Now, I want you all to take note of what I'm saying. I am sorting this one out alone and if any of yous starts your own war with Jimmy O'Hara or any of the others behind my back, you'll have me to answer to.'

No one argued. When Harry Mitchell gave out orders, he was always obeyed.

'How you gonna collar Butch on his own?' Eddie asked.

Harry smiled. 'Every Wednesday morning Butch travels alone up to Southhall horse market. It's his only day away from the boys. The horsebox he goes in isn't kept on the site, he keeps it in a lock-up around the corner. He leaves really early, about half-five and I'm gonna wait for him at the lock-up.'

Reg nodded. He loved the idea. 'What you gonna do? Frighten him or finish him off?'

Harry shrugged. 'I dunno. Butch is probably totally unaware that his boys have been performing on our territory. I might just shoot him in the foot, give him a little warning. Mind you, if we have any repercussions, I'll blow his fucking brains out.'

'Why don't you just blow his brains out anyway?' Ronny said, laughing.

Harry ignored his idiotic son. 'Oh, one more thing before we go. I'm gonna need a driver to come with me. You up for it, Eddie?'

'Sure, Dad. When do you wanna do it, this Wednesday coming?'

Harry pondered momentarily. 'I think we'll leave it till the following week. They might be waiting for repercussions and we want them to enjoy a nice little surprise.'

Ronny glanced at Paulie. Neither said anything, but both were thinking the same thing. At thirty-six, Paul was the oldest. Ronny was thirty-three, yet Eddie, the youngest, was the golden fucking boy.

Reg clocked Ronny's annoyance and looked away. He was Harry's younger brother and had always been in his shadow, yet it had never bothered him. He didn't mind Paulie, he was OK, but Ronny was a moron and Reg made a mental note to keep a close eye on him. For months, he'd noticed him becoming more and more jealous of Eddie and it wasn't on – they were brothers, for fuck's sake.

With the meeting over, everybody said their goodbyes and went their separate ways.

Joyce glanced at the clock and opened the oven door. She tested the knife in her fruit cake and, happy it was properly cooked, put it on the kitchen top to cool down. Eddie was due to pick her daughter up soon, and she'd baked it especially for him.

Sitting in his armchair, Stanley was unable to concentrate on *Hawaii Five-O*. Usually, he was glued to anything Steve McGarrett did, but today the only thing he could concentrate on was that smarmy bastard who would shortly be picking his daughter up.

Stanley hadn't been able to sleep properly the previous night and, when he had dozed off, he'd had nightmares about Harry Mitchell. He'd dreamt that Mitchell had taken out his eye instead of Roger Dodds'.

His nightmare had only come to an end when Joyce punched him in the side of the head. 'What you screaming out and fidgeting for? You silly old bastard,' she'd said.

Stan had ignored her and gone downstairs to make himself a cup of tea. He'd sat up the rest of the night, frightened to go back to sleep in case his nightmare returned.

Joyce heard her daughter coming down the stairs and yelled out to her to come into the kitchen.

'Well, how do I look?' Jessica asked.

Joyce stared at her. She was wearing a flowery top, white plastic boots and sexy yellow hotpants.

'You look sensational. Where did you get your shorts?' she asked.

Jess giggled. 'They're not called shorts, Mum, they're hotpants. They were only cheap, I got 'em down Petticoat Lane.'

'What time's Eddie picking you up? Where's he taking you tonight?' Joyce asked excitedly.

'He's picking me up at six, I'm not sure where we're going yet.'

Joyce smiled and pointed to the fruit cake. 'I made that for your Eddie. Are you gonna invite him in?'

33

'I wasn't planning to.'

Noticing her mum's disappointment, Jessica immediately changed her tune. 'I'm sure he'll have time to come in for a quick cup of tea,' she said.

Joyce urged Jessica to shut the kitchen door. Last night, she'd been so excited about her daughter's romance, she could barely sleep. She had thought of an idea and she really didn't want Stanley earwigging.

'What's the matter?' Jessica asked.

'You know what we were talking about last night? About you making sure you don't let go of Ed.'

Jessica nodded.

Moving nearer, Joyce continued. 'Why don't you trap him? You know, get pregnant on purpose. I mean, let's face it, Jess, blokes like him don't come along every day and I'm sure if you were carrying his child, he'd propose.'

Jessica looked at her mother in horror. She wanted Eddie to propose to her because he loved her, not because she had a bun in the oven. They'd done it twice without a rubber, but only because Ed had run out, and she had no intention of trapping him. She was about to tell her mum to mind her own bloody business when the doorbell rang.

'Quick, don't keep him waiting,' Joyce said.

'Don't you dare say anything about babies and stuff in front of him, Mum.'

Joyce pushed her towards the front door. 'Of course not, dear.'

Stanley felt himself flinch as Eddie walked towards him.

'Good evening, Mr Smith,' Eddie said, holding out his hand.

As Jessica stepped out from behind him, Stan glared

at her. 'Surely you're not going out like that? You've got no bloody clothes on.'

Jessica raised her eyebrows. She didn't know who she liked the least. Her domineering mother, who was always trying to run her life for her, or her old-fashioned father, who still thought she was twelve years old.

'It's the fashion, Dad. All the girls are wearing hotpants.'

'Well, I've never bloody well seen anyone wearing them.'

'That's probably because you spend half your life in the betting shop. No one's gonna be wearing them in there, are they?' Joyce shouted at him.

Desperate to get away from her warring parents, Jessica grabbed Eddie's arm. 'Come on, let's go,' she said.

Eddie let her lead him out of the living room. 'Nice to meet you both again,' he said politely.

'Hang on a minute,' Joyce shouted.

Seconds later she presented Eddie with an object wrapped in tin foil. 'That fruit cake you liked, I baked you one,' she said proudly.

Eddie pecked her on the cheek. 'You're a star, Joyce. I'll have that for me supper.'

Jessica felt relief wash over her as Eddie drove away from the house.

'What's up, babe?' he asked her.

Jessica sighed. 'Just parent trouble. They're always arguing and they make me feel like piggy in the middle. Both of them drive me mad and I don't know what to do about it.'

Eddie laughed. 'I know exactly what you can do about it.'

'What?' Jessica enquired.

Swinging the car onto a nearby kerb, Eddie got out,

walked round the other side and opened the passenger door. As he knelt on one knee, Jessica looked at him in amazement.

'What you doing?'

Eddie held both her hands and smiled. 'Jessica Smith, marry me?'

# FOUR

Jessica immediately accepted her boyfriend's marriage proposal, but at Eddie's insistence, she said nothing to either of her parents.

'I'm a big believer in doing things properly, Jess. Keep schtum for now and next weekend I'll come round your house and ask for your parents' blessing. I'm a very traditional geezer at heart and I'm sure your dad would expect me to ask his permission.'

Jess loved Eddie's morals, but with her head in the clouds, she was desperate for the world to know of her good fortune. 'Can't I just tell my mum, Ed? It will be so hard keeping it from her and I know she won't say anything to my dad.'

Eddie shook his head. 'No, it's not right, Jess. We'll tell them together and then I'll take you shopping for a ring. I'll take you up Hatton Garden and you can pick whatever you want.'

How Jessica kept her mouth shut that week, she would never know. She didn't tell a soul, not even the girls at work. The following Saturday, she could barely contain her excitement and was out of bed before the birds had even started singing. She was unable to eat any breakfast, but made her parents boiled eggs, toast and tea and took it into their bedroom.

'What's all this in aid of?' her mother said, as she handed her the tray.

Jessica smiled. 'Eddie's coming round at twelve and I need you both to be here.'

Stanley sat up and eyed his daughter suspiciously. 'What's going on, Jessica?'

'Nothing untoward, Dad. Ed just wants to speak to you both, that's all.'

Hearing her brother moving about, Jessica swiftly left her parents' room and knocked on Raymond's door.

'Enter,' he shouted.

Jessica sat on his bed while he got himself ready. Raymond was a vain little sod and took longer to get his hair looking right than she did.

'What you up to today?' she asked him.

'I've got band practice, then I'm taking some bird out tonight.'

'Anyone I know?' Jessica asked him.

Raymond laughed and shook his head. He had a different girl on his arm every week and it was a standing joke between him and Jessica.

'What you up to then, sis?'

Jessica smiled. 'Eddie's coming round at twelve and then he's taking me shopping. I wanted you to meet him, Ray. Can't you hang about and say a quick hello to him, then go out after?'

Raymond checked his appearance in the full-length mirror. 'Sorry Jess, no can do. I'm meeting the boys at half-ten and they can't exactly practise without their drummer.'

Jessica stood up and gave her younger brother a hug. 'You have a good day and I want you to promise me that you'll make time to have a drink with me and Ed soon.'

Raymond wriggled out of her arms and checked his

shirt for creases. 'I promise. Why are you being all soppy and emotional?'

Jessica giggled. 'You'll find out later.'

As the clock struck twelve, Stanley sat fidgeting in his armchair. He'd arranged to meet his mate Jock in the pub at one and he was sick of this poxy Eddie messing up his Saturdays.

'I'll give him till half-twelve and if he ain't here, I'm off out,' he mumbled.

'You will do no such thing. You'll go out when I say you can go out,' Joyce told him.

Stan looked at the telly and said nothing. Ever since Jess had said that Eddie wanted to see them, his stomach had been in knots. Stan had a feeling that Mr Fucking Charming Bollocks wanted to take his daughter away on holiday and, if that was the case, he'd be far from happy about it.

Hearing a car engine, Joyce jumped out of her chair and lifted the curtain. She'd been bubbling with excitement all morning and was dying to know what Eddie needed to see them for. With a bit of luck he wanted to ask their permission to marry Jess.

'Here he is,' Joyce said, as the posh gold Mercedes pulled up.

Eddie picked up the bouquet and bottle of Chivas Regal he'd bought, and strolled up the path.

'How lovely to see you again, Joyce,' he said, handing her the flowers.

'Awww, you shouldn't have, they're beautiful. Let me put them in a vase.'

Eddie gave Jessica a lingering kiss and then followed her into the living room.

'Jess said you liked a drop of Scotch,' he said, handing Stan the bottle.

'Thanks,' Stan said ungratefully. If Eddie had turned up bearing solid gold bars, he still wouldn't like the bastard.

'Go and keep your mum company while I have a little chat with your dad,' Eddie told his girlfriend.

Jess gave his hand a good-luck squeeze and left the room.

Not one to go round the houses, Eddie came straight to the point. 'I have fallen head over heels for your Jessica, Mr Smith. She means the world to me and I would like to ask for her hand in marriage.'

Stanley felt every hair on his body stand up on end. Aware of his heart racing and his hands shaking, he urged Eddie to pour him a drink. Aware that Stan had turned a whiter shade of pale, Eddie was quite concerned.

'You don't look very well. Are you OK?' he asked, as he handed him a large Scotch.

Stanley downed the drink in one and immediately asked for a refill.

Desperate for an answer from the shivering wreck of a man, Eddie continued talking. 'Look, I know how you must feel and I know Jessica is still very young. But, I promise you, Mr Smith, you have my word that I will cherish and take good care of her.'

Unable to think of anything nice to say, Stanley grabbed the bottle of Chivas Regal and poured himself yet another.

'It's not up to me. Go and ask her mother,' Stanley muttered.

Eddie stood up and walked into the kitchen. 'Go and see your dad, Jess, I need to have a chat with your mum.'

Joyce smiled as he closed the kitchen door. 'Would you like some fruit cake?' she asked.

Eddie shook his head and cut straight to the chase. 'I am totally in love with your Jessica and I want to marry her. I've had a little chat with your husband and he said it's up to you, Joyce. I know she's very young, but I promise you with all my heart that I'll take good care of her.'

To say Joyce was over the moon was putting it mildly. Unable to stop herself, she flung her arms around Eddie's neck.

'I am so happy,' she sobbed. 'Welcome to the family, Eddie. My Jessica is a very lucky girl and I'd be proud to call you my son-in-law.'

Eddie smiled. 'I've got a bottle of champagne in the car. I'll bring it in and we can have a toast.'

Joyce sorted out her best crystal glasses and took four into the living room. She hugged Jessica. 'Congratulations, darling. Eddie's a wonderful man – you've bagged yourself a good one there.'

Noticing Stanley had a face like a smacked arse, Joyce kicked his leg. 'For Christ's sake cheer up, you miserable old bastard.'

Stanley said nothing as he was handed a glass of champagne.

Eddie kissed Jessica gently on the forehead. 'I'm taking Jess to Hatton Garden to choose a ring this afternoon. She can have the biggest diamond in the shop.'

Joyce couldn't wipe the smile off her face. The only rock Stan had ever bought her was a poxy old topaz. 'You'll have to pop back and show me your ring,' she said to Jess.

'I'll show you tomorrow. Now we're engaged to be married, you don't mind if I stay round Ed's tonight, do you, Mum? We want to go out for a meal to celebrate and we won't be back till late.'

Joyce nodded. 'That's fine by me, love.'

Stanley looked at his wife in disgust. His daughter

wasn't even married yet and Joyce was encouraging her to hawk her mutton.

'To my beautiful wife-to-be,' Eddie said, holding his glass aloft.

'To Jessica and Eddie,' Joycie crowed.

Stan looked at the clock. It was nearly half-past one and he was late to meet Jock. Desperate to get away from the man who had led his daughter astray, he stood up. 'I'm going out now.'

'You can't go out yet. We're in the middle of a celebration,' Joyce said angrily.

Eddie decided to stick up for his future father-in-law. 'It's fine, Joyce. To be honest, me and Jess need to make a move now ourselves. I'll drop you at the pub, Stan, if you like?'

Stanley shook his head. He'd rather crawl there on all fours than get inside Eddie's car.

Joyce tutted as her husband slunk away and then hugged both Jessica and Eddie. 'Have a nice evening and if you can't be good, be careful,' she giggled.

Feeling herself going red, Jessica dragged Eddie out of the front door. 'My mum is just so embarrassing at times,' she moaned to her fiancé.

Eddie waved at Joyce as they drove away. The old girl would jump in the river if he asked her to, but he'd have to work a bit harder if he was to win over the old man.

A few days after his engagement to Jessica, Eddie picked his father up at four o'clock in the morning. Butch wasn't expected to pick up the horsebox till around half-five, but his dad was keen to get there well before his intended victim.

Harry got into the car with a sports bag in his hand. 'What's in there?' Eddie asked him.

42

'Bolt-cutters. There's a yard bang opposite where Butch keeps the box. We'll cut the lock off and hide in there.'

'We're a bit early, ain't we?' Ed said.

'Do a right here, son. We're not going in your motor, we'll pick up the old Bedford van. It's still registered to some cunt in Luton, so worst ways we can burn it out if we need to.'

Eddie followed his father's directions and they swapped motors. Driving towards Stratford, Eddie told him about Jessica. 'I proposed to her at the weekend, Dad. I dunno when we'll get married yet, but I bought her a nice engagement ring. You'll have to meet her soon. She's a right little cracker and I know you'll like her.'

Harry patted his favourite son on the shoulder. 'I'm pleased for you, boy, I really am. I knew straight away that your mother was the one. She was a right little cracker as well.'

Thinking about his beautiful dead wife plunged Harry into silence and he didn't utter another word throughout the rest of the journey.

'Left here,' Harry said, snapping out of his trance. 'Pull up over there. That yard's the one we're gonna hide in, the one with all the graffiti.'

Checking that no one was about, Eddie opened the driver's door. 'What we gonna do if the people turn up and we're in their yard?'

Harry laughed. 'The yard belongs to Terry O'Donnell. He ain't used it for years and he owes me more than a few favours anyway.'

Taking the bolt-cutters out of the bag, Harry handed Eddie a pair of leather gloves and put on a pair himself. 'Put on the gloves and cut the chain, son. I've got another chain and lock in the bag to replace it with when we're

43

done. I'd love to see Terry O'Donnell's face if he can't get in to his own yard. I'll send him the new key in the post.'

As Eddie opened the gate he came face to face with a massive rat. 'Fuck that! It frightened the fucking life out of me,' he said, as the rat scuttled away.

Harry laughed. 'Shut up, you big pansy.'

'What we gonna do with the van?' Eddie asked.

'Put it in here,' Harry said. 'I'll run across and, once I've shot the cunt, we can drive straight off.'

Eddie parked the van inside, then closed the gates. He stuck his hand through the large gap and loosely laid the broken chain back through the lock.

Harry sat down on an old tin drum. 'I had a drive down here earlier this week. There's no one about this time in the morning. As soon as we hear Butch pull up, I'll creep out and do him as soon as he opens his yard. When you hear the gun go off, start the van and pull out. Lock up the yard for us, then we're away.'

Eddie nodded. He was freezing his bollocks off and wished he'd put on warmer clothes.

The men sat in silence while they waited. Finally, at 5.23, they heard a diesel engine pull up outside. Harry peeped through the gate to check it was Butch. He waited until Butch opened the gates and went inside his yard, then he gently lifted the loose chain, crept out and followed him in.

Butch was just about to climb into his horsebox when he saw Harry Mitchell staring at him with a gun in his hand.

'What the fuck! What's going on, mush?'

Harry shook his head. 'I warned you, Butch, we had a deal. Your boys have taken a fucking liberty, yet again.'

Butch could feel himself shaking. 'What are me boys meant to have done?'

'Performed in the Flag the other night, they did. Smashed the bogs up, terrorised the bar staff. The Flag is our territory, you know it is, Butch. Your boys have no manners and I'm not putting up with it any more.'

'I didn't know, Harry. I'm sorry, I'll talk to 'em, I'll sort it.'

Harry smiled as he lifted the gun. 'It's a bit late for that. I warned you about all this once before.'

'Please, no, don't kill me,' Butch said, as he fell to the ground.

Harry moved deftly towards him. Butch had gone down before he'd even fucking shot him, the coward. Harry grabbed hold of the petrified man's right leg.

'No, please, no,' Butch begged.

Harry Mitchell ignored his pleas, pulled back the trigger and blasted him in the right foot. 'Take that as a warning, Butch. If I was you, I'd advise your family to move their caravans to a different fucking area.'

As blood poured from his foot, Butch was aware of shit running down his legs. He was in too much pain to speak any more; instead he just covered his head with his hands.

Harry walked away. 'Next time, I'll blow your brains out,' he said menacingly.

Eddie replaced the lock and jumped back in the van. 'Everything go OK?' he asked, as his father got into the passenger's side.

'All sorted, son. Now, I don't know about you, but I'm bloody well starving. Drop the van off, drive back to Canning Town and we'll have a nice little fry-up in Maureen's Café.'

# FIVE

A month after announcing her engagement, Jessica sat nervously in the doctor's surgery, clutching her best friend's hand. Jessica's periods were usually as regular as clockwork; she could never remember it being one day late, let alone two weeks. Taking her friend Mary's advice, Jess had gone to see her doctor the previous week. The receptionist had given her a container for a urine sample, of which she was now awaiting the results.

Anxiously biting her nails, Jessica turned to her friend. 'What am I gonna do if I am? I mean, Eddie's already got two kids and he's never mentioned wanting any more. Say he finishes with me? He might call off the engagement and make me have an abortion.'

Mary put her arm around Jessica. 'You're being silly now. Eddie loves you, so why on earth would he treat you like that? I bet if you are pregnant, he'll be as pleased as Punch.'

About to reply, Jessica froze as her name was called. Mary accompanied her into the surgery and they sat down opposite Dr Hunter.

'I have the results of your test back, Jessica, and I can confirm that you are indeed pregnant.'

Jessica burst into tears. She and Eddie had only done it twice without a rubber.

'I'm too young to be a mum. I won't know what to do,' Jessica cried.

Mary hugged her and spoke to the doctor at the same time. 'I think it's a bit of a shock for Jess. Can we book her another appointment for next week?'

Dr Hunter nodded. In his profession he was used to this reaction. It's a shame these young girls never thought about the consequences before they opened their legs.

Mary thanked the doctor for his time and led Jessica outside. 'You wait here and get some fresh air while I book you another appointment,' she told her.

A trip to a nearby café proved to be a turning point in Jessica's anxiousness and, after three cups of tea, she even managed a smile.

'Me mum'll be pleased, I know that. She's always banging on about having grandchildren one day. As for me poor old dad, he'll probably drop dead with the shock of it all.'

Mary giggled. 'I wish I'd met a nice man like you have, I'd love to be in your position. When are you gonna tell him?'

Jessica took a bite of her bacon sandwich. 'I'm seeing Ed tonight, so I'll tell him then. Keep your fingers crossed, eh?'

Mary squeezed her hand. 'Everything'll be fine, I just know it will.'

Eddie counted the takings for the second time. Satisfied that they were spot-on, he placed the money in a carrier bag and stuffed it in his jacket pocket. Although his family owned salvage yards, most of their money came from pub protection. They tried not to hit on their own doorstep too much, and concentrated more on the surrounding areas. Everybody, including the O'Haras, thought that John, the guv'nor in the Flag, paid them protection, but that wasn't the case. John was their mate, he looked after them and vice versa.

Eddie turned the radio on as he made himself a sandwich. He hated silence, it gave him the heebies. Hearing the croaky voice of Rod Stewart, he cranked up the volume. He loved that song, 'Maggie May'. It was all about a young boy having an affair with an older woman. Eddie thought back to his colourful past. He'd been in that position many a time in his youth, so much so that the song could have been written especially for him.

Smirking, Ed flopped onto the sofa and was just about to tuck into his doorstep special when the phone rang. 'Fucking nuisance,' he muttered, as he ran to the hallway to answer it.

'All right, Dad? What you up to?'

'I'm just leaving home. Have I got some news for you, Eddie, my boy. Meet me in the Flag, I'll be there in half an hour.'

Eddie could tell by his father's voice that whatever news he had was bloody good.

'Don't keep me waiting. Tell us now.'

Harry Mitchell laughed. 'No way. I need to see the expression on your face when I tell you. Be patient and move your arse.'

Eddie shook his head as he replaced the receiver. He was a funny bastard, his father, a proper fucking character.

Jessica had a bath, dried her hair and sat on the bed in her dressing gown. She was dreading telling her parents the news, but the quicker she told them the better. Her mum should be OK; it was her dad she was worried about. Jessica wasn't very good at lying.

'What's the matter with you?' her mum asked her earlier.

'Nothing,' Jessica lied. Her dad wasn't at home and she'd rather kill two birds with one stone than tell them separately.

Hearing the front door slam shut, Jessica chucked on some clothes and wandered downstairs.

'Any chance of a quick word with both of you?' she asked sheepishly.

Joyce and Stanley followed her into the living room.

'Sit down,' Jessica urged.

Stan said a silent prayer. Something was wrong and with a bit of luck Mr Fucking Charming Bollocks had kicked her into touch.

'What's up, love?' he asked hopefully.

Jessica felt too embarrassed to look them in the eye, so she focused on the carpet.

'Please don't have a go at me, but I found out today that I'm pregnant. I'm really sorry if I've let you both down.'

Joyce hugged her daughter. The timing wasn't perfect but, nevertheless, she was thrilled. She'd always fancied being a young grandma. She could barely wait to get dolled up and go out walking with the pram. As for babysitting, she would look after the child as much as Jess would allow her.

'I'm so pleased for you, darling. Now, don't you worry about being young and not being able to cope. Your old mum will teach you the ropes and I'll be there for you as much as possible. Perhaps Eddie will buy you a house nearby, so I'm always on hand to help out and babysit.'

Stanley sat paralysed in the armchair. He'd had so many high hopes for his beautiful daughter and now she was up the spout by that Mitchell bastard.

'Are you OK, Dad?' Jessica asked him.

Stan nodded and looked the other way. He didn't want her to see the tears in his eyes.

'What about the wedding? Will you bring it forward or get married after the baby's born?' Joyce asked.

Jessica shrugged. 'I'll speak to Eddie tonight. He doesn't even know that I'm pregnant yet. I don't really want a baby out of wedlock, so the sooner we tie the knot, the better. I'd rather do it before I start showing.'

Joyce nodded. She could understand where Jess was coming from. Walking down the aisle with a stomach like a rugby ball never looked good on anyone. She squeezed her daughter's hand.

'Whatever you and Eddie decide, me and your dad are right behind you, aren't we, Stanley?'

Stan said nothing. The quicker he got out of this bleeding nuthouse the better.

'Stanley, what do you think you're doing? Where you going?' Joyce shouted.

Ignoring his wife, Stan put on his checked cap and slammed the front door.

Eddie ordered another drink and glanced at his watch. His bloody father was late and he was doing buttons to know what had happened.

Five minutes later, a beaming Harry Mitchell strolled into the pub.

'Well, what's occurring?' Eddie asked him.

Ushering his son over to an empty corner of the pub, Harry sat opposite him. 'They've gone.'

Eddie shook his head, 'Who you on about? Who's fucking gone?'

Harry started laughing. 'The O'Haras. They've moved away, the whole lot of 'em. They've gone to Essex, by all accounts. Butch sent a message to me yesterday, via Ginger Mick. He told him to tell me that there won't be any repercussions and he wants an end to the feud for good. Ginger Mick said the old cunt was petrified and he can barely fucking walk. Yesterday they went – the site's completely fucking empty. Packed up their stuff and did a moonlight flit, apparently.'

Eddie couldn't stop smiling. He would never have to see Jimmy O'Hara's ugly boat race ever again.

'Bring us over a bottle of champagne, Betsy,' he ordered the barmaid.

Eddie shook his old man's hand. 'You know what this means, don't you? We can take over the Stratford boozers. I can't wait for us to bowl into the Chobham and demand money off that pikey-loving cunt of a guv'nor. I think we should stick the price up in there, charge him more than we charge anyone else.'

Harry laughed. 'My sentiments exactly. Apparently, they had seven boozers in Stratford on their payroll, all told. In the next couple of days we'll pay all of 'em a visit, get our foot in the door.'

Eddie sipped his drink. 'Are you sure that Ginger Mick can be trusted?'

Harry nodded. 'I've had him on me payroll since he was a young 'un. Safe as houses, he is. The O'Haras thought he was their Joey – what they didn't know was that I set it all up. We needed a spy in the camp, and Ginger Mick was perfect.'

Reg, Paulie and Ronny's arrival spelled the start of a glorified piss-up. Champagne corks went flying and there were pats on the back and handshakes all around.

'Come and join us, John,' Harry urged the guv'nor.

Ronny started the singalong and the rest of the lads joined in: 'When the inbred O'Haras go run, run, a-running

51

along, shoot the bastards, shoot the bastards, shoot, shoot, shoot the bastards.'

'What yous lot celebrating? Ain't won the bleedin' football pools, have yer?' Betsy asked, as she brought over yet another two bottles of champagne.

'We're celebrating being the kings of the East End,' Ronny shouted, grabbing her large backside.

'Keep yer dirty fucking hands to yerself, Ronny Mitchell,' Betsy said, laughing.

The raucous behaviour, jokes and songs continued for hours and, three sheets to the wind, Eddie completely lost track of time. 'Shit, I was meant to pick Jess up at seven,' he said, leaping out of his chair.

'Fuck her off, stay out with us tonight,' Ronny said.

'Yeah, let's go to a club and celebrate properly,' Paulie suggested.

Eddie shook his head. He was a gentleman and would never let Jess down at short notice. Realising he was in no fit state to drive, he asked John the guv'nor to call him a cab.

Five minutes later, he heard a bib outside and said his goodbyes.

'All of us will meet in here tomorrow at two o'clock. Then we can pay a nice friendly visit to the Chobham and the rest of them boozers in Stratford,' his father told him.

Eddie jumped into the cab and urged the driver to put his foot down.

Jessica, who had been standing looking out of the window for an hour, felt relief surge through her as Eddie got out of the cab. She ran to the front door.

'There you are.'

Eddie was full of apologies, 'I'm so sorry I'm late, babe. Something cropped up. It won't happen again, I promise.'

52

'I was so worried, I thought you'd had an accident or something,' Jessica said.

Eddie held her close and stroked her hair. 'I got stuck with some business, you know how it is.'

'Where's your car?' Jessica asked.

Eddie was saved from answering by Joyce's intervention.

'Would you like a beer, Eddie? Or a cup of tea and fruit cake?'

Eddie shook his head. 'The cab's waiting outside. I'm gonna take Jess out for a nice meal. Another time, eh, Joycie?'

Joyce could tell Eddie was a bit drunk, but boys would be boys. Her son Raymond was the same; he was always coming home tipsy.

Joyce winked at Jess and crossed two fingers on both hands. 'Good luck,' she mouthed, as they walked up the path.

Jessica sat in the restaurant and barely touched her food. 'Leave the chips if you like, but eat that fillet steak,' Eddie urged her.

'I'm not hungry,' Jessica said, as she slipped it onto his plate.

Having sobered up a bit, Eddie soon realised that Jess wasn't herself and obviously had something on her mind. He put down his knife and fork and took her hands in his.

'Come on, spit it out, what's a matter, babe? Are you having second thoughts about us getting married or something?'

Jessica shook her head. She just had to say it, there was no other way. 'I went to the doctor's today, Eddie. Please don't have a go at me, but I'm pregnant.'

Eddie's smile was that wide it almost lit up the restaurant. 'Are you sure? Have you had a proper test?'

Jessica nodded. 'The doctor gave me the results today. Look Ed, I'm so sorry. If you want me to get rid –'

Eddie leaned further across the table and kissed her on the lips. 'Get rid of it? Are you mad? Don't you get it, Jess? I love you and we can have as many babies as you want.'

Realising that he was telling the truth, Jessica smiled. 'What about the wedding, though? I'm not walking down the aisle with a bun in the oven, Ed. It will look awful, people will think I'm a tart.'

Eddie laughed. 'You ain't gotta walk down the aisle with a bun in the oven. Look, we'd have had trouble finding a vicar to marry us on the quick 'cause I've already been married. How about I book a register office? We can get married in the next couple of weeks if you want.'

Jessica's eyes shone. 'Really, Ed? Do you mean that?'

'Of course I do. Waiter, bring us over a bottle of champers,' Eddie said loudly.

Aware of all the other diners looking at him, Eddie smiled. He loved being the centre of attention, it was all part of his make-up.

He stood up and addressed the whole restaurant. 'You see this beautiful girl here,' he said, pointing at Jess.

'We, us two, are getting married and we're having a baby. Now, who fancies a glass of champagne to celebrate our happiness with us?'

'I'll have one,' said an old man with a bald head.

'We'll have a drink with you,' said a woman in a spotted dress.

Eddie ordered the waiter to get more bottles of champagne and share them between all the other diners. The restaurant was reasonably empty and, apart from themselves, there were only five other tables taken.

Jessica could feel herself blushing beetroot red. Eddie could be so bloody loud, especially when he'd been drinking.

'Nosy load of bastards. They were all looking at us,' he whispered to Jess.

Winking at her, Eddie carried on where he'd left off. 'Now come on, fucking stand up, I've just bought you all champagne.'

Well aware that he was probably a local villain, everybody leaped to attention. Eddie held his glass aloft.

'To Jessica, the most beautiful girl in the world,' he said.

Wary, but amused at the same time, everybody lifted their glasses.

'To Jessica,' they repeated after him.

Minutes later, Jessica's happiness partly disintegrated.

'I beg your pardon?' she said to Eddie. He was winding her up, he had to be.

'I said, I want you to pack your job up in the morning. Now we're getting married, things are different. I've got money – you don't need to work any more.'

Jessica looked at him in amazement. She liked her independence, enjoyed her little job and she had so many friends there.

'I'm not ready to give it up yet, Ed. I know when I've had the baby, I'll have to, but that's ages away yet.'

Eddie held her hands and gazed deep into her eyes. 'Look, if we're gonna get wed, you've got to get your priorities right. I mean what's more important, a poxy job in a shoe shop, or us and our baby's future? Marriage is

55

all about give and take, Jess, and if you can't do this one little thing for me, then maybe you're not ready for such a big commitment.'

Jessica bit her lip. She had just found the man of her dreams and she couldn't lose him over something so trivial. She squeezed his hand.

'You're so right, Ed. I mean, I'd have to give it up in a few months anyway, so I might as well do it now. I'll ring them first thing tomorrow, to tell them that I'm leaving.'

Eddie smiled. 'That's my girl. You know it makes sense.'

Joyce and Stanley were watching a late-night film when Jessica arrived home. 'Did you have a nice evening? How did Eddie react to the news?' Joyce asked excitedly.

'Oh, Ed was thrilled. He said we can have as many babies as I want,' Jess said happily. 'And I'm giving my job up. I'm gonna ring the shop tomorrow to tell them I won't be coming back.'

Stanley looked at his daughter in astonishment. 'You can't give up your job. I thought you liked working in the shoe shop.'

Jessica shrugged. 'Eddie said that I don't need to work any more. He said he'll look after me and the baby from now on.'

Aware that her dad was anything but happy, Jessica looked away from him. 'I'll make us all a nice cup of tea,' she said, as she swiftly left the room.

Stanley glared at Joyce. 'She loves that bloody job. That bastard's trying to manipulate her already. It ain't right, Joycie. Next thing you know, he'll have her shut in a fucking cupboard. These villains have different principles to the likes of me and you. They keep their women under lock and key, and we've got to put a stop to it before it's too late.'

Joyce threw her husband a look of contempt. 'Don't you dare spoil our daughter's happiness. If Eddie wants to support Jess, then good for her. I wish I hadn't had to work when I was pregnant. Do you know how hard it was for me, dragging myself to that bloody office every day? I had no choice, we couldn't survive on your measly wages. You leave our Jess alone and keep your idiotic opinions to yourself, Stanley. Unlike me, she's found a rich man, a good 'un.'

About to answer his wife back, Stanley was stopped from doing so by Jessica's reappearance. 'Thanks, love,' he said, as she handed him his cuppa.

Jessica sat down next to her mum. She had one more bombshell to drop and she knew her dad wasn't going to be happy. 'Oh, by the way, Eddie and I have decided to get married in a couple of weeks' time. We're not gonna bother with a church do, we've decided on a register office.'

As the horror of the situation hit Stanley, he spilt half of the contents of his favourite mug over his leg. 'Bollocks!' he yelled, as the hot tea scalded him.

'Silly old goat,' Joyce whispered.

Jessica felt sorry for her dad. She knew it had always been his dream to one day walk her down the aisle. 'Are you OK, Dad?' she asked kindly.

Stanley said nothing as he dabbed his trousers with his handkerchief. Whatever he said would make no difference, so what was the bloody point? Both his wife and daughter thought the sun shone out of Eddie Mitchell's arse. With a sense of foreboding, Stanley said goodnight, left the room and trudged dejectedly up the stairs.

He was sure that the day would come when his wife and daughter would wish they had listened to him. Until that day came, Stanley had little choice other than to smile, be polite and keep schtum.

# SIX

Joyce gasped in admiration as Jessica walked through the door.

'You look just like a model – so, so pretty. I am so proud of you, Jess, I really am.'

Not wanting her mother and father's arguments spoiling her big day, Jessica had opted to get ready over the road. Her friends, Ginny and Linda, lived next door to one another. Both worked as hairdressers and they had kindly offered to do her hair and make-up for free.

Noticing Jessica's hands shaking, her best friend, Mary, handed her a glass of wine. 'Your hair looks fabulous at the back. Whose idea was it to put those beads in it?'

Jessica smiled. 'It was Eddie's, actually. We saw a girl wearing white beads in her hair in a pub last week and Eddie said they'd look great for my wedding day. He likes me to wear my hair up.'

Jessica only had one set of grandparents still alive. Her dad's parents had both died in the last few years, but her mum's parents had recently retired to Norfolk. Her nan smiled at her. 'Beautiful dress, darling. Where did you get it from? Must have cost a fortune with that crochet and crystal trim.'

Jessica carefully sat down and took a sip of her wine. 'A shop in Knightsbridge. Eddie sent me there; his friend owns the place and I was allowed to choose whatever I wanted. Ed told me not to worry about the price, he wouldn't even let the man tell me how much it cost.'

Nanny Ivy pursed her lips. 'Sounds too good to be true, this Eddie,' she said curtly.

Joyce scowled at her mother. She saw very little of her parents, which suited Joyce just fine. They hadn't seen eye to eye for years and Joyce would never forgive her mum for forcing her to marry Stanley.

'No, he's not too good to be true, mother. He's a respectable gentleman, a lovely chap. In fact, he's the total opposite of what you made me end up with.'

Ivy knew when to shut up. There was nothing what-soever wrong with Stanley. Joyce had always had a high opinion of herself. Acted like Lady Dunabunk, she did, full of her own self-importance.

'Where is everybody?' Jessica asked.

Joyce looked at the clock and felt the first stirrings of annoyance. She'd been so wrapped up talking about the wedding, she'd forgotten Stanley had been due back ages ago.

'Christ knows where your father's got to. He was ready at ten o'clock this morning, had a bath and put his suit straight on, he did. Then he dragged your grandad and Raymond down the bookie's, said they'd only be half-hour. If he's in that pub, getting half-sozzled, I'll bleedin' well kill the bastard.'

Jessica felt her heart beating at double its usual pace. She was already nervous about the day ahead and the last thing she needed was her parents at one another's throats. Please God, not today, she prayed silently.

\* \* \*

60

Stanley Smith stood in the betting shop and watched in dismay as trap six came stone bollock last.

'Stupid fucking mutt, wants putting down,' he cursed, as he made the short walk back to his local. 'Give us another three bitters, three whisky chasers, and a lager for Raymond,' he told Anna, the barmaid.

Anna smiled. 'You're going for it today, Stanley. Who's that older man you're with? And why are yous all dressed up?'

Not in the mood for polite conversation, Stanley mumbled the words, 'Father-in-law, going to a wedding,' and walked away.

Stanley was dreading the day ahead of him. The thought of handing his beautiful daughter over to a bastard like Eddie Mitchell filled him with hatred and anger.

'What's the time, Stan? Hadn't we better be getting back soon?' asked Bill, his father-in-law.

'Mum'll have her broom out if you're late,' Raymond joked.

'It's OK, we've got time to drink these,' Stan replied confidently.

Jock, Stan's best mate, necked his whisky chaser and smiled. 'Well, did you have any luck with that dog you had the tip on?'

Stanley shook his head. 'I think the bastard mutt's still running. My luck's fucked at the moment, in every way you could think of.'

Seconds later, Stanley's luck got even worse as he spotted an angry-looking Joyce stomping into the pub. 'Shit, tell her I've already left,' he said, as he threw himself under the table.

Knowing her husband's cowardly behaviour of old, Joyce crouched down and immediately found him. 'Stanley, get up from under that table and get your arse home this minute!' she screamed.

Aware of the whole of the pub laughing at him, Stanley crawled out like a naughty schoolboy.

'I'm sorry, Joycie. Me, Ray and Bill lost track of time. We were just gonna –'

Joyce lifted her umbrella and repeatedly whacked him on the backside. 'Home, Stanley, now, and I mean now.'

With Joyce and her brolly on his tail, Stanley ran out of the pub, twice as fast as the mutt he'd lost his money on.

Eddie stood in Barking register office and glanced at his watch.

'Don't worry, she will be here,' his brother Ronny assured him.

Eddie smiled. Paulie had been his best man at his first wedding to Bev, so he'd felt it only right to even things up by asking Ronny this time round.

Ronny had been thrilled to be asked. He'd hugged him, with tears in his eyes. 'I'd be honoured, bruv, fucking honoured.'

Eddie wiped the palms of his hands on his smart grey suit. 'Get someone to open that door, I'm sweating me cobs off in here,' he ordered Ronny.

'She's arrived. They're here,' somebody shouted.

Eddie took a deep breath as Jessica walked towards him. Smiling, he squeezed her hand. 'You look beautiful, really beautiful.'

The vows might have been short and sweet, but they were filled with emotion and spoken with meaning.

Eddie slipped the ring on Jessica's finger and kissed her tenderly. 'I love you, Mrs Mitchell,' he whispered.

\* \* \*

With little time to organise the big event, Eddie had chosen a restaurant in Canning Town for a slap-up meal, followed by a knees-up back at his local pub. He'd booked a disco and had told John, the guv'nor, to serve free drinks all night. He hadn't invited too many people. Including Jessica's family and friends, there were about fifty at the wedding and meal, and another fifty or so invited to the reception at the boozer.

'I can't believe my best mate's married,' Mary said, smiling.

'You look so pretty, Jess,' Linda said.

'Beautiful,' Ginny agreed.

'Congratulations, darling,' Joyce said, hugging her daughter.

'I like Ed, he's a top bloke, sis,' Raymond said, kissing her.

Stanley felt his eyes water as he watched his daughter and Eddie gaze into one another's eyes. It would all end in tears, he just knew it would.

His mother-in-law felt the same way. 'I don't like him. Surely our Joyce must realise they're a family of villains? You've only got to look at them to see what they are.'

Stanley gave a defeated shrug. 'You know what Joycie's like, once she gets a bee in her bonnet. I never liked the flash bastard from day one, but as usual, my opinion counts for nothing in our house. I tried to tell Joycie, but she can't see the wood for the trees.'

Noticing her father's dismal expression, Jessica walked over and hugged him. 'I know you've got your doubts, Dad, but trust me, I love Eddie and I know what I'm doing.'

Stanley took a handkerchief out of his pocket and dabbed his eyes. 'I hope you're right, darling, for your sake I do.'

Covered in confetti, Jessica and Eddie posed for numerous photographs.

'Now all immediate family stand together,' the photographer shouted.

As the camera flashed, both families smiled – well, apart from Ivy and Stan, that was. Stanley flinched as he spotted Harry Mitchell glance his way. Please God, don't let him recognise me, he prayed.

Jessica felt nervous as she took her seat next to Eddie in the restaurant. Her own family were sitting at a different table and she'd have felt much more comfortable sitting with them.

She'd never met any of Ed's family, apart from Ronny and Paulie, until now. 'Where are Gary and Ricky? You said you'd bought them suits and they were coming.'

Eddie shook his head. 'Sore subject. They were meant to be here, but my cunt of an ex-wife had one of her tantrums and took 'em away on holiday. You wait till she gets home, I'll give her take my kids away without my permission.'

Not wanting to spoil his day, Eddie quickly changed the subject. 'This is my Auntie Joan that I told you about, who brought me up as a nipper, and this is my Auntie Violet, my dad's sister.'

'I'm very pleased to meet you both,' Jessica said shyly.

Auntie Joan patted the chair next to her. 'You sit next to me, my darling, and Ed can sit at the top of the table. Oh, look at her, Vi, ain't she pretty? Got the face of an angel, ain't she?'

'She's an absolute princess,' Violet replied.

As the two women showered her with compliments, Jessica felt her face redden. She wouldn't have felt so nervous if she could have had a proper drink, but obviously, she didn't want to make a show of herself in front of Eddie's relations.

Harry Mitchell smiled at her. 'You'll get used to our nutty family in time, honest you will. Now, where's your dad? I've been introduced to your mum, but I don't even know which one your father is.'

As Harry Mitchell strolled towards him, Stanley felt the colour drain from his skin. Memories of the past came flooding back and all he could picture was Roger Dodds covered in blood with his eye hanging out. Unable to swallow the lump of fillet steak in his mouth, Stanley began to make choking noises.

'For goodness' sake, Stanley, why do you always have to show me up?' Joyce yelled, as she punched him on the back.

As the meat flew out of his mouth and landed on Harry Mitchell's lapel, Stan felt his bowels loosen.

Raymond burst out laughing and, luckily for Stan, Harry Mitchell was in a jovial mood. 'Fucking hell, I've had a few bullets aimed at me in me time, but never a lump of meat,' he joked.

Jessica was mortified. 'Dad, this is Harry, Eddie's father.'

'Pleased to meet you,' Stanley mumbled, shaking his hand.

There was no recognition on Harry's face, and Stan breathed a sigh of relief.

'Christ, you're shivering. Shall I get them to turn the heating up?' Harry asked kindly.

Stanley shook his head. 'No, I'm fine thanks. I've got a bit of a chill, I think.'

Aware that her father was making a total penis of himself, Jessica quickly dragged Harry towards her brother. 'And this is Raymond, my younger brother.'

Raymond stood up and shook Harry Mitchell's hand. 'Nice to meet you, sir,' he said politely.

'I'm sure we'll all catch up again later in the pub,' Harry said, bemused by his new in-laws. The brother was a proper kid with a handshake like a man's. As for the father's limp hand, the less said the better. 'You can always tell a man's soul by his handshake,' his old mum used to tell him and Harry had learned over the years that she was spot on.

After everybody had finished their meals, champagne was poured freely all round. Harry Mitchell was the first to give a speech. He kept it short and sweet, but ended it by giving Jessica an envelope to open.

'My wedding present to both of you,' he said.

Jessica gasped as she looked inside. There were flight tickets and a stay in a five-star hotel in Italy. 'It's booked for next week. I've never flown before!' she yelled gleefully.

As the best man, Ronny was the next to stand up. He spoke about Ed as a kid and ending it by saying, 'Bev, my brother's ex-wife, was as thick as two short planks. She was ugly, a monster, and I'm sure that everyone will agree that this time Ed's got it right. Jessica is everything his first wife wasn't and I'm sure they'll be extremely happy together. Raise your glasses everybody. To Eddie and Jessica.'

Eddie locked eyes with his dad and Uncle Reg. All three shook their heads. Ronny had the brains and decorum of a fucking rat. Eddie quickly stood up, made a couple of jokes and glossed over his brother's comments. He ended his speech by handing Jess yet another envelope.

'You've made me so happy by becoming my wife, Jess. This is my present to you,' he told her.

Jess couldn't believe her eyes as she tore it open.

A few days ago they'd viewed a beautiful house not far from where her parents lived. Jess had fallen in love with it on sight. It was in a private road and was beautifully decorated.

'We can't afford it yet, Jess. Let's get the wedding out of the way and we'll find somewhere after we're married,' Eddie had told her.

Now she had the deeds and keys in her hand and could scarcely believe her luck. 'I can't believe it. Thank you, I love you so much,' she said, as she threw her arms around Eddie's neck.

Overcome by excitement, Jess lifted up the hem of her dress and ran over to her mum's table. 'Look, Mum, it's only ten minutes' walk from you. That's the house I told you about. There's a picture of it there.'

Eddie stood proudly behind his wife. 'I knew she wanted to live near you and what Jess wants, she will always get,' he told Joyce.

Joyce grabbed Eddie's face and planted a smacker on his forehead. 'I can pop round when you're at work and, when the baby arrives, I'll babysit whenever you want. I knew you'd make a great son-in-law the moment I saw you, Eddie. I can't thank you enough for buying her a house near her mum. Look, Stanley, isn't it wonderful?'

Stanley glanced at the piece of paper and nodded dumbly. As much as he hated Eddie, he was pleasantly surprised by this strange turn of events. Knowing Eddie's type, he'd have fully expected him to whisk Jessica miles away from him and Joycie.

'A young girl needs to be near her mum and dad. That's what families are all about,' Eddie said, smiling at Stan.

'Don't expect me to come round and change shitty nappies, will you, sis?' Raymond said laughing.

Eddie ruffled Raymond's hair. Jessica's little bro was a proper character. In fact, he reminded Ed of himself at sixteen. Eddie allowed himself a wry smile. Neither Jess nor Ray were fuck-all like their father, so surely at least one of them had to belong to the milkman.

With the speeches and surprises all over, Eddie started to organise cabs to get to the reception.

As Joyce went off to powder her nose, Ivy shifted herself next to Stan. 'I know I said this earlier, but I really don't like him, Stan. Whatever was my Joycie thinking of, encouraging Jess to get involved with the likes of him?'

Stanley shook his head. 'I've no idea, but I'm glad it ain't just me. I don't trust him, Ivy. He's got eyes like dead fish.'

Ivy shuddered. She'd noticed Eddie's cold, calculating stare from the moment she'd set eyes on him and the thought of her beautiful granddaughter sharing her life and bed with him sent shivers down her spine.

'She won't find happiness with him, Stanley. I've seen his sort before. He'll mould Jess into what he wants and, before she knows it, he'll suck the fucking life out of her.'

# SEVEN

## *Seven years later – 1978*

Aware of the commotion in the back of her car, Jessica turned down the radio. 'Will you two stop mucking about while Mummy's trying to drive? What are you doing in the back?'

'Frankie's took one of my new trainers and she's put it out the window,' Joey said, trying to grab his sister's arm.

As she stopped at a red light, Jessica glanced around. 'You'd better not have thrown his trainer out, Frankie. Now where is it?'

'I haven't, Mum,' her daughter said, showing her the proof.

'Give it back to Joey, now,' Jess ordered.

Giggling, Frankie gave the trainer back to its rightful owner.

Jessica sighed as she turned up the radio volume. Her children certainly drove her doolally at times, but she loved them more than life itself. She'd been horrified when the doctor had first told her that she was expecting twins.

'I'm only seventeen, I'll never cope,' she had cried to Eddie.

Eddie had put his strong arms around her and washed

away her fears. 'You'll be a natural, Jess. Remember, we're in this together. I'll help out as much as I can and your mum'll be brilliant, I know she will.'

As usual, Eddie was right and, once she had got over the initial shock, Jess had never looked back. She remembered the day she'd given birth as though it was yesterday. The pain was unbearable and, due to the size of the babies and her small frame, the doctors had given her an emergency caesarean.

'We think the babies could be in trouble,' they had said.

Eddie and her mum had both been by her side when she'd finally come round. 'Where are the babies? Are they OK?' were her first words.

Eddie had tears in his eyes as he gently lifted them out of their cots. 'We've got one of each, Jess. A boy and a girl.'

As rough and sore as she felt, Jess could barely believe her luck. The twins were a decent weight and absolutely perfect. To be blessed with one of each was a sheer gift from God.

Eddie and Jessica had spoken about baby names for months leading up to the birth. They hadn't known what they were having, so they had chosen two names for a boy and two for a girl.

Francesca was Jessica's choice. She thought it was the prettiest name she'd ever heard. Eddie chose Joseph. He wanted the name to be a tribute to his deceased grandfather. Their names were shortened within the first few years of their lives. Everybody referred to them as Frankie and Joey. They adored one another, and everything they did, they did together.

Jessica's thoughts were interrupted by her son.

'Mum, I think I'm gonna be sick.'

Unable to find her usual supply of sick bags, Jessica urged him to try and hold on for a minute. 'Open the window, Joey. I can't stop in the middle of the A13. Let me get round this corner and I'll –'

The sound of retching mixed with the smell of sick stopped Jess in mid-sentence.

'Urgh! Mum, open the roof.' Frankie said, holding her head out of the window.

Spotting a lay-by, Jessica pulled over to inspect the damage. It was everywhere – all over Joey, the seats and the bloody carpet. With nothing but a box of tissues, Jess did her best to clean up both her son and the car. She daren't tell Ed. He'd only recently bought her the red Mercedes convertible as a birthday present and he wouldn't be impressed to know it was now covered in spew.

'Make sure you've got a sick bag with you when you take Joey out,' Ed insisted.

Jessica had carried a couple originally, but Joey had already used them and, with a brain like a sieve, she had forgotten to replace them.

'Now, come on, don't cry,' Jessica said, wiping away her son's tears.

Poor little sod, it wasn't his fault that he was a terrible traveller. Frankie loved being in the car and was fine, but Joey, unfortunately, was the opposite.

Jessica put down the roof and continued her journey towards Tesco. Her parents and brother were coming over this evening and she had promised to cook them a slap-up meal. She couldn't wait to show her dad and brother around her new house. Her mum had already visited and had fallen head over heels with it, but her dad and brother hadn't yet seen the finished article.

'Oh, Jess, it looks like a mansion. It reminds me of

71

one of them posh houses in them American films your father watches.'

Jessica was thrilled with her new surroundings. The house was any woman's dream. Eddie had had it built from scratch by some pals of his. He'd bought the land, got planning permission and, even though it had taken ages to finish, it was well worth the wait. The area, in the country lanes of Rainham, Essex, was perfect for the kids.

Before they had moved, they'd still lived in Upney, near Jessica's parents, and Eddie had hated the area. 'It's a fucking shit-hole round here, Jess. Now the kids are nearing school age, we need to move somewhere nicer,' he had told her a couple of years back.

Jessica had been reluctant to move at first but, within a month, Eddie had persuaded her. Eddie had forbidden Jessica to see the new house until it was all finished, and when she had, she was gobsmacked. Set in an acre of ground, it had four bedrooms, two bathrooms, a big dining room, a luxury lounge and the most enormous, modern kitchen she had ever seen.

Jessica whooped with delight when she saw the garden. Eddie had made it into a playground for the kids. They had swings, slides, a trampoline, and he'd even had their own tree-house built for them.

'Well, what do you think?' he'd asked her.

'I absolutely love it. It's the nicest house I've ever seen in my life,' Jessica said, overwhelmed.

Eddie might be a rough diamond, but his good points definitely outweighed his bad. Jessica was sort of aware of how her husband earned his money, but she never asked any questions. Eddie had a dark side to him sometimes, especially when he drank Scotch. They were the times Jessica chose to forget. Many a time Ed's eyes would blacken and he'd lose his rag over the most trivial thing.

Jessica always forgave him. She loved him too much not to, but he did frighten her. He'd never hit her or anything like that, but there were occasions when she'd feared he would.

Overall though, Ed was a fantastic husband, a good dad and a wonderful provider. Jess had never wanted for anything since the day she'd met him and she had never seen him so much as glance at another woman. On the whole, their marriage was extremely happy and everyone had their faults, didn't they?'

'Mum, Mum, I need a wee-wee,' Joey said, snapping Jess out of her daydream.

Jessica quickly stopped the car. Her son had a weak bladder at the best of times.

'Go behind that bush over there,' she ordered.

Frankie laughed as her brother disappeared into the undergrowth. 'Joey is funny, isn't he, Mummy?'

Jessica ruffled her daughter's hair. Frankie and Joey might be twins, but in many ways they were chalk and cheese. They looked nothing like one another and their personalities were extremely different. Frankie had dark hair and was more like Eddie. She was a proper tomboy, a little daredevil, who would try anything once. Joey was the opposite. He had blond hair and was more like herself. He hated heights, was petrified of insects and cried every time he watched *Lassie*.

Eddie would get really annoyed with Joey sometimes. 'You're meant to be a boy. Stop acting like a fucking wimp,' he would shout at his son.

Jessica would comfort Joey, wipe away his tears, and then Eddie would have a go at her. 'You're to blame for the way he is. You mollycoddle the fucking kid. It's a hard life out there, Jess, and he needs to shape up before it's too late. Ricky and Gary were never like him, they

73

were proper little boys. Joey acts like a sissy and if you don't knock it out of him, then I fucking will.'

Jessica smiled as her son got back into the car. 'You OK now, love?'

Joey nodded. 'Can me and Frankie have an ice cream from the shop, Mum?'

'No, because you won't eat your dinner,' Jessica said sternly.

'Please, Mum, we promise we will eat our dinner,' Frankie whinged.

Jessica could never say no to her kids and both of them knew it. 'OK, but don't tell your dad,' she said.

Frankie and Joey locked eyes. 'Thank you, Mummy,' they said, smiling at one another.

In the heart of London's East End, tempers were starting to fray. As Eddie Mitchell stared at the shivering wreck of a man, he felt nothing but contempt. 'What do you mean, you ain't got the fucking money? You know the rules,' he shouted menacingly.

'I'm really sorry. My car broke down and I had to get that repaired, then my fridge-freezer went wrong. I'll pay you next week, I promise I will,' the man pleaded.

Eddie turned to his two brothers. 'What do you reckon lads? Should we give him another week or cut the cunt's ear off?'

Ronny Mitchell gave a sadistic grin. 'I don't think we should chop off his ear. How 'bout we do his little finger instead?'

The shivering man fell onto his knees. 'Please don't hurt me. You know my wife is ill, she's disabled. I had to get the car fixed to take her to the hospital. If you hurt me she'll have no one to look after her.'

As Ronny licked his lips and pulled the knife out of his

pocket, Eddie ordered him and Paulie to wait in the car. 'But I thought you wanted us to do him?' Ronny argued.

'Just get in the fucking car, will you?' Eddie yelled.

Hearing the front door slam, Eddie helped the man up and sat him on the sofa. 'The thing is, mate, I know that you're lying to me. You never got no car fixed or brought no fucking fridge-freezer. You spunked my money in the pub and the bookie's, didn't you?'

'No, I never. I swear I –'

Annoyed at being lied to, Eddie stopped the man in mid-sentence by grabbing him around his scrawny neck. 'Don't lie to me, you cunt, 'cause I'll kill you.'

The man started to sob. 'I'm sorry, I didn't mean to spend it. It's so hard looking after my Elaine, a drink and a bet is my only release.'

Eddie looked at the man with pure disgust. He knew for a fact that he fucked off out every day and left his poor disabled wife indoors to fend for herself. The grapevine was a funny old thing and there wasn't much went on that didn't reach his ears.

Eddie knelt down and moved his face inches away from the man. 'Now listen to me and listen very carefully. I'll waive the money you owe me, on one condition.'

'What? I'll do anything, I promise,' the man said.

'I want you to look after your wife properly. If I hear that you've left her sitting in her own piss and shit for hours while you're larging it in the pub or betting shop, I swear I'll come back and personally fucking cut you to shreds.'

The man started to sob. 'Thank you Mr Mitchell. You have my word.'

Over in Upney, Joycie Smith was busy showing her friends the new machine that Eddie and Jessica had bought her for her birthday.

Rita crouched down and stared at the object in question. 'What's it called again? And what does it do?'

'I've already told you twice. It's called a video recorder and you can record programmes off the telly and watch them at a later date.'

'But how can it do that?' Rita asked, bemused.

'You have to put a tape inside and pre-set it. I recorded *Corrie* the other night and I only watched it this morning.'

Hilda looked at her in awe. 'It's marvellous, ain't it? Bleedin' marvellous.'

Joyce went into her peacock mode. She could almost feel her feathers spreading out like a fan. 'It's modern technology, ain't it? Because Jessica and Eddie are so wealthy now, they know all about these things before anybody else does. You should see their new house – like a palace, it is.'

Hilda and Rita glanced at one another. They wouldn't upset Joycie for the world, but they'd already heard about Jessica's new house a thousand times before. So much so, the pair of them felt that they knew every tile, carpet and room inside out.

'Cooking a posh dinner tonight, my Jess is. All the family will be there. Me and Stan could have done without it, but Eddie adores us, insists that we come,' Joyce lied.

Bored as arseholes, Hilda furtively nudged her friend. Rita quickly clocked on and cleverly changed the subject.

'Where is your Stan? We haven't seen him for ages. My Arthur said he rarely goes down the bookie's any more.'

Joyce sighed. 'Out the back with them bleedin' pigeons of his. Thinks more of them birds than he does of me. Keeps talking about getting himself a new cock.'

Hilda and Rita roared with laughter. Eddie had bought Stanley his first racing pigeon a couple of years back and he'd been hooked from day one. Joyce had hated his new hobby from the word go, but had put up with it because it was Eddie's idea.

'Dirty bastard things they are. Full of shit me garden is and I'm sure it's them that's killed me roses,' Joyce moaned.

Rita smiled politely. 'Well, I suppose it gives Stanley an interest. The only interest my Arthur's got is the pub and the horses,' she moaned.

'Maybe you're right. My Stanley don't even bother going to the pub that much any more,' Joyce said proudly, knowing full well that Rita's Arthur was a borderline alcoholic.

Glancing at the clock, Joyce realised the time was getting on. 'Please don't think I'm being rude, but I'm gonna have to start sprucing meself up in a minute. Jess's mansion is in the country and it takes us about half-hour to get there. She's expecting us at seven, so I'd best get me skates on.'

Rita and Hilda immediately stood up. Talk about outstaying your welcome, they both thought.

'Thanks for the tea and cake. See you soon, Joycie,' Hilda said.

Joyce did her queen wave at the door. 'Don't forget, anything you want to watch, come and see me and I'll record it for you.'

Slamming the front door, Joyce marched into the back garden. 'Stanley, stop cuddling your cock and get yourself bathed and changed.'

'Just give me ten minutes, dear, and I'll be with you,' Stanley said.

'No, Stanley. Put your cock away now, pronto.'

# EIGHT

'So when is that cheeky old cunt gonna pay up then?' Ronny asked Eddie.

Eddie pulled into the pub car park. 'Next week. I'll go round and collect it myself,' he lied.

'Ain't you coming in for a quickie?' Paulie asked him.

Eddie shook his head. 'Got the in-laws coming round for dinner. I promised Jess I'd be home early.'

Eddie sighed as his two brothers walked away. He daren't tell Paulie and Ronny that he'd just wiped the geezer's debt. They wouldn't understand his reasons, they'd think he'd lost his marbles. It was only a monkey and Ed would rather ensure that the disabled wife was properly cared for than worry about a pittance.

Financially, Eddie was doing very nicely indeed and five hundred quid was no more than loose change to him. It hadn't always been plain sailing. When his dad had first retired and handed him the reins a few years back, he'd worked his plums off to get where he was now.

Becoming a loan shark had never entered Eddie's mind, but with the pub protection game becoming harder than ever, he'd sort of fallen into it by accident. A chance meeting with an old pal of his, who was coining it in, had put the idea in his head. Obviously, he'd consulted his father first. Although Harry had retired by then, Eddie still looked to him as head of the family and respected his wisdom.

Within months of becoming a loan shark, business was booming. They lent to any bastard they could. Businessmen, builders, milkmen, dustmen: as long as they could afford their weekly repayments and agreed to the hefty interest charges, they could borrow.

With the Mitchells' reputation, the majority of their clients paid up on time, and it was an easy life compared to smashing up boozers. There were the odd one or two who needed time to pay, or a couple of clever dicks who tried to knock them, but they always got their dough back eventually. A bullet lodged in the kneecap or the odd finger chopped off always seemed to do the trick and, like magic, their money would reappear within days. 'Abrafuckingcadabra,' Eddie would say, laughing his head off.

Both Paulie and Ronny had had their noses put out of joint when their father had retired and insisted on Eddie taking control. But their whingeing fell on deaf ears.

'I make the decisions in this fucking family and if I decide that Eddie's the man to take over, then that's how it's gonna be. If yous two don't like it, tough shit – you know what you can do,' their dad told them bluntly.

Eddie could sense the resentment, especially Ronny's, at the way things had turned out. Eddie was the baby of the family and should have been bottom of the pecking order. Now a couple of years on, all was forgiven. Eddie's loan-shark idea had turned up trumps and made him and his brothers very wealthy indeed. They still did a bit of pub protection here and there, but a lot of boozers had been bought by bigger breweries, so they just stuck with their remaining handful of privately owned ones. Uncle

Reg was still working with them but, due to health problems, was on the verge of retiring. His walking was giving him gyp, and he was waiting to see a specialist. The poor old sod could barely get about any more and he certainly didn't need the money, as he'd earned plenty over the years.

'Uncle Reg wants to pack it in, so I think we need to take someone else on,' Eddie had told his brothers only yesterday.

'We don't need anybody else. The three of us is more than enough,' Ronny insisted.

Eddie disagreed. They needed a bit of young blood and he had just the right person in mind. All Ronny was worried about was his wallet. He was a greedy bastard and wouldn't want to share out any of his profits. Ronny had recently bought a house and moved in with Sharon, and all he did was brag about paying cash for it.

The Mitchell family still owned the salvage yard in Dagenham, but Harry had now sold off all the others. He'd made a handsome bit of dough on a couple of them. He'd flogged two to property developers and had come out with well over a million in profit.

Eddie put his foot down as he hit the A13. He'd recently treated himself to a Porsche 911 and loved the fact that its turbo engine left every other car on the road standing. He turned off at Barking and headed towards his old address. When he and Jessica had moved out, he'd allowed his ex, Beverley, and his two boys to move in. Gary and Ricky were now fourteen and twelve and had both been expelled from two schools in Canning Town, where they'd previously been living. Neither were particularly bad lads, but it had hit them hard when Eddie had left home. Without a man around they were forever getting into scrapes and fights, and trouble seemed to follow them.

Beverley had been an awkward bitch to deal with when Eddie had first remarried. She had stopped the boys going to the wedding, and many a time she had cancelled arrangements when Ed was supposed to be having them for the weekend.

Eddie had wanted to kill her with his bare hands on many occasions, but in the end he'd done the sensible thing and hit her where it hurt. 'I've got a right to see my boys every weekend and take 'em away in the summer. You'll not get another penny out of me, Bev, until you agree to my terms,' he'd told her.

It had almost killed him knowing that his kids were going without, but he had to be cruel to be kind. Bev held out for two months, then one day turned up in the Flag begging for money and forgiveness. Eddie had had regular contact with his boys ever since. He kept to his word and always saw Bev all right. Most of the money he gave her, she spunked on alcohol and takeaways. She'd only been eight stone when he'd first met her and now she weighed eighteen.

Eddie pulled up outside his old house. He always picked the boys up on a Friday and took them back home on the Sunday. They were doing much better at school since they'd moved to Barking and they loved spending their weekends at his new house.

'You got all your stuff? Where's your mother?' Eddie asked them.

'She's drunk. She's been drinking cider all day and she's asleep on the sofa,' Ricky said, giggling.

Eddie ordered the boys to go and sit in the car. Annoyed, he marched in the house and woke Beverley up.

'Whaddya want?' she asked, bleary-eyed.

'There's your money,' Eddie said, throwing an envelope at her. 'Look at the state of yourself, Bev. No wonder them boys have got problems, seeing you like this every day.'

Beverley sat up. 'I do my best. Anyway, what do you care? All you're bothered about is the wonderful fucking Jessica and your twins.'

Eddie shook his head. 'I wouldn't be letting you live here rent free if I weren't fucking bothered. Drop the bitter act, Bev, it don't suit you, love, and take my advice – sort yourself out before it's too late.'

Beverley burst into tears. She knew she'd let herself go and didn't need Ed to tell her. 'Go on, fuck off home to your other family and leave me alone!' she screamed.

Eddie stormed out and slammed the front door. There was no reasoning with Bev when she was pissed, so he might as well save his breath.

'Can we go in the swimming pool when we get there, Dad?' Gary asked.

'Not tonight, son. We've got guests coming over for dinner, but you can muck about in there all day tomorrow, if you want.'

Eddie smiled as he listened to the boys gabble away in the back. Since he'd married Jess he'd turned into a proper family man. He loved nothing more than spending his weekends with his beautiful wife and children. Over seven years they'd been married now, and he'd never so much as looked at another woman in that time. Marrying Jessica was one of the best decisions Ed had ever made and he worshipped the ground that she walked on. Like any other couple, they had their rows. Eddie knew he could be a Victorian bastard at times and, overall, Jessica suffered him well.

'Look, Dad. That house you always tell us to look at has got a sold sign up.'

Wondering if Gary had got it wrong, Ed swung the

Porsche around and drove back to be nosy. 'Fuck me, you're right son,' he said mystified.

The house in question was a beauty and, unlike his own, had needed nothing doing to it at all. Eddie had tried to buy the place himself. He had viewed it, but the price was way over the top. The owner lived abroad and wanted well over a quarter of a million for it. Ed had tried to barter with him, but the geezer was having none of it. The house had much more ground than the one Eddie had bought, at least another couple of acres.

Eddie turned the car back round and sped towards home. That house had been on the market for a couple of years and he was desperate to make a few phone calls, see if he could find out who had finally landed it.

'What are you doing, Stanley? You've done a left, ain't you meant to have done a right back there?'

Stanley glared at his wife. The only thing she had ever driven in her life was him – bloody mad. 'I do know where I'm going, dear. I have been here before, remember?'

Recognising certain landmarks, Joyce guessed that for once, her husband was right. 'Miserable old goat,' she mouthed to Raymond, who was sitting quietly in the back.

Raymond ignored his mum and stared out of the open window. His parents drove him crazy and he'd taught himself to switch off from them. He felt a bit sorry for his dad sometimes. His mum ruled his old man's life, but it was his own fault, as he should have put his foot down years ago. Raymond rested his head against the seat. The evening sun and cool breeze felt lovely against his skin. He shut his eyes, deep in thought.

Eddie had rung him earlier at the scrapyard. He'd told him to make sure he definitely came tonight, as he wanted to have a chat with him about work.

'Don't worry, you ain't done nothing wrong. What I've got to say is all good,' Eddie assured him.

Raymond had been employed by Eddie since he was eighteen years old and he'd always worked bloody hard. He had left school at sixteen with medium qualifications and high hopes of getting a record deal with his band. It hadn't happened and, with his dreams shattered, Raymond had given up his music career and taken on a job as a trainee butcher. From the word go, he hated the job. The smell was disgusting, the sawdust they put on the floor got down his throat and the sight of dead animals turned his guts. Listening to his complaints one day, Eddie had offered him a lifeline.

'I need someone to work in the salvage yard. I'll give you the address – go down there first thing Monday morning and ask for Pete. I'll tell him to expect you.'

Raymond had started work there that day and had never looked back since. He no longer resembled a skinny little rock star. The physical nature of the job had given him muscles he had never known existed. His mother had been embarrassing him lately whenever her friends came round.

'Look at my Raymond. Six foot tall and built like a brick shithouse, ain't he?' she'd say proudly. 'Nothing like his father.'

'Left here and then left again, Stanley,' Joyce yelled, making Raymond jump out of his skin.

Annoyed at yet again being told what to do, Stanley drove the Cortina along his daughter's drive at speed and then slammed his foot on the brake. Seeing Joyce's head nearly hit the dashboard, he chuckled as he got out.

'You silly old bastard, you've nearly bloody killed me. I bet I've got whiplash now because of you.'

Holding the door open for his wife, Stanley winked at

Raymond. 'I'm so sorry, dear. It's these new shoes you bought me, my foot must have slipped.'

As Frankie and Joey ran out to greet their nan, Joyce's whiplash was forgotten.

'Hello, my babies. Give your nanna a big kiss.'

Joey clung to one of her hands and Frankie the other. 'Have you brought us any presents, Nanny?' Frankie asked bluntly.

'Yep, but you can't have them till after your dinner.'

Playfully scolding her daughter, Jessica welcomed her family. 'So lovely to see you all. Cheekier by the day, my Frankie's getting. Take no notice of her,' she laughed.

Once inside the house, Joyce took it upon herself to give her husband and son the grand tour. Both of them had seen the house before, but not in its finished state. 'Look at the downstairs bathroom – marble them tiles are. Handsome, aren't they?'

Barely giving them a chance to look, Joyce dragged Stanley and Raymond into the lounge. 'Look at that chandelier, Stanley. Ain't it beautiful, Raymond? Cost an absolute fortune that did. Pure crystal, it is – ain't it, Jess?'

Hearing her husband come down from upstairs, Jessica quickly changed the subject. 'We're in the lounge. Can you get everybody a drink, Ed?'

Eddie beamed as he kissed Joyce and shook hands with both Stanley and Raymond.

'Sorry, I was on the phone, I didn't know you'd all arrived. Now, what can I get you?'

'I'll just have a lager, Ed,' Raymond said immediately.

'Can I have a sherry?' Joyce asked, with a silly giggle.

Eddie smiled at Stanley. 'I've got a nice twenty-year-old Scotch for me and you to crack open, Stan.'

'Lovely,' Stanley said, rubbing his hands together.

'You don't want that, Stanley. Scotch is too strong for you. Why don't you just have a beer?' Joyce piped up.

'He'll be fine having a drop of Scotch, Joyce. Jessica's made up the guest room for yer. Stan ain't gotta drive, has he?' Ed said, sticking up for him.

Not wanting to behave like an old dragon in front of Eddie, Joyce forced a smile. 'Go on then, but take it easy, Stanley. I don't want you getting drunk and showing me up, like you have in the past.'

'Can I sit on your lap, Grandad?' Joey asked him.

Stanley smiled as his grandson plonked himself on his lap. He loved the twins and prided himself on being a good grandad. He'd often taken them out for days with Joyce. They'd go for picnics, trips to the zoo and he'd teach them how to fly his pigeons.

It was just after the twins were born that Stanley had decided to make an effort with Eddie. Joyce had dragged him up the hospital and, as soon as he'd first laid eyes on Frankie and Joey, he'd gone all gooey, into grandad mode. Not wanting to miss out on their childhood, he'd had little choice other than to be polite to their father. It was hard at first, but over the years, he'd sort of got used to it.

As much as Stanley hated to admit it, Eddie did have some good points. He always stuck up for Stan when Joyce put her two penn'orth in, he'd given Raymond a half-decent job and he spent every weekend with Jessica and the children.

'Cheers, Stan,' Eddie said, handing him his Scotch.

Stanley thanked Eddie and watched him walk away. He could never go as far as to say he actually liked him or trusted him, but he'd learned to make the best out of a bad situation. Eddie was OK, in a very-small-dose kind of way.

Eddie lifted up Frankie and swung her around above his head. 'You ain't heard who's bought that big white house, have you, Jess?' he asked.

'Put me down, Daddy,' Frankie said giggling.

Jessica smiled at him. 'What, that massive place down the road here?'

'Yeah, that's the one. I've just made a few phone calls, but no one knows who's got it.'

Hearing a commotion out the back, Jessica stood up. 'I'll ask down the school, see if anyone knows. Ed, you'd better go out in the garden. Gary and Ricky are fully clothed in that swimming pool, they're fighting with one another, I think.'

Stanley and Joyce both looked at one another in horror. They didn't agree on much in life, but the one thing they both thought was what uncontrollable, rude little toerags Eddie's eldest sons were.

'I'm just gonna check on the meat,' Jessica said brightly.

Joyce stood up and looked out the back. 'I didn't know them little bastards were gonna be here,' she said to Stan.

Frankie smiled. 'What is a bastard, Nanny?'

Stanley stood up and picked up his granddaughter. 'Basket, Frankie. Nanny said she didn't know Mummy had a basket here.'

Hearing the voices of Gary and Ricky, Stanley handed Frankie to Joyce. 'I dunno about you Joycie, but I most certainly need another drink.'

Joyce smiled with rare affection at her husband. 'Me too, and make it a large one, Stanley.'

# NINE

Eddie carved up the roast beef, while his wife brought in the side dishes.

'I'll just serve up a little plate for Frankie and Joey and the rest of yous can help yourselves,' Jessica said.

Making sure everybody had enough meat on their plates, Eddie opened a couple of bottles of wine. 'Who wants red and who wants white?' he asked.

'I'll have red, but just a small one,' Joyce giggled. She'd already had three glasses of sherry and was feeling a little bit tipsy.

'Can me and Gary have a drop of wine, Dad?' Ricky asked innocently.

Still annoyed with his sons for arsing about in the swimming pool when he'd blatantly told them not to, Eddie glared at his middle son. 'No, you can't, and don't be so bloody cheeky.'

Ricky scowled and nudged his brother. 'Mum lets us have a drink indoors, don't she, Gary?'

'Well, I'm not your mother and you're not indoors now. You're in my house and you abide by my rules. As for your mother letting you drink alcohol, I'll be having a little word with her about that. Now, shut up the pair of you and eat your fucking dinner.'

Desperate to change the subject, Jessica picked up one of the dishes. 'More roast potatoes anyone?' she asked.

'I'll have some, sis,' Raymond said, grinning.

Joyce pointed towards Stanley. 'Your father will have a couple more as well,' she told Jess.

As the potatoes were put on his plate, Stanley looked up in amazement. He had obviously spoken without him moving his mouth.

Joey slid off his chair. 'Don't want no more, Mummy.'

Jessica looked at his plate. He'd barely touched a morsel. She knew she shouldn't have let him eat that ice cream he'd pleaded for earlier.

'Try and eat some more, darling, see if you can eat as much as your sister.'

Joey shook his head. 'I don't feel well, I got tummy-ache,' he lied.

Eddie shook his head as his youngest son left the table. All of his kids were good eaters, bar Joey, who was a finicky little waif. 'He'll be ill, that kid, if he don't start eating more. You wanna get him up the doctor's, find out what's wrong with him,' Eddie told Jess.

Jessica shrugged. 'He's OK, he's just fussy, that's all. He wasn't well earlier, maybe that's why.'

Frankie smiled as she took her brother's Yorkshire pudding off his plate. 'Joey was sick all over Mummy's new car,' she said, giggling.

Eddie looked at Jess in horror. 'He weren't, was he?'

Jessica stood up and began to clear the dinner plates. 'It wasn't his fault, Ed. I forgot to put some bags in there for him. The poor little sod can't help being travel sick.'

Eddie wanted to say plenty, but instead said nothing. A fortune he'd paid for that Mercedes convertible and already it must smell like a fucking hospital ward.

'Who wants dessert? I've got Black Forest gateau or fresh strawberries and ice cream,' Jessica asked gaily.

'I'll have some strawberries, love,' Stanley replied.

Joyce snatched the empty dish out of his hand. 'No, he won't. Fruit gives him terrible wind and I've got to sleep next to him tonight,' she told Jess.

Eddie burst out laughing. How poor old Stanley put up with Joyce, he would never know. He stood up. 'Come on Stan, I'll take you outside and show you me new car. We can go for a quick spin in it if you like?'

Stanley grinned. He'd always been a Ford man himself, believed in buying the best of British, but he wouldn't say no to a ride in that Porsche. Apart from his pigeons and horse racing, cars were his only other real passion. He leaped up from the dining table. 'I'm ready when you are, Ed.'

'You coming with us, Ray?' Eddie asked.

'No, Uncle Raymond. We want you to see Milky the Cow,' Frankie said, with her hands on her hips.

'Please don't go, Uncle Raymond,' Joey begged.

With two pairs of pleading eyes desperate for his company, Raymond decided to stay put.

'We'll have that chat when I get back,' Eddie told him.

Stanley followed Eddie out of the front door. 'What were the kids on about? Have you got a cow out the back?'

Eddie started to laugh. Stan didn't have a clue, bless his cotton socks. 'No, course not. They're talking about their new toys – Milky, the Marvellous Milking Cow. Drove me mad for 'em, they did. All the toy shops had sold out and I spent a whole day driving around looking for 'em. I got two in the end, had to drive all the way to Southend to pick the bastard things up. The things you do for kids, eh?'

Stanley said nothing. Eddie was a good dad, a good husband, but there was still something very sinister about him that Stan couldn't put his finger on.

Hearing the front door slam, Joyce and Jessica grinned at one another. No words were needed, but both of them were absolutely thrilled that Stanley and Eddie had got over their little differences and become friends.

'Is it OK if me and Ricky go out the back and play football? We won't go near the swimming pool, I promise.'

Jessica ruffled Gary's hair. 'Of course you can. Mind the flowerbeds, though.'

Joyce helped Jessica take the dirty dishes into the kitchen. 'I'll wash up for you, love,' Joyce insisted.

Jessica giggled. 'There's no need, Mum, I've got a dishwasher.'

Joyce looked at the metal machine with interest. She'd heard about dishwashers, but had never seen one up close before. 'You sure it cleans them properly, Jess? I mean, it ain't like human hands, is it?'

'Of course it cleans them properly. Now, if you wanna make yourself useful, Mum, pour us both another drink.'

Frankie poked her head around the kitchen door. 'Grandma, where's our presents? It's after dinner now.'

Topping up her glass with sherry, Joyce followed Frankie into the living room. She delved into her big black shopping bag. 'Here we go. You've got a jamboree bag each and me and Grandad clubbed together and bought you both a new toy.'

'What is it? Can we have it now?' the twins asked excitedly.

'Have the jamboree bag now and as soon as Grandad gets back, you can have your toys.'

'Oh, I want mine now,' Frankie said, sulking.

'Do as Nanny says,' Jessica shouted sternly.

Joey was a polite kid, but her daughter could be a stroppy little cow at times.

Ten minutes later, an ashen-faced Stanley walked back into the house, alone. 'Jesus Christ, drove like a lunatic, he did. Nearly killed us on that bend down the road there. I think I'm gonna bring me dinner up,' he moaned.

Raymond got himself a lager and poured his shell-shocked father a large Scotch. 'Eddie always drives fast. Get that down your neck, you'll be fine,' he told his dad.

As Stanley ran to the toilet and retched, Eddie was still sat in the car, laughing. Watching Stanley leap out looking like death warmed up and then stagger up the drive was one of the funniest things he'd ever seen. He knew deep down that Stanley only suffered him for the sake of the kids and driving like a maniac was payback time. Picturing Stan's face when he'd hit that bend, Eddie had to hold his bollocks to stop himself pissing on the seat. With his hand still clutched around his privates, Eddie walked towards the house. Unable to keep a straight face, he tried to think of something else.

'Dad feels ill – did you have to drive like a nutcase? He's just brought all his dinner up,' Jessica said angrily.

'Gotta go a loo,' Eddie said, running upstairs.

Locking the bathroom door, Eddie put his hand over his mouth. Stanley spewing his guts up had tipped him over the edge and, instead of just having the giggles, he was now on the verge of hysterics.

'Can we have our toys now?' Frankie asked impatiently.

'Grandad will give them to you,' Joyce said, handing them to her husband as he walked back into the room. Poor Stanley looked so ill, she wanted to lighten him up a bit. Remembering that he'd earlier jolted the car and nearly broken her neck, she quickly snatched them back from him.

'Nanny chose them so,on second thoughts, Nanny should give them to you,' she told the twins.

Having managed finally to compose himself, Eddie nodded to Raymond to follow him outside. 'Do you wanna cigar?' he asked him.

Raymond shook his head. 'No thanks, I'll have a fag.'

Staring at Raymond, Eddie put both hands on his shoulders and spoke in earnest. 'When I first gave you a job, Ray, I sort of did it for Jessica's sake. You were just a kid, her little brother, and I must admit, although I liked you, I had me doubts. Over the years you've proved me wrong. You've been honest, loyal, a real top-class employee. The thing is, Raymond, you're not a boy any more, you're now a man and that is why I want to offer you a handshake, a proper in.'

Raymond nodded. He'd learned to understand Eddie's lingo over the years and he knew exactly where the conversation was going.

Eddie smiled at him. 'My Uncle Reg is on the verge of retiring. We need another pair of hands and I want you to join the family properly. You're gonna be working with me, Paulie and Ronny. You're no fool, you know the set-up. What's your opinion on that?'

Unbeknown to Eddie, Raymond had been waiting for this moment for a long time. Unable to control his emotions, he grabbed the big man and hugged him.

'I'm honoured, Eddie, and I promise you faithfully that I will do you proud.'

Laughing, Eddie pushed him away and squared up to him. 'You'd better do me proud,' he said, as he lunged into a bit of play-fighting.

Gently pushing Raymond away, Eddie put his serious head on, once more. 'You won't be a gofer. You'll have a three-month trial, then you'll be on virtually the same cut as Paulie and Ronny are.'

Raymond could scarcely believe his luck. He'd prayed

for this day to happen and now it finally had. He could move out of his parents', buy his own property. If he played his cards right, the world could be his oyster. 'Thanks, Eddie. I'll do whatever you ask of me and I truly mean that.'

Eddie nodded. 'Good lad. Now, a few ground rules. You don't say a word to anyone about anything we do. Birds, mates, family – not a soul. If anyone asks, you're a debt collector.'

Raymond nodded. He understood perfectly.

Deep in thought, Eddie tilted his head. 'I think it's probably for the best that I lend you some dough and you get your own place. If any shit hits the fan, you don't want your parents involved, do you?'

'I've been wanting to leave home for ages anyway. I think the world of me mum and dad, but they do me head in,' Raymond said frankly.

'First thing on Monday, Ray, I'm gonna take you out, rent you somewhere and get you kitted out as well. Remember one golden rule: a man is always judged on what he wears. You've always got to look the part, wear good clobber. We'll go up Savile Row and get you a couple of suits from there.'

'Daddy, what are you doing out here? I want you to see my new toy.'

Eddie picked up Frankie and held her in his left arm. He held his right out to Raymond. 'Welcome to the family, son.'

After a couple more Scotches, Stanley's stomach had settled and he was now on the floor playing with the twins.

'What you got, then? What's Nanny and Grandad brought you?' Eddie said, kneeling down.

'I've got a Madame Alexander doll, and Joey's got a Tonka truck,' Frankie said proudly.

Eddie admired their gifts and, noticing Gary and Ricky sitting alone, he stood up and walked towards them. 'You all right, boys?'

'I'm OK,' Gary said.

'Me too,' said Ricky.

Eddie sat in between them and put an arm around each of them. He'd had the hump earlier when he couldn't find out who had brought the poxy house he'd wanted and he shouldn't have taken it out on them for having a dip. 'Sorry for shouting at you earlier. Listen, I'll do you a deal. Go and pour your old dad a drink and you can both have a can of lager.'

Gary smiled. 'Can we really?'

'Just the one, mind. Now move your arses, 'cause Daddy's thirsty.'

Eddie felt a pang of guilt as they ran excitedly from the room. They must feel left out sometimes with all the attention showered upon the twins. The poor little sods didn't have much of a home life and they were good kids at heart.

'Christ, you must have poured half the bottle in there,' Ed said to Gary, as he was handed a full glass of Scotch.

Urging the boys to sit down next to him, he told them about his plans for the following weekend. 'Grandad Harry is organising a surprise party for your Uncle Reg to celebrate his retirement, so we're going to that on Friday, and you know Pat Murphy who owns that old converted farmhouse not far from here?'

Ricky looked bemused, but Gary nodded. 'Is that the man you took us to see, he used to be a boxer?'

'Yep, that's the one. Well, every year he has this big bank-holiday party, where he invites all his family, all his mates and the neighbours. Well, as we're neighbours now, we've got an invite. I've never been before, but it's meant to be the bollocks. He has everything there, rides for the kids, a boxing ring, there's a barbecue, a disco. It's next Sunday, so do yous boys fancy it?'

'Yeah. Can I have a go at the boxing?' Gary asked.

'Me too. I wanna box as well,' Ricky said.

Eddie gently banged their heads together. 'Only if you behave yourselves in between.'

'We will, we promise,' they both said.

Gary and Ricky both loved boxing. Eddie had sent them up to Peacock Gym in Canning Town at quite a young age and they were both good little prospects, according to their trainer.

Hyped up, Gary and Ricky went out the back to practise their sparring.

'What party's that, then?' Jessica asked, sitting down next to Eddie.

'Pat Murphy's. The kids will love it. He has clowns, all sorts of entertainment for them, it'll give you a chance to meet some of the other wives as well. Next Sunday, it is.'

Jessica squeezed his hand. He was such a softie, her Ed. A real family man. 'It sounds wonderful. Roll on next week,' she said, kissing him gently.

'Mum, Dad, Joey won't give me my new doll back,' Frankie whinged.

Seeing his son cradle the doll, Eddie bent down and snatched it away from him. 'The Tonka truck's yours. Boys don't play with dolls, Joey.'

Lip trembling, Joey looked at his father. 'Sorry, Daddy.'

Eddie put on some music and the rest of the evening swam by.

'Do you want my body, am I really sexy?' Joyce sang, getting all Rod Stewart's lyrics wrong.

Aware that she was pointing at him, Stanley turned his back. 'Don't start all that, Joycie, will yer?'

Not used to drinking large amounts of alcohol, Joyce felt her legs go from under her. 'Oh dear, I think I'm drunk,' she said, as she clung on to the sofa for dear life.

'Are you OK, Mum?' Jessica said, helping her up.

'Yes, dear. Actually, I feel wonderful.'

Embarrassed, as he'd never witnessed either of his parents so pissed before, Raymond jumped into action. 'I think we should all call it a night now and get some shut-eye. Give me a hand, Dad, to help Mum up the stairs.'

Used to being told what to do, Stanley jumped to order. 'Goodnight all,' he yawned.

Eddie winked at Raymond. 'I hope the sofa's comfortable enough for ya. I'll put the kids to bed and we'll speak again in the morning,' he said.

The twins were crashed out on the floor, so Jessica lifted up Joey and Eddie grabbed Frankie. 'Where's Gary and Ricky?' she asked.

Eddie laughed. 'I told 'em they could have one can of lager and I'm sure the little bastards had about three. I had to help them into bed about an hour ago. I put 'em in Joey's room.'

Jessica giggled. It had been their first proper get-together in their new home and she had loved every single minute of it.

Whether it was due to the amount of sherry she'd drunk, Joyce wasn't sure, but for the first time in years, she felt amorous. 'Stanley, wake up,' she said, poking her husband in the ribs.

Receiving no response, she moved her hand around a bit. 'Stanley,' she said seductively.

Aware of a hand around his cobblers, Stanley jumped up like a bush kangaroo. 'What the fuck! What are you doing, woman? Have you gone mad?'

Jessica just happened to be passing the guest room as her father bolted out in his Y-fronts.

'Whatever's the matter?' she asked, noticing his shocked expression.

Stanley held his hand over his parcel. 'It's your mother – she's having a funny turn.'

'What, is she ill?' Jessica said, panicking.

'No, not that kind of funny turn,' Stanley said, embarrassed.

Realising what had happened, Eddie grabbed Jessica and dragged her into their bedroom. Hysterical, he could barely speak for laughing.

'Your mother's after a bunk-up.'

'Oh, don't say that,' Jessica said, mortified.

Hearing raised voices, Jessica poked her head around the bedroom door.

'I mean it, Joycie, if you touch me again in that way, I'll go and sleep downstairs in the armchair,' she heard her father say.

Hand over her mouth, Jessica stood in stupefied shock. 'I can't believe it,' she said to Eddie.

Unable to stop laughing, Eddie grabbed her and threw her onto the bed. 'You are so naive, Jessica Mitchell, and do you know what? I fucking well love you for it.'

# TEN

After dropping his two boys home early on Sunday evening, Eddie shot up to the Flag for a prearranged meet with his dad, brothers and uncle.

As he explained that he'd offered Raymond a place in the family firm, Ronny flew into one of his tantrums. 'He's a fucking outsider. How do you know he ain't a grass? He could rob us blind for all you know,' he screamed at Eddie.

Harry Mitchell did his best to defuse the situation. He took Ronny outside the pub and, knowing the best way to handle his son, spoke to him gently and respectfully.

'Look, Ronny, I know you've got your doubts about Ed taking on someone new, but he knows what he's doing. Raymond's no stranger to us. He's been working for Eddie on the scrap for years and seeing as he's Jessica's brother, he's got family ties with us, ain't he?'

'But I don't wanna share my cut of the profits. The fact is, Dad, we don't need anybody else, especially a fucking kid,' Ronny argued.

Harry put an arm around his shoulder. 'Look, Raymond's only on trial at first. Chances are, he might not be what Eddie's looking for and it won't work out anyway. If you're concerned about him being young and wet behind the ears, have a word with Eddie, get him to set up a task, see if Raymond's cut out for our line of work.'

The fact that his dad was taking him seriously for once was enough to make Ronny calm down. 'Maybe you're right, Dad. Testing the cunt out ain't such a bad idea. There's a couple of people been fucking around with us lately. That big skinhead geezer, Mad Dave, owes us a lot of wedge and ain't breaking his neck to pay it back. How about if the wonderful Raymond pays him a visit? Mad Dave's about six foot three. He's a massive bastard, with arms like tree trunks. Let's see how the dear little apprentice pits his wits against him, eh?'

Harry led his son back inside the pub. 'Don't rub Eddie up the wrong way now. Just put your idea forward sensibly,' he urged Ronny.

Eddie sat in silence as he listened to Ronny's plan.

'I think it's a great idea,' Paulie said immediately.

Reg glanced at Eddie and shrugged. 'I suppose even if the kid gets a pasting, it'll show us what he's made of.'

Eddie shook his head. 'For fuck's sake, Raymond's only twenty-three – can't we test him out on someone else? Making him confront Mad Dave on his tod is like slinging him into a cage of starved lions.'

Looking at his dad for support, Eddie was surprised when, for once, he didn't receive any.

'I was thrown in at the deep end when I was a lad. Never did me any harm,' Harry said honestly.

Aware that he was alone in fighting Raymond's corner, Eddie had no choice other than to agree to the ridiculous idea.

'Fine, it that's what everyone wants, then I'll sort it,' he said.

\*   \*   \*

100

Unaware of the big task he had coming his way, Raymond was up a 5 a.m. the following Monday morning.

'Christ, what's up with you? Shit the bed or something?' Stanley asked, as his son plonked himself down opposite him.

'I'm just really excited, Dad. Starting me new job today, ain't I? Couldn't sleep last night at all, so I thought I'd get up and pester you before you went to work.'

Stanley offered his son a piece of toast. 'What's this job all about then? I know you said you're going to be debt collecting, but what sort of people are you going to be dealing with?'

'I don't know yet. Eddie's picking me up at nine. He's taking me out to buy me some good clothes. He says I have to look the part for this kind of job.'

Suddenly losing his appetite, Stanley threw his toast in the bin and turned away from his overly enthusiastic son. He didn't like the sound of this new job, not one little bit and he feared for the safety of Raymond.

Stanley buttoned his shirt up and put on his uniform jacket. He sat down opposite Raymond and shook his hand. 'Good luck, son. I hope it all goes well for you, but will you promise me one thing?'

'What's that, Dad?'

'Promise me if the job turns out to be dangerous in any way, you'll walk away and look for something else.'

Raymond nodded. His father was such an old stick-in-the-mud, but he meant well. 'I promise, Dad,' he said untruthfully.

Whether the job was dangerous or not, Raymond had no intention of walking away from it. He had been waiting for an opportunity like this all his life, and he would do literally anything to impress Eddie and secure his place in the family firm.

'Goodbye son, see you tonight,' Stanley shouted.

Raymond sighed as his father shut the front door. How he could sit on that stinking bus every day, being abused by schoolchildren, Ray would never know. It was watching the old man come home moaning about his job every night that had given Raymond the determination to make something of his own life. He loved his dad dearly, but would rather die than end up like him.

'Morning, darling. I'm so excited for you. Now, let your old mum cook you a nice bit of egg and bacon. You need to keep your strength up if you're gonna be working with Eddie and his brothers.'

Raymond shook his head. 'Thanks, Mum, but I've already eaten. I haven't had a bath yet, so I'd best go and get meself ready.'

Joyce smiled as he bolted upstairs. Her Raymond working with Eddie and his brothers had made her the proudest mother in the universe and she couldn't wait to tell her friends. Hilda and Rita would be so jealous. Both their sons had crappy jobs and not much to show for their lives. Raymond had always been far too intelligent to end up like them.

Eddie picked Raymond up at nine on the dot. 'I've found you a flat. It belongs to a mate of mine who's doing a bit of bird. It's fully furnished and he only wants a score a week rent. I'll take you there now, it's in Dagenham, and it's only ten minutes away from me and Jess.'

Eddie said very little as Raymond walked around the flat and studied the joint. It was very basic, but clean and certainly liveable.

'Whaddya think?' Eddie asked, once Ray had looked in every room.

'Yeah, it's OK. Beats listening to me parents argue,' Raymond said bluntly.

'Once you find your feet, you can get yourself somewhere better. It'll do you until then, though. Get your stuff packed up tonight and I'll pick you up in the morning and help you move in,' Eddie told him.

Raymond looked at Eddie in amazement. He hadn't expected things to move this quickly; he thought he'd be moving in a month or so. He hadn't even told his parents that he was leaving home yet. 'It's a bit quick, ain't it, Ed? Can't I move in in a couple of weeks? It'll give me more time to sort stuff out.'

Eddie shook his head. 'If you're gonna be working with me, you definitely need your own space. Too many eyes, too many questions, Raymond.'

Raymond nodded. He could hardly argue with Eddie, could he now? He forced a smile. 'Tomorrow it is, then.'

The next step was Savile Row, where Eddie forked out on two suits, four shirts, three ties and a pair of black leather shoes. Eddie had known the guy who owned the tailor's shop for years.

'Seeing as my family are your best customers, how quick can you get one of them suits altered for me?' he asked.

'It'll be done by tomorrow afternoon, Mr Mitchell,' came the owner's reply.

'There's nothing like people showing you a bit of respect, Raymond. One day that will be you, son,' Eddie said, as he guided him towards a posh restaurant.

With the menu written in French, Raymond urged Eddie to order for the both of them.

'And bring over a bottle of your finest champagne as well,' Eddie told the waiter.

Sipping the bubbly, Eddie and Raymond chatted about Jessica and the kids until their food arrived.

Raymond, who was by now starving, bolted his down within minutes. 'Nice bit of grub, ain't it, Ed?'

Eddie laughed. 'It's OK, I've had better.'

Already loving his new life, Raymond gladly accepted the offer of another bottle of champagne.

Clearing his throat, Eddie decided it was time to drop the bombshell. In detail, he explained the conversation he'd had with his family and the task Raymond had been given.

'So where do I find this Mad Dave?' Raymond asked immediately.

'He owns a two-bob car lot on an industrial estate in Leyton. He's in a right remote spot at the back of it. There's a young bird works for him, calls herself his secretary, but really he's shafting her behind his old woman's back. I can't remember the bird's name, but she's about eighteen, a single mum and she leaves at three to pick her kid up from school. Mad Dave ain't got many friends – horrible cunt he is – so chances are, once she's gone, he'll definitely be on his Jack Jones.'

'How much does he owe you?' Raymond asked calmly.

Eddie was pleased, but also quite taken aback by the kid's attitude. He seemed keen to pass the task and Ed hoped that it wasn't just the champagne talking.

'Eight grand he's fucked me over for. He brought a load of hooky motors off of me. He owed ten altogether, but he paid back two, then he came out with some cock and bull about the Old Bill nicking the cars off him. It's a load of old bollocks, I know it is, but he's been fobbing me off ever since. I try and be fair with people, Ray, but I'll be honest with you, if I still hadn't got me dough by the end of this month, I was gonna do the cunt meself.'

'Can I take something with me to use if I need to?' Raymond asked.

'I'll give you something to carry. I've got a cosh, a baseball bat – you can take whatever you want. Anyway, you ain't gotta worry. Me and the boys will sit just outside the gate. Any agg, we'll be there like a shot, mate.'

Raymond smiled. He'd never suffered from having a nervous disposition and he wasn't about to get one now. He needed this job and he would do whatever he had to, to prove his worth. 'I've got me own tool, I'll use that, and thanks anyway, but I'm sure I won't need any help.'

Eddie was stunned by the boy's coolness. 'Be warned, Ray, Mad Dave's a big old lump. A wanker he is, but a pushover he ain't.'

Smiling, Raymond topped up both of their glasses. 'To me and Mad Dave. May the best man win, eh?'

Two days later, all Savile Rowed up, Raymond sat in the back of a white transit van alongside Eddie, Ronny and Paulie. Uncle Reg had donned his check cap and pipe, and had offered his services to drive.

'I wore this just in case we were seen. I look like some OAP on a jolly boys' outing, no one's gonna clock us with me driving,' he laughed.

'So you're ready to play with the big boys are you, Ray?' Ronny asked sarcastically.

Raymond could tell immediately that Ronny didn't want him in the firm and was determined to prove him wrong. 'More than ready,' he answered politely.

'Next on your right, Reg. You know where it is, don't you? Straight down the bottom of that road.'

'Don't worry, I know I've semi-retired meself, but I ain't fucking senile yet,' Reg said jokingly.

Ronny nudged Paulie as they pulled up outside Mad Dave's appalling-looking car site. 'I'd love to be a fly on the wall, wouldn't you?' he whispered.

Paulie ignored him. Whatever the end result, this kid had bigger bollocks than most.

'What tool did you bring?' Eddie asked, as he opened the back door.

From nowhere, Raymond pulled out the biggest butcher's knife Eddie had ever seen. 'Fucking hell. Where did you get that from?'

'I used to be a butcher, didn't I? And I know exactly how to use it. Now, are you sure his bird's gone home?'

Eddie urged Reg to poke his head around the gate.

'She drives a light-blue Ford Fiesta and parks it just on the right as you go in.'

Within seconds, Reg hobbled back, giving the thumbs up.

Ronny sat quietly as Raymond stepped out of the van and strolled into the car lot like he owned the place. Flash little cunt, I hope he comes unstuck, he thought to himself.

With the knife tucked firmly down the inside of his jacket, Raymond spotted the Portakabin and marched straight in.

Mad Dave was sat on a black leather chair. He had his feet on a wooden desk, a beer in one hand and a copy of the *Sun* newspaper in the other. 'Can I help you?' he said, without properly looking up.

'Yes, you can. I work for Eddie Mitchell and I'm here on his behalf to collect the eight thousand pound that you owe him.'

Mad Dave took a large gulp of beer, burped, then threw his head back with laughter. 'You're 'aving a giraffe, ain't yer, mate? So you're telling me that that mug Eddie Mitchell has sunk so low in his fuckin' business empire that's he's sent some teenage kid round to threaten me?'

Raymond grinned. 'I'm not a teenage kid and I'm not threatening you. I'm just asking for the dosh that you owe.'

Mad Dave cracked open another beer and downed it

within seconds. 'Do yourself a favour, kid, and fuck off home,' he told Raymond.

As Mad Dave stood up, Raymond felt a slight twinge of fear. The geezer was fucking ginormous. 'I don't want no aggro, just pay me the money and I'll leave,' Raymond urged him.

Laughing hysterically, Mad Dave walked towards Raymond and lifted him by his new shirt and tie. 'Go away, you silly little boy,' he said, as he dragged him towards the Portakabin door.

As fast as a greyhound chasing a hare, Raymond pulled the knife out and shoved it straight through Mad Dave's guts.

As he hit the floor, Mad Dave's eyes rolled straight into the back of his head. Raymond bent down to check on him; he had seen enough dead animals to know when someone was brown bread. Desperate not to get the man's blood on his new suit, Raymond knelt to one side as he searched through Mad Dave's pockets. He'd spotted the safe when he first came in and it was one of them cheapies that wasn't coded by numbers. Finding a massive bunch of keys, Raymond walked towards the safe and tried numerous ways to unlock it. 'Come on,' he said, as he turned key after key.

Finally, Ray felt the lock turn. He quickly grabbed all the money from inside, pocketed it, and washed the blood off his hands in the sink. Spotting a tea towel, he wiped the safe, the desk and the door. He hadn't touched anywhere else, he was sure he hadn't. Washing the blood off the knife, he put it back inside his jacket. His new suit was ruined. He'd caught his pocket with the knife and ripped it, and not only that, it was also sprayed with blood.

With the tea towel firmly attached to his hand, Raymond opened the cabin door. He then ran for his bloody life.

Waiting for Raymond to return was the longest wait of Eddie's life. Ronny hadn't helped with his stupid comments and jokes. Willing the kid to come through for him, Eddie smiled as he saw him running towards the van.

'Drive, quick, go,' Raymond said, as he leaped into the back.

Paulie and Ronny were stunned to see splashes of blood on Ray's suit. He didn't have a mark on him, so it couldn't be his.

'Are you OK? What happened?' Eddie asked nervously.

Raymond was aware of his arms shaking as he put his hand in his pocket and pulled out bundles of £20 notes wrapped up in elastic bands. 'There's ten bundles there. I should imagine there's a grand in each,' he managed to stutter.

Ronny couldn't believe his eyes. 'What the fuck? What did you do? Whose blood is it?'

Raymond put his head in his hands. 'I had to kill him, I had no choice.'

Uncle Reg nearly took the van straight up the kerb. He'd seen some newcomers over the years, but none like this kid. 'Don't worry, son. We'll get rid of the knife and your clothes and clean you up round mine.'

Seeing the shocked expression on the faces of his brothers, Eddie burst out laughing. 'I think Raymond's passed his little task, don't you boys?' he asked sarcastically.

Paulie immediately held his hand out to Raymond. 'Well done, mate. Welcome to the family.'

Ronny had no choice other than to do the same. 'I can't believe you killed the cunt. How did it happen?' he asked in awe.

Having by now composed himself a bit, Raymond repeated what had happened in full. 'I knew he was dead immediately. Remember, I know by the eyes, I used to chop up dead animals, didn't I?'

Thrilled by the way Raymond had come through for him, Eddie grabbed him in a playful headlock. 'Well you certainly chopped up a big animal back there, didn't you, eh?'

Uncle Reg lived in Bow, and within the hour, Raymond was as good as new. A bath had scrubbed the blood away, the knife was long gone and all his clothes, including his socks, pants and shoes, had been burnt to cinders. As he sat on the armchair wearing Uncle Reg's clothes, Raymond was enjoying being the centre of attention.

'You can't go out like that. You look like fucking Alf Garnett,' Paulie chuckled, as he handed the hero a large Scotch.

'Thank God you moved into your new flat. Can you imagine your mother's and father's faces if you came home from work looking like that?' Eddie said, ruffling his hair.

Raymond smiled. He had already got over the shock of what he'd done, but the adrenalin was like a drug and he felt high with all the excitement. His parents had been shell-shocked yesterday when he'd moved most of his stuff out.

'What will you eat? Who's gonna cook for you and wash and iron your clothes?' his mother had said.

'He's moving out to become a proper villain. He'll be locked up for murder before you know it,' he'd heard his father shout.

Raymond smiled to himself. If he had the choice of killing people and making loads of money or killing his own soul by driving around in a bus, then he'd definitely choose option A.

As Ronny counted the money, the Scotch flowed around the room. 'There was two grand in each bundle, there's twenty grand here, not ten,' Ronny shouted out.

Eddie filled Raymond's glass right up to the very top. 'I think you should come and stay with me and Jess for a few days, just in case the Old Bill come sniffing around.'

Raymond agreed immediately. He'd already been given an alibi and he knew exactly what to say. Auntie Joan was covering for him and she had already been briefed to say that he'd been round at hers.

A knock on the front door spelled the arrival of Harry Mitchell. Hearing the story in full, Harry shook Raymond's hand and hugged Eddie. 'I told you throwing him in at the deep end was the right thing to do,' he told his son.

Eddie laughed. 'So you're taking all the credit for our new addition, are you? I don't think so, Dad – in your dreams, mate.'

As the jokes and drinks flowed, Eddie stood up and ssshed everyone. 'Let's have a toast to our wonderful new family member.' He smiled at Raymond. 'I'm gonna change your name for you, boyo. Raymond don't really suit you, it sounds too wank. From now on, after your performance today, you are officially called Raymondo.'

Raymond laughed as all the men stood up. 'To Raymondo,' everybody said, toasting him.

Raymond's smile lit up the room. He may not have made it as a rock star, but life was all down to fate, and he had certainly made it now.

# ELEVEN

Jessica did her best to avoid attending Uncle Reg's surprise party, but Ed was having none of it.

'Why don't you just go with the boys and Raymond, Ed? I've got a bit of a headache and if we've got that party on Sunday, I'll be shattered.'

Eddie poured himself a Scotch. Jess pissed him off at times. For years, he'd fallen over backwards to entertain her family, yet when it came to his, it was an effort for Jess to give them the time of day.

Knocking his drink back in one, Ed glared at her. 'You can be such a selfish fucker at times. You've gotta come. All my family are gonna be there, and it ain't gonna look good if I turn up without you. Not only that, I want the kids to be there. My dad, aunts and brothers ain't seen 'em for fuck knows how long.'

'But I don't really know your family that well, and I won't know anyone else there. It's all right for you, Ed, you'll be stood up the bar with the boys all night, while I'm sat alone like a lemon,' Jess argued.

About to lose his rag, Ed stopped himself. 'I'll tell you what, why don't you ring your mum and dad and invite them. That way, you ain't sitting on your Jacks. Give us the phone, I'll ring 'em for you.'

Knowing when she was beaten, Jess reluctantly passed Ed the telephone. She'd never felt comfortable around Eddie's family. Ed always seemed to get drunk when they had a get-together and Jessica dreaded these odd occasions.

'Sorted,' Ed said, as he handed Jess the phone.

'What did Mum say? Is my dad coming as well?' Jessica asked.

Eddie laughed. 'Your mother nearly had a heart attack with the excitement of it all. Your dad's popped out, but your mum said he'll do as he's told. Right, you'd better get your arse in gear, I told me dad we'd be there at seven.'

About to walk out of the room, Jess saw Eddie pour himself a refill. 'Ed, promise me you won't get drunk tonight?'

Eddie shook his head in annoyance. 'Jess, you're me wife, not me keeper. Do yourself a favour, go and get ready and stop treating me like a fucking moron.'

Harry Mitchell had sworn everybody to secrecy. He didn't want Reg to clock on, so, instead of holding the party in the Flag, he'd booked the hall in the Marquis of Salisbury. He'd told Reg he was taking him out for a quiet meal with the boys.

'I don't want no fucking circus,' Reg warned him.

'You're not fucking getting one. What do you think I'm gonna do? Throw you a big party?' Harry lied.

Family and friends had been told to arrive at the Marquis at seven, half an hour before Reg was due there.

'For fuck's sake, cheer up a bit. You look like you're going to a funeral,' Ed hissed, as Jess got out of the cab.

Annoyed with his wife's demeanour, Eddie ushered Gary and Ricky inside and left Jess to deal with the twins.

'There you are. I wondered where you'd got to,' Joyce said, as she spotted her daughter.

'I've had the day from hell. Ed's been in a bad mood and the kids have driven me mad,' Jess moaned.

'Mum, can I have some crisps?' Frankie asked in a whining voice.

'You can have some when Daddy comes back from the bar. Now go and sit next to Grandad.'

'Mum, Mum,' Joey said, tugging her arm.

'What's the matter?' Jess asked, as she noticed Joey was crying.

'I think I've peed my pants.'

Ed reappeared at precisely the wrong moment. 'What's up?' he asked, handing Jess her drink.

'Nothing. I'm just going to take Joey to the toilet.'

'I'll take him. It's about time he started using the gents,' Eddie said, grabbing his son's hand.

'No. He thinks he's had a little accident, Ed. Leave it to me and I'll sort him out.'

Eddie looked at his son in disgust. 'What's the matter with you? You're not a baby, you're six years old. Why don't you ask if you wanna go to the fucking toilet?'

Jessica picked up her sobbing son. 'Don't shout at him, Ed. He can't help it.'

'He's a fucking embarrassment,' Eddie hissed, as he headed back to the bar.

Stanley glanced at Joyce as Eddie walked away. Neither of them had heard the conversation, but both of them got the gist that their son-in-law wasn't happy.

'I don't trust him as far as I can throw him, Joycie.'

'Stanley, just drink your drink and shut your cakehole,' Joyce ordered.

Uncle Reg arrived at quarter to eight.

'Surprise!' everyone shouted, as he shuffled in, embarrassed.

113

'Fuck you, Harry. You know how I hate anything like this.'

Sylvie, Harry's lady friend, had spent the morning decorating the hall with balloons, banners and old photographs of Reg.

'Oh, for fuck's sake,' Reg said as he clocked an enlarged image of himself as a spotty-faced teenager wearing an old army helmet.

Ed stood up the bar with Raymond, Ronny and Paulie. All four of them were in the mood for a party and were knocking the Scotch back like it was going out of style.

'Where's Jess?' Ronny enquired.

'Dunno, probably mollycoddling the fucking kids, as usual,' Ed replied arrogantly.

Seeing Gary and Ricky nick someone's beer, Eddie smiled. They were boys to be proud of. Not once had they ever shown him up by pissing themselves in public.

Stanley was frozen to his chair as he spotted Harry Mitchell strolling towards him with a bottle in his hand.

'Joyce, Stanley, lovely to see you again. And how are my beautiful grandchildren?' Harry said, patting the twins on the head.

Noticing Stanley flinch, Harry held up the bottle and smiled. 'Champagne, anyone?'

'Yes, please. I do like a drop of champers,' Joyce said, in a silly posh voice.

Harry poured her a glass and then turned to Stanley. 'And would you like a drop of the finest, Stanley?'

'No, not for me,' Stanley said, as he bolted to the toilet.

Frankie and Joey nudged one another as the strange man sat next to them.

114

'This is your grandad, Harry. Say "hello, Grandad Harry,"' Joyce said in a stupid, childlike voice.

Frankie giggled. She'd been in a naughty mood all day. 'My brother has peed his pants,' she said proudly.

'No, I didn't,' Joey shouted.

'Stop it, Frankie. She's only joking,' Joyce awkwardly informed Harry.

'No, I'm not. Joey always wets himself.'

As Joey burst into tears, Joyce burst into false laughter. 'Kids, eh? Say the funniest things don't they, Harry?'

Not sure what planet Joyce or his grandchildren were on, Harry stood up. 'Excuse me, Joycie. I have to answer a call of nature.'

'Bye Harry, lovely to see you again,' Joyce yelled, as he walked away.

Seeing Stanley hovering nervously by the doorway, Harry pretended not to notice him. He knew full well why Stanley was shit-scared of him. Harry never forgot the face of a victim or their friends, and he knew Stanley was the geezer who had been in the pub with Roger Dodds on the evening he'd unfortunately taken his eye out. Harry had recognised Stanley on the night of Eddie's wedding. He'd had him checked out afterwards, just to confirm that his mind was as sharp as ever. Harry smiled. The look on Stanley's face when he'd waved the champagne bottle towards him was a picture of pure fucking fear.

Auntie Joan and Auntie Vi were in their element. Harry had booked a duo, one singing and one on the piano, that were playing every war song that Joan and Vi had sung down the shelters.

Gee, it's great after bein' out late
Walkin' my baby back home

115

Arm in arm over meadow and farm
Walkin' my baby back home.

Eddie interrupted Joan and Vi's sing-song by plonking himself in the middle of them. 'How's my two favourite aunties?' he asked cheekily.

'Oi, go and get your bleedin' own,' Vi said, as he nicked a sausage roll off her plate.

Joan squeezed his hand. 'It's a wonderful evening, Eddie. Thoroughly enjoying ourselves, me and Vi are. Mustard this duo, ain't they?'

'Bit old hat for me. I prefer The Who or a bit of Rod Stewart meself,' Ed joked.

'Your mother loved all these songs, Eddie. There was no telly in them days, and we'd sit round your mum's coal fire singing these songs. Kept us amused, they did, especially when the sirens went off and we were stuck down them bloody shelters for hours on end,' Joan told him.

Eddie was overcome by emotion. 'I wish I could remember more about me mum. I can picture her face, but that's about it.'

Vi smiled at him. 'She was a kind, wonderful woman. Had a heart of gold, didn't she, Joan?'

Joan nodded. 'Give you her last ha'penny, she would. She was one of life's gentle souls.'

Aware that his eyes were starting to well up, Eddie stood up.

'Where's the little 'uns? We've seen Gary and Ricky, but we ain't seen the twins yet, have we, Vi?' Joan said.

'I'll tell Jess to bring 'em over in a minute,' Ed said, as he walked away.

Bowling over to the table where his wife was sitting, Ed could see no sign of her. 'Where's Jess?' he asked Stanley.

Stanley shrugged. 'Joyce has took the kids to the toilet, but I've no idea where Jess is.'

Eddie's eyes scanned the hall. He wasn't happy with Jessica's behaviour tonight. How could she not take the twins over to say hello to his two old aunts? She was out of fucking order.

Unable to see hide nor hair of Jess, Eddie walked back to the bar.

'What's up?' Paulie asked him.

'Nothing,' Eddie said, as he urged the barman to leave a bottle of Scotch on the counter.

Spotting Raymond chatting up a bird, Ed walked over to him. 'Where's Jess? You seen her?'

Raymond shrugged. 'She was sitting with me mum and dad. Don't worry, she won't go far without the twins. I'm gonna make a move now, Ed. This is Jane and we're going back to mine.'

As the singer took a toilet break, Ed smiled when his dad leaped on the stage and began one of his infamous speeches.

'Everyone knows why we're here tonight. We're celebrating the retirement of the oldest swinger in town. Reg, where are you? Now, I might be his brother, but I ain't giving you no old flannel. He was a horrible fucker when he was a kid. At six years old he . . .'

As Ed spotted Jess all cosied up with some good-looking geezer, he lost track of his father's speech. Fuming, Ed marched towards her, grabbed her arm, and pulled her away. 'Whaddya think you're fucking doing?'

Jessica looked at Eddie in horror. 'I beg your pardon. Are you drunk, Eddie? Don't embarrass me, please.'

Eddie sneered at the bloke. 'Who's that cunt?' he asked Jess.

'Lee Jones. You remember my old schoolfriend, Mary?

Well, Lee's her older brother. Please don't start, Ed. We're catching up on old times, that's all.'

'I am not a happy man, Jess. My aunt Joan and aunt Vi are sitting on that table near the door. You ain't said hello or fuck all to 'em. Asking me if the twins are here, they were. I want you to take the kids over to 'em, now, before I lose my temper with yer.'

'I'll take them over in a minute. Please don't show me up in front of Lee, Ed. I'd hate any bad stories to get back to Mary.'

Ed sneered. 'Fuck Lee and fuck Mary. I'm your husband and you'll do as I say.'

As Ed stormed back to the bar, Jess made her excuses to Lee and went off to find the twins. Sometimes her husband's temper was like a ticking time bomb and she would hate to create a scene.

'Who was that geezer Jess was all over? Got bored of you already, has she?' Ronny joked.

Eddie pushed Ronny up against the wall. 'Shut it, else I'll punch your fucking lights out.'

Ronny was taken aback. 'I'm only mucking about, Ed. I didn't mean it, honest I didn't.'

'What's going on?' Harry asked, pulling Eddie away.

'Nothing, Dad. It's him, he's off his fucking head,' Ronny said, feeling brave now his father had appeared.

Harry had a quiet word with Eddie. 'Look son, I don't know what's bugging you, but leave it tonight, eh? This is your Uncle Reg's party and I want him to have a good time.'

Eddie nodded. 'I'm fine, Dad. Ronny just needs to learn when to shut it, that's all.'

'Come on, twins. Say goodbye to Auntie Vi and Auntie Joan,' Jessica said, searching for her husband out of the corner of her eye. As she dragged the twins away, she clocked him. Ed was standing at the bar only yards away from Lee and his friends.

Jessica hadn't seen Lee Jones for years and was surprised to see him at Reg's party. Apparently, he was best friends with Ed's Uncle Albert's son, and he'd invited him. Jessica's heart was in her mouth as she sat back down with her parents. Unbeknown to Eddie, Lee had been her first love. She'd met him through his sister, Mary, and she'd had a crush on him for well over a year before he'd finally noticed she existed. They'd dated for two years on and off and Jess had lost her virginity to him. The relationship had ended when Jess had left school. It had run its course and both she and Lee amicably decided to go their separate ways.

Aware that Lee was talking about Jessica, Eddie edged towards him. Albert's son, John, had his back to Ed, otherwise he'd have warned Lee to shut up.

'Jess was always good-looking when we were kids, but she's a fucking stunner now. What a shame she's married. I wonder if she's up for a bit on the side? I'd give me right arm to fuck her again. You never know, she might even dump her husband for me,' Lee joked.

Like a madman, Eddie lunged towards Lee. 'That's my wife you're talking about. I'll kill you, you fucking cunt!' Ed shouted, as he rammed Lee's face repeatedly against the wooden bar post.

As Jessica screamed and ran towards the bar, Stanley felt the colour drain from his face.

'Stop it, Daddy, stop it,' Frankie cried, as she followed her mum from the table.

'Do something, Stanley,' Joyce shouted, as she tried to comfort Joey. Her grandson was trembling and had crawled under the chair.

It was Harry and Reg who managed to drag Eddie outside. His victim's face was smashed beyond recognition and somebody had already called for an ambulance.

Pushing his son against the wall, Harry glared at him. 'What the fuck was that all about?' he asked Ed.

Reg went back inside. He hated big parties at the best of times and had never wanted one in the first place. Now he had to somehow get to Lee and bribe him, to make sure he didn't involve the police.

'Why did you do it, Eddie? Why?' Jessica sobbed, as she ran over to her husband.

Using all of his strength, Ed pushed his old man flying and grabbed Jessica around the throat. 'What are you, some slag? How many other men have you fucking well slept with?' he roared, as he tightened his grip and slammed her head against the brick wall.

'I'm sorry, Ed. Stop it, please, you're hurting me,' Jess pleaded.

Harry grabbed Ed around the neck from behind. 'That's enough. Now get back inside.'

As Ed stormed off, Harry put a comforting arm around Jessica's shoulder. 'Are you OK, love?'

Jessica burst into tears. 'Ed frightens me when he drinks that Scotch. It turns him into a monster.'

Harry sat Jessica down on a nearby wall. He handed her his handkerchief and told her to dry her eyes. 'You leave Ed to me, I'll have a word with him. Is your head OK? You're not hurt, are you?'

Jessica shook her head. 'I love him so much, Harry. What am I gonna do?'

Squeezing her hand, Harry smiled. 'And my Ed loves you very much. I know he's a wild card at times, but he worships the ground you walk on, Jess. Tonight was just a one-off, he'd never intentionally hurt you, I know he wouldn't.'

For the first time ever, Jessica saw Harry Mitchell in a different light. She'd never had much to do with him in the past. Feeling guilty for all the years she'd tried to keep Harry away from the twins, she turned to face him. 'Why don't you come over for dinner one day, Harry? I'll cook us a nice roast and you can bring Sylvie with you.'

Harry winked at her. 'That sounds perfect.'

Stanley resembled a startled deer as he saw Harry clock him. He'd been rooted to the spot for the past five minutes and could barely believe what he'd witnessed. He'd seen Eddie with his hands around Jessica's throat, and was about to react before Harry had stepped in.

'Have a chat with your dad and I'll speak to Ed,' Harry said, walking away.

'Are you OK? He didn't hit you, did he?' Stanley asked.

Jessica stood up. 'No, he didn't. I'm fine, Dad, honest I am. It's cold out here, let's go back inside.'

'What's going on?' Joyce asked, as Stanley and Jessica sat down at the table.

As Jess hugged the twins, Stanley moved next to his wife. 'Thanks to you, our daughter's married to a fucking lunatic. As I walked outside, Ed had his hands around Jessica's throat and was trying to strangle her.'

'Why? What's she done wrong? Didn't you try and stop him, Stanley?'

'His father dragged him off of her. Anyway, what was I meant to do? They're villains, Joycie. They probably carry guns with them. They ain't gonna take no notice of a little man like me, are they?'

Lee had been carted off in the ambulance and had been told in no uncertain terms to say that he'd fallen down the stairs that led up to the hall, or else.

Eddie had now calmed down a bit. His dad had given him a good talking to and he was back at the bar having a drink with his brothers.

Most of the guests, including Auntie Joan and Auntie Vi, hadn't batted an eyelid when Ed had kicked off. Most family get-togethers ended up in a ruckus of some kind, and once you'd seen one poor bastard beaten to pulp, you'd seen them all.

Vi and Joan had been dancing to 'I've Got a Lovely Bunch of Coconuts', when the fight had erupted.

'Eddie's smashing some bloke's head against the bar,' Vi had said casually.

Joan carried on singing without even bothering to look round. She'd brought the boys up, and knew full well what cloth they were cut from.

Pissed off with Ronny and Paulie bombarding him with questions about Lee, Ed walked over to his dad. 'Can I have a quiet word?'

Harry excused himself from Sylvie and followed his son outside. 'I'm sorry for pushing you, Dad. I just lost it, you know how it is.'

Harry put a wise arm around his son's shoulder. 'Take my advice, Ed, talk to Jess and tell her you're sorry. Good women are hard to find and you'll be a fool to yourself if you lose her. I know I'm sort of courting Sylvie, but she'll never replace your mother, no one can.'

Ed nodded. He had no intention of taking his dad's advice, he was far too clever for that. Give women an inch and they take a mile. 'Thanks for the guidance,' he said, walking away.

'Oh, and by the way, Ed.'

Eddie turned around.

'If you ever push me like that again, I swear I'll knock your fucking block off.'

Eddie nodded, took a deep breath and strolled over to the table where Jess was sitting. 'Come outside, we need to have a little chat,' he told her.

'I've ordered a cab, Jessica wants to go home,' Stanley said curtly to Eddie.

'Cancel it. Jessica's going nowhere without me,' Eddie said, glaring at Stanley.

Stanley looked down at his feet. He knew when to shut up.

The twins were both asleep now, and Ed stroked their hair. 'We need to talk, Jess,' he said firmly.

As Jessica followed Eddie outside, Stanley turned to Joyce. 'If our Jess forgives him for tonight, she wants her bleedin' head tested.'

Joyce said nothing. For the first time ever, she had her doubts about Eddie. Trying to strangle Jessica was not something she had ever thought Ed would do.

'This is all your fault, Joycie, encouraging her to get involved with the likes of him. I tried to tell you but, as always, you wouldn't listen.'

Joyce stared at her husband. He was beginning to get on her nerves. He was forever blaming her for Jess getting involved with Eddie, and Joyce had had enough of it. 'Just shut up, Stanley. Jessica chose her own husband, it was nothing to do with me. All I did was support her choice, like any good mother should. I know Eddie was out of order tonight, but every couple has their arguments. Look at me and you, we don't stop arguing. The trouble with you, Stanley, is you never liked Eddie from day one. Ever since our Jess brought him home, you've been waiting for something like this to happen, just so you can say, "I told you so".'

Defeated, Stanley shook his head. 'It will all end in tragedy and tears, dear. You mark my words.'

Eddie lit a fag and leaned against the wall. 'You should have told me, Jess. If I'd known Lee was your ex, if you'd have said something, I wouldn't have lost it. How do you think I felt? Here I am at me uncle's retirement party and there's some geezer standing at the bar bragging about fucking me wife.'

Standing on tiptoe, Jessica cupped her husband's handsome face and gently kissed him. 'I'm sorry, Eddie. I can't believe Lee stood at the bar saying those things. We were only young when we dated, and he was a nice, quiet boy. He was my best friend Mary's brother.'

Eddie stared at the floor. 'It's ruined my night, Jess. I mean how would you like it, if some bird was giving it large about shagging me?'

With the memory of her husband trying to throttle her totally erased from her mind, Jessica apologised once again. 'I'll never keep anything from you again, Ed. I'm really sorry. Can't we go back and enjoy the rest of the party and forget all about it? I promise there'll be no more secrets.'

Ed shrugged then nodded. 'As long as you ain't got no more skeletons locked in the closet, I'm willing to forget about tonight.'

Jessica felt relief as she hugged him. 'I love you,' she whispered.

Eddie held her tight. 'Oh, and one more thing. I don't want you to have any more contact with that Mary.'

Jessica agreed. She rarely spoke to Mary now anyway. Eddie's feelings were far more important to her than those of some old schoolfriend.

The perfect gentleman, Ed held the door open for Jessica. As she walked through, Eddie smirked. The best form of defence was attack and, as usual, Ed had turned the situation around to his advantage.

# TWELVE

As Eddie Mitchell ended the phone call, he could barely wipe the grin off his face. His father had just rung him and, in undercover lingo, let him know that the Old Bill were officially treating Mad Dave's murder as a bungled burglary and were looking for two young black males who had been seen loitering around that area the previous week.

Desperate to tell Raymond the good news in person, rather than via the phone, Eddie picked up his car keys. Ray had been at it all weekend with the tart he'd met at Reg's party, and had only just got rid of her.

'Finish getting the kids ready, Jess. I'm just popping out for a bit, I'll be back in about half-hour.'

'Where are you going?' Jessica called, as he slammed the front door.

Flustered because she was running late and was not even ready herself, Jessica marched Joey and Frankie downstairs and ordered Gary and Ricky to keep an eye on them for her. 'I won't be long. I just want to have a quick shower and get changed. Make sure they don't go out in the garden. They're ready for the party and I don't want them to get covered in mud.'

'Where's me Dad?' Gary asked.

Jessica shook her head. 'How should I know? You know what your father's like, comes and goes as he pleases.'

'Can I come upstairs with you, Mummy?' Joey whined.

'No, stay down here with your sister. Mummy won't be long, be a good boy and Gary and Ricky will play a game with you.'

'Please, Mum,' Joey screamed, clinging on to her legs.

Dragging him up by his arm, Jessica smacked him gently on his bottom. 'Do as I say, or Daddy won't let you go to the party.'

Desperate for twenty minutes to herself, Jessica left her son bawling his eyes out and went upstairs to make herself glamorous. The argument between herself and Eddie was now well and truly forgotten. Jess had a big bump on the back of her head where Ed had thrown her against the wall, but she hadn't told him that he'd hurt her. After the Lee episode, she was just thankful he'd forgiven her.

Sipping the coffee Raymond had just made him, Eddie pulled a face and spat the contents of his mouth back into the mug.

'Fucking hell, that's rancid. I think the milk's gone off.'

Raymond ignored his complaint. He was more inter- ested in hearing about the Old Bill's findings than worrying about poxy milk.

'Right, tell me from the beginning what your dad said.'

Eddie explained the conversation in full. 'So, it looks like we're all off the hook. The filth always hated Mad Dave, he led 'em a merry dance for years, so they're not gonna pursue his death with five-star treatment.'

Raymond felt a surge of relief flow through his body. He'd been getting jumpy last night and hadn't slept too well. At least with the new information, he could now relax a bit. 'How does your old man know all this?' he asked Eddie.

Eddie smiled. 'The old man's had a couple of coppers on his payroll for years. One's a bent sergeant. The dodgy cunt demands a serious backhander for his info. It's worth it in the long run, though, we'll never get nicked with him on our side. He's tipped us off a few times in the past, when the filth were on our cases. An insider of that quality is worth his weight in gold.'

Raymond nodded in agreement. 'What you up to today, Ed? Is it all right if I come round to see Jess and the kids?'

Raymond loved having his new flat and independence, but he hated being alone for too long. That's why he'd let Jane, the bird he'd met, stay for two nights.

'We're going to a party down the road from me. This geezer has a big do every year. Pat Murphy his name is, he's an ex-boxer. Go and get yourself ready, Ray, and you can come with us. Jess won't mind, she'd love you to come,' Eddie told him.

Raymond didn't need asking twice. He was so used to his mum and dad constantly shouting at one another, he couldn't get used to the silence. 'I'll just run a quick bath. I'll be fifteen minutes, tops.'

Eddie laughed at his eagerness. 'Best you move your arse then, 'cause I told Jess I'd only be half an hour. Leave the door open, so you can give me the full lowdown on that little floozy you tugged.'

Jessica tried on a few outfits. She opted for her white linen trousers, red patent platform boots and a patterned vest top. She had originally chosen to wear her new dress, but had decided to keep it casual, as she had no idea what the other women would be wearing. Jess put a cardigan, a pair of denim hotpants and a pair of flip-flops in her bag. She might get changed later on and, if she wanted to dance, she could take her boots off and wear her flatties.

'I'm home, babe,' she heard Eddie shout.

Unable to walk properly in her new chunky footwear, Jessica held on to the stair rail for dear life as she plodded down the stairs.

'Fucking hell, sis! You look like Wonder Woman in them.'

Surprised, but pleased to see her brother, Jessica playfully punched him. 'This is all the rage, Ray. You wouldn't know about women's fashion if it smacked you over the head, so I'd keep quiet if I was you,' she joked.

'Ed said I could come to the party with you. You don't mind, do you?'

Jessica smiled. 'Not at all. The twins will be thrilled.'

With Frankie in one arm and Joey in the other, Eddie walked towards Jessica. 'You look fabulous, but you don't need all that make-up on,' he said, pecking her on the lips.

Jessica wiped off her eye shadow. 'I didn't know what to wear. It's so warm today, I was going to wear my hotpants, but I don't know what the other women will be wearing and I'd hate to turn up looking tarty.'

Eddie smiled. 'You could never look like a tart, Jess. We ready to make tracks then?'

Both Jessica and Raymond nodded.

'Gary, Ricky, move your arses. You've got one minute or I'm leaving you here,' Ed shouted.

Patrick Murphy was a big, flash, loud Irishman who loved nothing more than being the centre of attention. He'd been holding his legendary bank-holiday parties for over ten years now and every year he tried to push the boat out a couple of yards more. Over the years, Patrick had fathered six children by three different women. Like many a good man, he adored his own, but wasn't that keen on anybody else's. This year, to rectify his own little problem, he'd fenced off a great big part of the field just for the kids. He'd hired fairground rides, swings and slides. He'd even booked Bob the balloon man and a clown from Corringham to keep the little bastards occupied and well away from the adults.

Eddie had chosen to drive his Porsche to the party. He had no intention of driving it home drunk, but was determined to show off his wealth. Jess had urged him to get a cab, but he'd flatly refused. She was a woman and she didn't understand the method in a man's madness.

With the whole family unable to fit in the Porsche, Jessica had also brought her Merc. 'We'll get a cab home later and pick the cars up tomorrow,' Ed told her.

Parking on the packed field, Eddie suddenly wished he had got that cab after all. 'Jesus wept! Look at the motors here. Look at that Roller – I wonder who that belongs to?'

'I dunno, but the guests here are all obviously minted. Look at that green Bentley, Ed. Ain't it a beauty?' Ray said.

Annoyed that his motor paled into insignificance, Eddie quickly leaped out and urged Ray, Gary and Ricky to do the same. 'Come on, Jess has just parked up and I'm gagging for a drink.'

Walking towards the gates of the house, Eddie was surprised to see a big bloke in a suit vetting people.

'Names?' the guy asked bluntly.

Eddie gave him his name and explained who Raymond was.

'In you go,' the geezer told him.

'Eddie! Great to see you,' Pat Murphy said, shaking his hand.

Eddie introduced his family and gratefully accepted the glasses of champagne that a waiter appeared with.

'We're gonna get a hot dog, Dad,' Gary said, dragging Ricky away.

'Mummy, can I go and see the clown?' Frankie screamed.

'I wanna balloon. Get me a balloon,' Joey said, tugging Jessica's arm.

Patrick smiled at the two spoilt brats. 'Do you want to come with me? Uncle Patrick has booked childminders to look after you and keep you amused. We've got games, toys, even fairground rides – safe ones, of course.'

'Yes! Can we go Mummy, please?' Frankie screamed.

Jessica looked at her husband for guidance. 'I'm not sure, Ed. Shouldn't they stay with us for a bit?'

Joey burst into tears and threw himself onto the ground. 'I want a balloon and I want one now,' he sobbed.

Embarrassed by his son's behaviour, Eddie yanked him up by one arm. 'I'll give you more than a balloon in a minute, Joey. Stop behaving like a baby and act your fucking age.'

'I'll go over the play-area bit with 'em, if you want,' Raymond offered.

'No, you won't. As Pat says, they'll be fine. It's time they were let off the harness. If we didn't pamper them so much, they wouldn't make a show of us in public every time we took 'em out. I'm sick of 'em whingeing and crying every time they don't get their own way and I ain't putting up with it no more,' Eddie said, glaring at his wife.

Jessica looked away. Once Eddie got a bee in his bonnet, there was no point arguing with him. She knew he was having a dig at her, but she couldn't help the way she was. She hated letting the twins out of her sight. The

131

week they'd started school was the worst week of her life. She'd drop them off, drive straight home and sob her heart out until it was time to pick them up again.

'Go on, then. Uncle Patrick will show you the play area. Enjoy yourselves,' she said, as the twins skipped happily away.

Sensing Jessica's awkwardness, Raymond put an arm around her shoulder. 'If we stand over there by that bar, we can keep more of an eye on 'em,' he said.

Jessica nodded gratefully.

Seeing that Eddie was already surrounded by a fan club, Raymond tapped his arm. 'Me and Jess are gonna stand by that table next to the bar.'

'No probs. I'll be over in a bit,' Eddie replied.

Spotting Frankie and Joey joyfully running around hitting one another with plastic hammers, Jessica relaxed and took in the rest of her surroundings. There were two makeshift bars, about half a dozen waiters walking about with trays and right in the centre was the biggest barbecue that Jessica had ever seen.

Aware that his sister was clocking the grub, Raymond pointed towards the conservatory. 'They've got tons more food in there. There's sandwiches, seafood, everything. I saw it as we walked past. Are you hungry? Shall I get you something?'

Jessica shook her head. 'I'll have something later. What's that man doing with them boxes? And what's that big square thing over there?'

Raymond craned his neck. 'I think the geezer carrying the boxes is the DJ. He's probably setting his stuff up for later and I think that's the boxing ring over the back. From what Eddie was telling me, I think all the lads lark about in it later on.'

Noticing a crowd of women sitting together, Jessica

had a look to see what they were wearing. 'Good job I never wore my denim hotpants. No one is very dressed up. In fact, I feel silly in these boots now, I'm gonna put my flip-flops on.'

Raymond laughed as Jessica frantically tried to tug her boots off. Women were funny creatures. Blokes didn't give a shit what they were wearing – well, apart from Eddie, that was. He insisted on buying the best of everything.

Seeing Gary and Ricky bound towards her, Jessica asked them a favour. 'Don't tell your dad I asked you, but will you check on the twins for me? They're in that play area that's sectioned off.'

Gary and Ricky did as they were asked and were back within minutes. 'They're having a great time. Frankie is hitting the clown with a big plastic hammer and Joey's skipping about with some other little boy,' Gary told Jess.

'We told them where you're standing, so they know where to find you,' Ricky said to Raymond.

Seeing Eddie walk towards her with another couple, Jessica smiled at him.

'This is Dougie, an old pal of mine from way back and this is his girlfriend, Vicki,' said Eddie. 'Dougie, Vicki, this is Jessica, my wife, and my brother-in-law, Raymondo.'

As the men shook hands, Jessica grinned shyly at Vicki. Dougie looked well into his forties, but his girlfriend only looked about the same age as herself. Jessica liked her immediately. Vicki was very pretty with long dark hair, a warm smile and was a very trendy dresser.

As the waiter came up, both girls reached for the bubbly. 'I love your shoes – where did you get them from?' Jessica asked.

'Dougie bought them for me. He got them up the West End,' Vicki replied.

Overhearing their conversation, Eddie noticed that Jess had put on an old pair of flip-flops. He gently pulled her to one side. 'Put your boots back on, babe, I don't like you in them flip-flops. They make you look like a cleaner.'

Feeling a bit embarrassed, Jessica smiled at Vicki. 'Men, eh?' she muttered as she quickly did as Ed had asked.

Vicki did her best to put her at ease. 'Dougie's the same. He always tells me what to wear. Wow, them red boots are just fabulous.'

Eddie grinned. 'See,' he said nudging Jess. 'Your husband knows best.'

Jessica nodded and turned back to Vicki. 'So, are you and Dougie local? I take it you live together.'

Vicki nodded. 'Your husband was telling us where you live. We're about five minutes away. You'll have to come round one day. We can have lunch while the men are at work.'

'I'd love to,' Jessica replied, thrilled.

Ever since Jess had married Eddie, she'd lost touch with virtually all of her friends. She'd still heard from Mary, but Ed had even put a stop to that now. Eddie hated her going out of a night. Ginny had rung her recently and invited her out for a meal to celebrate their friend Linda's birthday. Eddie had made it perfectly clear that he didn't want her to go. 'Only old slappers go on girls' nights out when they're married with kids,' he told her. Jess didn't bother to argue. What was the point when she always came out second best?

'I won't be a sec. I'm just going to check on the kids,' Jess told Vicki.

'Where you off to?' Ed asked her.

'To make sure the twins are OK,' Jess replied.

Eddie sighed and turned back to Dougie and Raymond.

'What about that pikey that's bought that big house near you? He's fucking cakeo, he is,' Dougie said.

'What pikey? You talking about the big white gaff near the bend?' Ed asked.

'Yeah, that's the one. I don't know his name, someone pointed him out to me earlier. He's here at the party, pulled up outside in a Roller, he's a mate of Patrick's, apparently.'

Eddie felt his blood start to boil. He'd despised travellers ever since he was a teenager and he certainly didn't want them living near him. The O'Haras were the main cause of his hatred and, even though he hadn't seen them for years, he still hated Jimmy with a passion. Annoyed, Eddie snatched a couple more glasses off the waiter's tray and handed one to Dougie.

'I ain't fucking happy about a pikey living near me. You know what thieving bastards they are, I'll have to fucking nail everything down. See if you can spot the cunt and show me who he is.'

Dougie craned his neck and shook his head. 'Maybe he didn't stay long. I can't see him now.'

Raymond laughed at Eddie's annoyance. 'Whoever it is, if he's brought a house the size of that white one and is swanning about in a Rolls-Royce, I doubt you'll need to worry about him nicking your plant pots, Ed.'

Luckily for Raymond, Eddie saw the funny side and laughed. Maybe he was overreacting a bit. The feud with the O'Haras was now in the past, and it was wrong to tar every other traveller with the same brush.

Jessica returned with not only the twins, but two other little boys in tow as well.

'Fuck me, we only had two kids when they went in there,' Eddie joked.

Jessica smiled. 'They wanted you and Uncle Raymond to meet their new friends.'

135

Seeing Frankie holding hands with a little boy, Eddie smiled. Seeing that Joey was also holding hands with a little boy, Eddie knocked his arm away. 'Frankie can hold hands with boys. You can only hold hands with girls, Joey. Do you understand?'

'Yes, Daddy,' Joey said meekly.

Jessica felt sorry for her son. 'Don't have a go at him. He's only six, and at that age they hold hands with girls and boys,' she said to Eddie.

Feeling guilty, Eddie ruffled Joey's hair. 'What's your mate's name then?'

'Michael,' Joey mumbled.

Eddie smiled at Frankie. 'And what's your friend's name?'

Holding hands with the object of her affection, Frankie put her other hand on her hip. 'He's not my friend, Daddy, he's my boyfriend and his name is Jed.'

Eddie bent down and shook hands with both kids. 'Pleased to meet you Michael, pleased to meet you Jed,' he said, laughing.

'Can I take Frankie to play in the woods?'

'Cheeky little bugger,' Eddie said to Raymond and Dougie. 'No, you bloody well can't,' Eddie told him laughing.

'Yes, I can,' Jed said, pecking Frankie on the cheek.

Eddie couldn't believe the front of the kid. He wasn't even used to grown men answering him back, let alone an ankle-biter. Grabbing hold of Frankie, Eddie hoisted her into his arms. 'Off you go now, Jed. Go and find your own mum and dad.'

Jed shook his head. 'I wanna stay here with Frankie.'

'Please, Daddy, let me go and play in the woods with Jed,' Frankie cried.

Getting more annoyed by the second, Eddie handed his daughter over to Jessica and knelt back down to face the brat. 'Listen Jed, I'll tell you once more, go away, else I'll go and find your father and get him to drag you away.'

Jed stared into Eddie's eyes. 'No, you won't. My daddy knows you, he don't like you. He won't do as you tell him.'

Suddenly, an awful feeling washed over Eddie. Surely not? It couldn't be, could it?

Eddie felt his mouth go dry as he asked the question. 'Who is your father, Jed?'

Jed smiled. 'My dad is Jimmy O'Hara.'

# THIRTEEN

Realising that Eddie was anything but happy, Jed decided it was time for him to jog on.

'Bye Frankie,' he shouted as he ran away.

Petrified, little Michael bolted as well. Absolutely seething, Eddie vented his anger towards his six-year-old daughter. 'If I ever find out you've been playing in them woods with a gyppo, I'll break your fucking legs, Frankie.'

Sobbing, Frankie clung to her mum. She was far too young to understand what she had done so wrong. 'I'm sorry, Daddy,' she whispered.

Not used to seeing his sister so upset, Joey started to sob too. Jessica was furious. 'Pull yourself together, Ed. Your daughter's only six years old, for God's sake.'

Desperate to try and smooth things over, Raymond grabbed Eddie's arm. 'Come on, me and you will go and get another round of drinks,' he told him.

Still shell-shocked, Eddie allowed himself to be led away.

Embarrassed by her husband's behaviour, Jessica apologised profusely to Dougie and Vicki. 'I'm so sorry about that. Eddie's such a great dad usually, I don't know what's come over him.'

With both twins still sobbing and clamouring for her

attention, Jessica did her best to placate them. 'Now, come on, stop all that crying. Daddy didn't mean what he said, he just got angry, that's all. He is silly at times your daddy, isn't he?'

Holding one another's hands, Frankie and Joey nodded simultaneously.

Looking into their innocent little eyes, Jessica felt like crying herself. Picking on her was one thing, starting on the kids was another. Aware that Eddie was on his way back from the bar, she quickly pulled herself together. 'Shall Mummy take you to get an ice cream from that van over there?'

The word ice cream usually managed to stop the tears and Jessica was relieved as, once again, it worked wonders.

'Can I have a ninety-nine?' Frankie asked brightly.

'I want a screwball, Mummy,' Joey grinned.

As Eddie reappeared he tried to wrap his arms around her, Jessica scowled and walked away with the twins. Watching Jessica walk away, Eddie stood chatting to Raymond and Dougie. He wasn't really concentrating on the conversation – he couldn't. The party was pretty packed now and Ed had no idea where O'Hara was, but he couldn't get him out of his mind.

He'd never set eyes on any of the O'Haras since the day they'd moved off the site in Stratford. He'd heard rumours over the years that Jimmy was doing well for himself in the scrap game. He also heard that he'd originally moved to Basildon and then, more recently, to Kent. Finishing his Scotch, Eddie headed back to the bar to get himself another.

O'Hara being at the party was bad enough, but the fact that the cunt was swanning about in a Roller and had bought the fucking house that he'd wanted was far too much for him to swallow.

139

'All right, Dad? Can you get me and Ricky a beer?'

Eddie smiled at his eldest two boys. ''Course I can. What you been doing?'

Gary grinned. 'We've been sparring in the ring. I met this boy, Billy O'Hara. Same age as me, he is, and he thinks he's the bollocks. He wants to fight me later and I'll beat him, Dad, I just know I will.'

Eddie handed the boys their drinks. 'I need you to beat that boy, Gary. I know his father and I hate him. Now, don't let me down, son.'

Gary smiled confidently. 'I won't. I'll let you know when we're ready to fight and you can come and watch me,' he said, dragging Ricky away.

About to walk away from the bar, Eddie came face to face with his very worst nightmare.

'How you doing, mush?' Jimmy O'Hara asked him.

Not wanting to mug himself off, Eddie kept his voice calm. 'Fine. And you?'

Jimmy smiled. 'I'm cushti. Actually, I'm glad we bumped into one another. I dunno if you've heard, but I think we're about to become neighbours. Bought the place down the road to you, I have. I'm moving in this week.'

'So I hear,' Eddie said brightly. He was desperate to sound normal and hide the jealousy in his voice.

Jimmy O'Hara tilted his head to one side. 'Look, mush, I know we've been through a lot of shit in the past, but we've both moved on now, so can we call it quits?'

As Jimmy held out his right hand, Eddie had little option but to shake it. 'Suits me. I've got a family now, I don't want no grief,' Eddie replied.

Jimmy smiled. 'Same here. I'm putting a mobile home next to me new gaff, so me mum and dad can live there. Three chavvies I've got now, all boys. Actually, I think me youngest, Jed, has got a crush on your daughter. You never know, we might have a wedding on our hands, Eddie boy.'

Eddie made an effort to smile. If O'Hara thought for one minute that his beautiful daughter would ever be jumping over a broomstick, pissing in a bucket and eating a wedding banquet of baked hedgehog in clay, he could fucking think again.

'I best be getting these drinks back now, the lads'll be wondering where I've gone. I'll see you around, Jimmy.'

As Eddie walked away, Jimmy O'Hara smirked. The scar he'd given him was a pure work of art. He could sense that Eddie Mitchell was thoroughly pissed off with him buying the house and that pleased him immensely. Jimmy O'Hara wasn't as forgiving as he portrayed himself. As if he was ever going to forget his father being shot in the foot. His old man was a shadow of his former self and had walked with a limp ever since.

He and his brothers had all sworn to their father that they would let bygones be bygones. They had promised to forget about their feud with the Mitchells, once and for all. Knowing his dinlo brothers, they probably had forgotten about it. Jimmy didn't see much of them now. Ever since he'd given up the pub protection racket, he kept well away.

Opting to go legal was the best decision Jimmy had ever made. The month he'd spent in hospital after Eddie had beaten him to a pulp had given him food for thought. Jimmy had always been the brains of the family since he was a nipper, and he was now the proud owner of fifteen scrapyards in Kent and Essex. Millions he'd made, fucking millions, and he made sure his wife, chavvies and parents were all well provided for.

Ordering a round of drinks, Jimmy nodded to Eddie as he walked back past him. He would never break his promise to his dad while Butch was still alive. Jimmy grinned as he marched across the field. He would bide his time, play Mr Nice Guy and then, one day, when the time was right, he'd make Eddie Mitchell wish that he'd never been born.

'Please Mummy, can we go and play on the rides?' Joey asked.

'We'll be good, we won't be naughty,' Frankie added.

Jessica looked at Eddie with pleading eyes. 'Let them go and play, Ed. They'll only be bored standing here with us.'

Eddie shook his head. He was drunk now, very drunk. 'Fuck me, you've changed your tune. You didn't want to let them out of your sight a few hours ago. They ain't going nowhere, they're staying put.'

Seeing the twins faces crumple, Jessica stood her ground. 'If you won't let them go and play, I'm taking them home, Ed. It's too hot for them sitting here and I'm not gonna let them watch you drink yourself into a stupor again. They were petrified when you kicked off the other night. It's not fair on them, they're only babies.'

Furious at being spoken to like shit in front of Dougie and Raymond, Eddie grabbed Jessica by the arm and dragged her towards the bar.

'Ed, stop it, you're hurting me!' Jessica cried.

Dougie had had enough of Eddie's drunken behaviour by now. 'I've just spotted a pal of mine over by the entrance. Tell Eddie I'll see him later on,' Dougie told Raymond as he dragged Vicki away.

Raymond nodded. He could see that his sister was upset and he didn't know what to do for the best. His dad had told him about the row at Reg's party, but getting involved in other people's maritals just wasn't his scene.

'Can we go home now, Uncle Raymond?' Joey pleaded.

Raymond glanced back towards the bar. Seeing Eddie shouting at Jessica, he decided he had no choice but to step in. Blood was thicker than water, after all. 'Stay there, don't move,' he ordered the twins.

Running towards his sister, he pushed himself in between her and Eddie. 'For fuck's sake, can yous two stop arguing? You're upsetting the kids and everybody's looking at you. It's embarrassing.'

'Eddie's drunk, Ray. All I want to do is go home,' Jessica wept.

'I've told you, you're my missus and you'll go home when I say you can,' Eddie said nastily.

Raymond put a protective arm around his sister. 'Come on, Jess, let's go and stand over by the disco. The kids can have a dance and we can watch 'em.'

Eddie sneered as his wife and brother-in-law walked away. He knew deep down that he was in the wrong. As a rule, he was a good drinker, he could hold his own with the best of them. But on the odd occasion when he hammered the Scotch, he knew he turned into an arrogant arsehole.

'There is nothing worse than seeing a grown man drunk and acting like a fucking idiot. Watch your booze intake, Eddie, 'cause when you're steaming, that's exactly what you turn into,' his father had told him only recently.

Eddie ordered himself another large Scotch. He had every right to get pissed after the shock he'd had today. Jessica wouldn't understand. For years he'd only had to look in the mirror and see his scar to be reminded of Jimmy O'Hara.

'Dad, Dad. Quick, the boxing's about to start,' Gary said, tugging at his sleeve.

Putting his arm around his eldest, Eddie swaggered

over to the ring with him. 'Beat that O'Hara kid and I'll give you a score, Gary.'

'What about me?' Ricky asked.

'You win your bout and I'll give you a score as well,' Eddie said laughing.

'Are you OK?' Vicki asked, as she sat down on the grass next to Jessica.

Jessica nodded. 'Eddie's never usually like that, so please don't think badly of him, will you?'

Vicki squeezed her hand. 'I don't. I have to put up with a lot with my Dougie sometimes, believe me.'

Jessica smiled. 'Aren't you and Dougie going to get married or have children?'

A sudden look of sadness washed over Vicki. 'Dougie's ex-wife died of leukaemia and I think he still loves her. He don't wanna get married again, he says no one can ever take her place. He reckons he wants more kids, but I don't know if he's just bluffing. It's hard sometimes, Jess, I feel like I'm second best to a ghost.'

Noticing tears in Vicki's eyes, Jessica hugged her new friend. 'We're a right pair we are, aren't we?'

Their conversation was ended by an excited Frankie. 'Look Mummy, Joey's dancing.'

Jessica stood up to get a better look at her son. The DJ was playing the Village People's 'YMCA' and Joey stood in a circle full of adults. He was waving his arms and copying the funny dance they were doing.

Vicki linked arms with Jessica. 'Ah, look. He's just so gorgeous, both of your kids are. You're really lucky, Jess. I'd give my right arm for two kids like yours.'

Jessica smiled proudly. Everybody said how gorgeous her twins were and they were right, of course.

\* \* \*

144

Eddie's heart thumped with adrenalin as Gary stepped into the ring. He could see Jimmy O'Hara standing opposite and he just prayed that the training his son had been given at the Peacock Gym would pay off.

'Go on, Gary, I'm banking on you, son,' he yelled, as the fight started.

'Jab, jab, Gary. Hit him with your right,' Raymond urged.

As Gary swung a right hook and the O'Hara boy hit the canvas, Eddie and Raymond leaped up and down.

Not only was Patrick Murphy the referee, he also ran a book on these special occasions, and both Eddie and Raymond had stuck a oner on Gary to win. 'He's a good little boxer,' Patrick told Eddie, as he handed over their winnings.

Eddie smiled as Jimmy O'Hara approached him. 'Got a good right hook, won fair and square your boy. How old's your other one? My second one down, Marky, is thirteen.'

'My Ricky's twelve, but he can handle himself all right.'

'Get him in the ring, then,' O'Hara demanded.

Eddie and Raymond placed another oner bet each and watched as Ricky put on a pair of gloves. 'Hit him hard, son, as hard as you fucking can,' Eddie urged him.

'He's a lot taller than me,' Ricky said vulunerably.

'The bigger they are, the harder they fall,' Eddie told him.

'Go on, Ricky, you can do it,' Gary yelled as the bout began.

Desperate to make his dad proud of him, Ricky flew out of his corner. Within a minute he had knocked the O'Hara boy down.

'Marky's fine, let him carry on,' Jimmy O'Hara shouted.

Patrick Murphy waved his hands to signal the end of

the fight. 'And the winner is Ricky Mitchell,' he shouted, holding Ricky's right arm aloft.

Jimmy O'Hara was pissed off. He'd had £200 each on his boys and they'd both let him down. 'Why did you stop it? He slipped over,' he moaned to Pat Murphy.

Patrick shrugged. 'You know the rules, Jimmy. He never slipped, he was put down. One knock down, fight over. They're only kids, remember.'

Seeing the smarmy expression on Eddie Mitchell's face, Jimmy walked towards him. 'Let's put the little 'uns in there, then. How old's your youngest?'

'My Joey's six, but his mother won't be letting him get in there,' Eddie chuckled.

Jimmy tried to goad him, 'Does your wife wear the trousers, then? Five he is, my Jed. Come on, let the chavvies have a go. What are you? A man or a mouse?'

Eddie shrugged. Jed might only be five, but he certainly wasn't a wimp like Joey was. As it wasn't in his nature to back down, Eddie went off to find his youngest.

Seeing Jessica sitting with Vicki, he walked over to them. 'Where's Joey?'

Jessica smiled and pointed to the makeshift dancefloor. Eddie's blood boiled as he spotted his son. He looked a right pansy dancing in a circle with six little girls.

'He's coming with me. I've organised a little boxing match for him,' Eddie told Jessica bluntly.

Jess looked at her husband in horror. 'What do you mean? A boxing match?'

'He's going in the ring with that little Jed. They're only having a spar up, it's nothing dangerous,' Eddie said reassuringly.

'No, he is not,' Jessica said immediately. 'He's six years old, Eddie.'

146

Ignoring her, Eddie marched towards Joey and dragged him out of the circle.

'Leave him alone!' Jessica screamed, chasing after her husband.

'Daddy, no, leave Joey alone,' Frankie cried.

Vicki caught Jess by the arm and cuddled her. 'Leave it, Jess. You won't win. Men like ours, they don't listen, love.'

'Please, Daddy. I don't want to box, I want to dance,' Joey sobbed.

Picking up his son, Eddie marched him towards the boxing ring. 'Stop crying else I'll wallop you. Now, all you've got to do is get in that ring and land a few punches. Just hit him as hard as you can, Joey. You're older than him, you'll be fine.'

'I don't want to, Daddy,' Joey said, trying to wriggle out of his father's arms.

Eddie slapped his son gently around the face. 'Like it or not, you're doing it. Dancing is for girls, boxing's for boys. Now get in that ring and make your dad proud of you.'

Jessica was hysterical as her son was lifted into the ring. 'Do something, Raymond, please,' she screamed.

Grabbing hold of her and Frankie, Raymond hugged them both. 'It'll be fine, Jess. I can't do nothing, you know what Ed's like. Just face me and don't look. It'll be over within seconds.'

Joey shook like a leaf as the boy stared at him. 'Hit him, Joey, hit him!' Eddie screamed.

'I can't. I don't want to,' Joey sobbed, as Jed lunged towards him.

As the punch landed on Joey's chin, he hit the deck with an almighty thud.

Seeing Patrick Murphy wave his hands, Jimmy O'Hara

147

jumped into the ring and lifted Jed up in triumph. He'd had £500 on his youngest, so at least he was no longer out of pocket.

Eddie dashed into the ring to tend to Joey.

'Is he OK? I'm a first-aider,' he heard someone say.

'He doesn't look OK,' somebody else shouted.

Jessica pushed Raymond away and took in the pandemonium. Hysterical, she ran towards her son. 'Joey, Joey, Joey!' she cried.

Seeing her son's limp body, Jessica screamed louder than she had ever screamed before.

# FOURTEEN

'I've just examined Joey. He's absolutely fine, you can take him home now,' the doctor told Jessica.

Relieved, Jessica repeatedly thanked the doctor and hugged her mum. 'Ring Dad and get him to come and pick us up,' she told Joyce.

Joey had come round five minutes after he'd been knocked out cold. Petrified that he might have concussion or suffered permanent brain damage, Jessica had brought him to casualty. He'd been kept in overnight as a precaution and Jess was thankful that her prayers had been answered and he was OK.

She had used Patrick's phone to call her parents, who had been brilliant. Stanley had taken the hysterical Frankie home with him, while Joyce had stayed with Jessica and Joey at the hospital all night.

Eddie had turned up at the hospital late the previous night, but Jess had immediately sent him packing. 'Get away from me and my children,' she screamed.

'Please, Jess, let me see Joey. I'll make it up to him, I'll make it up to you and Frankie as well. Nothing like this will ever happen again, I promise,' Ed pleaded.

Jessica was having none of it. She had seen a side to her husband over the last couple of days that she'd never seen before. A nasty, vicious, drunken side, and she would never forgive him for what he had done to Joey. 'Just go, Ed. If you don't I shall scream blue murder and tell the nurses and doctors what really happened,' she told him.

With tears in his eyes, Ed walked away. Jess knew he felt terribly guilty – she could see it in his eyes – but she could never excuse what he had done.

She had told them in casualty that Joey had fallen off a swing. She could hardly tell them the truth, could she? Their faces would be a picture if she told them her husband had forced their six-year-old son to participate in a boxing match. She'd have social services knocking on her door if the doctors found out the truth..

'Hello, Mummy. Are we going home now? I want to play with Milky the Cow.' Joey said chirpily.

Jessica scooped her son into her arms. 'We're going to stay with Nanny and Grandad for a few days,' she told him.

Joey looked perplexed. 'But I haven't got any toys at Nanny and Grandad's house. Can't we go to our house, Mummy?'

Jessica stroked his thick blond hair. The innocence of his eyes tugged at her heart strings and she felt a tear run down her cheek. 'Frankie's round at Grandad's. You want to see your sister, don't you? And what about the pigeons? Grandad will take you out and you can help him fly them.'

Joey could tell that his mum was upset, but he wasn't sure why. 'OK,' he said, smiling.

'Hello, darling, how's Nanny's little soldier?' Joyce said, as Jessica walked towards her with Joey in her arms.

'I'm hungry, Nan. Can I have some chips?'

Joyce kissed Joey on the forehead. 'As soon as we get home, Nanny will cook you whatever you want.'

\* \* \*

As soon as Raymond opened his front door, Eddie walked inside and sat on the sofa with his head in his hands. He hadn't slept a wink and he was consumed with guilt and an aching heart. Ed knew he'd been bang out of order. Seeing O'Hara had made his blood boil. Overcome by jealousy, he'd got paralytic and the rest was history.

'I know Joey's all right. I rang up the hospital this morning. What am I gonna do, Ray? Say I've lost Jess? She might leave me and take the kids with her.'

Raymond shrugged. This was an awkward situation for him, and his loyalty really lay with his sister. Seeing tears in Eddie's eyes, he decided not to rub salt in his wounds. He obviously knew what he'd done was wrong, so there was no bloody point in making it worse for him.

'I dunno what you're gonna do, Ed. Is Joey still in hospital or have they let him out?'

'The nurse I spoke to said that he was OK and he'd be discharged this morning. I can't see Jess coming home, though. Your mum's up there with her and I reckon she'll take the kids round to hers.'

Raymond nodded. He'd shot up the hospital last night and spoken to Jessica and his mum, and he knew she wasn't planning on going home. 'Do you wanna drink? You're shaking,' Raymond said to Eddie.

Ed shook his head. 'It's drink that's fucking caused all this. If I hadn't been so pissed, none of it would have happened.'

Raymond opened a can of lager and sat down opposite Eddie. 'I really don't know what to say, Ed. The only advice I can give you is to let me sister calm down a bit. I wouldn't go round me mum's just yet. I mean, Jess has got to come home at some point, she's got no clean clothes for herself or the kids with her, has she? And what about school? She won't want the twins having too much time off, will she?'

Eddie stood up. 'I'm gonna go home and wait there in case she comes back. I might try and ring her at your mum's, see if she'll talk to me. I'll do anything to get her to forgive me, Ray. I love her, she's my life and without her I'm nothing.'

'Joey,' Frankie cried, throwing her arms around her brother's neck.

Stanley hugged Jessica. He'd always known that one day that bastard she'd married would show his true colours and he just hoped that his daughter had the courage to leave him now.

'I'm gonna have a lie-down on the sofa,' Jessica said.

'Let Mummy have a rest. Nanny's going to cook some of her special crinkled chips,' Joyce said, leading the kids into the kitchen.

Stanley sat in his armchair. He needed to have a chat with Jessica in private. 'You've got to leave him, Jess. I mean, if he's done what he's done to his son, it proves that he's capable of anything. It's not like it's a one-off. He nearly strangled you the other night, love. The man's a fucking monster.'

Jessica looked down at her hands and said nothing. Punishing her husband was one thing; leaving him was another.

Her dad carried on talking. 'You've got to put the kids first, Jess, and if their safety is at risk, you've no option but to leave him.'

Jessica felt her eyes welling up. 'I need to make this decision myself, Dad. I'll stay here for a few days, get me head straight and then I'll decide what to do.'

Stanley shook his head. 'If you stay with Eddie, you're

a fool, Jess. He's obviously an animal and you'd be far better off without him in your life.'

Pleased that the twins had run back into the room and ended such an awkward conversation, Jessica went outside to talk to her mum. 'Dad reckons Eddie's dangerous. He said I've got no choice other than to leave him.'

'Don't take no notice of that silly old bastard. What does he know, eh? Look, what Eddie did this weekend was wrong, very wrong, but you can't just walk away from an otherwise happy marriage because of two stupid mistakes. You said yourself, he was drunk both times. Lay the law down to him. The ball's in your court, Jess. Tell him you'll only come home if he promises not to drink Scotch in front of you and the kids any more.'

Jessica sighed. She had so much on her mind, she felt as if her head was about to burst. 'I really don't know what came over him, Mum. He's usually such a good husband and father, and I've never seen him as drunk as he was yesterday. There was some bloke at the party that he's had this feud with over the years. Eddie hates this O'Hara fella. I think he was the one that scarred his face and I just don't think Eddie could handle seeing him again.'

Joyce smiled. 'There's your answer, then. It was a one-off, Jess. Play hard to get, make him sweat for a few days before you go back home, but you must go back, dear. Look at your lovely house, you don't want to lose that and your nice lifestyle, do you now?'

Jessica nodded. The house and her lifestyle were the last of her bloody problems, but sometimes it was easier just to agree with her mum than to argue her point.

Eddie paced up and down the living-room carpet. He was desperate to speak to Jessica, but too nervous to ring her.

Debating whether to call his dad and ask for advice, he decided against it. His dad had got the pox of him the other night, so how could he admit he'd now allowed his six-year-old son to be knocked out cold?

Furious with himself, Eddie punched the wall. He was probably the laughing stock of Rainham. Gossip tended to travel at a hundred miles an hour in the circles he mixed in. Noticing one of Jessica's sweatshirts lying on the chair, Eddie picked it up and held it to his nose. As he took in her scent, he felt a comfort within.

'Forgive me, Jess. I love you so much,' he whispered.

Looking around the house he'd been so proud to have built, Ed decided that he now hated it. Without Jessica's constant chattering and the twins' happy laughter, it wasn't homely at all. He'd dropped Gary and Ricky home earlier and the silence was killing him. Desperate to make things right again, Eddie picked up his car keys. A phone call wasn't the answer. He needed to see his beautiful wife face to face, tell her how sorry he was. Even if he had to go down on his bended knee to get her back, so be it.

Jessica was upstairs freshening up when she heard the doorbell go.

'Mummy, Daddy's here,' Frankie shouted.

Feeling her body go rigid, Jessica stood rooted to the spot. She wasn't ready to face him yet – she couldn't.

'You're not going to answer the door, are you?' Stanley said to Joyce.

'Of course I'm going to answer it. You stay there, and mind your own business. I'll speak to Eddie in the kitchen.'

Joyce ushered the twins out of the room. 'Frankie, Joey, go upstairs with Mummy. Nanny needs to have a little chat with your dad.'

'Is Daddy angry with me because I lost at boxing?' Joey asked innocently.

Joyce stroked his head. 'Of course not, darling. Just go upstairs until Nanny calls you, then you can come down and say hello to your dad.'

As Joyce opened the front door, Eddie was standing there holding a massive bouquet. 'I am so sorry for what happened, Joyce. Where's Jess? I desperately need to talk to her.'

Joyce led him into the kitchen. 'She's very upset, Ed. I don't know if she's ready to have it out with you yet. Let me make us a brew and then I'll go upstairs and try and persuade her to talk to you.'

Eddie sat on a stool. 'I ain't slept all night. How's Joey? I take it he's here?'

Joyce nodded. 'The twins are both upstairs. Joey seems OK now, he's just eaten a big plate of chips, bless him.'

Eddie put his head in his hands. 'I feel so guilty, Joyce. I'll make it up to Joey, I promise I will. If Jess can find it in her heart to forgive me, I'll book us all a holiday. We can spend some proper time together as a family, it will do us all good.'

Joyce handed him his cup of tea.

'What do you want?' she asked, as Stanley peered around the door.

Ignoring Eddie, Stanley walked in. 'The pigeons need feeding,' he said curtly.

As Stanley shut the back door, Joyce locked it. The crafty old sod had only come out to be nosy. She smiled at Eddie. 'Stands out there for hours with his cock in his hand,' she joked.

Eddie did his best to force a smile. He wasn't in the mood for jokes, no matter how funny they were.

'Go upstairs and speak to Jess for me, Joyce. Ask her if I can go up and talk to her.'

Jessica was sitting on the bed with the twins either side of her.

'Are you angry with Daddy?' Frankie asked her.

'Can we go and see him now?' Joey pleaded.

Joyce opened the bedroom door. 'Ed wants to talk to you, Jess. I'll take the kids downstairs and send him up, shall I?'

Jessica shook her head. 'I don't want to see him, Mum. I'm not ready to go through all this yet.'

Joyce put her hands on her hips. 'Look dear, he's your husband, you have to talk to him and there's no time like the present.'

Jessica sighed. 'OK, but let the twins stay here for a minute. I'll send them down when he comes up. I'm not leaving them on their own with him.'

Joyce nodded and left the room.

'Go up, Eddie. She's in her old bedroom.'

Eddie felt his heart rate quicken as he carried the flowers up the stairs. He took a deep breath and walked into the room.

'Daddy!' Frankie and Joey exclaimed.

'Hello, kids. Can Daddy have a cuddle?' he said, with tears in his eyes.

Hugging them both tightly, Eddie crouched down and kissed them. 'You go downstairs and see your nan for a minute,' he told them.

They both nodded. 'Will you come and see Grandad's pigeons with me?' Joey asked him.

'Another time, son,' Eddie said, wiping his eyes on his sleeve.

As the twins left the room, Eddie handed the flowers to Jess. 'Peace offering,' he said.

Without looking at them, Jessica put them on the floor. 'It's gonna take a bit more than a bunch of flowers, Eddie.'

Eddie knelt down in front of her and tried to take her hands in his, but Jessica quickly snatched hers away.

'Jess, I'm so sorry for what happened. I was bang out of order and I promise you faithfully that nothing like that will ever happen again. Please, Jess, look at me. You and the twins mean the world to me, just give me another chance, let me make it up to you.'

Aware that Ed was crying, Jessica averted her eyes. If she looked at him she'd melt and she was desperate not to thaw that easily. 'What you did to Lee the other night was bad enough, but what you did to your own son was despicable, Eddie. How am I ever meant to trust you again? How can I live with a man who I'm frightened to leave alone with his own children?'

'Don't say that, please don't say that. You make me sound like a monster, Jess. I love my kids, you know I do. I made a mistake, one stupid mistake, that's all. Just give me another chance. I'll do anything you say, anything,' Eddie begged.

Jessica shook her head. 'It's not that easy, Eddie. I thought Joey was dead, I really did. How do you think that made me feel?'

'I'm sorry babe, I really am. Let's go home, we can talk indoors,' Eddie pleaded.

Jessica stood up and opened the bedroom door. 'I want you to leave now, Eddie. I need to think things through, decide what I want to do. I need you to bring some clothes here for me and the kids. Bring their school bags as well and Milky the Cow and some other toys.'

Shell-shocked, Eddie stood up. 'How much stuff shall I bring? Do you think you'll be back home by next weekend?'

Jessica kept her cool. She was damned if she was going to make this easy for him.

'Who says I'm coming home at all? I've got a massive bump on my head and my son nearly died. The way that I feel at this moment, Eddie, I never want to see you or that bloody house ever again.'

# FIFTEEN

Many visits, phone calls and apologies later, Jessica agreed to go out alone for a meal with Eddie to discuss their future.

Her mother had done her head in and just wouldn't let sleeping dogs lie. 'You can't keep messing your husband around, Jess. Two mistakes he's made and even though they were big mistakes, you can't keep punishing the man forever. There'll be women out there who will be waiting in the wings as we speak. I'd make things right with him, if I was you, before it's too late and some little dolly bird gets her claws into him.'

Not wanting the kids to see her going out with their father, Jessica had asked her dad to take them to the pictures. 'I don't want Frankie and Joey to see Ed. They're missing him and it might upset them. He's picking me up at seven, so don't bring them back until at least half past,' she told her father.

'Don't worry, I'll take them for a pizza after the film, but I'll tell you something, if you get back with that arsehole, you want your bloody head tested,' her dad said bluntly.

Jessica ignored his comments. It had been just over a week now since she'd moved back in with her parents and between them they'd driven her up the bloody wall. She did appreciate them both caring, but they wouldn't leave the subject of her marriage alone and the fact that their opinions differed so much made it all the worse.

Sighing, Jessica fished through her temporary wardrobe. She had very little to choose from because most of her clothes were still in Rainham. Not wanting Eddie to think she'd made too much of an effort, she decided to wear her faded jeans. Matched with her red bag, T-shirt and stilettos, she could still look nice without going over the top.

Pleased with her overall appearance, Jessica carefully applied her mascara and lipgloss. Knowing that Eddie hated her wearing too much make-up, she deliberately added some blusher and eyeliner. Sod him, Ed wouldn't have the guts to say anything about her appearance tonight, the bastard would be far too busy grovelling.

Jessica felt slightly apprehensive as she walked down the stairs. She had already decided where she wanted her future to lie, but there was a lot that needed ironing out first.

As Jessica walked into the kitchen, Joyce looked at her in horror. 'Christ, you could have made more of an effort. I thought you was going out for a nice meal. You can't sit in a posh restaurant in those old-looking denim jeans. You look like a bloody workman.'

'Mum, please don't start, I'm not in the mood. I feel a bundle of nerves as it is. Is there any of that wine left in the fridge?'

Joyce tutted as she poured her daughter a small glass. Every night this week Jessica had insisted on having some wine with her evening meal and Joyce was beginning to think she was turning into an alcoholic.

'Don't drink too much while you're out with Eddie tonight. You need a clear head on you – you don't want to act like an old lush. Men hate to see their women drunk, especially men like Eddie.'

Jessica snatched the glass and stomped out of the kitchen. The quicker she got out of this lunatic asylum, the better.

Eddie sat upstairs in his Auntie Joan's house. His father had called an urgent meeting and Ed knew by the look on his face that whatever news he had was good news.

'I heard what happened at the party last week, Gavin Smith told me. How's Joey? Recovered, has he?' Ronny said, laughing.

'Joey! What's a matter with the boy?' Harry Mitchell asked.

Eddie shot his brother a look of pure hatred. His dad knew nothing about what had gone on at the party and if anyone was going to tell him, he'd rather do it himself. 'I'll tell you later, Dad. Tell us your news first,' Eddie said, embarrassed.

Ronny was such a loudmouth prick. Now he knew, there was little point in hiding the truth from anyone else.

As Auntie Joan tapped on the door, Eddie jumped up to let her in. 'There's chicken and beef in the sandwiches. Now, are you sure you don't want me to make you a nice brew, Harry?'

Smiling, Harry shook his head. 'We've good news today, Joanie, so we'll be having a little celebratory tipple instead,' he told her.

Joan nodded and shut the door. The men had important business to discuss and they didn't need her hanging about like a mother hen.

Harry opened a bottle of expensive Scotch and urged Paulie to do the honours. Sipping his own, he smiled at Raymond. 'Well, Raymondo, I have some very good news

161

that is of particular interest to you. The police yesterday arrested a lad in connection with the murder of Mad Dave. I've since heard they've formally charged him. They'd been looking for two black boys who were already well known to them. One of them is called Rowan, I don't know his surname, but they found his fingerprints in the Portakabin. Apparently, Mad Dave reported a burglary down his yard a few weeks back, so chances are it was this Rowan kid and his mate, who are well-known thieves. I suppose the Old Bill have found the kids' prints and surmised it was him that came back and killed him. What a fucking result, eh? Leaves the rest of us in the clear.'

Raymond lifted his glass. 'To Rowan,' he chirped.

'To Rowan,' everybody else said, laughing.

Looking at his watch, Eddie realised it was gone half-six. 'Listen, I'm sorry to have to leave so quickly, but I've gotta be somewhere.'

'You ain't even drunk your drink yet, at least have that first,' Paulie told Eddie.

Eddie stood up. Fuck the drink – the last thing he needed was to turn up round Jessica's mum's smelling like a brewery.

'She's got you right where she wants you, that old woman of yours,' Ronny goaded.

Eddie chose not to rise to the bait. 'I'll catch up properly with you all next week or something.'

'What was you gonna tell us about Joey?' Harry enquired.

Shaking his head, Eddie walked towards the door. 'I'll give you a ring tomorrow, Dad, and don't listen to what anybody else says. Ronny's heard what happened through the rumour mill. At least if you hear it from me, you know it's kosher.'

Harry Mitchell nodded. 'Take care, son.'

\* \* \*

162

Jessica was annoyed as she lifted back the curtain and peered out of the upstairs window. Eddie was already a quarter of an hour late and if he didn't arrive before the kids got back, she would tell him to go and take a running jump. Furious with herself for having agreed to go out with her husband in the first place, Jessica lay down on the bed. Her mum's voice quickly made her stand up again.

'Jess, Eddie's here, love.'

Glancing in the mirror, Jessica ran down the stairs. 'I won't be late, Mum, and don't forget, if the kids ask, I'm out with Mary.'

'Aren't you going to invite him in?' asked a disappointed Joyce.

'No, I'm not,' Jessica said, as she opened the front door.

Eddie smiled as he saw his stunning wife walk towards him. 'I'd better say a quick hello to your mum,' he said.

'No, let's just go,' Jessica told him.

The conversation in the car was awkward, but polite.

'I haven't booked us anywhere yet. I thought I'd let you decide where you wanted to eat. How do you fancy that nice Italian we took me dad to on his birthday that time?' Eddie asked.

Jessica nodded. 'That'll do fine. I liked it there, the food was lovely.'

The restaurant was about ten minutes' drive away and, as Eddie led Jessica inside, he was relieved to find that it wasn't too busy. He pulled the waiter to one side. 'Can we have a table right at the back, we need a bit of privacy,' he told him.

Jessica chose a seafood dish and Eddie opted for the mouth-watering lasagne.

As the waiter topped their glasses up with wine, Eddie

leaned across the table and held Jessica's hand. 'I've missed you and the twins so much,' he told her.

Jessica nodded and averted her eyes. Eddie still gave her butterflies after all these years and the way that her heart was pounding reminded her of when they'd first got together. 'I have missed you too, Ed, but after what happened, if we do make another go of it, there have to be some changes.'

Relieved that she was softening towards him, Eddie smiled at her. 'Your wish is my command, Jess. I'll do whatever it takes to get you back. What is it you want me to do?'

Jessica took a deep breath. 'Firstly, I want you to apologise to the people from the party. I think we should both pop round to see Pat Murphy and Dougie and Vicki. You were so loud and argumentative, Ed, you upset everyone. We've only just moved into the area and I don't want people to think we're the dregs of society. Just tell them you was drunk and how awful you feel about forcing Joey into that boxing ring.'

Eddie nodded. 'I'll do it. I'll go and apologise first thing tomorrow.'

Jessica paused, before carrying on. 'I want to come with you. I don't want the women down the school making snide comments about us, so I want to show that we're united as a couple. Another thing I want you to do is knock at that O'Hara bloke's and shake his hand to show there's no bad feelings. We only live down the road from him, Ed, and I really don't want any aggravation. I can't live my life looking over my shoulder and if you and him have got this feud going on, it's not safe for me and the kids to live there.'

Eddie looked away from her. Apologising to Pat and Doug was one thing, making things all right with that cunt O'Hara was another. He turned back to Jess. 'The feud between my family and the O'Haras has been going on for years, Jess. It's complicated – you wouldn't understand.'

Jessica stood her ground. 'What's more important, Ed? Jimmy O'Hara, or me and the children? I'm not coming home until you do as I say, and if you don't, then I'm leaving you for good.'

Knowing his wife meant business, Eddie nodded once again. He hated the thought of swallowing his pride, but the thought of life without Jess was far worse. 'OK, I'll do it,' he said.

'I'm coming with you. I want us to go to the O'Haras' together. I don't want his wife and family to think that there's any ill feeling. I'll probably bump into the woman at some point and I don't want any awkwardness.'

Having little choice, Eddie reluctantly agreed. 'Is that it? When are you moving back – tomorrow?' he asked Jessica.

'I haven't finished yet. There's more,' Jessica told him, much to his dismay. 'I don't want you to stop drinking because I know you're usually fine, but I want you to promise me that you'll never get drunk like that in front of me and the children again. It's the Scotch, Eddie, it doesn't agree with you. You are a horrible drunk and I can't live like that. I also want you to lay off Joey. You're always picking on him because he's not as rough and ready as Gary and Ricky. He is what he is, Ed, and I love him for that and so should you. You favour Frankie and it shows. It's not fair, Ed, Joey's a little darling and he loves you very much.'

Eddie was shocked by his wife's comments. 'I don't favour Frankie, I love Joey just as much. With boys, Jess, it's a father's job to toughen 'em up a bit. My dad brought me and my brothers up that way and I did the same with Gary and Ricky. I mean, you want him to be able to stick up for himself, don't you? We don't want him getting picked on at school, do we?'

Jessica bit back. 'I just want you to leave him alone, Ed, you're always on his case. You go mad if he picks up one of Frankie's dolls or does something that you don't consider boyish. He's six years old, for God's sake. Gary and Ricky never had twin sisters – if they had, they'd have probably played with their toys as well.'

Eddie shrugged. In his eyes, he hadn't been doing anything untoward. All he'd been trying to do was teach the boy right from wrong. 'I'll promise I'll never get drunk like that again, and yes, I'll let Joey grow up in his own time. But Jess, don't ever say that I love any of my other kids more than him, 'cause it's untrue. You've hurt me saying that; he's my son and I'd fucking die for him.'

Realising that Eddie looked a bit choked up, Jessica felt awful. She wanted to say something about how he'd grabbed her round the neck and hurt her head, but perhaps this wasn't the right time. Maybe she had been too harsh on him, too brutal. 'So, when shall the kids and I move back home, then?' she said, squeezing his big, lifeless hand.

With tears in his eyes, Eddie managed a smile. Jess and the twins were coming home where they belonged and nothing else really mattered. 'How about tonight? It's only eight o'clock. Shall we bolt our dinner down, then go and pick the twins up?'

Jessica nodded. 'I'd like that very much.'

Because they were on their school holidays, Joey and Frankie were allowed to stay up later than usual. As the

166

front door opened, they ran to greet their mum and were surprised, but also delighted, to see their dad.

'Cuddles, Daddy, cuddles,' Frankie demanded.

Joyce poked her head around the door and beamed at the happy family atmosphere.

Eddie put Frankie down and held his arms out to Joey. 'Come and have a cuddle with your dad, eh?' he urged him.

Joey ran into his arms. 'Do you still love me, Daddy?' he asked solemnly.

Eddie held his son tighter than ever before. 'I love you more than you'll ever know, Joey,' he said, stroking his head.

Jessica ushered her mum back into the lounge and had a brief word with both of her parents. 'Mum, Dad, thanks ever so much for letting me and the kids stay here. You've been brilliant, both of yous have.'

Joyce hugged her. 'Everything sorted, love? You going back home?'

Jessica nodded. She was desperate to get back to her big house and taste her home comforts once more.

Stanley sat stony-faced staring at the telly. He had nothing to say, nothing at all.

'You don't mind if we shoot off now, do you, Mum? Our clothes and the kids' toys we can pick up tomorrow.'

Joyce smiled as Eddie walked into the room with a twin in each arm.

'I'll pack all your stuff up for you in the morning. Yous get yourselves home,' Joyce urged them.

Eddie grinned. 'I wouldn't mind a cup of tea first, Joycie. You make the best brew I've ever tasted, and I'm parched.'

Thrilled by her son-in-law's compliment, Joyce jumped up and almost ran to the kitchen.

Unable to take any more of Eddie's old bollocks, Stanley stormed out of the room.

'You OK, Dad? Where are you going?' Jessica shouted after him.

'To feed the pigeons. Take care, love,' Stanley shouted, as he slammed the kitchen door.

Relieved to be alone, Stanley spoke quietly to his birds. Ernie and Ethel were his pride and joy. They might only be pigeons, but they listened to him, they understood, and that was more than he could say about his family.

'It will all end in tears, Ernie. You mark my words, Ethel, that Eddie's no good. Jess'll never be happy with him,' he told them.

'Coo-coo, coo, coo-coo,' the pigeons replied.

Stanley felt a tear roll down his cheek. Even his pigeons could see through Eddie's charade. If only his family could do the same.

# SIXTEEN

Much to Eddie's dismay, Jessica insisted that the twins sleep in the king-size bed with her, and he sleep in the spare room.

'Please let's share a bed, Jess. I've missed your warmth, I need a cuddle,' Eddie pleaded.

Jessica shook her head. By the time they'd got home, both the twins were out for the count and they had had to carry them up the stairs. 'It's only for tonight, Ed. I don't want them waking up wondering where they are. Anyway, they've both had a bit of a tummy bug. I want them next to me, so I know they're all right.'

The following morning the twins were both full of beans. 'Can we go and play outside?' Frankie asked excitedly.

'You can play in the garden later. Firstly, you've both got to have a bath and then Daddy's gonna take us all out for lunch,' Jessica told them.

Frankie stuck her bottom lip out. 'I don't want to go out for lunch, Mummy. I want to have a picnic in the tree house.'

Jessica smiled. Trying to keep the kids from getting dirty in the garden could be a real pain sometimes, but she was glad to be back home. 'How about if we go to that pub that's got the big play area?' Jessica asked hopefully.

Joey and Frankie jumped up and down on the bed. They liked the pub with the play area, there were lots of other children there. 'Can we go now, Mummy?' Joey pleaded.

Jessica lifted them both off the bed. 'Bath first and then we can go,' she laughed.

Hearing Jess and the kids banging about, Eddie got up himself. 'Good morning, sexy,' he said, hugging his wife.

His touch felt good and Jessica returned the compliment. 'I've told the kids we'll take them to that Beefeater that's got the big play area. Get yourself ready, Ed, and we can stop on the way and deliver our apologies.'

'Can't we do that tomorrow? We can't take the kids with us, can we?'

Annoyed that he was trying to go back on his word, Jessica pulled away from him. 'Don't start breaking promises, Ed. We said we were gonna do it today and we will. The kids'll be fine – we'll only be a minute and they can sit in the car.'

Knowing he was still on a trial run, Eddie unwillingly agreed. He was dreading being marched up to people's houses like a naughty schoolboy. Him – Eddie Mitchell? Talk about making him look a cunt but, unfortunately, he didn't have much choice. He wanted his life with Jess to get back to normal and if a few apologies allowed that to happen, it was worth it.

An hour later, Eddie stood at Pat Murphy's front door and rang the musical bell. Hearing it play, 'When Irish Eyes are Smiling', Eddie couldn't help but laugh.

'Trust Patrick! Fuck knows where he got that from,' he said to Jessica.

Patrick immediately opened the door. 'My auntie who

170

lives in Limerick got hold of it for me. Good, isn't it?' he said chuckling.

Eddie held out his right hand. 'Patrick, I've just popped round to apologise for my drunken behaviour at your party. I was well sloshed and I probably upset a few people other than my wife.'

Patrick Murphy laughed loudly. 'Bejesus, Eddie, you were fine. I've had a lot worse than you here over the years, that I have, for sure.'

Spotting the twins waving at him from the car, Patrick nodded towards them. 'How's your son now?'

Eddie smiled at Jessica and squeezed her hand. 'He's absolutely fine. No thanks to his dad though, eh, babe?'

Jessica nodded. 'Well, we'd best be going now, Patrick, and once again, we're sorry for spoiling your party.'

Patrick waved them goodbye. 'I'll see you both soon,' he shouted.

The next stop was Dougie and Vicki's house. 'Hello yous two,' Vicki said, as she opened the front door.

'Is Dougie about?' Eddie asked her.

'He's in his office. Spends half his life in there, he does. Come in, I'll tell him you're here.'

Jessica gesticulated to the twins to tell them that they would only be a minute. 'Stay in the car, you're not to get out,' she shouted.

As Eddie stood apologising to an unfazed Doug, Vicki and Jessica swapped phone numbers. 'How about you and Doug come over to ours for dinner next week?' Jessica asked her.

'We'd love to, wouldn't we, Doug?' Vicki replied.

Dougie smiled. 'I've told Ed, the party's long forgotten. Christ, if I had a pound for every time I've got pissed and made a prick of meself, I'd be a very rich man, and yes, dinner sounds great,' he added.

Jessica and Eddie said their goodbyes and left. Driving towards Jimmy O'Hara's house, Eddie felt his stomach start to churn. Two down and one to go and this was the bastard he was dreading.

Pulling onto O'Hara's drive, Eddie was surprised to see that the beautiful grounds of the house he'd once been so keen to buy now resembled a shit-hole. There were two big, tatty mobile homes either side of the house, six lurchers, three Jack Russells and dog shit everywhere. There were a load of horses standing behind a wire fence and there was even a fucking goat staring at him.

'Typical fucking pikeys,' Eddie muttered as he got out of the car.

'Can we go and see the horses?' Frankie squealed with delight.

'Can we stroke them? Joey asked.

With dogs leaping up at him from all angles, Eddie did his best to stay calm. 'Yous two stay in that car and don't move,' he ordered the twins.

'Please, Daddy, let us see the horses,' Frankie whinged.

'No, Frankie, and I mean no. Do you wanna stay in the car with the kids, Jess? There's more animals running around than there is in a fucking circus.'

Jessica opened the car door. She needed to know that Eddie had said the right things to Mr O'Hara. 'I'm coming with you,' she insisted.

With a Jack Russell trying to shag his right leg, Eddie made his way towards the house. Seeing a miniature tractor drive past, he took little notice. Goats, horses, dogs, tractors – they all seemed to blend in with the territory.

With a heavy heart, he knocked on Jimmy O'Hara's front door.

Frankie looked in amazement as the tractor stopped

by the car and Jed, whom she'd met at the party, leaped off it.

'Frankie!' he exclaimed. He opened the door of the car and urged her to move over.

Unusually for Frankie, she came over all shy. 'Do you live here?' she mumbled, averting her eyes from the grinning Jed.

Joey could feel his heart pumping though his T-shirt. This was the boy who had hit him in the boxing ring and he was petrified of a repeat performance.

Aware of Joey's anxiety, Jed held his hand out to him. 'I'm really sorry for hitting you so hard. I didn't mean to hurt you. I had to do it, else my dad would have beat me.'

'Shake his hand then, like Daddy does,' Frankie urged her brother.

Joey did as he was told and sat quietly as Jed spoke to Frankie.

'Come for a ride on my tractor,' Jed urged her.

Frankie shook her head. 'My dad said I had to stay in the car. He'll tell me off if I get out.'

Jed laughed. 'You're a scaredy cat. Go on admit it, you're frit to death. You think I can't drive, but I can. I can even drive my dad's car – I can, honest I can,' Jed bragged.

Jimmy O'Hara smiled as he locked eyes with Eddie Mitchell. 'Well, well, well, this is a nice surprise,' he said, with a hint of sarcasm.

Embarrassed that the Jack Russell was still trying to mount him, Eddie gently pushed it away.

Jimmy O'Hara laughed as he picked the dog up. 'His name's Rocky; I named him after me cousin. He likes you, look. Got his cory out, for you, he has.'

Eddie ignored Jimmy's crude comment and held out his right hand. 'My wife and I were just passing and we thought it could be a good idea to stop by, just to say no hard feelings about last week. As you said at the party, we're neighbours now and all of us want a quiet life.'

Jimmy shook Eddie's hand and nodded towards his car. 'My little Jed's chatting up your daughter again. Ain't stopped talking about her since that party last week. I'd definitely say we're gonna be in-laws one day,' Jimmy said, chuckling.

Eddie glanced at the car in horror. 'We'd best be going now. Come on, Jess,' he urged.

'I appreciate you dropping by, Eddie. Goodbye, Mrs Mitchell,' Jimmy said, as he shut the front door.

'Who was that?' his wife Alice asked.

'Eddie dinlo fucking Mitchell,' Jimmy said, laughing his head off.

Breaking into a run, Eddie reached the car before Jess. 'What are you doing in there?' he shouted at Frankie.

'Nothing, Daddy. You said we wasn't allowed to get out of the car, so Jed got in to talk to us.'

'We're going now, so time for you to get out, boy,' Eddie told Jed.

Grinning from ear to ear, Jed leaned towards Frankie and pecked her full on the lips. 'I'm your boyfriend now, Frankie, and I'll come and see you soon,' he yelled, as he climbed back on his tractor.

Eddie waited for Jess to get in. Furious, he started the engine and put his foot down.

'Frankie's got a boyfriend, Frankie's got a boyfriend,' Joey sang to his sister.

Frankie felt herself go all weird again. 'No, I haven't,' she said shyly.

'Yes, you have and you kissed him,' Joey giggled.

Annoyed that some old dodderer was driving too slow, Eddie held his hand on the hooter and cursed as he overtook him.

'You stay away from that boy, Frankie, do you hear me?' Eddie demanded.

Aware that Jed was the boy who had knocked Joey down in the boxing ring, Jessica was more worried about her son. 'Are you OK, Joey? Did that boy frighten you, love?'

Joey shook his head. 'He said sorry, Mummy. He said that his dad made him hit me.'

'Sounds a bit like you, dear,' Jessica said, nudging her husband.

Eddie drove in stony silence. Shaking hands with Jimmy O'Hara had made him feel physically sick, and as for that cheeky fucking kid of his, he'd kill that little bastard if he ever came anywhere near his daughter again.

Seeing the expression on Eddie's face, Jessica guessed today had been hard for him. 'Thanks Ed, for doing that for me,' she said, stroking his arm.

'Are we going to the pub now, Daddy?' Joey asked.

Still in a foul mood, Eddie tried his hardest not to show it. 'Yep, we're going there now, son,' he replied, as cheerfully as he could.

An hour and a couple of pints later, Ed had finally calmed himself down. Sitting opposite Jessica on a wooden bench in the beer garden, he gently held her hand. 'This is what life's all about, eh? Me, you and the kids,' he said, nodding towards the twins, who were playing happily on the apparatus.

Jessica smiled as Frankie waved at her.

'Watch me, Mummy,' she yelled as she hurtled down the big slide.

Jessica turned her attention back to her husband. 'I know

we've had our ups and downs recently, but I do love you, Eddie Mitchell.'

Eddie winked at her. 'Does that mean we're gonna sleep in the same bed tonight and you're gonna let me have my wicked way with you?'

Jessica felt her cheeks redden. Even after all these years, Eddie still had the ability to make her blush. 'Yes, we will sleep in the same bed tonight and, if you behave yourself, I just might let you have your wicked way with me,' she told him shyly.

Their intimate moment was ended by a screaming Joey. Standing at the top of a climbing frame, he was bawling his eyes out.

'What's the matter?' Jessica asked, walking towards him.

Frankie giggled as she took stock of the situation. 'Joey's too scared to come down, Mummy,' she said, as she ran over to her dad.

Knowing her son didn't like heights, Jessica urged him to hold the metal rail and walk backwards. 'Just come down the way you went up, Joey,' she urged him.

'I can't, Mummy. I can't get down,' Joey sobbed.

Aware that some other children were laughing as him, Jessica had little option but to go up herself and carry Joey back down. 'It's all right, Mummy's here now. Come on, stop crying, there's a good boy.'

'Isn't Joey a crybaby, Daddy?' Frankie said laughing.

Eddie was embarrassed. There were other parents looking over at him and he was thankful that nobody knew him in this boozer.

Jessica walked towards him with Joey in her arms. 'I'm gonna take him to the toilet and sort him out. He's had a little accident. Give us your car keys, Ed, I've got a spare set of clothes for him in the boot.'

'What do you mean accident? Has he hurt himself?' Eddie asked, bemused.

'Don't tell no one, Mummy,' Joey begged his mother.

'He's wet himself,' Jessica mouthed to Eddie.

Annoyed, Eddie slung her his car keys. His youngest son was a total fucking embarrassment. That Jed might be a little bastard, but at least he was a kid for his father to be proud of. Joey was a total tart and showed himself and his family up wherever he went.

'I'm going on the swing now, Daddy,' Frankie said, as she climbed off his knee.

Eddie sipped his beer and watched his daughter swing higher than any of the other kids. At least Frankie had a bit of spirit about her; Joey had fucking none whatsoever. Seeing his wife and son walk towards him, Eddie forced a smile. He couldn't have a go at Joey or say anything about him, as he'd promised Jessica he wouldn't.

'Panic over. What shall we do, Ed? Shall we order some food now? The kids both want burger and chips.'

Eddie stood up. 'Keep an eye on Frankie. She's over there with some little boy, he keeps following her around,' he told Jessica, as he headed to the bar.

The little boy in question was quite taken with Frankie and had been trying to attract her attention for the last ten minutes. 'My name's Luke. What's yours?' he asked her.

'Not telling you,' Frankie shouted at him.

'Why not? I've told you my name,' Luke said, trying to hold her hand.

Frankie snatched her hand away. Placing her hands on her hips, she scowled at her stalker. 'Go away and leave me alone.'

As Eddie walked back from the bar, he saw Frankie clump the boy. Putting the drinks on the table, he went

177

over to rescue the poor little sod, who was now sprawled on the ground crying.

'I'm really sorry,' he told the boy's shocked parents.

Eddie lifted his daughter up and carried her back to the table. 'It's naughty to punch people. Why did you punch him, Frankie?'

'Because he wanted to be my boyfriend. I don't like him, Daddy. I want Jed to be my boyfriend.'

Tilting his daughter's chin towards him, Eddie stared at her coldly. 'Listen to me, Frankie, I'm only ever saying this once. If you ever, ever mention Jed's name again, I'm gonna wash your mouth out with soap and water. Do you understand what I'm saying to you?'

Shocked by her father's attitude, Frankie felt her eyes fill up with tears. She flung her arms around his neck and sobbed.

'I'm sorry, Daddy. I won't say Jed any more.'

Wiping her tears away, Eddie smiled at her. 'You promise me, Frankie?'

Thrilled that her father was no longer angry with her, Frankie smiled at him. 'Yes, Daddy, I promise.'

# SEVENTEEN

## *Nine years later – 1987*

Glancing at his watch, Eddie picked up his bunch of keys. 'I'm gonna make a move now, love. I've gotta go up north today to speak to some arsehole that's knocked me. I might be really late back, so don't wait up.'

Jessica brushed a bit of fluff off her husband's collar and hugged him tightly. 'Be careful, Eddie. I love you,' she told him.

As the front door slammed, Jessica resumed her house-work duties. Eddie had always tried to convince her to let him hire a cleaner, but she was having none of it. 'I like doing the housework myself, Ed. Anyway, I don't want a stranger poking around in my home. Vicki and Doug had to sack their cleaner, she was thieving off of them. We're OK as we are,' Jessica insisted.

Happy with the cleanliness of her kitchen, Jessica decided she had done more than enough to earn herself a brew and a biscuit. Dunking the chocolate digestive into her cup, she savoured its flavour and her thoughts returned to her husband. Eddie's job worried the life out of her sometimes. She knew he was still loan-sharking and even though he'd done very well out it, she wished he could find a profession that was less dangerous.

Over the years, Eddie's business had grown, but the

risks had grown with it. Ronny had been shot and was now confined to a wheelchair. He'd been blasted through the lower back and the doctors had since – unsuccessfully – carried out three operations to try to repair his spine.

The one thing that did please Jessica was that Gary and Ricky were now both working with their father. Twenty-three and twenty-one respectively, Gary and Ricky were into bodybuilding and Jessica worried a lot less knowing that they were with Eddie.

Paulie and Raymond were still in the firm, so there were five of them in all. The accident had made Ronny very miserable and bitter and, according to Eddie, he now spent his days drowning his sorrows in numerous pubs. The last time Jessica had seen Ronny was when she had been to visit him in hospital with Eddie. He had been really nasty towards her and she had run from the ward, crying.

'Take no notice. He's one bitter and twisted cunt. He's always been jealous of our relationship,' Eddie said soothingly.

Even though Ronny spoke to Eddie like shit, Eddie still included him in the family business and looked after him financially. Ronny still lived with Sharon, and Eddie did all he could for her sake.

Neither Jess nor the twins had a great deal to do with any of Eddie's family. In Jessica's heart, she knew what they were and she had never felt particularly comfortable or wanted the twins around them. Eddie wasn't like his brothers. He was the odd one out, the good guy. Eddie's family rarely bothered to come to their house in Rainham and that suited Jessica down to the ground. The odd cup of tea and a sand-wich around Auntie Joan's or an occasional meal out with Harry was the only contact she and the kids really had with them now.

'All right, Mum? What's for breakfast?'

Snapping out of her daydream, Jessica began fussing around her daughter. 'Look at your uniform – your skirt's all dirty. You can't wear that, Frankie. Go upstairs and change it.'

Frankie tutted and snatched at the dishcloth. Her skirt only had a tiny mark on it and it was easily wiped off.

'There, done. Now instead of getting on my case, do you think you can make me some breakfast? I'll have a fry-up, if that's OK.'

Jessica put the frying pan on and buttered some bread. 'Go and ask Joey if he wants one, too,' she ordered Frankie.

With a stomp of her feet and a flick of her hair, Frankie marched out of the kitchen. Jessica sighed and shook her head. The twins were her life, she adored them, but they were fifteen going on fifty. Frankie, in particular, drove her up the wall. She was her father's daughter all right, she was Eddie to a tee.

People who had never met the twins before always assumed that Frankie was older than Joey. They didn't even look like twins. Frankie was voluptuous, with dark hair and tanned skin like her father. Joey was as skinny as a beanpole, with blond hair and pale skin like herself. Their personalities were also very different. Frankie was hot-headed and impulsive, while Joey was laid-back and comical.

Frankie had always been Eddie's favourite out of the two and still was. Both fiery, they argued constantly, but adored one another at the same time. Joey's relationship with his father was more complex. They had nothing in common whatsoever, and although their conversations tended to be polite, they were also stilted.

'Joey just wants toast,' Frankie said, plonking herself down at the kitchen table.

Jessica pricked the sausage to make sure it was done properly, then dished up her daughter's breakfast.

'Morning, Mum,' Joey said, kissing her on the cheek.

'Toast won't fill you up. Why don't you let me make you a nice bacon sandwich?' Jessica asked him.

Joey sat opposite his sister. 'Toast is fine, Mum. What you up to today? You off out anywhere nice?'

Jessica smiled. Unlike Frankie, Joey was always so interested in her life. 'Yes, I am going out. Vicki's coming round and we're going clothes shopping together. We're gonna pop in and have lunch with Nan and Grandad on the way back.'

'Mum, see if you can get me a pair of bleached jeans with rips in them. Don't get me rubbish ones though, get a decent make. I'm bursting out of a size eight now, so you'd better get me a ten,' Frankie told her.

'OK, darling, I know the ones you mean. What about you, Joey, do you need anything?'

Joey smiled. 'I could do with some new trainers. Get me Nike, Mum, the ones with the light-blue tick down the side.'

Seeing time was getting on, Jessica urged the kids to finish their breakfast. Living in the lanes meant they needed a lift to and from school and she didn't want them to be late again. 'Come on, hurry up. You've got your exams soon and you don't want to fail them,' Jessica said sternly.

Frankie and Joey smirked at one another as they followed their mum out to the car. Little did she know, neither of them had any intention of spending their day studying for their exams. Joey and Frankie hated school and going through the school gates wasn't on their agenda.

Driving up the M1, Eddie was deep in thought. Ronny had just rung him, shouting and bawling and, for the second time that week, Ed had bitten his tongue.

No one, including Eddie, knew exactly what had happened to Ronny. Ed had apparently been owed a lot of money by a Scottish geezer called Jake Souness. 'I'm gonna fucking blow his brains out,' Ronny had drunkenly bragged one day.

Eddie had told his brother to stay away from Jake. 'Leave it to me. Souness is no fucking mug – he's heavy material. I'll have a word with Dad. He'll know how to play it,' Ed warned him.

As silly as arseholes, Ronny had ignored Eddie's advice and gone to see Jake Souness alone. He had been found half dead two days later and had no recollection of what had actually happened. All he had said was that Jake had poured neat bottles of vodka down his throat, forcing him to drink it. 'I don't remember anything after that. My next memory is waking up, being in agony and not being able to walk,' Ronny said.

Harry Mitchell had come out of retirement to get revenge for his son. He had tortured Jake Souness for three days and, when Jake's body could take no more, he had chopped his head off while he was still alive.

Eddie had been with his father that day and Jake Souness's screams would live with him forever.

'Take the next junction, Ed,' Raymond said, snapping Ed out of his daydream.

Eddie was heading towards a gypsy camp on the outskirts of Birmingham. Dickie Pearce had taken the right piss out of him. Fifteen grand, Eddie had lent him and the cunt had done a runner with it. Finding Dickie Pearce hadn't been easy. Eddie would never have lent him the cash in the first place if he had known he had links with the travelling community. Eddie thought Dickie was just your average guy, and he'd been shocked to find out that the piss-taking bastard was, in fact, a plastic pikey.

'Answer that,' Eddie ordered Raymond as his phone rang.

'It's your dad. Says it's urgent,' Raymond told him.

Knowing that he had his shooter in the Land Cruiser with him, Eddie swung into a lay-by. The Vodafone he owned weighed a ton, it was hard to hold while driving and he could do without causing an accident, today of all days.

'I'm driving. What is it, Dad?' he asked impatiently.

Listening to what his father had to say, Eddie's mood lifted like magic. 'No. When? How?' he asked joyfully.

As Eddie ended the phone call, he turned around in his seat and smiled at Paulie, Gary and Ricky.

Raymond nudged him. 'Come on, don't keep us in suspense. What's happened?'

'Dad's just heard that Butch O'Hara's brown bread. He ain't sure how he croaked it, but someone he knows said it was a heart attack. Apparently Jimmy's gonna set fire to his trailer with the body inside.'

'Why ain't they gonna have a proper funeral for him? Didn't they like him?' Ricky asked bewildered.

Eddie laughed. 'They like a bit of DIY, the old pikeys. I think it's custom for 'em to burn the dead in their own homes. Strange bastards, they are, I've always said that.'

Eddie whistled as he continued his journey. Lady Luck hadn't been very kind to Jimmy over the years, and every time he received yet another kick in the bollocks it pleased Eddie immensely.

Even though they lived near one another, Eddie saw very little of Jimmy. His wife, Alice, had left him years ago. Apparently, she had walked into one of his salvage yards and had caught her beloved Jimmy having his cock sucked by some little dolly bird.

Alice was a typical feisty travelling lass and, by all

184

accounts, had gone mental. Rumour had it, she had gone home and, on Jimmy's return, she had clumped him over the head with a claw hammer. The following day, Alice had packed her bags, shoved the kids in the car and left him for good.

Eddie was overjoyed by Jimmy's little mishap and dined out on it for months afterwards.

Jimmy was never the same man after Alice left him. Without his wife and kids by his side, he let his businesses slip, sold his Roller, and became a bit of a recluse.

Eddie grinned as he turned off the M1. Jimmy's mum had died a couple of years back and, now the old man had popped his clogs, he had no one living on his acres of land bar himself.

Eddie stifled a snigger. At least he had his dogs and horses. Maybe the fucking goat was still alive and that could keep poor Jimmy company on his big piece of land.

Frankie put her last fifty pence into the fruit machine. 'Poxy thing,' she said, kicking the base of it.

Joey laughed as she walked towards the table. 'Why do you waste your money on those things? I've told you before, gambling's for mugs,' he said as she sat down.

Spending their days in the café in Dagenham with a group of their friends was a regular pastime for Frankie and Joey. The café was owned by the sister of one of their best mates and she always allowed them to hang out there. Sometimes they went to school, but most days they couldn't face it. They would wave to their mum as she dropped them off and as soon as she drove away, they would cross the road and catch the bus to Dagenham.

Neither Joey nor Frankie were fans of their school uniform, so they always carried a spare set of clothes with them. They would get changed upstairs on the bus, then would change back into their school uniform on the return journey.

Neither of their parents were aware of what they got up to. Both the twins smoked and drank and sometimes they would stand on the corner totally wasted, waiting for their mum to pick them up. They were always careful, though, and only stuck to vodka, as it had no smell. Their mum would go apeshit if she knew, and their dad would probably rip their heads off.

Writing sick notes had become second nature to both of them. Joey wrote Frankie's, copying his mum's handwriting, and Frankie returned the favour for Joey, copying her dad's.

'What's the time?' Frankie asked her brother.

'Half-one,' Joey replied.

'I'm bored sitting here. Let's go to the park and drink our vodka, eh?'

Joey shrugged and turned to their friends. All of them were partial to a tipple, but Frankie was an absolute nightmare. Joey stood up and urged the others to do the same.

'Come on, Alkie Annie wants her daily fix,' he joked.

Laughing, the six good mates left the café together.

Stanley smiled as his daughter tucked into her ham-salad sandwich. She was a breath of fresh air, his Jessica, and even now, at thirty-three, she was still as beautiful as ever.

'So, how are your pigeons, Stanley? Are you still racing them?' Vicki enquired.

Stanley loved nothing more than discussing his birds and launched into a full account of their day-to-day activities. He liked Jessica's friend and was pleased that his daughter had someone local to turn to if she ever needed her help.

Stanley still didn't like or trust Eddie. His son, Raymond,

186

had turned into a clone of the man and he was extremely bitter about it. Stanley had little option but to play happy families. He loved his daughter and grandchildren so, all in all, Eddie had him by the bollocks.

When Jessica had left Eddie that time, Stanley had stuck to his guns. He hadn't spoken to Eddie for nine months, nor visited the house. He had eventually given in. He had missed Jess and the twins terribly and Joyce's constant moaning had forced him to change his mind. Since then, a happy medium had been met. He was polite to Eddie for the sake of his family, though inwardly he still hated him.

'We're gonna have to go now. I've gotta pick the kids up in an hour,' Jessica informed her parents.

Joyce stood up and cuddled her daughter. 'So will we see you before Christmas?'

'Of course, it's weeks away,' Jessica said smiling. 'I'll pop over next week. You and Dad will stay for a few days at Christmas, won't you? If you come over Christmas Eve in the afternoon, you can go home the day after Boxing Day.'

Joyce looked at Stanley. 'It all depends if Jock's around to feed the pigeons. If not, we can still stay, but I'll have to pop back to see to them every day,' Stanley said.

Joyce raised her eyebrows. 'Stanley's cock will be the death of me.'

Roaring with laughter, Jessica and Vicki left the house.

Eddie drove past the gypsy site and hid the Land Cruiser as best as he could down the end of a dirt track. It was two weeks since he'd found out where Dickie Pearce was actually living and he'd had him watched ever since.

Unfortunately for Eddie, he had no chance of getting his money back. Dickie had a gambling problem and was up to his eyeballs in debt. Eddie wasn't overly bothered about the dosh. He was cakeo and fifteen grand was peanuts to him. What Eddie was annoyed about was the fucking liberty Pearcey had taken. No one messed with the Mitchells, and Eddie couldn't be seen to be lapsing in his old age. Dickie had bragged to a lot of people that he'd knocked Eddie for the dough and, because of that, Ed had no option but to take the silly man out.

'It's gone six o'clock. What time did you say he was due?' Paulie asked.

Eddie knew that Dickie had been making ends meet by selling flowers from the roadside. He also knew that he drove a white Escort van down this road at approximately six o'clock every evening.

'He'll be here any minute,' Eddie told his brother.

'Can't you turn on the engine so we can have some heating? I'm freezing me bollocks off here,' Paulie moaned.

Eddie glared at him. Paulie had turned into Ronny, he was sure he had.

'Shall I put the music on as well? We can dance and have a party, then everyone will know we're here, you soppy cunt.'

Paulie quickly shut up. Ever since Ronny had left the firm and Eddie's boys had joined, he'd felt like a complete fucking outsider.

'Right, there's headlights coming our way,' Eddie said, starting the engine.

'It's him, I'm sure it's a white van,' Raymond told him.

Making sure no one else was about, Eddie crawled along the road. Nearing the van, he switched on his beam. Seeing a startled-looking Dickie put his hands over his face, Eddie pulled up alongside him. Dickie immediately spotted the gun.

'Drive down the end of the dirt track, then open the door and get out,' Eddie ordered him.

Dickie did as Eddie asked. Petrified, he squealed like a pig as he fell to his knees. 'Please don't shoot me. I'm sorry Eddie, I'll pay you back, I promise I will. I've got kids and a grandkid – you can't shoot me, you can't.'

Eddie got out of the Land Cruiser. He put his big foot on top of Dickie's head and pulled back the catch.

'Pull the car forward,' he urged Raymond. He'd only just bought his new Toyota Land Cruiser and he didn't want it covered in some scumbag's blood.

'Kids, grandkids! Shame you didn't think of them before you knocked me, you mug,' Eddie said, smiling at Dickie Pearce's fright.

Lifting Dickie's chin up with his boot, Eddie winked at him. 'Bye-bye Dickie,' he said, as he casually pulled the trigger.

Eddie got into the passenger seat. 'Do us a favour, Ray, find a McDonald's or something. I'm fucking starving.'

'Frankie! Joey! Your dinner's ready,' Jessica shouted up the stairs.

'We're not hungry yet. We'll warm it up later,' Frankie shouted back.

Jessica sighed and covered the plates with cling film. She had gone to a lot of trouble to cook for them and now they were too busy to eat. Not wanting to eat alone, Jessica covered her own up. She hated eating alone, always had done.

Bored, Jessica poured herself a glass of wine. The twins worried her at times. She knew they were working hard for their exams, but she didn't want them overdoing it. Whenever she picked them up from school lately, they seemed so knackered. They barely spoke on the way home because they were so worn out.

'We're going upstairs to do our homework,' they would say as soon as they got through the front door.

'But you've only just left school. You must have a break. Can't you do it later?' she would ask them.

'You don't understand, Mum. The school gives us tons of homework and if we don't do it, we'll get in big trouble,' Frankie told her.

A couple of times Jessica had gone upstairs to try to help them do their homework, but they'd both been fast asleep.

As she sipped her wine, Jessica made a decision. She would go to that school tomorrow and have a quiet word with the headmaster. She wouldn't tell Frankie and Joey her plans. They were typical teenagers and they'd get all embarrassed. She wouldn't even tell Eddie, he'd say she was being a drama queen. Jessica smiled as she topped up her glass. She was a good mum and good mums were protective of their brood. Joey and Frankie were only fifteen and they shouldn't be working like Trojans, bless them.

# EIGHTEEN

'Good morning sleepyhead.'

Jessica opened her eyes and smiled. She had slept like a log and wasn't even aware that Eddie had been lying beside her. 'What time did you get in? I didn't hear you come to bed,' she asked him.

'I got back about two, but I sat up for an hour. I was watching all the news programmes. That fire at King's Cross station was fucking terrible, wasn't it?' Eddie said.

Jessica propped herself up on one elbow. 'Mum rang and said something about a fire. To be honest, Vicki came round last night and we had a few glasses of wine. Doug was away on business, so she didn't leave till twelve. We sat in the kitchen playing tapes. I was gonna put the telly on, but by the time she left, I forgot all about it. What happened then? Did anybody get hurt?'

Eddie sighed and kissed Jessica on the forehead. His wife rarely watched or listened to the news and she didn't have a clue about current affairs. In fact, half the country could collapse in an earthquake and Jessica wouldn't be any the wiser.

'The escalator went up in flames. It was just after rush hour, so a lot of people got caught up in it. I think the death toll is about twenty-seven or something. They reckon it might turn out to be more, though, there are still a lot of people classed as critical.'

Jessica's eyes filled with tears. 'Oh Ed, that's awful! I feel so sorry for the poor people that died. How must their families feel, knowing they've been burned alive?'

Eddie held her tightly. 'Don't upset yourself, Jess. These things happen.'

Jessica wiped her eyes and changed the subject. 'How did you get on up north? Did you find that man and get your money back?'

Eddie nodded. 'Yeah, all sorted.'

'Did he pay you straight away?' Jessica asked.

Eddie smiled as he thought of Dickie with his brains blown out. 'Oh yeah, he paid all right,' he said.

Feeling himself getting hard, Eddie nibbled Jessica's earlobe. 'Stop it, Eddie. I've got to take the kids to school. What time is it?' Jessica said giggling.

'Sod the kids. Look what you've done to me,' Eddie told her, as he placed her hand on his erection.

Unable to resist her handsome husband, Jessica urged him to enter her. Arching her body, she gasped as he sped up his rhythm.

As Eddie orgasmed and rolled onto his back, Jessica sat up and stroked the hairs on his chest. 'What do you want for breakfast?' she asked him.

Eddie smiled at his beautiful wife. He had never been a selfish lover and unless Jessica was satisfied, then neither was he. 'I want you,' he said, as he moved down the bed and pleasured her with his tongue.

Aware of the animal-like noises coming out of her parents' bedroom, Frankie got out of bed and crept next door to wake Joey.

'What time is it?' her brother mumbled.

Frankie pulled the quilt from over his head. 'Forget the time. Mother and Father are at it again. They're just so embarrassing. When I hear 'em making them noises, it puts me off me breakfast.'

Joey smiled and sat up. 'They are married, Frankie – they're entitled to have a bunk-up, you know.'

Frankie pulled a face. 'I'm never gonna have sex after listening to them two. No wonder I'm still a virgin, they've put me off for life.'

Joey couldn't help but laugh. She could be a funny girl, his sister, at times. 'You'll have sex when the time's right. You just ain't met the right person yet, that's all.'

Frankie playfully punched his arm. 'Hark at you, the expert. You've never been out with a girl for more than a couple of weeks.'

'So?' Joey answered.

'So, how come you're so knowledgeable? Both Leanne and Sarah said you never slept with them. So, who have you slept with, then?'

Joey laughed as he forcefully but playfully removed Frankie from his bedroom. 'That's for me to know and you to find out,' he told her.

Jessica stood over the cooker with a smile on her face. 'Do you want mushrooms and beans?'

'I'll have whatever you're offering,' Eddie replied suggestively.

Jessica giggled. 'So what are you up to today? Will you be home late tonight?'

Eddie shook his head. 'I've got a few people to visit, all local, and I'll probably poke me head in the Flag and see if Ronny's in there. I won't be late, I'll be home before teatime. What about you? You doing anything?'

Debating whether to tell him she was worried about

the twins and was off to see the headmaster, Jess heard Frankie and Joey's footsteps and decided to keep quiet. 'I've not planned anything, although I might pop into Romford and get some more Christmas presents.'

'What's a matter with you? Too old to give your dad a kiss now, are you?' Eddie asked Frankie.

Frankie politely kissed him then, screwing up her face, smiled at her brother.

'You didn't kiss him on the lips, did you? You don't know where his tongue's been,' Joey whispered in Frankie's ear.

Frankie punched Joey and laughed.

Eddie finished his breakfast and put the plate in the dishwasher. 'I'm off now, babe,' he said to Jess.

'See you later, kids. I'm back early tonight. Shall we all go out for a Chinese or shall I order a takeaway?'

Frankie nudged Joey. They'd already decided not to attend school today and they didn't want to drink vodka all afternoon, then have to sit in a restaurant with their parents. 'We've got tons of homework, Dad. Me and Frankie would prefer a takeaway,' Joey replied.

Eddie put on his jacket. 'I'll see you all later, then. Pick what you want off the menu and I'll order it as soon as I get home,' he said.

Jessica fed the twins, tidied up the kitchen, then went upstairs to get changed. Usually, she drove the children to school in a tracksuit or jeans, but she couldn't do that today. How could she expect the headmaster to take her seriously if she looked like a tramp?

'What you all done up for?' Frankie asked, as she came down the stairs.

Feeling flustered, Jessica searched for her handbag. 'I'm going Christmas shopping after I've dropped yous two off,' she lied.

\* \* \*

Due to heavy traffic, the journey to the school took about twenty minutes.

'Bye, Mum,' the twins said, as they slammed the car door.

Jessica waved and drove away. She'd already hatched her plan. She would park a couple of streets away, then drive back once they were inside their classroom.

Half an hour later, Jessica made her way into the school gates. She had been to the headmaster's office a couple of years ago, when Joey had been taken ill and, as luck would have it, she remembered where it was.

'Can I help you?' asked a stuffy-looking woman sitting at a typewriter.

'I'd like to speak to the headmaster about my children,' Jessica stated.

'And who shall I say wants to speak to him?'

'Mrs Mitchell. I'm Francesca and Joseph's mother.'

The woman smirked. 'Take a seat. I'll let Mr Redknapp know that you're waiting.'

Jessica sat nervously tapping her fingers. She wasn't very good at confrontation and she was beginning to wish that she hadn't come alone. Eddie was much more businesslike than she was, he would have known exactly what to say.

'Mr Redknapp's ready for you to go in now,' the woman told her.

As Jessica walked in, the headmaster smiled. 'Please sit down, Mrs Mitchell,' he said.

'I've come to see you because I'm very worried about Joseph and Francesca,' Jessica rambled.

The headmaster nodded. 'I'm very pleased you have come to see me. In fact, I was going to contact you next week. We at the school are also very worried about Joseph and Francesca. They seem to be catching one illness after another and it's seriously affecting their schoolwork.'

Jessica looked at the headmaster in amazement. 'What illness? They're not ill. I've come to talk to you about the amount of homework they've been given. I don't understand, what do you mean?'

Picking up his phone, Mr Redknapp pressed a button. 'Margaret, could you bring in the Mitchells' file with the children's letters, please?'

Jessica was bemused. 'What's going on? Why have the twins been telling you they're ill?'

Mr Redknapp smiled. Parents could be so naive at times, especially mothers. 'Thank you, Margaret,' he said, as his secretary left the office.

Throwing the letters onto the desk, Mr Redknapp urged Jessica to take a look at them. 'Is that your or your husband's handwriting, Mrs Mitchell?'

Jessica recognised the writing immediately. It belonged to Joey and Frankie. Reading the letters, she felt herself go cold. 'How long has this been going on?' she asked Mr Redknapp.

'About eight months. I'm surprised no one mentioned it to you at the parents' evening.'

'I never came to the last one. The kids told me that ten of the teachers had the flu and parents' evening had been cancelled.'

The headmaster sighed. 'Joseph and Francesca obviously have very inventive imaginations, don't you think?'

Jessica wished the ground would open up and swallow her. 'Where are they? Can you go and get them out of their classroom for me?'

The headmaster chuckled. 'I'm afraid they're not here today, Mrs Mitchell. In fact, we've only seen them twice in the last three weeks.'

'But I dropped them off at the gates this morning.

I drop them off here every morning and I pick them up in the afternoon.'

Mr Redknapp shrugged. 'Well, I'm afraid your children have been pulling the wool over everybody's eyes. Maybe you can have a word with your husband, Mrs Mitchell. With their exams coming up, the situation needs to be sorted as soon as possible.'

Seething and red-faced, Jessica stood up. 'Thank you for telling me, Mr Redknapp. I will speak to my husband and I can assure you that both Francesca and Joseph will be attending on a regular basis in future. It is my duty as a mother to march them into their classrooms if I have to.'

Mr Redknapp nodded. 'I'll leave the problem in your more than capable hands, then, Mrs Mitchell.'

Unaware that their mother was talking to their headmaster about them, Frankie and Joey were having a little tipple. 'Give us a swig of yours, Joey. Mine's all gone,' Frankie demanded.

Joey handed her the vodka bottle. 'You're such a greedy cow, Frankie. Don't drink it all, give us it back,' he said, snatching at it.

Frankie giggled and let out a burp. 'You're such an old woman, Joey. Make yourself useful and light me a fag.'

Glancing at his watch, Joey jumped off the park bench. 'Shit, it's half-past two. Come on, Frankie, let's run to the bus stop, else Mum'll be waiting for us.'

Frankie laughed and gently pushed him. 'I'll race you. Last one to the bus stop is a retard.'

Not wanting to upset Eddie at work, Jessica decided not to call him on his mobile, and, instead, wait for him to get home. Unable to concentrate on any Christmas shopping, Jessica went home and got stuck into the housework. To say she was furious was an understatement. The twins had taken her for a complete and utter fool and they needed to be punished. She wondered where they were spending their days and what they were doing. Maybe they were walking the streets or sitting round at a friend's house, or maybe they were up to worse.

Feeling as though she no longer knew them, Jessica picked Frankie and Joey up from school at their usual time. As hard as it was, she decided not to let them know she'd cottoned on. Eddie was a much better disciplinarian than she was and he would know exactly how to handle the situation. Filled with fury, Jessica did her best to act normal. 'How was your day?' she asked.

'Oh, the usual, Mum,' Joey replied.

'I got top marks in maths today,' Frankie added.

Jessica felt like screaming. Part of her wanted to stop the car and swing for the devious little toe rags, but somehow she managed to stop herself.

'We're going upstairs to do our homework,' Frankie said as soon as they got indoors.

Jessica was glad. Keeping her temper was difficult and the further out of her sight the pair of them were, the better.

Eddie arrived home at half-past five. 'Hello, darling, I'm starving. Shall I order the grub? Have the kids picked out what they want?' he asked Jessica.

'You'd better sit down,' Jessica told him.

Explaining the story in full, Jessica expected Eddie to go ballistic and was surprised when he didn't.

'I'll go up and speak to 'em. They've got to be punished. I think we should ground them till the New Year. What do you think?' Eddie said calmly.

Jessica was flummoxed. 'Is that all you've got to say? Aren't you even annoyed with them?'

Not wanting to cause an argument, Eddie held Jessica in his arms. 'Of course I'm annoyed and I'll let them know that. But the thing is, Jess, kids will be kids. I used to bunk off school, me brothers did it too. Gary and Ricky were the same – it's what kids do, ain't it?'

Jessica shook her head. 'I never did it. I was too frightened to do anything like that, I was worried I'd get caught.'

Eddie laughed. 'You wasn't a Mitchell though, was you?'

Eddie went upstairs and spoke to the kids, calmly, but firmly. 'Now, I want to know where you've been hanging out. And what you've been doing. And don't lie to me, because I will find out the truth.'

Frankie nudged Joey. 'We've been changing out of our school uniform and going to the café in Dagenham,' Joey mumbled.

'And sometimes we sit in the park,' Frankie added.

'Well, from now on you're going to school every day. And you're both grounded until New Year,' Eddie told them. He was sure they were telling the truth. He could see it in their eyes.

'Oh, but Dad. What about our Christmas disco?' Frankie whinged.

Eddie winked at her. 'You should have thought of that before you played hookey. Now, get your devious little arses downstairs. I'm starving and I wanna order some dinner.'

Jessica wasn't quite as forgiving as her husband and she ignored the twins as they sat down to eat.

'Would you like some more rice, Mum?' Frankie asked her.

'No, eat it yourself,' Jessica replied angrily.

At nine o'clock the twins both yawned. 'We're going to bed now,' they said.

They knew they had got off lightly and they didn't want to push their luck.

Once her deceitful offspring were out of her sight, Jessica began to relax a bit. 'Shall we have another glass of wine?' she asked Eddie.

Eddie stood up to fetch another bottle and was interrupted by the phone ringing. 'All right, Doug? How's tricks?'

'OK, mate. I want you and Jess to come round for dinner on Saturday night. It's Vicki's birthday and I've got a surprise planned for her. She'll definitely want your Jess to be there, I know that,' Dougie said.

'Yeah, that's fine. What time do you want us round?' Eddie enquired.

'About eight.'

'So, what you got planned then?' Eddie asked, intrigued.

Dougie lowered his voice. 'I'm gonna propose and, as long as she says yes, I've booked a holiday for us to go on next week. It's in the Caribbean, I've arranged for us to get married out there. I'm not gonna tell her till we get there. I thought I'd be spontaneous and shock her, for once.'

Eddie laughed. 'You're a fucking boy, you are.'

''Ere, talking of shocks, you heard about Jimmy O'Hara?' Dougie asked.

'I know the old man popped his clogs,' Eddie replied.

'Yeah, that's right, and Jimmy's got back with his old woman. Moved back in yesterday, Alice did, with his youngest kid, Jed.'

'Fuck me, that's a turn-up for the books. You can tell me more on Saturday,' Eddie said, gutted that Alice had forgiven the bastard.

Eddie ended the call, poured the wine and snuggled up next to his wife.

'Put the news on, Ed. I still haven't seen anything about that fire,' Jessica said.

As Ed switched channels, he was shocked to see a picture of Dickie Pearce flash up on the screen.

'A man has been found dead in a gangland-style shooting in Birmingham. Fifty-one-year-old Richard Pearce, a father of two, was found in the early hours of this morning. Police are appealing for witnesses.'

'Poor man. How awful for his children,' Jessica said sadly.

Eddie felt like bursting out laughing, but instead put on his most solemn voice. 'I don't know what this world's coming to, Jess – my life, I don't!'

# NINETEEN

As Christmas approached, Jessica was like a dog with two tails. The festive season was her favourite time of year and she always went to town with it.

'You're a fucking girl, you are,' Ed had told her only last week, as she'd arrived home with yet more lights and decorations.

Jessica sighed. When the kids were young, they had got into the Christmas spirit with her. Now they were fifteen, they had no interest in it whatsoever. They didn't even want presents any more, they just wanted money. Frankie and Joey had both been spoilt and were more interested in receiving rather than giving and Jessica blamed herself for that. Ever since they were toddlers, she had always given them anything they asked for, and now she was older and wiser, she wished she had been stricter with them.

'Right, I'm off now, babe. Are you sure you don't fancy coming with me?'

Jessica shook her head. Eddie was going to visit his family to drop their presents off and she'd managed to wangle her way out of going with him. 'Honestly, Ed, I would have loved to have come, but I've got far too much to do. Mum and Dad are coming at three and I haven't even tidied the guest room yet. I've got to cook that big lump of ham, vac, polish, prepare dinner and –'

Ed stopped her mid-sentence. 'OK, I get the message. You do what you've got to do and I'll see you when I get back. I'll probably pop in the Flag for a Christmas tipple with me dad and brothers this afternoon, but I won't be late home.'

Jessica hugged him. 'Don't rush back. You enjoy yourself, I'm sure I can manage to entertain Mum, Dad and the kids without you.'

Eddie kissed her on the forehead. 'Oh, you've just reminded me, the kids want to go out tonight. It's only round a mate's house. It's OK with me if it's OK with you.'

Jessica was dubious. 'I'm not sure, Ed. I want to have a drink tonight and I'm not drinking and driving. Anyway, I'm not sure I trust them any more.'

Eddie disagreed. 'They'll be fine. I'll give 'em the money to get a cab. They've been stuck in for nearly six weeks, Jess, we can't keep 'em locked up forever. We'll tell 'em they've got to be back by eleven.'

Reluctantly, Jessica agreed. Ever since her trip to the school, Frankie and Joey had attended regularly and worked very hard. She had been in touch with Mr Redknapp, their headmaster, and he had organised a homework rota to enable them to catch up for their exams. They were still way behind their classmates, but Jessica couldn't fault their efforts. They'd worked tirelessly most evenings, so a little break might do them good.

The roads weren't as busy as Eddie expected them to be and it didn't take him long to get to his aunt's house.

'How's my favourite nephew? Come inside and warm yourself up by the fire. Bleedin' taters out there, ain't it?

I've made you a nice bread pudding – it's just cooling down,' Auntie Joan said, thrilled to see him.

Eddie made himself comfortable. 'What you doing tomorrow? You off to your friend's, as usual?'

Auntie Joan spent every Christmas and Boxing Day at her friend Ada's house. 'Yep, Ada's son is picking me up this evening. I've got me little case packed. What about you? Have you and Jess got a house full this year?'

'Not really, no. Jessica's parents are coming to stay and that's about it. Gary and Ricky have sodded off to Tenerife and Raymondo is spending Christmas Day round his new girlfriend's house. We'll probably have a house full Boxing Day. Our friends Dougie and Vicki are coming over. They're the ones that I told you about, the ones that have just got married abroad and I think Raymondo is bringing his posh bit of skirt round to meet us.'

Auntie Joan laughed. 'I'll go and pour you a nice cuppa. The bread pudding should be cool enough to cut now.'

Eddie smiled as she handed him a plate and put his tea on the table.

'What's your dad and brothers doing?' Joan asked him.

'Dad's going round to Paulie's for dinner and I'm not sure, but I think Ronny and Sharon are going as well. Reg is going round Uncle Albert's, I know that. You're always welcome to come over to mine, Auntie Joan. I know I'm wasting me breath, 'cause I've asked you a thousand times, but the offer's always there. I can pick you up Boxing Day and drop you back home whenever.'

Auntie Joan shook her head. 'It's nice of you to ask, love, but you know how set in me ways I am. I like me East London, I don't do Essex, I'm afraid.'

Eddie smiled. When they made his aunt, they broke the bloody mould.

'There is something you can do for me though, boy.

You remember old Molly? Lives in the flat over the back here. Molly Jenkins – little woman with grey hair, walks with a limp.'

Eddie nodded. 'I know who you mean.'

'Well, I'm really worried about her. Michael, her son, is a bastard to her. Got a drink and drug problem he has, and he keeps turning up at her door asking for money. Poor old Molly only lives on a pension and she's petrified of him. Twice he's clumped her now and it's not on, Eddie. He drinks in the Grave Maurice, always in there, he is. He'll definitely be in there now. Somebody needs to have a little chat with him, if you know what I mean.'

Eddie knew exactly what she meant. 'Leave it with me,' he told her.

An hour later, Eddie stood up. Fishing in his jacket pocket, he pulled out an envelope and handed it to Auntie Joan. 'I want you to treat yourself to something nice, Auntie,' he told her.

Embarrassed, Joan flapped her arms about. 'I don't want your bleedin' money. What do I need money for at my age?'

Eddie chuckled. They had this same argument every Christmas. 'Please don't insult me. If you don't want it, give it to the fucking dogs' home or something.'

Auntie Joan hugged him. 'Me old winter coat's going home a bit, maybe I'll treat meself to a new one,' she told him.

Wishing her a happy Christmas, Eddie jumped into his Land Cruiser and headed towards the pub. The Grave Maurice was literally minutes away on Whitechapel Road. Eddie had no idea who Michael Jenkins was, but he knew Alan, the landlord.

'Eddie! What a lovely surprise,' Alan said, shaking his hand.

Eddie accepted his offer of a drink and sat down on a bar stool next to him.

'What can I do for you, son?' Alan asked him.

'I'm looking for a Michael Jenkins. He drinks in here, apparently.'

Alan nodded towards a scruffy-looking geezer who was standing alone at the opposite end of the bar. 'Local pisshead, he is.'

Eddie nodded. Shame it wasn't his own fucking money he was getting pissed on, he thought, anger rising inside him. He turned back to Alan. 'His mother's a mate of my Auntie Joan. Apparently, the lovely Michael has been knocking her about for his beer money. She's seventy-odd, his poor old mum, Al. He needs a little wake-up call, don't you think?'

Alan nodded. 'Be my guest, Eddie. I don't like the bloke and he's a fuckin' nuisance in here at times.'

Eddie finished his drink. 'Thanks, Al. I'll take him outside and speak to him. Take care, mate, and have a nice Christmas.'

Michael Jenkins didn't like the look of the man who approached him and he certainly didn't fancy going outside with him.

'Do as I say, else I'll break your fucking legs,' Eddie whispered in his ear.

'I can't go anywhere, I've gotta meet me mate in a minute,' Michael pleaded.

Eddie's eyes clouded over. 'If you don't walk outside now and get in the Land Cruiser, I swear I will come back with a gun and blow your fucking brains out.'

Like a lamb being led to the slaughter, Michael Jenkins did as he was told.

Eddie started the engine. 'Where are you taking me? What am I supposed to have done?' Michael said nervously.

Eddie said nothing. He knew of a dead-end turning a few streets away that was always deserted. Reaching his destination, Eddie opened both doors. 'Get out,' he ordered Michael.

Petrified, Michael started to flinch. 'What am I meant to have done? You've got the wrong person. I swear it's not me. You're Eddie Mitchell, aren't you?'

Eddie dragged Michael into the alleyway. Pulling a knife out of his pocket, he pointed it at him. 'You are one piece of fucking shit. And if I ever find out you've laid one finger on your mother again, I will personally fucking kill you. You leave her be, you keep away from her. Do you get my meaning, cunt?'

'I promise I won't go near her again. She offered me money, she gave it to me,' Michael said sobbing.

Despite his odd fib to Jessica, Eddie hated liars. Unable to control his temper, he threw Michael to the floor and stood on his wrist. 'You lying fucking scumbag,' he said, as he positioned the knife on his thumb. Hacking away, Ed realised that the job wasn't complete and the thumb was hanging on by a thread of skin. Determined to chop the bastard thing off, he brought the knife down once again.

Eddie kicked the thumb down the alleyway. Smiling, he left Michael screaming and wriggling and walked back to his motor. 'You say one word or mention my name to anyone, then I'll come back and chop your cock off,' he shouted to his victim.

Reversing out of the dead end, Eddie rang his dad. Reg, Ronny and Paulie were all in the Flag with him and Ed was pleased, as it meant he could kill four birds with one stone.

Turning on the radio, Eddie smirked as he heard the song being played. 'Little Lies' by Fleetwood Mac was very appropriate for poor Michael. Eddie smiled as he thought of what he'd just done to him. Years ago when he was a little boy, his dad used to take him to the fishmonger's. Eddie was obsessed with the live eels wriggling about in the big bowls of water and he loved watching the man chop them up alive. Eddie grinned. That's what Michael Jenkins' thumb had reminded him of today, a live fucking eel. Laughing out loud, Eddie put his foot on the accelerator and sped off.

'Joey, Frankie, your nan and grandad are here,' Jessica shouted up the stairs.

Thrilled that their mother had agreed to them going out later, the twins bounded down stairs with smiles on their faces. Staying in every night doing tons of homework had been soul-destroying for them, so much so that they'd climbed out of the window last week and gone out for the evening. It had nearly all ended in tears, as Joey had struggled to climb back up, lost his balance and fallen backwards onto the drive. Frankie had had to creep downstairs and let him in at the front door. It was a miracle he was just bruised and not badly injured. It was also a miracle that their parents hadn't heard the commotion.

Joyce and Stanley made a real fuss of the twins. 'What you done to your face? You've got a big bruise. You ain't been fighting, have you?' Joyce asked Joey.

'No, I fell out of bed, Nan.' Joey told her sincerely. He'd got the bruise when he'd fallen off the roof.

Frankie backed him up. 'It's true, Nan. He went to bed one night and woke up like that the next morning. I can vouch for him, honest I can.'

Frankie glanced at her brother and he winked at her.

'How's school? You must have your exams soon.' Stanley asked both of them.

Jessica shot the twins a look. She'd warned them not to tell their nan and grandad about the fiasco at the school.

'We've been working really hard, Grandad. We take our exams very seriously,' Frankie said cheekily.

Jessica felt her lip curl. She could swing for that girl sometimes, she really could.

Eddie tutted as Paulie brought over another drink. He already had three lined up on the table and was struggling to get through them. 'What you trying to do – get me pissed? I've already had about six. I can't drink all of them, I've got the motor outside,' he joked.

Ronny was in a quiet mood. He hated being stuck in a wheelchair and he couldn't stand other people being happy. No one knew what his life was like. Being treated like a cripple made him feel so inferior that sometimes he wished he was dead.

'Looking forward to Christmas around Paulie's?' Eddie asked him cheerfully.

'Yeah, can't wait. I'm gonna dress up as fucking Santa and slide down the chimney while singing "Rudolph the Red-Nosed Reindeer",' Ronny answered sarcastically.

Eddie glanced at Sharon. She had just turned up to take Ronny home and Eddie felt truly sorry for her. Years ago, he'd never been a massive fan of his brother's bird, but just lately his heart went out to her. Most women would have run a mile after Ronny's accident, but Sharon had stuck by him through thick and thin. Ronny showed her no love at all, he spoke to her like shit and Eddie didn't know how she put up with him. It wasn't as though they had kids or anything to keep her there.

'Come up the bar; let me get you a drink, Sharon,' Eddie said.

'Yeah, go on. Fuck off with him, I dunno why you

turned up so early – I ain't going nowhere yet,' Ronny said nastily.

With tears in her eyes, Sharon followed Eddie up to the bar.

'What do you want, love?' Eddie asked her.

Sharon shrugged. 'I'll just have an orange juice, please.'

Eddie smiled at her. 'Why don't you have something stronger? Have a glass of wine or something. One won't hurt you.'

Sharon shook her head. 'Living with Ronny has put me off drink for life.'

Eddie shouted up an orange juice and handed it to her. 'Listen, if you ever need any outside help, just let me know. I can pay for a carer or someone who will give you a break.'

Sharon felt her eyes well up again. She wasn't used to kindness. 'I can manage all right. I just wish he was more grateful and didn't drink so much. When he's drunk, he says the most terrible things to me.'

Eddie nodded sympathetically. 'My offer will always be there for you, Sharon. You know my number. If things get too much for you, then ring me.'

Sharon smiled sadly. 'Thanks Ed, I will.'


'What's for dinner, love?' Stanley asked his daughter.

'I've done a nice cold-meat buffet with crusty bread, pickles, jacket potatoes, cheese and coleslaw. I thought it best that we don't overeat tonight – we don't want to spoil ourselves for tomorrow, do we?'

Joyce agreed. 'Any chance of another glass of Baileys, dear?'

'We're going out now, Mum,' Frankie said, as she walked into the room all dolled up in a denim miniskirt.

Jessica looked at her in astonishment. 'It's only ten to

six – your dad's not even back yet. Why are you all dressed up? You're only going round your friend's house, aren't you?'

Joey stepped out from behind his sister. He was also dressed smartly. 'We've gotta make an effort, Mum. All our school friends are going to be there. We can't look like tramps at Christmas,' he said.

'Whose house are you going to? Are their parents going to be there?'

Frankie spoke earnestly. 'We're going round Joey's friend David's house. And I'm not going to lie to you, Mum, his parents are going out for a meal, but David said they'll be back by ten o'clock.'

Jessica nodded. She had met David a couple of times and he was a pleasant enough boy. At least Frankie had been honest with her about his parents going out for the evening, so maybe she'd learned her lesson.

'How are you getting there?' she asked the twins.

'Cab. We've already ordered it. It's double fare after six; that's why we're going out early,' Frankie answered.

Hearing a toot outside, Jessica smiled at them. 'Go on, off you go. Have a good time and no getting drunk.'

'We won't, Mum, I promise,' Frankie said, nudging her brother.

'And don't forget to be back by eleven,' Jessica shouted out.

As Frankie slammed the door, Joey smiled. 'Do you think she believed us?'

Frankie giggled. 'Course she did. Especially when I said that David's parents weren't gonna be at home. I saw the gleam in her eye at my honesty.'

Joey laughed. 'You're such a cow at times, Frankie.'

Frankie and Joey got into the minicab.

'Where are you going?' the driver asked.

Frankie laughed. It was Christmas, the season of good-will and it was about time her brother knew that she was aware of his interesting little secret.

'We're gonna be ending up at the Angel pub in the village. But can you go to Cherry Tree Lane first?' Joey said.

'Are we picking someone up?' the driver asked.

Frankie smiled. 'Yes, my brother's boyfriend.'

# TWENTY

Astonished that his sister knew his secret, Joey urged her to shut the fuck up. He didn't want the cab driver knowing his business; he couldn't take that risk.

'Change of plan, mate. Drop us at the Cherry Tree lights. We've gotta get some fags and stuff, we'll walk from there,' Joey told the driver.

'So, you're not going to the Angel now?' the bewildered cabbie asked.

Joey shook his head. 'Nah, we're not, mate.'

'That'll be three-eighty,' the cabbie said, giving Joey a strange look and the once-over.

Joey handed him a fiver and told him to keep the change. 'I haven't really got a boyfriend, mate. My sister has a lot of mental issues and tends to blurt out these things,' he said, as he shoved Frankie out of the cab.

Seeing the driver's bemused expression, Frankie couldn't stop laughing. 'Your face was a picture, Joey. I bet he goes back to his office and tells his colleagues he's just picked up a shit-stabber and a nutcase.'

Joey didn't share her warped sense of humour. He lit up two fags and handed her one. 'How do you know?' he asked bluntly.

Frankie took a long drag and blew the smoke in his

face. 'I've known for ages, you idiot. Don't you remember that time around Simon's house? You and David were upstairs going through his record collection and I sneaked up. I saw you leap apart from one another. It was obvious you'd been kissing!'

Joey didn't know whether to laugh or cry. He felt awkward that Frankie knew, but was also relieved that she did. 'Does anybody else know? You won't say anything to Mum and Dad, will you?' he asked her.

Frankie threw him a sarcastic look. 'Of course, I'm gonna tell 'em tomorrow. I'll wait till we're eating our Christmas dinner and hold a sausage on me fork while screaming out "Joey likes willies," shall I?'

Joey laughed. He trusted Frankie and knew she wouldn't dob him in it.

'Have you, you know, done anything with him?' Frankie pried.

Joey smirked. 'Well, sort of.'

Frankie was perplexed. 'Like what?'

'I'll tell you all about it another time. Now come on, we'll be late. I'll race you to David's house. Last one there's a plonker.'

Jessica waited for Eddie to arrive home, and then brought out the buffet. 'Mum, Dad, help yourselves,' she urged.

Eddie pecked his little homemaker on the cheek. 'What time did the kids go out?'

'Just before six. They didn't want to pay double fare. How was your day, love?'

Eddie smiled. Best he didn't mention that he'd chopped someone's thumb off. 'It was good. I went to see me Auntie Joan, then popped in the Flag to have a drink with the rest of the family.'

'Did you see your dad?' Jessica asked.

'Yeah. He looked tired, the old man. Said he's had some agg with a few kids knocking on the door late at night. Reckons they're potential burglars, knocking to see if there's anyone at home. The silly little bastards obviously don't know who me father is, do they? If they set one foot inside his property, me dad'll fucking kill 'em,' Eddie replied, laughing.

The buffet was beautifully presented and went down a treat.

'That's me done. Bleeding handsome, love,' Joyce said, rubbing her stomach.

'Can I get you anything else, Dad?' Jessica asked, picking up her father's empty plate.

'I'm absolutely bloated. I could manage another Scotch though,' Stanley said cheekily.

Joyce pursed her lips. 'You've had four already, Stanley. Can't you have a cup of tea instead?'

'Whatever you say, dear,' Stanley said calmly.

'Do you want a cuppa as well, Mum?' Jessica asked.

'Oh, no! I'll have a Baileys, love.'

Eddie and Jessica looked at one another and burst out laughing. Joyce couldn't understand why they were laughing at her. 'What's the matter?' she asked annoyed.

Eddie handed his father-in-law a Scotch. 'Thanks, Eddie,' Stanley said gratefully.

Joyce took the glass of Baileys from Eddie and downed it in one. She scowled at Stanley. Her husband was one greedy bastard at times, he really was.

'Bye, Mrs Hughton, bye, Mr Hughton. Have a lovely Christmas,' Joey shouted to David's parents as they left the house.

Frankie laughed at his politeness. 'I'll leave you and lover boy to it,' she said, as she skipped on ahead.

David looked at Joey in amazement. 'You ain't told her, have you?' he asked horrified.

Joey shook his head. 'She knew. She's known for ages, apparently. Do you remember that time we were round at Simon's and we thought she'd caught us? Well, she did.'

David was much more macho than Joey and was desperate to keep his confusion over his sexuality a secret. 'Well, that's fucking great, Joey. She won't say nothing, will she? I mean, I am captain of the football team. Can you imagine what the lads would say?'

'She's my twin – of course she ain't gonna fucking say anything,' Joey told him.

As Frankie strolled on ahead, the two lads walked in silence. David's attitude annoyed Joey at times. Joey wasn't ashamed of fancying boys, and if it wasn't for his father finding out and probably burying him alive, he'd have shouted it from the rooftops. David was the opposite. He'd always claimed that he was straight. He was adamant that he was just experimenting and, one day, would marry and have children.

Joey had no intention of following in his so-called boyfriend's footsteps. He'd known from a very early age that he only liked boys, and was 100% positive that he was gay. He'd been out with a couple of girls, but kissing them had turned his stomach over.

'Sorry if I snapped at you. Are you OK, Joey?' David asked him.

Joey nodded. 'Let's catch up with Frankie, eh?'

As Eddie left the room to make a few phone calls, Jessica switched on the television. Her mum and dad were both having forty winks and the house seemed so quiet all of a sudden. Flicking through the channels, Jessica spotted a programme where a mother was holding a newborn baby. 'Aah,' Jessica murmured as she realised that the baby looked just like Joey had when he was born. Sighing, Jessica switched channels. The twins were all grown up now. They didn't need her any more and she didn't want to depress herself.

'What's up? You look sad,' Eddie said, as he sat down next to her.

Forcing herself to stop being sentimental, Jessica smiled. 'Nothing's wrong. I'm fine.'

Hours later, Joey grabbed his sister's arm. 'Frankie, hurry up, the cab'll be waiting outside.'

Frankie was tipsy and in no rush to leave the pub. 'Tell the cab to go away and come back after twelve. Mum and Dad'll be all right; they'll probably be pissed by now anyway.'

Joey shook his head. His sister could be such a pain in the arse sometimes. 'Look, if we're late, Mother'll probably ground us again. You might be willing to take that chance, but I bloody well ain't. Sod not being allowed out on New Year's Eve. I wanna celebrate the start of 1988 in style.'

Seeing Joey getting annoyed, Frankie poked her tongue out at him. 'OK, you win. I'm coming. Just let me say goodbye to the girls.'

'Where's David?' Frankie asked, as she walked outside. 'He's staying for a bit. He ain't gotta be home till after twelve,' Joey said.

Frankie laughed. 'No kisses for you tonight then, dear.'

'Just shut up and get in the car, will you?' Joey told her sternly.

As the front door slammed, Jessica nudged Eddie and smiled. 'They're bang on time. It's one minute to eleven, bless 'em,' she said.

Frankie bounded into the lounge. 'As it's Christmas, can me and Joey have a proper drink, Mum?' she asked boldly.

Jessica looked at Eddie. 'I don't see why not,' he said.

'We'll both have a vodka and Coke then,' Frankie said, sitting in between her grandparents.

Joey sat down next to his mum. 'How was your evening, love? Did you have a nice time with David?' she asked.

Frankie laughed. 'He always has a nice time with David, don't you, Joey?'

Joey scowled at his sister and quickly changed the subject.

Tanked up on Baileys, Joyce was in a playful mood. 'Why don't we have a little game? Who fancies playing *Give Us a Clue*?' she asked.

Eddie laughed. 'You mean charades, Joyce?'

'Whatever.' Joyce laughed. 'Never been the same, that programme, since Michael Aspel left and Parky took over.'

'Who's going first?' Jessica enquired.

Joyce leaped up and waved her hands.

'TV, two syllables,' Joey said.

Crossing her legs, Joyce urged her family to guess the first syllable.

'You look like you're busting for a piss, the way you're standing, Joycie,' Eddie said, taking the mickey.

Joyce turned to Stanley.

'Knees? Legs?' he asked.

Unable to control her annoyance, Joyce let rip at him. 'Didn't you notice me crossing me legs? It's *Crossroads*, you silly old bastard,' she said, flopping down in the armchair.

Eddie stood up to take his turn.

'Film, two words. The something,' Jessica said.

'*The Godfather*,' Frankie shouted correctly.

'Clever girl,' Stanley said, impressed.

Frankie smiled. 'That was easy, it's Dad's favourite film.'

'Sounds about right,' Stanley mumbled, as he nodded politely.

Already bored with Christmas, Joey stood up. 'I'm really tired. I'm gonna go to bed, if that's OK.'

Frankie nodded. 'Me too,' she said, finishing her drink.

'Do you want waking up early to open your presents?' Jessica asked them.

'Leave it out, Mum. We asked for just money; we're fifteen, not five,' Frankie replied, laughing.

Seeing Eddie yawn, Jessica smiled. 'Shall we finish this game tomorrow and go to bed now?' she said.

Eddie nodded. 'Are yous two staying up for a bit?' he asked his in-laws.

Joyce stood up. 'No, we've had enough as well. Come on, Stanley, leave that drink, you've had enough. Come on, chop-chop.'

Having little alternative, Stanley left the glass of Scotch and followed his wife up the stairs.

Jessica felt glum as she pulled the quilt over herself. She had been in a funny mood all night, and was struggling to snap out of it. Eddie got undressed and snuggled up next to her. Planting kisses on the back of her neck, he asked her what was wrong.

'I'm fine, honest I am,' Jessica insisted.

'No, you're not. We've been married for a long time, Jess, and I know when something's wrong.'

Jessica turned to face him. 'You're gonna think I'm ever so silly if I tell you.'

Eddie leaned over her and moved her fringe out of her eyes. 'Tell me, I promise I won't think you're silly.'

Jessica struggled for the right words. 'It's just that now

219

the kids are older, it doesn't really feel like Christmas any more. I've noticed it this year more than any other. They'll soon be leaving school and it's as though they don't need me, Ed. I feel like I've been made redundant all of a sudden.'

Eddie saw a tear roll down her cheek and held her close. 'Ssh, don't cry, Jess,' he whispered.

He didn't really know what to say to her. He was glad the kids were nearly off their hands, but he tried to put himself in her shoes. From the time they were babies, Jess had been stuck indoors, nurturing them. He'd always been out working and, although he hated admitting it, he'd barely noticed them growing up. Eddie had always been an impulsive bastard and tonight was no exception. It broke his heart to see his wife look so sad. He loved her so much, he would literally do anything in his power to make her happy.

'Let's have another baby,' he said to her.

Jessica turned over and looked at him with an incredulous expression. 'What? We can't – I'm thirty-three and you're forty-six.'

Eddie laughed. 'So? Me dick still works, don't it?'

Jessica shook her head. 'Oh, we can't, Ed. What will me mum and dad say? And the twins would be horrified.'

Smiling, Eddie straddled her and refused to move until she agreed. 'Fuck your parents and fuck the kids. This is all about me and you, Jess. It's our future, no one else's.'

'Are you really serious or are you just winding me up?' Jessica asked him.

'I'm as serious as the day I asked you to marry me. Come on, Jess, let's go for it, eh?'

Jessica thought over his suggestion. She'd thought her nappy-changing days were well and truly finished and she hadn't expected this bombshell to be dropped on her.

'We'll have to talk about it properly, weigh up the pros and cons,' she said.

Eddie smiled. Unlike him, Jess was sensible. 'Go on, say yes, you know you want to. Just think about that pitter-patter of tiny feet.'

Jessica grinned. It would be lovely to have a focus and be needed once more.

Knowing how she hated being tickled, Eddie did exactly that. 'Go on, let's be devils. You know I've got super-sperm, don't ya? Well, this time next year, we could have a cot in that corner and it could be our baby's first Christmas.'

Laughing hysterically, tears ran down Jessica's face as she begged him to stop tickling her.

'Say yes and I'll stop,' Eddie told her.

'Yes,' Jessica yelled. 'Yes, yes, yes!'

# TWENTY-ONE

On Christmas morning, Jessica woke early with a big smile on her face. Desperate to check that her husband had meant what he'd said the previous evening, she gently prodded him until he opened his eyes.

'What time is it?' Eddie mumbled.

'It's half-past six. You did mean what you said last night, didn't you? It wasn't the drink talking, was it?'

Eddie smiled at her. 'Of course I meant it. Why don't we have a little practice now. No time like the present, eh?'

Jessica giggled as Eddie leaped on top of her. 'Be quiet, Ed. I don't want me mum and dad to hear us.'

'Well, in that case, I'll make as much fucking noise as possible,' Eddie told her laughing.

Unable to put up with Joyce's snoring any longer, Stanley decided to get up and have a shower. At home, he and his wife slept in separate bedrooms. When they stayed at Jessica's, they were forced to share, unfortunately.

Not wanting to wake Joyce up, Stanley decided to tiptoe towards the en-suite bathroom in the dark. Seconds later, he caught his leg on the chair and fell flat on his face.

Joyce woke with a fright and switched on the light.

'What are you doing, you senile old goat?' she screeched at him.

Stanley stood up. 'And a happy Christmas to you too, dear,' he said, slamming the bathroom door.

After making love to his wife, Eddie had a quick shower and went downstairs to make breakfast. Smoked salmon and scrambled eggs washed down with a glass of champagne was a Christmas-morning ritual. The festive season was the one time of the year when Eddie mucked in with the cooking to give his long-suffering wife a break.

'Morning, Stanley. Do you fancy some smoked salmon and scrambled eggs?' he asked.

Stanley pulled a face. 'Makes me feel ill, that bleedin' salmon. Ain't got any bacon, have you?'

Eddie smiled as his father-in-law shuffled into the living room. Poor old Stanley had never been high up in the class stakes, bless him.

The twins ambled downstairs as the rest of the household were eating. 'Where's ours?' Frankie said, annoyed that no one had called them.

Eddie chuckled. 'Go and make something yourself, you lazy pair of sods.'

Jessica put on the Christmas CD and began to sort through the many presents under the tree.

'Do we have to listen to this rubbish, Mum? Can't we put on some house music or something?' Frankie complained.

'No, this is staying on,' Jessica said, grinning at Eddie. Jess was so excited about their baby plans, she couldn't stop thinking about it. It was the best Christmas present Eddie could have given her.

As all the gifts were being opened, Eddie studied his son. Joey was nothing like Gary and Ricky at all. Dressed in bleached jeans with a pink jumper, he looked and acted like a poof. Even the way he opened his gifts was done in a feminine way; he kept squealing like a fucking girl. Eddie sighed. Thank Christ Joey had brought a couple of girlfriends home earlier this year. Eddie was relieved that his son was actually into birds, as over the years he'd had his doubts. Can you imagine? Eddie Mitchell's son, the poof: he'd never have lived that one down.

'This is for you, Dad. It's from me and Joey,' Frankie yelled, handing him a present.

'Sorry, angel, I was in a dream world there,' Ed said, as he unwrapped the Pringle jumper. 'Thanks, kids,' Eddie said, handing his wife a small velvet box.

Jessica opened it and squealed with delight. 'Oh, Ed, it's beautiful,' she said, as she studied the diamond ring.

Joyce snatched it from her and showed it to Stanley. 'Look, dear, a diamond ring. Better than them poxy slippers you bought me, don't you think?'

With all the giving and receiving over, Eddie stood up. 'I'm just gonna give my family a ring, then I'll pour us some more drinks.'

Busy putting the wrapping paper into black bin liners, Jessica looked up. 'Ring Ray for us, Ed, and bring the phone in here so Mum and Dad can talk to him.'

Eddie rang his dad first, but got no answer. He then rang Paulie. 'Is the old man there yet?' he asked his brother.

'Nah. If he ain't at home, then he's probably over Mum's grave or on his way,' Paulie told him.

About to ring Raymond, Eddie was thrilled when the phone rang and it was Gary and Ricky in Tenerife. 'Merry Christmas, Dad. Gary's pissed already,' Ricky said, laughing.

Eddie chuckled. 'How you getting on? What's the weather like?'

'It's fucking well hot, Dad. The apartment is the nuts and there's plenty of crumpet out here. We're gonna spend today on the beach with two little sorts we met yesterday,' Ricky told him.

Gary snatched the phone from his younger brother. 'I ain't pissed, Dad, take no notice of him. He was well gone last night, you know what a lightweight he is.'

'Where you having your Christmas dinner? Have you booked anywhere?' Eddie asked Gary.

'Nah. We ain't gonna bother. It's too hot for a roast, so we'll have a barbecue on the beach instead. Listen, Dad, the pips are going, we'll call you in a couple of days. Have a good one and give our love to –'

Eddie smiled as the money ran out. Gary and Ricky were obviously having a whale of a time, the lucky bastards.

Punching in Raymond's mobile number, Eddie could tell that he was already at his girlfriend's house. 'What you talking all posh for, you wanker?' he ribbed him.

'I'm not. Don't start all that tomorrow when we come over,' Raymond whispered.

Eddie chuckled as he took the phone into the living room. Polly, Raymondo's new bird, was a posh bit of stuff, by all accounts, and came from an extremely wealthy family.

'The prodigal son,' Eddie said, handing the phone to Joyce.

'Hello, Raymond. Are you having a nice time, love? What's their house like?'

'Yep, I'm having a lovely time thanks, Mum,' Raymond replied, ignoring her second question.

'What's the house like?' Joyce prompted him once again.

'Yes, happy Christmas, Mum. Can I say hello to Dad and Jess now?' Raymond asked.

Disappointed she hadn't got any more out of him, Joyce handed the phone to Stanley. 'He obviously can't talk properly; her parents must be in the room,' she said to Jessica.

'Looking forward to seeing you tomorrow, son,' Stanley said, handing the phone to Jessica.

Jessica wished Ray happy Christmas and asked what time he would be arriving the following day.

'About four o'clock, sis, if that's all right? Polly's dad wants us to go for a quick drink in his local before we leave.'

'That's fine. Well, give our love to Polly and her family and tell her we'll look forward to meeting her tomorrow.'

Jessica smiled as she ended the call. 'He sounds so loved-up for the first time in his life,' she said.

'What did he say, then? Did he say what the house was like?' Joyce said, getting more agitated by the minute with the lack of information she was receiving. All Raymond had told her was that Polly's parents were well off and lived in Chelsea. Joyce couldn't wait to meet them. If their daughter was getting serious with her son, then she had every right to check out the in-laws.

The rest of the morning and early afternoon passed pleasantly and at half-past two, Jessica ordered Eddie to start carving the turkey, ham and beef.

'Frankie, can you give me a hand with the vegetables?' she asked her daughter.

'Can't Nan help you?' Frankie whinged.

Joyce stood up and Joey ordered her to sit back down. 'You're a guest, Nan. I'll help Mum,' he said, glaring at Frankie. She was a lazy cow, his sister, and she only got away with it because she was his dad's favourite.

The dinner looked delicious and, as Jessica brought in the stuffing balls, cauliflower cheese and sausages rolled in bacon, she urged everybody to tuck in. 'Help your-selves. I'm just gonna make a drop more gravy,' she said, as the phone rang.

'Leave that or give it to me and I'll tell whoever it is to fuck off,' Eddie shouted out.

Jessica answered it and was surprised to hear Paulie's voice on the other end. 'Jess, is Eddie there?' he asked her.

'We're just eating our dinner. Can he call you back, Paulie?'

'No, it's urgent, Jess, I need to speak to him now,' Paulie replied.

Sighing, Jessica took the phone into the dining room. She had no time for either of Eddie's brothers; they were both arrogant bastards. 'It's Paulie. He says it's urgent,' she said, handing the phone to Eddie.

Cursing, Eddie put down his knife and fork. Snatching the phone, he stormed out of the room. 'This had better be important. What's the fucking problem?' he asked his brother.

'No one knows where Dad is. He was meant to be here hours ago and he ain't showed. I've rung Reg and he ain't heard a dickie bird from him. I wondered if he'd rung you.'

Eddie felt his pulse quicken. His dad was Mr Reliable and he instinctively knew that something was wrong. 'He ain't rung me. Maybe he's still over at Mum's grave. What time was he due at yours? Have you been round to the house?'

'He said he'd be here by twelve. I sent Sharon round there at two, but she said there was no answer. I've rung the Flag, but he's not in there. I ain't got a key to his house. Joan's got one, but she's away.'

'I've got a key,' Eddie said immediately. 'I'll leave now. Can you meet me there?'

'Course. Shall I bring Ronny as well?'

'No, just bring yourself. I'll be about twenty minutes, if I put me foot down.'

Replacing the receiver, Eddie noticed that his hands were unsteady. 'Please God don't make him have had a stroke or heart attack or something,' he mumbled to himself.

Poking his head around the dining-room door, Eddie urged Jessica to come outside.

'Whatever's the matter?' she asked concerned.

'It's me dad. He ain't turned up round Paulie's for dinner. It ain't like him. I reckon he might have had an accident or a funny turn indoors. I've got a spare key, I'm gonna shoot round, make sure he's OK.'

Jessica nodded understandingly. 'I'll warm your dinner up for you when you get back. Will you be OK? Do you want me to come with you?'

Eddie shook his head. 'I've got me mobile. I'll call you when I've found out what's happened.'

Jessica was worried as she heard Ed's Land Cruiser zoom away. Eddie was very close to his dad and it would be awful for him if he'd fallen seriously ill on Christmas day.

'What's up?' her mother asked, as she walked back in the room.

'Nothing. Ed's just had to pop out for a bit.' Jessica said awkwardly. She didn't want to spoil everybody's day and there might be no reason to panic yet.

Frankie glared at her mother. 'Well, you must know where Dad's gone. It must be important or he wouldn't have left his dinner.'

Jessica pushed her plate away. Suddenly, she didn't feel hungry any more. 'He's popped round your grandad's. Apparently, Grandad was meant to go to your Uncle Paulie's for dinner, but he never turned up.'

Frankie shrugged. 'Knowing Grandad, he's probably out on the lash with his mates and Dad's had a wasted journey,' she said.

With Eddie's unexpected absence, the mood at the dinner table became sombre. 'Do you want some more meat or potatoes, Dad?' Jessica asked, trying to keep things normal.

'No thanks, love,' Stanley replied.

'I'll have some,' Frankie said.

'Have you got any more sausages in the kitchen, Mum?' Joey asked.

With only Frankie and Joey still eating, Jessica began to clear the plates away. 'Who wants Christmas pudding and who wants banoffee pie?' she asked brightly.

'Why don't we wait till Eddie gets back, dear?' her mother said soothingly.

Joey and Frankie nudged one another. 'I'm bored. Shall we get pissed?' Frankie whispered.

Joey replied with a wink.


Paulie was already waiting outside his dad's house when Eddie pulled up. 'I've knocked again and rung the bell,' he told Eddie.

With a heart that felt like lead, Eddie fumbled for the key in his pocket .

'Dad! Dad!' he shouted, as he opened the front door. His legs were like jelly.

'Fuck! No!' Paulie whispered as they walked into the lounge. The place had been ransacked.

There was no sign of their father, so Eddie ran up the stairs. 'Dad!' he screamed. 'Dad!'

Walking into his father's bedroom, the first thing Eddie saw was splattered blood. 'No, fucking God, no!' he screamed, as he cradled his battered father.

Hearing his brother's screams, Paulie galloped up the stairs. 'Oh no! Tell me he's alive, Eddie. Please tell me he's still alive.'

Tears running down his face, Eddie could barely bring himself to speak. 'Who's done this to you, Dad? Who's done this?' he cried.

Taking a closer look, Paulie saw that his father's head was pummelled to a pulp. 'I'll call the police, I'll ring an ambulance,' he shouted.

Kneeling in his father's blood, Eddie cradled his father's face in his hands and sobbed. 'It's too late. We're too fucking late. He's dead, Paulie, Dad's dead!'

# TWENTY-TWO

Paulie made the 999 call. Within seconds of the Old Bill arriving, Eddie washed his father's blood off his hands and his shock turned to fury. He couldn't show himself up in front of these mugs – it wasn't an option. 'When I find out who's responsible for this, I'll torture the cunt for so long, he'll wish he'd never been born,' he said to his brother.

Approached by a DS, Eddie distractedly shook his hand.

'I know this has been an awful shock for you, but are you able to answer a few questions for us, Mr Mitchell?' asked the copper.

Still in a trance, Paulie poured two large brandies, handed one to Eddie and urged him to do all the talking. Eddie explained exactly what had happened. 'So when me dad never turned up for dinner, me and Paulie came round to check on him, and that's how we found him.'

The DS nodded sympathetically. 'Can you think of anyone who might have a grudge against your dad? Maybe someone he's recently had an argument or some kind of falling-out with?'

Eddie shrugged his shoulders. His father had probably upset hundreds of people over the years, but he could hardly tell the filth that, could he?

'What about them young kids dad was having grief with? You know, the kids he was talking about on Christmas Eve?' Paulie said, remembering the conversation in the pub.

Eddie repeated the story, and then told the copper that he'd had enough. 'Me head's all over the place. I've just found me father with his brains hanging out, for fuck's sake. Any other questions are gonna have to wait.'

Topping up his brandy, Eddie dragged Paulie out into the garden. 'I bet the O'Haras have got something to do with this. Seems funny it's happened just after Butch died.'

Paulie shook his head. 'It's too unprofessional for them. They'd have just shot Dad through the head; they wouldn't have bothered to ransack the place.'

Eddie shrugged. 'I wouldn't put anything past them pikey scumbags. How do you know they ain't just made it look like a burglary to cover it up?'

Paulie handed his brother a cigarette. 'You're barking up the wrong tree, Ed. I mean, Dad told us about them kids he'd had grief with and, if you want my opinion, it looks like the work of young 'uns.'

Eddie disagreed. 'Dad might have been knocking on, but he was still as strong as an ox. He'd have killed a couple of kids with his bare hands. This is the work of men, strong men, you mark my words.'

'Excuse me, Mr Mitchell.'

Eddie dobbed out his fag and walked towards the DS.

'We're going to do some house-to-house enquiries. In such a residential area, we're sure somebody must have seen or heard something.'

Eddie nodded and looked at Paulie. Fuck the police: he would be doing his own house-to-house enquiries. 'Me and you had better start making some phone calls. You ring Ronny, then Uncle Albert and get hold of Reg. I'll ring Raymond and I'll have to try and contact Gary and Ricky, somehow. Don't let anyone tell Auntie Joan, Paulie. The shock'll fucking kill her. I'll wait till she gets back from her friend's and go and tell her in person. Don't let anyone tell Sylvie either. She was courting the old man for years, and it's only right that I tell her meself. It's what Dad would have wanted.'

Paulie nodded. His dad was barely cold and already he felt like a spare part. Eddie gave out the orders and, like a mug, he just obeyed.

Jessica was frantic. She had been constantly trying to call her husband's mobile for the past three hours and was still unable to get hold of him.

'Try not to worry too much, Mum. Dad's battery is always flat – they don't last very long on them mobiles, you know,' Joey said soothingly.

Stanley and Joyce glanced at one another. Christmas was absolutely ruined and they didn't know what to do or say.

'Why don't I warm up some mince pies and pour everyone a drink?' Frankie said helpfully.

Jessica looked at her in amazement. She was surprised her lazy daughter even knew how to use the oven. 'Go on then, love,' she told her. Until they knew what had happened, they had to try and carry on as normal.

The shrill of the phone diminished any hope of normality. 'Eddie, where are you? What's happened? I've been so worried,' Jessica asked frantically.

Her husband's reply knocked her for six. Feeling the colour drain from her face, she clung on to the armchair to stop herself from falling.

'Listen Jess, I've got to go. The police want to speak to me again. I'll call you back as soon as I can,' Eddie told her.

Unable to breathe properly, Jessica felt her legs buckle underneath her. Joyce and Stanley leaped off the sofa and rushed to her aid. 'Go and get your mum some water, Joey,' Stanley shouted.

'What's the matter, Mum? What's happened to Dad?' Frankie asked.

Managing to sit up, Jessica sipped from the glass that her mother was holding.

'Don't just stand there, Stanley! She's in shock, go and get her some brandy,' Joyce bellowed.

Not able to cope with all the dramatics, Joey burst into tears.

Desperate to pull herself together for the sake of her children, Jessica downed the brandy in one. 'It's OK. Dad's OK,' she told the twins.

'What's happened, Mum?' Frankie asked fearfully.

Urging her father to top her glass up, Jessica took a deep breath. 'It's G-g-grandad, he's been m-m-murdered,' she stammered.

Relieved that it wasn't their father, the twins breathed a sigh of relief.

Raymond walked towards Eddie and grabbed him in a bear hug.

'You didn't have to come straight over, Ray. I bet your girlfriend weren't too pleased,' Eddie said to him.

'Her parents didn't look too happy, but Polly was OK. Now, tell me everything from the start. I loved your old man, Ed, I can't fucking believe this has happened.'

With tears in his eyes, Eddie repeated the story. 'He was bludgeoned to fuck, Ray. Paulie thought he'd been done with a hammer, but I'm sure it was a baseball bat. I could see the marks engraved on his face.'

Again, Raymond hugged Eddie. What could he say?

No one would know what to say in a situation like this, there were just no words of comfort.

Pulling away, Raymond looked him in the eye. 'Who do you think's responsible?'

Eddie shook his head. 'I really don't know. It's a novice's job, but my guess would be that Jimmy O'Hara ordered it. I swear, Ray, if I find out it's him, I'll skin the pikey cunt alive. My poor dad. Gutted I am, Ray, fucking heartbroken.'

Raymond nodded. 'If it is O'Hara, I'll help you get revenge, Ed.'

Seeing Ronny hurtling towards him like a paraplegic Speedy Gonzales, Eddie sighed. 'Talk to this cunt for me, Ray. He's pissed out of his brains, been spouting all sorts in front of the filth, he has. I can't be doing with him right now, I really can't.'

Leaving Raymond with his brother, Eddie walked over to his Uncle Reg. 'Is Albert not with you?' he asked him.

Reggie shook his head. Albert was his and Harry's younger brother. Albert was a nice enough geezer, but had never been involved in the family firm and instead had spent his life working as a greengrocer. 'He wanted to come, but I told him to wait at home. You know our Albert, he's about as useful as a one-legged fucking donkey in situations like these.'

Eddie nodded. He was desperate to get home to Jessica. He needed her arms around him and her soothing voice telling him everything was going to be OK. Seeing Ronny was now annoying the life out of the neighbours, Eddie walked back over to Raymond. 'Why don't you, Paulie and Reg come back to mine? There's no point us standing here, is there? We can't do anything, can we?'

Raymond agreed and pointed to a house across the street. 'The old boy opposite, Mr Miller, wants a word with you.'

Eddie strolled across the road and knocked on the door. He hadn't seen old Cyril Miller for years and was surprised by how frail he had become. He used to be a hefty lump, but had lost so much weight that he was virtually unrecognisable.

'Sorry to hear about your dad, son, he was a good neighbour. The Old Bill knocked earlier and I told 'em what I saw. There was three lads out here last night, about ten o'clock it were, 'cause I was watching the news. They were kicking up a din, I saw your old man come out, have a go at 'em. He chased 'em and they ran off down the road. I didn't see their faces, but they looked like young 'uns – I'd say about thirteen, at a guess.'

Eddie shook Cyril's hand. 'Get a pen and take down my phone number. If you remember anything else or see 'em round here again, call me, not the police.'

Cyril nodded and went into the hallway to fetch a pen and paper. Thanking him, Eddie walked towards Paulie and told him the plan. 'It's depressing me, standing here – let's go to mine,' he told him.

Paulie nodded. 'Ronny'll have to come as well, though. We can't pack him off on his own if we're all going back to yours.'

Full of reluctance, Eddie agreed.

Jessica took the phone call and hugged the twins. 'Dad's on his way home. Raymond's with him and Uncle Ronny and Paulie are coming back as well.'

Choking on his glass of whisky, Stanley thumped his chest and put the glass on the table. He felt as if he was in *The Godfather* movie and part of him expected to see Marlon Brando walk through the door with his colourful son-in-law.

'What's the matter with you? You need to see a doctor

236

about that continuous choking of yours,' Joyce told him.

Stanley nodded. This was the worst Christmas he'd ever had and, with Eddie's family on their way, it was about to deteriorate even more.

'Is it OK if me and Joey have another drink, Mum?' Frankie asked. Joey and herself had been drinking with the adults all day.

Jessica nodded. Her children's alcohol consumption was the least of her problems at this particular moment in time.

Hearing the scrunch of gravel outside, Jessica ran to the front door. She wasn't overly pleased that Ronny and Paulie were coming back, but what could she say at such a terrible time?

'Come in, you must be freezing. Make yourselves at home,' she said awkwardly to Eddie's brothers.

Frankie ran to the front door and threw her arms around her father. Eddie kissed her and then locked eyes with his beautiful wife. She was the only one who could console him. 'Go and pour the lads a drink, Frankie. I need to talk to Mum alone for a minute.'

Eddie walked upstairs and nodded towards Jessica to follow him. He took off his coat, sat on the marital bed and put his head in his hands. Everything seemed like a bad dream and he wished it was just that. Jessica crept into the room.

'Oh, Eddie, I'm so sorry about your dad. It's awful – what a terrible thing to happen to him. He was such a nice man.'

Eddie stood up and held her tight. Jessica was his rock and he needed her more now than ever. 'You didn't mind me bringing the boys back, did you?' he whispered.

'Of course not. Don't be so silly,' Jessica replied.

Eddie stroked her long blonde hair and found comfort as he took in the scent of her coconut shampoo. 'I really love you, Jess. Me dad's death won't change anything. We'll still try for that little baby, everything will be OK, I promise you.'

Jessica's eyes welled up. 'The baby can wait Eddie, but I'll tell you something now – if it's a boy, we'll call him Harry as a tribute.'

'Do you mean that?' Eddie asked.

'Yes, I do,' Jessica said adamantly.

Downstairs, Joyce was rather enjoying all the drama. Unfortunately, Stanley wasn't.

'I think we should go to bed soon, dear, give the family some space,' he whispered to his wife.

Joyce had no intention of going anywhere. She was upset over what had happened to Harry Mitchell, but would dine out on the excitement for weeks. Being part of a notorious gangster's family suited Joyce down to the ground. She didn't even bother to read her Mills & Boon books any more. 'So did you say it was a baseball bat or a hammer, Ronny?' she asked again.

Extremely drunk, Ronny spilt his guts. 'It was a baseball bat. The lifestyle we lead, I suppose something like this was always bound to happen,' he bragged.

Desperate to get his grandchildren away from the wheelchair psycho, Stanley ordered them to follow him into the kitchen. This was no conversation for such young ears. 'Take no notice of Uncle Ronny. He's very drunk and talking nonsense,' he told them.

Frankie and Joey were unfazed. They had known what their family was for years. Insisting that they were fine, they got rid of Stanley and went outside for a sneaky smoke.

'I bet it'll be a big funeral,' Frankie said to Joey.

Joey nodded. 'Be every villain for miles there. I wonder if it'll be televised.'

Frankie laughed. Her brother did love the camera. 'It won't be on telly. Grandad weren't Al Capone, you know.'

Joey hugged his sister. 'I dunno about you, Frankie, but I need to get out of this house tomorrow. I wish I could meet a boy I liked. David's started to bore me now.'

Frankie slipped her arm into his. 'Let's get New Year out the way and then I'll take you to a gay club. We look old enough to get in and you'll find a decent bloke there.'

Joey squeezed her hand. 'I'm so glad you know, Frankie. You're the only one I can really talk to.'

Frankie smiled. She often wound Joey up – she always had – but she loved her brother more than anyone. 'Are you upset about Grandad Harry?' she asked him.

Joey shrugged. 'I suppose so. He was our grandad, but we never really saw him, did we? I'd be much more upset if it was Grandad Stanley.'

'Me too. Grandad Harry never seemed like a proper grandad. I don't remember him hugging us or playing games with us, or anything, do you?'

Joey shook his head. 'He was sort of invisible in our lives, so I doubt I'll really miss him.'

'So why did you do your dramatics and burst out crying earlier, then?' Frankie teased.

'I didn't know what was going on. I thought something had happened to Dad and I hated seeing Mum so upset,' Joey told her.

'Joey, Frankie. What you doing? You'll catch pneumonia out there,' Jessica shouted.

'Best we look upset again now for Mum and Dad's sake,' Frankie told her brother.

239

Joey smiled. 'I can burst out crying again if you want. It's probably a gay thing – you wouldn't understand.'

Giggling at their own wit, the twins raced one another back to the house.

# TWENTY-THREE

The TV crews and reporters started to arrive on Boxing Day morning and this infuriated Eddie. His father might have been a notorious villain, but he had always tried to keep Jessica and the kids out of the spotlight. 'If them parasites think they're camping outside my gates, they've got another fucking think coming,' he yelled.

'Any chance of a lager or something?' Ronny asked bluntly.

Eddie looked at his brother in disgust. Ronny had been that pissed last night, he'd slept in his wheelchair and shit himself. Now, at nine o'clock in the morning, he wanted to start all over again. Throwing Ronny a look that could kill, Eddie dragged Paulie out to the kitchen. 'I'm gonna have to get Ronny out of the house. I had to wipe the cunt's arse this morning while you were asleep. Take him home, do whatever you like with him, as long as he's out of my face. He's a fucking arsehole, spouting his mouth off like there's no tomorrow and it ain't fair on Jess and the kids.'

Paulie nodded. 'I'll take him home now. I dunno how we're gonna get past the press though, they're mob-handed out there.'

Eddie shrugged. 'Just drive your car at the cunts, they'll

soon move out the way. Make sure Ronny keeps his trap shut. Take Reg with you, he can sit in the back with Ronny and keep him under control.'

Stanley got showered and sat watching his wife put her slap on. 'I really think we should go home this morning, dear. Maybe we can take Frankie and Joey back with us for a couple of days. They shouldn't be in this environment, it's not right. I always knew our Jess shouldn't have got involved with Eddie. Something like this was always bound to happen, and say there's repercussions? I'm worried for Jess' and the twins' safety, I really am.'

Zipping up her make-up bag, Joyce turned to her husband. 'It wasn't a gangland-style killing. You do over-react, Stanley. Harry was burgled by the sound of it, by yobs who then murdered him. I don't want to go home. We've got to stay here; our daughter needs us.'

'Well, I need to pop home to check on the pigeons. I know Jock's looking after them, but I need to make sure they're OK.'

'Can't you bloody well ring him?' Joyce asked, annoyed.

'You know the way I feel about me hen and me cock, dear. I need to see Ethel and Ernie with me own eyes. I won't be long, I just need to put me mind at rest.'

Joyce smirked at her husband's turn of phrase. She hadn't seen his actual cock for years, thank God.

Slightly hungover, Joey opened his sister's bedroom door. 'Frankie, wake up. There's loads of cars and people at the bottom of our drive.'

Yawning, Frankie wandered over to the window to see what the fuss was all about. 'I think it's the press. They've got cameras and that, I think.'

Joey squealed with delight. 'Quick, get dressed, we'll go out there. You never know, we might get our pictures on the front page of one of the nationals tomorrow.'

Frankie smiled at her brother's excitement. He'd always loved a bit of drama and having his picture taken. 'I'll be ready in half-hour,' she giggled.

Eddie slammed the front door and breathed a huge sigh of relief. His brothers and uncle had just left and he was glad to see the back of them.

'Why don't you let me make you some breakfast, Ed? You need to eat, love,' Jessica told him.

Eddie shook his head. All he kept seeing was his poor old dad with his brains hanging out, and he didn't fancy a morsel. 'I'm gonna try the hotel again, see if I can get hold of the boys.'

He had tried to ring Gary and Ricky the previous evening, but had not been able to track them down. The receptionist had promised to get an urgent message to them, asking them to call home, but so far, Eddie had heard nothing.

Eddie dialled the number. Not in a good mood, he found his patience running out within seconds. 'Ain't you got someone there that can speak fucking English, mate?' he shouted. As Eddie was passed to someone else, he immediately slammed the phone down. 'They ain't been back to the hotel all night, Jess. I dunno how I'm gonna get hold of them. They're the ones I need here, not Paulie and fucking Ronny.'

Jessica put her arms around her husband's waist and laid her head on his muscular shoulder. 'The boys will probably ring later. Everything will be OK, Ed. Please let me make you a sandwich and a coffee. I'm so worried about you.'

Eddie held her close to him. 'Go on then, make me a bacon sarnie and I'll eat it just because I love you so much.'

The doorbell made Eddie nearly jump out of his skin. Peeping through the glass to check it wasn't another reporter, he was relieved to see Dougie and Vicki standing there.

'I'm so sorry, mate, I've only just heard,' Dougie told Eddie.

Eddie sent Vicki into the kitchen to see Jessica and ushered Dougie into his office. 'I will find out who murdered me dad and I'll treat them to the most painful death possible. I can't do anything at the moment; the Old Bill are coming round later to take a statement. I'm gonna wait till the boys get back from Tenerife, let it die down a bit and then I'll start me own investigation. I'd put money on it that Jimmy O'Hara was involved in some way, shape or form.'

'When did the police say your dad was murdered?' Dougie asked.

'They ain't said yet, but he was as dead as a dodo when I got there. He was freezing cold he was, looked like he'd been dead for hours. It was awful, Doug, really awful. At least if someone had shot him in the head, the poor cunt wouldn't have suffered. He must have had a terrible death and I swear I'll get revenge for him, if it's the last thing I ever do.'

'Mickey Finley rang me and told me what had happened. He said Harry's house had been burgled and there was no sign it was gangland.'

Eddie shook his head. 'I reckon some cunt's made it look that way on purpose. There'd been some kids hanging around the area outside me old man's house. He told me on Christmas Eve, said they were being a fucking nuisance. I reckon it was a set-up, my life, I do.'

244

Dougie shrugged. 'Jimmy O'Hara's back with his old woman now. Apparently, he had a big bash at his gaff on Christmas Eve that lasted late into the early hours. Patrick Murphy told me. He went round there, by all accounts, so it couldn't have been Jimmy.'

Eddie felt deflated. O'Hara had been his only suspect. 'I'll find out who it was, Doug, don't worry about that. I can't get dad's face out of my mind. Half of his brains were hanging out over the carpet, I was smothered in me own father's blood. Can you imagine how that feels? Dougie, can you?'

Dougie hugged his pal. 'The truth will raise its ugly head. It always does, Ed.'

Frankie and Joey put on their most solemn expressions as they came face to face with their mother. 'How are you, Mum, and how's Dad?' Joey asked sympathetically.

'I'm OK, but your dad's devastated,' Jessica said sadly.

'Can we go out for a while, Mum? It's doing mine and Joey's heads in, all this. We'd like to spend some time with our friends, chill out a bit,' Frankie said.

Jessica didn't know what to say. She didn't want the twins' Christmas to be any worse than it already was, but she was worried about the hordes of press outside. 'I don't know if you can leave the house. Your dad's in his office with Dougie, I'll ask him when he comes out. Go and see Nan and Grandad for a minute – they're sitting in the lounge on their own.'

Vicki smiled as Frankie and Joey wandered off obediently. 'They're such good kids, they really are. Actually, I know this isn't the right time, but I've gotta tell you. I'm pregnant, Jess, I did the test yesterday.'

Thrilled for her friend, Jessica forgot about her own problems and embraced her. 'I am so pleased for you,

Vicki, I really am. I'll let you into a little secret as well. Chances are we might be new mums together. Eddie and I have decided to try for another baby.'

Vicki squeezed her friend's hand. 'That's wonderful. We can go shopping for baby clothes together and our kids can be best friends.'

Jessica nodded. 'I'm just so worried about Ed, Vick. Finding his dad murdered like that must have been such a shock for him. I can't imagine how he must feel.'

Vicki nodded sympathetically. 'Was you close to Harry? You never saw him that much, did you?'

Jessica shrugged. 'When me and Ed first got together, I saw him a fair bit. He used to come round sometimes when the kids were young, but once we moved to Essex, the visits sort of dwindled. I wasn't really close to him but, at the end of the day, I loved him because he was Eddie's dad. I preferred him to Eddie's brothers and uncles, I never liked them very much and still don't. I do remember once, though, when Harry was very kind to me. It was at Reg's retirement do. Me and Ed had had a massive row and Harry calmed things down. I returned the favour by inviting him and Sylvie round for dinner. They came the once, but after that I didn't see Harry for yonks.'

Seeing her husband and Dougie walk into the kitchen, Jessica quickly changed the subject. 'The twins want to go out to see their friends, Ed. I think it will do them good to get out of the house, don't you?'

Eddie nodded. He had been so wrapped up in his father's death, he hadn't given Frankie and Joey much thought. 'Me and Dougie are gonna pop out to see a few people, so I'll drop 'em off on the way. You'll be OK here with your Mum, Dad and Vicki, won't you? If the Old Bill turn up, just fuck 'em off till later. If Gary and Ricky ring, tell 'em to get the first flight home.'

Jessica was worried. She knew how hot-headed Eddie could be and she didn't want him doing anything stupid. 'Where are you going? You won't be long, will you?'

Eddie shook his head. 'Couple of hours, tops. Gonna go for a couple of pints with Dougie and Pat Murphy.'

Relieved that he was only going to the pub, Jessica called Frankie and Joey. 'Your dad's going out and he's gonna drop you off at your friend's,' she told them.

Frankie and Joey glanced at one another. Friend's my arse – they were going straight to the pub.

Opening the front door, Eddie spotted a geezer in a bush with a camera. Furious, he lost his rag and chased him. 'Get off my land, you cunt. I told you earlier, this is private fucking property. You step one foot in here again and I'll chop your fucking bollocks off.'

'I just want to ask you a few questions, Mr Mitchell. Is it true that –'

Picking the paparazzo up by the throat, Eddie snatched his camera from him and jumped up and down on it. The petrified man fell to the floor and curled himself up in a ball. 'Please don't hurt me – I'm sorry,' he pleaded.

Dougie grabbed hold of Eddie. There were flashbulbs going nineteen to the dozen and his pal wasn't doing himself any favours. 'Get back indoors, kids. Come on, Ed, leave it – he's not worth it,' Dougie urged.

Hearing the commotion outside, Jessica let out a scream. Stanley tried to comfort his daughter. 'Ssh, Jess, it's all finished now, love. Eddie's coming back inside,' he told her.

'Good for Eddie. They want locking up, them press,' Joyce said boldly.

Dougie dragged Eddie into the house and told Jessica to pour him a strong drink. 'He don't need all this shit with them knobs out there,' he said, sticking up for his friend.

Stanley put on his jacket. 'I'll drop the kids off at their mate's. I've got to go home to see to me pigeons,' he offered.

Jessica nodded. The further away from all this upset the children were, the better.

'I will come with you, after all. I could do with a bit of fresh air,' Joyce told her husband. She had suddenly realised how wonderful it would be if her photo appeared in a newspaper. Her friends were already in awe of her underworld connections and they would be so, so jealous if they opened their newspaper tomorrow and saw her face smiling back at them.

'Come on, then,' Stanley said angrily. He knew his wife better than she knew herself and he guessed her intentions were not entirely honourable.

Joyce gave a royal wave as the electronic gates opened. On their father's orders, Joey and Frankie hid their faces under a blanket in the back of the car.

'Stop waving at them, you stupid old bat,' Stanley screamed.

'Just shut up and drive,' Joyce replied, still waving.

Relieved that they weren't being followed, Stanley told the twins to uncover themselves. He felt so sorry for his grandchildren. 'Where do you want me to drop you?' he asked sympathetically.

'In the town centre, by the clocktower, Grandad,' Frankie replied.

'What one of your friends lives by the clocktower?' Stanley pried.

'Stacey,' Frankie said, nudging her brother.

Five minutes later, Stanley put his indicator on and stopped the car. 'Now are you sure you're going to be all right? Me and Nanny will watch you go into your friend's house,' said a concerned Stanley.

'We're fine, Grandad. Stacey's mum owns that pub across the road. It's called the Angel.

'Stacey and her family live upstairs,' Joey lied.

Stanley watched the twins walk into the pub. Worried sick, he turned to Joyce. 'Them kids won't grow up to be normal, not in an environment like that, they won't.'

'Jessica and Eddie are wonderful parents. Them kids have never wanted for a thing in their lives,' Joyce said angrily.

Stanley scowled at his superficial wife. 'A bit of normality wouldn't go amiss for them. Everything's about money with you, isn't it, Joycie? What do you know about parenting anyway? You was the one that encouraged your own daughter to take up with a villian in the first place.'

Joyce was shocked by the change in Stanley's attitude. 'Turn the car around and drop me back at Jessica's, immediately. How dare you talk to me like that, Stanley? How dare you?'

Furious, Stanley swung the car around. 'I'm trying to make you see sense. Something bad will happen to our Jess or them kids. I can feel it in me bones, Joycie, on my life I can. One day you'll be sorry you never listened to me.'

# TWENTY-FOUR

## *1988*

Eddie knotted his black tie and glanced at himself in the mirror. Greasing his hair back with Brylcreem, he put on a pair of dark sunglasses to enhance his image. Today was his father's funeral, God rest his soul. The police had kept hold of Harry's body for six weeks and they would have kept it longer, had Eddie not intervened. He'd threatened to blow the whistle on a couple of his dad's old acquaintances just to get things moving.

'You want us to catch your father's killer, don't you?' the bent DS asked Eddie sarcastically. The bent DS was nothing to do with Harry's case and wasn't keen to intervene.

Unable to function properly while his father was lying on a cold slab in the mortuary, Eddie gave it to him. 'If you don't get my dad's body released by next week, I will personally ensure that the shit hits the fan. I know every dodgy deal my father did with you and your pals and I'm sure it would make interesting reading for the Chief of Police. The mugs leading the hunt are no nearer to finding his killers now than they were the day he died. Useless cunts, the lot of them. Just release me dad's body so he can get the send-off he deserves and then I'll find the killer me fucking self.'

The threat worked wonders and the following day Eddie received a phone call allowing him to organise the funeral. The six weeks since Harry had been murdered had been the hardest in Eddie's life. Many a night he'd woken up in a cold sweat as a nightmare had brought it all back to him. The images of his father's battered face and body seemed to torture him every time he closed his eyes.

Ed had finally got hold of Gary and Ricky the day after Boxing Day. They had flown home within twenty-four hours and, along with Raymond, had been a great support to him ever since.

With the Old Bill about as much use as a chocolate fucking teapot, Eddie had started his own line of investigation. He, Ray and the boys had spoken to every underworld connection they knew, but nobody had heard so much as a whisper.

Frustrated, Eddie had turned his attention towards his dad's neighbours. The young lads that had been harassing his father had been spotted by all of them and Eddie managed to get a description. The problem was, seeing as they'd always worn their hoods up, the description was rather vague.

The one thing that did prick Eddie's ears was something that Iris next door had said. Annoyed with the boys making a racket outside, she had confronted them and chased them with her rolling pin. 'They were laughing at me, Eddie, taking the right piss, they were. The one that spoke to me – called me a silly old cow and told me to fuck off – wasn't a Cockney. He had an accent, a strange accent. I couldn't say where it was from, but his voice had a country lilt to it.

From day one, Eddie was positive that the O'Haras were behind his dad's untimely death and Iris's bit of info

251

only confirmed his belief. Jimmy O'Hara and his motley crew all originated from the Cambridgeshire area and their accents were just how Iris had described. With no actual proof, all Eddie could do was sit back and bide his time. He was positive that the young boys had been sent to his father's as a ploy. He was also sure that somebody much bigger and stronger had committed the actual murder.

The police had told Eddie the reason why none of the neighbours had heard his father's screams. The coroner said Harry had been gagged at the time of his death, which had occurred between midnight and 2 a.m. on the morning of Christmas Day. His official report stated that Harry had eleven serious injuries, among which were a broken jaw, bones and a fractured skull. A baseball bat had been used on Harry's head and the rest of his body had been kicked around like a football. With so many injuries, the actual cause of death wasn't properly identified. The coroner had said he was 90% certain that Harry had died of head injuries, but couldn't be absolutely positive. The only thing everybody could be sure about was that Harry Mitchell had died in one of the worst ways imaginable.

Picturing Jimmy O'Hara and his cronies gloating, Eddie smashed his fist against the bedroom wall. O'Hara had held a party round his on Christmas Eve to give himself an alibi, Eddie was certain of that. He obviously hadn't committed the murder himself, but he must have organised it.

Seeing Jessica walk into the room, Ed tried to pull himself together. 'Are you OK, love? What have you done to your hand?' she asked, noticing his knuckles were bleeding.

'I caught it in the drawer,' Eddie lied.

Jessica stood on tiptoes and put her slender arms around his shoulders. 'Me and the kids are ready. Shall we make a move now?'

Eddie nodded. He just wanted the day to be over.

Joyce stood in Harry Mitchell's front garden. The flowers and tributes that kept arriving completely took her breath away. A keen gardener, she had never seen so many flowers. Hundreds and hundreds there were, and she had just seen another enormous arrangement arrive that spelled out the word LEGEND. Aware of a photographer standing over the road, Joyce patted her hair into place. Ever since she had got her picture on page seven of the *Sun* newspaper, she had felt like a local celebrity. People were still stopping her in the street now and the article had appeared six weeks beforehand.

As more and more people arrived to pay their respects, Stanley became increasingly uncomfortable. Most of them were obviously well-known villains and he felt like a spare prick at a wedding. Noticing Roy Shaw, the notorious prize-fighting champion, looking his way, Stanley quickly averted his eyes. He didn't feel at ease around these people and he couldn't wait to get home to his pigeons.

As the horse-drawn hearse arrived carrying Harry's body, all the neighbours came out of their houses. The street was heaving with mourners and it was more like a carnival than a funeral.

Eddie got into the first car. He was joined by Paulie, Ronny, Reg, Albert, Auntie Joan, Auntie Vi and his dad's distraught long-term lady-friend, Sylvie. Gary and Ricky got into the second car with Jessica, the twins, Raymond, Joyce and Stanley. The other cars were filled with more distant relations.

The funeral was to take place at East London Cemetery in nearby Plaistow. Harry had purchased his own plot years before, insisting he wanted to be laid to rest next to his beautiful wife.

Frankie nudged Joey as the procession made its way through the crowded streets. Hundreds of people had made the effort. Some were waving banners and flags, but most were bowing their heads as a mark of respect. Jessica pointed a flag out to the twins. 'Look at that. "Harry Mitchell, simply the best", it says. Your grandad was very popular, wasn't he?'

'Shame we never saw him,' Joey whispered to Frankie.

Stanley felt his face redden as the TV crews pointed a camera in his direction. He could just imagine all his old pals down the bus depot watching the news tonight and seeing him on there. Thank God I took early retirement, Stanley thought. He was embarrassed to be a part of such a family.

'Will you stop fucking waving,' Stanley shouted at Joyce, who was milking it. Her outfit looked awful. She had a massive black-netted hat on her head and Stanley thought she looked like a fucking witch. The only thing she was lacking was a broomstick.

Due to the horrific circumstances surrounding Harry's death, the service itself was a very solemn affair. The vicar who presided over the proceedings was an old pal of the Mitchells. He had married Harry and his wife many moons ago.

Eddie stood up to say a few words, but was too choked up to go through with it. Seeing Ronny race towards him in his wheelchair, Eddie handed him the piece of paper.

'My Dad was the best and, I swear on God's life, we'll get revenge for you, Dad. Whoever did this to you,

254

we'll do a hundred times worse to them,' Ronny slurred, ignoring what was written down in front of him.

Eddie cringed. Trust Ronny to be pissed and say something like that in the house of God. Frantically waving his hands, Eddie urged the organist to play the song that he had chosen. Harry's all-time favourite was the old war time classic, 'Heart of My Heart'.

'When I pop me clogs, I want that played at me funeral. It was me and your mother's favourite song, Eddie,' his dad had told him.

Lots of tears flowed as everybody joined in with the words.

> When we were kids on the corner of the street,
> We were rough and ready guys,
> But oh, how we could harmonise!

Feeling his eyes well up, Eddie did his best to hold back the tears. Every villain in London was here and he was desperate not to make a tit of himself in front of the world's finest. Pulling himself together, Eddie joined in with the singing:

> I know a tear would glisten,
> If once more I could listen,
> To the gang that sang
> 'Heart of My Heart'.

As the chapel began to empty, Jessica squeezed Eddie's hand. 'It was a lovely send-off. Your dad would have been proud,' she told him.

Eddie stood by the graveside, amazed by the number of people in attendance. There had been hundreds unable to fit inside the chapel and they had listened outside to the service on a loudspeaker. Eddie stood between Sylvie and Auntie Joan. Both women were beside themselves and he had to nigh-on physically support them.

As his father's body was finally laid to rest, Eddie breathed a sigh of relief. 'God bless, Dad,' he whispered, as he threw earth on top of the coffin.

Desperate to be seen as an important member of the family, Joyce grabbed Eddie's arm. 'Come and look at the beautiful flowers,' she insisted.

Eddie let her drag him away and listened as she rattled on about who had sent what. 'Look at that beauty that says BIG H; Freddie Foreman sent that. I love the LEGEND one, don't you? That's from the Krays. Look at that boxing glove, Ed, it's massive, ain't it?'

'Who sent that?' Eddie asked, completely disinterested.

'Er, I can't remember. Here we go: the card says Jimmy O'Hara and family.'

Eddie felt the blood in his veins run cold, 'Give us that fucking card,' he yelled.

Wondering what she had done so wrong, Joyce nervously handed it to him. Eddie stared at it. 'To Eddie and family. Our thoughts are with you at this sad time. Jimmy O'Hara and family.'

Eddie was livid. He left Joyce standing with her mouth open and stomped over to his brothers. 'The cheeky pikey cunt, he's taking the fucking piss out of us,' he yelled.

Raymond ran over and tried to calm him down. 'Don't say nothing here, Ed. If Jimmy's done it to wind you up, you don't want him to think he's succeeded. There's too many eyes and ears around. Just forget about it for now and we'll discuss it tomorrow.'

Eddie brushed Raymond's arm away. 'Let's get away from here. Tell the undertakers we're ready. I need a fucking drink.'

As Jessica ran over to see what their father was upset about, the twins nudged one another. 'I think our family is really weird, don't you?' Joey whispered.

Frankie burst out laughing. 'I wouldn't say they're weird, but they're definitely not normal.'

Joey smiled as he saw Auntie Joan, Auntie Vi and another lady heading their way.

'Look at yous two. Ain't you all grown up, and such handsome kids. Look Sylvie, these are Harry's grandchildren. This is Frankie, who's a ringer for her father, and doesn't Joey look like his mother?' Vi said.

Sylvie shook hands with the twins. 'We have met before, but it was years ago and I'd never have recognised you now.'

Frankie and Joey both kissed her politely.

'Kids, come on, we're going!' Eddie yelled.

'Goodbye Sylvie, bye Auntie Joan, bye Auntie Vi. Are you all coming back to the pub?' Joey asked.

'No, lovey. It's been a long day. Me, Vi and Sylvie are gonna toast your grandad indoors. We're going back to mine for a drink,' Joan told him.

Joey linked arms with his sister and led her back to where the cars were parked.

'Dad didn't look too happy, did he?'

Frankie giggled. 'I shouldn't fucking think so. He has just buried his father who happened to be brutally murdered in his own bed.'

'I didn't mean that – you know what I meant,' Joey said, annoyed.

Frankie laughed. 'Come on, I'll race you. Last one back buys the fags later.'

Eddie had no other option than to book the Flag for the wake. His father had spent so many hours of his life in there, he would have come back and haunted Eddie if it had been held anywhere else. Obviously there was a free bar, but the size of the pub was a problem. With so many mourners, there weren't enough staff behind the bar or enough room for people to stand comfortably. Eddie made a quick phone call and organised another free bar in the Ordnance Arms, which was also an old haunt of his dad's. People could make their own mind up where they wanted to go. If they weren't happy being squashed like sardines in a tin, they could have a drink in Harry's memory down the road.

Jessica stood in the corner of the pub with Vicki. Dougie was up at the bar with the men. Neither Vicki nor Jessica were annoyed that their husbands had deserted them. On this type of occasion the men always clubbed together and the women were left to their own devices.

'Where are the twins? Can you see them? I have to keep my eye on them, as they do like a drink, you know,' Jessica said to her friend.

Vicki craned her neck. 'I can't see them, but I'm sure they're fine. How old are they now? Nearly sixteen, aren't they? I was drinking in pubs at their age, weren't you? I wouldn't worry about them too much.'

Jessica nodded. The twins were a bit too streetwise for her liking and she couldn't help but worry about them.

Eddie stood up at the bar with all the old school.

'Can I have a quick word with you, Eddie?' Patrick Murphy asked him.

Eddie followed the big Irishman outside the pub and they found a quiet spot. 'Please don't think I'm sticking my nose in your business, Eddie, but I'm telling you now, your father's murder had nothing to do with the O'Haras. I was round at Jimmy's on Christmas Eve. His sons were there, his brothers, his cousins. I didn't leave there till three in the morning. I know this must be awful for you, Ed, but you've gotta look somewhere else for your answers. You know as well as I do that when Alice left Jimmy, he lost his swagger. I know you've had a feud with him in the past, but he's a changed man now. He don't want any grief, especially now Alice has agreed to give him another chance.'

Eddie put his thinking cap on. Maybe the stress of what had happened to his father had caused him to bark up the wrong tree. If the whole of the O'Hara clan were at Jimmy's, then maybe, just maybe, it wasn't them. Rubbing his tired eyes, Eddie looked at Patrick for answers. 'Apart from the O'Haras, I can't think who else had a massive grudge against my dad. I mean, if someone would have blasted his brains out, I could have dealt with it, understood it. But battering the life out of him – who would do a thing like that? It ain't exactly our style, is it?'

Patrick handed Eddie a cigar. 'No, it's not the work of people like us, Eddie. This is what I'm trying to tell you. I know Jimmy's a traveller, but he's a family man and, like us, he has rules. I know your old man shot his, but if he wanted revenge, he would have returned it the same way. Can you honestly see him ransacking your dad's house and torturing him? Jimmy ain't a bad geezer deep down and that ain't his style. He has standards, for fuck's sake.'

Eddie accepted a light and urged Patrick to go back inside. 'Shout me up a large Scotch. I just need five minutes to meself,' he told him.

Patrick nodded. 'Promise me you'll think about what I've said, Eddie. I'm friendly with both you and Jimmy and I'd hate to see your feud reignited for no reason. You've got to think of your wife, Eddie, your children. Do you really want to put them in danger?' If you start a war, how do you know your family won't be caught up in the crossfire? You've got to let sleeping dogs lie on this one, Ed. Jimmy O'Hara never killed your father.'

Eddie watched the big man walk away. Patrick Murphy was no man's fool and deep down, Eddie knew that what he was saying made sense. Waiting for the police to release his dad's body had made his brain go all wonky. It couldn't have been Jimmy O'Hara, it wasn't his style and he had a cast-iron alibi.

As Jessica walked towards him, Eddie smiled at her.

'Are you OK? I was worried about you. Why are you out here on your own?'

Eddie held his arms out and hugged his wife tightly. Jessica was his life and he'd never do anything to endanger the welfare of her and the kids, not in a million years.

# TWENTY-FIVE

In the weeks that followed Harry's funeral, Eddie got himself back into his usual routine.

As he and the police had drawn a blank on the identity of his father's killer, Eddie had little option other than to throw himself into his work. Since Christmas, he had let things slip, but he was determined not to fuck up the Mitchell reputation his dad had fought so hard to create in the first place.

The nightmares of what had happened still haunted Eddie. Many a night, he would get up about 3 or 4 a.m. and sit downstairs drinking endless cups of tea. Jessica had been a real star. She was very supportive and, if he was having a black day, she was gentle and understanding.

'For fuck's sake, Dad. Three times I've asked you the same question and you still ain't answered me.'

'Sorry, Rick, I was miles away, son. What were you saying?'

Ricky stood up. 'Forget it. It's my round. Same again?'

Eddie nodded. It was his forty-seventh birthday today. Jessica was at home preparing for a dinner party for him. It would be the first time they'd entertained at home since his dad's untimely death.

Gary and Ricky had declined the invitation of a quiet

night in. 'We're going to a rave up town, Dad, but we'll take you out for a beer in the day,' they'd told him.

Eddie hadn't minded. They were only in their early twenties and he had been exactly the same himself at their age.

Ricky handed his brother and father their drinks.

'What exactly is all this rave shit you keep on about?' he asked his sons.

Gary laughed. 'If you ain't heard of raves, Dad, then you must be getting old.'

'They're a new thing out. Word has it, they're gonna sweep the country this summer. The music's blinding, Dad. They play house music. Everyone gets out of their nuts and they go on all night long,' Ricky added.

'You two ain't fucking taking drugs, are you?' Eddie asked.

Gary shook his head. 'We just get pissed and pull all the birds, Dad,' he lied.

Neither Gary nor Ricky were really into drugs, but ecstasy tablets were a new thing out, and they liked to drop an occasional one. They liked the ones called American burgers. They were proper happy pills and you could dance all night on them. These raves went on for hours and without something in your system to keep you going, you'd be as out of place as a pig in a synagogue.

'So, who's coming round yours tonight?' Ricky asked his father.

'Raymondo's bringing Polly, his bit of posh, round. We ain't met her yet. He was bringing her round Boxing Day but, obviously, when Grandad was found dead, he didn't. Vicki and Dougie are coming and I've also invited Patrick Murphy and his old woman.'

'Well, I hope you have a good night, Dad. How are the twins? Will they be there?' Gary asked.

Eddie smiled. 'They're OK. They didn't wanna sit in with their old dad, either, so they're pissing off out. Jess worries when they go to these parties and stuff, but they're nearly sixteen and all their friends are allowed to go and come home late. I always give 'em cab money to get themselves home, mind. I've told them the day I find out they've been pocketing the money and walking home is the day I put me foot down.'

As their dad went to the toilet, Ricky turned to Gary. 'Shall we give him the present now?'

Gary took the black velvet box out of his pocket. The lads had clubbed together and brought their father a new watch. It was a Rolex and had cost them a fucking fortune.

'Happy birthday, Dad. That's from the two of us,' Gary said, as Eddie returned to the table.

Eddie was choked as he opened the box. 'Fucking hell! It's beautiful, but you shouldn't have spent that kind of dough. A shirt would have done me. I'd rather see yous spend your money on yourselves.'

'You've always been a great dad to us and this is the first year we've been in a position to buy you something decent,' Gary insisted.

Eddie took his old watch off and put the new one on. 'I love it,' he said truthfully.

Ricky glanced at his brother. 'We're gonna have to go in a minute, Gal. We promised Mum we'd be there by three.'

'How is your mother?' Eddie asked.

Gary sighed. 'She ain't been well, Dad. The doctor's told her she'll be dead in two years if she don't knock the drink on the head. She's so thin now and her skin looks kind of yellow.'

Eddie shook his head sadly. 'I know me and your mother were never Romeo and Juliet, but I'm sorry to

263

hear that. Go on, yous get going, and tell your mum, if she needs money or anything, she knows where I am.'

Gary and Ricky said their goodbyes and left. Eddie ordered himself another drink and sat at the table alone. He'd met his sons in a pub in Aveley where no one knew him. It was nice to have a quiet bevvy and be anonymous for once. Glancing at his new watch, Eddie smiled. Gary and Ricky had always been thoughtful and generous. From the age of five upwards, they'd made or bought him nice presents. Frankie and Joey were the opposite. The twins had been given far too much from an early age and they'd grown up in their own little world. They rarely remembered his or Jessica's birthdays and, even though they received plenty of pocket money, they never bothered spending it on anyone other than themselves.

Deep in thought, Eddie didn't notice the man walk towards him.

'Eddie, how are you, mush? I was sorry to hear about your father. Our families might never have been muckers, but your old man didn't deserve to die like that. This is Alice, my wife. Can I get you a drink?'

Looking at Jimmy O'Hara's outstretched hand, Eddie didn't know whether to break it or shake it. Not wanting to make a scene, he did neither. 'I can't stop. My Jess is expecting me back. We're having people round for dinner later,' he said abruptly.

As Eddie stood up, Jimmy nodded to Alice to make herself scarce. 'Go and get the drinks,' he ordered.

Alone with Eddie, Jimmy faced up to him. 'I know you probably think your old boy's death was something to do with me, but it weren't. Life's too short to hold grudges and if I was gonna retaliate for your father shooting mine, I'd have done it in an honourable way. At one point, I was desperate to get my revenge, but

264

I'm not fiery like I used to be, Eddie. Losing my Alice gave me the kick in the bollocks I needed. My family come first now and I don't want no feud with anyone. I would never jeopardise losing Alice and my kids again, ever.'

Eddie stared into Jimmy's eyes. He was quite an expert on reading people by their behaviour and expressions and he came to the conclusion that O'Hara was either telling the truth or was a fucking top-drawer liar. More confused than ever about his father's death, Eddie said his good-byes and left the pub.

Later that evening, Jessica smiled as Eddie launched into yet another one of his anecdotes. She'd been worried that tonight might be too much for him but, thankfully, she had been wrong. Eddie was on top form and she was relieved he was back to his old self.

'There's plenty more to eat in the kitchen. Is anyone still hungry?' she asked.

With everyone telling her they were full to the brim, Jessica started to clear the table. She had chosen an Italian menu for the dinner party and the food had gone down a treat.

Eddie poured his friends another drink. He was a bit unsure about Polly, Raymond's bird. The girl was pleasant enough, but spoke with a plum in her chops.

'No more for me, thanks, Eddie. Three is my limit,' Polly told him firmly.

With everybody sorted, Eddie took a glass of wine out to Jessica in the kitchen. 'She's a funny one, Raymondo's bird, ain't she?'

Jessica smiled. 'I wouldn't put her with our Raymond in a million years, but as long as she makes him happy, that's all that matters.'

'Do you reckon he's fucking her? I can't imagine her in the sack, can you? Oh, Raymond, please hurry up and shoot your load, the butler will be here soon,' Eddie said, mimicking Polly's posh tones.

'Sssh, they might hear you,' Jessica scolded him.

Eddie could be such a piss-taker at times and she didn't want him upsetting the wonderful evening they were having. Eddie tilted her chin and kissed her. 'I think we should up our baby-making sessions from this week onwards – what do you say?'

Jessica sighed. Tonight, she was more worried about the two she'd given birth to than about creating another. 'I don't like Frankie and Joey being allowed to stay out round their friends' houses. It worries me sick. I mean, we don't even really know the parents.'

Frankie and Joey had gone to a sixteenth birthday party. The party was miles away, in Fulham, and Jessica had been dead against them going from the start.

'But Mum, Dionne, was my best friend throughout most of my school years. It's not her fault that her parents have moved to Fulham. I'm not going on my own, am I? I've got Joey to take care of me. Her mum said we can stay in the guest room and she's going to call you to confirm,' Frankie whinged.

Jessica discussed it with Eddie and, in the end, they had decided to let the twins go. She hadn't been able to get hold of Dionne's mum, but had spoken to her older sister, who had confirmed the arrangements.

'Shall I give them a call? Make sure they got there all right,' Jessica asked Eddie.

She had insisted that they take their father's mobile phone so she could contact them to put her mind at rest.

Eddie shook his head. 'They're nearly sixteen, Jess. We

need to learn to trust them, not check up on them all the time. They're good kids: they'll be fine, trust me.'

Joey and Frankie stood near the bar. The gay club was an eye-opener for both of them and they were overwhelmed by the atmosphere. The Dionne story had been a cover-up and their friend, Paige, had done a wonderful job pretending to be Dionne's sister.

'He's nice. Look, the tall one with the blond hair who's looking over.'

Joey shook his head. 'Nah, he ain't my type.'

Frankie smiled. She had promised Joey months ago that she would come to a gay club with him and this was their first visit. She could sense her brother's excitement; he was like a kid in a sweet shop, bless him.

'Talk to me Joey, quick. I've got some meaty lesbian making eyes at me.'

Joey slung his arm around Frankie's shoulder and ordered another drink. 'Maybe you're really into a bit of pussy. I mean, you don't seem to get very far with boys, do you, Frankie?' he said, winding her up.

Frankie glared at him. 'Fuck you, I'm not into women. I'm just fussy. I mean, look at the boys around our way, the ones that have asked me out. Would you fancy them?'

Joey shook his head. He had finished with David a while back and, apart from him, there'd been no one else local to catch his eye. In a way, he could understand Frankie's dilemma. 'What type of bloke do you actually want?' he asked his sister.

Frankie shrugged. 'We've been brought up with a certain lifestyle, Joey, so I'm hardly liable to date some mug. I want a bloke that's gonna make me laugh, treat me like a princess, like Dad always has. To be honest,

267

I suppose I'm looking for someone who is a bit like Dad. You've always been closer to Mum, but I ain't.'

Joey laughed. 'So you're looking for a scar-faced, top-class villain. That should be easy – why don't I just place an ad in the local paper for you?'

As usual, Frankie appreciated her brother's wit. The pair of them had realised at an early age what sort of family they were part of, and often had a joke about it.

'Joey, you've pulled again and this one is nice. He's that gorgeous, if it turns out he ain't a woofta, then I'll have him. Look, standing over there, to your left.'

Looking around, Joey spotted the bloke who was staring his way. The guy was older than him, probably well into his twenties. 'Wow,' Joey mumbled, as he felt his stomach lurch.

Mr Gorgeous was well over six feet. He was wearing light stonewashed jeans and a tight-fitting white T-shirt. He had a perfect body, face and physique and was an absolute out-and-out sort. Aware of Mr Gorgeous smiling at him, Joey turned away. He felt like a fox startled by headlights. 'He's a lot older than me. I dunno,' he said dubiously.

Frankie burst out laughing. 'He's fucking amazing, what is wrong with you? Please don't tell me you've dragged me all the way here and now you're shit-scared to go for it.'

Glancing back at the mystery bloke, Joey quickly looked away. 'Go and get us another drink – and get me a double,' he ordered his sister.

Waving her money at the barman, Frankie couldn't stop smiling. Her brother was such a funny bastard at times.

'All right? My name's Lisa. First time here, is it?' asked a hefty woman with a skinhead.

Frankie nodded. 'I'm here because of my brother. He's gay, not me.'

The woman smiled. The newcomers all said that. In denial, the lot of them. 'Let me buy the drinks,' the skin-head bird said.

Frankie refused. 'Thanks, but no thanks,' she said curtly.

The woman smiled at her. 'It's not unusual to be curious. You're only young and sometimes it takes a while to come to terms with what you was born to be.'

Frankie snatched the drinks off the barman. 'I am not a fucking dyke, so will you sod off and pester someone else,' she said angrily.

Realising that his sister wasn't happy about something, Joey went to her rescue. 'Is everything OK? What's the matter?'

The shaven-haired woman scowled at him. 'Your sister's got issues, love,' she said, walking away.

As Frankie repeated the conversation, Joey couldn't stop laughing. 'Don't laugh – it ain't fucking funny. She thought I was a lesbo,' Frankie said, fuming.

Too busy winding Frankie up, Joey didn't notice Mr Gorgeous walking his way.

'Hi, my name's Dominic. Can I buy you a drink?'

Her brother's startled expression amused Frankie immensely. 'His name's Joey and, yes, he'll have a large vodka and orange. I'm Frankie, his twin sister, by the way.'

Dominic shook Frankie's hand and smiled. 'And what would you like?' he asked.

'I'd just like my brother to meet someone as handsome as you and get himself laid,' Frankie replied, grinning at Joey.

Joey was horrified. Frankie could be such a cow at times. 'Take no notice. My sister can't help having a mouth like a sewer,' he said awkwardly.

269

Dominic squeezed Joey's arm. 'Your sister can shout up the drinks. Come and dance with me,' he said.

Joey was petrified as he followed Dominic onto the dancefloor. His silly liaison with David was nothing compared to the way this guy made him feel. Dominic was a man, not some confused schoolboy.

Chatting to a transvestite at the bar, Frankie watched her brother with interest. He and Dominic had been dancing for over ten minutes now and were getting on like a house on fire.

As the DJ changed the tempo, Dominic took Joey in his arms. 'Are you OK?' he asked gently.

Joey nodded. Truthfully, he felt anything but OK. His heart was beating like a drum, his palms were sweaty and he was talking rubbish. 'I think I'm a little bit nervous. I've never done anything like this before,' he admitted.

Dominic smiled at him. This boy was so different from any of the others he had ever met. He was innocent and gorgeous. Aware that Dominic had an erection, Joey didn't know whether to laugh or cry.

Conscious of Joey's predicament, Dominic brushed his lips against his. He smiled and spoke softly. 'Relax Joey. I'll be gentle with you, I promise.'

# TWENTY-SIX

Joey and Dominic's relationship developed quickly and, within a few weeks of meeting, both of them were head over heels in love. The situation was awkward. Dominic lived near the Angel in Islington. He had a demanding job working as a money broker in the city. Joey was studying for his GCSEs and finding time to see one another regularly was virtually impossible.

On a healthy wage, Dominic had his own property, a two-bedroom flat. He kept begging Joey to stay over, but Joey had only been able to do so twice.

Dominic had a very manly voice, so Joey had given him his home telephone number and had told his parents that he and Frankie had met a new mate. Desperate not to arouse suspicion, he told Dominic to ask for either him or his sister if his dad or mum answered the phone.

'Oi, oi! So how was last night, then, lover boy?'

Joey smiled as his sister entered his room and sat on the edge of his bed. He had spent the previous night at Dominic's and told his parents he was staying at David's to revise for his exams. 'It was wonderful,' Joey said, beaming.

'Well, give us the gory details, then.'

Joey ordered Frankie to shut the bedroom door. He had stayed around Dominic's once before, but his nerves had got the better of him. Last night, he had actually done it and had enjoyed every second. 'It was fantastic, Frankie. Dom's got a body to die for and his willy is absolutely enormous.'

Inquisitive by nature, Frankie was desperate for more detail. 'So, what exactly happened then? I mean it ain't like a girl and a boy, is it?'

Joey felt his cheeks redden. 'What are you like, you nosy cow? I'm not discussing the ins and outs – it's private.'

Frankie laughed at Joey's embarrassment. 'Go on, tell me more. Did you go all the way this time?'

'Yes, and that's all I'm telling you, so don't bother asking me no more questions.'

Joey being gay didn't bother Frankie one iota. She enjoyed winding him up, but was also genuinely pleased that he had met someone he liked. She had always got on better with boys than girls and would have hated Joey to have gone out with some bimbo she hated. That would have made her extremely jealous.

'So, did you come?' Frankie asked, desperate to know more. They had always had such a close, open relationship. Joey told her everything and vice versa.

'Yes, of course. Now, can we shut up about it now, 'cause Mum's calling us.'

Jessica smiled as the twins bounded down the stairs. 'What are you laughing at?' she asked Frankie.

'Nothing important. Joey was just telling me about the biology homework he was doing last night.'

Jessica tutted. 'You wasn't being rude, Joey, was you?'

'Of course not, Mum,' Joey replied, kicking his smirking sister under the table.

'I wanted to talk to yous about your birthday. You're

sixteen soon and Dad and I asked you ages ago what you wanted to do. Have either of you decided yet?'

Joey nudged Frankie. Their parents had wanted to throw a big party at home and invite all of their friends. The twins were totally against the idea. There was no way Joey could chance inviting Dominic, and Frankie reckoned it would be as boring as hell. There was a new place where everyone was going called the Berwick Manor. It had started a rave night on a Friday and the twins were desperate to go there.

Frankie smiled at her mum. 'We have thought about it and we've decided we want to go out with our friends on the Friday, which is our actual birthday, then maybe have a smaller party here with you, Dad, Nan, Grandad and the rest of the family on the Saturday.'

Jessica found it hard to hide her disappointment. 'Why don't you want the big party for all of your friends? Dad could have done a barbecue and all your mates could have brought their costumes and had a swim.'

Frankie decided to be truthful. 'Our friends like drinking, not swimming, Mum. They'll laugh at us if they come here and only get offered soft drinks. We can still have a barbecue – we can do that on the Saturday with the family.'

Defeated, Jessica shrugged. She didn't mind the twins having the odd drink or two, but she wasn't about to let their friends do the same. Say one of them got drunk and was ill, how would she explain that to their parents? It would make her and Eddie look awful and tarnish their responsible reputation. 'OK, I'll let your dad know,' Jessica said miserably. The twins were at an age now where they wanted to do their own thing.

'Where is Dad?' Frankie asked. He never worked weekends and was usually glued to her mother's side.

'He's popped out to see a mechanic. There's a problem with the Land Cruiser and he wants to get it repaired. I should imagine he'll be home soon – he's already been gone ages,' Jessica said.

Aware that his mum was upset about the birthday party, Joey stood up and hugged her. 'Frankie and I aren't doing anything today. How about when Dad gets back, we all go out for something to eat? Frankie and I will treat you and Dad for once. Because we've been so busy doing homework, we've saved loads of pocket money.'

Jessica smiled. 'That would be lovely, Joey.'

Eddie Mitchell sat in the car park of the Robin Hood pub in Dagenham. He was looking for a geezer called Tommy Trott. Trottsy, as he was better known, was out of Canning Town and had borrowed five grand from Eddie six months ago. He had paid back the first three instalments, then had disappeared off the face of the earth.

Eddie had received a phone call only yesterday, telling him that the cheeky bastard had resurfaced in Dagenham and was larging it in the Robin Hood. Usually Eddie dealt with the mugs who tried to knock him alone, but Trottsy had annoyed him more than most, so he'd brought Raymond with him. Eddie had known Trottsy for years and had helped him out on many occasions in his younger days. That's why Trottsy's deception was that much worse.

Raymond looked at his watch. 'What time did this geezer say Trottsy normally gets here?'

Eddie tapped his fingers on the steering wheel in annoyance. Twelve o'clock was the information he had received and it was now quarter to one. 'He'd better hurry up. I told Jess I wouldn't be long, she thinks I'm getting the car fixed. Twelve, I was told. We'll give it another half-hour and if there's still no sign of him, we'll have another bash tomorrow.'

'I can't make tomorrow, Ed. Polly's dad has a boat and we're all going sailing,' Raymond said awkwardly.

Eddie nodded. He was a good boss and didn't expect any of the lads to work at weekends, unless it was unavoidable, of course. 'Don't worry, Gary and Ricky will have to get their lazy arses out of bed or, worst ways, I'll bring Paulie with me. So, how's things going with Polly? It sounds serious.'

Raymond smiled. He was a deep person at times and didn't like to give much away, especially when it came to relationships and stuff. His mum was brain damage and Eddie was a piss-taker, so he always kept his cards close to his chest. 'It's going all right. She's a nice girl,' was all he said.

About to pry some more, Eddie was stopped by the appearance of Trottsy walking towards them. 'Here he is, the low-life cunt, just crossing the road. Go and grab him, Ray, put your arm around his shoulder and lead him over here. There's tons of traffic about, so be careful. Any probs, show him the gun under your jacket.'

Raymond had never met Tommy Trott before. 'Is that him? The geezer in the denim jacket?' he asked.

'Yeah, go on, quick as you like,' Eddie replied.

Whistling as he walked, Tommy Trott crossed the busy road and stopped to spark up a Rothmans. He didn't see Raymond approach him – he was too busy trying to shield his lighter from the gusty wind.

'Who are you? What the fuck do you want?' he yelled, as Raymond grabbed hold of him.

'Shut the fuck up and walk with me. A mate of mine wants a little word with you,' Raymond said calmly.

'I ain't going nowhere. I'm –'

The gun being thrust into his ribs stopped Tommy in mid sentence. Immediately, he realised that Eddie Mitchell must be involved.

'I'm gonna pay Eddie back, I've just been a bit short. I lost me job, I was paying him up until then,' Tommy whinged.

'Shut up and tell him yourself,' Raymond said coldly.

As Raymond and Tommy walked towards the motor, Eddie smiled as he switched on the ignition. Trottsy's face was a picture of panic, the fucking moron.

Longbridge Road was far too busy at this time of day for Eddie to do the business, so he ordered Raymond to put his prey in the back and sit beside him.

'Long time no see, Tommy boy,' he said sarcastically.

'Ed, I'm so sorry, I lost me job. I'll get your money. Next week I'll pay you, I promise,' Tommy pleaded.

Ignoring his pleas, Eddie did a left out of the pub car park. He knew a quiet little spot, a couple of miles away. Ever since his father's cruel death, Eddie had found that his violent streak had worsened. He had always enjoyed a bit of rough and tumble and an odd finger or thumb dismembered, but finding his father the way he did had made him more brutal than ever.

Eddie drove down to the bottom of a road that led only to high-grass wasteland and turned off the engine. Relieved that there wasn't anyone in sight, Eddie opened the driver's door. 'Get out,' he ordered the shivering wreck previously known as big, bold Tommy Trott.

'I will pay you back, Eddie. Please don't hurt me,' Trottsy begged.

Eddie laughed as his expensive black leather shoe repeatedly made contact with Trottsy's head. As Tommy's front teeth flew onto a nearby rock, the blood running down his throat hampered his speech.

'Please, Eddie, please! I'm sorry,' he slurred in pain.

Realising that Eddie was losing the plot, Raymond tried to drag him away. 'Come on, Ed, you've made your point. Give him a chance to pay up,' Ray shouted.

'Made me point, made me fucking point! I've known this cunt for years. Taken the right piss out of me, he has. Fuck the money, I want him dead.'

Hearing a dog bark, Raymond grabbed Eddie and shook him. 'There's someone coming. Let's go, come on. Think of Jess, for fuck's sake.'

The mention of his wife's name and a Rottweiler bounding towards him was enough to snap Eddie out of his violent trance. Tommy Trott's face was barely recognisable as Eddie aimed a farewell kick at it. 'Next week I want my money or you're dead, you cunt,' he spat.

Raymond bundled Eddie into the passenger side of the Land Cruiser. Both men had clocked that the Rottweiler was sniffing around Trottsy, licking his wounds. 'Buster, Buster!' its owner was yelling in the distance.

Raymond jumped into the driver's seat and did a speedy three-point turn. Putting his foot down, he pulled away just as the dog's owner came into full view. 'That was close. You don't think Trottsy will say ought, do you?'

Eddie smirked. 'What do you think? The mug's jaw is smashed to smithereens. Would you say ought? I bet he can't even speak for a month.'

Raymond headed towards his new house. He had recently purchased a property in Gidea Park, Romford. Meeting Polly had prompted him to move out of his previous address. Polly had class and he wanted to show her that he had it, too. 'We'll go to my house. You're covered in claret, you can't go home like that. You can borrow something of mine, it'll save Jess having kittens.'

Having now calmed down, Eddie couldn't stop laughing.

'Did you see that fucking Rotty? I'm sure it swallowed Trotty's teeth. It was sniffing at them and then I saw them disappear. They were lying on that big bit of rock beside him.'

Eddie's laugh was infectious and Raymond quickly joined in. 'The funniest bit was when the dog was licking his face and then had a shit not two yards from his head.'

Eddie had been too focused on his victim to see the dog have a dump. 'How fucking funny is that? Top dog! I must invest in a Rottweiler, Raymondo, I really must.'

'Ring Dad again, Mum. Me and Joey are starving,' Frankie whinged.

Jessica tried her husband's mobile for the umpteenth time. 'It's still switched off,' she said worriedly.

Bored out of her brains, Frankie urged Joey to follow her upstairs. 'We're going to listen to some music, Mum.'

'Give us a shout when Dad gets home,' Joey shouted out.

Frankie put the radio on. House music was a new thing out and she and Joey loved listening to the local pirate radio stations that were playing it.

Frankie shut her bedroom door. 'Thanks, Joey. Now we're stuck going out with Mum and Dad tonight and, if that ain't bad enough, you've said we'll pay for it.'

Joey shrugged. 'I felt sorry for Mum. You could have explained about the party in a kinder way.'

'Well, what was I meant to say? You know as well as I do that she would have embarrassed us. Can you imagine our friends drinking lemonade, playing pass the parcel and eating jelly and fucking ice cream? Well, no, neither can I. I explained it the best way I could. You always leave it to me, Joey, so best you do it in future.'

Joey sighed. He had always been the coward out of

the two of them and left Frankie to it. 'Sorry, sis,' he said kindly. He and Frankie rarely argued, and on the odd occasions they did, they were friends again within the hour.

Frankie hugged him. 'I wish Dad would hurry up, I'm ravenous.'

Joey smiled. 'Me too.'

By the time Eddie arrived home, Jessica was a bag of nerves. 'Where have you been? I was so worried!' she exclaimed, breathing a sigh of relief.

'Sorry, babe. The car needed a new part and the mechanic had trouble getting it. I should have called, but me battery on me mobile went dead and I couldn't find a phone box that worked,' Eddie hated lying to her, but on odd occasions like these, he had little choice.

'Why are you wearing different clothes? You had your grey trousers on and your white shirt earlier.'

Eddie smiled at his wife's bemused expression. She was so naive and he fucking loved her for it. 'I had to help the mechanic fix the bastard motor. The boy that normally works with him phoned in sick. Covered in oil, I was. Raymondo popped down to keep me company, so I went back to his to get changed. You know how I hate being dirty.'

Jessica smiled. 'You'll never guess what. The kids are taking us out for a meal tonight and they're paying for it.'

Eddie laughed. 'Well, that's a first. Are they fucking ill? Or are they hiding a terrible secret?'

A couple of hours later, Eddie was sitting in a restaurant with his wife and kids. 'Ain't this nice? Me, you and the twins,' he said, squeezing his wife's hand.

Jessica smiled. 'It's lovely.'

The waiter approached the table. 'Are we all ready to order?' he asked.

Ever the gentleman, Eddie urged Jessica and the kids to order first.

'And you, sir?' the waiter asked.

Usually, Eddie liked his steak medium rare. Thinking of the state he had made of Trottsy's face earlier, he smiled. 'I'll have a T-bone. I want it cooked rare, and bring us over a bottle of your finest champagne, please.'

Jessica and the kids all turned their noses up as Eddie's steak arrived.

'That looks like a live animal, Dad,' Frankie complained.

'Your plate's smothered in blood,' Joey moaned.

'You don't normally have your steak like that, dear,' Jessica commented.

Eddie savoured the taste as the steak mixed with blood slipped down his throat. Now he knew just how that Rottweiler had felt earlier.

# TWENTY-SEVEN

On the morning of the twins' sixteenth birthday, Eddie was up at the crack of dawn.

'Where you going? You promised you weren't working today,' Jessica said sleepily.

'I'm not. I've gotta go out and pick up a surprise for the twins,' Eddie replied.

Jessica sat up with a bolt. 'But they wanted money and I've already got them a load of surprises to open.'

Eddie put on his tracksuit. 'I won't be long, probably about an hour or so. I'll have a shower and shave when I get back. What time are your parents coming?'

Jessica was bemused. 'They're not coming till tomorrow, about one. What have you got to pick up for the kids?'

Eddie laughed. 'That's for me to know and you to find out.'

Jessica was annoyed as he ran down the stairs and slammed the front door. She hated being kept in the dark and she hoped he wasn't bringing home something impractical. He had a devious glint in his eye and that was never a good sign with Eddie.

Jessica had a quick shower, then woke the twins up. 'Come on, birthday boy and girl. I haven't allowed you to have a day off school so you can lie in bed all day.'

'Oh, leave off, Mum, I'm tired,' Frankie moaned.

Joey jumped out of bed. Filled with excitement, he ran into his sister's room and leaped on top of her. 'Come on, Frankie, let's go and open our presents,' he pleaded.

'Drop dead, Joey,' Frankie mumbled.

Knowing how his sister hated being tickled, Joey did just that. 'Come on, sweet sixteen and never been kissed. Get your miserable arse out of bed, you boring cow.'

Fully awake by now, a defeated Frankie got up.

Tutting, Jessica went downstairs to cook the twins a nice birthday fry-up. The way they spoke to one another was beyond belief at times, but she knew they didn't really mean what they said. They had inherited their father's warped sense of humour, unfortunately.

Frankie plonked herself down at the kitchen table. 'Where's Dad?'

'Gone to pick up your birthday surprise and don't ask me what it is, because I haven't a clue,' Jessica told her.

'Can't we open our presents before breakfast?' Joey pleaded with his mum.

'No, Joey, wait till your dad gets back. He'll be upset if you open them and he's not here. Now, do you both want a sausage as well as some bacon?'

Frankie threw her brother a sardonic look. 'Let Joey have mine, Mum, he likes a nice juicy sausage.'

Joey aimed a sly kick Frankie's way. 'Bitch,' he whispered.

Eddie smiled as the two new additions to the family sat quivering on Raymond's lap.

'Fucking hell, Ed, slow down, will you? One's just pissed all over me.'

Eddie dropped his speed. Raymondo had a nice wet patch on the leg of his trousers.

'What time is Polly coming? Is she staying with you tonight or arriving tomorrow?' Eddie said, struggling to contain his laughter.

'I'm picking her up early tomorrow morning. She's working today,' Raymond replied, annoyed that his £100 trousers were covered in slash. He was dreading tomorrow. Eddie and Jessica had already met Polly, but his mother and father hadn't.

'Be warned, my mother's absolute brain damage. If she starts asking you loads of questions, don't feel you have to answer them. Me dad's OK, but him and me mother don't stop arguing,' he had warned Polly on the phone the previous night.

Eddie read Raymond's thoughts and smiled. 'I bet Joycie will have a field day. She's been dying to interrogate Polly ever since you first mentioned her.'

'I don't need reminding, Ed. Ouch! That little fucker just bit me,' Raymond exclaimed.

Chuckling, Eddie put his foot down and sped towards home.

'Dad's been gone ages. Can't we just open a few presents, Mum?' Joey begged.

'At least let us open one,' Frankie whinged.

Hearing her husband's tyres scrunch against the gravel outside, Jessica was relieved. The twins hadn't stopped moaning since the moment they had opened their eyes. 'He's here now. Go out and see what he's got for you,' she told them.

Jessica wiped the kitchen top down and, hearing whoops of delight, went outside to see what all the fuss was about. 'What the hell?' she said, as she spotted their presents bounding towards her.

Eddie smiled at her. He hadn't asked Jessica's

permission, as he knew she would say no. 'The kids have always wanted a dog. Ain't they gorgeous?' he said anxiously.

Jessica glared at her husband and her brother. She kept her house spotless and didn't want it any other way.

'Nothing to do with me,' Raymond declared.

She walked towards Eddie. 'You should have asked me first. What breed are they? They won't get big, will they?'

Eddie slung his arm around Jessica's shoulder. 'Ahh, look. The kids love 'em. It is their sixteenth, ain't it? They'll look after 'em, walk 'em and that.'

Jessica repeated her previous question.

'They're Rottweiler puppies. They don't grow that big,' Eddie lied.

Desperate to get the smell of the dog's piss off his new trousers, Raymond went into the house to clean himself up. Eddie could be an impulsive bastard at times and he could tell his sister wasn't amused.

'Look, Mum, isn't he cute?' Frankie said, lifting one of the dogs up.

'Can I have this one, Frankie? That one's mental like you, this one's the quiet one, like me,' Joey asked, his eyes shining. When he was little, he'd hated dogs, been petrified of them. These were adorable, though.

Jessica clocked the twins' elation. How could she say no? She could hardly tell them they couldn't keep the pups now that they'd seen them. Frankie and Joey would be heartbroken and she would feel like the Wicked Witch of the West.

Aware that Jessica was mellowing, Eddie told the kids to let their mother hold the puppies.

'Aren't they meant to be dangerous, Rottweilers? I mean, say I get pregnant. We can't have them around a newborn,' Jessica whispered to Eddie.

'They'll be fine. I'll train 'em up as guard dogs. Since me dad died, I worry about you and the kids being alone in the house. They'll be protection for you when I'm at work,' Eddie assured her.

'Yeah, but what about the baby?' Jessica whispered again.

'We'll worry about that when the time comes. I can build a kennel outside,' Eddie replied.

'Do you wanna hold them, Mum?' Joey asked.

Not wanting to be a spoilsport, Jessica had little choice. Peering down at the two little funny faces, she smiled as they both licked her hands. 'Aw, they are sweet. What are you going to call them?' she asked the twins.

'What about calling one Buster? That's a good name for a dog,' Eddie spouted.

'I like Bruno,' Frankie said immediately.

'I don't mind mine being called Buster, Dad. You did buy them for us,' Joey said gratefully.

Eddie ruffled his son's hair. 'That's sorted then. Let me have a shower and some breakfast and then we'll take a drive down to the pet shop. We'll buy them a bed and some toys. I've brought 'em some food already.'

Jessica smiled at the twins. 'Bring Buster and Bruno inside and you can open your other presents,' she said.

The rest of the day passed by in a happy bubble. The twins were thrilled with the acid-washed denims Jessica had brought them and excitedly pocketed the £200 each that was in their cards. Frankie and Joey had begged their dad for mobile phones and couldn't believe their luck when they received one each.

Jessica cooked spaghetti bolognese for dinner, the twins' favourite. By teatime, Buster and Bruno were flaked out in their doggy beds, looking pleased with their new surroundings.

At six o'clock, Frankie elbowed Joey. They were meant to be going out at eight and needed to get their arses in gear. 'Mum, Dad. Is it OK if we stay round our friend's tonight? We told you we're going to the pub in Rainham, didn't we? Well, Stacey said we can go back to hers and stay there after,' Frankie asked politely.

'No, you're lucky you're allowed to go to the pub. You can come home at twelve,' Jessica said sternly.

Frankie poked Joey. 'But, Mum, we are sixteen now. Dad has already charged our mobile phones and we'll carry them with us,' Joey said, doing his bit for once. He had arranged to meet Dominic later and, along with Frankie, they were going to a rave, then planned to stay in a nearby hotel.

'Say something, Eddie. They've only just got them dogs and already they want to leave us to look after them.'

Eddie shrugged. He would never let Frankie stay out all night alone, but Joey wasn't exactly a wild one, and he knew he would look after his sister. 'If you stay out, I want you back here by eight in the morning. I also want you to ring home when you're in safely from the pub. I know everyone around this area and if I find out either of you were drunk, you're grounded,' Eddie told them.

As the twins skipped happily upstairs to get ready, Jessica turned to her husband. 'We don't even know this Stacey's parents. The kids could be up to all sorts for all we know,' she said.

'Look, they're leaving school in a couple of months and then they'll be working, Jess. They can fucking leave home the age they are now, if they want. We can't wrap 'em in cotton wool – we've gotta give 'em some leeway. I mean, they ain't bad kids, are they? I know we caught 'em out playing hookey that time, but other than that, they've never given us major reasons not to trust 'em.'

As Buster and Bruno walked towards her, Jessica picked their little bodies up and sat them on her lap. 'I know you're right, Ed. I just worry about them, that's all.'

Eddie laid her head on his shoulder. 'Frankie and Joey will cause us no problems. They ain't the type – trust me!'

Joey and Frankie met Dominic in the Albion pub in Rainham.

'A couple of Frankie's friends will be here soon, so we must be discreet,' Joey warned his boyfriend.

Dominic nodded understandingly. He knew Joey didn't want anyone to know about their relationship. Joey hadn't told him an awful lot about his father, but the few bits he had told him were enough to make him wary, and Dom guessed this was the reason why Joey insisted that they keep things secret. The more people that knew, the better chance of his dad finding out.

'Happy birthday to you, Your arse smells of poo,' sang Frankie's friends.

Frankie giggled as she hugged Stacey, Demi and Paige. She didn't have that many girl mates, but these three were a bit tomboyish, like herself. Along with David and Wesley, the girls were the crowd that she and Joey had bunked off school with and they had all known one another for years.

'Where's David and Wesley?' Paige enquired.

'Wesley's meant to be coming, but David can't make it,' Frankie said, glancing at her brother. The relationship between Joey and David had never repaired itself since their couple of fumbles. David didn't even come out any more if Frankie and Joey were going to be there.

'Who's that? He's a sort. How old is he?' Demi whispered to Frankie.

Realising Demi was pointing at Dominic, Frankie laughed. 'His name is Dominic, he's twenty-six and I'm positive he ain't got a girlfriend.'

Stacey, Paige and Demi all had their tongues hanging out. 'Where do you know him from? Does he live round here?' Stacey asked.

'He lives in north London. He's a mate of Joey's. Now, shall we get drunk?' Frankie said, trying to change the subject.

With the vodka and pineapple going down nicely, the girls talked excitedly about the night ahead. This rave lark was new to all of them and they couldn't wait to try the experience.

'Do you think we're dressed right?' Demi asked.

Frankie shrugged. 'Dunno. Joey's mate, Dom, said he's been to one up his way. He said it's casual, everyone wears jeans and trainers and stuff.'

Joey smiled as Dominic bent over to pick some money up he'd dropped. He only had to look at the muscles in Dominic's buttocks to experience a feeling of butterflies. 'So, did you book the hotel?' he asked him.

Dominic nodded. 'There's nothing decent around here, so I got us into a little B&B. There's no bar, but I dropped me stuff off there and stocked the room up with drink. I booked two rooms, one for us and one for your sister and her mates. I asked for single beds, obviously. Don't worry, it won't look suspicious.'

Joey smiled. He had been on double vodkas and already felt merry. 'Fuck it – come to me family barbie tomorrow. I'll get Frankie to invite her mates as well. If there's a crowd of us there, no one will bat an eyelid.'

Dominic was unsure. Joey's father sounded a bit too heavy for his liking. 'I dunno, say someone says something, Joey?'

Checking none of the girls were watching, Joey squeezed Dominic's hand. 'There's only me, you, and Frankie that knows. No one's gonna say anything. Come on, please say yes.'

Unable to say no to the beautiful blond boy who had knocked him for six, Dominic nodded his head.

The Berwick Manor was set in the country lanes in the middle of nowhere. It didn't look like a nightclub, more like a massive country home.

'Weird-looking, ain't it?' Frankie said, as she climbed out of the taxi.

'Frankie, you've left your phone under the seat,' her brother shouted.

Frankie hated taking out a handbag – she felt like a right girlie – so had shoved her phone and fags into a carrier bag. The phone weighed a bloody ton and was a poxy nuisance to lug around, especially if she wanted to dance later on. She snatched at the carrier bag. 'Look after it for me Joey, please?' she pleaded.

Dominic laughed. He liked Joey's sister, she was a top girl. ''Ere, give it to me. I'll keep it safe for you,' he told her.

Frankie smiled. 'If he weren't queer, I'd have gone for him meself,' she whispered to Joey.

'Shut up,' Joey said, as he pushed her towards the entrance.

Inside the place was rocking and Frankie's eyes lit up. 'This is amazing,' she said as she stared at the funky, trendy people cluttering the dancefloor. The music was different, amazing, and there was a handsome-looking guy with dreadlocks spinning the tunes. Everyone looked so relaxed and happy and Frankie had never seen anything like it.

'Shall I get a drink? Everyone seems to be on water,' Joey said to Dominic.

Older and wiser, Dominic laughed. 'They take Es at these places; water's all they drink.'

Joey stood with a confused expression plastered across his face. 'What's an E?'

'Ecstasy tablets. New things out, they are. They've all been taking them in the City, where I work.'

With ears like a bat, Frankie turned to Dominic. 'What do Es do? Have you tried one? Are they any good?'

Dominic smiled. 'No idea, I've never taken one, but judging by the looks on the faces on the dancefloor, they're all right. The guys I work with reckon they're wicked. Apparently, you get this euphoric feeling when you take them and you just love everybody.'

Wandering back to her friends, Frankie ordered another round. 'Four vodkas with pineapple and two vodkas with orange,' she shouted to the barman.

'Oi, stop pushing in. I was before you,' a voice said.

About to let rip at the lad standing next to her, Frankie looked at him and, for the first time in her life, was totally lost for words. He was as fit as a fiddle, had dark, floppy hair and the brightest green eyes she had ever seen.

'What's up? Cat got your tongue?' he asked her, laughing.

'Go on, you go first,' Frankie mumbled. She couldn't look him in the eye – he was drop-dead gorgeous and making her insides go all funny.

'I'll have two lagers mate, four bottles of water and whatever this lady wants,' the lad said.

Struggling to find her voice, Frankie turned to him. 'I'm fine. I have my own money and I've got to get a round,' she mumbled.

The lad laughed as he waved a big wad at her. 'Can't a man buy a lady a drink? I'll get the round,' he insisted.

With her eyes desperately searching for her brother and their mates, Frankie was annoyed that she couldn't see them. 'Whatever, just hurry up, I've lost the people I'm with,' she told him.

The lad chuckled. 'Ungrateful little filly you are, ain't ya?'

As his face broke into a cheeky smile, Frankie smiled back. He had the most perfect teeth and appealing face she had ever seen.

'I definitely recognise you from somewhere. Do you come down here all the time?' he asked her.

Frankie shook her head. 'Nah, first time I've been here. I like it though, it's proper.'

The lad laughed. 'Hark at you – proper! I bet you're a right little handful, ain't ya?'

Frankie swallowed her drink and then necked her brother's double. Suddenly full of Dutch courage, she gave it back to the lad. 'Who do you think you are, you cheeky bastard? Actually, you do look familiar, like something out of a horror movie,' she said giggling.

'You all right?' Joey said reappearing.

Frankie handed him the drinks. 'Sorry, I forgot to get your one. Where are Dominic and the girls?'

'We're over by the dancefloor. I've still got a drink, so don't worry about mine. Are you sure you're OK?' Joey asked, looking at the boy standing next to her.

Frankie nodded. 'I'm fine. I'll be over in a minute.'

The lad smiled as Joey walked away.

'That ain't your boyfriend, so who is it? Your brother?'

Frankie nodded. 'How did you know he weren't my boyfriend?'

The boy smirked. 'Too normal. You go for tough boys, a bit like meself!'

291

Frankie grinned at his cheekiness. 'You're so full of yourself. Has anyone ever told you that?'

The lad chuckled. 'Every day, sugar pie. I swear I know you from somewhere. What's your name?'

'Me name's Frankie. What's yours?'

The lad shook her hand. 'Extremely pleased to meet you, Frankie. I'm Jed. Jed O'Hara.'

# TWENTY-EIGHT

As the recognition hit her, Frankie nearly dropped her glass in shock. 'I think we have met before, at a party when we were young,' she mumbled.

'What party? Where?' Jed asked her.

'I'm Frankie Mitchell. Eddie Mitchell's daughter. I can't remember where the party was, but I think your dad and my dad made you and my brother fight with one another in a boxing ring. I can't remember exactly what happened, but I think you beat my brother, 'cause my mum was hysterical.'

Jed laughed. 'I know your face, but I don't remember the fight. My father made me spar with so many kids over the years, I sort of lost count.'

With her heart pounding, Frankie gratefully accepted Jed's offer of another drink. 'Let me take these drinks back to me mates – they'll think I've gone missing,' she said.

'You go and tell your brother that you're OK, and we'll meet back here in five minutes. I'll buy you another drink then. The music's proper loud, ain't it? We can go outside and talk,' Jed said, grinning at her.

'Who's that boy? How do you know him?' Joey asked, as Frankie appeared by his side.

'We've met before,' Frankie replied casually.

This was neither the time nor the place to mention the name Jed O'Hara. Joey was a drama queen at the best of times. 'Where are the girls?' Frankie asked Joey.

Joey pointed towards the dancefloor. 'Dom's such a show-off, he's teaching them some new moves. I'm gonna join 'em – you coming?'

Frankie shook her head. 'I'm gonna stand at the bar and have a drink with that boy I know.'

Joey smirked. 'You like him, don't you? It's written all over your face.'

'No, I don't. I'm just chatting, that's all,' Frankie said agitated.

Joey was full of suspicion as he watched his sister walk away. They knew all the same people and he wondered where Frankie knew the lad from.

'Are you OK?' Dominic asked, as Joey joined him on the dancefloor.

'Yeah, sort of. Do us a favour, Dom, you're taller than me. Keep an eye on Frankie, she's standing up the bar with some bloke with dark hair. I don't like the look of him. I don't know why, but keep watch for me.'

'Frankie will be fine. You're just being overprotective, as any decent brother should,' Dominic whispered in his ear.

Frankie felt like an idiot as she stood up at the bar alone.

'Wanna dance?' some spotty-faced jerk in dungarees asked her.

'Fuck off,' she replied angrily.

'Worried I'd forgotten about ya, was ya?' said a voice beside her.

Jed's confidence was appealing and Frankie couldn't help but giggle. 'I was hoping you had. I prefer him over there,' she said, pointing at Mr Dungarees.

Jed laughed. 'Let's go outside, we can have a proper chat. I can't hear meself think in here.'

As she followed Jed outside, Frankie was nervous, but also excited. The Berwick Manor was remote and, apart from a few revellers and a mass of parked cars, the outside was a kind of ghost town.

'Follow me,' Jed said, leading her away from the car park.

After a five-minute walk, Jed grabbed her hand and sat down by a tree. Not backwards in coming forwards, he pinned Frankie down on the sweet-smelling grass and plunged his tongue down the back of her throat.

Frankie succumbed to his kiss and then, as realisation kicked in, pushed him away. 'I thought you wanted to talk,' she said defensively.

Jed smiled. Her face was even prettier when she was angry. His mum was always trying to fix him up with fellow travelling girls, but he preferred gorgers. He'd slept with loads, but none of them had captured his heart. They were too common and tarty for him. Not like Frankie – she was feisty and beautiful.

Jed held her hand. 'Sorry about that. I didn't mean to be forward, but I had to kiss you. I remember you now. You were the little rawnie who stole my heart at Pat Murphy's party. Memory like an elephant, me. I think you came to me dad's house once and I sat in a car with ya.'

Frankie didn't remember going to his house. 'How comes we ain't bumped into one another over the years, then? Your dad lives near me, don't he?' she asked.

'I moved away. Me old mum caught me father at it, so we went to live in Basildon. Didn't like it there much, although there was a good nightclub down the A127. Elliot's it was called, but I think it's shut down now. Shame, I could have taken you there for our first date.'

Frankie smiled. This boy was gorgeous. 'What you trying to say? Do you want me to go out with you?' she asked shyly.

Trying his luck again, Jed chuckled as he held her down. As he lay on top of her, he knew she was aware of his erect penis rubbing against her. 'I'll take you anywhere you want. I'll treat you like a proper princess. Come out with me tomorrow.'

Frankie had never felt so sexual in her life. Richard Jones at school had tried to rub himself against her once. She had frozen and then punched him in the cock. Richard had screamed in agony and had never spoken to her again. With Jed it was different. His eyes, his cheeky smile, his erection – she was hooked by it all.

'I can't come out tomorrow. It's mine and Joey's sixteenth birthday today and me parents have organised this boring family barbecue for us.'

Feeling himself getting a little bit too excited, Jed rolled off her. 'What about Sunday? Meet me Sunday.'

Frankie nodded. 'OK. Where and when?'

Jed laughed. She wanted him and he knew it. 'I've gotta mobile phone. I'll give you me number and you can ring me tomorrow. Anyway, tonight's not over yet.'

As he kissed her again, Frankie felt an unusual sensation wash over her. She had always known she wasn't gay, like her brother, but most of the boys she had met had done nothing for her.

'Just stroke it for me,' Jed panted, placing her hand on his big, hard cock.

Frankie felt the fullness of it through his jeans. She had

296

never really touched one before and it was massive, like a snake.

'Do you wanna see it?' Jed asked her.

'Frankie, are you out here? Frankie, where are you?'

'Shit – it's me brother,' Frankie said. She pushed Jed away, stood up and pulled herself together.

'I'm over here, Joey. Just having a chat. I'm coming back in now.'

Joey glared at Frankie as she reappeared looking dishevelled. 'What have you been doing?' he whispered accusingly.

'Nothing. Don't fucking start on me. You bat the other way, remember?' she spat back at him.

Annoyed, Joey grabbed Dominic's arm. 'Come on, leave her to it. We're going back inside,' he said.

Jed held Frankie's hand as they walked towards the entrance of the club. 'Dordie! Is he the other way, your brother?'

Frankie shook her head. 'Not as far as I know. He's had loads of girls,' she lied.

Chuckling, Jed tilted her chin and kissed her with a passion. 'I'll think you'll find he is, Frankie. I reckon that geezer with him is his boyfriend.'

Frankie shrugged. She wasn't about to start discussing her brother's private life with anyone.

As soon as they re-entered the Berwick, Jed went to get some more drinks and Frankie searched for Joey. 'What you got the hump about? Where have the girls gone?' she asked as she caught sight of him.

Joey spoke abruptly to her. 'The girls have all gone to a party in Dagenham. They met some lads they knew. What was you doing with that boy? You were doing something, Frankie.'

'Having a fucking kiss and cuddle, is that all right? Don't go all psycho on me, Joey. I'm sure if I can accept the way you are and what you get up to, then you can accept that I'm only human, too.'

Feeling a bit silly, Joey hugged her. 'I'm sorry, Frankie. You've never really had much track with boys and I was just worried about you. Who is he, anyway? He don't come from round here, does he? He's got a funny accent.'

Too frightened to spill the beans, Frankie lied. 'His name's John and I know him through an old friend of mine. I'm not sure where he comes from, but I think he's from up north or somewhere.'

'Me and Dom have had enough of it here now. We might go back to the B&B. Are you coming? You can bring John if you like. Dom's got some drink,' Joey said, hoping she had forgiven him.

Frankie smiled. 'Give us five minutes and I'll ask him if he wants to come.'

Jed laughed as Frankie repeated the story. 'So I've gotta pretend I'm called fucking John, now, have I?'

'Please. I've been thinking about that party years ago, and you knocked Joey out, if I remember rightly. I don't want him to remember who you are.'

Desperate to get the beautiful Frankie alone in a bedroom, Jed promised he would keep his trap shut. 'I'll just say goodbye to me mates, give us a minute,' he told Frankie.

'Where are your mates? Shall I come with you?' Frankie asked him.

'My mates are vultures. They'll take one look at you and they'll all want you for themselves. Stay here and wait for me,' Jed told her.

'Are you ready?' Joey said, spotting his sister standing alone.

Frankie looked around. Jed had been gone ages now and she was worried he'd had a change of heart. As she saw him bowling towards her, relief flooded through her body. 'Here he is,' she told her brother.

Outside the Berwick, Dominic jumped in a taxi.

'I've got me pick-up truck here. Come with me,' Jed told Frankie.

Unable to say no, Frankie told Dominic and Joey to go on ahead and climbed into the Toyota Hilux.

As Jed expertly swung out of the car park and followed the taxi, she smiled at him. 'How old are you? When did you pass your test?' she asked him, impressed.

Jed laughed. 'I'm younger than you, you dinlo. Us travelling boys don't need driving licences. We're taught from an early age how to drive. I've been tugged before – got away with it, I did. I told the gavvers I was me brother. Me cousin gets hold of bent insurance certificates. Filled it out meself, I did. The gavvers are mugs, they know nothing.'

'What's gavvers mean?' Frankie asked, bemused by his slang.

'The police, you dinlo,' Jed said laughing.

The B&B was a shit-hole bang opposite the A13. It wasn't built to be paradise, but to serve a purpose for workmen and party-goers.

'We'll go in me brother's room. His mate, Dom, has got a load of drink in there,' Frankie informed Jed.

'You go and grab the drink off them. I wanna spend some time alone with you, Frankie. We can't chat properly in front of your brother.'

Dominic handed Frankie a bottle of vodka and two cartons of orange juice.

'Are you sure you're gonna be OK, Frankie? Please

don't do anything you'll regret in the morning,' Joey begged her.

Headstrong, Frankie waved away her brother's fears. 'Yous two have a good time. Don't make the walls shake,' she giggled as she shut their door.

Taking a deep breath, she entered the other room.

'Come here, sexy,' Jed said, smiling at her.

As Frankie got under the flimsy quilt, she realised that Jed had taken his jeans and pants off. 'Stop it,' she squealed as he put her hand on his penis. She had never felt a naked one before and it reminded her of the raw jumbo sausage that her dad cooked at barbecues.

Laughing, Jed poured out two large vodkas and handed her one. 'You ever tried an E?' he asked her.

Frankie shook her head. 'I've heard about them, though,' she replied casually.

She had to sound knowledgeable; she didn't want Jed to think she was some stupid schoolgirl.

Jed lent out of the bed and pulled a small plastic bag out of his jeans. 'I've gotta couple here. Shall we do one?' he asked her.

'I dunno. I've got to be home early,' Frankie said awkwardly.

Jed put one on his tongue and washed it down with vodka. 'Come on. It's your birthday – enjoy yourself,' he urged her.

Desperate not to look boring, Frankie took the white tablet from him and swallowed it.

'There's my girl. American burger, that is. They're the bollocks, they are. Make you feel horny, they do.'

Frankie poured herself another vodka and orange. The tablet looked just like a paracetamol, and she was sure it wouldn't do much to her.

Jed had a portable radio in the front of his truck and

had brought it up to the room with him. 'I need a slash, find a station,' he asked Frankie, as he put his jeans back on.

Frankie got off the bed and felt herself go all weird. She felt happy, but very sick at the same time. As Jed came out the toilet, she raced towards it. 'I feel funny, I think I'm gonna be sick,' she mumbled.

Jed chuckled. 'Bring it up. Looks like seaweed, it does. Once you've spewed, you'll feel fine.'

Frankie's heart was pounding as she looked at the weird-coloured stuff that had come from her stomach. 'Wow,' she said out loud. Jed wasn't wrong, she now felt amazing.

Bounding out of the bathroom, Frankie grabbed his hand. 'Turn the music up, let's dance,' she screamed.

Frankie and Jed's high lasted all night.

At 6 a.m. Jed urged Frankie to lie on the bed with him. 'I want you to be my woman, Frankie,' he told her earnestly.

As his tongue connected with hers, Frankie let out a moan.

'Let me fuck you,' Jed whispered in her ear.

Frankie shook her head. She might be high, but she still knew what was right and wrong. 'I do like you, Jed, but not tonight, not yet. I've only just met you.'

Jed couldn't help himself. He usually got his own way with every bird he went for. He held his penis in his hand and tried to guide it inside Frankie.

'No! I said no,' Frankie said angrily.

'Just let me put it in. If you don't like it, I'll pull it straight back out again,' Jed pleaded with her.

As he tried to enter her, Frankie pushed him away. She wasn't ready for this; it wasn't right.

301

'Please, let me do it,' Jed begged her.

'No. I said no and I mean fucking no,' Frankie told him.

'Just wank me off then, please,' Jed said, grabbing Frankie's hand.

Fuming, Frankie squeezed his balls as hard as she could.

Jed let out an almighty yelp. 'Why did ya do that?' he shouted.

'I've had enough now, Jed. I'm going home,' Frankie said, as she jumped out of the bed

'I'm sorry. I couldn't help meself. You make me so horny. Let me drive you home,' Jed begged her. He liked this girl: she was so different from the others who always spread their legs so easily.

Frankie shook her head. 'You stay here. I have to go home with Joey. My parents will go mad if we come home separately.'

Searching for the pen he always carried on him, Jed grabbed Frankie's hand and wrote his number on her arm. 'Please ring me, Frankie. I'm sorry if I was a bit forward, but it was only because I like you so much. Come out with me on Sunday? I'll treat you like a princess, I promise.'

Frankie's emotions were out of control. Meeting Jed had blown her mind, and her sensible side told her he was very wrong for her indeed. 'I don't know, Jed. My dad and your dad don't get on. It ain't gonna work,' she told him bluntly.

Jed walked towards her and hugged her in a way she had never been hugged before. 'Trust me, we'll make it work. Fuck our dads, who cares what they think? I like you, you like me and nothing else matters. Let's try and make a go of it, eh? What do you say?'

As Jed grinned, Frankie's heart pounded. He wasn't just trying it on – he actually was into her. With the E frazzling her brain, Frankie didn't know if she was coming or going. How could she be with Jed? He had just tried to shag her without her consent. Desperate to get away from him, she picked up her jacket.

'Goodbye, Jed. It was nice meeting ya. Take care of yourself.'

# TWENTY-NINE

Jessica breathed a sigh of relief as she heard the front door close and the twins creep up the stairs. Joey had rung home last night, as promised, but it still hadn't lessened her worry. She could never relax when the kids stayed out, and she'd lie awake imagining all sorts. Hearing a strange whining noise, she nudged her husband.

'Ed, wake up. One of the dogs sounds like it's crying. Go and make sure it's OK.'

'All dogs whine. It'll be fine, Jess,' Eddie said grumpily. He had been in a deep sleep and wasn't happy being woken.

'Ah, listen to the poor little mite. Go and see to 'em, Ed. They might want to go out to do toilets. You brought them home. Go on, up you get.'

Mumbling obscenities to himself, Eddie threw on his trackie bottoms and stomped downstairs.

The twins lay top-to-toe in Joey's bed. Neither of them were sleepy and they were whispering excitedly about the previous evening. As Frankie gabbled on, Joey sat up and stared at her. 'You've taken something, ain't you? Your pupils look massive and you're talking all weird.'

'No, I ain't,' Frankie said defensively. She could still

304

feel the effects of the ecstasy tablet, and still felt quite high.

'You're lying. Did that fucking John give you drugs?' Joey asked, his temper rising.

'Sssh, Mum and Dad will hear. Do you wanna cause a riot? If you must know, I had half of one of them Es in the Berwick. Jed never gave it to me, somebody else did.'

Joey couldn't believe how stupid she had been. If their parents found out, the pair of them would be grounded for life. 'Don't ever do that again, Frankie. You don't know what's in the bloody things. And who's Jed? I thought the bloke you was with was called John.'

Frankie took a deep breath. She couldn't tell anyone who Jed was – not yet, anyway. 'I said John. You must be hearing things,' she told Joey.

'Are you gonna see him again?' Joey asked.

'I don't know. I need to get some sleep now, I'm going back to me own room,' Frankie replied haughtily.

Joey grabbed her arm. 'You haven't told me what happened yet. Did you do anything with him? You didn't have sex with him, did you?'

'No, of course I didn't,' Frankie replied, pulling her arm away. Joey questioning her was making her feel paranoid and she needed to be left alone. 'I'll tell you all the gory details later,' she whispered, as she shut his bedroom door.

Frankie walked into her own room and quietly closed the door. She sat down at her dressing table and studied herself in the mirror. She looked out of it; her eyes were the give-away. 'Shit,' she mumbled, as she remembered the barbecue that was planned for later.

She cursed herself for having taken the bloody tablet in the first place. How was she meant to sit and be normal

305

in front of her parents and grandparents when she felt totally out of her nut? She crawled into bed and shut her eyes. Jed's face was at the forefront of her mind. He had been too forward for her liking, but no boy had ever made her feel the way he had.

Frankie had taken Jed's number, but she hadn't given him hers. She shut her eyes and pictured Jed's face. He had eyes that twinkled when he smiled. She loved his lopsided grin, his dark, wavy hair. Even his funny accent set her pulse racing.

Thinking of his rock-hard penis, Frankie shuddered with excitement. Jed might be bad news, but she had to see him again. It was the only way to get him out of her system.

Joyce and Stanley arrived promptly at one on the dot. 'Are Raymond and Polly here yet?' were the first words out of Joyce's mouth.

'No, they're coming later,' Jessica said, ushering her parents into the lounge.

'Where are the twins?' Stanley asked.

'In bloody bed. Went out with their friends last night, they did, and they're still in the land of nod,' Jessica replied in annoyance.

'What the hell is that?' Joyce screamed as two bundles of fluff jumped onto her lap.

Eddie smiled at his mother-in-law's horrified expression. 'Meet Buster and Bruno, Joycie, the new additions to the Mitchell household.'

Begrudgingly stroking their heads, Joyce was appalled as Buster got a little overexcited and urinated on her dress. 'Oh, look at me new frock! Get 'em off of me. Quick, take 'em away!' she screamed.

Stanley and Eddie looked at one another and burst out laughing.

'Don't worry, Mum, I'll get a cloth. It'll come out – it's only a little splash,' Jessica said, glaring at the men.

Eddie followed Jessica into the kitchen. 'I've got a bit of a confession to make, babe. I rang me Uncle Reg yesterday and invited him over for the barbie. I felt a bit guilty 'cause I ain't seen much of him recently. I didn't think he'd accept, but he rang me back and said Paulie and Ronny are coming too.'

Jessica was not impressed. 'Oh, Ed, it's meant to be the kids' birthday party. They barely know your family.'

Eddie hugged his wife and kissed her on the forehead. 'I'm sorry, it just escalated and I could hardly say no. Come on, cheer up. I picked another few trays of meat up, so we've got plenty of grub. It's only one day, Jess, we can get through it, me and you.'

Jessica sighed. Eddie's family turning up was the last thing she needed, but she could hardly tell him to uninvite them at this late stage. For years, Eddie had welcomed her family with open arms, so it wouldn't exactly hurt her to entertain his for once. She smiled at him. 'Don't worry, Ed. We'll all have a great day. Can you pour Mum and Dad some drinks while I go and wake our lazy children?'

Joey got showered and dressed, then sat on Frankie's bed while she got ready.

'Do my eyes look OK now?' she asked him. She had managed to doze off for a few hours and felt a damn sight better than she had earlier.

'You don't look as bad as before. In fact, you look much better,' Joey told her honestly.

'What time did you tell Dom to arrive?' Frankie asked him.

Joey felt himself shudder. Inviting Dominic had seemed a good idea last night when he was inebriated, but in the

307

cold light of day, he was now shitting himself. 'Wesley's picking him up in a cab from the B&B. I wish I hadn't invited him now. You don't think Mum or Dad or our mates will clock on, do you, sis?'

Frankie shook her head. 'Dominic looks as straight as a die and if he's coming with Wesley, no one will bat an eyelid.'

Joey breathed a sigh of relief. 'Who did you invite? I asked a couple of other boys in the Berwick. I hope they don't turn up – I barely know them.'

Frankie laughed. 'I invited Stacey, Demi and Paige. I can't remember who else, I was a bit pissed. We better warn all of them not to mention the Berwick Manor. Mum and Dad think we went to Stacey's after the pub, remember?'

'You tell the girls to keep schtum and I'll tell the lads. Did you invite that John?' Joey asked.

Shaking her head, Frankie applied some lipgloss. 'Nah. I'm not even sure if I'm gonna see him again.'

'Frankie, Joey, everyone's waiting for you down here.' Jessica yelled. She was getting more annoyed by their no-show by the minute.

'Come on,' Joey said, dragging his sister away from the mirror.

Considering it had poured with rain the day before, the weather was glorious. There wasn't a cloud in the sky and the sun was scorching.

Eddie sat out in the grounds with his uncle, brothers and Dougie.

'Where's Raymondo?' Paulie asked.

'He'll be here soon, so will Gary and Ricky,' Eddie replied.

Desperate to meet her son's posh girlfriend, Joyce was up and down like a yo-yo.

'Will you sit down and come away from that bloody window, woman,' Stanley scolded her.

Joyce gave him one of her looks. 'No, I won't. Now shut your face, you miserable old goat, and drink your bleedin' beer.'

Gary and Ricky arrived and handed Jessica a big bunch of flowers. 'We brought the twins something, but these are for you,' Ricky told her.

'You shouldn't have. Your dad's in the garden. Thanks, boys,' she said, kissing them both on the cheek.

Joey hovered nervously in the hallway.

'What's the matter, love?' Jessica asked him.

'Nothing. Just waiting for my friends to arrive,' he replied anxiously.

'You're acting like a right twerp. Have a couple of drinks, for fuck's sake, else you'll give yourself away,' Frankie whispered to him.

'All right if me and Joey have another drink, Mum?' Frankie said, already topping up their glasses.

'I suppose so. It is your birthday party, but don't go too mad. How was your night out? You haven't said much about it,' Jessica asked.

As she screwed the lid back onto the vodka bottle, Frankie smiled. 'It was a bit boring, to be honest, Mum.'

The ringing of the doorbell stopped Jessica from prying any more. 'Get that, Joey!' she yelled.

Joey's heart leaped as he answered it. 'Come in, Dom. All right, Wes? Say hello to me mum, boys,' he said, as calmly as he could.

Jessica kissed Wesley, then turned her attention to Dominic. 'Nice to meet you, at last. I know my Joey spends hours talking to you on the phone, but we haven't met before, have we?'

'No, Mrs Mitchell,' Dominic answered politely.

Jessica was shocked by Dominic's appearance. He was obviously into bodybuilding or something and looked years older than Joey or Wesley.

Dominic had been in this situation in the past with other boyfriends' parents. He knew exactly how to play it. 'Your Joey likes coming out with me, Mrs Mitchell. We pull so many girls, we're babe magnets, aren't we Joey?' he joked.

Joey nodded dumbly.

Frankie's pals arrived shortly after Joey's. 'Where did yous sneak off to last night? Joey said you went to a party in Dagenham,' Frankie asked them.

'Our night was probably boring compared to yours. The party was crap. Who was that boy you were with?' Stacey pried.

'He was gorgeous,' Demi added.

'I've never seen you behave like that before, Frankie. You looked well loved-up with him, you did,' Paige giggled.

'Oh, I've known him for years. It's a long story, I'll tell you later. Don't mention him in front of my parents and don't mention the Berwick Manor. If any one asks, we went to the pub, then back to yours, Stacey.'

Joyce heard a car engine and almost flew towards the window. 'Here they are. She's pretty, Stanley. Looks posh, she does. A bit thin. I'll have to get Raymond to bring her around ours. I can soon fatten her up – looks like she needs a good dinner, she does.'

Stanley scowled at his wife. She had just moved quicker than his bloody pigeons could. 'For Christ's sake, Joycie, don't start with your comments and embarrass our Raymond, will you?'

Joyce looked at Stanley as though he were something

310

on the bottom of her shoe. 'Since when have I ever embarrassed anyone?' she asked innocently.

As her son and Polly walked towards her, Joyce smiled at the girl and, unable to stop herself, did a little curtsy.

'Whatever are you doing, Mother?' Raymond asked her.

Joyce ignored him. 'Pleased to meet you, Polly. My Raymond's told me so much about you. This is my husband, Stanley. Stanley, stand up and shake Polly's hand.'

Jessica stood in the doorway with Vicki. Unable to stifle their laughter, they fled back to the kitchen. Raymond followed them.

'Mother's off her fucking head. Pour Polly a glass of red wine, sis. I'll have a beer. This is gonna be a nightmare, I just know it.'

'Get us another lager, Ed. You got any stronger than five per cent?' Ronny asked his brother.

Eddie had put a load of cold beers in a black dustbin in the garden and filled it with blocks of ice. 'I dunno what's in there. I'll have a look for you,' he said.

Ronny raced towards the bin in his wheelchair. 'I'll have the Stella. Five point two, that is,' he said snatching two cans.

Eddie sat back down. He and Paulie had just been discussing their father's murder.

'So, where do we go from here? I've chased up Dad's old contacts in the filth and they still reckon they ain't got nothing. They said they never found as much as a fingerprint,' Paulie said.

Eddie felt the usual fire in his belly as he discussed his father's death. He had spoken to every underworld contact he knew ten times over, and no one had heard anything. The Old Bill still reckoned it was something to do with the kids that had been hanging around the area, being a nuisance, but Eddie wasn't so sure. How could a bunch of kids bludgeon to death a gangland legend and not leave a fucking clue?

Eddie swallowed his beer in one go. 'I'll pop round to see all Dad's neighbours again this week. I'll knock on every door for miles if I have to. Some cunt must know, or at least have heard something.'

Paulie nodded. 'It just don't seem fucking feasible, none of it, does it?'

Eddie stood up. He needed a refill. The conversation was making him thirsty. Face etched with anger, he faced his brother. 'Don't worry, Paulie. I'll find out who did it and, when I get me hands on the cunt, I will torture him for weeks. I'll starve him, burn him, cut him, then pull all his teeth and fingernails out, one by one. By the time I've finished, whoever did it will wish they'd never been born!'

Jessica was sweating in the dress she had on. She went upstairs to get changed into a vest top and shorts. She would have liked to have put on her bikini and jumped into the swimming pool, but didn't feel comfortable in front of Eddie's family. She had noticed Ronny leering at her in the past, and was sure he was a pervert.

Vicki giggled as Jessica sat down next to her. She had mixed them up some cocktails and they had been having a right old laugh at the expense of Eddie's family. 'Shut your legs, Jess. Quick, the pervert's looking over,' Vicki said laughing.

Jessica glanced at Ronny out of the corner of her eye. She had dark sunglasses on, so he couldn't see her looking at him. 'I never liked him when I first got with Eddie. He was really jealous of our relationship,' she told Vicki.

'Is his wife here?' Vicki asked.

'No, of course not. Sharon's not his wife, she's his girlfriend, the poor cow. Neither Paulie nor Reg have brought their other halves, either. I reckon they keep all their women shut in cupboards indoors. The only time I've ever seen 'em out is at weddings or funerals.'

Vicki smiled. 'I wouldn't put up with that, would you? I mean, I know Dougie usually leaves me and stands with the men, but that doesn't bother me. I wouldn't be left indoors all the time, though, would you?'

Jessica shook her head. 'That's one thing I must say about my Eddie. He can be a sod at times, but he's always put me and the kids first. He's a real family man, he is.'

Glancing back at Ronny, Vicki started to giggle again. 'Do you reckon his todger works if he's paralysed?'

Jessica burst out laughing. 'Shut up, Vicki, for Christ's sake. You've just put me off me piña colada.'

Joyce couldn't help herself. Every time Polly and Raymond walked away, she reappeared by their side like a shadow. 'So, how long has your father been in the jewellery business, Polly? Raymond says he has lots of shops. How many exactly has he got?'

Sighing at Polly, Raymond linked arms with his mother and gently led her away. 'Mum, you're going a bit over the top now. Polly's come here to socialise, not be interrogated. Sit down and have a drink with Dad. You can meet Polly another time. Perhaps I'll bring her round yours one day or something.'

'That'll be nice, dear,' Joyce said, smiling.

Spotting what her husband had done, Joyce's smile disappeared. 'What the bloody hell have you got on your bonce? Take it off, Stanley.'

'It's only me handkerchief. The sun's burning me scalp. It's all right for you, you've got hair,' Stanley moaned.

Joyce snatched the handkerchief off his head. 'What

313

will Polly think? You look like something out of *It Ain't Half Hot Mum*, you silly old bastard!'

Stacey, Demi and Paige sat with their mouths wide open as Frankie told them all about her liaison with Jed.

'So, was his willy big?' Demi asked.

'I suppose so. I dunno – I've never seen a real one before,' Frankie replied giggling.

Seeing her brother, Dominic and Wesley heading their way, she told the girls to say no more.

'I really like that Dominic. Can't you put a word in for me?' Stacey begged her.

If only she knew, Frankie thought as she nodded her head. 'I'm going to the toilet and then I'll get me dad to put some music on,' she told the girls.

Eddie was busy on barbecue duty. 'All right, sweetheart? Tell yours and Joey's mates that the food's ready now,' he told Frankie.

Frankie gave him a hug. 'What's that for?' he asked.

'Dunno. 'Cause I love you, I suppose,' Frankie replied guiltily.

'Who's that geezer standing over there with you? The tall one with the dark hair. Looks older than your crowd,' Eddie asked. He didn't trust strangers, especially in his house.

'Oh that's Wesley's mate, Dominic. Me and Joey know him well, he's a really nice person, Dad.'

Satisfied with Frankie's explanation, Eddie winked at his daughter and held up a burnt-looking steak on a large fork. 'Grub's up, everybody,' he bellowed.

Frankie went upstairs, sat on her bed and searched through her purse. When she'd come in this morning, she'd written Jed's number on a piece of paper, then washed it off her arm. She was tempted to ring him and arrange a date for the following day. Staring at his number, she switched on her mobile. Should she? Shouldn't she?

'Hello, yous two,' she said, as Buster and Bruno came tottering towards her.

Shoving the piece of paper into her bedside drawer, she switched off her phone and went back to the party.

Jessica had prepared three massive bowls of salad. She had also made coleslaw and warmed up lots of garlic bread. 'Help yourselves – there's plenty more in the kitchen,' she urged everybody.

As Jessica sat down to eat hers, she studied her son from behind her glasses. She was intrigued by what she saw. The way he and Dominic were looking at one another wasn't normal. They looked at each other the way she looked at Eddie.

As the two lads walked towards the barbecue, Jessica noticed Joey slyly pinch Dominic's bum.

'Oh my God,' she said out loud.

'Whatever's wrong? Are you OK, Jess?' Vicki asked concerned.

Jessica chucked her plate on the grass and jumped out of her seat. 'No, I'm not. In fact, I think I'm gonna be sick.'

# THIRTY

Eddie waved goodbye to the last of the guests and shut the front door.

'Are you OK? You've been ever so quiet and you look really pale,' he asked Jessica.

'I've got a terrible migraine. Are Gary and Ricky still here?' Jessica replied.

Eddie nodded and gave his wife a big cuddle. 'I thought it was a great party. Even Ronny behaved himself and that's a first.'

Jessica nodded. 'I was enjoying it earlier, before I came over bad.'

'The twins got some nice presents, didn't they? Did you see their faces when your mother brought the cake out and made everybody sing "Happy Birthday". They were well embarrassed and their friends were taking the right piss out of 'em.'

Jessica kissed Eddie on the lips. 'I'm going to bed now. You sit up and have a nightcap with Gary and Ricky. I'll tidy up in the morning, when I feel a bit better.'

'Sweet dreams,' Eddie whispered lovingly.

Jessica barely slept at all that night. Her mind was in turmoil as she tried to convince herself that Joey was straight and she was wrong. She pictured herself at Joey's age. She had been knocking about with her old friend, Mary, then. Had they ever pinched one another's bottoms for a laugh, or looked at one another romantically. No, they hadn't.

As much as she hated to admit it, Jessica wondered if, deep down, she had always known that Joey was different. He had brought girls to the house over the years and had even introduced them as his girlfriends, but Jessica had never been fooled.

Seeing him with Dominic earlier – the closeness between them, the affectionate glances – was proof of something she had desperately tried to avoid. Joey was still her son. She would love him whatever he was, but Eddie certainly wouldn't. One sniff of her son's sexuality coming out into the open and there would be murders, literally.

Two doors away, Frankie was also unable to sleep properly. Every time she shut her eyes, Jed O'Hara's face disrupted her thoughts.

At 8 a.m., she got out of bed and took the piece of paper out of the drawer. She switched on her mobile phone. It was so early, he probably wasn't even awake yet. Punching in his number, she held her breath. Her heart was beating like a drum and, as he answered, she could barely speak through nervousness.

'All right? It's Frankie,' she mumbled.

Jed laughed. 'You took your time ringing me, didn't ya?'

'You're awake, then?' Frankie said stupidly.

'Of course I'm awake, you dinlo. I'm talking to you, ain't I?'

Sensing her apprehension, Jed smiled. He often had this effect on women and he was used to it. 'What you up to? Meet me in half-hour,' he told her.

Frankie nearly dropped the phone in shock. 'It's only

317

just gone eight. I haven't had a shower yet. I need some time to get ready.'

'Well, make it an hour then. Shall I pick you up from outside your house?' Jed asked.

'No. Don't pick me up from here. Where else can I meet you?'

Jed chuckled. He was dying to see Frankie again. 'You know where my house is, don'tcha? Just before you get there, in the direction you're coming from, there's a lay-by on the left. I'll meet you there, say half-nine.'

Frankie smiled. 'See you then.'

'And Frankie, don't put on too much make-up. I wanna see that pretty face of yours.'

Frankie felt faint as she ended the phone call. She didn't have a clue what to wear and had very little time to get ready.

Hearing Frankie switch the shower off, Jessica got out of bed. Joey and Frankie were as close as close could be, and if anyone knew his sordid secret, it was Frankie.

She gently tapped on her daughter's bedroom door.

'This is all I fucking need,' Frankie muttered, as she chucked half her wardrobe onto the floor.

'Can I come in, love?' Jessica whispered.

'Yes,' Frankie replied angrily.

Jessica sat on the edge of Frankie's bed. Her daughter wasn't the earliest riser on earth and she wondered what was so special about today. 'You're up early. Going somewhere nice, are you?'

With time running out, Frankie decided her acid-washed jeans and denim jacket would have to do. Her black suede ankle boots and black basque were enough to tart the outfit up. She didn't want to look like a tomboy. 'I'm going out with the girls. It's Stacey's cousin's birthday and she's having a barbecue,' Frankie lied.

Jessica knew when Frankie was lying, but said nothing. Whatever she was hiding couldn't be any worse than Joey's little secret, and Jessica was more worried about her son than her daughter. 'Has, erm, Joey said anything to you recently about his life? He hasn't confided in you about anything unusual, has he?'

'Like what? What you talking about?' Frankie replied casually.

Jessica was a bit lost for words. Say Joey hadn't said anything to Frankie, or she had made a mistake. 'Has he got a girlfriend?' Jessica blurted out.

Aware that her mum was on her brother's case, Frankie said very little. 'I dunno. We're not together all the time, Mum. He ain't said nothing to me, but if you're so interested in Joey's love life, you best ask him yourself.'

Jessica nodded. The twins were as thick as thieves and, chances were, even if Frankie did know something, she wouldn't tell anyone. 'So where does Stacey's cousin live, then?' she asked, changing the subject.

Frankie let out a bored sigh. 'I don't know. Stacey never told me. Now, can you leave me alone, Mum? I'm trying to get ready and you're making me late.'

With a heart full of worry, Jessica apologised and walked away.

Frankie checked her appearance, grabbed her purse and ran down the stairs. She wanted to warn Joey about the conversation she had had with her mother, but he was fast asleep and she didn't have time to arse about. Debating whether to take her phone with her and ring him, she decided against it. The poxy thing was a nuisance to lug around and she had nearly lost it twice the other night.

Running into the kitchen, Frankie took a large gulp of vodka out of the bottle. 'No, doggies, no,' she said, as Buster and Bruno tried to clamber up the leg of her jeans.

'All right, Frank? What you doing?' Ricky asked.

Startled, Frankie dropped the vodka bottle and it smashed to smithereens on the stone kitchen floor. 'You scared me. I didn't realise you were still here,' Frankie replied.

'Me and Gal slept in the lounge. Drinking a bit early, ain't ya, girl?'

Shooing the dogs out of the kitchen so they didn't cut their paws, Frankie looked at Ricky with pleading eyes. 'Look, I'm meeting a boy and I don't want Mum and Dad to know. Can you clean that mess up for me? I'm running late.'

'What's going on? Was something smashed?' Jessica shouted out from upstairs.

Ricky smiled at Frankie. 'Sorry, Jess, it was me. I went to make a coffee and knocked a bottle of vodka off the kitchen top. You go back to bed, I'll clean it up.'

Frankie hugged her half-brother.

'Do you wanna lift?' he asked her.

'No, I'm fine. Thanks Ricky, you've just saved my life.'

As Frankie ran down the drive, she nervously glanced back at the house. She usually got cabs wherever she went and prayed that no one was watching her.

Frankie's heart leaped as she heard a loud tooting coming from behind her. She was afraid to look around. Surely it wasn't her dad?

Aware of a gold four-wheel drive pulling up beside her, she glanced apprehensively at it.

'Get in, Frankie,' Jed ordered her.

Frankie did as he asked. 'Sod you, you frightened the bloody life out of me. Whose car's this? Where's your pick-up truck?'

'At home. Can't take a beautiful girl out in a pick-up truck, can I? This Shogun's mine as well. Bought it off some old mush me dad knows. Got it for a good price, I did.'

Frankie was impressed. None of the boys she had ever mixed with could even reach the pedals on a motor like this, let alone own one or drive one. 'Where are we going?' Frankie asked, trying to sound relaxed.

'Cambridgeshire,' Jed replied coolly.

Frankie looked at him in amazement. He had to be joking, surely. She didn't even know where Cambridgeshire was, but it sounded a long way away. 'You are having a laugh, aren't you?'

Jed stopped at the red traffic light. He leaned towards her and softly kissed her on the lips. 'No, I'm not having a laugh. It's where my family comes from. You'll love it. It's absolutely beautiful, Frankie, just like you are.'

As his piercing green eyes gently teased her, Frankie looked away. The effect he had on her was abnormal and she barely knew what day it was.

'I'm just gonna fill up with diesel. You want anything to eat or drink?' Jed asked her.

Frankie shook her head. Sod the food and drink, all she wanted was him.


Eddie, Gary and Ricky did most of the tidying up. 'You have a break, Jess, we'll do all the dirty work and you can add your magic touch at the end,' Eddie insisted.

With her mind in no-man's-land, Jessica politely asked her parents if they would mind if they didn't stay for dinner.

'Of course not. We know you're not yourself, love,' Stanley said kindly.

Joyce wasn't so understanding. She loved being in this nice big house and was in no rush to head back to her own rabbit hutch. 'Me and your dad will stay here, Jess. You have a lie down. I'll cook the dinner today.'

Jessica blatantly refused. She had enough problems without having her mother driving her bloody mad. 'Look, I'm sorry, Mum, but go home, please. I'm really not up to it today. You can come over again next week, and I'll do you dinner then.'

Annoyed, Joyce stomped upstairs to pack her overnight bag. 'I've got no meat out the freezer, so me and you will have to starve, Stanley,' she shouted loudly.

Stanley hugged his daughter. 'Take no notice. You know what she's like.'

The drive to Cambridgeshire didn't take as long as Frankie thought it would. Jed took her down by the Fens and showed her where his dad and grandfather had both been brought up.

'I really miss my grandad. He was a good old boy,' Jed said, urging Frankie to sit down next to him. He wondered if she knew that her grandad had shot his grandad, but he said nothing. He didn't want to pry, unsettle her; it wasn't the done thing.

Frankie sat with her back against the bark of the tree and smiled. 'It is lovely here. It's so peaceful,' she said.

Telling Frankie to lie across his knees, Jed ran his fingers through her hair. 'We can live here one day. Imagine, me, you and our chavvies. It would be proper, wouldn't it?'

'What's a chavvie?' Frankie asked him.

'Kiddies. Our babies,' Jed said, laughing.

Wrapping her arms around his neck, Frankie pulled him towards her and kissed him passionately.

'No trying it on with me and don't you dare touch me cory. I'm not that type of boy, you know,' Jed said teasing her.

Frankie giggled. 'Is your cory what I think it is?'

Jed pointed at his erection. 'It's a big cory, ain't it? Ere cacker, I'm sorry about trying it on with you the other night. Them Es make me horny, I shouldn't have done that. I was out of order.'

As Jed took her in his arms, Frankie clung to him for dear life. He had a wonderful smell, a manly aroma, and she couldn't get enough of him.

Jed stood up and grabbed her by the hand. 'Come on, before I get overexcited. Let's go to a pub, I'll buy you a roast dinner.'

Joey was still in bed and Jessica was desperate for time alone with him. 'Ed, you and the boys have worked so hard this morning. Take Gary and Ricky to the pub and buy them a few beers. Go on, I insist.'

Eddie put an arm around Jessica's shoulder. 'This is the type of woman you wanna end up with, lads. She's one in a million,' he said proudly.

Gary laughed. 'Come on Dad, quick, before she changes her mind.'

As soon as the men had left the house, Jessica took a deep breath and went upstairs. 'Joey, wake up love,' she said, as she knocked and then entered her son's bedroom.

'All right, Mum? What's the time?' Joey mumbled, his eyes still half shut.

'It's gone one. Can I have a little chat with you, darling?'

The seriousness of his mum's voice made Joey's eyes open wide. 'What's the matter? Has something happened? Where's Frankie?'

Jessica sat on his bed and clutched his hand. 'Nothing's wrong. Frankie's gone out with her friends. You dad's not in, he's up the pub and Nanny and Grandad have gone home. It's just me and you, Joey, and we need to have a little talk, love.'

Joey wasn't silly. He sat himself up. She knew; he knew that she knew. 'What about, Mum?' he asked nervously.

Jessica smiled. 'About you and Dominic. About what's going on.'

Joey tore his eyes away from her. What was he meant to say. It was embarrassing. He could talk to Frankie about his sexuality, but not his mum.

Understanding his dilemma, Jessica spoke softly to him. 'It's OK. I'm not annoyed. Whatever you are, or might be, is fine by me. I love you, Joey, you're my son, and I'll always love you, no matter what.'

Shocked by his mum's understanding attitude, Joey's lip wobbled, then the tears came. 'I'm really sorry, Mum. I've tried to like girls, but I can't. I've always known I liked boys, ever since I was little. Even when I was about nine or ten, I remember fancying that bloke out of *The Dukes of Hazzard*,' he admitted.

'Sssh, it's all right, baby. Don't cry, Joey, please, or you'll make me cry, too.' Jessica handed him a tissue. 'So how long have you been seeing this Dominic? Is it serious between you? Or is it just casual?'

'We haven't been seeing one another long. I really like him, though, Mum. It's the first proper relationship I've had. I'm not going through a phase, I know I'm not.'

Jessica smiled. 'And Dominic likes you, too. That's how I found out, I saw the way you were with one another yesterday. It reminded me of how me and your dad were when we first got together.'

Joey gave a half-smile. 'You and Dad are still like that now. So, Frankie never told you, then?' he asked.

'No. I did ask her earlier, but she denied all knowledge. I take it that she knows?'

324

Joey smiled. 'She's the only one who does know. I haven't told anyone else, I swear I haven't.'

Tilting Joey's chin towards her, Jessica stared into his eyes. 'Now listen, my darling, and listen carefully. You must never bring Dominic to the house again and you must never go out with him around this area. If anyone finds out, Dad will lose the plot. Where does Dominic live?'

'The Angel, Islington,'

'Well, from now on, you'll have to meet him where he lives or somewhere miles away from here.'

Joey nodded. 'What will happen in the long run, though, Mum? I mean, if we stay together, I can't keep Dominic a secret for ever, can I?'

'You can and you will, Joey. You have to, you have no choice. Believe me, son, if your dad finds out, he will not accept it, not in a million years.'

Feeling anxious, Joey squeezed his mother's hand. 'Be truthful with me, Mum. Please don't lie. If Dad did find out, what do you think he would do to me?'

Jessica felt her eyes well up. 'My guess would be, he'd disown you. As for Dominic – remember, your dad's got a temper. Who knows what he might do to him? Your guess is as good as mine, Joey.'

# THIRTY-ONE

The following morning, Jessica felt under the weather, so Eddie offered to run the kids to school.

'You look peaky. Stay in bed. I've gotta go out anyway. Dad's solicitor rang me, he wants to see me urgently and I promised Auntie Joan I'd take her shopping. Her old legs are playing her up a bit, bless her heart.'

'Thanks, Ed,' Jessica mumbled, as she ran to the toilet to be sick.

Joey poked his head around Frankie's bedroom door. His sister had got in late the previous evening and she knew nothing about the conversation with his mum. 'Take some normal clothes in your bag. I need to talk to you. Let's bin school today and go to the pub instead. We'll just tell Mum we got our days mixed up and thought we didn't have to go in,' he whispered.

Frankie smiled as she stuffed her jeans and T-shirt into her school bag. Thinking of Jed, she tucked her mobile phone in as well. She would ring him later and, if he wasn't busy, maybe they could meet up again.

Eddie dropped the twins off at school and headed straight towards Whitechapel. He had arranged to meet his dad's solicitor at two o'clock, so had plenty of time to take Joan shopping beforehand.

'Eddie! Come in, boy. I've made you a nice bread pudding, your favourite.'

Eddie kissed her. Joan was looking ever so old and frail these days. Making a mental note to visit her more often, he followed his aunt into the kitchen. 'So how's tricks? What you been up to?' he asked.

'Not a lot, love. Don't get out much now, to be honest. So many muggings and stuff round here now. Old Maisy Miller got followed into the post office and had her pension snatched last week. Three blacks it was. Wicked bastards they are. We should never have let 'em into the country, you know.'

Realising she was about to get on to the famous Enoch Powell speech, Eddie cleverly changed the subject. 'How's that mate of yours doing now, Auntie? Molly something or other. You know, the one whose son was giving her grief?'

'Molly Jenkins, you mean. Yeah, she's fine. Keeps well away from her now, her Michael. Had an unfortunate accident, he did. Rumour has it, he got beaten up and lost his thumb in the process. Makes you wonder if someone knew what he was doing to his poor old mum, doesn't it?' Joan said, with a twinkle in her eye. She wasn't stupid. She had known when she told Eddie about Molly that Michael would soon experience a nasty little accident of some kind.

As the kettle on the stove began to whistle, Eddie smiled. 'When I take you shopping, I'll buy you a new kettle, Auntie, something a bit more modern.'

'No, you won't. Nothing wrong with this one. The tea don't taste the same when the water's boiled by them bleeding electric things. Tastes like fucking rat's piss, it does.'

Eddie chuckled. Joan might be looking old and frail, but she certainly hadn't lost her spirit.

\* \* \*

Frankie and Joey sat at a corner table in the Albion. 'So, is that it? Didn't she say anything else?' Frankie asked, amazed.

Joey shook his head. He had just been telling his sister about the chat he'd had with his mum the previous day. 'She just said that Dom must never come to the house again and not to meet him in Rainham any more. She said I'd be better seeing him in Islington.'

Frankie smiled. 'Well at least you ain't gotta worry about Mum finding out any more. One down, one to go, eh? When you gonna tell Dad?'

'Don't take the piss, Frankie, it's not a bloody joke,' Joey said, annoyed.

Frankie went up to the bar to get some more drinks. As she returned, Joey turned the tables.

'Well, what about you then? Where was you all day yesterday? Sucking Johnny-Wonny's cock, was we?' he asked her.

Desperate to unload the burden of who she was really seeing, Frankie leaned towards him. 'If I tell you something, Joey, you must promise me that you'll never breathe a word to anyone. Not even Mum must know this.'

Joey was intrigued. 'Go on,' he urged his sister.

'John ain't who I said he is. His name's Jed and I didn't wanna tell you because he's Jimmy O'Hara's son.'

Astonished, Joey stared at her and waited for her to laugh. It was a joke, surely – it had to be.

'Well, say something then,' Frankie urged.

Realising Frankie wasn't mucking about, Joey shook his head. 'Ain't that the boy who beat me up when I was little?'

'Don't be a drama queen, Joey. He didn't beat you up. I'm sure Nan or Grandad told me once that Dad forced you to get into a boxing ring with him. It wasn't Jed's fault, you were both little kids. It was Dad's fault if it was anyone's.'

Joey didn't know an awful lot about his father's business, but one thing he did know was there was a long-running feud between the O'Haras and his family. 'Frankie, you've gotta stop seeing him. Dad will go mental – he'll kill you if he finds out.'

Frankie shrugged. 'Well, he'll kill you if he finds out about Dominic, won't he? At least we'll both be dead, eh?'

Joey sipped his drink. 'It can't be serious, you only met Jed on Friday. Why don't you just nip it in the bud while you still can. You're a pretty girl, Frankie, there's plenty of other boys to choose from.'

Frankie shook her head vehemently. 'I don't want any other boy, I want Jed. I spent the whole day with him yesterday and it was fantastic. I know I ain't known him long, but I love him, Joey, I know I do.'

Knowing how strong-minded Frankie was, Joey nodded dumbly. She had always stuck by him. She had accepted his sexuality and accepted Dominic. 'Look, Frankie, I'm your brother and I love you. If this Jed makes you happy, then I'm happy for you.'

Frankie pulled her phone out of her bag. 'If I ring him and tell him to come down here, will you mind? I really want yous two to get on. Jed's brilliant, honest, he's a scream and I know you'll just love him, Joey.'

Joey nodded. 'Love him' was a bit strong. He had already met Jed on Friday night and wasn't over impressed by what he saw. 'Was it him that gave you that E, Frankie?' Joey asked.

'No. I got it off someone in the Berwick. Please don't start with all the questions, Joey. You won't get on with him if you start accusing him of things he hasn't done.'

Frankie put the phone to her ear. 'Jed, it's me. What you up to? I'm in the Albion.'

Joey guessed by the big grin that spread across his sister's face that Jed was coming to meet them.


After being dragged around the supermarket by his aunt, Eddie dropped her off and headed to Wanstead. His dad's solicitor, Larry, had been a friend of the family for years. As bent as a nine-bob note, Larry knew every trick in the book and was the perfect brief for anybody not quite legit.

Walking into the restaurant, Eddie asked the waiter if Larry had arrived yet. 'No sir, but your table's ready. Would you like to sit down or have a drink at the bar?'

Eddie ordered a drink and sat at the table. Larry had attended his dad's funeral, but had then sodded off on a three-month cruise. 'Look, there's no rush. We'll sort me old man's estate out when you get back,' Eddie had told him.

Unbeknown to Eddie, his dad had paid for the cruise and ordered Larry to book it as and when he died. Harry's orders were, 'Don't let Eddie know immediately. Leave it three to six months, at least.'

'Eddie, how are you? Any news yet? Larry asked him as he sat down opposite.

Shaking his head, Eddie shouted for a bottle of champagne to be brought over. 'No news at all. Fucking useless, the filth are. They couldn't catch a cold, the cunts. I'm gonna start rooting around meself again, see if I can do a better job. I've asked around the underworld, but no one's heard a dickie. It's a mystery, Lal, it really is.'

Feeling a bit melancholy, Larry quickly changed the subject. He had liked Harry Mitchell very much. He was one of life's characters. His death was an awful shock and Larry hated talking or thinking about it.

Eddie studied the menu.

'The lobster's good in here,' Larry told him.

Eddie ordered them both lobster and sipped his champagne. His father had always told him that he hadn't bothered making a will. 'What's the point? I've got three sons and it will all be split equally. I know you'll look after Reg and Joanie for me and I want the grandkids to be seen all right,' Harry had instructed Eddie.

Bored with listening about Larry's holiday, Eddie spoke bluntly. 'So, have you found out what the old man's estate was worth?'

'I sure have. All in all, including the house your dad was living in, it's worth around the three-million-pound mark.'

Eddie didn't bat an eyelid. The old man had always had an eye for a pound note and three mill didn't shock him at all. In fact, knowing his dad, he wouldn't be surprised if there was more. When he was a kid, he had once caught his dad digging a hole and putting big silver tins in it. 'What's that, Dad?' he'd asked innocently.

'Money, son. Never let the authorities know what you've got. Always bury the bastard. You might not understand now, Eddie, but you will one day, when you're older,' was his dad's reply.

'You don't seem very shocked, Eddie. I mean, considering the size of the house your dad lived in, it's a rather large amount, don't you think?'

'The old man could have bought a big fuck-off mansion years ago, Lal. If I had a pound for every time I tried to persuade him to move, I'd be the richest man in England. He would never leave that house in Canning Town because me mother had lived there with him. Said it made him feel close to her, he did. When he got murdered that night, do you know what the bastards did? Dad kept the house as a shrine to Mum. Whoever done him in smashed every photo he had of her, and Paulie reckons they even took a couple as souvenirs. That's what makes me think it wasn't kids. I'll catch whoever it was one day, Lal, and I swear on my parents' grave, I will fucking kill 'em with me bare hands.'

Over in Rainham, Joey felt uncomfortable as his sister and Jed behaved like the lovesick teenagers they were. He had never really seen his sister kiss a boy before, and watching Jed stick his tongue down her throat was making him shudder. 'Are we ready to order?' he asked, agitated.

Jed laughed. 'You're not jealous, are ya? Don't wanna kiss me yourself, do ya?'

Joey looked at Frankie in horror. Surely she hadn't told him.

Jed stood up. 'I'll go and get another round of drinks and order some food,' he said.

'You ain't fucking told him, have you?' Joey spat at Frankie.

'Of course not, you idiot. He asked if you and Dominic were at it the other night and I denied it. I told him you've had loads of girlfriends. He's just mucking about with you, 'cause you shared the room with Dom.'

'If you ever tell him, I will never speak to you again,' Joey hissed.

Jed swaggered back to the table. 'I ordered about ten different dishes. You can just take your pick,' he said, laughing.

Frankie thought Jed was joking until the barmaid kept

332

coming up with plates of food. 'Why did you buy all this? It's such a waste of money,' she told Jed.

Jed put his arm around her shoulder and gave her a penetrating stare. 'You didn't know what you wanted, so I bought you the lot. Anyway, I've got loads of wonga. Next weekend, I'll take you shopping and buy you some gold. Whaddya want? Earrings? Bracelet? A chain? I'll even buy you a diamond if you want one.'

About to eat a chip, Joey clocked his sister's gooey expression. She was putting him off his lunch. In fact, he felt physically sick. As the happy couple locked tongues once more, he voiced his opinion. 'You're so embarrassing – the whole pub is looking at us. Instead of mauling one another in public, go and get a fucking room.'

Back in Wanstead, Larry savoured the last mouthful of lobster and wiped his mouth with a serviette. He waited for Eddie to finish his meal, then cleared his throat. 'The reason I asked you to meet me here today is because I have something to tell you, Eddie.'

Delving into the inside pocket of his jacket, Larry handed him a letter. 'Your dad gave me strict instructions that you were to read this. He told me to leave it a certain length of time before I gave it to you. I need to pop outside to make a few phone calls, so I'll leave you alone for a few minutes.'

Eddie tore the letter open. His dad's handwriting had never been the best and he hoped he could understand the bastard thing. As luck would have it, it was typed.

Dear Eddie,
Obviously, if you're reading this, it means I've popped me clogs. Sorry if this letter feels like

333

I've come back to haunt you, but there are a few things I need to tell you, son.

Firstly, I want to tell you how much I love you and how proud I am of you. Paulie and Ronny never quite made the grade and, even from an early age, I knew you were gonna be the star of the show. You didn't let me down. Everything I had worked so hard for, you improved on, and that pleased me more than you'll ever know. You may wonder why I'm telling you this, now I'm brown bread, but I couldn't say it while I was alive. I was never very good with words and, apart from when I was with your mother, I've never been able to show my feelings.

Aware of getting emotional, Eddie paused and took a sip of his drink. He took a deep breath, then continued to read.

The second thing I want to say to you son, is don't end up alone. You and Jessica are the equivalent of me and your mum. Look after her, boy, and don't ever let her down.

Thirdly, I have some instructions for you. Dig about six-foot deep under the apple tree at the bottom of my garden and you'll find plenty of hidden treasure. I want you to keep this to yourself. Don't tell your brothers or anyone, as it's all meant for you.

Last, but not least, I made a will in 1987. I've left a substantial amount for Paulie, Ronny, Gary and Ricky, but the bulk I've left to you. You're the only one I can trust to do the right thing with it, Eddie, and I want you to look after the following people for me:

Reg
Auntie Joan
Auntie Vi
Sylvie (she was a good friend to me)
all the grandchildren
Uncle Albert
Raymondo
and John (from the Flag)

Make sure all me old neighbours are OK, Ed. Especially old Iris next door and Cyril Miller over the road. (Them two ain't got a pot to piss in, bless 'em.)

Well, that's about it, son. You look after yourself now and make sure you look after that wonderful family of yours.

Love always, Dad

P.S. Hopefully, Ed, my death was a quick heart attack in the Flag or I croaked it in my sleep. If by any chance it wasn't natural and some bastard took me out, I put my trust in you to get revenge for me.

With tears streaming down his face, Eddie kissed the piece of paper and put it in his pocket. 'I will, Dad, I promise,' he whispered.

# THIRTY-TWO

Eddie instructed Larry to inform his brothers of his father's wishes. He then sat back and waited for the inevitable fall out.

It was Ronny who rang first. 'A hundred fucking grand! That's all me and Paulie have been left. It ain't fair, Ed, we know he's fucking left it all to you. You're some snake in the grass, you are, ain't ya?'

Eddie did his best to calm his brother down. 'Look, none of this is my fault, Ronny. I didn't even know Dad had made a will.'

Ronny was spitting feathers. 'Didn't know! Don't lie to me, you cunt. I bet the two of yous cooked it up between you. What about his house? He left you that and all, has he? There's me ended up in a fucking wheelchair because of him and you're the one reaping the rewards.'

Not wanting to have this conversation over the phone, Eddie told Ronny that he would meet him and Paulie later that evening in the Flag.

'Cunt!' Ronny screamed as he slammed the phone down.

Guessing what the phone conversation was all about, Jessica wrapped her arms around her husband's toned waist. Harry's wealth and generosity had been a shock to her, but she was thrilled for Eddie and the children's sake. 'You won't have to work so much now. Why don't you stop doing what you're doing, Ed? I'm always afraid that one day you might not come home again. With all that money, you can set up a legitimate business. If you get someone else to run it for you, you can spend more time with me and the kids,' she told him.

Eddie waved away her fears. 'No one's gonna hurt me, Jess. Anyway, I like what I do and I'm not a man who can sit on his arse all day. The kids are all grown up now and me and you spend every weekend together as it is.'

Kissing his wife on the forehead, Eddie gently released her arms from around his waist. 'I'll probably be home late tonight, babe. I've got some business to attend to with Raymond and I've gotta face the wrath of Pinky and Perky down at the Flag.'

Eddie's humour never failed to make Jessica smile. 'Love you,' she shouted, as he closed the front door.

Hearing their father's car pull off the drive, Joey and Frankie came downstairs. Their exams had now started and, as neither of them were taking very many, they only had to attend school on certain days.

'Yous two are all glammed up. Where you off to today?' Jessica asked them.

'Southend,' the twins replied in unison.

Jessica smiled. She loved the hustle and bustle of Southend on a sunny day. When she was young, her mum and dad used to take her and Raymond there for a day trip. 'Now be careful. Are you going with all your friends? How are you getting there?'

'There's a big crowd of us going, Mum. We're all travelling together by train, so we'll be fine. I'll look after Frankie,' Joey said reassuringly.

Jessica smiled. Joey was such a sensible boy. She had

now got over the initial shock of his little secret, and loved him more than ever. A beautiful person inside, he was just different, that was all.

'Do you need any money?' Jessica asked. She had forbidden Eddie to tell the twins about his windfall. They were leaving school soon and she wanted them to get a job and make their own way in life.

'We don't need no money, Mum. We've got a load left from our birthday,' Frankie replied honestly.

As the cab tooted outside, Jessica gave them both a kiss. 'Don't forget to bring me back a stick of rock,' she shouted as she waved them off.

Shutting the front door, Jessica sighed. She had been desperate for some time alone all morning. Riffling through her handbag, she found the pregnancy test. Three mornings in a row she had been as sick as a dog. At first, she had thought it was the shock of finding out about Joey, but now she wasn't so sure. Jessica took the white stick out of the box and studied the instructions. When she was pregnant with the twins, this type of technology probably hadn't even existed.

Realising that the test only took five minutes, Jessica smiled. The quicker she got the answer she wanted so badly, the better.

'Oi, oi!' Jed shouted, as he picked up Frankie in the lay-by near his house.

Frankie smiled as she got in his red pick-up truck. 'Where's your Shogun?' she asked him.

'Me dad's got to drive up north. His motor's been playing up, so he borrowed mine.'

Cupping Frankie's face with his hands, Jed gently kissed her. 'Whaddya wanna do today then?'

Lying to her mum had given Frankie ideas. 'Can we

338

go to Southend? I haven't been there for ages and it's a lovely day for the seaside.'

Jed laughed at her way with words. 'I'd take you to the moon and back if you asked me to, Frankie.'

With the help of Raymond and a JCB, Eddie set to work at digging up his dad's garden. Apart from Jessica and her brother, Eddie hadn't told a soul about his dad's letter and its contents.

'You all right, boys? I've got some cold Guinness in the fridge if you want one,' shouted Iris from next door.

Sweating his cobbs off, Eddie gratefully accepted her offer.

'Your turn, Raymond, I'm fucked,' he said.

Eddie had thought it would only take a couple of hours to find what he was looking for. He had been wrong. The ground was rock hard and the digger he had borrowed was pony.

'Thanks, Iris,' Eddie said, as he grabbed the two cold cans.

'Why you digging up the apple tree?' Iris asked nosily.

'Me dad planted it for me mum when she was alive. He always said to me, "When I die, son, I want you to dig up the tree and replant it in your own garden,"' Eddie lied.

He had concocted the story earlier. 'If any of the neighbours ask, we're digging up the tree and replanting it at mine. After we've found what we're looking for, I'll ring up Davey Brown, get him to pick it up and dump it somewhere for us,' Eddie told Raymond.

'It will die if you dig up its roots. It won't grow properly again,' Iris said suspiciously.

Eddie smiled. 'It was me dad's final wish, so I'll do me best to save it,' he assured her.

* * *

In the trendy Liverpool Street wine bar, Joey smiled as Dominic excused himself to make an important phone call. Joey had come up to meet him for lunch and his boyfriend was taking the rest of the afternoon off so they could spend some time together.

As Dominic returned to the table, he tenderly rubbed Joey's leg. 'I've just booked us a posh hotel for the afternoon,' he said, as he brushed his hand teasingly over Joey's thigh.

Thrilled that he was in an area where nobody knew him and he could be himself, Joey squeezed Dominic's hand. 'Let's finish our drinks and go there now,' he said excitedly.

Standing not twenty feet away was an extremely interested spectator. Darren Palmer was the son of one of Ronny Mitchell's friends. He recognised Joey, knew exactly who he was – they had been at junior school together. He also knew who Dominic was, as his mate worked with him in the City and referred to him as the bum boy. Watching the two queers walk out of the pub, Darren almost flew to the phone box.

''Ere, Dad, you'll never guess who I've just seen. Eddie Mitchell's son, Joey, was all over some bender called Dominic. They were virtually at it in the pub – they were fondling and all sorts.'

As they ended the call, Terry Palmer couldn't stop smiling. He had never liked that flash bastard, Eddie Mitchell. Paulie and Ronny were good lads, but Eddie was too far shoved up his own arse. Joey Mitchell, a poofta. Whoever would have thought it, eh? You just couldn't make it up!

Punching in Ronny Mitchell's number on his mobile, Terry Palmer could barely speak through laughing.

\* \* \*

340

Southend was heaving with people and Frankie wished she had suggested somewhere else.

'What's up? Not bored with me already, are ya?' Jed teased, knowing full well she wasn't.

Frankie smiled. They had played in the amusement arcades, strolled along the beach, eaten fish and chips and Jed had even won a big teddy bear for her, which they were carrying with them. 'Shall we go somewhere quieter, where we can be alone?' Frankie asked him.

'We can get some booze and I'll book us a room, if you like,' Jed suggested.

Desperate to get intimate with him, Frankie grinned. 'I'd like that Jed, I really would.'

Unable to lift the large silver chest, Eddie urged Raymond to give him a hand.

'Christ almighty! It looks like something out of *Gulliver's Travels* – the bastard thing's fucking heavy,' Raymond moaned.

'Quick, cover it over with them sacks,' Eddie ordered, as he spotted Iris in her garden again.

Lugging it into his father's house, Eddie noticed the nosy old cow peering over the fence. 'Just clearing up all the branches, Iris,' he shouted.

Once inside the house, Eddie flicked the lid of the chest open.

'Well, fuck me,' Raymond said, looking at Eddie in astonishment.

Lifting the guns out one by one, Eddie studied them. Hand, machine, shot: there was every gun going. He stared at the jewellery. Sovereigns, ingots, rings, chains: there were hundreds of different pieces.

Raymond picked up a black velvet bag and opened it. 'Jesus, Ed, you've got a load of diamonds 'ere, mate.'

Eddie smiled. His old man was a wily old bastard and he didn't know whether to laugh or cry. 'Pick out something for yourself, Ray, and take something nice for Polly.'

Raymond shook his head. 'They're yours mate, don't be silly. I don't want nothing.'

'Take it, Ray. Me old man wanted you to have something, I know he did,' Eddie insisted.

Knowing how forceful Eddie could be, Raymond picked out a pretty ring for Polly and a chunky one for himself. He put them in his pocket and turned to Eddie. 'What you gonna do with the guns? You can't leave 'em here.'

Eddie shrugged. 'I'll take the diamonds and jewellery home and put them in the safe. The guns can be hidden down the salvage yard for now. Let's shoot straight there. We can come back here tomorrow and tidy stuff up. I've gotta come back anyway; I wanna ask around, see if anyone's got any more information about Dad's murder.'

'What shall we do about the digger? Have you gotta take it back today?'

Looking at his watch, Eddie cursed. He had told Ronny he would meet him and Paulie at seven and it was already six o'clock. 'The digger's fine, it can stay here till tomorrow. I think I'm gonna ring Paulie and Ronny and meet 'em tomorrow instead. If we clean up here in the morning, it'll give us plenty of time to talk to the neighbours, then we'll go to the Flag after that.'

Raymond agreed.

'I'll tell you what. I dunno about you, but I could kill a couple of beers. Why don't we drop the guns off, then stop at a boozer where no one knows us?' Eddie suggested.

Raymond laughed. 'We could walk into a boozer in Timbuktu and people would know us, Ed.'

Eddie chuckled. 'Come on you tosser, help me get this chest in the motor.'

Frankie laughed as Jed pressed the 'play' button. He was such a sod. In the hotel reception, he had seen a girl carrying a tape recorder. 'Oi, pretty lady, let me buy that off you,' he'd said.

The girl had looked at Jed in amazement. 'It's only a cheap one,' she'd replied.

'How much do ya want for it?' Jed had asked.

'I don't really want to sell it,' the girl had said.

Jed had put his hand in his pocket and waved some money in her face. ''Ere you go. Take fifty quid for it.'

The girl had snatched the money, handed him the battered old tape recorder and disappeared before Jed could change his mind. Jed had then gone outside to his truck and reappeared with a selection of cassettes, which they were now playing.

'Why did you pay all that money for this rubbish?' Frankie asked him. She loved it really. Jed was so impulsive, and the way he was filled her with intense excitement.

''Cause I didn't want you to be bored. You don't wanna be stuck in a room all day with no music, do ya? My old tape recorder's fucked. Dropped it on the floor, I did, and now it won't work any more.'

Frankie smiled. Christ knows where Jed got all his money from. He had plenty and chucked it about like there was no tomorrow. 'Do you mind if I ask you something?'

'Ask away,' Jed replied, grabbing her hand.

'Where do you get all your money from? Does your dad give it to you or do you sometimes go to work?'

Jed turned the music up, took Frankie in his arms and made her dance with him. 'I never went to school. Been

343

working since I was eight years old. I'll never be poor, I can turn me hand to lots of things.'

'Like what?'

'I sell horses, motors, caravans, diggers. You name it, I can get it and sell it. I'll be cakeo one day, Frankie. You stick with me and you'll be rich as well.'

Frankie tightened her grip on him. 'What is this rubbish music? Ain't you got any acid house?' she asked him.

Jed tilted her chin towards his. 'Who needs all that house music crap when you've got country and western? That shit's only all right if you stick a pill down your throat, but country music is proper. You listen to the words. Every song tells a story, Frankie.'

Frankie listened and by the time Tammy Wynette had reached the chorus of 'Stand By Your Man', she and Jed were in bed together.

Unaware of what his daughter was up to, Eddie was on his way home. 'I won't be long, darling. I've just gotta drop Raymondo off first. I'll be about fifteen minutes,' he told Jess.

Jessica ended the call. Grinning, she put Eddie's dinner in the oven. She had been doing buttons all day waiting for her husband to get home. Desperate to tell someone her news, Jessica had rang Vicki and told her. 'Please don't say a word to Doug. I only found out this morning and I haven't had a chance to tell Eddie yet,' she begged.

Vicki was thrilled for herself and her friend. She was over five months now, and it was great that she and Jess would both be mums together.

As the Guns N' Roses song was played on the radio, Jessica turned it up full blast. She wasn't usually a fan of

344

rock music, but the song was called 'Sweet Child O' Mine', and Jess couldn't resist joining in with the chorus.

Back in Southend, Jed was having trouble inserting his penis inside Frankie. 'Are you OK?' he whispered as he finally entered her.

'I'm fine,' Frankie lied. She felt as if her insides were being ripped to shreds.

'I love you, Frankie,' Jed told her as his movements got faster and faster.

'I love you, too,' Frankie replied, wincing.

Suddenly he made a groaning noise and rolled off her. 'What's up? Have I done something wrong?' she asked, concerned.

Propping himself up on his elbow, Jed rubbed her clit with his finger. 'Nothing's up. I've already come, you dinlo,' he said laughing.

As Frankie's breathing started to quicken, Jed moved his finger faster and faster. 'Ahh, Jed,' Frankie panted, as she grabbed his head with both hands. This felt nice, much more pleasurable than him being inside her. She reached her orgasm, yanking his head.

'Fucking hell. You nearly broke me neck,' Jed teased.

Frankie let out a happy sigh. She really had found the man of her dreams.

Hearing Eddie's car pull up on the gravel, Jessica flung open the front door.

'What's this, a welcome committee?' Eddie joked.

Jessica took his hand and dragged him into the lounge. She handed him the glass of champagne she'd already poured and told him to sit down and drink it.

As Buster and Bruno bounded into the room, Jessica shooed them out. This was her and Eddie's moment.

'What's occurring?' Eddie asked. He had sort of already guessed, but didn't want to spoil her plans to tell him herself.

'You'll never guess what I found out today,' Jessica said excitedly.

'I've no idea,' Eddie lied.

'I'm pregnant, Eddie. We're having that baby,' Jessica screamed.

Still caked in mud from earlier, Eddie stood up and lifted her into his arms. 'I love you so much, Jessica Mitchell. I really, really do.'

# THIRTY-THREE

At seven o'clock the following evening, Eddie and Raymond pulled up outside the Flag in Canning Town.

Eddie had asked around half the neighbourhood earlier but, apart from what he already knew, no one had any more information about the night his dad died. Frustrated by the lack of progress he'd made, Eddie wasn't in the best of moods.

'There must have been bangs, crashes and fucking screams. Me poor fucking dad was tortured. Some cunt must have heard something, surely,' he said to Raymond.

Raymond shrugged. He had no answers. Poor old Harry's death was a complete mystery to all and sundry. 'How's Jess?' Raymond asked, changing the subject.

The mention of his wife's name lifted Eddie's mood. Jessica had told him to keep her pregnancy quiet until she had seen her doctor and knew how far gone she was. She didn't even want the twins or her parents to know just yet. Desperate to tell at least one person, Eddie smiled.

'Keep it to yourself, but we're gonna be parents again. Found out yesterday, Jess did. She's over the bloody moon; we both are.'

Thrilled at the prospect of becoming an uncle once more, Raymond grabbed Eddie around the neck with his right arm. 'You're a dark horse, you are. I'm surprised at your age you can still get it up, you cunt.'

Laughing, Eddie pushed him away. 'Remember, not a word to anyone. Jess ain't told your mum and dad yet, so don't put your foot in it, for fuck's sake.'

Paulie and Ronny were sitting at their usual table. Both had faces like smacked arses. As Eddie walked in, he heard a few sniggers. He took no notice, walked up to the bar and ordered himself and Raymond a drink.

'What you having?' he shouted over to his brothers.

'Are you sure you can afford it?' Ronny asked sarcastically.

Eddie sat down and tried to make the two of them see sense. 'Look, I know you're both upset, but I'll always see you all right. If you need any money, just ask me and I'll give it to you. Dad left me strict instructions: he wants me to look after a few people, make sure they're comfortable. He left me the bulk, 'cause he knew he could trust me to carry out his wishes.'

'You're a lying cunt. Don't take me and Paulie for mugs. You can stick your handouts where the sun don't shine,' Ronny spat at him.

Eddie turned to Paulie. He had always been the more sensible one out of the two. 'Is that your opinion as well, Paulie? Is it?'

Not able to hold Eddie's gaze, Paulie stared at his lap. 'I want out, Ed. I want out of the business and out of your life. We're meant to be brothers and all you've ever done is stitch me and Ronny up. Well, it's gone too far now. Me and Ronny have discussed things and neither of us want any more to do with you.'

Eddie looked at Paulie in amazement. He guessed that he might have a cob on, but he had never expected this. They had always worked together; how could he even think of walking away? 'Don't be so childish, Paulie. Dad wouldn't have wanted this. We're Mitchells, we're meant to stick together. What do you wanna leave the firm for? It's stupid, I knew fuck-all about Dad's will. It was his wishes, not mine.'

Desperate to say his pre-planned speech, Ronny piped up. 'For years we've lived in your shadow, Ed. You were always the old man's favourite – you spent half your life licking his arse. Why should you dish out the orders, eh? What makes you so fucking special? Me and Paulie have had it with you. We're setting up on our own. We'll find our own clients and do a bit of sharking ourselves.'

Eddie looked at Ronny with contempt. As usual, his eyes were gone and his speech was slurred. Unable to stop himself, Eddie laughed in Ronny's face. 'Well, I wish you every success, Ronny. I'm sure people will be quaking in their boots when they're threatened to pay up by an alcoholic cripple.'

Overcome by jealousy and hatred, Ronny picked up an empty beer bottle and aimed it at Eddie's head. As the bottle brushed against his hair and whizzed past him, Eddie jumped up to retaliate.

'Leave him – he ain't worth it. Come on, Ed, let's get out of here,' Raymond said, holding Eddie back.

Sitting back down, Eddie looked at Paulie with pleading eyes. 'You're making a big mistake, bruv, you really are.'

As Paulie looked at the floor, Eddie shook his head, stood up and walked away.

Ronny called Eddie's name. He hadn't played his ace card yet and he was gagging to do so. 'Oh, and by the way, big man. Your son Joey's a fucking bum boy. Got a boyfriend, he has. Sucks cock and takes it up the arse regularly, by all accounts.'

As Eddie lunged at Ronny, the barmaid let out a

piercing scream. John, the guv'nor, was on holiday, and she didn't know how to deal with such violence.

Picking Ronny up by the neck, Eddie lifted him out of his wheelchair and threw him as hard as he could against the wall. 'You fucking lying cunt, I'm gonna kill you!' he shouted.

To save Ronny's sorry arse, Paulie and Raymond joined forces. When angry, Eddie was so strong he was almost impossible to control.

Eddie bent down and held Ronny around the throat as if to strangle him. 'How dare you fucking bring my kids into this, you cunt!' he screamed.

'It's true. Ask Terry Palmer. Ask his son. I'm not lying, Ed, I'm not,' Ronny said, choking. He was frightened now, really frightened.

Managing to pull Eddie away, Raymond dragged him outside the pub. 'Let's get out of here, mate. I think the barmaid's called the filth,' Ray told him.

Eddie said nothing. Chucking his keys at Raymond, he got in the passenger side and slammed the door. 'Are you OK?' Raymond asked him as they drove along in silence.

'No, I fucking ain't,' Eddie yelled. 'As for my so-called brothers, I hope they both rot in hell. I never wanna see either of them ever again!'

Jessica sat in the kitchen with a massive smile on her face. She and Vicki were discussing baby names and they had completely different ideas on the subject.

'Angel's a lovely name for a little girl,' Vicki insisted.

Giggling, Jessica put the kettle on. Eddie would have a fit if she called their kid Angel.

'I think you should opt for an American name if you have a boy. Me and Dougie quite like Troy, so what about you calling yours Travis?' Vicki suggested.

Jessica smiled. 'I've already promised Ed that if we have a boy, we'll call it Harry in memory of his dad.'

As the front door slammed, Jessica ran into the hallway. 'Oh, it's you, Ed. You're early, love. Do you want a cup of tea?'

'Where's Joey?' Eddie shouted.

Jessica's heart went over as she noticed that Eddie's face looked as black as thunder. She knew, without a doubt, that he had been told something. 'Vicki's in the kitchen,' she said, as brightly as she could.

'Get rid of her,' Eddie spat.

Jessica ushered her friend outside and apologised profusely.

'I wouldn't like to be in Joey's shoes. What's he done?' Vicki whispered.

'I bet he's been bunking off school again and Ed's just found out,' Jessica lied.

As she shut the front door, Jessica felt physically sick. She had to play it cool; it was her duty as a mother to protect her son. 'Whatever's the matter?' she asked Eddie.

'Where is he? Is he out with his fucking boyfriend, is he?' Eddie screamed, grabbing his wife by the shoulders.

'Boyfriend? What are you talking about? You're hurting me, Ed, stop it, please.'

Eddie let her go. Leaning with his back against the wall, he put his head in his hands and slumped to the floor. 'He's gay. Our Joey's a fucking queer, that's what the word on the street is. Do you know anything about it, Jess? If you do, tell me. I want the fucking truth.'

Jessica shook her head furiously and proclaimed her son's innocence. 'Don't be so ridiculous, Eddie. Our Joey's got a new girlfriend – he really likes her, he does. He was only telling me about her yesterday. He wants

351

us to meet her. He asked me if she could come round for tea.'

'Are you sure he ain't fucking lying to you?' Eddie asked.

'Of course he's not lying. Someone's winding you up, Eddie. Who told you? Who's spreading these lies?'

'Ronny told me. Terry Palmer told him. Everyone's been told. As I walked in the Flag earlier, every bastard was sniggering at me.'

Jessica knelt in front of her devastated husband. 'How can you believe anything that comes out of Ronny's mouth? He's jealous of you, he always has been. He's making up these awful lies because he can't deal with your dad leaving you all that money. He wants to get back at you, Ed, and he'll resort to anything to do so.'

Eddie shrugged. 'I'll go and see Terry Palmer, see what he has to say. Don't look so worried, I ain't gonna hurt him. I just want solid proof.'

'It's all lies. I know my own son, Eddie,' Jessica insisted.

Eddie shrugged. Joey had always been different – too different for his liking. 'He is fucking effeminate, Jess. Let's face it, Joey's never been like Gary and Ricky, has he? Even as a kid, he was frightened of his own shadow. I mean, he dresses strange and sometimes I look at him and think that he should have been the girl and Frankie the boy. She's got bollocks, Frankie has, but not Joey. He's not normal, Jess, I've always known it, but I kept me trap shut for years for your fucking sake.'

With tears rolling down her cheeks, Jessica did her best to hold her own. 'Of course he's not like Gary and Ricky, or you and your brothers. I didn't want him to end up in your world, it was me that forced him to be different. I mean, come on, as much as I think the world of Gary and Ricky, their mum was an alkie, that's why they're rough around the edges. I brought Joey up differently. He's soft, gentle, with a heart of gold, and I instilled that into him. He might be unusual, but that doesn't mean he's gay, Ed. It's just different mothers, different upbringings, that's all.'

Holding out his arms, Eddie snuggled up to his wife. 'I'm sorry if I hurt you. I just lost me rag.'

'Promise me, Eddie, that you won't say anything to Joey. He's in the middle of his exams, it's not fair on him. You know how he takes things to heart – he'll be traumatised.'

'I swear I won't say anything to him,' Eddie said honestly. He had no intention of giving Joey a warning. If what was being said was true, he would catch him at it and when he did, he would throttle both him and his fucking boyfriend.


Terry Palmer lived alone in a council flat in Beckton. Terry had once been a man of substance, but since his wife had stung him for all he had, his life had gone completely downhill.

Opening another can of Special Brew, Terry focused on the television. He was watching the film *Once Upon a Time in America*. 'Go on, get in there,' Terry said, laughing.

Terry fancied himself as a Robert De Niro type. He and Rob were two of a kind, they sang from the same hymn sheet.

As the buzzer rang, Terry opened the security door automatically. His son, Darren, often stayed of a night, so he left the front door on the latch for him and sat back down. Engrossed in the bit where De Niro actually rapes the bird, Terry barely looked up as the front door closed. 'I'm starving – you brought any grub home with you, Dal?' he shouted out.

'The Chinese was shut, so I brought this round to fill you up,' Eddie whispered, as he yanked Terry's head back and stuck the barrel of a gun down the back of his throat.

Not knowing that her husband was currently playing cowboys and Indians, Jessica tried Joey's mobile number repeatedly. Eddie had popped out to take the dogs for a run and she desperately needed to warn her son. 'Please answer, son, please answer,' she prayed out loud.

Finally, God looked down on her.

'Whatever's wrong, Mum? Has something happened? I'm busy,' Joey exclaimed in annoyance.

Joey had just been having a bit of the other and the constant ringing of the phone was preventing him from reaching a climax.

'Joey, you need to come home right now, son. Your dad knows. Someone told him about Dominic. Now, don't worry, I've got you out of it, but I've told him you've got a new girlfriend. Ring up a girl mate and bring her round tomorrow for tea.'

Joey's hands shook so much he could barely hold the weight of his phone. 'Who am I gonna ring? Apart from Frankie's mates, I don't really mix with any girls.'

Jessica spoke forcefully to him. 'I don't care who you ring or who you know, Joey, but make sure you bring a girl round here tomorrow. I've just stuck my neck out for you and if your father finds out I'm lying, he'll throttle the pair of us.'

Joey stared at his penis. His erection had deflated so

much that it now resembled a burst balloon. 'OK, Mum, I'll find a girl. I'll do it,' he promised.

With eyes as wide as flying saucers, Terry Palmer tried to speak, but couldn't. The gun was hurting his throat and was choking him. Aware of his own urine running down his legs, he began to beg.

Eddie slowly withdrew the gun from Terry's throat. Smiling, he pointed it at his bollocks instead. 'You got something to tell me about my Joey, have you, Terry?'

Petrified, Terry shook his head. 'I don't know anything, honest I don't. Please don't hurt me, Eddie, please.'

Eddie pulled back the catch. 'Tell me what your son saw, else I'll kill you. I want the truth and I'll know if you're lying, you cunt.'

Terry's mouth was as dry as a bone. It was a struggle to swallow, let alone talk. 'I need a drink,' he gasped.

With the gun still fixed on Terry's meat and two veg, Eddie handed him his can of Special Brew. 'Drink that and talk, you prick,' he ordered.

Covering his prized possessions with both hands, Terry blurted out all he knew. 'Darren saw Joey. He was with a bloke called Dominic in a wine bar in Liverpool Street. Him and your Joey were groping and kissing and stuff. Please don't hurt me, Eddie, none of this is my fault. My son saw them, not me.'

Eddie stared deep into Terry's eyes. 'Why did you tell Ronny? You knew what would happen.'

'I'm sorry, Eddie. I'd had too much to drink. I didn't think. I'll ring Ronny now, tell him Darren got it all wrong. I'll say it was someone who looked like your Joey.'

Eddie took the silencer out of his pocket and attached it to the gun.

Realising what Eddie was doing, Terry fell to his knees

355

and begged. 'I am so sorry. Don't kill me, Eddie. I'll move – you'll never see me again – but please, I beg you, please don't shoot me.'

Eddie Mitchell had never been a man to be dissuaded by tears and apologies. With little emotion, Eddie held the gun to the right side of Terry's temple.

Seconds later, he pulled the trigger.

# THIRTY-FOUR

The twins took their last exam in June and both Joey and Frankie whooped with joy as they walked through the school gates for the very last time. They had never really caught up from all the time they'd had off, but had completed all their homework and done their very best.

'How do you think you did?' Frankie asked her brother.

'Shit,' Joey replied. He had always hated maths and, even if he hadn't have bunked off, was sure he'd have still failed.

Noticing her brother looking a bit downcast again, Frankie did her best to cheer him up. Ever since their mum had warned Joey that his father was on his case, Joey had been down in the dumps. 'Why does life have to be so awkward, sis? I've only been able to see Dominic three times in the last month.'

Frankie linked arms with her brother. 'Look, it won't be for ever. You said you want to work in an office. If you get a job up town as an office junior or something, you can see Dom all the time. You can meet for lunch, then shag his brains out after work.'

Joey smiled. 'I suppose so.'

The twins had taken four exams each. Academically, Frankie was probably the brighter of the two. Trouble was, she had never particularly liked school, which resulted in her never fulfilling her potential.

'Look, if you're missing Dominic that much, why don't you invite him out tonight? Dad ain't gonna know anyone in the Berwick Manor, is he? Mum and Dad think we're staying round our friend's anyway. You and Dom can book a room somewhere. Having a bit of the other might cheer you up a bit.'

Joey playfully thumped her. He was tempted, but unsure. 'It's too dangerous, Frankie. I promised Mum I wouldn't see Dom locally and if she finds out, she'll kill me.'

Frankie had always been the daredevil out of the two of them. 'Don't be such a wuss. Ring Dominic, enjoy yourself. Live dangerously, Joey, I most certainly do.'

Joey laughed. Dangerous was his sister's middle name. 'How are things going with Jed? Is it still serious?'

Frankie's face broke into a big, silly grin. She had seen Jed almost every day since they had met and she worshipped the ground he walked on. 'I love him so much, Joey. When I'm old enough, I'm gonna marry him and have loads of kids.'

'That'll please, Dad,' Joey said sarcastically.

'I don't care. Sod Dad! It's my life and I'll do what I want with it.'


Walking around Tesco, Jessica smiled as she checked her shopping list. Positive she hadn't forgotten anything, she made her way to the checkout.

Sunday was to be a special day for her and all the family. Her parents, Raymond, Polly, Gary and Ricky were coming over for dinner. Jessica had chosen to do a roast. She had bought two big ribs of beef and all the trimmings to go with it. It was going to be a double celebration.

358

Her parents and everybody else thought they were coming just to celebrate the twins leaving school, but Jessica was now ready to announce that she was pregnant.

Apart from Eddie and Vicki, Jessica still hadn't told a soul, not even the twins. She had been desperate to get over the dreaded twelve-week mark before she announced it to the world.

Jessica thanked the cashier and walked towards her car. She loaded her shopping into the boot and leaned against it for a breather. The sun was shining, life was good and she was so excited about her future. Thankfully, the Dominic episode had now blown over with Eddie. Joey had brought a girl round for tea and Ed had believed their relationship was kosher. Jessica smiled. She couldn't wait for the new baby to arrive and at times like these she felt like the luckiest woman alive.

Eddie stood in the hallway of the pub's living quarters. He counted the money and nodded. 'All right, Alec, it's all here. See you same time next month.'

With all debts and protection money collected, Eddie gave Gary and Ricky a ring to see if everything had gone smoothly their end. Since Paulie had left the firm, Eddie had split the collections in two. He and Raymond did one half of their patch and Gary and Ricky the other.

'All done, Dad. Everything went as sweet as a nut,' Gary told him.

'Good lads. You and Ricky out on the town again tonight?'

Gary laughed. 'Going to a rave out Watford way.'

Eddie raised his eyebrows at Raymond. He was far too old to understand all this rave lark. Sometimes Gary and Ricky would go to one and not come home for two days.

'Well, have a good time, and don't forget Sunday, Gal,

will you? Jessica's cooking a special meal. It's a double celebration. Make sure you and Ricky are there by three at the latest.'

'What's the other celebration, then? I thought we were just celebrating the twins leaving school,' Gary asked.

Eddie chuckled. 'There's more to it than meets the eye. You and Ricky behave yourselves and I'll see you both on Sunday.'

Ending the phone call, Eddie turned to Raymond. 'Shall we have a couple of pints somewhere?'

Raymond shook his head. 'Polly's off work today, so I'm gonna meet her up town. She wants to do a bit of shopping.'

Smirking, Eddie nudged him. 'Ain't shopping for engagement rings, are we, Raymondo?'

'Not yet. Don't worry, you'll be the first to know if and when we do,' Raymond replied, chuckling.

Desperate to cure his dehydration, Eddie passed his house and carried on through the lanes. He had a couple of phone calls to make and couldn't make them indoors.

The Optimist was a pub only a few minutes from his home. He pulled into the car park and strolled inside. 'Pint of Kronenberg,' he said to the barmaid.

Taking his drink outside, Eddie sat at one of the wooden tables. He was sweltering, but there was no way he would take his shirt off. He hated it when he saw geezers in pubs with no tops on. People had no decorum these days, no respect. Ed had a fit body and he wouldn't do it. These arseholes that chose to strip half naked were always big fat pricks with bellies like darts players.

Eddie rang home first. He needed to make sure all was OK. 'All right, Jess? I'll be home soon, love. I bet the twins are happy, aren't they? Are they home yet?'

'Yeah, they're playing with the dogs in the garden.'

360

'Give 'em a shout, Jess, I wanna talk to 'em.'

Bewildered, Jessica called the kids. Eddie never usually asked to speak to them on the phone.

'What's up, Dad?' Frankie asked.

'Bet you and Joey are over the moon, ain't ya? No more school, eh? You still going out celebrating with your mates tonight?'

Frankie giggled. 'Over the moon's putting it mildly. Yeah, we're still going out. There's loads of us, so it should be a really good night.'

'Where you off to – the pub?'

'Yeah, probably the Albion,' Frankie replied. She didn't want him knowing that they were hanging out at the Berwick Manor.

'Ask your mum if she wants me to bring home a take-away.'

Frankie did as she was told. 'No, it's OK, Dad. Mum's already cooked something.'

Eddie ended the call and quickly made the other. When he had first heard the rumours about Joey, he had done nothing, apart from blowing Terry Palmer's brains out.

Palmer's murder had been all over the local news. The Old Bill had even come to the house, but Jessica had given him an alibi by saying he was at home all evening and hadn't left her side. When the police left, Jessica had questioned him herself. 'You were just out with the dogs, weren't you, Eddie? Swear to me that you didn't kill that man.'

'I swear on our unborn baby's life, I was out with the dogs,' Eddie insisted.

He actually wasn't lying. When he had murdered Terry Palmer, Buster and Bruno were in his motor outside Palmer's flat. The dogs were his accomplices.

Jessica never mentioned the incident again and neither

did he. He had no worries about Paulie or Ronny saying anything to the filth. His brothers might be jealous wankers, but they were no snitches. Grasses didn't exist in the Mitchell empire; never had and never would.

Eddie had bided his time, watching Joey closely. He had never mentioned his son's sexuality to Jessica, Raymond or anyone since that day. Jessica must have thought he had forgotten all about it, especially since Joey had brought the pretend girlfriend home, but nothing could be further from the truth.

The thought of his son being a raving iron was eating away at Eddie's insides and he needed to know if it was true. After a lot of thought, he had scoured through the Yellow Pages and hired a private detective. He had been careful. He picked one miles away, a woman called Gina, and provided her with a false name. He called himself John Smith.

'A mate of mine's got this problem. His daughter's dating some kid called Joey and he thinks the lad could be playing her about. My pal's got a few bob and his daughter's quite a plain girl. He reckons this Joey's only with her because she's worth money. He's even heard a rumour that this Joey lad's gay.'

Gina had guessed that Eddie's pal was actually himself. She often had clients come to her with cock and bull stories. At the end of the day it was none of her business. Her only concern was doing her job properly and getting paid. Gina had had more John Smiths on her books than she could remember. It was a very common name that people chose to use. She had never had a John Smith like this one, though. This one was mind-blowingly handsome, with sexuality oozing from every pore.

As Gina answered the phone, Eddie spoke quietly but clearly. 'Me pal's just rung me. Joey's blown his daughter out tonight, so can you follow him? If you see him looking intimate with another geezer, he wants you to follow them wherever they go. He needs you to get Joey's mate's full name and address.'

Gina smiled at the gruff, sexy voice. 'OK, Mr Smith. Does your friend want me to follow Joey from his house in Rainham?'

'Yeah, he does,' Eddie replied. He had already given Gina £500 quid upfront to gain her confidence. He had promised her another £1,500 once she came up with the information he wanted. 'If me mate owes you any more dough, let me know and I'll run it down to your office.'

'No, it's fine at the moment. Tell your friend that he's still in credit, Mr Smith.'

Eddie arranged to call her the following day and went to get another pint. So far Gina had followed Joey three times, but had come up with nothing. It was only a matter of time, Ed thought, as he sat back down. He would even-tually find out the truth and when he did, there would be murders – literally!


Frankie was having a fantastic time in the Berwick Manor. She and Jed had swallowed ecstasy tablets earlier and, after feeling sick, she had just come up on it.

As Inner City's 'Good Life' came pumping out of the speakers, she dragged Jed onto the dancefloor.

Seeing Dominic talking to his school friends, Joey quickly dragged him away. 'Are you OK?' Dominic asked, concerned.

'Not really. I'm paranoid in here. It's too close to home for my liking.'

Dominic smiled. 'I've stacked our room up with alcohol. I've got some puff as well. Shall we take a rain check?'

Desperate to kiss Dom more than anything else in the world, Joey managed to stop himself. 'I'll just go and find Frankie, tell her we're leaving,' he said excitedly.

Joey found his sister on the dancefloor. Whispering his plans in her ear, he returned to Dominic and ushered him out of the packed, smoky club. Outside was desolate and Joey had the devil inside as he dragged Dom around the side of the building. It had been over two weeks since he had touched or even kissed him.

Both boys were totally unaware of the dark-haired woman sitting in the black Nissan Micra. Seeing the boys get into a minicab, Gina put her camera on the passenger seat. Mr Smith would be thrilled with the photographs she had just taken. All she had to do now was find out Joey's friend's full name and address, and her work would be complete.


Jed O'Hara had his own trailer on his father's land. He had often asked Frankie to stay there in the past, but she had always refused. Tonight, however, with the ecstasy tablet clouding her judgement, Frankie was up for an adventure.

As Jed parked his Shogun on his father's drive, he took Frankie by the hand.

'Oh, my God! What the fuck is that?' Frankie said, as she spotted an animal with horns walking towards her.

Jed giggled. The Es they had taken were fucking strong. 'It's a ram, you dinlo. What the fuck did you think it was? An elephant?'

Frankie was laughing hysterically as they traipsed across the field. Jed opened the door of his trailer and they fell into one another's arms. The sex on an E was sensational, and they were at it hammer and tongs for hours.

Finally, Frankie gently pushed Jed away. She was sore down below and needed a break. 'Can I have a look around?' she asked him. So far, all she had seen of the trailer was the bedroom.

Jed poured them both a pint of water and smiled as she took in the surroundings. Frankie had no knowledge of travellers before she had met Jed and the way they lived intrigued her. 'Why have you got so much china?' she asked him.

Jed laughed. ''Cause me mother decorated it for me. She collects china and because she's run out of room indoors, she now stores it in mine.'

Frankie stared intently at the plates decorating the wall. They were beautiful and had horses pulling pretty little gypsy carts.

'You ever been on a horse and cart?' Jed asked her.

Frankie smiled. 'No. Why? Have you?'

Jed chuckled. 'Course I have, you dinlo. I used to race the bloody things. I tell you what, daylight's breaking now. Shall I harness one up and take you out for a ride?'

Frankie burst out laughing. 'Go on, then, let's do it.'

At 5.30 a.m., Jed and Frankie trotted off down the road. 'Hey up,' Jed shouted as he whipped the filly on the arse.

'I love where you live. Your life's so exciting, Jed. My house is so boring – it's nothing like yours.'

Jed held both reins in his right hand. He put his left arm around Frankie. 'Move in with me?'

'I can't. My dad will kill me,' Frankie replied immediately.

'Tell him about us. I ain't frightened of your father and neither should you be. He's gonna find out we're together one day, ain't he?'

Frankie sighed. 'Yeah, I know, but not yet. You don't know my dad – he'll go mental, I know he will.'

Approaching a bend, Jed held the reins back in both hands. 'Trot on,' he said, making a funny clicking noise with his mouth.

Thinking of her dad gave Frankie the heebie-jeebies. Say he drove along and saw her? Feeling worried all of a sudden, she laid her head on Jed's shoulder. 'I'm cold. Can we go back now? I haven't got to be home yet. We can go back to bed if you like.'

Jed turned his head and kissed her gently on the lips. 'I bet you marry me within a year. I'll bet you anything you like.'

Frankie burst out laughing. Jed oozed so much confidence. He had such a glow, you could almost warm your hands on him. Poking her tongue out, Frankie snatched the reins out of Jed's hands.

'Trot on,' she yelled. 'Trot on!'

Jimmy O'Hara had never been a man to lie in bed of a morning. His Alice was the same and they had their own little routines. Alice would get up like a good wife should and clean the house till it sparkled. Jimmy would feed the animals and do the dirty jobs, which men were supposed to do.

As he saw the horse and cart pull onto the drive, Jimmy's eyes widened. He had been aware of a horse trotting about earlier, but thought he had dreamed it. Seeing Jed jump off the cart, he threw down the bucket he was holding and moved nearer to see who the pretty little filly was. He had seen the girl before, she definitely looked familiar, but she didn't look like a travelling girl. His Jed was a dark horse. Jimmy had guessed by Jed's recent behaviour that he had met a bird he liked, but Jed had said very little about her.

Jimmy sneaked around the back of his house so he

could get a closer peek. Seeing Frankie not twenty yards from him, realisation crept in and Jimmy smiled with such gusto, it nearly pushed his teeth out. 'It's fucking Eddie Mitchell's girl,' Jimmy whispered as he ducked down, desperate not to be seen.

As Jed shut the door of his trailer, Jimmy stood up. Unable to stop himself, he laughed out loud. Eddie Mitchell was one flash bastard, and wiping the smile off his smarmy face would make Jimmy the happiest man in the universe.

# THIRTY-FIVE

Eddie was in a foul mood the following day. 'Where's the twins?' he asked Jess.

Jessica shrugged. 'They're not back yet. I think they stayed round their friend's house.'

Ed glared at her. 'Whaddya mean, you think? It's your duty to know where they are. I've told you time and time again to keep tabs on 'em. You're far too fucking lenient, Jess.'

'I do keep tabs on them, but just lately they've been a bit secretive. I've a feeling our Frankie's got a boyfriend and Joey's covering up for her,' Jessica said honestly.

'Your parenting skills leave a lot to be desired. Best you find out what Frankie's up to, 'cause if she comes home pregnant, I'll crucify her and fucking blame you,' Ed shouted as he slammed the kitchen door.

The twins finally arrived home at Saturday teatime. Desperate to know the truth about Joey, Eddie tried to call Gina, but her mobile was switched off. 'Bollocks,' Ed shouted, chucking his phone against the wall. The not knowing was torture. At least once he had some proof, he could do something about it.

On the Sunday morning, Jessica had a list of jobs for Ed to do and it wasn't until lunchtime, when her parents arrived, that Eddie had a chance to escape. 'Right, I've vacced your car and tidied up the garden. You're OK with your parents for a bit, ain't ya? I'm gonna take the dogs out for a run.'

Jessica gave him a dubious look. He never usually took Buster and Bruno for a run. The last time he had, there had been a murder and the police had come knocking on the door. 'You're not going far, are you? How long will you be?' Jessica asked him suspiciously.

'I dunno. For fuck's sake, Jess, I've worked me bollocks off all morning. Give us a break, will ya?'

Jessica felt uneasy as he left the house. She could always tell when Eddie had something on his mind and she was sure he was up to no good. He'd been in a funny mood for days now and certainly wasn't his chirpy self.

Bored with sitting with Stanley, Joyce walked into the kitchen. 'Let me help you, dear. Shall I peel some potatoes or veg for you?'

'You go and sit in the lounge with Dad. Everything's under control, Mum.'

'I can't sit in there with your father. Been doing my head in all weekend, he has. Just got himself a new cock, ain't he? It's all he talks about. Called it Willie, he has, as a tribute to Willie Carson. I mean, how can you call a cock Willie? Ain't normal, is it, Jess?'

Jessica burst out laughing. Her mother was hilarious and she didn't even realise it.

'There you are! Is Joey still in bed?' Jessica asked, as Frankie suddenly appeared.

Kissing her nan, Frankie flopped onto a chair. She

didn't want to be stuck in all day – she wanted to be out with Jed, but wasn't sure how to broach the subject. 'Joey's getting up now, Mum. I know we're having dinner and all that, but do you mind if I go out afterwards?'

Jessica felt her hackles rise. Frankie was always out lately and Jessica barely saw her. Sometimes she stayed out all night and Jessica had a feeling that she had met a boy and was up to Christ knows what. 'Will it hurt you to stay in for one day? Gary and Ricky are coming over, so are Raymond and Polly. This is meant to be a celebration for you and Joey leaving school.'

'Yeah, I know and I do appreciate it, but it's one of my friend's birthdays today and we're all meant to be going bowling. Please say I can go, Mum. I haven't got to go till after dinner.'

'Do as you like, Frankie, I don't care any more,' Jessica said bluntly. Her daughter was a selfish little cow and she was beginning to lose patience with her behaviour.

As Joey walked in, Frankie slunk into the lounge to see her grandfather.

'Mum, Joey, go and sit in the front room. I'll be in meself in a minute,' Jessica said. Her kitchen was enormous, but somehow people still managed to get under her feet.

Stanley told the twins all about his new cock. 'My Willie's a beauty. Faster than the speed of light, he is. My mates down at the pigeon club are so jealous. Two of 'em have already tried to buy him off me. They say he's the best cock they've ever seen.'

Frankie giggled. 'I'm sure Joey would like to see him, Grandad. He likes pigeons, especially cocks. Don't you, Joey?'

'Really? Why don't I pick you up in the week, Joey? You can come round and see him,' Stanley enthused.

'That would be lovely, Grandad,' Joey lied, glaring at his sister.

Deciding to get his own back, Joey turned to his nan. 'Do you think our Frankie looks like a gypsy, Nan? We was in a pub the other day and this travelling girl came up to us. She said she was positive that our Frankie had a bit of gypsy in her.'

Joyce was furious. 'Of course she don't. Christ, she don't wanna look like one of them tinkers. Never trusted the bastards, I ain't. Years ago, when your mum was little, I had one knock on me front door. She was selling lucky heather and when I refused to buy any, she told me that bad luck was coming my way. The next morning, I got up, tripped down the stairs and broke me bloody arm. Even to this day, I swear she put a curse on me. Evil bastards they are. If you have the misfortune of meeting one again, don't have nothing to do with 'em, will you?'

Joey smirked at his sister. 'Of course not Nan. We wouldn't dream of having any dealings with gypsies, would we Frankie?'

Eddie Mitchell tied the dogs to the wooden table and went inside the Optimist to get a drink. His mouth was as dry as a nun's crotch and he didn't know whether it was due to the hot weather or the impending phone call he had to make.

Eddie thanked the barmaid and went back outside. Buster and Bruno were lying on their backs having their stomachs tickled by some old boy in a trilby hat.

'Good guard dogs you're gonna be,' Eddie muttered, as he walked towards the table. He had been training them to growl and bark at strangers, not lie on their backs with their legs up in the air.

'Beautiful day, isn't it?' the man in the hat commented to Eddie.

'Wonderful, mate,' Eddie replied sarcastically. He was too worried about his gay son to get involved in pointless small talk.

As the man walked away, Eddie downed his whisky chaser in one. His heart was pumping nineteen to the dozen at the thought of what he might be about to hear. He rang Gina's number and took a deep breath as she answered.

'Well?' he asked, trying to sound calm.

'I have all the information you wanted, Mr Smith, including photographs.'

'What did you find out?' Eddie asked abruptly.

'I'll tell you everything when we meet up. I did an eighteen-hour stint to find out all the information you required. I now need to arrange collection for the remainder of the money I'm owed.'

'Can I meet you now? Please, my mate's desperate to find out the score,' Eddie pleaded

'Well, it's a bit awkward. I have to attend a function at three o'clock at a friend's house.'

'I'll meet you now. Anywhere that suits you. I'll pay you extra, make it worth your while.'

Gina sighed. Mr Smith was a very generous but difficult client and, due to her crush on him, she couldn't say no. 'My friend lives in Benfleet. Do you know the Tarpots? I can meet you there at two-forty-five.'

'I'll be there,' Eddie responded immediately.

Overcome by anxiety, Eddie got himself another pint and a whisky chaser. He didn't know what he was going to say to Jessica. With everyone due around for dinner, she was bound to go apeshit at him.

As Buster and Bruno tried to clamber up his leg, he

sipped his drink and stroked their heads. 'Why is my life so fucking difficult, boys? Yous two have got it easy. When I die, I'm coming back as a fucking dog!'

Jessica basted the roast potatoes and slammed the oven door shut. Where the bloody hell had Eddie got to?

'All right to get another beer, Jess?' Gary asked.

'Help yourself, love. Can you make sure everyone's got a drink for me? Christ knows where your father is. He was only taking the dogs for a run and he's been gone nearly two hours. I can't do everything, Gary. I'm trying to cook the bloody dinner.'

Gary squeezed Jessica's arm. 'You just concentrate on the food and I'll deal with everything else. Once I've sorted the drinks out, I'll give the old man a ring, see where he's got to.'

'Thanks, love. I already tried to ring him twice, but he's not answering his phone,' Jessica said gratefully.

Shouting at the dogs to stop yelping, Eddie sped down the A13. Aware that his phone was ringing yet again, he answered it. 'Where are you, Dad? Jess has got the right needle,' Gary informed him.

Eddie didn't want anyone to know where he was going. 'I've lost one of the dogs, Gal. Buster bolted into the woods and I'm hunting for him now.'

'Me and Ricky'll come and help you find him,' Gary offered.

'No, don't worry. I've got a couple of dog walkers helping me. Look, do us a favour, son. I don't wanna upset the kids, so tell Jess on the quiet. I won't come back till I've found him – he can't have gone far.'

Gary ended the call and went to find Jessica to explain. 'I can't understand why he took 'em out in the car in the first place. We're inundated with fields around here. Where has he taken them?'

Gary shrugged. 'He didn't exactly say, but he mentioned the woods.'

Jessica thanked Gary and began cutting the meat. Her husband's story sounded a little bit too far-fetched for her liking.

Not sure where they were supposed to be meeting, Eddie rang Gina as he drove into Benfleet.

'Follow the road straight down and the pub comes up on your right. I'm sitting in the car park in a black Nissan Micra,' Gina told him.

Eddie spotted her immediately and parked right next to her. 'What have you got?' he asked, as he squeezed his big frame into her small passenger seat.

Gina handed him Dominic's name and address. 'Your friend's suspicions were correct,' she said, getting straight to the point.

'Where's the photos?' Eddie asked, his heart feeling like a lump of lead.

Gina handed him a sealed envelope. 'Your friend might want to look at these in private, Mr Smith,' she said diplomatically.

Eddie nodded and handed her a wad of money. 'There's sixteen hundred quid there. Fifteen that I promised you and a oner on top for meeting me today.'

'You've paid me far too much. Please, take some back,' Gina urged. Her heart was beating like a drum, as she'd never been so close to him before.

Eddie opened the car door. 'You keep it, love, but promise me: what you saw, you'll never breathe a word. My pal's an important geezer and he wouldn't be happy if any of this got out.'

'You have my word and my word is my bond. I can guarantee you, your friend has nothing to worry about. I work in a very clandestine manner, Mr Smith.'

Watching Gina drive away, Eddie decided to head back nearer to home before he opened the envelope. He would probably write his Land Cruiser off down the A13 if he opened it in Benfleet. Dreading what the contents held, Eddie started the engine and sped off like a loony.

Annoyed that her day had been thoroughly spoilt, Jessica barely touched her dinner.

'You not hungry, Mum?' Joey asked, concerned.

'No, love. Has everyone finished? I'll take the plates out.'

'Would you like me to give you a hand?' Polly asked politely.

'That's a first. You don't usually lift a cup,' Raymond joked.

With Polly's help, Jessica cleared the table and organised the dessert. If Ed wasn't home by the time the strawberry pavlova was eaten, then sod him, she would announce her good news alone.

'I don't want afters. Is it all right if I go out now, Mum?' Frankie whinged.

'No, it's not. Sit down and shut up for five minutes,' Jessica spat back.

'I don't think I like that, dear. What's it called?' Stanley asked, pointing to the dessert.

'Pavlova! You always have to be awkward, Stanley, don't you?' Joyce said.

'Don't worry, Dad. I've got a blackberry crumble as well. Just waiting for it to warm up. I forgot to turn the oven back on again.'

375

Half an hour later, everybody was full to the brim.

'Thanks, Jess, that was lovely,' Ricky remarked as he helped his stepmum take the dishes out to the kitchen.

'So, how's your father's business doing, Polly? Has he been affected by this recession at all?' Joyce asked nosily.

Stanley felt sorry for his son's girlfriend. For the past hour, all Joyce had done was give her the third degree. 'For goodness' sake, woman. Can't you change the subject?' he said bravely.

'Shut up and mind your own business,' Joyce snapped back.

Jessica handed two bottles of champagne to Ricky and told him to open them. Handing everybody a champagne flute, Jessica topped up their glasses.

'Is this to toast my wonderful grandchildren?' Stanley asked, winking at the twins.

Jessica smiled. She felt sad that Eddie wasn't here to join in, but Frankie was waiting to go out, so what could she do?

Urging Joey and Frankie to stand up, Jessica grinned at them. 'My little babies have now left school and are about to start looking for jobs. To Frankie and Joey – we all wish you every success in your future,' she proclaimed.

'To Frankie and Joey,' everyone repeated.

Frankie knocked her champagne straight back. She was aching to see Jed. 'Can I go out now, Mum?' she asked cheekily.

Jessica hated giving speeches. Eddie was good at them, but she wasn't, and even felt nervous in front of her close family. Urging Frankie to sit back down, Jessica cleared her throat. 'I've got some news of my own. I know Mum and Joey have both commented on me putting on a bit of weight recently. Well, there is a reason for this. I'm pregnant! Eddie and I are going to be parents again, and

Joey and Frankie are going to have a little brother or sister.'

An expert at overacting, Joyce leaped up and down like a kangaroo. 'That's wonderful. Oh Stanley, we're gonna be grandparents again,' she squealed with delight.

'Congratulations, dear,' Stanley said in a monotone voice. He still didn't like Eddie – never had and never would. He loved his grandchildren, though, and would certainly welcome another.

Joey turned to Frankie and pretended to put his fingers down the back of his throat.

'It's disgusting. How old are they? I hope they don't expect us to wipe its arse and babysit, 'cause I won't,' Frankie whispered to her brother.

Aware that the twins' reaction hadn't been one of utter joy, Jessica spoke softly to them. 'You'll always be Mummy's favourites. You were my first born,' she assured them.

'Ain't you a bit old?' Joey asked her bluntly.

'Don't expect me to look after it,' Frankie chipped in.

Jessica smiled. They were probably a bit jealous, bless them. She was sure they would get used to the idea once the baby was born, and would make wonderful siblings for him or her.

'Go on, you can go out now, Frankie. Are you going out as well, Joey?'

'Yep,' Joey said, as he shoved Frankie out of the room. A screaming brat in the house was the last thing either of them needed.

Raymond hugged his sister. 'Me and Polly are thrilled for you,' he said kindly.

'Who wants more champagne? Me and Ricky are gonna be bruvvers again and that deserves a celebration on its own, don't it, bruv?' Gary said.

Ricky agreed and gave Jessica a squeeze. 'Gal, ring Dad again, see where he is,' he ordered his brother.

Not wanting anyone listening in, Gary wandered out into the garden and rang his dad's number. Unbeknown to Jessica, he had been ringing him for the last hour, but couldn't get any response. The more he thought about the Buster story, the more he knew his dad had been lying. 'What the fuck is going on?' Gary said out loud, as once again he received no answer. Unbeknownst to Gary, Eddie was back in the Optimist. Finishing his fourth pint, Ed untied the dogs' leads. He was dreading looking in that envelope. He knew by Gina's voice and face that the contents were bad news, but it was now or never and he had to know the truth.

Lifting the dogs into the back of the Land Cruiser, he sat in the driver's seat and ripped the envelope open. As Eddie stared at the picture of his son kissing Dominic, he repeatedly smashed his fist against the steering wheel. Taking a deep breath, he looked at the rest. The worst one was the last one. His son, his own flesh and blood, had his hand placed on Dominic's cobblers.

Aware of a watery taste in his mouth, Eddie opened his door and retched his guts up.

Conscious of a couple looking at him, Eddie started the engine and sped off. He stopped in a lay-by in the middle of nowhere and got out of the motor again. Furious, he banged his head against the passenger door.

'Fuck, fuck, fuck!' he screamed.

Distraught, Eddie got back into the motor. Fishing through his pockets, he found Dominic's address. Islington, the bastard lived, and his name was Dominic King.

Eddie restarted the engine. 'More like Queen, not fucking King,' he mumbled.

Heading towards another pub, Eddie took deep breaths. He couldn't go home yet; he needed to calm himself down first. He musn't let Jessica, Raymond or anyone clock onto his findings. He had to act normal, it was the only way.

Tomorrow he would pay this Dominic a visit. He would give him King – he would dethrone the cunt.

# THIRTY-SIX

Jessica was furious with her husband's behaviour and, as he made an appearance the following morning, she neither glanced at nor spoke to him. He had eventually come home around midnight. She had been in bed, but had heard the dogs barking and him staggering about downstairs.

She knew he was drunk. It wasn't often Eddie got like that now, but she could always tell when he was by the amount of noise he made and the length of time it took him to reach the top of the stairs.

Something was troubling him, she knew that. Eddie hadn't been himself for weeks and Jessica wondered if he had raked up some new information about his father's murder. He hadn't even slept in their bedroom, but had gone into the spare room.

As Jessica banged the kettle against the worktop, Eddie stopped eating his cereal and tried to cuddle her. 'I'm sorry about yesterday. It took me hours to find Buster and then something else cropped up. I'll make it up to your mum and dad, I promise. Got a lot on me plate at the moment, I have, Jess.'

Jessica was angry. Men were so full of themselves at times. 'And so have I, Ed. I've got a lot on my plate, as well. Have you forgotten that I'm carrying our third child? I'm sick of clearing up after everyone here. The twins don't lift a finger and since you brought them dogs home, the place is a tip. Full of hairs, it is, and I now have to clean twice a day, instead of once. Also, I'm worried about Frankie. I know she's turned sixteen now, but I don't like her staying out all night. I'm sure she's got a boyfriend she's not telling us about. I asked her outright the other day, but she denied it, of course.'

Eddie felt the hairs on the back of his neck stand up. He had enough problems with Joey without Frankie being at it as well.

Joey walking into the kitchen stopped the conversation dead. 'Morning Mum, morning Dad,' Joey said brightly.

The sight of his son put Eddie off the remainder of his cornflakes. Joey disgusted him and he would never forget those photographs as long as he lived.

'Do you want me to make you some breakfast, love?' Jessica asked Joey.

'Not really hungry, Mum. You got any fruit? I fancy a banana.'

Remembering the snap where Joey had his hand around his boyfriend's nether regions, Eddie threw his cornflakes into the bin and stomped upstairs.

'What's up with him? Yous two had a row?' Joey asked his mum.

Jessica shrugged. 'I don't know what's the matter with him. Don't worry, it can't be anything to do with you, Joey. If Dad had found out anything about Dominic, he'd have said something to me, I know he would. Maybe it's to do with Grandad Harry. Perhaps he's heard some rumours about what happened to him, or something.'

Joey hugged his mum. He had always been closer to

her than he had to his father, and since she had supported him over his sexuality, he loved her more than ever.

'If I ask you something, Joey, will you tell me the truth?'

'Of course, what do you want to know?'

'I know Frankie's got a boyfriend and I want to know why she's being so secretive about him.'

Joey didn't know what to say. He couldn't drop Frankie in it, so made up the first excuse he could think of. 'Frankie gets embarrassed, Mum. All she's told me is his name. She's never had a proper boyfriend before, so I think it's all new to her. His name's John, apparently, and I'm sure in time she'll bring him home so we can all meet him.'

Jessica pushed Joey's hair off his forehead. He was such a sensitive boy and had a gift for putting her mind at rest. 'Where you off to today?' she asked him.

'I'm going shopping in Romford. Its Dom's birthday next weekend and he's taking me to a posh restaurant to celebrate. He bought me a lovely bracelet for my birthday, Mum. I've hidden it upstairs, but I'll show you it later,' Joey whispered.

Jessica smiled. Her son was in love and, in her own way, she was pleased for him. She would rather Joey be in love with a girl, but he was sixteen now and old enough to make his own choices in life. 'I wish you every happiness, Joey, I really do,' Jessica whispered back.

Aware of Eddie's footsteps approaching, Jessica told Joey to sit down and eat his banana.

'I'm going out now. Got a lot of work on today, so I dunno what time I'll be home,' Eddie growled.

Not able to be in the same room as his son, Eddie turned on his heel without waiting for an answer. The quicker he got out of the house, the less physically sick he would feel.

\* \* \*

Frankie woke up feeling like nothing on earth. She was meant to be going over to Kent with Jed to drop off a horse that he'd sold, but she felt too ill to do so. She rang him up to explain. 'I'm so sorry, Jed. I've been as sick as a pig. Do you feel OK? I think that Chinese we ate last night was a bit dodgy.'

Jed laughed. 'You see me, Frankie – never had a day's illness in me life. I ain't even on no doctor's books. I've told you before, you don't eat enough meat. Meat makes you strong, makes you healthy, it does. Fit as a fiddle, I am.'

'How long will you be in Kent for? Can I see you when you get back?' Frankie asked, changing the subject. Talking about meat was making her feel worse than ever.

'Well, if you ain't coming, I might have to take me other bird with me, so I might not be back till tomorrow,' Jed goaded her.

Knowing he was only winding her up, Frankie managed a smile. 'Don't muck about, you tosser.'

'I'll be back this afternoon. I'll ring you when I'm through the tunnel. Tell your mum and dad you're staying at your mate's tonight and stay at mine.'

'OK,' Frankie said immediately. Even though things were getting awkward at home, with her mum asking all sorts of questions, she still couldn't resist spending the night with him. Waking up with Jed in the morning was the best feeling in the whole wide world. Frankie said goodbye to him and struggled onto the landing.

'Mum, I feel really ill. I've been sick twice, I think I've got food poisoning. Bring me up some medicine, will you?' she shouted.

When the kids were younger, Jessica used to be frantic if they had any kind of illness. Since they had got older, she didn't worry too much. She was sure that alcohol played a part in many of their little off days. They drank like fish indoors, so Christ knows what they were sinking when they were out gallivanting with friends.

Fishing through the cupboards, Jessica took a box of tablets upstairs. 'I've got some Setlers. Take two of them,' she said, handing Frankie the box.

Seeing how washed-out her daughter looked, Jessica sat down on the edge of her bed. 'You're having too many late nights and you're drinking too much, that's your trouble. You're only sixteen, Frankie, your body can't cope with being abused on a regular basis.'

Frankie took the tablets, and then lay flat on her back. She felt like death warmed up and a lecture from her mother was the last thing she needed. 'I'm staying round Stacey's tonight, but I promise I won't drink,' Frankie lied.

Jessica squeezed her daughter's hand. 'Don't fib to me, Frankie. I know you've got a boyfriend and I know you've been spending a lot of time with him. If I've accepted Joey's relationship, what makes you think that I wouldn't accept yours? You've left school now, so you're entitled to have a boyfriend. Why don't you bring him round for tea one day, so me and your dad can meet him?'

Overcome by anxiety, Frankie burst into tears and put her head under the quilt. 'Just leave me alone and go away,' she yelled.

Shaking her head in disbelief, Jessica said no more. She stood up and left her daughter to her tantrum.

Sitting outside the pub in Islington, Eddie sipped his drink and stared at the flats across the road. For the last hour he had been watching every bastard that entered the building and there was still no sign of gay boy Dominic. He had buzzed number fourteen earlier, but there was no

384

reply. He guessed Dominic was working. He was a lot older than Joey and, from what he could remember of seeing him at his house, the boy seemed intelligent and well dressed.

Eddie sighed. If Frankie had brought Dominic home, he would have been reasonably happy about it, but not fucking Joey.

Thinking back to when his son was young, Eddie knew that the signs had always been there. He had wanted to stick his oar in years ago and toughen the kid up but, frightened Jessica would leave him again, he had kept his trap shut. Ed had let Jessica bring the twins up in the way she thought was right and now he could have kicked himself.

A son needed a dad to take him in hand, show him what the world was all about. Eddie had missed out on all that with Joey. He had been out working a lot and Jessica had cracked the whip, not him. Trouble was, she hadn't cracked it hard enough. Lost in his thoughts, Eddie almost did a double take as he saw the tall, dark-haired geezer letting himself in the security door.

'Who's a pretty boy then?' Eddie mumbled as he walked back into the pub for a refill.

Dominic had been indoors just over an hour when the buzzer sounded. He hated travelling on the underground; all those sweaty people made him feel grubby and he had just got out of the bath. Throwing on his white dressing gown, Dominic rushed to answer the door.

'Hello, who is it?'

'Royal Mail, mate. I've got a delivery for you.'

Dominic was perplexed. He had nothing on order, to his knowledge. Suddenly it came to him. Joey must have sent him an early birthday present. His boyfriend was such a sweetie sometimes, he really was.

As Dominic opened the front door, the force of Eddie's fist sent him the full length of the hallway. As his dressing gown flew open, he quickly tried to cover his glory. 'What do you want? Please don't hurt me.' he sobbed as he recognised Joey's father.

Eddie shut the door. 'You got a stereo, Pretty Boy?' he asked.

'It's in the l-l-living r-r-room,' Dominic stammered. It wasn't just his voice that was shaking, his whole body was quivering like an unset jelly.

Eddie made Dominic get up and turn the stereo system on. 'Find a decent radio station, like that new one, Capital Gold. Turn it up loud, then kneel on the floor,' he ordered.

'I don't k-k-know the frequency,' Dominic whimpered.

Eddie forced Dominic to lie flat on his face next to the stereo. Ed liked to whistle while he worked and Capital Gold played all the oldies that he liked. Putting his boot on the back of Dominic's neck to stop him from moving, Eddie found what he was looking for.

'A Whiter Shade of Pale' by Procol Harum was playing and as Eddie turned Dominic over, he thought how appropriate the song was. The colour of Pretty Boy's face was whiter than fucking snow.

'Please d-don't kill me. I p-p-promise I will never see Joey again, if that's what you w-w-want,' Dominic begged, terrified.

Eddie smiled. 'Got any beers?' he asked.

'In the f-f-fridge.'

'If you move, I'll kill you,' Eddie told him.

Bringing in a pack of four, Eddie handed one to his son's lover. 'Drink it,' he said, as he sat on the sofa.

As Dominic got up to sit on the armchair opposite, Eddie threw an unopened can at his head. 'Get down on the floor, you cunt. I never said you could get up, did I now?'

'Sorry. I'm so sorry,' Dominic pleaded, as he lay on his front.

Eddie sipped his lager. Trust Pretty Boy to only have Carlsberg. Weak person, weak lager.

'Turn over on your back,' Eddie ordered him.

Shivering, Dominic clutched his dressing down around himself and did as he was told. He was so petrified that his voice had temporarily gone on holiday.

Finishing the lager, Eddie crushed the can in his right hand and smiled as Dominic flinched. 'Do you know what this song's about?' Eddie asked him.

Capital Gold was now playing the Bee Gees' classic, 'Gotta Get a Message to You'.

'No. I don't k-k-know m-many oldies,' Dominic managed to whisper.

'It's about someone who's gonna die and wants to send a message to their loved ones,' Eddie informed him.

'Please d-d-don't kill me. I bbeg you,' Dominic pleaded. 'I p-p-promise, I'll do whatever you ask.'

Knowing that Dominic was telling the truth, Eddie decided to give him just one last little scare. He had no intention of killing him. After the unfortunate Terry Palmer incident, he had to let his bullets lie low for a while. Eddie didn't fancy a stretch inside. Not only that, Jess leaving him would break his heart, and she was worth more to him than Pretty Boy was.

Taking the carving knife out of the inside pocket of his leather jacket, Eddie bent down. 'Open your dressing gown,' he demanded.

Dominic's hand shook like a leaf as he tried to undo the belt, but couldn't. Not one to see a man struggling, Eddie did the honours for him.

'Please, no!' Dominic screamed, holding his hands over his penis and shaking his head from side to side in fright.

As Eddie looked at Dominic's flaccid dick, he tried to erase his son from his mind. One thought of Joey wanking it or sucking it, he would chop the bastard thing off in a flash.

As Dominic screamed in anticipation, Eddie turned the radio up a bit louder. The geezer was a typical weasel, and Eddie didn't want the neighbours knocking on the door.

Lifting Dominic's cock up with the knife, Eddie held the blade to it and stared deeply into his victim's eyes. 'You ring Joey tomorrow and you tell him it's all over. I want you to let him down as kindly as possible, just say he's too young or something. If he won't accept that, you tell him you've met someone else.'

'I will, I will, I p-p-promise,' Dominic wept.

Eddie smiled at Dominic's anguish. Unable to resist terrorising Dominic even more, Ed flopped his penis over and made the slightest of cuts on the tip. 'You see that? Look, it's your blood.'

'I can't look. I c-c-can't, I've got a phobia of b-b-blood,' Dominic whispered.

'Well, I'll tell you something, shall I? If you ever set foot within a hundred yards of my son again, I will hunt you down and chop that little knob of yours off for you. Then I'll pick it up with me bare hands and ram it straight down the back of your throat until you choke on it. Now, do we understand one another?'

'I u-u-understand. I'll tell Joey t-tomorrow. You h-h-have my w-word,' Dominic sobbed.

With a wry grin on his face, Eddie wiped the blood off his knife onto Dominic's dressing gown. He then turned the radio up full blast and calmly left the flat.

# THIRTY-SEVEN

From the moment Joey received the phone call from Dominic, he was totally inconsolable. He couldn't eat or sleep, and for the next forty-eight hours refused to get out of his bed.

By day three, Jessica was really worried about her son. She had told Eddie that Joey had the flu, but with his constant tantrums and tears, it was getting harder for her to cover for him. As luck would have it, Eddie had been at work for the last couple of days and hadn't asked too many questions. Today, he was at home and Jessica was dreading him being there.

A while back when Eddie had hit the roof over the Dominic rumours, Jessica had told her husband that Joey had a new girlfriend. Fortunately, Joey had taken her advice and brought a girl around for tea. The doubts about Joey's sexuality had ceased to exist since that day and Jessica didn't want the worry of anything fresh coming out into the open.

Having now forgiven Eddie for disappearing last Sunday, Jessica smiled as he sat down at the kitchen table next to Frankie. 'Who's hungry? I've got a fresh crusty loaf and a nice bit of butcher's ham if anyone wants a sandwich,' Jessica said.

'I'll have ham and tomato,' Frankie said immediately.

'I'll have the same,' Eddie said, tickling his daughter to annoy her.

'Stop it, Dad. You're hurting me,' Frankie giggled.

'I'm not stopping till you tell me and your mother who this new boyfriend of yours is. What's the big secret? He ain't my age, is he?'

As Frankie wriggled on the floor to get away from her father, Eddie kneeled on her arms so she couldn't move. 'Seize,' he ordered Buster and Bruno, who tried to lick her to death.

'Get off, Dad,' Frankie yelled as the dogs slobbered all over her face.

'Not until I know who this geezer is. I'm your father, I have every right to know. If it weren't for me, you wouldn't even be here,' Eddie taunted her.

'He's not your age and his name's John. I met him down the Albion. Now, get off me, Dad, seriously, you're hurting my arms.'

Joining in the fun, Jessica repeatedly hit Eddie with the tea towel. 'Come on, enough's enough,' she said laughing.

Frankie ate her sandwich in silence. Life was becoming more awkward by the day for her.

'Why don't you ask your boyfriend if he wants to come round for dinner tonight, love?' Jessica enquired.

Sick of being interrogated and not having a good enough answer, Frankie stood up. 'Just leave me alone, the pair of you. John and I aren't even serious yet, so why do you have to poke your noses in and try and spoil everything for me?' she yelled, running up the stairs.

Eddie ran into the hallway. 'Best you and that brother of yours stop going out partying all the time and look for a fucking job instead,' he shouted up the stairs after her.

Ed had only been mucking about with her, the miserable little cow.

'Don't shout at her, Eddie. I think she's got her period or something,' Jess told him.

'I couldn't give a fuck what she's got! I'm not having all this for much longer, Jess. They both wanted to leave school at sixteen, so now they can go and get a fucking job. I was ten years old when I started work and I've always worked since. They're a lazy pair of bastards. All they do is doss about – they don't lift a finger in here. Going out on the piss all the time ain't gonna get 'em far in life. Once they've spent their birthday money, that's it, they ain't getting no more. They expect continuous handouts and it's as much as they can do to say thank you. Well, I'm putting me foot down from now on. Too soft we've been with 'em, and this is the fucking result of it.'

Aware that Ed's eyes had started to cloud over, Jessica quickly changed the subject. 'I'm sure I felt the baby moving this morning, Ed. It's the first time, I've really felt it. Shall we go shopping tomorrow? We can get the cot and a few other bits.'

The mention of his unborn child put a smile back on Eddie's face. He put his arms around Jessica from behind and gently fondled her stomach. 'How about we choose some wallpaper and stuff and I'll make a start on changing the spare room into a nursery.'

Jessica turned around and threw her arms around his neck. 'Oh, Ed, that sounds wonderful.'

Frankie sat on the edge of her brother's bed. 'You can't carry on like this, Joey. Why don't you ring Dom? Talk to him.'

Joey's eyes filled up with tears once again. 'I've tried. He keeps putting the phone down on me. I can't understand it, we were getting on OK. Dominic always treated me well. He loved me, I know he did, and last week he even spoke about me moving into his flat sometime soon. It doesn't make sense, Frankie. He hasn't even been out to meet anyone else, yet he said he's fallen for some other bloke.'

'You don't reckon it's got anything to do with Dad, do you? Maybe he found out and threatened him or something.'

Joey shrugged. 'I doubt it. Surely Dad would have gone mental at me if he knew something. I wonder if Dom's met someone at work; maybe a new bloke's just started there or something.'

'Why don't you go up to where he works. Wait outside the building, you can see for yourself then. I'll even come with you, if you want.'

Joey and Frankie's conversation was ended by a gentle tapping on the bedroom door.

'I've made you a nice ham sandwich and cup of tea. You can't keep starving yourself, Joey, you need to eat something, love,' Jessica said, walking into the room.

Jessica was as surprised as anyone that her son's relationship had fallen to pieces but, in a way, she was relieved. At least she didn't have to worry about Eddie finding out now.

Joey refused the sandwich. 'Go away, Mum. I'm not hungry,' he cried.

He couldn't bear to speak to anyone apart from Frankie.

Eddie crept up the stairs and stopped halfway, listening to the conversation.

Jessica lifted up the plate and handed it to Joey. 'Please, just eat half for Mummy.'

'Stop treating me like a fucking child. I don't want the poxy sandwich. Go away and leave me alone. If you keep on at me, I'm gonna kill myself.' Joey screamed as he knocked the plate out of her hand.

Hearing the plate smash, Eddie saw red. How dare he talk to his mother like that? The queer little ponce. Opening Joey's bedroom door, Eddie picked up half the sandwich off the floor.

'Eat it, you cunt,' he ordered.

'Stop it, Ed!' Jessica screamed.

'Leave him alone, Dad,' Frankie yelled.

Overcome by a vision of Joey having a big dick in his mouth, Eddie held back his son's head and shoved the sandwich in there. 'Eat it, fucking eat it!' he yelled.

As Joey began to make choking noises, Jessica pummelled Eddie with her fists. 'If you hurt him, I'm leaving you,' she screamed hysterically.

Frankie jumped on top of her brother to shield him from their father. 'Get off him, you bully,' she shouted.

'You're no son of mine. Never was and never will be,' Eddie spat as he left the room.

Making sure that Joey was not hurt in any way, Jessica left him with Frankie and chased her husband down the stairs. 'How dare you treat our son like that? What's got into you, Eddie? If you ever lay your hands on him again, we're finished.'

'What's got into me? I'll tell you what's got into me, shall I? How do you think that him sucking blokes' cocks makes me look, eh? Every time I look at him, he makes me feel sick. I'm ashamed to call him my son. You knew all about it, didn't you? You knew he was at it with that Dominic and you allowed it to continue. What type of mother does that make you, eh?'

Jessica looked at Eddie in amazement. He had obviously known about Dominic all along. 'It was you that ended their relationship, wasn't it? What did you do, beat

Dominic up? Threaten to kill him? Violence is all you know, isn't it, Eddie? Well, that might be part of your world, but it's not part of mine. I'm a good mother and I love my children whatever they are.'

Eddie gave a sarcastic laugh. 'Yeah, and you've done a fantastic job, ain't ya? We've got a daughter out on the piss all night, shagging Christ knows who and a son who's away with the fucking fairies. Well done, Jess, what a wonderful job you did. You see, when our next baby is born, I'm taking over the parenting and I mean that, Jess. Our next kid will be raised my way.'

Jessica burst into tears, 'You can be such a nasty bastard at times, Eddie, you really can.'

Eddie picked up his keys. Usually, whenever Jessica turned on the waterworks, it tugged at his heartstrings, but not today. He was furious with her for allowing Joey to carry on seeing Dominic, fucking furious. 'I'm going down the pub, don't wait up,' he said, as he slammed the front door.

Hearing their dad's car pull off the drive, Joey and Frankie both ran downstairs. They had been earwigging and had heard every word.

'Well, at least I now know why Dominic finished with me. I'm just relieved he's not in love with someone else. I'm gonna meet him from work next week, tell him I know that my dad paid him a visit. Maybe we can sort things out. What do you think, Mum?'

Jessica smiled sadly. Joey had caused all this fracas, yet he was only bothered about himself. Frankie was the same – in fact, she was probably even more selfish than Joey was. Perhaps Eddie was right. Maybe she was a terrible mother and should let him bring up the next child, the way that he saw right.

'Are you OK, Mum?' Joey asked, aware that she was looking at him strangely.

'Not really. I'm going to have a lie down.'

Without even glancing back at her children, Jessica tearfully left the room.

Not that far away, someone else was planning to cause a spot of bother. Jimmy O'Hara was well aware that Eddie Mitchell had been creeping into one of their local pubs recently. Michael Murphy was a cousin of Patrick's and he spent half his life propping up the bar of the Optimist.

Three days ago, on finding out his son was dating Frankie Mitchell, Jimmy had given Michael a ring. 'As soon as Eddie Mitchell comes into that pub again, call me. I'll make it worth your while, Mickey boy,' Jimmy told him.

Jimmy was feeding his chickens when his mobile phone rang.

'Jimmy, it's Michael. Eddie Mitchell has just walked in.'

Jimmy smiled as he dropped the food and ran towards his pick-up truck. It was finally time for a bit of action.

Eddie munched on a packet of dry-roasted peanuts and gulped back his pint. As his phone rang, he answered it and was surprised to hear Jessica on the other end. 'What's up?' he asked abruptly.

'Oh, Ed, I'm sorry. I'm having a lie down and I've been thinking about what you said. I have been too easy on the twins, I know I have. I'm gonna toughen up, you know. What you said this morning about them getting a job makes sense. They have too much time on their hands and I think a bit of responsibility would do them the world of good.'

Eddie smirked. He just loved being proved right. 'No more hiding things from me about Joey, Jess. He either starts dating girls or he stays fucking celibate. I'm not having him make a fool out of me again. I'll disown him next time and sling him out the house, I swear on my life, I will.'

'Please don't say things like that, Ed. Things are awkward for Joey, and I still think you were out of order earlier. You nearly choked the poor little sod. He's probably just going through a phase, I'm sure he'll grow out of it.'

'Well, if he don't, he'll be moving to the fucking Hebrides or somewhere,' Eddie said angrily.

'All right, Eddie? Can I get you a drink, mush?'

Telling Jessica they would talk later, Eddie ended the call and stared at Jimmy O'Hara's ugly face. 'No, I'm all right, thanks,' Eddie replied.

As O'Hara walked to the bar, Eddie cursed himself for drinking locally. 'This is all I fucking need,' he muttered. He couldn't just get up and walk out – he would make himself look like a right mug. Letting the pikey bastard know that he bothered him was the last thing Eddie wanted.

'So, how's business?' Jimmy asked as he sat down opposite Eddie.

'Yeah, going well. What about you?'

Jimmy smiled. 'Good. I don't do so much meself now. I'm happy pottering about at home doing a bit of buying and selling.'

'How's your wife?' Eddie asked politely.

'My Alice is fine. She's a good woman, she is. What about your Jess?'

'Pregnant,' Eddie said smugly.

'Well, I'll be blowed. So is my Alice,' Jimmy told him, smirking back.

About to make his excuses and leave, Eddie was shocked to see the barman bring over a bottle of champagne and plonk it on the table. 'I never ordered this,' Ed said immediately.

'I did. With our families getting it together, I thought me and you should have a little celebration,' Jimmy said grinning.

Eddie looked at him in bewilderment. Surely Ronny and Paulie hadn't joined forces with the O'Haras. If they had, it would be the worst mistake they had ever made. He would be straight up the Flag and would kill the pair of them with his bare hands. 'Whaddya talking about?' Eddie asked.

'Don't you know?' Jimmy asked, chuckling.

Eddie was getting annoyed now. He hated being in the dark about anything, least of all with Jimmy O'Hara. With his expression getting darker by the second, Eddie felt his bottom lip curl up. 'Know fucking what?'

Jimmy was loving every minute of it. Mitchell was already losing his rag and he didn't even know the full story yet, the mug.

Jimmy smiled. 'Your Frankie and my Jed. Well loved-up, they are. Your daughter's always staying on my land in his trailer. Probably at it like rabbits as we speak – you know what these kids are like.'

Unable to stop himself, Eddie leaped up and grabbed O'Hara by the throat. 'Don't lie. This ain't fucking funny, Jimmy. Whatever problems we've had in the past, it's nothing to do with my daughter.'

Michael Murphy walked over. 'Are you OK, Jimmy? What's the problem?'

Jimmy knocked Eddie's hand away and poured two glasses of champagne. He hated the stuff, but had bought it out of devilment. Sipping the shit, Jimmy smiled. 'On my Alice's life, I'm not joking. My Jed and your Frankie are inseparable. They was even out five o'clock the other morning riding up and down on the horse and cart. Let's not argue, Eddie. I mean they'll probably end up getting married, so we have to try to get along for their sake!'

Eddie picked up his glass of champagne and threw the contents into Jimmy O'Hara's unsightly face. 'Over my dead fucking body,' he spat, as he stormed out of the pub.

Approaching his Land Cruiser, Eddie took his frustrations out on the driver's-side door. 'I'll kill the little pikey cunt, I'll fucking kill him,' Ed yelled as he repeatedly kicked the metal as hard as he could.

Aware of Jimmy watching him out of the window, Eddie jumped in his motor and zoomed off.

Eddie was absolutely livid. O'Hara had almost creamed himself while telling him the story. Loved it, the arsehole had, and Eddie sensed that it was probably true. It all made sense. The secrecy, the lies and an invisible boyfriend with a fucking pseudonym.

As he drove for miles, Eddie felt like he had taken a dozen punches from a heavyweight boxer. He had no idea where he was going, the thought hadn't entered his head. Spotting a pub, Eddie swung into the car park. He had to catch Frankie red-handed before he could do anything about it, but there was no point in him following her. She was too cute and he couldn't risk alerting her that he knew.

Making up his mind, Eddie took the business card out of his pocket and punched the number into his phone. 'Gina, it's John Smith. I've got another job for you, but I need you to do it first thing tomorrow.'

'I can't do it tomorrow, Mr Smith. I have another assignment I'm working on, but I can probably do it on Wednesday for you.'

Eddie hated people saying no to him. When he wanted something done, he wanted it immediately. 'Look, this is urgent. I'll give you a thousand pound a day for however long it takes. The house you followed the boy from, I need you to follow his sister.'

Unable to resist the money or the handsome Mr Smith, Gina succumbed to his persuasion. 'OK, I'll do it.'

# THIRTY-EIGHT

Unable now to stand the sight of either of his kids, Eddie rang Jessica to check whether they were at home or not.

'They've gone out and both of them said they won't be back till late. Why are you asking, Eddie? What's wrong?' Jessica could tell by the sound of his voice that something terrible had happened.

As Eddie walked into the house, Jessica noticed the look of despair etched across his face. 'Get me a drink and pour yourself one, too. Trust me, you're gonna need it,' Ed told her.

Jessica poured Eddie a large brandy and herself a white-wine spritzer. She had never been a fan of drinking alcohol while pregnant, but she told herself that one wouldn't hurt.

Eddie downed his drink in seconds and immediately got up and poured another. He turned to Jessica, his face contorted with pain. 'I've just found out why our daughter has been so secretive about this boyfriend of hers. Talk about fraternising with the enemy. Guess who she's dating, Jess. Go on, fucking guess.'

Worried, Jessica shrugged. Frankie told her very little and she didn't have a clue. 'I don't know, love, honest I don't. Who is it?'

Walking towards the fireplace, Eddie picked up Frankie's latest photograph and smashed it against the wall. 'Jed O'Hara. Our wonderful fucking daughter has been staying on Jimmy's land while shagging his pikey cunt of a son. I'm not having it, Jess, I won't fucking allow it, and tomorrow, when I have the proof in my hands, I will fucking do something about it.'

A couple of miles down the road, Joey had cheered up immensely since finding out that Dominic had only binned him because of his father's interference.

'So, what do you reckon, Frankie? Shall I wait outside Dom's office tomorrow? Or should I give him a few more days to calm down? What would you do if you were me?'

Not hearing a word her brother was saying, Frankie stared vacantly out of the pub window.

'Frankie, whatever's the matter with you today? You're staring into thin air like a tit in a trance.'

'I'm sorry, Joey, I was miles away. What were you saying?'

Knowing his sister better than she knew herself, Joey moved next to her and put a comforting arm around her shoulder. 'What's up? I know you're not yourself. Have you had a row with Jed?'

Frankie shook her head. 'No, it's not that.'

'Well, what is it, then? You know we can tell one another anything.'

Without warning, Frankie burst into tears. 'Oh, Joey, I'm in a right mess. Please don't tell anyone, but I think I might be pregnant.'

Joey looked at his sister in astonishment. 'For fuck's sake, Frankie, please tell me you're joking.'

'I'm not joking. My period's late, and after we were chatting in your room this morning, I was sick twice.'

Joey held her in his arms. Frankie had always been there for him throughout his dramas, and now she needed him to do the same for her. 'Sssh, stop crying. We'll sort this, Frankie, I promise.'

'How? I can't tell Mum and Dad – they'll kill me,' Frankie wailed.

Joey wiped her eyes with his cuff. 'You stay in here and get us another drink and I'll walk down the road and find a chemist. I take it, you haven't done a test yet?'

Frankie shook her head. 'It was only when I was sick earlier that I thought about it. I checked my diary and my period is over three weeks late. I'm so frightened, Joey. I can't tell Jed – say he says he don't want a baby? He might finish with me or something, and I can't lose him. I love him too much.'

Joey soothed her until she finally stopped crying. 'Don't cry, Frankie. You're probably worrying over nothing and it's just coincidence. I mean, you're not stupid. You and Jed have been using something, haven't you?'

Embarrassed, Frankie averted her eyes and stared at her lap. 'Not all the time. Jed didn't like using the rubbers – he said they made his cory itch,' she mumbled.

Annoyed by his sister's naivety, Joey stood up. The quicker he went and got this bloody test, the better. 'I'll tell you something, Frankie, Jed will have more than an itchy cory to worry about if the test's positive. Can you imagine Dad finding out that him and Jimmy O'Hara are about to become family? There'll be murders, Frankie, fucking murders and I hope, for your sake, it's a false alarm, I really do.'

As Eddie knocked back drink after drink, Jessica vacced up the broken glass. The photograph of Frankie was ruined and she had slung it in the bin. 'I know this is hard for you, Eddie, but you won't find your answers in the bottom of a glass. Who told you all this, anyway? It wasn't Ronny again, was it?'

'No, it wasn't fucking Ronny. I haven't heard from him or Paulie since that day in the Flag when I found out our son likes taking it up the arse. What have we done so wrong, Jess, tell me? We've got two kids, one gay and the other screwing pikeys. They've had a privileged upbringing and this is how they repay us. Well, not any more, Jess. I'm putting my fucking foot down from now on and if they don't do as I say, I want the pair of them out of this house immediately.'

Jessica didn't know what to do for the best. There was no reasoning with Eddie when he was in this kind of mood and she was afraid what he might do when the kids came home.

'So, who told you then?' she asked solemnly.

'Jimmy fucking O'Hara. I got it straight from the horse's mouth. I'll kill that boy of his, on our baby's life, if he's touched our Frankie. I'll fucking kill him, Jess.'

Frightened by Ed's demeanour, Jessica tried to hug him, but he pushed her away. 'Please don't talk like that, Eddie. You're scaring me. I'll have a chat with Frankie when she gets home. For all we know, it might not even be true.'

Eddie stood up and snatched at his keys that were on the table. 'Frankie needs a good hiding, not one of your little chats. All this is your fault, Jess. You've been so fucking lenient with 'em, they've ended up with no morals whatsoever. I'm off out and don't expect me home tonight. I'm sick of the sight of this house and I'm sick of the sight of everyone that lives in it.'

As Eddie slammed the front door, Jessica and the glass both shuddered.

*   *   *

Frankie did the pregnancy test in the pub toilets. Too nervous to get the result for herself, she came out and thrust the stick into Joey's hands.

'Urgh, it's all wet. It ain't got your piss on it, has it?' Joey whinged.

'Stop being such a fucking pussy! It only takes five minutes. You check the result for me, I can't do it – I'd do it for you.'

The twins sat in silence. The five minutes seemed more like an hour to both of them. Frankie glanced at her watch. 'Go on, then, check it now.'

'What exactly have I got to look for?' Joey asked.

'If there's a blue line, I'm pregnant and if it's clear, then I ain't.'

As Joey studied the stick, Frankie shut her eyes and said a silent prayer. Her brother's voice interrupted her before she even had time to finish her conversation with God.

'Fucking hell, it's got a blue line. You're pregnant, Frankie, you're pregnant!'

Jessica sipped a cup of tea and weighed up all her options. She could stay at her mum and dad's house, but she didn't want to involve them in this. Her mum always gave unwanted advice and Jessica knew deep down that her dad had never really taken to Eddie. Another option was to stay around Vicki's, but again, Jess didn't want to involve her and Doug either. The problems with the twins were bad enough without the whole world finding out about them.

Finishing her cuppa, Jessica chose option number three. She would ring Raymond and ask him to stay round at hers. Jessica trusted her brother more than anyone and if he came over, at least she wouldn't be alone in the house.

Raymond was having a meal with Polly and her parents when his phone rang. He excused himself and took the call outside. 'What's up, sis?'

'Oh, Raymond. Please can you come round? Something bad's happened and I don't know what to do.'

Raymond sighed. He'd had to shoot away often recently and he didn't want Polly getting sick of his lifestyle and dumping him.

'I'm a bit busy at the moment, Jess. Can't I come round tomorrow?'

Jessica started to cry. 'I don't know how to handle this alone, Raymond. Eddie's found out that Frankie's been seeing Jimmy O'Hara's son and he's gone off his head. I'm frightened to stay here on my own, in case Ed comes back drunk and starts trouble.'

Raymond knew only too well that anything to do with Jimmy O'Hara was enough to tip Eddie over the edge. 'Stay calm, sis. I'll be round within the hour,' he told her.

Ignoring her brother's advice not to tell Jed about the baby, Frankie rang her boyfriend and told him to meet her at the pub. Finding out the test was positive had prompted her to be straight with him. She loved him and just hoped Jed loved her as much as he said he did.

'Just get rid of it, Frankie. We've still got some of our birthday money left. I'll help you pay for an abortion. Mum and Dad will never have to know,' Joey begged her.

Frankie shook her head. 'No, it's not fair, Joey. This is as much Jed's baby as it's mine. I can't get rid of it without telling him. I love him and I couldn't do that to him. For all I know and you know, he might want me to keep it.'

About to plead with Frankie once again, Joey saw Jed walk in and quickly shut up. As her boyfriend walked towards her, Frankie felt her whole body shake from head to toe. She couldn't tell him here. The pub had been almost empty earlier, but now was quite busy.

Jed was more perceptive than most boys his age and he immediately clocked the twins' serious demeanour. 'Blimey, what's up with yous two? Look like you've seen a ghost, the pair of yous do,' he said, smiling.

Telling Joey to stay put, Frankie dragged Jed outside. 'Can we talk in the motor? Where you parked?' she asked him.

Jed led her to his new pick-up truck and opened the door for her. 'Do you like it? Four grand, I give for this. Bought it yesterday, I did, off some old grunter.'

Barely noticing the black metal monster on wheels, Frankie nodded dumbly.

Lifting her chin up, Jed was surprised to see tears in her eyes. 'What's a matter? Not dumping me, are ya?'

Frankie shook her head. She had never felt so nervous in her life and Joey looking out of the pub window wasn't helping matters.

'Jed, I'm pregnant,' she whispered.

Jed burst out laughing. 'Is that why you're crying, you dinlo?'

'I'm scared, Jed. We're so young, what are we gonna do?' Frankie asked, crying even more.

Jed took her into his arms and kissed her tears away. 'Look at me, Frankie,' he ordered her.

Frankie did as he asked and was surprised to see him grinning. 'It's not funny. You're acting as though you want the baby.'

Jed chuckled. 'Of course I want the baby. I love you, Frankie, and we'll get married, if you want.'

'Married!' Frankie exclaimed excitedly.

Jumping out of his seat, Jed ran around the other side

of the truck and dragged Frankie out. He sat her on the tail of the truck and got down on one knee.

'There's people watching now, so don't make me look a cory. Marry me, Frankie – I love you.'

Young, naive and hopelessly in love, Frankie said an immediate yes, without thinking about the consequences.

As Jessica finished explaining the full story, Raymond sat silently, sipping his beer. He knew more than anyone how much Eddie hated Jimmy O'Hara and he couldn't believe, if true, how Frankie could have been so bloody stupid.

'He swore on our baby's life that if it was true, he'd kill this Jed. What am I gonna do, Ray?' Jessica sobbed.

Hugging his sister, Raymond was more worried about his brother-in-law. Eddie was the most hot-headed person he had ever come across and he dreaded what he was capable of doing to the O'Haras. The problem was, they were no mugs themselves, and if another feud broke out between the two families, everybody's lives, including his own, would be in danger.

'Let me have a drive around, see if I can find him, Jess. I tried to ring him on the way here, but his phone was switched off.'

Jessica grabbed hold of her brother's hand for dear life. 'Please don't leave me here alone, Raymond. The twins will probably be back soon and if Ed comes back and you're not here, I'm frightened of what he'll do. He could be anywhere. He said he wasn't coming home tonight, so you won't know where to find him, anyway.'

Seeing how shaken up Jessica was, Raymond agreed to stay. None of this shit could be doing her pregnancy any good and he was worried if he left and Eddie came home and created a scene, she might have a miscarriage.

\* \* \*

Unaware of what was happening at home, Joey looked at his sister in total and utter disbelief. 'You can't get married! You're only sixteen.'

Frankie smiled at Jed as he came back from the bar with a bottle of champagne and three glasses. ''Ere you go. Get this down your neck,' Jed said, as he handed a glass to Joey.

Joey had always been frightened of his sister's lover, so he chose his words very carefully. 'I'm sorry, Jed, I've nothing against you, mate, but my parents are gonna go mental. It's bad enough Frankie's pregnant, but marriage – there's no way my dad's gonna let that happen.'

Jed didn't seem worried in the slightest as he threw a loving arm around his wife-to-be. 'It's got fuck-all to do with your dad. If he don't like it, it's tough shit. Me and your sister wanna be together, and that's all that matters,' Jed said, smiling at him.

'But if you say you're getting married, Frankie, Mum and Dad will chuck you out,' Joey pleaded. He was desperate to make her see sense.

'Look, Joey, as much as I love you, I think I'm gonna have to move out anyway. Jed said I can live in his trailer with him on his dad's land until he buys us somewhere of our own,' Frankie told him.

Seeing her brother's eyes well up, Frankie squeezed his hand. 'Don't get upset, Joey. I'll only be five minutes away and you can come over whenever you want.'

'Course you can,' Jed chipped in. Frankie's brother wasn't his cup of tea. It was obvious the mush was as queer as a nine-bob note, but if Joey visiting made Frankie happy, then it was OK by him.

The thought of life indoors without Frankie was unbearable for Joey. 'When are you thinking of moving out?' he asked.

Frankie was adamant as she answered. 'I'm gonna go home in the morning and tell Mum and Dad everything. If it all kicks off, which it's bound to, then I'm going straight away. I'm sorry, Joey, but this is my life and if Mum and Dad can't accept Jed or the baby, then I'm leaving tomorrow, for good.'

# THIRTY-NINE

The following morning, Eddie woke up with a sore head, stiff neck and a mouth like a camel's arse. He had spent the night at his salvage yard and had slept on the uncomfortable leather chair. Annoyed with himself for getting so drunk, he walked over to the sink, cupped some water in his hands and washed his face. He'd had the day from hell yesterday, but was now feeling guilty for taking it out on Jessica.

Spotting his car keys lying on the floor, Eddie turned the cabin upside down searching for his mobile. Gina would be ringing at some point today and he needed to find the bastard thing. With no joy, he ran out to his motor and was relieved to see it lying on the passenger seat. He tried to switch it on, but the bloody thing was dead. 'You stupid fucking cunt,' he said, cursing himself.

Still in a complete daze, Eddie nearly forgot to lock the Portakabin up, but remembered just in time. He needed to get home to sort things out with Jessica. Maybe Jimmy O'Hara had been winding him up, although he doubted it very much. Too cocksure of himself, O'Hara was, to be lying.

Eddie started the motor and glanced at his watch. Today would probably drag on forever, but at least by nightfall he should know the truth.

Jessica had lain awake all night and had got up at the crack of dawn. Neither Eddie nor Frankie had come home last night and she was worried sick about both of them. Not knowing what to do with herself, Jessica made Raymond a fry-up, then busied herself with the housework. In times of need, she always turned to her chores to help her; she found them therapeutic.

At 7 a.m., Jessica could stand the suspense no longer and gently tapped on Joey's bedroom door. Her son had arrived home late last night and informed her that Frankie was staying at a friend's house. Jess had tried to question him, begged him to talk to her, but Joey had burst into tears, then locked himself in his bedroom and refused to come back out.

'Joey, it's Mum. I desperately need to talk to you, love. It's not about you, it's about Frankie. She could be in a lot of trouble and I need your help to stop anything silly from happening.'

Joey got out of bed and unlocked his bedroom door. He was furious with Frankie for what she had done and was planning to do. He was also annoyed with her for leaving him in the shit to deal with the aftermath of her stupidity.

Noticing her son was all puffy-eyed, Jessica tenderly rubbed his arm. 'Are you still upset over Dominic?' she asked kindly.

Joey said nothing as he flopped back on his bed. Every time Dominic's name was mentioned, it felt as if a dagger was being jabbed through his heart. He missed him dreadfully and with all that had happened with Frankie, he needed to see him and be comforted by him, not talk about him.

Jessica cleared her throat. 'I know about Frankie and Jimmy O'Hara's son. Your dad knows as well and, as you can imagine, he's none too pleased. For your sister's sake, Joey, I need to know everything. Is it serious? Does she see him much? Are they sleeping together? Tell me all you can, Joey, it's important that you do.'

Joey looked away from her. It was Frankie's job to tell their mum, not his. 'She's coming back this morning, Mum. You can ask her for yourself.'

'So, it is true, then? Jimmy O'Hara told your dad yesterday and I wasn't sure if he was winding him up. What's his name, Joey?' Jessica asked softly. She had to bluff to get the truth out of him.

'His name's Jed. You should remember him, Mum, he's the one that Dad stuck me in the boxing ring with when I was little. Now, if you don't mind, I'm busy. I have to go somewhere myself. Anything else you need to know, Frankie will tell you. This is none of my business.'

Jessica sat with her mouth open. She hadn't realised Jed was that terror of a child who had knocked her son out cold. 'Are you going anywhere nice?' she asked. She couldn't think straight, this was all too much for her.

'Nowhere special. Please, Mum, just leave me alone. I need to have a shower and get out of this house.'

With the weight of the world on her shoulders, Jessica closed Joey's bedroom door and went downstairs.

Aware that his sister looked upset, Raymond hugged her. 'Shall I see if I can find Eddie?' he asked her.

About to answer, Jessica ran to the window as she heard a car pulling up outside.

'Speak of the devil, eh, sis?' Raymond joked, as he went outside to speak to his brother-in-law.

'Is everything OK?' Raymond asked him.

'Not really, but I'll know for definite later. Did you stay here with Jess last night?' Eddie enquired.

Raymond nodded. 'She was a bit upset and rang me. Listen, Ed, I know the score, Jess told me about Frankie and O'Hara's boy. If anything kicks off and you need backup, I'm there for you, you know that.'

Eddie put his arm around Raymond's shoulder. 'Cheers, mate, much appreciated.'

Raymond laughed as Eddie lifted a massive bouquet out of his boot. 'Fucking hell, they ain't for me, are they?'

'Get over yourself, you fucking tosser. Listen, Ray, can you do me a big favour? I've got a gut feeling today's gonna be a bad day. I've got a bit of running around to do, but do you think you can stay here? I don't wanna leave Jess and the kids on their own.'

Raymond immediately agreed. 'Frankie ain't here though, Ed. She never came home last night.'

Eddie felt his pulse start to quicken. 'If I find out she's in that pikey's fucking caravan, I'll kill him, then kill her,' he told Raymond.

Aware that Eddie's eyes had turned cloudy and angry, Raymond led Eddie back to the house. 'Just calm down and go and see Jess. You going off your head ain't gonna do her pregnancy any good, is it?'

Eddie handed Raymond his phone and he told him to put it on charge and make himself scarce for five minutes.

Jessica was in the front room and didn't look up as her husband walked in.

'Jess, I'm so sorry for having a go at you. None of this is your fault, I know it's not. You know the old saying, "You always hurt the ones you love"? Well, I don't mean

413

to, but I suppose because we're so close I take my frustrations out on you.'

Jessica had never been one to carry on an argument. She had only ever done that once with Eddie, when he had shoved Joey into that boxing ring and she had gone back to her mother's for a few days.

As Eddie knelt in front of her, Jessica smiled. 'Look, I'm on me fucking hands and knees, begging your forgiveness. Don't tell anyone, will ya? Got me reputation to think of, ain't I?'

Jessica looked at the beautiful flowers and hugged Eddie as he sat down next to her. 'I've been so worried about you. I thought you'd gone round the O'Haras and done something stupid. Please don't drink that Scotch any more. I can smell it on your breath,' she pleaded, burying her head in his neck.

Eddie stroked her long blonde hair. 'I'm sorry, babe, and I swear I won't touch another drop of Scotch. Raymond said Frankie never came home last night. Do you know where she was?'

'Joey came back and said she stayed at her friend's house. She was probably round Stacey's,' Jessica answered, trying to smooth the situation over.

'Listen, Jess. I promise you that whatever Frankie's up to, I'll try and deal with it in the nicest way I can, but if that don't work, then I'm gonna have to go one step further. Do you understand what I'm saying?'

Jessica clung to her husband for dear life. 'Yes, Eddie, I understand,' she whispered.

Not too many miles away, in Upney, Stanley was in a deep sleep and totally oblivious of his wife prodding and poking him.

Annoyed that he was glued to that stinking armchair

of his and snoring like a pot-bellied pig, Joyce bent down so that her mouth was only an inch away from his ear. 'Stanley', she screamed as loudly as she could.

Stanley shot up in such shock that he lost his balance and fell head first out of the chair. 'You stupid bloody woman. What did you do that for?' he grumbled as he rubbed his right elbow.

Joyce couldn't help but giggle. Stanley looked so funny lying on the carpet in a heap. 'I want you to get yourself ready, Stanley. We need to drive over to our Jessica's. Something's not right, she's got problems, I know she has. Our Raymond was over there last night and Jess barely spoke to me on the phone this morning.'

'Probably something to do with that dodgy old man of hers. Ain't got himself nicked, has he?' Stanley muttered, standing up.

'Now, don't start all that. We've no idea what's wrong yet. I know my Jess and she sounded to me like she'd been crying. For all we know, Stanley, it could be something to do with the baby,' Joyce told him.

'Shouldn't we ask if it's OK for us to visit? We can't just turn up,' Stanley said. Fortunately, he wasn't as nosy as his wife.

'No, because Jess'll say no and then we'll never find out what was wrong in the first place. Now go and get changed, quick as you like,' Joyce said.

'I'm all right. I'll go like this,' Stanley said miserably.

'No, you bloody well won't. Them trousers have got pigeon shit all over 'em. Go upstairs and put your nice grey ones on.'

Stanley tutted, but knew better than to argue. 'What am I meant to say to Jock? I'm meant to be meeting him at eleven to fly our pigeons,' he moaned.

Joyce shook her head furiously. 'You and Jock can get

your cocks out any day. Now, chop-chop, Stanley. I'm not one to be kept waiting, you know that.'

'Wicked old witch,' Stanley spouted as he stomped up the stairs.

Back in Rainham, Frankie's heart was beating nineteen to the dozen as she crouched down behind the big bush in her next-door neighbour's front garden. 'Move over a bit, Jed. Your legs are sticking out, someone will see you,' she told her boyfriend.

Jed shook his head in disbelief. He loved his woman very much, but sometimes she had the brains of a rocking horse. 'I'm telling you, Frankie, this is a stupid idea. Does it matter if your dad's there? He's gonna find out when your mum tells him, anyway. We should have done things my way, instead of sitting here like a pair of dinlos.'

Frankie said nothing. Jed had wanted to drive over to her parents, face them and tell them the news together, then load all her belongings onto his truck. Petrified of the fracas that was bound to happen, Frankie put her foot down. She had no doubt whatsoever that her dad would barricade her in the house, then smash both Jed and his new pick-up truck to smithereens.

Hearing the sound of an engine starting up, Frankie peered through the bushes just in time to see her dad's Land Cruiser pull off the drive. 'Right, me dad's gone out. The only people in the house are me mum and possibly me Uncle Raymond. His car's on the drive and I don't think he was with me dad,' she told Jed. She knew Joey was out, as she had seen him jump into a cab about half an hour ago.

'Please let me come with you, Frankie. We're getting married; your mother's gonna think I'm a right div if

416

I don't face her like a man,' Jed pleaded, as Frankie stood up.

Frankie shook her head. 'You don't wanna come in while me Uncle Raymond's there. He's me father's henchman, so he's bound to kick off. I promise you, once the initial shock's worn off, you can meet me mum. Today, though, I need to talk to her alone.'

Watching Frankie walk away, Jed made a decision. He didn't like the sound of Uncle fucking Raymond and if Frankie weren't back in half an hour, he was going in there, whether his girlfriend liked it or not.

As Frankie walked up the drive, her mind was a whirlwind of emotion. She felt guilty at letting her parents down, but her love for Jed was far too strong for her to put her parents first.

Frankie let herself in with her key.

'There you are. Where have you been?' her mum asked, obviously relieved to see her.

'Mum, I need to talk to you,' Frankie mumbled.

'You OK?' Raymond asked, poking his head into the hallway.

Frankie nodded. 'Fine, thanks. I just need to talk to Mum in private.'

Knowing when he wasn't wanted, Raymond retreated back into the lounge.

'Come on, we'll sit in the kitchen, I'll shut the door,' Jessica said. She knew by Frankie's face that whatever she had to say was very serious and she was dreading hearing it.

Not usually one to eavesdrop, Raymond knew he had little choice. Eddie would want to know what was going on and, for all their sakes, he had to find out. Taking his shoes off, Raymond crept into the hallway and placed his ear against the door.

417

'What is it, love?' Jessica asked as Frankie began to cry.

'You know that boy I've been seeing? Well, I didn't bring him home because his dad's Jimmy O'Hara. His name's, Jed, Mum, and he makes me so happy.'

'Don't cry. I sort of already knew,' Jessica said, cuddling her.

'There's more, Mum, and you're not gonna like the rest.'

'Go on,' Jessica said, her heart in her mouth.

'I'm pregnant and we're getting married,' Frankie stated. Blurting it out was the only way she could say it.

Feeling her legs turn to jelly, Jessica grabbed one of the wooden chairs and slumped down on it. 'Oh, my God! You can't be, Frankie. You're only a baby yourself.'

Frankie fiercely wiped her tears away. She needed to stand up for herself, be strong, not weak.

'I'm not a baby, Mum. I'm sixteen and I know my own mind. Dad's gonna hate me, I know he is. That's why I'm leaving home today.'

Unable to stop himself, Raymond burst into the kitchen. 'You're going nowhere, Frankie. Your dad'll be home soon and he'll sort this mess out.'

Frankie stood up, her eyes blazing. 'You can't tell me what to do. I'm sixteen and I can legally leave home if I want to.'

She turned to her mother. 'Let's not forget, Mum, you were only one year older than me when you got pregnant with me and Joey. You married Dad and had us, didn't you? Why should things be different for me? I love Jed and I will always love him.'

Raymond glared at his niece. Without knowing it, the stupid, brainless girl had just revived the feud that he and everybody else had been dreading. 'I'll tell you why things are different for you, Frankie – because you're with Jimmy O'Hara's son, you idiot. This is gonna break your dad's heart and cause so much fucking trouble. Don't you realise what you've done? Are you that fucking stupid?' Raymond yelled.

'Please stop arguing,' Jessica sobbed.

Having changed lookout positions, Jed was now in Frankie's back garden and could hear almost every word.

'Who do you think you are? Go fuck your grandmother, you cheeky cunt,' Jed shouted, flinging open the back door.

As Raymond went for her boyfriend, Frankie screamed.

Jessica tried to grab hold of her brother. 'Stop it, will you? Violence isn't the answer,' she wailed.

'Come on, Frankie, leave your stuff here, I'll buy you more. We're going,' Jed said, grabbing her hand.

Raymond took hold of Frankie's other arm. 'She's going nowhere, not till her dad gets home. Get upstairs, Frankie, your boyfriend's leaving now.'

Frankie was hysterical as her uncle got Jed into a head-lock and marched him out of the front door. As Raymond slammed the door and walked back inside, he tried to stop a hysterical Frankie following Jed.

'You're going nowhere, you stupid little cow,' he spat at her.

Jed had never been frightened of anyone in his life and he certainly wasn't frightened of Uncle fucking Raymond. 'I'm not leaving here without Frankie,' he shouted, as he repeatedly booted the front door.

'Lock the back door and shut all the windows,' Raymond ordered his tearful sister.

Like a raging bull, Jed tore a big branch off a tree and

put it straight through one of the windows. 'Frankie, Frankie! Don't take no notice of your wanker of an uncle. Come on, hurry up,' he yelled.

Ordering Jessica to make sure her daughter stayed inside, Raymond ran out to his motor. He always carried a baseball bat for emergencies and this was definitely one of them.

'I ain't frightened of you, you fucking dinlo,' Jed shouted at him.

Confident that he could fight Raymond off, Jed changed his mind as soon as he spotted the baseball bat coming his way.

'You go near Frankie again and I'll fucking kill you,' Raymond screamed, as he chased Jed down the driveway.

Streets ahead of him, Jed couldn't resist turning round and doing a wanker sign. 'Shut up, you muggy cunt,' he said, smirking.

Incensed, Raymond carried on chasing him.

Never ones for perfect timing, Joyce and Stanley chose that exact moment to turn into the driveway. Joyce looked at Stanley to make sure her eyes weren't deceiving her. 'Was that our Raymond chasing someone with a baseball bat?'

Stanley nodded dumbly. He was far too shocked to speak.

Joyce got out of the car and did a little jog back to the entrance of the driveway. 'Raymond! It's your mother. Get your arse back here. What do you think you're doing?' she screamed.

With her son nowhere to be seen, a furious Joyce stomped back to the car. 'Come on, Stanley. Don't just sit there, we need to find out what's going on.'

As Stanley got out of the car, he felt nauseous. He hated trouble of any kind and certainly didn't want to be involved in it.

Jessica opened the front door. 'What's going on?' Joyce asked, as her daughter fell sobbing into her arms.

Frankie knew that this was probably her only opportunity to escape. Desperate to get away, she sprinted past her mum and nan and sent her grandfather flying as he tried to walk through the front door.

Losing his balance for the second time that day, Stanley landed on his arse. 'Gordon Bennett!' he exclaimed as he tried to get up again.

Jessica could barely speak for crying. 'Frankie's pregnant. Eddie's gonna kill her. What am I gonna do, Mum?' she said between sobs.

Joyce sat Jessica on the sofa. 'Now, come on, dear, stop all that crying. Everything will sort itself out,' she said gently.

'It won't. She's pregnant by the gypsy boy down the road and Eddie's had a feud with that family all his life,' Jessica wept.

Aware of his balance letting him down once more, Stanley fell onto the sofa in utter shock.

'Gypsy? What do you mean? Is that who our Raymond was chasing?'

Jessica nodded. 'Jed's a gypsy boy. All his family are travellers.'

Seeing her husband's face go deathly white, Joyce felt her own turn the same colour. 'Oh, my Gawd. I feel ill,' she gushed.

With his baseball bat still in his hand, Raymond ran back to the house. He had chased Jed for about a mile, but the cocky little bastard was as fast as a whippet and he hadn't got anywhere near him. Out of breath, Raymond ran into the house and put his hands on his knees.

'Where's Frankie?' he asked panting.

421

Jessica burst into tears again. 'She's gone. She ran off and I couldn't stop her.'

Ignoring his parents, Raymond picked his mobile phone up off the table and ran out the back. Willing the phone he was ringing to answer, he breathed a sigh of relief when it did.

'Ed, it's me. Something terrible's happened. You need to come home right now.'

# FORTY

At ten to one, Joey left the coffee shop and crossed the busy main road. Dominic took his lunch break at one o'clock and, although dreadfully nervous, Joey couldn't wait to see him.

Joey had travelled up by train and, while pretending to read the paper, he'd had a long, hard think about his future. Living at home without Frankie by his side really didn't appeal to Joey. He loved his mum, but his sister was the only one who really understood him.

As Dominic walked through the huge glass doors, Joey's heart skipped a beat.

'What are you doing here?' Dominic hissed at him.

'I need to talk to you,' Joey pleaded.

'I've already told you, I've met someone else. Now please just leave me alone,' Dominic told him.

Upset by his ex-lover's reaction, Joey followed him as he walked off in the opposite direction. 'I know you're lying, Dom. I found out the truth and I know my dad came to see you. Please, let's go for a drink so I can say my piece. Ten minutes of your time, that's all I ask.'

Dominic had never felt so petrified in his entire life as the night Joey's father had paid him a little visit. He still couldn't sleep even now, and every time he closed his eyes, he could feel the tip of that knife on the base of his helmet.

Deep down, Dominic still adored Joey, but he wasn't about to tell him that. He couldn't – it was too dangerous. 'Ten minutes, then I want you and your thug of a father out of my life for good,' he said venomously.


Eddie took the phone call from Gina, which confirmed what he had already been told.

'I'm still in the vicinity. I've taken loads of photographs. Do you want me to meet you now, Mr Smith?'

Guessing that Raymond's phone call had something to do with Frankie, Eddie asked Gina to do him a big favour. 'Look, I don't care how much this costs. I want you to keep my friend's daughter and the bloke she's with in your sights. Anywhere they go, I want you to follow 'em. Can you do that for me?'

Gina smiled. She would literally do anything for the gorgeous Mr Smith. 'Of course I will,' she told Eddie.

Desperate to get home, Eddie ended the call and pressed his foot hard against the accelerator. He had been on his way to pick up some money off a geezer in Kent, when Raymond rang him. He had immediately turned around and headed back towards Rainham. Unfortunately, it had taken him ages, as there'd had been an accident at the Dartford Crossing.

Eddie breathed a sigh of relief as he finally pulled into his driveway. Raymond had been reluctant to talk on the phone and all the way home Eddie had been going over what might have happened. Eddie had never been a person to be kept in the dark and the suspense was fucking killing him.

Eddie opened the front door. 'Well, what's going on?'

he yelled, as he saw Jessica, Joyce, Stanley and Raymond sitting in the living room with faces like ghosts.

Jessica burst into tears. 'You tell him, Ray, I can't do it,' she sobbed.

'Fucking tell me then!' Eddie screamed at Raymond.

'Sit down, let me pour you a brandy,' Raymond said.

Eddie was getting more wound up by the second. 'Fuck sitting down and fuck the brandy. Just spit it out, will ya?'

'Frankie's pregnant. She's left home and says her and Jed O'Hara are getting married,' Raymond told him.

Eddie couldn't have been more shocked if an elephant had walked into the lounge. 'What? Over my dead body. Who told you this?'

Seeing the cold, calculating look in his son-in-law's eyes, Stanley felt his bowels loosen, and made a quick exit.

'Where you going, Stanley? Why are you walking funny?' Joyce yelled at him.

'I need the toilet,' Stanley replied, as he did a clenched-arse shuffle down the hallway.

'There's something wrong with that man,' Joyce commented.

Raymond glared at her. 'For fuck's sake, Mother, shut up,' he said as he turned to Eddie.

'Frankie told us. She came home after you went out. He was with her, that Jed, cocky little bastard he is. I chased him off with a baseball bat. I'd have mullered him if I'd have caught him, Ed, but he ran as fast as a grey-hound chasing a rabbit.'

Unable to stop himself, Eddie flew into one almighty rage. 'I will fucking kill that scumbag pikey cunt. Come on Ray, me and you are going over to the house. I want my daughter home and I want her home now!'

Eddie stormed into the kitchen like a bull in a china shop. 'This should do the trick,' he spat, as he grabbed hold of a carving knife.

'Please, Eddie, don't go round there,' Jessica screamed, as she got down on her hands and knees and clung to his legs.

'Jess, get off of me. This is our daughter we're talking about, and I need to put a stop to this shit right now. May God be my judge, she ain't having that pikey cunt's kid. I'll rip it out of her with me bare hands if I have to,' Eddie shouted.

'You'll get arrested. Please, Raymond, do something. You're the only one he'll listen to,' Jessica screamed.

As Eddie stormed out of the house, Raymond caught up with him and grabbed him by the shoulders. 'Listen to me. Jess is right, this ain't the way to do things. For fuck's sake, use your brain. It's broad daylight. If you go round there and stab the cunt, you'll spend the rest of your life in the nick. Think about Jess. You've got a baby on the way.'

Realising Raymond was right, Eddie threw the knife on the gravel, sank to his knees and cried tears of pure anger.

Less than half a mile away, Jed paced nervously up and down his trailer. His old man had gone away to a horse fair for the weekend and his mother was staying at her sister's.

'What's the matter, Jed?' Frankie asked, giving him a hug.

'Us travellers are psychic, Frankie, and I've got a bad feeling about us staying here alone. If me dad was here, we'd be all right, but he ain't.'

'What we gonna do then? I need some clothes, Jed, and underwear.'

Jed squeezed Frankie and rocked her from side to side. 'I think we should get out of here. Me dad's got a trailer in his salvage yard in Tilbury. We can stay there till he gets back from the horse fair. I'm not frightened of no one, Frankie, but we should get away and let things calm down a bit. Don't worry about clothes and stuff. I'll stop on the way there and take you shopping. Trust me, my nan sensed stuff happening and I'm the same.'

Frankie smiled. Life was one big adventure with Jed and he made her feel so safe and loved. 'Are you sure everything's gonna turn out all right, Jed?' she asked him.

Jed tilted her chin. 'I know everything's gonna be OK, but I also know the quicker we get out of here the better.'

As they drove out the gates, neither Jed nor Frankie noticed the woman clocking them in the little black Micra.

Oblivious to what was happening to his sister, Joey was trying to iron out his own problems. Unable to stop his emotions, he hugged Dominic for what would probably be the last time and could only watch as he walked away. As Dominic turned around and waved, Joey stood rooted to the spot for a few minutes. Devastated, he then found the nearest pub to down his sorrows.

'I want a triple vodka, with ice and a dash of lemonade,' he told the barman.

Finding a quiet table, Joey flopped onto a seat. What his father had done to Dominic was despicable and unforgivable.

Joey had never been that close to his dad. He had always known deep down that his dad preferred Gary and Ricky. It didn't really bother him. Even when he was a child, he had sensed that his dad saw him as a disappointment, the weakest link, and he had just got on with things in his own little way.

Another thing that Joey was always aware of was that his father was a villain. Frankie and he had both clocked on when they were about ten years old and spent many a night giggling about what their school teachers might say.

Although not a big fan of his father, Joey had never imagined him as a violent, nasty, vicious bully. Dominic wasn't lying, Joey knew that, and he was flabbergasted by his dad's behaviour. To force his way into Dom's flat with a knife was bad enough on its own. But then, to make him lie naked on the floor while threatening to chop his penis off was the most callous act that Joey had ever heard of.

'You will always hold a special place in my heart and I will always love you, Joey. But, promise me, for my safety, you won't contact me again,' Dominic had begged him.

Finishing his drink, Joey slammed the glass on the table and stormed out of the pub. He couldn't wait to get home and tell his mum the story. She was married to an animal who had a screw loose and she had every right to know the truth.

As Joey got on the train, his thoughts turned to his sister. If his dad was capable of doing what he had done to Dom, Christ only knows what he was capable of doing to Frankie's boyfriend. Joey had no idea if Frankie had told their parents after he had left this morning, but he knew he had to warn her. He didn't particularly like Jed, but at this moment in time he preferred him to his sadistic headcase of a father.

As the train stopped in a tunnel, Joey listened intently as an announcement was made: 'Due to signal failure, there will be a short delay.'

'Shit,' Joey muttered. He needed to get home – and

fast. Jed could be in serious trouble and he had to warn Frankie immediately.

After his minor show of emotion, Eddie had now got his act together. Just in case things turned sour, he needed to get anything dodgy off the premises. 'Right, stick the jewellery and diamonds in that sports bag, Ray. Get that picture down from in the front room as well. That's hooky – came out of an art gallery, I think.'

As his son reached above his head to take the painting off the wall, Stanley looked at his wife in horror. 'I always said Eddie was a crook, didn't I?' he whispered.

'Why don't you just shut the fuck up,' Joyce said, punching him in the arm.

Jessica was having a lie on the bed and Joyce was worried about her. She had almost fainted earlier with bad stomach pains, but had begged her mum not to tell Eddie.

Joyce turned to Stanley. 'I think him and our Raymond are going out somewhere. Do you think I should tell Eddie that Jess ain't well?' she said in hushed tones.

Stanley shrugged. He hated this house, hated Eddie and couldn't wait to get home to his pigeons.

As Buster and Bruno came in from the garden and leaped on him with muddy paws, Stanley stood up. 'Our son and son-in-law are probably just popping out to rob a bank, dear. I'm going outside to have a cigar. I need some fresh air and I can be lookout for the police arriving,' he said sarcastically.

'You are one miserable old bastard,' Joyce told him, as he left the room.

Upstairs, Jessica was wide awake and crying on her pillow. She had had pains and twinges all day. Unbeknown to her family, she had rung the hospital earlier.

'You haven't lost any blood at all?' the nurse had enquired.

'No, but I sort of passed out,' Jessica had replied.

'You'll be fine. You've just been overdoing it. All you need is rest,' the nurse insisted.

Hearing the front door slam and an engine start up, Jessica got up and walked over to the window. Seeing her husband's Land Cruiser roar away, she ran downstairs. 'Mum, where's Eddie gone? Is Raymond with him?' she asked, panicking.

Joyce smiled and patted the seat next to her. 'Sit down and I'll make you a nice cup of tea. Raymond's with Eddie, they've gone to the pub. Ed wanted to come up and tell you but I told him not to. I thought you were asleep.'

Picking up the house phone, Jessica rang her husband's mobile, just to check her mother's story.

'I'm fine, Jess. I've calmed down now, honest. Me and Raymond are going out for a few pints,' Eddie assured her.

Jessica was relieved. He sounded OK. 'Promise me, Ed, you won't get on the Scotch,' she begged him.

'I promise, and I love you,' Eddie replied.

Jessica felt her body relax as she sipped the strong, sugary tea.

As Joey burst into the room, Jessica knew her day was destined to end as badly as it had begun. 'Mum, I need to talk to you alone,' her son insisted.

Jessica stood up. Joey was visibly upset, so she led him upstairs, away from his grandparents.

Stanley, who had followed his grandson into the house, looked at Joyce. 'No wonder them kids have got problems. There's more dramas going on than *Dallas* in this family. Our Jess should never have married Eddie,

430

I told you that years ago, but you wouldn't listen, would you?'

Joyce pursed her lips. 'I should have never married you, but I did. Now, just sit down and shut your bastard trap.'

As Joey sobbed his heart out, Jessica did her best to comfort him.

'I can't understand what you're saying. What did Dad do?'

'He broke into Dominic's flat, made him lie on the floor naked and threatened to chop his penis off and shove it down his throat. Dom won't see me no more, Mum, he's too scared. And now I'm worried about Frankie. If Dad did that to Dominic, what will he do to Jed?'

Jessica felt the hairs on her body stand on end. She suddenly didn't feel as if she knew her loving husband at all. 'We need to ring Frankie and warn her, Mum. Dad's capable of anything, I just know he is. Dominic told me that Dad even made a little cut on the end of his penis, then he laughed as he wiped the blood all over his dressing gown.'

Jessica felt physically sick as she told Joey to search his sister's bedroom. Frankie hadn't taken her mobile with her and they needed to find Jed's number to ring him. As Jessica felt a sharp twinge in her stomach, she lay on her bed and prayed. 'Please God, keep me and my children safe. Amen,' she whispered.

A few miles down the road, Eddie and Raymond were doing a bit of digging. After leaving home, they had purchased a bottle of Scotch and a bag of ice, and headed straight to Ed's salvage yard.

'That's deep enough,' Eddie said, handing Raymond the haul they had dug up from his father's house. Eddie

431

knew it was about to all go off, and he didn't want anything dodgy indoors in case the rozzers came sniffing around.

'What about the painting?' Raymond asked.

'I'll deal with that. You OK for a minute? I've gotta make a couple of phone calls. If you need me, I'll be in the cabin.'

Pouring himself a large Scotch, Eddie drank it, then rang Gina's number. 'Well, are they still in Rainham?' he asked.

Gina smiled when she heard Eddie's voice. 'No, they're in Tilbury. Earlier they went shopping, bought clothes and a sleeping bag and now they're in an old trailer on what looks like some kind of scrapyard.'

'Get yourself home now. Can you get back there first thing tomorrow? I might need you to watch them all day. Money's no object, you know that.'

Gina was usually very professional, but couldn't resist letting her guard down for once. 'I'll do it on one condition, Mr Smith.'

'What?' Eddie asked.

'That you buy me dinner as a thank you.'

'You've got a deal,' Eddie lied. He had no intention of taking Gina anywhere. Not once had he ever even thought of cheating on Jess, and he wasn't about to start now.

'I've gotta go now. Get there at six,' he said, ending the call.

Eddie refilled his glass and studied the guns that he and Raymond had dug up earlier. He had no idea where his father had got the machine gun from. He held it in his hand and smiled. It felt good, it felt right and, providing everything went to plan, it would spell the end of Jed O'Hara, once and for all.

# FORTY-ONE

Opening her eyes, Frankie nudged Jed. They were snuggled up together in a sleeping bag, but the bed they were lying on smelt musty and damp. 'Jed, I need to get up. Move over, will you? The smell of this bed's making me feel sick.'

Jed unzipped the bag so Frankie could climb over him. Unbeknown to her, the trailer they were staying in used to be his little shagging den. When his mum and dad split up, Jed had kept in close contact with his old man and when he was thirteen, his dad had given him the key to this place.

'It's got everything you need in there, boy. Anytime you wanna pull yourself a little gorger bird, take her back there,' he told him.

Within a month of being given the key, Jed was making regular use of the trailer. He had been knocking about with his cousin, Sammy Boy, at the time and, between them, they must have brought a thousand birds back. Jed smiled. He and Sammy boy had had some good times here. None of the birds had meant anything to them, it was all just a bit of fun. Jed had changed since he'd met Frankie. He had never been in love before, but Frankie had cast her magic spell over him. He was

433

content now and other girls didn't interest him in the slightest.

'Jed, what's in this little box room that's locked? Have you got the key? Can I have a look in it?'

About to say yes, Jed remembered what was in there. 'Shit. I've gotta get rid of that stuff,' he mumbled. 'It's a load of old rubbish in there, Frankie. It's me dad's stuff, he don't like anyone going in there,' Jed lied. Frankie would have a fit if she knew what was really in there. If she ever saw those photographs, that would be the end of their relationship. Cursing himself for being so slap-dash, Jed made a mental note to burn the photos as quickly as possible. He had only kept them as souvenirs and should have got rid of them yonks ago.

He got out of bed and slung on his clothes. Frankie smiled as Jed put his masculine arms around her. 'What we gonna do today? Can we get something to eat? I'm starving,' she asked.

'I'll tell you what, why don't we go and get a Maccy D's? And then later, when it's dark, I'll clear me dad's shit out of that spare room and we can make ourselves a nice romantic campfire to sit round.'

Frankie kissed him. She had not sat around a camp-fire since she was a kid. Her dad used to make a big thing of Bonfire Night when she and Joey were little. 'Perfect,' she said.

As he shut the trailer door, Jed smiled. Later, those photos would go up in smoke and then his beautiful girl-friend would never be any the wiser.

With his brain doing overtime, Eddie got out of bed as soon as the birds began to sing.

'Can't you sleep, love?' Jessica asked softly.

Eddie sat on the edge of the bed and held his arms

434

out for a hug. 'Listen, I can't rest not knowing what our Frankie's up to. Today I'm gonna bring her home, Jess, and I need you to do me a favour. I don't think there'll be any trouble, but I don't want you here until she's home. I want you to take Joey and stay at your parents' for a couple of days.'

Jessica moved from her husband's grasp. 'How are you gonna bring her home? You're not gonna do anything silly, are you, Eddie?'

'Of course not. Me and Raymond know exactly what we're doing. I swear to you, Jess, all I want is our baby home, safe and sound.'

Unable to stop thinking about what Joey had told her, Jessica got more involved than usual. 'What about Jed? What are you planning to do to him? I know you better than you think, Eddie, and if you hurt that boy, then I'm leaving you for good.'

Eddie looked at Jessica in amazement. Her leaving him was never going to happen. 'What the hell are you talking about? Has someone been telling tales about me, or what?'

Jessica shook her head. She had promised Joey that she would never repeat what he had told her. 'If you say one word, Dom will be as good as dead, Mum,' Joey had begged her.

'I'm just worried, Ed. No one's said anything to me, but I know what you're like. When you're on that Scotch you're a different person. Just promise me that you won't hurt Jed.'

Eddie crouched down, took her hands in his and looked as sincere as a child. 'I swear to you, all I'm gonna do is buy off that boy. I want Frankie home and him out of her life. If I pay him enough, he'll move on and he won't come back. These pikeys are fly-by-nights, Jess. They ditch one bird, then they're with another five minutes

435

later. He won't return searching for our Frankie, not if the money's good enough, I bet ya.'

Jessica sighed. She wanted to believe Eddie, but didn't know if she could any more. 'It's not as easy as that, Eddie. What about the baby? You seem to have forgotten that Frankie's pregnant. If Frankie wants to keep the child, Jed's bound to want to see it at some point.'

Every time Frankie's baby was mentioned, it was a struggle for Eddie to keep his temper intact. 'That pikey piece of shit probably already has about ten kids dotted about the country. That's what they're like, all fucking inbred. None of 'em go to school and the only thing they learn is to fuck one another. Pat Murphy reckons Jimmy O'Hara's wife, Alice, is his cousin, so that says it all! I dunno about you, Jess, but I refuse to let my daughter live in that community. Now, are you going to your mother's with Joey, or what?' Ed asked angrily.

'Yes. I'll get up now, wake Joey and we'll get going.' Jessica said sadly.

Annoyed with himself for shouting at her, Eddie held Jessica tightly. 'I'm sorry, babe. You know what I'm like. I'll ring you when I've sorted things, then you can come home.'

Staring into his cloudy eyes, Jessica knew he had bigger plans for Jed than he had admitted. She was worried now, really worried. The last thing she wanted to do was betray Eddie, but she knew she had to do something. Feeling terribly guilty, she pecked him on the lips. 'I love you,' she told him.

Thankful she was OK about his plans, Eddie smiled at her. 'And I love you too, babe.'

Jed laughed as Frankie polished off her second egg and bacon muffin. 'Sure sign you're eating for two. You'll be as fat as a bull soon, you will.'

436

Frankie playfully punched him. When she had first got with Jed, his warped sense of humour used to give her the hump. Now she just joined in with him. 'I don't care if I get big and fat. If you don't want me, Jed, there's loads of others that will.'

Jed grabbed Frankie's face and, not caring about the other diners watching, stuck his tongue down the back of her throat.

'Do you mind? That's disgusting,' said a grey-haired woman sitting nearby.

Jed grabbed Frankie's hand. They had eaten all their food and were ready to leave, anyway.

Never able to resist a parting shot, Jed grabbed the woman's hand as he walked past her, and guided it towards his penis. 'You're only jealous, you old grunter. You want me and me cory for yourself, don't ya?' he taunted her.

'Management! I demand you call the police. Never in my life have I been so insulted,' the woman screamed.

Pissing themselves with laughter, Jed and Frankie ran from the restaurant.

Eddie was sitting opposite Raymond in Rosie's Café along the A13.

'Yous two are looking as handsome as ever, may I say,' Rosie shouted out to them.

Rosie was a plump woman in her late fifties and Eddie always had a laugh with her. Rosie had a personality to die for and the biggest pair of tits he had ever seen in his life. 'Rosie, put them knockers away, shut your trap and cook my fucking bacon,' he shouted back.

Turning back to Raymond, Eddie filled him in on the plan. 'So what we're gonna do is turn up there when darkness falls in two separate motors. I want you to run in with a baseball bat and, if Jed starts, clump him over the head with it. Then I need you to drag Frankie out the trailer, shove her in the car and take her home.'

Raymond shook his head. 'That ain't gonna work. Your Frankie's like a wild fucking cat. You don't honestly think she's gonna come out gracefully and sing to the radio on the way home, do ya?'

'I've brought a load of rope with me. I know she's my daughter, but you're gonna have to tie her up. There's a gag in me boot: stick that on her as well,' Eddie told him.

Raymond's face was a picture. 'So where do you come into all this? And what am I meant to do with her when I get her home? What's Jess gonna say when I bring her daughter home looking like an escape artiste?'

Eddie smirked. Raymond had cottoned on to his sense of humour over the years – so much so that he could probably give Eddie a run for his money now. 'I've sorted everything. When you get home, Gary and Ricky will be there. I didn't really want to get 'em involved in this one, but I had no choice. You can leave Frankie with them, they'll take care of her. Then I want you to drive back to Tilbury to help me clear up what's left of Jed.'

'Surely Frankie's gonna realise you've killed him. She's got a will of her own, that girl. Say she starts blabbing to someone?'

'She won't. I'm gonna tell her I gave Jed ten grand to get out of her life. He put it in his pocket and ran like a racehorse, I'll tell her,' Eddie said confidently.

Raymond had his doubts about the story. 'She ain't stupid, your Frankie. You don't wanna underestimate her, Ed.'

'She'll be fine in time. Obviously, she's gonna be upset at first, but once I persuade her to get rid of the baby, she'll get over it. Hopefully, one day she'll meet a nice bloke, have his kids and thank me for her lucky escape.'

438

Not agreeing with Eddie's way of thinking, Raymond changed the subject. 'If you shoot Jed in the trailer, we're gonna have to burn it.'

Eddie smiled. He was clever and had thought of everything. 'I'm gonna burn the trailer, but not Jed. You know what the filth's like, they'll find his teeth and work out it's him. When you drive off with Frankie, I'm gonna kill him, then wrap his body up in plastic. I've got a hooky motor to use. When you come back, we're taking the body over to Flatnose Freddie. Freddie disposed of many bodies for me dad over the years, and our pikey friend, Jed, is going into his big cement mixer. "Freddie," I said, "the boy's a traveller, he's used to open space." "Don't worry, Eddie, I'll prop him up in one of the flyovers I'm building. He's out in the open for ever then," Freddie assured me. Then Ray, we'll burn the motor.'

Raymond said nothing as he sipped his tea. Eddie's plan was good, but not infallible and Raymond had a terrible feeling that something was about to go very, very wrong.


A couple of miles away, Jessica paced up and down the living room. Joey had just left to stay with his grandparents. 'Please, Mum, I wanna stay with you. What are you gonna do? Please tell me,' her son begged her.

Jessica had waved away his fears. 'Mummy's not doing anything for you to worry about. All I'm going to do is ring Jed and speak to him and Frankie. If I can meet up with them, maybe between us we can sort things out,' she told Joey honestly.

'Please let me come with you. I miss Frankie so much,' her son pleaded.

Knowing that Joey was an emotional wreck and certainly no tough cookie, Jessica refused. 'You stay at

Nan and Grandad's and as soon as I've met up with Frankie, I promise I'll ring you and tell you everything.'

With Joey now safely out of the house, Jessica rang Jed's number. Joey had found it the day before; it was written on a piece of paper in Frankie's bedside cabinet.

As Jed answered the phone, Jessica spoke calmly and rationally. 'Please don't put the phone down, Jed. It's Frankie's mum and I want to help you.'

'We're fine. We don't need your help,' Jed said coldly.

'Listen, Jed, and listen carefully. I need to meet up with you. Eddie's on the warpath and I'm worried about your safety. I swear he doesn't know that I'm ringing you and if you see him, please don't tell him.'

Jed swerved onto a kerb and, holding his phone between his legs, repeated the conversation to Frankie. Although Frankie used to be a daddy's girl, she knew that her mum was the one she could trust. 'Let me speak to her,' she urged Jed.

Reluctantly, Jed handed her the phone. 'Mum, what's up?'

Jessica repeated what she had already told Jed. 'I'm really worried, Frankie. Your dad's planning something stupid, I saw it in his eyes.'

'Well, he won't find us,' Frankie said adamantly.

'Aren't you at Jed's house?' Jessica asked surprised.

'No, we're miles away. It's remote where we're staying, sort of in the middle of nowhere.'

'Please Frankie, tell me where you are and I'll come over and sort things out. I understand how you feel about Jed and the baby, I really do. I felt the same about your dad and you and Joey when I fell pregnant. I want you to be happy, Frankie, and if you want to marry Jed and have his baby, then it's fine by me. We still need to convince your father, but if I can come over and speak to you and Jed, between us we can make things right.'

Frankie held her hand over the phone and spoke to Jed. 'Look, I know she's not setting us up, my mum's not like that. We can't stay away forever, Jed. I miss Joey and I'm gonna want contact with him. If anyone can make my dad see sense, it's my mum. Please, give her the address and let her come over.'

Against his better judgement, Jed told Jessica where they were staying and told her not to drive there until it got dark. 'And don't come in your own car. Borrow one off someone else, or we ain't got a deal,' Jed told her as he abruptly ended the call.

'Thanks, Jed,' Frankie said, squeezing his hand.

Jed snatched his hand away. ''Ere, cacker, you've done a wrong 'un there, Frankie, I'm telling ya. I've got a terrible gut feeling that tonight is gonna be one almighty disaster. Things ain't gonna go cushti, I just know they ain't.'

# FORTY-TWO

Eddie and Raymond sat in a grotty pub in Tilbury. The weather was awful. It was meant to be midsummer, but the rain was bouncing off the ground.

'How did you know that Frankie and Jed were in Tilbury?' Raymond asked, sipping his pint.

'I hired a private detective. I need you to go and pay her for me tomorrow. She's got the hots for me, so I ain't going meself. I can't anyway – I'll be too busy indoors sorting Frankie out. I'll ring Jess tomorrow morning, get her to come home. She'll know what to do.'

'Are you gonna tell Jess the same story as you're telling Frankie?' Raymond enquired.

'Of course. No one must ever find out the truth. I'm not even gonna tell Gary or Ricky. The less anyone knows, the better with this one.'

'Do you want another pint?' Raymond asked.

'Nah. I'll just have an orange juice. We've got a big night ahead of us and we need our wits about us,' Ed replied.

Raymond felt himself shudder. Kidnapping Frankie, murdering Jed – something didn't feel right. Even the weather seemed against them. 'Be careful, Ed. Something feels wrong about all this to me.'

Eddie laughed. 'You know your trouble? You worry too much, Raymondo.'

Jessica sat in Vicki's house drinking a strong black coffee. Her nerves had been shattered last night, which had led to her feeling faint and weak.

'So, is Joey at home?' Vicki asked concerned.

'No, me dad picked him up earlier. He didn't want to go – he wanted to stay with me – but what could I do, Vicki? It's not right, him being in the house with all this going on.'

Vicki gave her best friend a hug. Jessica told her everything and vice versa. They trusted one another implicitly and what was said between them, was never repeated to either of their husbands. 'So, how exactly is Ed going to get Jed to stay out of Frankie's life?'

Jessica shrugged. 'Ed says he's going to offer Jed money to stay away. The thing is, Vicki, I think Jed and Frankie are truly in love. If Jed knocks back Eddie's offer, then I'm petrified of what might happen next. I need to sort it, but Jed said I can't take my own car.'

Vicki said nothing. She had heard loads of rumours about Eddie Mitchell over the years and knew he was ruthless and dangerous. 'Look, you can take my car. If anyone can sort this mess out, then it's you, Jess. And don't worry too much about Eddie – he'll be too frightened of losing you to do anything stupid.'

Jessica's face momentarily lit up. 'Do you really think so, Vicki?'

Vicki smiled. 'Of course I do.'

Lying was Vicki's only option. She could hardly tell her best friend that Eddie would stop at nothing to get what he wanted. What Jessica didn't know couldn't hurt her, and as her friend, it was Vicki's job to protect her from the awful truth.

Back in Tilbury, the bonfire was burning brightly.

'Do us a favour, Frankie. Most of this wood's wet. Go and see if you can find some dry bits,' Jed told her.

Frankie stared at the fire. 'It's burning OK. Do I have to, Jed?' It gave Frankie the heebies where they were staying and she didn't fancy walking around in the dark on her own.

'No one's gonna abduct you, you dinlo. The only reason the fire's burning is 'cause I cleared some of me dad's old tut out of that room. I've got nothing left to burn now.'

As Frankie walked off, Jed ran into the trailer, grabbed the incriminating photographs and threw them onto the fire. 'Burn, you bastards,' he mumbled, prodding them with a stick.

By the time Frankie ran back, the evidence was in ashes. 'All right? Where's the wood?' Jed asked her.

Frankie fell into his arms. 'I saw a rat and I hate them. It was staring at me, Jed.'

Jed held her tightly. 'I can't stand 'em either. Longtails, I call 'em. Evil little bastards, they are.'

'You don't think there's any watching us now?' Frankie asked him.

'Look, there's one there,' Jed yelled, making Frankie jump out of her skin.

Jed laughed. 'Come on, let's go inside and have something to eat. You can tidy up a bit before your mum gets here.'

Two miles down the road, Eddie could feel his adrenalin levels rising. 'This orange juice is making me feel queasy. Get us a large Scotch, Raymondo. Get yourself one an' all.'

As Raymond went up to the bar, Eddie gave Gina a call. 'Well, are they still there?'

'Yes. They've lit a fire outside, so I think they're settled for the night.'

'You can pull off now. My colleague will settle up with you tomorrow. I know we agreed on a price, but I've stuck a few hundred quid in extra for all your hard work.'

'Thank you, Mr Smith, that's very kind of you, but I would rather be taken out for dinner,' Gina said boldly.

'I'm very busy at the moment, but as soon as I get a bit of free time, I'll call you,' Eddie lied. He had to keep her sweet, as he didn't want her blabbing. 'And Gina, not a word to anyone. My friend's a very violent man and if any of this got out, it would make him very angry,' Eddie said threateningly.

'I understand,' Gina replied.

'Well, I've gotta go now. It's been a pleasure doing business with you,' Eddie said, before ending the call.

Raymond handed Eddie his drink. 'Who was that on the blower?'

'The private detective. I've just sent her home. It's getting dark now, so I suggest we have a couple more drinks, then make our move.'

Oblivious of what was about to happen, Jed and Frankie were munching crisps and discussing baby names. 'Whaddya think of Chantelle for a girl?' Frankie asked.

Jed turned his nose up. 'Don't like it, sounds like a fucking porn star.'

'Well, you think of some, then. You ain't liked any of mine so far,' Frankie said sulkily.

445

Jed pushed her onto the bench settee. 'Getting the hump, are we?' he said, tickling her.

As he kissed her passionately, Frankie immediately responded. 'I really do love you,' she told him as he pulled away.

Jed smiled. He needed to butter her up to ask his next question. 'Frankie, if we have a boy, can we call him Butch, after my grandad? I know you never met him, but he was a good old mush and I was always close to him.'

Frankie paused before answering. She didn't particularly like the name, but it obviously meant a lot to Jed. 'I don't see why not, but let's decide for definite nearer the time,' she said smiling.

Jed grinned as he cuddled her. Baby Butch would be the most idolised kid in the travelling community. His grandfather had been a legend amongst their own and by giving his son the same title, the name Butch O'Hara would carry on for years to come.

Frankie stood up and peered out of the window. 'I'm sure I just saw headlights. Go outside and have a look, Jed, it might be my mum.'

Seeing a figure walk towards her, Jessica turned the beam down and squinted. She had had terrible trouble finding her way here and had stopped on numerous occasions to ask for directions.

Jessica breathed a sigh of relief as she realised the boy must be Jed. At one point, she had wondered if he and Frankie had sent her on a wild goose chase, and was so glad that they hadn't.

'Just park down the road somewhere. It's a bit muddy, but you'll be OK, won't ya?'

Jessica looked at her feet. In her frantic state of mind, she had forgotten to put her shoes on and was only wearing carpet slippers. 'I've got me slippers on,' she told Jed awkwardly.

'Wait there,' Jed said, as he legged it back to the trailer.

'What's up? Was it me mum?' Frankie asked. She had been looking out of the window, but it had started raining heavily again and she couldn't see a thing.

'Yeah, it is. Give us your trainers, Frankie. Your mum's got her slippers on and it's like a swamp out there.'

Frankie giggled. 'I'm a size three and me mum's a size six. They won't fit her.'

Jed took them off of her anyway and ran back out to Jessica. 'Try them,' he said.

Unable to get them on, Jessica handed them back to him. 'Don't worry. If my feet get soaked it won't kill me, will it?'

Jed gave a half-smile. 'Just follow me and run. I've got a heater inside. I'll try and get the slippers dry for ya before you drive back.'

Frankie felt nervous as her mother stepped into the trailer. 'This is cosy,' Jessica said politely, hugging her daughter.

''Ere, put these on,' Jed said, handing her his socks and dealer boots to wear.

'Thanks, love,' Jessica said gratefully, as he put her slippers on top of the heater.

'Make Mum a cup of tea,' Frankie urged Jed.

Jessica squeezed her daughter's hand. 'So, how are you? Why aren't you staying at Jed's house?'

'Jed's dad and mum aren't there. His dad's gone to a horse fair and his mum's at her sister's. We was gonna stay there, but Jed said we'd be safer staying here until his dad gets back.'

'Were you worried about your dad?' Jessica asked.

Frankie nodded. 'What we gonna do, Mum? Me and

447

Jed don't wanna have to live like this. I'm happy and I want everybody to be happy for me. I want you, Joey and dad to all be part of me and my baby's life.'

Seeing tears roll down Frankie's face, Jessica felt her own eyes well up. 'Frankie, I promise you that I'll do my utmost to make your dad see sense. I can see that you and Jed are in love and I want to support both of you and the baby. With me being pregnant as well, our babies can be playmates, Frankie. I can babysit whenever you want. If you and Jed want to go out, I can –'

Handing Jessica her tea, Jed shut her up in mid-sentence. 'Look, I know you mean well, Mrs Mitchell, but unless you sort that husband of yours out, none of that shit's gonna happen, is it? I ain't having Frankie upset while she's carrying my child, so if things ain't smoothed out fast, I'm taking Frankie away and none of yous will ever see her again!'

Crawling along in the rain, Eddie stopped the motor, got out and jumped in the passenger seat of Raymond's motor. 'Right, that's the place down there on the left. You know what you've gotta do, don'tcha?'

Raymond nodded. 'Take this just in case,' Eddie urged as he handed him a small gun.

'Whaddya want me to do with that?' Raymond asked.

'Nothing, it's just for back-up. Now remember, Ray, be as threatening as you can when you get there. If the door ain't open, then smash the fucking windows. You'll have to hit 'em hard, 'cause it's probably that plastic shit. That cocky pikey cunt is bound to stick up for himself and I want you to clump him as hard as you can with the bat. Knock him out, so he don't wake up. Now, you go first and when I see you've got Frankie and driven off, I'll go in and finish off the job.'

Raymond felt sick as he drove towards the trailer. Usually violence didn't bother him. He could kill a man in the blink of an eye, but not when it involved his own family. He didn't like Eddie's plan one little bit, but he was too frightened to argue. When Eddie Mitchell made his mind up to do something, there wasn't a man in the world who could change his mind.

As the tyres screeched to a halt outside, Frankie screamed, grabbed her mother and got down on the floor. Jed took the knife he always carried out of his pocket and stood by the door.

'Open this fucking door – now!' Raymond screamed menacingly as he smashed the baseball bat against it.

'Oh, my God! It's Raymond. Your dad's gonna kill me. What am I gonna do?' Jessica whispered, sobbing.

'Quick, hide in that room, Mum. There's a gap under the bed,' Frankie urged her.

As Jessica crawled into the bedroom, she shuddered as she heard the window go through. 'Please God, don't let anyone get hurt. Please God, don't let anyone get hurt,' she repeated over and over again.

Frankie screamed as Raymond threw himself against the door and it flew open. 'Leave us alone. Go away!' she screamed.

Desperate to be the big hero, Jed lunged at Raymond with the knife. 'You fucking mug!' Raymond yelled, easily knocking it out of Jed's hand.

As Jed picked the kettle up, Raymond obeyed Eddie's orders and clumped him over the head with the baseball bat. He could have hit him harder, but guilt stopped him from doing so. All he wanted to do was stun Jed; it was Eddie's job to do anything else.

Jed wasn't stupid, so he fell on the floor and played dead.

'Jed! Jed!' Frankie screamed hysterically.

As Raymond walked towards her, Frankie went for him. 'Get off of me! I hate you and my dad. I wish you were both dead,' she yelled, pummelling her fists against his chest.

Raymond took the rope out of his pocket and carried out the instructions he had been given. 'It's all right, Frankie, all I'm doing is taking you home,' he said, as she repeatedly kicked and punched him.

'Jed, wake up, please wake up,' Frankie cried.

As Raymond bent over with his back towards him, Jed held his forefinger to his mouth to tell Frankie to be quiet and to let her know he was all right. I love you, he mouthed to her.

Frankie bit Raymond's hand, as he tried to gag her. Raymond felt terrible. He was cut out for most things, but not this shit. He was mad to have let Eddie talk him into this. He should have been a man and refused.

Jed lay still as Raymond finally managed to tie and gag Frankie. He cursed himself for not bringing a proper weapon with him. Pretending he was knocked out cold was all he could do. Raymond was double his size and was armed with his infamous baseball bat, and Jed knew that Frankie needed him alive, not dead.

Jessica was frozen with shock. She couldn't breathe, move or anything. Her daughter's screams had been awful. She had wanted to get up and help her, but she had been paralysed by fear and couldn't. She felt faint again, really ill.

Seeing Raymond bundle Frankie towards the car, Eddie picked up the machine gun and studied it. He had never used one of these things before, but he was sure he could handle it.

As Raymond's car pulled away, Eddie got out of his

car and took a pop at one of the nearby squashed cars. Perfect, he thought, as the bullets landed exactly where he aimed them.

Hearing the gun being fired, Jed quickly got up. It was obvious what was coming next and he knew he had no choice other than to leg it. Raymond had smashed a couple of windows in the trailer and, realising the gunshots were coming from the front, Jed squeezed himself out of a back window and literally ran for his life.

At the sound of the gun being fired, Jessica lost consciousness. Out for the count, she was totally unaware of her husband's footsteps nearing.

In the back of Raymond's car, Frankie was desperately trying to pull the gag off her mouth. She had seen her father waiting in the shadows as Raymond had lifted her into his motor, and not only was she worried about Jed, she was also concerned about her mother.

Realising Frankie was making all sorts of funny noises, Raymond stopped the car. He had to check she was all right in case she couldn't breathe properly. 'Are you OK? Can you breathe?' he asked as he pulled the gag off her.

'You stupid fucking idiot. I saw me dad outside and Mum's in that trailer.'

'What?' Raymond asked incredulously. Frankie was winding him up – she had to be.

'I swear on my baby's life, Mum's in there. She came to see me to sort stuff out. When she heard your voice, she hid under the bed.'

Realising that Frankie was telling the truth, Raymond felt all the hairs on the back of his neck stand up. 'Jesus! No!' he screamed, as he spun the car around and raced back to the scene of the crime.

\* \* \*

451

Eddie smiled as he saw the dealer boots poking out from under the bed. He would have liked to have tortured the little fucker for a while, but he really didn't have the time. Poor little Jed must have crawled in here after Raymond clumped him over the bonce. Smiling, Eddie prepared his speech.

'Bye-bye, Jeddy boy. This is what you get for crossing me,' he said as he let fly with the machine gun.

With blood splattered all over himself and the walls, Eddie decided enough was enough. He was extremely thirsty and decided he needed to have a little refreshment before Raymond got back. The cleaning-up process was much harder work than just killing people, unfortunately.

Eddie went to the fridge and was pleased to find a can of lager. 'Cheers, you little gyppo cunt,' he toasted, as he sat down on the old sofa.

Sipping his beer, Eddie took a good look at the surroundings. 'So this is how pikeys live, is it?' he said cuttingly.

Smirking, Eddie slurped his beer. Frankie wouldn't thank him for a while, but he had literally saved his daughter from a life of hell. Any man in his position would have done the same as he had. Every father in the world only wants the best for their daughter, don't they?

As the sound of brakes screeched outside, Eddie shot up like a jack-in-the-box. Raymond wasn't due back yet, so who the fuck was this?

Eddie picked up the machine gun and lifted back the old net curtain. As he saw Raymond running towards him, Eddie guessed there had been a hitch, but still breathed a sigh of relief. Flatnose Freddie would have thought he was taking the right piss if he had turned up with a boot full of bodies instead of just one.

'What's up?' he asked as Raymond let himself in.

'Where's Jessica? Have you seen her?' Raymond asked frantically.

'Of course I ain't seen her. She's round her fucking mother's,' Ed replied, looking at him as though he was mental.

'No, she ain't. Frankie said she was here, she came to see her,' Raymond said nervously.

'Well, she ain't here now, is she?' Eddie said, fuming that his wife had gone behind his back.

'Where's Jed?' Raymond asked, as a sudden feeling of dread washed over him.

'Having a little rest under the bed. Don't worry, Ray, I've put about two hundred bullets in him, so he's hardly likely to jump out on us,' Eddie said, laughing.

Raymond yanked open the bedroom door and breathed a sigh of relief as he saw a pair of boots poking out from underneath the bed. 'Thank God. You did see his face, didn't you, Ed?' Raymond asked confused. He could have sworn that Jed was barefoot when he had left.

'You ain't losing the plot, Ray, are you? You clumped him, he crawled under the bed. I came in, shot the cunt, job done. So what is your problem?'

Raymond felt ill as he turned to Eddie. 'Ed, Frankie reckons Jess crawled under the bed and was hiding there.'

Eddie stood up. 'My old woman don't walk around in dealer boots,' he said, as he strolled into the bedroom.

Grabbing hold of the ankles, Eddie was shocked as the boots came off in his hand. Seeing a pair of perfectly manicured feet, Eddie sank to his knees. 'No, no, it can't be! No!' he shouted.

Raymond pushed him out of the way, grabbed the legs and dragged the body out. As Eddie screamed out his wife's name, Raymond started to sob.

'Jessica, Jessica. I'm so sorry, I love you. Why did you come here? Why?' Eddie howled, cradling her bullet-ridden body in his arms.

Raymond was too stunned to speak. He could barely believe that his beautiful, vivacious sister was the bloodied corpse he was looking at. Jessica's body was lacerated beyond recognition. Her beautiful blonde hair was matted with blood and her face looked contorted with shock.

'Oh my God, Eddie. What have you done?' Raymond whispered.

Sobbing like a baby, Eddie clung to his wife's lifeless limbs. Raymond tried to drag Eddie off his sister and, as he did so, Ed started to yelp like a wounded animal. Raymond stared at Jessica's face once more, then bent over and vomited.

As Raymond's gun fell out of his pocket, Eddie immediately picked it up. Without Jessica, his life was nothing and he knew he could never forgive himself or get over what he had done. 'It's all right, darling. I'll look after you and our baby. I'm coming with you,' he said, as he pointed the gun towards his temple.

'No, Ed! No!' Raymond yelled, as he lunged towards Eddie.

Outside in the car, Frankie was still tied up. She was frightened, thirsty and desperate to know what was going on. As she heard the gunshot echo in the wind, she let out a piercing scream.

'Jed! Mum! Where are you?' she sobbed.

# FORTY-THREE

Raymond crouched down. He had managed to knock the gun away from his brother-in-law's head, but it had still gone off and had whizzed through Eddie's shoulder. 'Stay with me, Ed. I'm calling an ambulance right now,' Raymond urged him.

Eddie lay moaning and groaning. He was conscious, but not really with it. 'Let me die. I want to die,' he muttered.

Ignoring his pal's wishes, Raymond dialled 999. 'Get me an ambulance. Two people have been shot,' he yelled, as the woman asked him which service he wanted.

Taking off his jacket, Raymond laid it over his sister's mutilated body. 'I love you, Jess,' he said, tears rolling down his face.

Knowing that the police were going to have a field day, Raymond's instincts kicked in and he ran outside to untie Frankie.

'What's happened? Is Jed alive?' his niece screamed.

By now Frankie was absolutely hysterical and Raymond had never felt so guilty in his life as he tried to calm her down. 'Jed's fine, he got away. Now listen Frankie, and listen carefully. The police and ambulance will be here in a minute. You say nothing to them, OK? All I'm gonna say is me and you drove over here to look for your mum.'

'I'm telling them everything. You and Dad are animals and I hate you both,' Frankie bellowed.

Raymond slapped his hand around her face. She was in terrible shock and needed to snap out of it, else they were all going down. 'You say nothing, Frankie, do you hear me? Nothing.'

'Where's my mum? I want my mum,' Frankie sobbed.

Untying the last bit of rope, Raymond held his distraught niece in his arms. How was he meant to tell her that her dad had killed her mum? As the sound of sirens approached, he pleaded with Frankie to do as he had asked. 'There's been an accident, Frankie. I'll explain later. Don't say anything to the police,' he said, as he jumped out of the car.

Both the police and paramedics were taken aback by the sight that greeted them. They were obviously trained to deal with these situations, but neither service had ever seen a woman with so many bulletholes in her body. Eddie was now out for the count, and was bleeding profusely.

'Is he still alive?' Raymond asked, as Eddie was rushed into the ambulance.

'He's still got a pulse, but we need to get him to hospital immediately. He's lost a lot of blood,' the paramedic replied.

Seeing the stretcher being brought out of the trailer, Frankie lost the plot. 'What's going on?' she screamed, as she got out of the car and ran towards the amubulance.

As Frankie tried to dart inside the trailer, a policeman grabbed hold of her. The police had been so shocked by the scene they had encountered, they hadn't even realised Frankie was there. 'Where's Jed? Where's my mum?' Frankie yelled.

'You can't go inside. It's a crime scene,' the policeman told her gently.

Raymond led his inconsolable niece back to the safety of the car. He had to tell her the truth before the coppers did the honours. Sitting Frankie in the passenger seat, Raymond crouched down and held her hands. 'Mummy's dead, Frankie. I'm so, so sorry,' he said, as another ambulance and more police back-up arrived.

'Mum's not dead. What about her baby? She can't be dead,' Frankie whimpered.

'It was an accident, Frankie. I'm sorry,' Raymond responded, hugging her fragile body in his arms.

As white as a ghost, Frankie shook like a leaf. 'I want my mum, I need to see her!' she screamed hysterically.

The police came over to tell Raymond and Frankie that the ambulance was waiting to take them to hospital. 'You'll be treated for shock. We're going to need to take statements from both of you later,' an officer informed Raymond.

Raymond nodded. He had already told the police that he had brought Frankie here to see her mum and found Jessica and Eddie both shot. 'It's obvious someone wanted to kill them, and thought they'd succeeded,' he told the shell-shocked copper.

'I want Joey. Ring Joey for me,' Frankie wailed, as she was helped into the ambulance.

Raymond sat opposite her with his head in his hands. How the hell was he meant to tell his mum and dad that both Jessica and the baby were dead?

Unaware of the carnage, Jed was sat drinking a beer and soaking his sore feet in a trailer over in Basildon. Fearful of losing his life, he had run for miles barefoot. He had heard the gunshots as he had scarpered across the fields, but had no idea of what had actually happened. Finally, he had come to a main road, had found a phone box and rung his cousin, Sammy Boy. His feet were ripped to pieces and when Sammy arrived to collect him, he could barely speak through the pain.

'Do you want another beer? How do ya feel now?' Sammy asked him.

Gratefully accepting the can, Jed opened it and drank most of the lager in one go. 'I feel like shit, but I need to find Frankie. I want you to drive me to her house and if she ain't there, then you'll have to take me back to Tilbury.'

'It's a bit risky if they've got shooters, ain't it?' Sammy asked him.

'If Frankie ain't indoors, I'll go to mine and get one of me dad's guns,' Jed replied.

Sammy handed him a fresh pair of socks and some trainers. 'Come on then, let's go.'

Many miles away, Joyce, Joey and Stanley were all of a panic as they headed towards Basildon Hospital.

'There's been a terrible accident – you need to come quick. Frankie's asking for Joey, so bring him with you,' was all Raymond had told them.

Joey couldn't stop crying, 'Whaddya think has happened, Nan?' he wept.

'I don't know, darling,' Joyce said, squeezing his hand.

Raymond was pacing the corridors when he spotted his parents walking towards him. The doctors were worried about Frankie. She had been that hysterical, her blood pressure had shot through the roof and they had now given her a sedative to calm her down.

Joyce and Stanley glanced fearfully at one another as they spotted the huge police presence. 'Is it Jess? Has she lost the baby?' Joyce sobbed, as she was led into a nearby relatives' room.

A sombre-looking policewoman urged them all to sit down.

'Where's Frankie? Is she OK?' Joey asked, shaking.

Raymond begged the policewoman to let him break the terrible news to his family.

'What's going on, son?' Stanley asked, his face stern.

Raymond let out a cry. 'Jessica's dead,' he sobbed.

'Dead! What do you mean, she's dead?' Joyce asked incredulously.

'There was a shooting. No one knows exactly what happened, but Jessica's dead and Eddie's being operated on as we speak.'

As Joey let out a piercing scream, Joyce collapsed with shock. Stanley stood up and, as his legs buckled, sank to his knees. 'I always knew that bastard would be the death of my Jessica, I always knew it,' he howled.

Nearby, in the operating theatre, Eddie's heart had just stopped beating. 'Cardiac arrest. Start resuscitation,' shouted one of the surgeons.

Everybody crowded round. It was touch and go for Eddie Mitchell.

Still unaware of the chaos, Jed and Sammy Boy headed straight to Frankie's house and were surprised to see her driveway swarming with police officers. Jed told Sammy to stay in the car.

'Wait here while I ask the gavvers what's going on,' he said as he slammed the car door.

'You can't go in there. No one's allowed in there,' said a copper, standing by the gate. He had been ordered to guard the property while his superiors searched for clues.

'What's happened? I need to see my girlfriend, she lives here,' Jed said bluntly.

'There's been an accident, that's all I can tell you,' the copper replied.

Jed was never one to be fobbed off. 'Me and my girlfriend are getting wed. She's having my baby, so I need to know she's all right. Can you try and find out where she is for me?'

Turning his back to Jed, the young officer spoke into his walkie-talkie. His girlfriend was also pregnant, so he felt some empathy towards Jed. 'Your girlfriend's OK. She's at Basildon Hospital.'

Jed sprinted back to the car. 'Basildon Hospital, as quick as you like,' he yelled at his cousin.

Back at the hospital, Joyce had been treated for shock. Seeing Joey and his father in absolute pieces, Raymond left the room. Their tears were pure and raw and Raymond felt as guilty as hell.

Outside, he punched the wall. He couldn't live this life any more. He pictured Jessica's face. It seemed so surreal that he would never see her or hear her infectious laugh ever again. Memories of the past came flooding back to Raymond. He remembered Jess struggling to learn to ride her bike without stabilisers. How she took the piss out of his obsession with Marc Bolan. She'd been so supportive when he'd joined that band, and even stuck up for him when he'd worn eyeliner. Raymond sat on a plastic chair and toyed with his emotions. Grassing Eddie up to the police was a no-go. Many people would have done, but not Raymond – he was too loyal. He knew how much Eddie had loved Jessica. It was an accident, a mistake. Ed's life would be destroyed after this. It was a pure mishap and Raymond would never tell a soul about the horrendous true happenings. As long as Frankie and Jed kept quiet, the police would just think that Jessica and Eddie had been attacked by somebody else.

Seeing a copper staring at him, Raymond went back

inside the hospital. Joey was curled up on the floor like a baby. 'Get up, Joey, come on, mate,' Raymond said, crouching down next to him.

'Leave him alone. This is all your fault, you and that other fucking hoodlum. With the lives you and him led, something like this was always bound to happen and it did, to my beautiful Jessica, who did nothing to deserve it. I hate what you've become, Raymond, and I'm ashamed to call you my son. Get out. Go on, get out, I never want to see your face again,' Stanley shouted, pushing his son towards the door.

Shocked at the venom in his usually mild-mannered father's voice, Raymond ran from the room.

With no room in the hospital car park, Sammy parked his motor in one of the spaces marked for staff only.

Jed had had his thinking cap on during the journey. He guessed from the police presence at Frankie's that something sinister had happened, so he had prepared himself a story. 'If the gavvers say anything, then I'm gonna say that you picked me up from Tilbury at six o'clock this morning. Me dad'll go mental, 'cause he owns that fucking land. Me truck's there and it's registered in his name, so the gavvers are bound to wanna question him. Thank God I burnt them photos yesterday, Sam. Can you imagine the can of worms they could have opened?'

'Are you sure you burnt 'em properly?' Sammy asked worried.

'Positive. I checked,' Jed replied confidently.

'Can I go and see my Joycie?' asked a red-eyed Stanley.

'And can I see Frankie now?' Joey asked, distraught.

Neither asked about Eddie, as neither really cared how he was.

461

The nurse nodded. 'Take no notice if they're still woozy. It will just be the medication we've given them,' she told them.

Joey sat down next to his sister's bed. 'What happened, Frankie? Talk to me,' he pleaded, as he stared into his sister's haunted eyes.

Frankie squeezed his hand. She wanted to tell him the truth, tell him that Raymond had kidnapped her, but she was still sedated, in shock, and unable to speak properly.

A few doors away, Stanley clutched Joyce's hand. She was still sound asleep, but Stanley was sure she could hear him. 'You should have listened to me all them years ago, Joycie. If Jess hadn't married Eddie, we wouldn't be mourning our daughter's death. We should have put our foot down when she was seventeen and she first met him. I always knew he was a villain, a wrong 'un, and still I let her marry him. How are Frankie and Joey ever gonna get over this, eh, Joycie? Their lives are ruined and so are ours. I hope that bastard doesn't wake up. He deserves to die, not our Jess. I hate him, Joycie, I really do.'

Joyce's eyes flickered open. 'You were right all along about him, Stanley. I'm just sorry I didn't listen to you,' she mumbled.

Unable to read properly, Jed kept stopping staff to ask them whether he was going in the right direction.

'Go straight down the end of this corridor, then turn left,' a nurse told him.

As Jed and Sammy ran around the corner, they came face to face with Raymond. 'Where's Frankie? What's happened?' Jed asked him.

Raymond led Jed away from the Old Bill.

'This is all your fault, you pikey cunt. My sister's dead

462

because of you. What are you doing up here anyway? Just do one, will ya?' Ray said viciously.

'If you don't tell me what's happened, I swear I'll cause a fucking riot,' Jed yelled.

Seeing the Old Bill had reappeared, Raymond realised that he had no option but to tell him. 'Frankie's not injured, but her mum's dead. Eddie's been shot as well. I don't know how he is 'cause no one will tell me.'

Jed looked at Raymond in astonishment. 'What happened? How did Jess die?'

'I don't fucking know,' Raymond spat.

Seeing a copper walk over to them, Raymond put his arm around Jed's shoulder. 'Say nothing about what went on. Go and see Frankie and make sure she keeps schtum as well,' he whispered.

Jed nodded and went in search of his girlfriend. The copper walked up to Raymond. 'Your brother-in-law's OK. I think he's in recovery.'

Raymond took a deep breath. 'Thanks for letting us know.'

'How is she, Joey?' Jed asked as he sat on a chair next to Frankie.

'She's sedated. She's still in shock. What are we gonna do, Jed? My mum's dead,' Joey sobbed.

As Jed stood up, Joey threw himself into his arms. Jed didn't know what to do. He was positive Frankie's brother was an iron and he didn't really want to touch him. 'Move out the way, Joey. I wanna talk to Frankie,' he said awkwardly.

As Jed held her hand, Frankie opened her eyes. 'I'm sorry about your mum. I'll look after you from now on, I promise I will. Is the baby OK? Have they checked you out?'

463

'I'm having a scan in the morning. Please don't leave me, Jed, stay here with me,' she whispered.

'I'm going nowhere,' Jed assured her.

Eddie Mitchell woke up in the early hours. At first his brain was fuzzy, but within minutes he remembered everything. 'Jessica! Jessica!' he cried, the tears rolling down his cheeks.

The Irish nurse walked over to him. 'You're going to be OK, Mr Mitchell. You had a nasty bullet wound and lost a lot of blood, but you're in the best place here. We'll have you back on your feet in no time.'

'Are the police still here?' Eddie asked groggily.

The nurse nodded. Eddie was in a private room and the police were waiting outside the door. 'Can you tell 'em to come in. I have a confession to make,' Eddie whispered.

Raymond stood outside smoking another cigarette. The whole episode had been a nightmare and had made him take stock of his life. He had already planned what he was going to do. He was going to propose to Polly, settle down and go straight. What he had seen in that trailer had put him off violence for life and he would never forget the sight of his sister's mutilated body lying on that floor for the rest of his days.

'Are you OK, Uncle Raymond?' Joey asked, as he walked up to him.

Joey felt like a spare part now that Jed had arrived, and he couldn't wait to leave the hospital and grieve in peace. Raymond put his arm around Joey's shoulder. 'I think I should ring your uncles Paulie and Ronny to tell 'em what's happened. They can tell Reg and Auntie Joan. They're all gonna find out, anyway.'

Joey nodded dumbly. His mum was dead and nothing else really mattered any more.

Sergeant Lineker could barely believe his ears as Eddie Mitchell confessed to murdering his own wife.

'So, it was mistaken identity? You thought that Mrs Mitchell was somebody else?'

Propped up against his pillow, a tearful Eddie nodded. 'My daughter's pregnant. She's only sixteen and I went there to shoot her boyfriend. I didn't know that my wife was there and when I saw this big pair of dealer boots poking out from under the bed, I assumed it was Jed, Frankie's fella. My Jessica and me were so happy. She was pregnant again and we were over the moon. I loved her more than anyone or anything,' Eddie said.

Sergeant Lineker glanced at his colleague. A full confession was the last thing they had expected to come out of Eddie Mitchell's mouth. 'You get some rest. You need to speak to your solicitor tomorrow. We'll set the wheels in motion.'

As the two coppers left the room, Eddie covered his face with his hands and howled. He had never admitted to a crime before in his life, but this was different. He had murdered his own wife and unborn child in cold blood, and spending the rest of his life in prison was what Eddie felt he deserved.

Stanley walked back into the room where his wife was. 'The doctor said that we can go home soon,' he told her.

Joyce sat up and clung on to her husband for dear life.

'Come on, let it all out,' Stanley said, as she sobbed on his shoulder. He felt like crying himself, but had to be strong for her sake.

465

'What are we gonna go without her, Stanley? She was my life,' Joyce wept.

Stanley felt his eyes welling up. 'I really don't know, but we'll manage somehow, darling.'

'I'm gonna pop outside with Sammy to have a fag. Shall I bring you a coffee back?' Jed asked Frankie.

Frankie nodded. 'See if you can find Joey for me. He can sit with me while you're gone.'

Jed nodded and left the room.

'Your sister wants you,' he told Joey as he walked past him.

Outside, Sammy handed Jed a cigarette. 'I might shoot off in a minute. Will you be all right here on your own?'

'I'll be fine. Frankie will probably be allowed to go home in the morning, so I'll stop here with her,' Jed replied.

Sammy shook his cousin's hand. 'You know where I am if you need me. Ring me tomorrow,' he said, as he went to walk away.

Jed grabbed hold of him. 'Sam, that thing we done, you must never tell anyone, especially not now. Promise me you won't?'

'I swear, you have my word,' Sammy replied.

Jed leaned against the wall as his cousin walked away. Thank God he'd had the brains to burn them photos he'd stolen as souvenirs. No one but him and Sammy knew the truth. He hadn't even told his dad.

Jed smiled as he thought back to that night. Murdering Harry Mitchell had been all his idea. He had planned it with precision and, due to his cleverness, they'd got away with it.

In Jed's eyes, Harry Mitchell had deserved to die. Butch, Jed's grandfather, had had his life ruined by

466

Mitchell. Butch had never recovered from being shot in the foot. He walked with a severe limp from that day onwards and spent the latter part of his life living as a recluse.

Jed had plotted the operation from start to finish. He'd recruited Sammy's younger brother, Billy, and his pals to act as decoys. Six times Jed had driven them over to Harry's and paid them fifty quid to cause mayhem. The boys had no idea what Jed was up to. He'd told them that the man had knocked him for money.

'See that house over there, number thirty-one? I want you to hang about outside and make a nuisance of yourselves. Make sure all the neighbours see and hear you, but keep your hoods up at all times so they can't see your faces. You've gotta shout, scream, throw stones, knock on the doors. I need you to be as noisy as you can,' Jed ordered.

On the night of the murder, Jed had paid the boys their money, driven them back to Essex, then he and Sammy Boy had returned to Canning Town. They knew Harry was in, as they'd seen the lights go on and off earlier.

Jed had chosen Christmas Eve for a reason. He knew there'd be loads of noise on the streets, therefore Mitchell's shouts and screams would blend in with those of drunken revellers.

At eleven o'clock, Harry's house was in complete darkness.

'Let's give it an hour, make sure the old shit-cunt's asleep,' Jed told Sammy.

Sitting across the road in the back of a hooky van, Jed and Sammy amused themselves by secretly poking fun at the merry worshippers heading off to midnight mass. At a quarter to twelve, Jed checked the coast was clear and told his cousin to follow him.

'Right, put your gloves on and your hood up. Time to give old Harry boy his Christmas present,' Jed whispered, as they crept through the alleyway that led to Harry Mitchell's back garden.

Jed knew they'd have no problem gaining entry. He'd done his homework and was aware that Mitchell left the louvres open in the conservatory to let his cat in and out. Jed then expertly removed the louvres one by one, climbed in, then urged Sammy to do the same.

Jed waited until he got to the lounge before he switched his torch on. Spotting the photos of young Harry with a pretty woman, Jed smiled. 'Once we've finished him off, we'll take a couple of them pictures as souvenirs. We need to rough the place up a bit, make a mess, but we'll have to do it quietly,' Jed whispered.

Gesticulating for Sammy to follow him up the stairs, Jed clutched his baseball bat tightly in both hands. He'd waited a long time for this moment and felt high on adrenalin.

Harry's snoring sounded like a pig snorting and Jed grinned as he tiptoed towards his bedroom. The door was open, and as Jed stood over the sleeping man, he was filled with a mixture of excitement and hatred. Glancing at Sammy, he lifted the bat in the air and smashed it as hard as he could over Harry's head.

Instinct took over and a dazed Harry staggered out of the bed and lunged at Jed. 'Who are you? What the fuck do you want?' he shouted, as his feeble punches failed to connect.

Jed hit Harry once more and laughed as he fell to the floor. 'Not as strong as you thought you were, eh?' he goaded.

'Tie up his arms and legs then shine the torch on him,' Jed told Sammy.

Recognising the accent was that of a traveller, Harry knew he was in trouble. For many years he'd slept with a gun under his bed and his only hope now was to make a grab for it. With the two blows he'd received to his head, Harry was no match for his fit young attacker. Clocking Harry's hand creeping under the bed, Jed repeatedly stamped on it with his right foot.

As Harry felt his wrist snap, he screamed out in pain. Sammy tied Harry's arms up, 'Who are you? One of the fucking O'Haras? I'm warning you – you kill me and my Eddie will break every bone in your useless pikey body,' Harry shouted.

Jed laughed as Sammy tied Harry's legs up. Harry reminded him of an oven-ready chicken, 'Sorry, did I forget to introduce myself? I'm Jed O'Hara, Butch's grandson, and this is my cousin, Sammy. I take it you remember my grandfather?'

Annoyed that Harry didn't reply, Jed booted him in the head. 'Answer me, you old shit-cunt.'

Harry was in so much pain he could barely speak. 'What happened with your grandfather was business, nothing personal,' he croaked.

'I'll give you fucking personal,' Jed spat, tying the gag around Harry's mouth.

Jed could sense Harry's despair. Watching him choking, trying to say something, Jed loosened the gag.

'Please don't kill me. I beg you not to. If you kill me, you're signing your own death warrant. The feud between our families ended years ago. To start it up again now will cause an absolute bloodbath.'

Jed tightened the gag once more. He had to finish what he'd come here to do. 'My grandfather turned into a hermit because of you. You killed his spirit and now I'm gonna kill yours. So go fuck your grandmother.'

As Jed lifted up the baseball bat, Harry began to wriggle like a fish out of water.

'Hurry up, Jed. Finish him off and let's get out of here,' Sammy urged his cousin.

Jed looked into Harry's petrified eyes and smiled. 'Happy Christmas. I hope you rot in hell,' he whispered, repeatedly smashing the bat over Harry's skull.

As blood sprayed everywhere, Sammy felt queasy. 'Come on, Jed, that's enough,' he said.

Even though he knew Harry was dead, Jed couldn't stop. His victim's head was already bashed to a pulp, so Jed started to smash the bat against his teeth.

Frightened, Sammy grabbed Jed and pushed him against the wall. 'Whaddya doing? The old cunt's been dead five minutes. We need to get out of here, Jed. If we don't, we're both looking at prison.'

The word prison seemed to snap Jed out of his violent trance. Checking he'd left no clues in the bedroom, Jed followed Sammy downstairs.

'Open a few drawers and throw some stuff on the floor. It has to look like a burglary,' Jed said, as he stuffed some photos inside his jacket.

Ten minutes later, with the house looking completely ransacked, Jed and Sammy climbed out the same way they'd got in.

'Excuse me. Do you know what the visiting hours are?'

Jed's daydream was ended by the woman standing in front of him. 'Sorry. What did you say?'

The woman repeated her question.

'I've no idea. Ask a nurse,' Jed told her.

Taking the last drag on his fag, Jed flicked the butt into the air. Everything had turned out OK in the end. Harry was long gone, Jessica was dead, Eddie was looking at a life sentence, which meant Frankie and the baby were all his.

Unable to stop himself, Jed began to laugh. He couldn't wait to tell his father that Eddie Mitchell had tried to shoot him, but instead had killed his own wife. For years his dad had banged on about getting his own back on the Mitchells and now, without his dad even knowing, he'd done it for him.

Jed grinned as he strolled back into the hospital. Thanks to him, the feud was finally over.

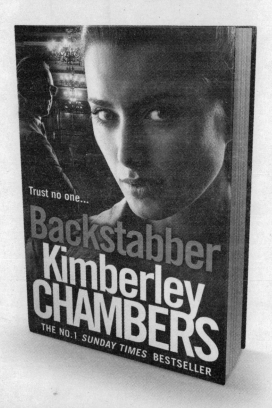

Born in Barcelona in 1964, Carlos Ruiz Zafón moved to Los Angeles in his twenties where he worked as a screenwriter. Before the publication of *The Shadow of the Wind* in 2001, Zafón had already published four successful novels for young adults. He now works full time as a novelist and is currently at work on his second novel, set in nineteenth-century Barcelona, part of a planned set of four based in the city, of which *The Shadow of the Wind* is the first.

# The Shadow of the Wind

CARLOS RUIZ ZAFÓN

Translated by Lucia Graves

PHOENIX

A PHOENIX PAPERBACK

First published in Great Britain in 2004
by Weidenfeld & Nicolson
This paperback edition published in 2005
by Phoenix,
an imprint of Orion Books Ltd,
Orion House, 5 Upper St Martin's Lane,
London WC2H 9EA

First published in Spain by Editorial Planeta, S.A., 2002

11 13 15 17 19 20 18 16 14 12

The present edition has been translated with the aid
of a grant from the General Directorate for Books,
Archives and Libraries, Spanish Ministry
for Education, Culture and Sport.

A CIP catalogue record for this book
is available from the British Library.

ISBN-13 978-0-7538-2025-4
ISBN-10 0-7538-2025-0

Typeset by Deltatype Ltd, Birkenhead, Wirral

Printed and bound in Great Britain by
Clays Ltd, St Ives plc

The Orion Publishing Group's policy is to use papers that
are natural, renewable and recyclable products and
made from wood grown in sustainable forests. The logging
and manufacturing processes are expected to conform to
the environmental regulations of the country of origin.

www.orionbooks.co.uk

*For Joan Ramon Planas,*
*who deserves better*

# The Cemetery of Forgotten Books

I still remember the day my father took me to the Cemetery of Forgotten Books for the first time. It was the early summer of 1945, and we walked through the streets of a Barcelona trapped beneath ashen skies as dawn poured over Rambla de Santa Mónica in a wreath of liquid copper.

'Daniel, you mustn't tell anyone what you're about to see today,' my father warned. 'Not even your friend Tomás. No one.'

'Not even Mummy?'

My father sighed, hiding behind the sad smile that followed him like a shadow all through his life.

'Of course you can tell her,' he answered, heavy-hearted. 'We keep no secrets from her. You can tell her everything.'

Shortly after the Civil War, an outbreak of cholera had taken my mother away. We buried her in Montjuïc on my fourth birthday. The only thing I can recall is that it rained all day and all night, and that when I asked my father whether heaven was crying, he couldn't bring himself to reply. Six years later my mother's absence remained in the air around us, a deafening silence that I had not yet learned to stifle with words. My father and I lived in a modest apartment on Calle Santa Ana, a stone's throw from the church square. The apartment was directly above the bookshop, a legacy from my grandfather, that specialized in rare collectors' editions and secondhand books – an enchanted bazaar, which my father hoped would one day be mine. I was raised among books, making invisible friends in pages that seemed cast from dust and whose smell I carry on my hands to this day. As a child I learned to fall asleep talking to my mother in the darkness of my bedroom, telling her about the day's events, my adventures

1

at school, and the things I had been taught. I couldn't hear her voice or feel her touch, but her radiance and her warmth haunted every corner of our home, and I believed, with the innocence of those who can still count their age on their ten fingers, that if I closed my eyes and spoke to her, she would be able to hear me wherever she was. Sometimes my father would listen to me from the dining room, crying in silence.

On that June morning, I woke up screaming at first light. My heart was pounding in my chest as if my very soul was trying to escape. My father hurried into my room and held me in his arms, trying to calm me.

'I can't remember her face. I can't remember Mummy's face,' I muttered, breathless.

My father held me tight.

'Don't worry, Daniel. I'll remember for both of us.'

We looked at each other in the half-light, searching for words that didn't exist. For the first time, I realized my father was growing old. He stood up and drew the curtains to let in the pale glint of dawn.

'Come, Daniel, get dressed. I want to show you something,' he said.

'Now? At five o'clock in the morning?'

'Some things can only be seen in the shadows,' my father said, flashing a mysterious smile probably borrowed from the pages of one of his worn Alexandre Dumas romances.

Night watchmen still lingered in the misty streets when we stepped out of the front door. The lamps along the Ramblas marked out an avenue in the early morning haze as the city awoke, like a watercolour slowly coming to life. When we reached Calle Arco del Teatro, we continued through its arch toward the Raval quarter, entering a vault of blue haze. I followed my father through that narrow lane, more of a scar than a street, until the glimmer of the Ramblas faded behind us. The brightness of dawn filtered down from balconies and cornices in streaks of slanting light that dissolved before touching the ground. At last my

2

father stopped in front of a large door of carved wood, blackened by time and humidity. Before us loomed what to my eyes seemed the carcass of a palace, a place of echoes and shadows.

'Daniel, you mustn't tell anyone what you're about to see today. Not even your friend Tomás. No one.'

A smallish man with vulturine features framed by thick grey hair opened the door. His impenetrable aquiline gaze rested on mine.

'Good morning, Isaac. This is my son, Daniel,' my father announced. 'He'll be eleven soon, and one day the shop will be his. It's time he knew this place.'

The man called Isaac nodded and invited us in. A blue-tinted gloom obscured the sinuous contours of a marble staircase and a gallery of frescoes peopled with angels and fabulous creatures. We followed our host through a palatial corridor and arrived at a sprawling round hall where a spiralling basilica of shadows was pierced by shafts of light from a high glass dome above us. A labyrinth of passage-ways and crammed bookshelves rose from base to pinnacle like a beehive, woven with tunnels, steps, platforms and bridges that presaged an immense library of seemingly impossible geometry. I looked at my father, stunned. He smiled at me and winked.

'Welcome to the Cemetery of Forgotten Books, Daniel.'

Scattered among the library's corridors and platforms I could make out about a dozen human figures. Some of them turned to greet me from afar, and I recognized the faces of various colleagues of my father's, fellows of the secondhand-booksellers' guild. To my ten-year-old eyes, they looked like a brotherhood of alchemists in furtive study. My father knelt next to me and, with his eyes fixed on mine, addressed me in the hushed voice he reserved for promises and secrets.

'This is a place of mystery, Daniel, a sanctuary. Every book, every volume you see here, has a soul. The soul of the person who wrote it and of those who read it and lived and dreamed with it. Every time a book changes hands, every time someone runs his eyes down its pages, its spirit grows and strengthens. This place was already ancient when my father brought me here for the first time, many years ago. Perhaps as old as the city itself. Nobody knows for certain how long it has existed, or who created it. I will tell you what my father told me, though. When a library disappears, or a bookshop closes down, when a book is consigned to oblivion, those of us who know this place, its guardians, make sure that it gets here. In this place, books no longer remembered by anyone, books that are lost in time, live forever, waiting for the day when they will reach a new reader's hands. In the shop we buy and sell them, but in truth books have no owner. Every book you see here has been somebody's best friend. Now they only have us, Daniel. Do you think you'll be able to keep such a secret?'

My gaze was lost in the immensity of the place and its sorcery of light. I nodded, and my father smiled.

'And do you know the best thing about it?' he asked.

I shook my head.

'According to tradition, the first time someone visits this place, he must choose a book, whichever he wants, and adopt it, making sure that it will never disappear, that it will always stay alive. It's a very important promise. For life,' explained my father. 'Today it's your turn.'

For almost half an hour, I wandered within the winding labyrinth, breathing in the smell of old paper and dust. I let my hand brush across the avenues of exposed spines, musing over what my choice would be. Among the titles faded by age, I could make out words in familiar languages and others I couldn't identify. I roamed through galleries filled with hundreds, thousands of volumes. After a while it occurred to me that between the covers of each of those books lay a boundless universe waiting to be discovered, while beyond those walls, in the outside world, people allowed life to pass by in afternoons of football and radio soaps, content to do little more than gaze at their navels. It

4

might have been that notion, or just chance, or its more flamboyant relative, destiny, but at that precise moment, I knew I had already chosen the book I was going to adopt, or that was going to adopt me. It stood out timidly on one corner of a shelf, bound in wine-coloured leather. The gold letters of its title gleamed in the light bleeding from the dome above. I drew near and caressed them with the tips of my fingers, reading to myself.

*The Shadow of the Wind*
JULIÁN CARAX

I had never heard of the title or the author, but I didn't care. The decision had been taken. I took the book down with great care and leafed through the pages, letting them flutter. Once liberated from its prison on the shelf, it shed a cloud of golden dust. Pleased with my choice, I tucked it under my arm and retraced my steps through the labyrinth, a smile on my lips. Perhaps the bewitching atmosphere of the place had got the better of me, but I felt sure that *The Shadow of the Wind* had been waiting there for me for years, probably since before I was born.

That afternoon, back in the apartment on Calle Santa Ana, I barricaded myself in my room to read the first few lines. Before I knew what was happening, I had fallen right into it. The novel told the story of a man in search of his real father, whom he had never known and whose existence was only revealed to him by his mother on her deathbed. The story of that quest became a ghostly odyssey in which the protagonist struggled to recover his lost youth, and in which the shadow of a cursed love slowly surfaced to haunt him until his dying breath. As it unfolded, the structure of the story began to remind me of one of those Russian dolls that contain innumerable diminishing replicas of themselves inside. Step by step the narrative split into a thousand stories, as if it had entered a gallery of mirrors, its identity

5

fragmented into endless reflections. The minutes and hours glided by as in a dream. When the cathedral bells tolled midnight, I barely heard them. Under the warm light cast by the reading lamp, I was plunged into a new world of images and sensations peopled by characters who seemed as real to me as my surroundings. Page after page I let the spell of the story and its world take me over, until the breath of dawn touched my window and my tired eyes slid over the last page. I lay in the bluish half-light with the book on my chest and listened to the murmur of the sleeping city. My eyes began to close, but I resisted. I did not want to lose the story's spell or bid farewell to its characters just yet.

Once, in my father's bookshop, I heard a regular customer say that few things leave a deeper mark on a reader than the first book that finds its way into his heart. Those first images, the echo of words we think we have left behind, accompany us throughout our lives and sculpt a place in our memory to which, sooner or later – no matter how many books we read, how many worlds we discover, or how much we learn or forget – we will return. For me those enchanted pages will always be the ones I found among the passageways of the Cemetery of Forgotten Books.

# DAYS OF ASHES
## 1945–1949

# 1

A secret's worth depends on the people from whom it must be kept. My first thought on waking was to tell my best friend about the Cemetery of Forgotten Books. Tomás Aguilar was a classmate who devoted his free time and his talent to the invention of wonderfully ingenious but bizarre contraptions such as the aerostatic dart or the dynamo spinning top. I pictured us both, equipped with torches and compasses, uncovering the mysteries of those bibliographic catacombs. Who better than Tomás to share my secret? Then, remembering my promise, I decided that circumstances advised me to adopt what in detective novels is termed a different 'modus operandi'. At noon I approached my father to quiz him about the book and about Julián Carax – both of which must be famous, I assumed. My plan was to get my hands on the complete works and read them all by the end of the week. To my surprise, I discovered that my father, a natural-born librarian and a walking lexicon of publishers' catalogues and oddities, had never heard of *The Shadow of the Wind* or Julián Carax. Intrigued, he examined the printing history on the back of the title page for clues.

'It says here that this copy is part of an edition of two thousand five hundred printed in Barcelona by Cabestany Editores, in June 1936.'

'Do you know the publishing house?'

'It closed down years ago. But, wait, this is not the original. The first edition came out in November of 1935, but was printed in Paris.... Published by Galiano & Neuval. Doesn't ring a bell.'

'So is this a translation?'

'It doesn't say so. From what I can see, the text must be the original one.'

'A book in Spanish, first published in France?'

'It's not that unusual, not in times like these,' my father put in. 'Perhaps Barceló can help us. . . .'

Gustavo Barceló was an old colleague of my father's who now owned a cavernous establishment on Calle Fernando with a commanding position in the city's secondhand-book trade. Perpetually affixed to his mouth was an unlit pipe that impregnated his person with the aroma of a Persian market. He liked to describe himself as the last romantic, and he was not above claiming that a remote line in his ancestry led directly to Lord Byron himself. As if to prove this connection, Barceló fashioned his wardrobe in the style of a nineteenth-century dandy. His casual attire consisted of a cravat, white patent leather shoes, and a plain glass monocle that, according to malicious gossip, he did not remove even in the intimacy of the lavatory. Flights of fancy aside, the most significant relative in his lineage was his begetter, an industrialist who had become fabulously wealthy by questionable means at the end of the nineteenth century. According to my father, Gustavo Barceló was, technically speaking, loaded, and his palatial bookshop was more of a passion than a business. He loved books unreservedly, and – although he denied this categorically – if someone stepped into his bookshop and fell in love with a tome he could not afford, Barceló would lower its price, or even give it away, if he felt that the buyer was a serious reader and not an accidental browser. Barceló also boasted an elephantine memory allied to a pedantry that matched his demeanour and the sonority of his voice. If anyone knew about odd books, it was he. That afternoon, after closing the shop, my father suggested that we stroll along to the Els Quatre Gats, a café on Calle Montsió, where Barceló and his bibliophile knights of the round table gathered to discuss the finer points of decadent poets, dead languages, and neglected, moth-ridden masterpieces.

*

Els Quatre Gats was just a five-minute walk from our house and one of my favourite haunts. My parents had met there in 1932, and I attributed my one-way ticket into this world in part to the old café's charms. Stone dragons guarded a lamplit façade. Inside, voices seemed to echo with shadows of other times. Accountants, dreamers, and would-be geniuses shared tables with the spectres of Pablo Picasso, Isaac Albéniz, Federico García Lorca, and Salvador Dalí. There any poor devil could pass for a historical figure for the price of a small coffee.

'Sempere, old man,' proclaimed Barceló when he saw my father come in. 'Hail the prodigal son. To what do we owe the honour?'

'You owe the honour to my son, Daniel, Don Gustavo. He's just made a discovery.'

'Well, then, pray come and sit down with us, for we must celebrate this ephemeral event,' he announced.

'Ephemeral?' I whispered to my father.

'Barceló can only express himself in frilly words,' my father whispered back. 'Don't say anything, or he'll get carried away.'

The lesser members of the coterie made room for us in their circle, and Barceló, who enjoyed flaunting his generosity in public, insisted on treating us.

'How old is the lad?' inquired Barceló, inspecting me out of the corner of his eye.

'Almost eleven,' I announced.

Barceló flashed a sly smile.

'In other words, ten. Don't add on any years, you rascal. Life will see to that without your help.'

A few of his chums grumbled in assent. Barceló signalled to a waiter of such remarkable decreptitude that he looked as if he should be declared a national landmark.

'A cognac for my friend Sempere, from the good bottle, and a cinnamon milkshake for the young one – he's a growing boy. And bring us some bits of ham, but spare us

11

the delicacies you brought us earlier, eh? If we fancy rubber, we'll call for Pirelli tyres.'

The waiter nodded and left, dragging his feet.

'I hate to bring up the subject,' Barceló said, 'but how can there be jobs? In this country nobody ever retires, not even after they're dead. Just look at El Cid. I tell you, we're a hopeless case.'

He sucked on his cold pipe, eyes already scanning the book in my hands. Despite his pretentious façade and his verbosity, Barceló could smell good prey the way a wolf scents blood.

'Let me see,' he said, feigning disinterest. 'What have we here?'

I glanced at my father. He nodded approvingly. Without further ado, I handed Barceló the book. The bookseller greeted it with expert hands. His pianist's fingers quickly explored its texture, consistency, and condition. He located the page with the publication and printer's notices and studied it with Holmesian flair. The rest of us watched in silence, as if awaiting a miracle, or permission to breathe again.

'Carax. Interesting,' he murmured in an inscrutable tone.

I held out my hand to recover the book. Barceló arched his eyebrows but gave it back with an icy smile.

'Where did you find it, young man?'

'It's a secret,' I answered, knowing that my father would be smiling to himself. Barceló frowned and looked at my father. 'Sempere, my dearest old friend, because it's you and because of the high esteem I hold you in and in honour of the long and profound friendship that unites us like brothers, let's call it at forty duros, end of story.'

'You'll have to discuss that with my son,' my father pointed out. 'The book is his.'

Barceló granted me a wolfish smile. 'What do you say, laddie? Forty duros isn't bad for a first sale.... Sempere, this boy of yours will make a name for himself in the business.'

The choir cheered his remark. Barceló gave me a triumphant look and pulled out his leather wallet. He ceremoniously counted out two hundred pesetas, which in those days was quite a fortune, and handed them to me. But I just shook my head. Barceló scowled.

'Dear boy, greed is most certainly an ugly, not to say mortal, sin. Be sensible. Call me crazy, but I'll raise that to sixty duros, and you can open a retirement fund. At your age you must start thinking of the future.'

I shook my head again. Barceló shot a poisonous look at my father through his monocle.

'Don't look at me,' said my father. 'I'm only here as an escort.'

Barceló sighed and peered at me closely.

'Let's see, junior. *What* is it you want?'

'What I want is to know who Julián Carax is and where I can find other books he's written.'

Barceló chuckled and pocketed his wallet, reconsidering his adversary.

'Goodness, a scholar. Sempere, what do you feed the boy on?'

The bookseller leaned towards me confidentially, and for a second I thought he betrayed a look of respect that had not been there a few moments earlier.

'We'll make a deal,' he said. 'Tomorrow, Sunday, in the afternoon, drop by the Ateneo library and ask for me. Bring your precious find with you so that I can examine it properly, and I'll tell you what I know about Julián Carax. Quid pro quo.'

'Quid pro what?'

'Latin, young man. There's no such thing as a dead language, only dormant minds. Paraphrasing, it means that you can't get something for nothing, but since I like you, I'm going to do you a favour.'

The man's oratory could kill flies in midair, but I suspected that if I wanted to find out anything about Julián Carax, I'd be well advised to stay on good terms with him. I proffered my most saintly smile in delight at his Latin outpourings.

'Remember, tomorrow, in the Ateneo,' pronounced the bookseller. 'But bring the book, or there's no deal.'

'Fine.'

Our conversation slowly merged into the murmuring of the other members of the coffee set. The discussion turned to some documents found in the basement of El Escorial that hinted at the possibility that Don Miguel de Cervantes had in fact been the nom de plume of a large, hairy lady of letters from Toledo. Barceló seemed distracted, not tempted to claim a share in the debate. He remained quiet, observing me from his fake monocle with a masked smile. Or perhaps he was only looking at the book I held in my hands.

## 2

That Sunday, clouds spilled down from the sky and swamped the streets with a hot mist that made the thermometers on the walls perspire. Halfway through the afternoon, the temperature was already grazing the nineties as I set off towards Calle Canuda for my appointment with Barceló, carrying the book under my arm and with beads of sweat on my forehead. The Ateneo was – and remains – one of the many places in Barcelona where the nineteenth century has not yet been served its eviction notice. A grand stone staircase led up from a palatial courtyard to a ghostly network of passageways and reading rooms. There, inventions such as the telephone, the wristwatch, and haste, seemed futuristic anachronisms. The porter, or perhaps it was a statue in uniform, barely noticed my arrival. I glided up to the first floor, blessing the blades of a fan that swirled above the sleepy readers melting like ice cubes over their books.

Don Gustavo's profile was outlined against the windows of a gallery that overlooked the building's interior garden.

Despite the almost tropical atmosphere, he sported his customary foppish attire, his monocle shining in the dark like a coin at the bottom of a well. Next to him was a figure swathed in a white alpaca dress who looked to me like an angel.

When Barceló heard the echo of my footsteps, he half closed his eyes and signalled for me to come nearer. 'Daniel, isn't it?' asked the bookseller. 'Did you bring the book?'

I nodded on both counts and accepted the chair Barceló offered me next to him and his mysterious companion. For a while the bookseller only smiled placidly, taking no notice of my presence. I soon abandoned all hope of being introduced to the lady in white, whoever she might be. Barceló behaved as if she wasn't there and neither of us could see her. I cast a sidelong glance at her, afraid of meeting her eyes, which stared vacantly into the distance. The skin on her face and arms was pale, almost translucent. Her features were sharp, sketched with firm strokes and framed by a black head of hair that shone like damp stone. I guessed she must be, at most, twenty, but there was something about her manner that made me think she could be ageless. She seemed trapped in that state of perpetual youth reserved for mannequins in shop windows. I was trying to catch any sign of a pulse under her swan's neck when I realized that Barceló was staring at me.

'So are you going to tell me where you found the book?' he asked.

'I would, but I promised my father I would keep the secret,' I explained.

'I see. Sempere and his mysteries,' said Barceló. 'I think I can guess where. You've hit the jackpot, son. That's what I call finding a needle in a field of lilies. May I have a look?'

I handed him the book, and Barceló took it with infinite care. 'You've read it, I suppose.'

'Yes, sir.'

'I envy you. I've always thought that the best time to read Carax is when one still has a young heart and a blank soul. Did you know that this was the last novel he wrote?'

I shook my head.

'Do you know how many copies like this one there are on the market, Daniel?'

'Thousands, I suppose.'

'None,' Barceló specified. 'Only yours. The rest were burned.'

'Burned?'

For an answer Barceló only smiled enigmatically while he leafed through the book, stroking the paper as if it were a rare silk. The lady in white turned slowly. Her lips formed a timid and trembling smile. Her eyes groped the void, pupils white as marble. I gulped. She was blind.

'You don't know my niece, Clara, do you?' asked Barceló.

I could only shake my head, unable to take my eyes off the woman with the china doll's complexion and white eyes, the saddest eyes I had ever seen.

'Actually, the expert on Julián Carax is Clara, which is why I brought her along,' said Barceló. 'In fact I think I'll retire to another room, if you don't mind, to examine this tome while you get to know each other. Is that all right?'

I looked at him aghast. The scoundrel gave me a little pat on the back and left with my book under his arm.

'You've impressed him, you know,' said the voice behind me.

I turned to discover the faint smile of the bookseller's niece. Her voice was pure crystal, transparent and so fragile I feared that her words would break if I interrupted them.

'My uncle said he offered you a good sum of money for the Carax, but you refused it,' Clara added. 'You have earned his respect.'

'All evidence to the contrary,' I sighed.

I noticed that when she smiled, Clara leaned her head slightly to one side and her fingers played with a ring that looked like a wreath of sapphires.

'How old are you?' she asked.

'Almost eleven,' I replied. 'How old are you, Miss Clara?'

Clara laughed at my cheeky innocence.

16

'Almost twice your age, but even so, there's no need to call me Miss Clara.'

'You seem younger, miss,' I remarked, hoping that this would prove a good way out of my indiscretion.

'I'll trust you, then, because I don't know what I look like,' she answered. 'But if I seem younger to you, all the more reason to drop the "miss".'

'Whatever you say, Miss Clara.'

I observed her hands spread like wings on her lap, the suggestion of her fragile waist under the alpaca folds, the shape of her shoulders, the extreme paleness of her neck, the line of her lips, which I would have given my soul to stroke with the tip of my fingers. Never before had I had a chance to examine a woman so closely and with such precision, yet without the danger of meeting her eyes.

'What are you looking at?' asked Clara, not without a pinch of malice.

'Your uncle says you're an expert on Julián Carax, miss,' I improvised. My mouth felt dry.

'My uncle would say anything if that bought him a few minutes alone with a book that fascinates him,' explained Clara. 'But you must be wondering how someone who is blind can be a book expert.'

'The thought had not crossed my mind.'

'For someone who is almost eleven, you're not a bad liar. Be careful, or you'll end up like my uncle.'

Fearful of making yet another faux pas, I decided to remain silent. I just sat gawking at her, imbibing her presence.

'Here, come, get closer,' Clara said.

'Pardon me?'

'Come closer, don't be afraid. I won't bite you.'

I left my chair and went over to where she was sitting. The bookseller's niece raised her right hand, trying to find me. Without quite knowing what to do, I, too, stretched out my hand towards her. She took it in her left hand and, without saying anything, offered me her right hand.

Instinctively I understood what she was asking me to do, and guided her to my face. Her touch was both firm and delicate. Her fingers ran over my cheeks and cheekbones. I stood there motionless, hardly daring to breathe, while Clara read my features with her hands. While she did, she smiled to herself, and I noticed a slight movement of her lips, like a voiceless murmuring. I felt the brush of her hands on my forehead, on my hair and eyelids. She paused on my lips, following their shape with her forefinger and ring finger. Her fingers smelled of cinnamon. I swallowed, feeling my pulse race, and gave silent thanks that there were no eyewitnesses to my blushing, which could have set a cigar alight even a foot away.

# 3

That afternoon of mist and drizzle, Clara Barceló stole my heart, my breath, and my sleep. In the haunted shade of the Ateneo, her hands wrote a curse on my skin that was to hound me for years. While I stared, enraptured, she explained how she, too, had stumbled on the work of Julián Carax by chance in a village in Provence. Her father, a prominent lawyer linked to the Catalan president's cabinet, had had the foresight to send his wife and daughter to the other side of the border at the start of the Civil War. Some considered his fear exaggerated, and maintained that nothing could possibly happen in Barcelona. In Spain, both the cradle and pinnacle of Christian civilization, barbarism was for anarchists – those people who rode bicycles and wore darned socks – and surely they wouldn't get very far. But Clara's father believed that nations never see themselves clearly in the mirror, much less when war preys on their minds. He had a good understanding of history and knew that the future could be read much more clearly in the streets, factories, and barracks than in the morning press.

For months he wrote a letter to his wife and daughter once a week. At first he did it from his office on Calle Diputación, but later his letters had no return address. In the end he wrote secretly, from a cell in Montjuïc Castle, into which no one saw him go and from which, like countless others, he would never come out.

Clara's mother read the letters aloud, barely able to hold back her tears and skipping paragraphs that her daughter sensed without needing to hear them. Later, as her mother slept, Clara would convince her cousin Claudette to reread her father's letters from start to finish. That is how Clara read, with borrowed eyes. Nobody ever saw her shed a tear, not even when the letters from the lawyer stopped coming, not even when news of the war made them all fear the worst.

'My father knew from the start what was going to happen,' Clara explained. 'He stayed close to his friends because he felt it was his duty. What killed him was his loyalty to people who, when their time came, betrayed him. Never trust anyone, Daniel, especially the people you admire. Those are the ones who will make you suffer the worst blows.'

Clara spoke these words with a hardness that seemed grown out of years of secret brooding. I gladly lost myself in her porcelain gaze and listened to her talk about things that, at the time, I could not possibly understand. She described people, scenes, and objects she had never seen yet rendered them with the detail and precision of a Flemish master. Her words evoked textures and echoes, the colour of voices, the rhythm of footsteps. She explained how, during her years of exile in France, she and her cousin Claudette had shared a private tutor. He was a man in his fifties, a bit of a tippler, who affected literary airs and boasted he could recite Virgil's *Aeneid* in Latin without an accent. The girls had nicknamed him 'Monsieur Roquefort' by virtue of the peculiar aroma he exuded, despite the baths of eau de cologne in which he marinated his Rabelaisian anatomy.

Notwithstanding his peculiarities (notably his firm and militant conviction that blood sausages and other pork delicacies provided a miracle cure for bad circulation and gout), Monsieur Roquefort was a man of refined taste. Since his youth he had travelled to Paris once a month to spice up his cultural savoir faire with the latest literary novelties, visit museums, and, rumour had it, allow himself a night out in the arms of a nymphet he had christened 'Madame Bovary', even though her name was Hortense and she limited her reading to twenty-franc notes. In the course of these educational escapades, Monsieur Roquefort frequently visited a secondhand bookstall positioned outside Notre Dame. It was there, by chance, one afternoon in 1929, that he came across a novel by an unknown author, someone called Julián Carax. Always open to the *nouveau*, Monsieur Roquefort bought the book on a whim. The title seemed suggestive, and he was in the habit of reading something light on his train journey home. The novel was called *The Red House*, and on the back cover there was a blurred picture of the author, perhaps a photograph or a charcoal sketch. According to the biographical notes, Monsieur Julián Carax was twenty-seven, born with the century in Barcelona and currently living in Paris; he wrote in French and worked at night as a professional pianist in a hostess bar. The blurb, written in the pompous, mouldy style of the age, proclaimed that this was a first work of dazzling courage, the mark of a protean and trailblazing talent, and a milestone for the entire future of European letters. In spite of such solemn claims, the synopsis that followed suggested that the story contained some vaguely sinister elements slowly marinated in saucy melodrama, which, to the eyes of Monsieur Roquefort, was always a plus: after the classics what he most enjoyed were tales of crime, boudoir intrigue, and questionable conduct.

*The Red House* tells the story of a mysterious, tormented individual who breaks into toyshops and museums to steal dolls and puppets. Once they are in his power, he pulls out their eyes and takes them back to his lugubrious abode, a ghostly old conservatory lingering on the misty banks of the Seine. One fateful night he breaks into a sumptuous mansion on Avenue Foch determined to plunder the private collection of dolls belonging to a tycoon who, predictably, had grown insanely rich through devious means during the industrial revolution. As he is about to leave with his loot, our *voleur* is surprised by the tycoon's daughter, a young lady of Parisian high society named Giselle, exquisitely well read and highly refined but cursed with a morbid nature and naturally doomed to fall madly in love with the intruder. As the meandering saga continues through tumultuous incidents in dimly lit settings, the heroine begins to unravel the mystery that drives the enigmatic protagonist (whose name, of course, is never revealed) to blind the dolls, and as she does so, she discovers a horrible secret about her own father and his collection of china figures. At last the tale sinks into a tragic, darkly perfumed gothic denouement.

Monsieur Roquefort had literary pretensions himself and was the owner of a vast collecton of letters of rejection signed by every self-respecting Parisian publisher in response to the books of verse and prose he sent them so relentlessly. Thus he was able to identify the novel's publishing house as a second-rate firm, known, if anything, for its books on cookery, sewing, and other handicrafts. The owner of the bookstall told him that when the novel appeared it had merited but two scant reviews from provincial dailies, strategically placed next to the obituary notices. The critics had had a field day writing Carax off in a few lines, advising him not to leave his employment as a pianist, as it was obvious that he was not going to hit the right note in literature. Monsieur Roquefort, whose heart and pocket softened when faced with lost causes, had decided to invest half a franc on the book by the unknown Carax and at the same time took away an exquisite edition of the great master, Gustave Flaubert, whose unrecognized successor he considered himself to be.

The train to Lyons was packed, and Monsieur Roquefort was obliged to share his second-class compartment with a couple of nuns who had given him disapproving looks from the moment they left the Gare d'Austerlitz, mumbling under their breath. Faced with such scrutiny, the teacher decided to extract the novel from his briefcase and barricade himself behind its pages. Much to his surprise, hundreds of miles later, he discovered he had quite forgotten about the sisters, the rocking of the train, and the dark landscape sliding past the windows like a nightmare scene from the Lumière brothers. He read all night, unaware of the nuns' snoring or of the stations that flashed by in the fog. At daybreak, as he turned the last page, Monsieur Roquefort realized he had tears in his eyes and a heart that was poisoned with envy and amazement.

That Monday, Monsieur Roquefort called the publisher in Paris to request information on Julián Carax. After much insistence a telephonist with an asthmatic voice and a virulent disposition replied that Carax had no known address and that, anyhow, he no longer had dealings with the firm. She added that, since its publication, *The Red House* had sold exactly seventy-seven copies, most of which had presumably been acquired by young ladies of easy virtue and other regulars of the club where the author churned out nocturnes and polanaises for a few coins. The remaining copies had been returned and pulped for printing missals, fines, and lottery tickets.

The mysterious author's wretched luck won Monsieur Roquefort's sympathy, and during the following ten years, on each of his visits to Paris, he would scour the secondhand bookshops in search of other works by Julián Carax. He never found a single one. Almost nobody had heard of Carax, and those for whom the name rang a bell knew very little. Some swore he had brought out other books, always with small publishers, and with ridiculous print runs. Those books, if they really existed, were impossible to find. One bookseller claimed he had once had a book by Julián Carax in his hands. It was called *The Cathedral Thief*, but this was a long time ago, and besides, he wasn't quite sure. At the end of 1935, news reached Monsieur Roquefort that a new novel by Julián Carax, *The Shadow of the Wind*, had been published by a small firm in Paris. He wrote to the publisher asking whether he could buy a few copies but never got an answer. The following year, in the spring of 1936, his old friend at the bookstall by the Seine asked him whether he was still interested in Carax. Monsieur Roquefort assured him that he never gave up. It was now a question of stubbornness: if the world was determined to bury Carax, he wasn't going to go along with it. His friend then explained that some weeks earlier a rumour about Carax had been doing the rounds. It seemed that at last his fortunes had improved. He was going to marry a lady of good social standing and, after a few years' silence, had published a novel that, for the first time, had earned him a good review in none less than *Le Monde*. But just when it seemed that the winds were about to change, the bookseller went on, Carax had been involved in a duel in Père Lachaise cemetery. The circumstances surrounding this event were unclear. All the bookseller knew was that the duel had taken place at dawn on the day Carax was due to be married, and that the bridegroom had never made it to the church.

There was an opinion to match every taste: some maintained he had died in the duel and his body had been left abandoned in an unmarked grave; others, more optimistic, preferred to believe that Carax was tangled up in some shady affair that had forced him to abandon his fiancée at the altar, flee from Paris, and return to Barcelona. The nameless grave could never be found, and shortly afterwards a new version of the story begin to circulate:

Julián Carax, who had been plagued by misfortune, had died in his native city in the most dire straits. The girls in the brothel where he played the piano had organized a collection to pay for a decent burial, but when the money order reached Barcelona, the body had already been buried in a common grave, along with beggars and people with no name who had turned up floating in the harbour waters or died of cold at the entrance to the subway.

If only because he liked to oppose general views, Monsieur Roquefort did not forget Carax. Eleven years after his discovery of *The Red House*, he decided to lend the novel to his two pupils, hoping, perhaps, that the strange book might encourage them to acquire the reading habit. Clara and Claudette were by then teenagers with hormones coursing through their veins, obsessed by the world winking at them from beyond the windows of the study. Despite the tutor's best efforts, the girls had until then proved immune to the charms of the classics, Aesop's fables, or the immortal verse of Dante Alighieri. Fearing that his contract might be terminated if Clara's mother discovered that he was miseducating two illiterate, feather-brained young women, Monsieur Roquefort presented them with Carax's novel dressed up as a love story, which was, at least, half true.

# 4

'Never before had I felt trapped, so seduced and caught up in a story,' Clara explained, 'the way I did with that book. Until then, reading was just a duty, a sort of fine one had to pay teachers and tutors without quite knowing why. I had never known the pleasure of reading, of exploring the recesses of the soul, of letting myself be carried away by imagination, beauty, and the mystery of fiction and language. For me all those things were born with that novel. Have you ever kissed a girl, Daniel?'

My brain seized up; my mouth turned to sawdust.

'Well, you're still very young. But it's that same feeling, that first-time spark that you never forget. This is a world of shadows, Daniel, and magic is a rare asset. That book taught me that by reading, I could live more intensely. It could give me back the sight I had lost. For that reason alone, a book that didn't matter to anyone, changed my life.'

By then I was hopelessly dumbstruck, at the mercy of this creature whose words and charms I had neither means nor desire to resist. I wished that she would never stop speaking, that her voice would wrap itself around me forever, and that her uncle would never return to break the spell of that moment that belonged only to me.

'For years I looked for other books by Julián Carax,' Clara went on. 'I asked in libraries, in bookshops, in schools. Always in vain. No one had ever heard of him or of his books. I couldn't understand it. Later on, Monsieur Roquefort heard a rumour, a strange story about someone who went around libraries and bookshops looking for works by Julián Carax. If he found any, he would buy them, steal them, or get them by some other means, after which, he would immediately set fire to them. Nobody knew who he was or why he did it. Another mystery to add to Carax's own enigma. In time, my mother decided she wanted to return to Spain. She was ill, and Barcelona had always been her home. I was secretly hoping to make some discovery about Carax here, since, after all, Barcelona was the city in which he was born and from which he had disappeared at the start of the war. But even with the help of my uncle, all I could find were dead ends. As for my mother, much the same thing happened with her own search. The Barcelona she encountered on her return was not the place she had left behind. She discovered a city of shadows, one no longer inhabited by my father, although every corner was haunted by his memory. As if all that misery were not enough, she insisted on hiring someone to find out exactly what had happened to him. After months of investigation, all the detective was able to recover was a broken wristwatch and the name of the man who had killed my father in the moat of Montjuïc Castle. His name was Fumero, Javier Fumero. We were told that this individual – and he wasn't the only one – had started off as a hired gunman with the FAI anarchist syndicate and had then flirted with the communists and the fascists, tricking them all, selling his services to the highest bidder. After the fall of Barcelona, he had gone over to the winning side and joined the police force. Now he is a famous bemedalled inspector. Nobody remembers my father. Not surprisingly, my mother faded away within a few months. The doctors said it was her heart, and I think that for once they were right. When she died, I went to live with my uncle Gustavo, the sole relative of my mother's left in Barcelona. I adored him, because he always gave me books when he came to visit us. He has been my only family and my best friend through all these years. Even if he seems a little arrogant at times, he has a good heart, bless him. Every night, without fail, even if he's dropping with sleep, he'll read to me for a while.'

'I could read to you, if you like, Miss Clara,' I suggested courteously, instantly regretting my audacity, for I was convinced that, for Clara, my company could only be a nuisance, if not a joke.

'Thanks, Daniel,' she answered. 'I'd love that.'

'Whenever you wish.'

She nodded slowly, looking for me with her smile.

'Unfortunately, I no longer have that copy of *The Red House*,' she said. 'Monsieur Roquefort refused to part with it. I could try to tell you the story, but it would be like describing a cathedral by saying it's a pile of stones ending in a spire.'

'I'm sure you'd tell it much better than that,' I spluttered.

Women have an infallible instinct for knowing when a

man has fallen madly in love with them, especially when the male in question is both young and a complete dunce. I fulfilled all the requirements for Clara Barceló to send me packing, but I preferred to think that her blindness afforded me a margin for error and that my crime – my complete and pathetic devotion to a woman twice my age, my intelligence, and my height – would remain in the dark. I wondered what on earth she saw in me that could make her want to befriend me, other than a pale reflection of herself, an echo of solitude and loss. In my schoolboy reveries, we were always two fugitives riding on the spine of a book, eager to escape into worlds of fiction and secondhand dreams.

When Barceló returned wearing a feline smile, two hours had passed. To me they had seemed like two minutes. The bookseller handed me the book and winked.

'Have a good look at it, little dumpling. I don't want you coming back to me saying I've switched it, eh?'

'I trust you,' I said.

'Stuff and nonsense. The last man who said that to me (a tourist who was convinced that Hemingway had invented the *fabada* stew during the San Fermín bull run) bought a copy of *Hamlet* signed by Shakespeare in ballpoint, imagine that. So keep your eyes peeled. In the book business you can't even trust the index.'

It was getting dark when we stepped out into Calle Canuda. A fresh breeze combed the city, and Barceló removed his coat and put it over Clara's shoulders. Seeing no better opportunity, I tentatively let slip that if they thought it was all right, I could drop by their home the following day to read a few chapters of *The Shadow of the Wind* to Clara. Barceló looked at me out of the corner of his eye and gave a hollow laugh.

'Boy, you're getting ahead of yourself!' he muttered, although his tone implied consent.

'Well, if that's not convenient, perhaps another day or . . .'

'It's up to Clara,' said the bookseller. 'We've already got seven cats and two cockatoos. One more creature won't make much difference.'

'I'll see you tomorrow, then, around seven,' concluded Clara. 'Do you know the address?'

# 5

There was a time, in my childhood, when, perhaps because I had been raised among books and booksellers, I dreamed of becoming a novelist. The root of my literary ambitions, apart from the marvellous simplicity with which one sees things at the age of five, lay in a prodigious piece of craftsmanship and precision that was exhibited in a fountain pen shop on Calle Anselmo Clavé, just behind the Military Government building. The object of my devotion, a plush black pen, adorned with heaven knows how many refinements and flourishes, presided over the shop window as if it were the crown jewels. A baroque fantasy magnificently wrought in silver and gold that shone like the lighthouse at Alexandria, the nib was a wonder in its own right. When my father and I went out for a walk, I wouldn't stop pestering him until he took me to see the pen. My father declared that it must be, at the very least, the pen of an emperor. I was secretly convinced that with such a marvel one would be able to write anything, from novels to encyclopaedias, and letters whose supernatural power would surpass any postal limitations. Written with that pen, they would surely reach the most remote corners of the world, even that unknowable place to which my father said my mother had gone and from where she would never return.

One day we decided to go into the shop and inquire

about the blessed artefact. It turned out to be the queen of all fountain pens, a Montblanc Meisterstück in a numbered series, that had once belonged, or so the shop attendant assured us, to Victor Hugo himself. From that gold nib, we were informed, had sprung the manuscript of *Les Misérables*.

'Just as Vichy Catalán water springs from the source at Caldas,' the clerk swore.

He told us he had bought it personally from the most serious collector in Paris, and that he had assured himself of the item's authenticity.

'And what is the price of this fountain of marvels, if you don't mind telling me?' my father asked.

The very mention of the sum drew the colour from his face, but I had already fallen under its spell. The clerk, who seemed to think we understood physics, began to assail us with incomprehensible gibberish about the alloys of precious metals, enamels from the Far East and a revolutionary theory on pistons and communicating chambers, all of which contributed to the Teutonic science underpinning the glorious stroke of that champion of scrivening technology. I have to say in his favour that, despite the fact that we must have looked like two poor devils, the clerk allowed us to handle the pen as much as we liked, filled it with ink for us, and offered me a piece of parchment so that I could write my name and thus commence my literary career in the footsteps of Victor Hugo. Then, after polishing it with a cloth to restore its shiny splendour, he returned the pen to its throne.

'Perhaps another day,' mumbled my father.

Once we were out in the street again, he told me in a subdued voice that we couldn't afford the asking price. The bookshop provided just enough to keep us afloat and send me to a decent school. The great Victor Hugo's Montblanc pen would have to wait. I didn't say anything, but my father must have noticed my disappointment.

'I tell you what we'll do,' he proposed. 'When you're old enough to start writing, we'll come back and buy it.'

'What if someone buys it first?'

'No one is going to take this one, you can be quite sure. And if not, we can ask Don Federico to make us one. That man has the hands of a master.'

Don Federico was the local watchmaker, an occasional customer at the bookshop, and probably the most polite and courteous man in the whole of the Northern Hemisphere. His reputation as a craftsman preceded him from the Ribera quarter to the Ninot Market. Another reputation haunted him as well, this one of a less salubrious nature, related to his erotic proclivity for muscular young men from the more virile ranks of the proletariat, and to a certain penchant for dressing up like the music-hall star Estrellita Castro.

'What if Don Federico doesn't have the right tools for the job?' I asked, unaware that to less innocent ears, the phrase might have had a salacious echo.

My father arched an eyebrow, fearing perhaps that some foul rumours might have sullied my innocence.

'Don Federico is very knowledgeable about all things German and could make a Volkswagen if he put his mind to it. Besides, I'd like to find out whether fountain pens existed in Victor Hugo's day. There are a lot of con artists about.'

My father's zeal for historical fact checking left me cold. I believed obstinately in the pen's illustrious past, even though I didn't think it was such a bad idea for Don Federico to make me a substitute. There would be time enough to reach the heights of Victor Hugo. To my consolation, and true to my father's predictions, the Montblanc pen remained for years in that shop window, which we visited religiously every Saturday morning.

'It's still there,' I would say, astounded.

'It's waiting for you,' my father would say. 'It knows that

one day it will be yours and that you'll write a masterpiece with it.'

'I want to write a letter. To Mummy. So that she doesn't feel lonely.'

My father regarded me. 'Your mother isn't lonely, Daniel. She's with God. And with us, even if we can't see her.'

This very same theory had been formulated for me in school by Father Vicente, a veteran Jesuit expert at expounding on all the mysteries of the universe – from the gramophone to a toothache – quoting the Gospel According to Matthew. Yet on my father's lips, the words sounded hollow.

'And what does God want her for?'

'I don't know. If one day we see Him, we'll ask Him.'

Eventually I discarded the idea of the celestial letter and concluded that, while I was at it, I may as well begin with the masterpiece – that would be more practical. In the absence of the pen, my father lent me a Staedtler pencil, a number two, with which I scribbled in a notebook. Unsurprisingly, my story told of an extraordinary fountain pen, remarkably similar to the one in the shop, though enchanted. To be more precise, the pen was possessed by the tortured soul of its previous owner, a novelist who had died of hunger and cold. When the pen fell into the hands of an apprentice, it insisted on reproducing the author's last work, which he had not been able to finish in his lifetime. I don't remember where I got that idea from, but I never again had another one like it. My attempts to re-create the novel on the pages of my notebook turned out to be disastrous. My syntax was plagued by an anaemic creativity, and my metaphorical flights reminded me of the advertisements for fizzy footbaths that I used to read in tram stops. I blamed the pencil and longed for the pen, which was bound to turn me into a master writer.

My father followed my tortuous progress with a mixture of pride and concern.

'How's your story going, Daniel?'

'I don't know. I suppose if I had the pen, everything would be different.'

My father told me that sort of reasoning could only have occurred to a budding author. 'Just keep going, and before you've finished your first work, I'll buy it for you.'

'Do you promise?'

He always answered with a smile. Luckily for my father, my literary dreams soon dwindled and were minced into mere oratory. What contributed to this was the discovery of mechanical toys and all sorts of tin gadgets you could find in the bric-a-brac stalls of the Encantes Market, at prices that were better suited to our finances. Childhood devotions make unfaithful and fickle lovers, and soon I had eyes only for Meccano and wind-up boats. I stopped asking my father to take me to see Victor Hugo's pen, and he didn't mention it again. That world seemed to have vanished, but for a long time the image I had of my father, which I still preserve today, was that of a thin man wearing an old suit that was too large for him and a secondhand hat he had bought on Calle Condal for seven pesetas, a man who could not afford to buy his son a wretched pen that was useless but seemed to mean everything to him.

When I returned from Clara and the Ateneo that night, my father was waiting for me in the dining room, wearing his usual expression of anxiety and defeat.

'I was beginning to think you'd got lost somewhere,' he said. 'Tomás Aguilar phoned. He said you'd arranged to meet. Did you forget?'

'It's Barceló. When he starts talking there's no stopping him,' I replied, nodding as I spoke. 'I didn't know how to shake him off.'

'He's a good man, but he does go on. You must be hungry. Merceditas brought down some of the soup she made for her mother. That girl is an angel.'

We sat down at the table to savour Merceditas's offering.

She was the daughter of the lady on the third floor, and everyone had her down to become a nun and a saint, although more than once I'd seen her with an able-handed sailor who sometimes walked her back to the shop. She always drowned him with kisses.

'You look pensive tonight,' said my father, trying to make conversation.

'It must be this humidity, it "dilates" the brain. That's what Barceló says.'

'It must be something else. Is anything worrying you, Daniel?'

'No. Just thinking.'

'What about?'

'The war.'

My father nodded gloomily and quietly sipped his soup. He was a very private person, and although he lived in the past, he hardly ever mentioned it. I had grown up convinced that the slow procession of the postwar years, a world of stillness, poverty, and hidden resentment, was as natural as tap water, that the mute sadness that seeped from the walls of the wounded city was the real face of its soul. One of the pitfalls of childhood is that one doesn't have to understand something to feel it. By the time the mind is able to comprehend what has happened, the wounds of the heart are already too deep. That evening in early summer, as I walked back through the sombre, treacherous twilight of Barcelona, I could not blot out Clara's story about her father's disappearance. In my world death was like a nameless and incomprehensible hand, a door-to-door salesman who took away mothers, beggars, or ninety-year-old neighbours, like a hellish lottery. But I couldn't absorb the idea that death could actually walk by my side, with a human face and a heart that was poisoned with hatred, that death could be dressed in a uniform or a raincoat, queue up at a cinema, laugh in bars, or take his children out for a walk to Ciudadela Park in the morning, and then, in the afternoon, make someone disappear in the dungeons of

Montjuïc Castle or in a common grave with no name or ceremony. Going over all this in my mind, it occurred to me that perhaps the papier-mâché world that I accepted as real was only a stage setting. Much like the arrival of Spanish trains, in those stolen years you never knew when the end of childhood was due.

We shared the soup, a broth made from leftovers with bits of bread in it, surrounded by the sticky droning of radio soaps that filtered out through open windows into the church square.

'So tell me. How did things go with Gustavo today?'

'I met his niece, Clara.'

'The blind girl? I hear she's a real beauty.'

'I don't know. I don't notice things like that.'

'You'd better not.'

'I told them I might go to their house tomorrow, after school, to read to her for a while – as she's so lonely. If you'll let me.'

My father looked at me askance, as if he were wondering whether he was growing old prematurely or whether I was growing up too quickly. I decided to change the subject, and the only one I could find was the one that was consuming me.

'Is it true that during the war people were taken to Montjuïc Castle and were never seen again?'

My father finished his spoonful of soup unperturbed and looked closely at me, his brief smile slipping away from his lips.

'Who told you that. Barceló?'

'No. Tomás Aguilar. He sometimes tells stories at school.'

My father nodded slowly.

'When there's a war, things happen that are very hard to explain, Daniel. Often even I don't know what they really mean. Sometimes it's best to leave things alone.'

He sighed and sipped his soup with little relish. I watched him without saying a word.

'Before your mother died, she made me promise that I would never talk to you about the war, that I wouldn't let you remember any of what happened.'

I didn't know how to answer. My father half closed his eyes, as if he were searching for something in the air – looks, silences, or perhaps my mother – to corroborate what he had just said.

'Sometimes I think I've been wrong to listen to her. I don't know.'

'It doesn't matter, Dad. . . .'

'No, it does matter, Daniel. Nothing is ever the same after a war. And yes, it's true that lots of people who went into that castle never came out.'

Our eyes met briefly. After a while my father got up and took refuge in his bedroom. I cleared the plates, placed them in the small marble kitchen sink, and washed them up. When I returned to the sitting room, I turned off the light and sat in my father's old armchair. The breeze from the street made the curtains flutter. I was not sleepy, nor did I feel like trying to sleep. I went over to the balcony and looked out far enough to see the hazy glow shed by the streetlamps in Puerta del Ángel. A motionless figure stood in a patch of shadow on the cobbled street. The flickering amber glow of a cigarette was reflected in his eyes. He wore dark clothes, with one hand buried in the pocket of his jacket, the other holding the cigarette that wove a web of blue smoke around his profile. He observed me silently, his face obscured by the street lighting behind him. He remained there for almost a minute smoking nonchalantly, his eyes fixed on mine. Then, when the cathedral bells struck midnight, the figure gave a faint nod of the head, followed, I sensed, by a smile that I could not see. I wanted to return the greeting but was paralysed. The figure turned, and I saw the man walking away, with a slight limp. Any other night I would barely have noticed the presence of that stranger, but as soon as I'd lost sight of him in the mist, I felt a cold sweat on my forehead and found it hard to breathe. I had read an identical description of that scene in *The Shadow of the Wind*. In the story the protagonist would go out onto the balcony every night at midnight and discover that a stranger was watching him from the shadows, smoking nonchalantly. The stranger's face was always veiled by darkness, and only his eyes could be guessed at in the night, burning like hot coals. The stranger would remain there, his right hand buried in the pocket of his black jacket, and then he would go away, limping. In the scene I had just witnessed, that stranger could have been any person of the night, a figure with no face and no name. In Carax's novel, that figure was the devil.

# 6

A deep, dreamless sleep and the prospect of seeing Clara again that afternoon persuaded me that the vision had been pure coincidence. Perhaps that unexpected and feverish outbreak of imagination was just a side effect of the growth spurt I'd been waiting for, an event that all the women in the building said would turn me into a man, if not of stature, at least of a certain height. At seven on the dot, dressed in my Sunday best and smelling strongly of the Varón Dandy eau de cologne I had borrowed from my father, I turned up at the house of Gustavo Barceló ready to make my début as personal reader and living-room pest. The bookseller and his niece shared a palatial apartment in Plaza Real. A uniformed maid, wearing a white cap and the expressionless look of a soldier, opened the door for me with theatrical servility.

'You must be Master Daniel,' she said. 'I'm Bernarda, at your service.'

Bernarda affected a ceremonial tone that could not conceal a Cáceres accent thick enough to spread on toast. With pomp and solemnity, she led me through the Barceló residence. The apartment, which was on the first floor, circled the building and formed a ring of galleries, sitting rooms, and passageways that to me, used as I was to our modest family home on Calle Santa Ana, seemed like a miniature of the Escorial palace. It was obvious that, as well as books, incunabula and all manner of arcane texts, Don Gustavo also collected statues, paintings, and altarpieces, not to mention abundant fauna and flora. I followed Bernarda through a gallery that was full to overflowing with foliage and tropical species. A golden, dusky light filtered through the glass panes of the gallery, and the languid tones from a piano hovered in the air. Bernarda fought her way through the jungle brandishing her docker's arms as if they were machetes. I followed her closely, examining the surroundings and noticing the presence of half a dozen cats and a couple of cockatoos (of a violent colour and encyclopaedic size) which, the maid explained, Barceló had christened Ortega and Gasset, respectively. Clara was waiting for me in a sitting room on the other side of this forest, overlooking the square. Draped in a diaphanous turquoise-blue cotton dress, the object of my confused desire was playing the piano beneath the weak light from the rose window. Clara played badly, with no sense of rhythm and mistaking half the notes, but to me her serenade was liquid heaven. I saw her sitting up straight at the keyboard, with a half smile and her head tilted to one side, and she seemed like a celestial vision. I was about to clear my throat to indicate my presence, but the whiff of cologne betrayed me. Clara suddenly stopped her playing, and an embarrassed smile lit up her face.

'For a moment I thought you were my uncle,' she said. 'He has forbidden me to play Mompou, because he says that what I do with him is a sacrilege.'

The only Mompou I knew was a gaunt priest with a tendency to flatulence who taught us physics and chemistry at school. The association of ideas seemed to me both grotesque and downright improbable.

'Well, I think you play beautifully.'

'No I don't. My uncle is a real music enthusiast, and he's even hired a music teacher to mend my ways – a young composer who shows a lot of promise called Adrián Neri. He's studied in Paris and Vienna. You've got to meet him. He's writing a symphony that is going to premiere with the Barcelona City Orchestra – his uncle sits on the management board. He's a genius.'

'The uncle or the nephew?'

'Don't be wicked, Daniel. I'm sure you'll fall for Adrián.'

More likely he'll fall on me like a grand piano plummeting down from the seventh floor, I thought.

'Would you like a snack?' Clara offered. 'Bernarda makes the most breathtaking cinnamon sponge cakes.'

We took our afternoon snack like royalty, wolfing down everything the maid put before us. I had no idea about the protocol for this unfamiliar occasion and was not sure how to behave. Clara, who always seemed to know what I was thinking, suggested that I read from *The Shadow of the Wind* whenever I liked and that I might as well start at the beginning. And so, trying to sound like one of those pompous voices on Radio Nacional that recited patriotic vignettes after the midday Angelus, I threw myself into revisiting the text of the novel. My voice, rather stiff at first, slowly became more relaxed, and soon I forgot myself and was submerged once more into the narrative, discovering cadences and turns of phrase that flowed like musical motifs, riddles made of timbre and pauses I had not noticed during my first reading. New details, strands of images and fantasy appeared between the lines, and new shapes revealed themselves, like the structure of a building looked at from different angles. I read for about an hour, getting through five chapters, until my throat felt dry and half a dozen clocks chimed throughout the apartment, reminding me that it was getting late. I closed the book and observed that Clara was smiling at me calmly.

'It reminds me a bit of *The Red House*,' she said. 'But this story seems less sombre.'

'Don't you believe it,' I said. 'This is just the beginning. Later on, things get complicated.'

'You have to go, don't you?' Clara asked.

'I'm afraid so. It's not that I want to, but . . .'

'If you have nothing else to do, you could come back tomorrow,' she suggested. 'But I don't want to take advantage of you. . . .'

'Six o'clock?' I offered. 'That way we'll have more time.'

That meeting in the music room of the Plaza Real apartment was the first of many more throughout the summer of 1945 and the years to follow. Soon my visits to the Barcelós became almost daily, except for Tuesdays and Thursdays, when Clara had music lessons with Adrián Neri. I spent long hours there, and in time I memorized every room, every passageway, and every plant in Don Gustavo's forest. *The Shadow of the Wind* lasted us about a fortnight, but we had no trouble in finding successors with which to fill our reading hours. Barceló owned a fabulous library, and, for want of more Julián Carax titles, we ambled through dozens of minor classics and major bagatelles. Some afternoons we barely read, and spent our time just talking or even going out for a walk around the square or as far as the cathedral. Clara loved to sit and listen to the murmuring of people in the cloister and guess at the echoes of footsteps in the stone alleyways. She would ask me to describe the façades, the people, the cars, the shops, the lampposts and shop windows that we passed on our way. Often she would take my arm and I would guide her through our own private Barcelona, one that only she and I could see. We always ended up in a milk bar on Calle Petritxol, sharing a bowl of whipped cream or a cup of hot chocolate with sponge fingers. Sometimes people would look at us askance, and more than one know-all waiter referred to her as 'your older sister', but I paid no attention to their taunts and insinuations. Other times, I don't know whether out of malice or morbidity, Clara confided in me, telling me far-fetched secrets that I was not sure how to take. One of her favourite topics concerned a stranger, a person who sometimes came up to her when she was alone in the street and spoke to her in a hoarse voice. This mysterious person, who never mentioned his name, asked her questions about Don Gustavo and even about me. Once he had stroked her throat. Such stories tormented me mercilessly. Another time Clara told me she had begged the supposed stranger to let her read his face with her hands. He did not reply, which she took as a yes. When she raised her hands to his face, he stopped her suddenly, but she still managed to feel what she thought was leather.

'As if he wore a leather mask,' she said.

'You're making that up, Clara.'

Clara would swear again and again that it was true, and I would give up, tortured by the image of that phantom who found pleasure in caressing her swan-like neck – and heaven knows what else – while all I could do was long for it. Had I paused to reflect, I would have understood that my devotion to Clara brought me no more than suffering. Perhaps for that very reason, I adored her all the more, because of the eternal human stupidity of pursuing those who hurt us the most. During that bleak postwar summer, the only thing I feared was the arrival of the new school term, when I would no longer be able to spend all day with Clara.

By dint of seeing me so often around the house, Bernarda, whose severe appearance concealed a doting maternal instinct, became fond of me and, in her own manner, decided to adopt me.

'You can tell this boy hasn't got a mother, sir,' she would say to Barceló. 'I feel so sorry for him, poor little mite.'

Bernarda had arrived in Barcelona shortly after the war, fleeing from poverty and from a father who on a good day would beat her up and tell her she was stupid, ugly, and a slut, and on a bad one would corner her in the pigsty, drunk, and fondle her until she sobbed with terror – at which point he'd let her go, calling her prudish and stuck up, like her mother. Barceló had come across Bernarda by chance when she worked in a vegetable stall in the Borne Market and, following his instinct, had offered her a post in his household.

'Ours will be a brand-new *Pygmalion*,' he announced. 'You shall be my Eliza and I'll be your Professor Higgins.'

Bernarda, whose literary appetite was more than satisfied with the church newsletter, glanced over him. 'I might be poor and ignorant, but I'm decent too,' she said.

Barceló was not exactly George Bernard Shaw, but even if he had not managed to endow his pupil with the eloquence and spirit of a literary lady, his efforts had refined Bernarda and taught her the manners and speech of a provincial maid. She was twenty-eight, but I always thought she carried ten more years on her back, even if they showed only in her eyes. She was a serial churchgoer with an ecstatic devotion to Our Lady of Lourdes. Every morning she went to the eight o'clock service at the Basilica of Santa María del Mar, and she confessed no less than three times a week, four in warm weather. Don Gustavo, who was a confirmed agnostic (which Bernarda suspected might be a respiratory condition, like asthma, but afflicting only refined gentlemen), deemed it mathematically impossible that the maid could sin sufficiently to keep up that schedule of confession and contrition.

'You're as good as gold, Bernarda,' he would say indignantly. 'These people who see sin everywhere are sick in their souls and, if you really press me, in their bowels, too. The endemic condition of the Iberian saint is chronic constipation.'

Every time she heard such blasphemy, Bernarda would make the sign of the cross five times over. Later, at night, she would say a prayer for the tainted soul of Señor Barceló, who had a good heart but whose brains had rotted away due to excessive reading, like that fellow Sancho Panza. Very occasionally Bernarda had boyfriends who would beat her, take what little money she had stashed in a savings account, and sooner or later dump her. Every time one of these crises arose, Bernarda would lock herself up in her room for days, where she would cry an ocean and swear she was going to kill herself with rat poison or bleach. After exhausting all his persuasive tricks, Barceló would get truly frightened and call the locksmith to open the door. Then the family doctor would administer a sedative strong enough to calm a horse. When the poor thing woke up two days later, the bookseller would buy her roses, chocolates, a new dress and would take her to the pictures to see the latest from Cary Grant, who in her book was the handsomest man in recorded history.

'Did you know? They say Cary Grant is queer,' she would murmur, stuffing herself with chocolates. 'Is that possible?'

'Rubbish,' Barceló would swear. 'Dunces and blockheads live in a state of perpetual envy.'

'You do speak well, sir. It shows that you've been to that Sorbet university.'

'The Sorbonne,' he would answer, gently correcting her.

It was very difficult not to love Bernarda. Without being asked, she would cook and sew for me. She would mend my clothes and my shoes, comb and cut my hair, buy me vitamins and toothpaste. Once she even gave me a small medal with a glass container full of holy water, which a sister of hers who lived in San Adrián del Besós had brought all the way from Lourdes by bus. Sometimes, while she inspected my head in search of lice and other parasites, she would speak to me in a hushed voice.

'Miss Clara is the most wonderful person in the world, and may God strike me dead if it should ever enter my head to criticize her, but it's not right that you, Master Daniel, should become too obsessed with her, if you know what I mean.'

'Don't worry, Bernarda, we're only friends.'

'That's just what I say.'

To illustrate her arguments, Bernarda would then bring up some story she had heard on the radio about a boy who had fallen in love with his teacher and on whom some sort of avenging spell had been cast. It made his hair and his teeth fall out, and his face and hands were covered with some incriminating fungus, a sort of leprosy of lust.

'Lust is a bad thing,' Bernarda would conclude. 'Take it from me.'

Despite the jokes he made at my expense, Don Gustavo looked favourably on my devotion to Clara and my eager commitment to be her companion. I attributed his tolerance to the fact that he probably considered me harmless. From time to time, he would still let slip enticing offers to buy the Carax novel from me. He would tell me that he had mentioned the subject to colleagues in the antiquarian book trade, and they all agreed that a Carax could now be worth a fortune, especially in Paris. I always refused his offers, at which he would just smile shrewdly. He had given me a copy of the keys to the apartment so that I could come and go without having to worry about whether he or Bernarda were there to open the door. My father was another story. As the years went by, he had got over his instinctive reluctance to talk about any subject that truly worried him. One of the first consequences of that progress was that he began to show his obvious disapproval of my relationship with Clara.

'You ought to go out with friends your own age, like Tomás Aguilar – you seem to have forgotten him, though he's a splendid boy – and not with a woman who is old enough to be married.'

'What does it matter how old we each are if we're good friends?'

What hurt me most was the reference to Tomás, because it was true. I hadn't gone out with him for months, whereas before we had been inseparable. My father looked at me reprovingly.

'Daniel, you don't know anything about women, and this one is playing with you like a cat with a canary.'

'You're the one who doesn't know anything about women,' I would reply, offended. 'And much less about Clara.'

Our conversations on the subject rarely went any further than an exchange of reproaches and wounded looks. When I was not at school or with Clara, I devoted my time to helping my father in the bookshop – tidying up the storeroom at the back of the shop, delivering orders, running errands, or even serving regular customers. My father complained that I didn't really put my mind or my heart into the work. I, in turn, replied that I spent my whole life working there and I couldn't see what he could possibly complain about. Many nights, when sleep eluded me, I'd lie awake remembering the intimacy, the small world we had both shared during the years following my mother's death, the years of Victor Hugo's pen and the tin trains. I recalled them as years of peace and sadness, a world that was vanishing and that had begun to evaporate on the dawn when my father took me to the Cemetery of Forgotten Books. Time played on the opposite team. One day my father discovered that I'd given Carax's book to Clara, and he rose in anger.

'You disappoint me, Daniel,' he said. 'When I took you to that secret place, I told you that the book you chose was something special, that you were going to adopt it and had to be responsible for it.'

'I was ten at the time, Father, and that was a child's game.'

My father looked at me as if I'd stabbed him.

'And now you're fourteen, and not only are you still a child, you're a child who thinks he's a man. Life is going to deal you some hard knocks, Daniel. And very soon.'

In those days I wanted to believe that my father was hurt because I spent so much time with the Barcelós. The bookseller and his niece lived a life of luxury that my father could barely dream of. I thought he resented the fact that Don Gustavo's maid behaved as if she were my own mother, and was offended by my acceptance that someone could take on that role. Sometimes, while I was in the back room wrapping up parcels or preparing an order, I would hear a customer joking with my father.

'What you need is a good woman, Sempere. These days there are plenty of good-looking widows around, in the prime of their life, if you see what I mean. A young lady would sort out your life, my friend, and take twenty years off you. What a good pair of breasts can't do . . .'

My father never responded to these insinuations, but I found them increasingly sensible. Once, at dinnertime, which had become a battleground of silences and stolen glances, I brought up the subject. I thought that if I were the one to suggest it, it would make things easier. My father was an attractive man, always clean and neat in appearance, and I knew for a fact that more than one lady in the neighbourhood approved of him and would have welcomed more than just his reading suggestions.

'It's been very easy for you to find a substitute for your mother,' he answered bitterly. 'But for me there is no such person, and I have no interest at all in looking.'

As time went by, the hints from my father and from Bernarda, and even Barceló's intimations, began to make an impression on me. Something inside told me that I was entering a cul-de-sac, that I could not hope for Clara to see anything more in me than a boy ten years her junior. Every day it felt more difficult to be near her, to bear the touch of her hands or to take her by the arm when we went out for a walk. There came a point when her mere proximity translated into an almost physical pain. Nobody was unaware of this fact, least of all Clara.

'Daniel, I think we need to talk,' she would say. 'I don't think I've behaved very well towards you—'

I never let her finish her sentences. I would leave the room with any old excuse and flee, unable to face the possibility that the fantasy world I had built around Clara might be dissolving. I could not know that my troubles had only just begun.

# AN EMPTY PLATE
## 1950

# 7

On my sixteenth birthday, I spawned the most ill-fated idea that had yet occurred to me. Without consulting anybody, I decided to host a birthday party and invite Barceló, Bernarda, and Clara. In my father's estimation, the whole thing was a recipe for disaster.

'It's my birthday,' I answered sharply. 'I work for you every other day of the year. For once, at least, you could try to please me.'

'Suit yourself.'

The preceding months had been the most bewildering in my strange friendship with Clara. I hardly ever read to her anymore. Clara would systematically avoid being left on her own with me. Whenever I called by her apartment, her uncle popped up, pretending to read a newspaper, or else Bernarda would materialize, bustling about in the background and casting sidelong glances. Other times the company would take the form of one or several of Clara's friends. I called them the 'Sisterly Brigade'. Always chaste and modest in appearance, they patrolled the area around Clara with a missal in one hand and a policeman's eye, making it abundantly clear that I was in the way and that my presence embarrassed Clara and the entire world. Worst of all, however, was Neri, the music teacher, whose wretched symphony remained unfinished. He was a smooth talker, a rich kid from the snobby San Gervasio district, who, despite the Mozartian airs he affected, reminded me more of a tango singer, slick with brilliantine. The only talent I recognized in him was a badly concealed mean streak. He would suck up to Don Gustavo with no dignity or decorum, and he flirted with Bernarda in the kitchen, making her laugh with his silly gifts of sugared almonds and his fondness for bottom pinching. In short, I hated his guts. The dislike was mutual. Neri would turn up with his scores and his arrogant manner, regarding me as if I were some undesirable little cabin boy and making all sorts of objections to my presence.

'Don't you have to go and do your homework, son?'

'And you, maestro, don't you have a symphony to finish?'

In the end they would all get the better of me and I would depart, crestfallen and defeated, wishing I had Don Gustavo's gift of the gab so that I could put the conceited so-and-so in his place.

On my birthday my father went down to the bakery on the corner and bought the finest cake he could find. He set the dinner table silently, bringing out the silver and the best crockery. He lit a few candles and prepared a meal of what he thought were my favourite dishes. We didn't exchange a word all afternoon. In the evening he went into his room, slipped into his best suit, and came out again holding a packet wrapped in shiny cellophane, which he placed on the coffee table in the dining room. My present. He sat at the table, poured himself a glass of white wine, and waited. My invitation specified that dinner would be served at eight-thirty. At nine-thirty we were still waiting. My father glanced at me sadly. Inside, I was boiling with rage.

'You must be pleased with yourself,' I said. 'Isn't this what you wanted?'

'No.'

Half an hour later, Bernarda arrived. She bore a funereal expression and a message from Miss Clara, who wished me many happy returns. Unfortunately she would be unable to attend my birthday dinner. Señor Barceló had been obliged to leave town on business for a few days, and she'd had to change her music lesson with Maestro Neri. Bernarda had come because it was her afternoon off.

'Clara can't come because she has a music lesson?' I asked, astounded.

Bernarda looked down. She was almost in tears when she handed me a small parcel containing her present and kissed me on both cheeks.

'If you don't like it, you can exchange it,' she said.

I was left alone with my father, staring at the fine crockery, the silver, and the candles that were quietly burning themselves out.

'I'm sorry, Daniel,' said my father.

I nodded in silence, shrugging my shoulders.

'Aren't you even going to open your present?' he asked.

My only response was to slam the front door as I left the apartment. I rushed furiously down the stairs, my eyes brimming with tears of rage as I stepped outside. The street was freezing, desolate, suffused in an eerie blue radiance. I felt as if my heart had been flayed open. Everything around me trembled. I walked off aimlessly, paying scant attention to a stranger who was observing me from Puerta del Ángel. He wore a dark suit, right hand buried in the pocket of his jacket, eyes like wisps of light in the glow of his cigarette. Limping slightly, he began to follow me.

I wandered through the streets for an hour or more, until I found myself at the base of the Columbus monument. Crossing over to the port, I sat on the stony steps that descended into the dark waters next to the dock that sheltered the pleasure boats. Someone had chartered a night trip, and I could hear laughter and music wafting across from the procession of lights and reflections in the inner harbour. I remembered the days when my father would take me on that very same boat for a trip to the breakwater point. From there, you could see the cemetery on the slopes of Montjuïc, the endless city of the dead. Sometimes I waved, thinking that my mother was still there and could see us going by. My father would also wave. It was years since we had boarded a pleasure boat, although I knew that sometimes he did the trip on his own.

'A good night for remorse, Daniel,' came a voice from the shadows. 'Cigarette?'

I jumped up with a start. A hand was offering me a cigarette.

'Who are you?'

The stranger moved forward until he was on the very edge of the darkness, his face still concealed. A puff of blue smoke rose from his cigarette. I immediately recognized the black suit and the hand hidden in the jacket pocket. His eyes shone like glass beads.

'A friend,' he said. 'Or that's what I aspire to be. A cigarette?'

'I don't smoke.'

'Good for you. Unfortunately, I have nothing else to offer you, Daniel.'

He had a rasping, wounded voice. He seemed to drag his words out and they sounded muffled and distant like the old 78s Barceló collected.

'How do you know my name?'

'I know a lot about you. Your name is the least of it.'

'What else do you know?'

'I could embarrass you, but I don't have the time or the inclination. Just say that I know you have something that interests me. And I'm ready to pay you good money for it.'

'I'm afraid you've mistaken me for someone else.'

'No, I hardly think so. I tend to make other mistakes, but never when it comes to people. How much do you want for it?'

'For what?'

'For *The Shadow of the Wind*.'

'What makes you think I have it?'

'That's beyond discussion, Daniel. It's just a question of price. I've known you had it for a long time. People talk. I listen.'

'Well, you must have heard wrong. I don't have that book. And if I did, I wouldn't sell it.'

'Your integrity is admirable, especially in these days of

sycophants and toadies, but you don't have to pretend with me. Say how much. A thousand duros? Money means nothing to me. You set the price.'

'I've already told you: it's not for sale, and I don't have it,' I replied. 'You've made a mistake, you see.'

The stranger remained silent and motionless, enveloped in the blue smoke of a cigarette that never seemed to go out. I realized he didn't smell of tobacco, but of burned paper. Good paper, the sort used for books.

'Perhaps you're the one who's making a mistake now,' he suggested.

'Are you threatening me?'

'Probably.'

I gulped. Despite my bravado, the man frightened me.

'May I ask why you are so interested?'

'That's my business.'

'Mine too, if you are threatening me about a book I don't have.'

'I like you, Daniel. You've got guts, and you seem bright. A thousand duros? With that you could buy a huge amount of books. Good books, not that rubbish you guard with such zeal. Come on, a thousand duros and we'll remain friends.'

'You and I are not friends.'

'Yes we are, you just haven't realized it yet. I don't blame you, with so much on your mind. Your friend Clara, for instance. A woman like that ... anyone could lose his senses.'

The mention of Clara's name froze the blood in my veins. 'What do you know about Clara?'

'I dare say I know more than you, and that you'd do best to forget her, although I know you won't. I have been sixteen too....'

Suddenly a terribly certainty hit me. That man was the anonymous stranger who pestered Clara in the street. He was real. Clara had not lied. The man took a step forward. I moved back. I had never been so frightened in all my life.

'Clara doesn't have the book; you should know that. Don't you ever dare touch her again.'

'I'm not in the least bit interested in your friend, Daniel, and one day you'll share that feeling. What I want is the book. And I'd rather obtain it by fair means, without harming anyone. Do you understand?'

Unable to come up with anything better, I decided to lie through my teeth. 'Someone called Adrián Neri has it. A musician. You may have heard of him.'

'Doesn't ring a bell, and that's the worst thing one can say about a musician. Are you sure you haven't invented this Adrián Neri?'

'I wish I had.'

'In that case, since you seem to be so close, maybe you could persuade him to return it to you. These things are easily solved between friends. Or would you rather I asked Clara?'

I shook my head. 'I'll speak to Neri, but I don't think he'll give it back to me. Perhaps he doesn't even have it anymore. Anyhow, what do you want the book for? Don't tell me it's to read it.'

'No. I know it by heart.'

'Are you a collector?'

'Something like that.'

'Do you have other books by Carax?'

'I've had them at some point. Julián Carax is my specialty, Daniel. I travel the world in search of his books.'

'And what do you do with them if you don't read them?'

The stranger made a stifled, desperate sound. It took me a while to realize that he was laughing.

'The only thing that should be done with them, Daniel,' he answered.

He pulled a box of matches out of his pocket. He took one and struck it. The flame showed his face for the first time. My blood froze. He had no nose, lips or eyelids. His face was nothing but a mask of black scarred skin, consumed by fire. It was the same dead skin that Clara had touched.

'Burn them,' he whispered, his voice and his eyes poisoned by hate.

A gust of air blew out the match he held in his fingers, and his face was once again hidden in darkness.

'We'll meet again, Daniel. I never forget a face, and I don't think you will either,' he said calmly. 'For your sake, and for the sake of your friend Clara, I hope you make the right decision. Sort this thing out with Neri – a rather pretentious name. I wouldn't trust him an inch.'

With that, the stranger turned around and walked off toward the docks, a shape melting into the shadows, cocooned in his hollow laughter.

# 8

A reef of clouds and lightning raced across the skies from the sea. I should have run to take shelter from the approaching downpour, but the man's words were beginning to sink in. My hands were shaking, and my mind wasn't far behind. I looked up and saw the storm spilling like rivers of blackened blood from the clouds, blotting out the moon and covering the roofs of the city in darkness. I tried to speed up, but I was consumed with fear and walked with leaden feet, chased by the rain. I took refuge under the canopy of a newspaper kiosk, trying to collect my thoughts and decide what to do next. A clap of thunder roared close by, and I felt the ground shake under my feet. A few seconds later, the weak current of the lighting system, which lit up the shapes of buildings and windows, faded away. On the flooding pavements the streetlamps blinked, then went out like candles snuffed by the wind. There wasn't a soul to be seen in the streets, and the darkness of the blackout spread with a fetid smell that rose from the sewers. The night became opaque, impenetrable, as the rain folded the city in its shroud.

'*A woman like that . . . anyone could lose his senses.*'

I started to run up the Ramblas with only one thought in mind: Clara.

Bernarda had said Barceló was away on business. It was her day off, and she usually spent the night with her aunt Reme and her cousins in the nearby town of San Adrián del Besós. That left Clara alone in the cavernous Plaza Real apartment and that faceless, menacing man unleashed in the storm with heaven knows what in mind. As I hurried under the downpour towards Plaza Real, all I could think was that I had placed Clara in danger by giving her Carax's book. By the time I reached the entrance to the square, I was soaked to the bone. I rushed to take shelter under the arches of Calle Fernando. I thought I could see shadowy forms creeping up behind me. Beggars. The front door was closed. I searched my pockets for the keys Barceló had given me. One of the tramps came up, petitioning me to let him spend the night in the entrance hall. I closed the door before he'd time to finish his sentence.

The staircase was a well of darkness. Flashes of lightning bled through the cracks in the front door, lighting up the outline of the steps for a second. I groped my way forward and found the first step by tripping over it. Holding onto the banister, I slowly ascended. Soon the steps gave way to a flat surface, and I realized I had reached the first-floor landing. I felt the marble walls, cold and hostile, and found the reliefs on the oak door and the aluminium doorknobs. After fumbling about for a bit, I managed to insert the key. When the door of the apartment opened, a streak of blue light blinded me for an instant and a gust of warm air graced my skin. Bernarda's room was at the back of the apartment, by the kitchen. I went there first, although I was

56

sure the maid wasn't home. I rapped on the door with my knuckles and, as there was no answer, allowed myself to enter. It was a simple room, with a large bed, a cupboard with tinted mirrors, and a chest of drawers on which Bernarda had placed enough effigies and prints of saints and the Virgin Mary to start a holy order. I closed the door, and when I turned around, my heart almost stopped: a dozen scarlet eyes were advancing towards me from the end of the corridor. Barceló's cats knew me well and tolerated my presence. They surrounded me, meowing gently. As soon as they realized that my drenched clothes did not give out the desired warmth, they abandoned me with indifference.

Clara's room was at the other end of the apartment, next to the library and the music room. The cats' invisible steps followed me through the passageway. In the flickering darkness of the storm, Barceló's residence seemed vast and sinister, altered from the place I had come to consider my second home. I reached the front of the apartment, where it faced the square. The conservatory opened before me, dense and impassable. I penetrated its jungle of leaves and branches. For a moment it occurred to me that if the faceless stranger had managed to sneak into the apartment, this was where he would probably choose to wait for me. I almost thought I could perceive the smell of burned paper he left in the air around him, but then I realized that what I had detected was only tobacco. A burst of panic needled me. Nobody in the household smoked, and Barceló's unlit pipe was purely ornamental.

When I reached the music room, the glow from a flash of lightning revealed spirals of smoke that drifted in the air like garlands of vapour. Next to the gallery, the piano keyboard displayed its endless grin. I crossed the music room and went over to the library door. It was closed. I opened it and was welcomed by the brightness emanating from the glass-covered balcony that encircled Barceló's personal library. The walls, lined with packed bookshelves, formed an oval in whose centre stood a reading table and two plush armchairs. I knew that Clara kept Carax's book in a glass cabinet by the arch of the balcony. I crept up to it. My plan, or my lack of it, was to lay my hands on the book, get it out of there, give it to that lunatic and lose sight of him forever. Nobody would notice the book's absence, except me.

Julián Carax's book was waiting for me, as it always did, its spine just visible at the end of a shelf. I took it in my hands and pressed it against my chest, as if embracing an old friend I was about to betray. Judas, I thought to myself. I decided to leave the place without making Clara aware of my presence. I would take the book and disappear from Clara Barceló's life forever. Quietly, I stepped out of the library. The door of her bedroom was just visible at the end of the corridor. I pictured her lying on her bed, asleep. I imagined my fingers stroking her neck, exploring a body I had conjured up from my fantasies. I turned around, ready to throw away six years of daydreaming, but something halted my step before I reached the music room. A voice whistling behind me, behind a door. A deep voice that whispered and laughed. In Clara's room. I walked slowly up to the door. I put my fingers on the doorknob. They trembled. I had arrived too late. I swallowed hard and opened the door.

# 9

Clara's naked body lay stretched out on white sheets that shone like washed silk. Maestro Neri's hands slid over her lips, her neck and her breasts. Her white eyes looked up to the ceiling, her eyelids flickering as the music teacher charged at her, entering her body between pale and trembling thighs. The same hands that had read my face six years earlier in the gloom of the Ateneo now clutched the maestro's buttocks that were glistening with sweat, digging her nails into them and guiding him towards her with desperate, animal desire. I couldn't breathe. I must have stayed there, paralysed, watching them for almost half a minute, until Neri's eyes, disbelieving at first, then aflame with anger, became aware of my presence. Still panting, astounded, he stopped. Clara grabbed him, not understanding, rubbing her body against his, licking his neck.

'What's the matter?' she moaned. 'Why are you stopping?'

Adrián Neri's eyes burned with rage. 'Nothing,' he murmured. 'I'll be right back.'

Neri stood up and threw himself at me, clenching his fists. I didn't even see him coming. I couldn't take my eyes off Clara, wrapped in sweat, breathless, her ribs visible under her skin and her breasts quivering. The music teacher grabbed me by the neck and dragged me out of the bedroom. My feet were barely touching the floor, and however hard I tried, I was unable to escape Neri's grip as he carried me like a bundle through the conservatory.

'I'm going to break your neck, you wretch,' he muttered.

He hauled me toward the front door, opened it, and flung me with all his might onto the landing. Carax's book slipped out of my hands. He picked it up and threw it furiously at my face.

'If I ever see you around here again, or if I find out that you've gone up to Clara in the street, I swear I'll give you such a beating you'll end up in hospital – and I don't give a shit how young you are,' he said in a cold voice. 'Understood?'

I got up with difficulty. In the struggle Neri had torn my jacket and my pride.

'How did you get in?'

I didn't answer. Neri sighed, shaking his head. 'Come

on,' he barked barely containing his fury. 'Give me the keys.'

'What keys?'

He punched me so hard I collapsed. When I got up, there was blood in my mouth and a ringing in my left ear that bored through my head like a policeman's whistle. I touched my face and felt the cut on my lips burning under my fingers. A bloodstained signet ring shone on the music teacher's finger.

'I said the keys.'

'Piss off,' I spat out.

I didn't see the next blow coming. I just felt as if a jackhammer had torn my stomach out. I folded up like a broken puppet, unable to breathe, staggering back against the wall. Neri grabbed me by my hair and rummaged in my pockets until he found the keys. I slid down to the floor, holding my stomach, whimpering with agony and anger.

'Tell Clara that—'

He slammed the door in my face, leaving me in complete darkness. I groped around for the book. I found it and slid down the stairs, leaning against the walls, panting. I went outside spitting blood and gasping for breath. The biting cold and the wind tightened around my soaking clothes. The cut on my face was stinging.

'Are you all right?' asked a voice in the shadow.

It was the beggar I had refused to help a short time before. Feeling ashamed, I nodded, avoiding his eyes. I started to walk away.

'Wait a minute, at least until the rain eases off,' the beggar suggested.

He took me by the arm and led me to a corner under the arches where he kept a bundle of possessions and a bag with old, dirty clothes.

'I have a bit of wine. It's not too bad. Drink a little. It will help you warm up. And disinfect that . . .'

I took a swig from the bottle he offered me. It tasted of diesel oil laced with vinegar, but its heat calmed my stomach and my nerves. A few drops sprinkled over my wound, and I saw stars in the blackest night of my life.

'Good, eh?' The beggar smiled. 'Go on, have another shot. This stuff can raise a person back from the dead.'

'No thanks. You have some,' I mumbled.

The beggar had a long drink. I watched him closely. He looked like some grey government accountant who had been sleeping in the same suit for the last fifteen years. He stretched out his hand, and I shook it.

'Fermín Romero de Torres, currently unemployed. Pleased to meet you.'

'Daniel Sempere, complete idiot. The pleasure is all mine.'

'Don't sell yourself short. On nights like this, everything looks worse than it is. You'd never guess it, but I'm a born optimist. I have no doubt at all that the present regime's days are numbered. All intelligence points towards the Americans invading us any day now and setting Franco up with a peanut stand down in Melilla. Then my position, my reputation, and my lost honour will be restored.'

'What did you work at?'

'Secret service. High espionage,' said Fermín Romero de Torres. 'Suffice it to say that I was President Maciá's man in Havana.'

I nodded. Another madman. At night Barcelona gathered them in by the handful. And idiots like me, too.

'Listen, that cut doesn't look good. Someone's given you quite a tanning, eh?'

I touched my mouth with my fingers. It was still bleeding.

'Woman trouble?' he asked. 'You could have saved yourself the effort. Women in this country – and I've seen a bit of the world – are a sanctimonious, frigid lot. Believe me. I remember a little mulatto girl I left behind in Cuba. No comparison, eh? No comparison. The Caribbean female draws up to you with that island swing of hers and whispers

61

"*Ay, papito*, gimme pleasure, gimme pleasure." And a real man, with blood in his veins . . . well, what can I say?'

It seemed to me that Fermín Romero de Torres, or whatever his true name was, longed for lighthearted conversation almost as much as he longed for a hot bath, a plate of stew, and a clean change of clothes. I got him going for a while, as I waited for my pain to subside. It wasn't very difficult, because all the man needed was a nod at the right moment and someone who appeared to be listening. The beggar was about to recount the details of a bizarre plan for kidnapping Franco's wife when I saw that the rain had abated and the storm seemed to be slowly moving away towards the north.

'It's getting late,' I mumbled, standing up.

Fermín Romero de Torres nodded with a sad look and helped me get up, pretending to dust down my drenched clothes.

'Some other day, then,' he said in a resigned tone. 'I'm afraid talking is my undoing. Once I start . . . Listen, this business about the kidnapping, it must go no further, understand?'

'Don't worry. I'm as silent as the grave. And thanks for the wine.'

I set off towards the Ramblas. I stopped by the entrance to the square and turned to look at the Barcelós apartment. The windows were still in darkness, weeping with rain. I wanted to hate Clara but was unable to. To truly hate is an art one learns with time.

I swore to myself that I would never see her again, that I wouldn't mention her name or remember the time I had wasted by her side. For some strange reason, I felt at peace. The anger that had driven me out of my home had gone. I was afraid it would return, and with renewed vigour, the following day. I was afraid that jealousy and shame would slowly consume me once all the pieces of my memory of that night fell into place. But dawn was still a few hours away, and there was one more thing I had to do before I could return home with a clean conscience.

Calle Arco del Teatro was there waiting for me. A stream of black water converged in the centre of the narrow street and made its way, like a funeral procession, toward the heart of the Raval quarter. I recognized the old wooden door and the baroque façade to which my father had brought me that morning at dawn, six years before. I went up the steps and took shelter from the rain under the arched doorway. It reeked of urine and rotten wood. More than ever, the Cemetery of Forgotten Books smelled of death. I didn't recall that the door knocker was shaped as a demon's face. I took it by its horns and knocked three times. The cavernous echo dispersed within the building. After a while I knocked again, six knocks this time, each one louder than before, until my fist hurt. A few more minutes went by, and I began to fear that perhaps there was no longer anyone there. I crouched down against the door and took the Carax from the inside of my jacket. I opened it and reread that first sentence that had entranced me years before.

> That summer it rained every day, and although many said it was God's wrath because the villagers had opened a casino next to the church, I knew it was my fault, and mine alone, for I had learned to lie and my lips still retained the last words spoken by my mother on her deathbed: 'I never loved the man I married but another who, I was told, had been killed in the war; look for him and tell him my last thoughts were for him, for he is your real father.'

I smiled, remembering that first night of feverish reading six years earlier. I closed the book and was about to knock one last time, but before my fingers touched the knocker, the large door opened far enough to reveal the profile of the keeper. He was carrying an oil lamp.

'Good evening,' I mumbled. 'Isaac, isn't it?'

The keeper observed me without blinking. The glow

from the oil lamp sculpted his angular features in amber and scarlet hues, conferring on him a striking likeness to the little demon on the door knocker.

'You're Sempere junior,' he muttered wearily.

'Your memory is excellent.'

'And your sense of timing is lousy. Do you know what time it is?'

His sharp eyes had already detected the book under my jacket. Isaac stared at me questioningly. I took the book out and showed it to him.

'Carax,' he said. 'I'd say there are at most ten people in this town who know of him, or who have read this book.'

'Well, one of them is intent on setting fire to it. I can't think of a better hiding place than this.'

'This is a cemetery, not a safe.'

'Exactly. What this book needs is to be buried where nobody can find it.'

Isaac glanced suspiciously down the alleyway. He opened the door a few inches and beckoned me to slip inside. The dark, unfathomable vestibule smelled of wax and dampness. An intermittent drip could be heard in the gloom. Isaac gave me the lamp to hold while he put his hand in his coat and pulled out a ring of keys that would have been the envy of any jailer. When, by some imponderable science, he found the right one, he inserted it into a bolt under a glass case full of relays and cogwheels, like a large music box. With a twist of his wrist, the mechanism clicked, and levers and fulcrums slid in an amazing mechanical ballet until the large door was clamped by a circle of steel bars that locked into place in the stone wall.

'The Bank of Spain couldn't do better,' I remarked, impressed. 'It looks like something out of Jules Verne.'

'Kafka,' Isaac corrected, retrieving the oil lamp and starting off towards the depths of the building. 'The day you come to realize that the book business is nothing but an empty plate and you decide you want to learn how to rob a bank, or how to set one up, which is much the same thing, come and see me and I'll teach you a few things about bolts.'

I followed him through corridors that I still remembered, flanked with fading frescoes of angels and shadowlike creatures. Isaac held the lamp up high, casting a flickering bubble of red light. He limped slightly, and his frayed flannel coat looked like an undertaker's. It occurred to me that this man, somewhere between Charon and the librarian at Alexandria, seemed to belong in one of Julián Carax's novels.

'Do you know anything about Carax?' I asked.

Isaac stopped at the end of a gallery and looked at me with indifference. 'Not much. Only what they told me.'

'Who?'

'Someone who knew him well, or thought so at least.'

My heart missed a beat. 'When was that?'

'When I still had use for a comb. You must have been in swaddling clothes. And you don't seem to have come on much, quite frankly. Look at yourself: you're shaking.'

'It's my wet clothes, and it's very cold in here.'

'Is it? Well, next time pray send advance notice of your call, and I'll turn on the fancy central heating system to welcome you, little rosebud. Come on, follow me. My office is over there. There's a stove and something for you to wrap yourself in while we dry your clothes. And some Mercurochrome and peroxide wouldn't go amiss either. You look as if you've just been dropped off by a police van.'

'Don't bother, really.'

'I'm not bothering. I'm doing it for me, not for you. Once you've passed through this door, you play by my rules. This cemetery is for books, not people. You might catch pneumonia, and I don't want to call the morgue. We'll see about the book later. In thirty-eight years, I have yet to see one that can run away.'

'I can't tell you how grateful I am—'

'Then don't. If I've let you in, it's out of respect for your father. Otherwise I would have left you in the street. Now, follow me. If you behave yourself, I might consider telling you what I know of your friend Julián Carax.'

Out of the corner of my eye, when he thought I couldn't see him, I noticed that, despite himself, he was smiling mischievously. Isaac clearly seemed to relish the role of sinister watchdog. I also smiled to myself. There was no doubt in my mind as to whom the face on the door knocker belonged.

# 10

Isaac threw a couple of blankets over my shoulders and offered me a cup of some steaming concoction that smelled of hot chocolate and some sort of alcohol.

'You were saying about Carax . . .'

'There's not much to say. The first person I heard mention Carax was Toni Cabestany, the publisher. I'm talking about twenty years ago, when his firm was still in business. Whenever he returned from one of his scouting trips to London, Paris, or Vienna, Cabestany would drop by and we'd chat for a while. We were both widowers by then, and he would complain that we were now married to the books, I to the old ones and he to his ledgers. We were good friends. On one of his visits, he told me how, for a pittance, he'd just acquired the Spanish rights for the novels of Julián Carax, a young writer from Barcelona who lived in Paris. This must have been in 1928 or 1929. Seems that Carax worked nights as a pianist in some small-time brothel in Pigalle and wrote during the day in a shabby attic in Saint-Germain. Paris is the only city in the world where starving to death is still considered an art. Carax had published a couple of novels in France, which had turned out to be total flops. No one gave him the time of day in Paris, and Cabestany had always liked to buy cheap.'

'So did Carax write in Spanish or in French?'

'Who knows? Probably both. His mother was French, a music teacher, I believe, and he'd lived in Paris since he was about nineteen or twenty. Cabestany told me that his manuscripts arrived in Spanish. Whether they were a translation or the original, he didn't care. His favourite language was money, the rest was neither here nor there. It occurred to Cabestany that perhaps, by a stroke of luck, he might place a few thousand copies in the Spanish market.'

'Did he?'

Isaac frowned as he poured me a bit more of his restorative potion. 'I think the one that sold most, *The Red House*, sold about ninety copies.'

'But he continued to publish Carax's books, even though he was losing money,' I pointed out.

'That's right. Beats me. Cabestany wasn't exactly a romantic. But I suppose everyone has his secrets. . . . Between 1928 and 1936, he published eight of Carax's novels. Anyway, where Cabestany really made his money was in catechisms and a series of cheap sentimental novels starring a provincial heroine called Violeta LaFleur. Those sold like hot cakes. My guess is that he published Carax's novels because it tickled his fancy, or just to contradict Darwin.'

'What happened to Señor Cabestany?'

Isaac sighed, looking up. 'Age – the price we all must pay. He became ill and had a few money problems. In 1936 his eldest son took over the firm, but he was the sort who can't even read the size of his underpants. The business collapsed in less than a year. Fortunately, Cabestany never saw what his heirs did with the fruit of his life's work, or what the war did to his country. A stroke saw him off on All Souls' Night, with a Cuban cigar in his lips and a 25-year-old girl on his lap. What a way to go. The son was another breed altogether. Arrogant as only idiots can be. His first grand idea was to try to sell the entire stock of the company backlist, his father's legacy, and turn it into pulp or something like that. A friend, another brat with a house in Caldetas and an Italian sports car, had convinced him that photo romances and *Mein Kampf* were going to sell like crazy, and, as a result, there would be a huge demand for cellulose.

'Did he really do that?'

'He would have, but he ran out of time. Shortly after he took over the firm, someone turned up at his office and made him a very generous offer. He wanted to buy the whole remaining stock of Julián Carax novels and was offering to pay three times their market value.'

'Say no more. To burn them,' I murmured.

Isaac smiled. He looked surprised. 'Actually, yes. And here I was thinking you were a bit slow, what with so much asking and not knowing anything.'

'Who was that man?'

'Someone called Aubert or Coubert, I can't quite remember.'

'Laín Coubert?'

'Does that sound familiar?'

'It's the name of one of the characters in *The Shadow of the Wind*, the last of Carax's novels.'

Isaac frowned. 'A fictional character?'

'In the novel Laín Coubert is the name used by the devil.'

'A bit theatrical, if you ask me. But whoever he was, at least he had a sense of humour,' Isaac reckoned.

With the memory of that night's encounter still fresh in my mind, I could not see the humorous side of it, from any angle, but I saved my opinion for a more auspicious occasion.

'This person, Coubert, or whatever his name is – was his face burned, disfigured?'

Isaac looked at me with a smile that betrayed both enjoyment and concern. 'I haven't the foggiest. The person who told me all this never actually got to see him, and only knew because Cabestany's son told his secretary the following day. He didn't mention anything about burned faces. Are you sure you haven't got this out of some radio show?'

I threw my head back, as if to make light of the subject.

'How did the matter end? Did the publisher's son sell the books to Coubert?' I asked.

'The senseless dunce tried to be too clever by half. He asked for more money than Coubert was proposing, and Coubert withdrew his offer. A few days later, shortly after midnight, Cabestany's warehouse in Pueblo Nuevo burned down to its foundations. And for free.'

I sighed. 'What happened to Carax's books, then? Were they all destroyed?'

'Nearly all. Luckily, when Cabestany's secretary heard about the offer, she had a premonition. On her own initiative, she went to the warehouse and took a copy of each of the Carax titles. She was the one who had corresponded with Carax, and over the years they had formed a friendship of sorts. Her name was Nuria, and I think she was the only person in the publishing house, probably in all of Barcelona, who had read Carax's novels. Nuria has a fondness for lost causes. When she was little, she would take in small animals she picked up in the street. In time she went on to adopt failed authors, maybe because her father wanted to be one and never made it.'

'You seem to know her very well.'

Isaac wore his devilish smile. 'More than she thinks I do. She's my daughter.'

Silence and doubt gnawed at me. The more I heard of the story, the more confused I felt. 'Apparently, Carax returned to Barcelona in 1936. Some say he died here. Did he have any relatives left here? Someone who might know about him?'

Isaac sighed. 'Goodness only knows. Carax's parents had been separated for some time, I believe. The mother had gone off to South America, where she remarried. I don't think he was on speaking terms with his father since he moved to Paris.'

'Why was that?'

'I don't know. People tend to complicate their own lives, as if living weren't already complicated enough.'

'Do you know whether Carax's father is still alive?'

'I hope so. He was younger than me, but I go out very little these days and I haven't read the obituary pages for years – acquaintances drop dead like flies, and, quite frankly, it puts the wind up you. By the way, Carax was his mother's surname. The father was called Fortuny. He had a hat shop on Ronda de San Antonio.'

'Is it possible, then, do you think, that when he returned to Barcelona, Carax may have felt tempted to visit your daughter, Nuria, if they were friends, since he wasn't on good terms with his father?'

Isaac laughed bitterly. 'I'm probably the last person who would know. After all, I'm her father. I know that once, in 1932 or 1933, Nuria went to Paris on business for Cabestany, and she stayed in Julián Carax's apartment for a couple of weeks. It was Cabestany who told me. According to my daughter, she stayed in a hotel. She was unmarried at the time, and I had an inkling that Carax was a bit smitten with her. My Nuria is the sort who breaks a man's heart just by walking into a shop.'

'Do you mean they were lovers?'

'You like melodrama, eh? Look, I've never interfered in Nuria's private life, because mine isn't picture perfect either. If you ever have a daughter – a blessing I wouldn't wish on anyone, because it's sod's law that sooner or later she will break your heart – anyhow, as I was saying, if you ever have a daughter, you'll begin, without realizing it, to divide men into two camps: those you suspect are sleeping with her and those you don't. Whoever says that's not true is lying through his teeth. I suspected that Carax was one of the first, so I didn't care whether he was a genius or a poor wretch. To me he was always a scoundrel.'

'Perhaps you were mistaken.'

'Don't be offended, but you're still very young and know as much about women as I do about baking marzipan pastries.'

'No contest there,' I agreed. 'What happened to the books your daughter took from the warehouse?'

'They're here.'

'Here?'

'Where do you think your book came from – the one you found on the day your father brought you to this place?'

'I don't understand.'

'It's very simple. One night, some days after the fire in Cabestany's warehouse, my daughter, Nuria, turned up here. She looked nervous. She said that someone had been following her and she was afraid it was the man called Coubert, who was trying to get hold of the books to destroy them. Nuria said she had come to hide Carax's books. She went into the large hall and hid them in the maze of bookshelves, like buried treasure. I didn't ask her where she'd put them, nor did she tell me. Before she left, she said that as soon as she managed to find Carax, she'd come back for them. It seemed to me that she was still in love with him, but I didn't say anything. I asked her whether she'd seen him recently, whether she'd had any news. She said she hadn't heard from him for months, practically since he'd sent her the final corrections for the manuscript of his last book. I can't say whether she was lying. What I do know is that after that day Nuria didn't hear from Carax again, and those books were left here, gathering dust.'

'Do you think your daughter would be willing to talk to me about all this?'

'Could be, but I don't know whether she'd be able to tell you anything that yours truly hasn't told you already. Remember, all of this happened a long time ago. The truth is that we don't get on as well as I'd like. We see each other once a month. We go out to lunch somewhere close by, and then she's off as quick as she came. I know that a few years ago she married a nice man, a journalist, a bit harebrained, I'd say, one of those people who are always getting into trouble over politics, but with a good heart. They had a civil wedding with no guests. I found out a month later. She has never introduced me to her husband. Miquel, his name is. Or something like that. I don't suppose she's very proud of her father, and I don't blame her. Now she's a changed woman. Imagine, she even learned to knit, and I'm told she no longer dresses like Simone de Beauvoir. One of these days, I'll find out I'm a grandfather. For years she's been working at home as an Italian and French translator. I don't know where she got the talent from, quite frankly. Not from her father, that's for sure. Let me write down her address, though I'm not sure it's a very good idea to say I sent you.'

Isaac scribbled something on the corner of an old newspaper and handed me the scrap of paper.

'I'm very grateful. You never know, maybe she'll remember something. . . .'

Isaac smiled with some sadness. 'As a child she'd remember everything. Everything. Then children grow up, and you no longer know what they think or what they feel. And that's how it should be, I suppose. Don't tell Nuria what I've told you, will you? What's been said here tonight should go no further.'

'Don't worry. Do you think she still thinks about Carax?'

Isaac gave a long sigh and lowered his eyes. 'Heaven knows. I don't know whether she really loved him. These things remain locked inside, and now she's a married woman. When I was your age, I had a girlfriend, Teresita Boadas, her name was – she sewed aprons in the Santamaría textile factory on Calle Comercio. She was sixteen, two years younger than me, and she was the first woman I ever fell for. Don't look at me like that. I know you youngsters think we old people have never fallen in love. Teresita's father had an ice cart in the Borne Market and had been born dumb. You can't imagine how scared I was the day I asked him for his daughter's hand and he spent five long minutes staring at me, without any apparent reaction, holding the ice pick in his hand. I'd been saving up for two years to buy Teresita a wedding ring when she fell ill. Something she'd caught in the workshop, she told me. Six months later she was dead of tuberculosis. I can still remember how the dumb man moaned the day we buried her in the Pueblo Nuevo cemetery.'

Isaac fell into a deep silence. I didn't dare breathe. After a while he looked up and smiled.

'I'm speaking of fifty-five years ago, imagine! But if I must be frank, a day doesn't go by without me thinking of her, of the walks we used to take as far as the ruins of the 1888 Universal Exhibition, or of how she would laugh at me when I read her the poems I wrote in the back room of my uncle Leopoldo's grocery shop. I even remember the face of a Gypsy woman who read our fortune on Bogatell beach and told us we'd always be together. In her own way, she was right. What can I say? Well, yes, I think Nuria still remembers that man, even if she doesn't say so. And the truth is, I'll never forgive Carax for that. You're still very young, but I know how much these things hurt. If you want my opinion, Carax was a robber of hearts, and he took my daughter's to the grave, or to hell. I'll only ask you one thing: if you see her and talk to her, let me know how she is. Find out whether she's happy. And whether she's forgiven her father.'

Shortly before dawn, with only an oil lamp to light my way, I went back into the Cemetery of Forgotten Books. As I did so, I imagined Isaac's daughter wandering through the dark and endless corridors with exactly the same determination as guided me today: to save the book. I thought I remembered the route I'd followed the first time I visited that place with my father, but soon I realized that the twists and turns of the labyrinth bent the passages into spirals that were impossible to recall. Three times I tried to follow a path I thought I had memorized, and three times the maze returned me to the same point. Isaac waited for me there, a wry smile on his face.

'Do you intend to come back for it one day?' he asked.
'Of course.'
'In that case you might like to cheat a little.'
'Cheat?'
'Young man, you're a bit slow on the uptake, aren't you? Remember the Minotaur.'

73

It took me a few seconds to understand what he was suggesting. Isaac pulled an old penknife out of his pocket and handed it to me.

'Make a mark on every corner, a notch only you will recognize. It's old wood and so full of scratches and grooves that nobody will notice it, unless the person knows what he's looking for. . . .'

I followed his advice and once more penetrated the heart of the structure. Every time I changed direction, I stopped to mark the shelves with a C and an X on the side of the passage that I was intending to take. Twenty minutes later I had lost myself in the depths of the tower and then, quite by chance, the place where I was going to bury the novel was revealed to me. To my right I noticed a row of volumes on the disentailment of church property penned by the distinguished Jovellanos. To my adolescent eyes, such a camouflage would have dissuaded even the craftiest mind. I took out a few tomes and inspected the second row that was concealed behind those walls of marble prose. Among little clouds of dust, various plays by Moratín and a brand-new *Curial e Güelfa* stood side by side with Spinoza's *Tractatus Theologico Politicus*. As a coup de grâce, I resolved to confine the Carax book between the 1901 yearbook of judicial minutiae from the civil courts of Gerona and a collection of novels by Juan Valera. In order to make space, I decided to remove and take with me the book of Golden Age poetry that separated them, and in its place I slipped in *The Shadow of the Wind*. I took my leave of the novel and put the Jovellanos anthology back in its place, walling in the back row.

Without further ado I left the place, finding my route by the marks I had made on the way in. As I walked in the dark through the tunnels and tunnels of books, I could not help being overcome by a sense of sadness. I couldn't help thinking that if I, by pure chance, had found a whole universe in a single unknown book, buried in that endless necropolis, tens of thousands more would remain unexplored, forgotten forever. I felt myself surrounded by millions of abandoned pages, by worlds and souls without an owner sinking in an ocean of darkness, while the world that throbbed outside the library seemed to be losing its memory, day after day, unknowingly, feeling all the wiser the more it forgot.

Dawn was breaking when I returned to the apartment on Calle Santa Ana. Opening the door quietly, I slipped in without switching on the light. From the entrance hall, I could see the dining room at the end of the corridor, the table still decked out for the party. The cake was there, untouched, and the crockery still waited for the meal. I could make out the motionless silhouette of my father in his armchair, as he observed the scene from the window. He was awake and still wearing his best suit. Wreaths of smoke rose lazily from a cigarette he held between his index and ring fingers, as if it were a pen. I hadn't seen my father smoke for years.

'Good morning,' he murmured, putting out the cigarette in an ashtray that was full of half-smoked butts.

I looked at him without knowing what to say. The light from behind him concealed his eyes.

'Clara phoned a few times last night, a couple of hours after you left,' he said. 'She sounded very worried. She left a message for you to call her, no matter what time it was.'

'I don't intend to see or speak to Clara again,' I said.

My father nodded but didn't reply. I fell into one of the dining-room chairs and stared at the floor.

'Aren't you going to tell me where you've been?'

'Just around.'

'You've given me one hell of a fright.'

There was no anger in his voice and hardly any reproach, just tiredness.

'I know. And I'm sorry,' I answered.

'What have you done to your face?'

'I slipped in the rain and fell.'

'That rain must have a good right hook. Put something on it.'

'It's nothing. I don't even notice it,' I lied. 'What I need is to get some sleep. I can barely stand up.'

'At least open your present before you go to bed,' said my father.

He pointed to the packet wrapped in cellophane, which he had placed on the coffee table the night before. I hesitated for a moment. My father nodded. I took the packet and felt its weight. I handed it to my father without opening it.

'You'd better return it. I don't deserve any presents.'

'Presents are made for the pleasure of the one who gives them, not for the merits of those who receive them,' said my father. 'Besides, it can't be returned. Open it.'

I undid the carefully wrapped package in the dim light of dawn. It contained a shiny carved wooden box, edged with gold rivets. Even before opening it, I was smiling. The sound of the clasp when it unlocked was exquisite, like the ticking of a watch. Inside, the case was lined with dark blue velvet. Victor Hugo's fabulous Montblanc Meisterstück rested in the centre. It was a dazzling sight. I took it and gazed at it by the light of the balcony. The gold clip of the pen top had an inscription.

Daniel Sempere, 1950

I stared at my father, dumbfounded. I don't think I had ever seen him look as happy as he seemed to me at that moment. Without saying anything, he got up from his armchair and held me tight. I felt a lump in my throat and, lost for words, fell utterly silent.

# TRUE TO CHARACTER
## 1951–1953

# 11

That year autumn blanketed Barcelona with fallen leaves that rippled through the streets like silvery scales. The distant memory of the night of my sixteenth birthday had put a damper on my spirits, or perhaps life had decided to grant me a sabbatical from my melodramatic woes so that I could begin to grow up. I was surprised at how little I thought about Clara Barceló, or Julián Carax, or that faceless cipher who smelled of burned paper and claimed to be a character straight out of a book. By November, I had observed a month of sobriety, a month without going anywhere near Plaza Real to beg a glimpse of Clara through the window. The merit, I must confess, was not altogether mine. Business in the bookshop was picking up, and my father and I had more on our hands than we could juggle.

'At this rate we'll have to hire another person to help us find the orders,' my father remarked. 'What we really need is someone very special, half detective, half poet, someone who won't charge much or be afraid to tackle the impossible.'

'I think I have the right candidate,' I said.

I found Fermín Romero de Torres in his usual lodgings below the arches of Calle Fernando. The beggar was putting together the front page of the Monday paper from bits he had rescued from a waste bin. The lead story went on about the greatness of national public works as yet more proof of the glorious progress of the dictatorship's policies.

'Good God! Another dam!' I heard him cry. 'These fascists will turn us all into a race of saints and frogs.'

'Good morning,' I said quietly. 'Do you remember me?'

The beggar raised his head, and a wonderful smile suddenly lit up his face.

'Do mine eyes deceive me? How are things with you, my friend? You'll accept a swig of red wine, I hope?'

'It's on me today,' I said. 'Are you hungry?'

'Well, I wouldn't say no to a good plate of seafood, but I'll eat anything that's thrown at me.'

On our way to the bookshop, Fermín Romero de Torres filled me in on all manner of escapades he had devised during the last weeks to avoid the Security Services, and in particular one Inspector Fumero, his nemesis, with whom he appeared to have a running battle.

'Fumero?' I asked. That was the name of the soldier who had murdered Clara Barceló's father in Montjuïc Castle at the outbreak of the war.

The little man nodded fearfully, turning pale. He looked famished and dirty, and he stank from months of living on the streets. The poor fellow had no idea where I was taking him, and I noticed a certain apprehension, a growing anxiety that he tried to disguise with incessant chatter. When we arrived at the shop, he gave me a troubled look.

'Please come in. This is my father's bookshop. I'd like to introduce you to him.'

The beggar hunched himself up, a bundle of grime and nerves. 'No, no, I wouldn't hear of it. I don't look presentable, and this is a classy establishment. I would embarrass you. . . .'

My father put his head around the door, glanced at the beggar, and then looked at me out of the corner of his eye.

'Dad, this is Fermín Romero de Torres.'

'At your service,' said the beggar, almost shaking.

My father smiled at him calmly and stretched out his hand. The beggar didn't dare take it, mortified by his appearance and the filth that covered his skin.

'Listen, I think it's best if I go away and leave you,' he stammered.

My father took him gently by the arm. 'Not at all, my son has told me you're going to have lunch with us.'

The beggar looked at us amazed, terrified.

'Why don't you come up to our home and have a nice hot bath?' said my father. 'Afterwards, if that's all right, we could walk down to Can Solé for lunch.'

Fermín Romero de Torres mumbled something unintelligible. Still smiling, my father led him towards the front door and practically had to drag him up the stairs to the apartment while I closed the shop. By dint of honeyed words and underhand tactics, we managed to remove his rags and get him into the bath. With nothing on, he looked like a wartime photograph and trembled like a plucked chicken. Deep marks showed on his wrists and ankles, and his trunk and back were covered with terrible scars that were painful to see. My father and I exchanged horrified looks but made no comment.

The beggar allowed himself to be washed like a child, frightened and shivering. While I searched for clean clothes, I could hear my father's voice talking to him without pause. I found him a suit that my father no longer wore, an old shirt, and some underwear. From the pile of clothes the beggar had taken off, not even the shoes could be rescued. I chose a pair that my father seldom put on because they were too small for him. Then I wrapped the rags in newspaper, including a pair of trousers that were the colour and consistency of smoked ham, and shoved them in the bin. When I returned to the bathroom, my father was shaving Fermín in the bathtub. Pale and smelling of soap, he looked twenty years younger. From what I could see, the two had already struck up a friendship. It may have been the effects of the bath salts, but Fermín Romero de Torres was on overdrive.

'Believe me, Señor Sempere, if fate hadn't led me into the world of international intrigue, what I would have gone for, what was closest to my heart, was Humanities. As a child I felt the call of poetry and wanted to be a Sophocles or a Virgil, because tragedy and dead languages give me goose pimples. But my father, God rest his soul, was a pigheaded man without much vision. He'd always wanted one of his

81

children to join the Civil Guard, and none of my seven sisters would have qualified for that, despite the facial-hair problem that characterized all the women on my mother's side of the family. On his deathbed my father made me swear that if I didn't succeed in wearing the Civil Guard's three-cornered hat, at least I would become a civil servant and abandon all my literary ambitions. I'm rather old-fashioned, and I believe that a father, however dim-witted, should be obeyed, if you see what I mean. Even so, don't imagine that I set aside all intellectual pursuits during my years of adventure. I've read a great deal, and can recite some of the best fragments of *La Divina Commedia* from memory.'

'Come on, chief, put these clothes on; your erudition is beyond any doubt,' I said, coming to my father's rescue.

When Fermín Romero de Torres came out of the bath, sparkling clean, his eyes beamed with gratitude. My father wrapped him up in a towel, and the beggar laughed from the sheer pleasure of feeling clean fabric brushing his skin. I helped him into his change of clothes, which proved to be about ten sizes too big. My father removed his belt and handed it to me to put around him.

'You look very dashing,' said my father. 'Doesn't he, Daniel?'

'Anyone might mistake you for a film star.'

'Come off it. I'm not what I used to be. I lost my Herculean muscles in prison, and since then ...'

'Well, I think you look like Charles Boyer, at least in build,' objected my father. 'Which reminds me: I wanted to propose something to you.'

'For you, Señor Sempere, I would kill if I had to. Just say the name, and I'll get rid of the man before he knows what's hit him.'

'It won't come to that. What I wanted to offer you was a job in the bookshop. It consists of looking for rare books for our clients. It's almost like literary archaeology, and it would be just as important for you to know the classics as basic black-market techniques. I can't pay you much at present, but you can eat at our table and, until we find you a good *pensión*, you can stay here with us, in the apartment, if that's all right with you.'

The beggar looked at both of us, dumbfounded.

'What do you say?' asked my father. 'Will you join the team?'

I thought he was going to say something, but at that moment Fermín Romero de Torres burst into tears.

With his first wages, Fermín Romero de Torres bought himself a glamorous hat and a pair of galoshes and insisted on treating me and my father to a dish of bull's tail, which was served on Mondays in a restaurant a couple of blocks away from the Monumental bull ring. My father had found him a room in a *pensión* in Calle Joaquín Costa, where, thanks to the friendship between our neighbour Merceditas and the landlady, we were able to avoid filling in the guest form required by the police, thus removing Fermín Romero de Torres from under the nose of Inspector Fumero and his henchmen. Sometimes I thought about the terrible scars that covered his body and felt tempted to ask him about them, fearing that perhaps Inspector Fumero might have something to do with them. But there was a look in the eyes of that poor man that made me think it was better not to bring up the subject. Perhaps he would tell us one day, when he felt the time was right. Every morning, at seven on the dot, Fermín waited for us by the shop door with a smile on his face, neatly turned out and ready to work an unbroken twelve-hour shift, or even longer. He had discovered a passion for chocolate and Swiss rolls – which did not lessen his enthusiasm for the great names of Greek tragedy – and this meant he had put on a little weight, which was welcome. He shaved like a young swell, combed his hair back with brilliantine, and was growing a pencil moustache to look fashionable. Thirty days after emerging from our bathtub, the ex-beggar was unrecognizable. But despite his spectacular change, where Fermín Romero de Torres had really left us openmouthed was on the battlefield. His sleuthlike instincts, which I had attributed to delirious fantasies, proved surgically precise. He could solve the strangest requests in a matter of days, even hours. Was there no title he didn't know, no stratagem for obtaining it at a good price that didn't occur to him? He could talk his way into the private libraries of duchesses on Avenida Pearson and horse-riding dilettantes, always adopting fictitious identities, and would depart with the said books as gifts or bought for a pittance.

The transformation from beggar into model citizen seemed miraculous, like one of those stories that priests from poor parishes love to tell to illustrate the Lord's infinite mercy – stories that invariably sound too good to be true, like the ads for hair-restorer lotions that were plastered over the trams.

Three and a half months after Fermín started work in the bookshop, the telephone in the apartment on Calle Santa Ana woke us up one Sunday at two o'clock in the morning. It was Fermín's landlady. In a voice choked with anxiety, she explained that Señor Romero de Torres had locked himself in his room and was shouting like a madman, banging on the walls and swearing that if anyone dared come in, he would slit his own throat with a broken bottle.

'Don't call the police, please. We'll be right there.'

Rushing out, we made our way towards Calle Joaquín Costa. It was a cold night, with an icy wind and tar-black skies. We hurried past the two ancient hospices – Casa de la Misericordia and Casa de Piedad – ignoring the looks and words that came from dark doorways smelling of charcoal. Soon we reached the corner of Calle Ferlandina. Joaquín Costa lay there, a gap in the rows of blackened beehives, blending into the darkness of the Raval quarter. The landlady's eldest son was waiting for us downstairs.

'Have you called the police?' asked my father.

'Not yet,' answered the son.

We ran upstairs. The *pensión* was on the second floor, the staircase a spiral of grime scarcely visible in the ochre light shed by naked bulbs that hung limply from a bare wire. Doña Encarna, the landlady, the widow of a Civil Guard corporal, met us at the door wrapped in a light blue dressing gown, crowned with a matching set of curlers.

'Look here, Señor Sempere, this is a decent house. I have more offers than I can take, and I don't need to put up with this kind of thing,' she said as she guided us through a dark corridor that reeked of ammonia and damp.

'I understand,' mumbled my father.

Fermín Romero de Torres's screams could be heard tearing at the walls at the end of the corridor. Several drawn and frightened faces peeped around half-open doors – boardinghouse faces fed on watery soup.

'And the rest of you, off to sleep, for fuck's sake! This isn't a variety show at the Molino!' cried Doña Encarna furiously.

We stopped in front of the door to Fermín's room. My father rapped gently with his knuckles.

'Fermín? Are you there? It's Sempere.'

The howl that pierced the walls chilled me. Even Doña Encarna lost her matronly composure and put her hands on her heart, hidden under the many folds of her ample chest.

My father called again. 'Fermín? Come on, open the door.'

Fermín howled again, throwing himself against the walls, yelling obscenities at the top of his voice. My father sighed.

'Dõna Encarna, do you have a key to this room?'

'Well, of course.'

'Give it to me, please.'

Doña Encarna hesitated. The other guests were peering into the corridor again, white with terror. Those shouts must have been heard from the army headquarters.

'And you, Daniel, run and find Dr Baró. He lives very close, in number twelve Riera Alta.'

'Listen, wouldn't it be better to call a priest? He sounds to me as if he's possessed,' suggested Doña Encarna.

'No. A doctor will do fine. Come on, Daniel. Run. And you, please give me that key.'

Dr Baró was a sleepless bachelor who spent his nights reading Zola and looking at 3-D pictures of young ladies in racy underwear to relieve his boredom. He was a regular customer at my father's bookshop, and, though he described himself as a second-rate quack, he had a better eye for reaching the right diagnosis than most of the smart doctors with elegant practices in Calle Muntaner. Many of his patients were old whores from the neighbourhood or poor wretches who could barely afford to pay him, but he would see them all the same. I heard him say repeatedly that the world was God's chamber pot and that his sole remaining wish was for Barcelona's football team to win the league, once and for all, so that he could die in peace. He opened the door in his dressing gown, smelling of wine and flaunting an unlit cigarette.

'Daniel?'

'My father sent me. It's an emergency.'

When we returned to the *pensión,* we found Doña Encarna sobbing with fear and the other guests turned to the colour of old candle wax. My father was holding Fermín Romero de Torres in his arms in a corner of the room. Fermín was naked, crying and shaking. The room was a wreck, the walls stained with something that could have been either blood or excrement – I couldn't tell. Dr Baró quickly took in the situation and gestured to my father to lay Fermín on the bed. They were helped by Doña Encarna's son, a would-be boxer. Fermín moaned and thrashed about as if some vermin were devouring his insides.

'But for goodness' sake, what's the matter with this poor man? What's wrong with him?' groaned Doña Encarna from the door, shaking her head.

The doctor took his pulse, examined his pupils with a torch and, without saying a word, proceeded to prepare an injection from a bottle he carried in his bag.

'Hold him down. This will make him sleep. Daniel, help us.'

Between the four of us, we managed to immobilize Fermín, who jerked violently when he felt the stab of the needle in his thigh. His muscles tensed like steel cables, but after a few seconds his eyes clouded over and his body went limp.

'Be careful, that man's not very strong, and anything could kill him,' said Doña Encarna.

'Don't worry. He's only asleep,' said the doctor as he examined the scars that covered Fermín's starved body.

I saw him shake his head slowly. 'Bastards,' he mumbled.

'What are these scars from?' I asked. 'Cuts?'

Dr Baró shook his head again, without looking up. He found a blanket amid the wreckage and covered his patient with it. 'Burns. This man has been tortured,' he explained. 'These marks are from a soldering iron.'

Fermín slept for two days. When he awoke, he could not remember anything; he just thought he'd woken up in a dark cell, that was all. He felt so ashamed of his behaviour that he went down on his knees to beg for Doña Encarna's forgiveness. He swore he would paint the *pensión* for her and, knowing she was very devout, promised she would have ten masses said for her in the Church of Belén.

'What you have to do is get better and not frighten me like that again. I'm too old for that sort of thing.'

My father paid for the damages and begged Doña Encarna to give Fermín another chance. She gladly agreed. Most of her guests were dispossessed people who were alone in the world, like her. Once she had got over the fright, she felt an even greater affection for Fermín and made him promise that he would take the tablets Dr Baró had prescribed.

'For you, Doña Encarna, I'd swallow a brick if need be.'

In time we all pretended we'd forgotten what had happened, but never again did I take the stories about Inspector Fumero lightly. After that incident we would take Fermín with us almost every Sunday for an afternoon snack at the Novedades Café, so as not to leave him on his own. Then we'd walk up to the Fémina Cinema, on the corner of Calle Diputación and Paseo de Gracia. One of the ushers was a friend of my father's, and he would let us sneak in through the fire exit on the ground floor during the newsreel, always when the Generalissimo was in the act of cutting the ribbon to inaugurate some new reservoir, which really got on Fermín's nerves.

'What a disgrace,' he would say indignantly.

'Don't you like the cinema, Fermín?'

'Between you and me, this business of the seventh art leaves me cold. As far as I can see, it's only a way of feeding the mindless and making them even more stupid. Worse than football or bullfights. The cinema began as an invention for entertaining the illiterate masses. Fifty years on, it's much the same.'

Fermín's attitude changed radically the day he discovered Carole Lombard.

'What breasts, Jesus, Mary, and Joseph, what breasts!' he exclaimed in the middle of the film, beside himself. 'Those aren't tits, they're two schooners!'

'Shut up, you degenerate, or I'll call the manager,' muttered a voice straight from the confessional, a few rows behind us. 'People have no shame. What a country of pigs we live in.'

'You'd better lower your voice, Fermín,' I advised him.

Fermín Romero de Torres wasn't listening to me. He was lost in the gentle swell of that miraculous bosom, with an enraptured smile and unblinking eyes. Later, walking back along Paseo de Gracia, I noticed that our bibliographic detective was still in a trance.

'I think we're going to have to find you a woman,' I said. 'A woman will brighten up your life, you'll see.'

Fermín sighed, his mind still dwelling on charms that seemed to defy the laws of gravity.

'Do you speak from experience, Daniel?' he asked in all innocence.

I just smiled, knowing that my father was watching me.

After that day Fermín Romero de Torres took to going to the movies every Sunday. My father preferred to stay at home reading, but Fermín would not miss a single double feature. He'd buy a pile of chocolates and sit in row seventeen, where he would devour them while he waited for the appearance of that day's diva. As far as he was concerned, plot was superfluous, and he didn't stop talking until some well-endowed lady filled the screen.

'I've been thinking about what you said the other day, about finding a woman for me,' said Fermín Romero de Torres. 'Perhaps you're right. In the *pensión* there's a new lodger, an ex-seminarist from Seville with plenty of spirit, who brings in some impressive young ladies every now and then. I must say, the race has improved no end. I don't know how the lad manages it, because he's not much to look at; perhaps he renders them senseless with prayers. He's got the room next to mine, so I can hear everything, and, judging by the sound effects, the friar must be a real artist. Just shows what a uniform can do. Tell me, what sort of women do you like, Daniel?'

'I don't know much about them, honestly.'

'Nobody knows much about women, not even Freud, not even women themselves. But it's like electricity: you don't have to know how it works to get a shock. Come on, out with it. How do you like them? People might not agree with me, but I think a woman should have a feminine shape, something you can get your hands on. You, on the other hand, look like you might be partial to the skinny type, a point of view I fully respect, don't misunderstand me.'

'Frankly, I don't have much experience with women. None, to be precise.'

Fermín Romero de Torres looked at me carefully, intrigued by this revelation.

'I thought that what happened that night, you know, when you were beaten up . . .'

'If only everything hurt as little as a blow to the face . . .'

Fermín seemed to read my mind, and smiled supportively. 'Don't let that upset you, then. With women the best part is the discovery. There's nothing like the first time, nothing. You don't know what life is until you undress a woman the first time. A button at a time, like peeling a hot, sweet potato on a winter's night.'

A few seconds later, Veronica Lake made her grand entrance onto the scene, and Fermín was transported to another plane. Taking advantage of a reel in which Miss Lake was absent, Fermín announced that he was going to pay a visit to the sweet stall in the foyer to replenish his stocks. After months of starvation, my friend had lost all sense of proportion, but, due to his metabolism, he never quite lost that hungry, squalid postwar look. I was left alone, barely following the action on the screen. I would lie if I said I was thinking of Clara. I was thinking only of her body, trembling under the music teacher's charges, glistening with sweat and pleasure. My gaze left the screen, and only then did I notice a spectator who had just come in. I saw his silhouette moving to the centre of the stalls, six rows in front of me. He sat down. Cinemas are full of lonely people, I thought. Like me.

I tried to concentrate on picking up the thread of the story. The hero, a cynical but good-hearted detective, was telling a secondary character why women like Veronica Lake were the ruin of all sensible males and why all one could do was love them desperately and perish, betrayed by their double dealings. Fermín Romero de Torres, who was becoming an adept film scholar, called this genre 'the

praying mantis paradigm'. According to him, its permuta-
tions were nothing but misogynist fantasies for constipated
office clerks or pious women shrivelled with boredom who
dreamed about turning to a life of vice and unbridled
lechery. I smiled as I imagined the asides my friend the
critic would have made had he not gone to his meeting with
the sweet stall. But the smile froze on my face. The spectator
who sat six rows in front of me had turned around and was
staring at me. The projector's misty beam bored through
the darkness of the hall, a slim cloud of flickering light that
revealed only outlines and blots of colour. I recognized
Coubert, the faceless man, immediately. His steely look,
shining eyes with no eyelids; his smile as he licked his nonexistent lips in the dark. I felt cold fingers gripping my
heart. Two hundred violins broke out on screen, there were
shots, shouts, and the scene dissolved. For a moment the
hall plunged into utter darkness, and I could hear only my
own heartbeat hammering in my temples. Slowly a new
scene glowed on the screen, replacing the darkness of the
room with a haze of blue and purple. The man without a
face had disappeared. I turned and caught a glimpse of a
silhouette walking up the aisle and passing Fermín, who was
returning from his gastronomic safari. He moved into the
row, took his seat, and handed me a praline chocolate.

'Daniel, you're as white as a nun's buttock. Are you all
right?' he asked, giving me a worried look.

A mysterious breath of air wafted through the hall.

'It smells odd,' Fermín remarked. 'Like a rancid fart,
from a councilman or a lawyer.'

'No. It smells of burned paper.'

'Go on. Have a lemon Sugus sweet – it cures everything.'

'I don't feel like one.'

'Keep it, then, you never know when a Sugus sweet might
get you out of a pickle.'

I put the sweet in my jacket pocket and drifted through
the rest of the film without paying any attention to
Veronica Lake or to the victims of her fatal charms. Fermín

Romero de Torres was engrossed in the show and the chocolates. When the lights went on at the end of the film, I felt as if I were waking from a bad dream and was tempted to imagine that the man in the stalls had been a mere illusion, a trick of memory. But his brief glance in the dark had been enough to convey his message. He had not forgotten me, or our pact.

# 12

The first effect of Fermín's arrival soon became apparent: I discovered I had much more free time. When Fermín was not out hunting some exotic volume to satisfy a customer's request, he spent his time organizing stocks in the bookshop, dreaming up marketing strategies, polishing the shop sign and windows till they sparkled, or buffing up the spines of the books with a rag and a bit of alcohol. Given this windfall, I decided to devote my leisure time to a couple of pursuits I had lately put aside: attempting to unravel the Carax mystery and, above all, spending more time with my friend Tomás Aguilar, whom I greatly missed.

Tomás was a thoughtful, reserved boy whom other children feared because his vaguely thuggish features gave him a grave and threatening look. He had a wrestler's build, gladiator's shoulders, and a steely, penetrating gaze. We had met many years before in the course of a fistfight, during my first week at the Jesuit school in Calle Caspe. His father had come to pick him up after lessons, accompanied by a conceited girl who turned out to be Tomás's sister. I had the brilliant idea of making some tasteless remark about her, and before I could blink, Tomás had thrown himself on me and showered me with a deluge of blows that left me smarting for a few weeks. Tomás was twice my size, strength, and ferocity. During our schoolyard duel, surrounded by boys who were thirsty for a bloody fight, I lost a tooth but gained an improved sense of proportion. I refused to tell my father or the priests who had inflicted such a thundering beating on me. Neither did I volunteer the fact that the father of my adversary had watched the thumping with an expression of sheer pleasure, joining in the chorus with the other schoolchildren.

'It was my fault,' I said, closing the subject.

Three weeks later Tomás came up to me during the break. I was paralysed with fear. He is coming to finish me off, I thought. I began to stammer, but soon I understood that all he wanted to do was apologize for the thrashing, because he knew the fight had been uneven and unfair.

'I'm the one who should say sorry for picking on your sister,' I said. 'I would have done it the other day, but you'd given me such a hammering, I couldn't speak.'

Tomás looked down, ashamed of himself. I gazed at that shy and quiet giant who wandered around the classrooms and school corridors like a lost soul. All the other children – me included – were scared stiff of him, and nobody spoke to him or dared look him in the eye. With his head down, almost shaking, he asked me whether I'd like to be his friend. I said I would. He held out his hand, and I shook it. His handshake hurt, but I didn't flinch. That afternoon he invited me to his house for an after-school snack and showed me his collection of strange gadgets made from bits of scrap metal, which he kept in his room.

'I made them,' he explained proudly.

I was incapable of understanding how they worked or even what they were supposed to be, but I didn't say a word. I just nodded in admiration. It seemed to me that this oversized, solitary boy had constructed his own tin companions and I was the first person he was introducing them to. It was his secret. I shared mine. I told him about my mother and how much I missed her. When my voice broke, Tomás hugged me, without saying anything. We were ten years old. From that day on, Tomás Aguilar became my best – and I his only – friend.

Despite his aggressive looks, Tomás was a peaceful and good-hearted person whose appearance discouraged confrontations. He stammered quite a bit, especially when he spoke to anyone who wasn't his mother, his sister, or me, which was hardly ever. He was fascinated by outlandish inventions and mechanical devices, and I soon discovered that he carried out autopsies on all manner of instruments, from gramophones to adding machines, in order to discover their secrets. When he wasn't with me or working for his father, Tomás spent most of his time secluded in his room, devising incomprehensible contraptions. His intelligence was matched by his lack of practicality. His interest in the real world centred on details such as the synchronization of traffic lights in Gran Vía, the mysteries of the illuminated fountains of Montjuïc, or the clockwork souls of the automatons at the Tibidabo amusement park.

Every afternoon Tomás worked in his father's office, and sometimes, on his way out, he'd stop by the bookshop. My father always showed an interest in his inventions and gave him manuals on mechanics or biographies of engineers like Eiffel and Edison, whom Tomás idolized. As the years went by, Tomás became very attached to my father and spent ages trying to invent an automatic system with which to file his bibliographic index cards, using parts of an old electric fan. He had been working on the project for four years now, but my father still showed great enthusiasm for its progress, because he didn't want Tomás to lose heart.

When I first introduced Tomás to Fermín, I was concerned about how Fermín would react to my friend.

'You must be Daniel's inventor friend. It's a great pleasure to make your acquaintance. Fermín Romero de Torres, bibliographic adviser to the Sempere bookshop, at your service.'

'Tomás Aguilar,' stammered my friend, smiling and shaking Fermín's hand.

'Watch out, my friend, for what you have there isn't a

hand, it's a hydraulic press. I need violinist's fingers for my work with the firm.'

Tomás let go of his hand and apologized.

'So tell me, where do you stand on Fermat's theorem?' asked Fermín, rubbing his fingers.

After that they became engrossed in an unintelligible discussion about arcane mathematics, which was all Greek to me. From that day on, Fermín always addressed him with the formal *usted* or called him 'doctor', and pretended not to notice the boy's stammer. As a way of repaying Fermín for his infinite patience, Tomás brought him boxes of Swiss chocolates stamped with photographs of impossibly blue lakes, cows parading along Technicolor-green fields and camera-ready cuckoo clocks.

'Your friend Tomás is talented, but he lacks drive and could benefit from a more winning demeanour. It's the only way to get anywhere,' Fermín said to me one day. 'Alas, that's the scientist's mind for you. Just consider Albert Einstein. All those prodigious inventions, and the first one they find a practical application for is the atom bomb – and without his permission. Tomás is going to have a hard time in academic circles with that boxer's face of his. In this world the only opinion that holds court is prejudice.'

Driven by a wish to save Tomás from a life of penury and misunderstanding, Fermín had decided that he needed to develop my friend's latent conversational and social skills.

'Like the good ape he is, man is a social animal, characterized by cronyism, nepotism, corruption and gossip. That's the intrinsic blueprint for our "ethical behaviour",' he argued. 'It's pure biology.'

'Aren't you exaggerating?'

'Sometimes you're so naïve, Daniel.'

Tomás had inherited his tough looks from his father, a prosperous property manager with an office in Calle Pelayo, close to the sumptuous El Siglo department store. Señor Aguilar belonged to that race of privileged minds who are always right. A man of deep convictions, he believed, among other things, that his son was both faint-hearted and mentally deficient. To compensate for these shameful traits, he employed all sorts of private tutors in the hope of improving his firstborn. 'I want you to treat my son as if he were an imbecile, do you understand?' I would often hear him say. Teachers tried everything, even pleading, but Tomás addressed them only in Latin, a language he spoke with papal fluency and in which he did not stammer. Sooner or later they all resigned in despair, fearing he might be possessed: he might be spouting demonic instructions in Aramaic at them, for all they knew. Señor Aguilar's only hope was that military service would make a man of his son.

Tomás had a sister, Beatriz. I owed our friendship to her, because if I hadn't seen her that afternoon, long ago, holding onto her father's hand, waiting for the classes to end, and hadn't decided to make a joke in very bad taste at her expense, my friend would never have rained all those blows on me and I would never have had the courage to speak to him. Bea Aguilar was the very image of her mother and the apple of her father's eye. Redheaded and exquisitely pale, she always wore very expensive dresses made of silk or pure wool. She had a mannequin's waist and wandered around straight as a rod, playing the role of princess in her own fairy tale. Her eyes were a greeny blue, but she insisted on describing them as 'emerald and sapphire'. Despite her many years as a pupil at the strict Catholic school of the Teresian mothers, or perhaps for that very reason, when her father wasn't looking, Bea drank anise liqueur from a tall glass, wore silk stockings from the elegant shop La Perla Gris, and dolled herself up like the screen goddesses who sent my friend Fermín into a trance. I couldn't stand the sight of her, and she repaid my open hostility with languid looks of disdain and indifference. Bea had a boyfriend who was doing his military service as a lieutenant in Murcia, a slick-haired member of the Falangist Party called Pablo Cascos Buendía. He belonged to an aristocratic family who owned a number of shipyards on the Galician *rías* and spent half his time on leave thanks to an uncle in the Military Government. Second Lieutenant Cascos Buendía wasted no opportunity to lecture people on the genetic and spiritual superiority of Spanish people and the imminent decline of the Bolshevik empire.

'Marx is dead,' he would say solemnly.

'He died in 1883, to be precise,' I would answer.

'Zip it, bonehead, or I'll kick you all the way to the Rock of Gibraltar.'

More than once I had caught Bea smiling to herself at the inanities that her boyfriend came out with. She would raise her eyes and watch me, with a look I couldn't fathom. I would smile back with the feeble civility of enemies held together by an indefinite truce but would look away quickly. I would have died before admitting it, but in my heart of hearts, I was afraid of her.

# 13

At the beginning of that year, Tomás and Fermín decided to pool their respective brains on a new project that, they predicted, would get us both out of being drafted. Fermín, in particular, did not share Mr Aguilar's enthusiasm for the army experience.

'The only useful thing about military service is that it reveals the number of morons in the population,' he would remark. 'And that can be discovered in the first two weeks; there's no need for two years. Army, Marriage, the Church, and Banking: the Four Horsemen of the Apocalypse. Yes, go on, laugh.'

Fermín Romero de Torres's anarchist-libertarian leanings were to be shaken one October afternoon when, in a twist of fate, we had a visit from an old friend. My father had gone to Argentona, to price a book collection, and would not be back until the evening. I was left in charge of the counter while Fermín insisted on climbing up a ladder like a tightrope walker to tidy up the books on the top shelf, just inches from the ceiling. Shortly before closing time, when the sun had already set, Bernarda's profile appeared at the shop window. She was dressed in her Thursday clothes – Thursday was her day off – and she waved at me. My heart soared just to see her, and I signalled to her to come in.

'My goodness, how you've grown!' she said from the entrance. 'I would hardly have recognized you ... why, you're a man now!'

She embraced me, shedding a few tears and touching my head, shoulders, and face, as if to make sure I hadn't broken anything during her absence.

'You're really missed in the house, Master Daniel,' she said, with downcast eyes.

'I've missed you, too, Bernarda. Come on, give me a kiss.'

She kissed me shyly, and I planted a couple of noisy kisses on each cheek. She laughed. In her eyes I could see she was waiting for me to ask her about Clara, but I had decided not to.

'You're looking very pretty today, and very elegant. How come you've decided to pay us a visit?'

'The truth is, I've been wanting to come for a long time, but you know how things are, we're all busy, and, for all his learning, Señor Barceló is as demanding as a child. You just have to rise above it and get on with things. But what brings me here today is that, well, tomorrow is my niece's birthday, the one from San Adrián, and I'd like to give her a present. I thought I could get her a good book, with a lot of writing and few pictures, but as I'm such a dimwit and don't understand—'

Before I could answer, a whole hardback set of the complete works of Blasco Ibáñez plummeted from on high, and the place shook with a ballistic roar. Bernarda and I looked up anxiously. Fermín was sliding down the ladder, like a trapeze artist, a secretive smile lighting up his face, his eyes filled with rapturous lust.

'Bernarda, this is—'

'Fermín Romero de Torres, bibliographic adviser to Sempere and Son, at your service, madam,' Fermín proclaimed, taking Bernarda's hand and kissing it ceremoniously.

'You must be confused, I'm no madam—'

'Marquise, at the very least,' interrupted Fermín. 'I should know. I have stepped out with the finest ladies on Avenida Pearson. Allow me the honour of accompanying you to our classics section for children and young adults, where I notice that by good fortune we have an anthology of the best of Emilio Salgari and his epic tale of Sandokan.'

'Oh dear, I don't know, I'm not sure about the lives of the saints. The girl's father used to be very left wing, you know. . . .'

'Say no more, for here I have none other than Jules Verne's *The Mysterious Island*, a tale of high adventure and great educational content, because of all the science.'

'If you think so. . . .'

I followed them quietly, noticing how Fermín was drooling over Bernarda and how she seemed overwhelmed by the attentions showered upon her by the little man with scruffy looks and the tongue of a stallholder. He was devouring her with his eyes as greedily as if she were a piece of chocolate.

'What about you, Master Daniel? What do you think?'

'Fermín Romero de Torres is the resident expert here. You can trust him.'

'Well, then, I'll take the one about the island, if you'd be kind enough to wrap it for me. What do I owe you?'

'It's on the house,' I said.

'No it isn't, I won't hear of it.'

'If you'll allow me, madam, it's on me, Fermín Romero de Torres. You'd make me the happiest man in Barcelona.'

Bernarda looked at us both. She was speechless.

'Listen, I'm paying for what I buy, and this is a present I want to give my niece—'

'Well, then, perhaps you'll allow me, in exchange, to invite you to afternoon tea,' Fermín quickly interjected, smoothing down his hair.

'Go on, Bernarda,' I encouraged her. 'You'll enjoy yourself. Look, while I wrap this up, Fermín can go and get his jacket.'

Fermín hurried off to the back room to comb his hair, splash on some cologne and put on his jacket. I slipped him a few duros from the till.

'Where shall I take her?' he whispered to me, as nervous as a child.

'I'd take her to Els Quatre Gats,' I said. 'I know for a fact that it's a lucky place for romance.'

I handed Bernarda the packet and winked at her.

'What do I owe you then, Master Daniel?'

'I'm not sure. I'll let you know. The book didn't have a price on it, and I have to ask my father,' I lied.

I watched them leave arm in arm and disappear down Calle Santa Ana, hoping there was somebody on duty up in heaven who, for once, would grant the couple a lucky break. I hung the CLOSED notice in the shop window. I had just gone into the back room for a moment to look through my father's order book when I heard the tinkle of the doorbell. I thought Fermín must have forgotten something, or perhaps my father was back from his day trip.

'Hello?'

A few seconds passed, and no answer came. I continued to leaf through the order book.

I heard slow footsteps in the shop.

'Fermín? Father?'

No answer. I thought I heard a stifled laugh, and I shut the order book. Perhaps some client had ignored the CLOSED sign. I was about to go and serve whoever it was when I heard the sound of several books falling from the shelves. I swallowed. Grabbing hold of a letter opener, I slowly moved towards the door of the back room. I didn't dare call out a second time. Soon I heard the steps again, walking away. The doorbell sounded, and I felt a draft of air from the street. I peered into the shop. There was no one there. I ran to the front door and double-locked it, then took a deep breath, feeling ridiculous and cowardly. I was returning to the back room when I noticed a piece of paper on the counter. As I got closer, I realized it was a photograph, an old studio picture of the sort that were printed on thick cardboard. The edges were burned, and the smoky image seemed to have charcoal finger marks over it. I examined it under the lamp. The photograph showed a young couple smiling at the camera. The man didn't look much older than seventeen or eighteen, with light-coloured hair and delicate, aristocratic features. The woman may have been a bit younger, one or two years at the most. She had pale skin and a finely chiselled face framed by short black hair. She looked drunk with happiness. The man had his arm round her waist, and she seemed to be whispering something to him in a teasing way. The image conveyed a warmth that drew a smile from me, as if I had recognized two old friends in those strangers. Behind them I could make out an ornate shop window, full of old-fashioned hats. I concentrated on the couple. From their clothes I could guess that the picture was at least twenty-five or thirty years old. It was an image full of light and hope, rich with the promise that only exists in the eyes of the young. Fire had destroyed almost all of the area surrounding the photograph, but you could still discern a stern face behind the old-style counter, a suggestion of a ghostly figure behind the letters engraved on the glass.

Sons of

# ANTONIO

## FORTUNY

Established in 1888

The night I returned to the Cemetery of Forgotten Books, Isaac had told me that Carax used his mother's surname, not his father's, which was Fortuny. Carax's father had a hat shop in Ronda de San Antonio. I looked again at the portrait of that couple and knew for sure that the young man was Julián Carax, smiling at me from the past, unable to see the flames that were closing in on him.

# CITY OF SHADOWS
## 1954

# 14

The following morning Fermín came to work borne on the wings of Cupid, smiling and whistling boleros. In any other circumstances, I would have inquired about his outing with Bernarda, but that day I was not in the mood for his poetic outbursts. My father had arranged to have an order of books delivered to Professor Javier Velázquez at eleven o'clock in his study at the university. The very mention of the professor made Fermín wince, so I offered to take the books myself.

'That sorry specimen is nothing but a corrupt pedant. A fascist buttock-polisher,' Fermín declared, raising his fist and striking the pose he reserved for his avenging moods. 'He uses the pitiful excuse of his professorship to seduce women. I swear he would even have it off with Gertrude Stein, given the chance.'

'Calm down, Fermín. Velázquez pays well, always in advance, and besides, he recommends us to everyone,' my father said.

'That's money stained with the blood of innocent virgins,' Fermín protested. 'For the life of God, I hereby swear that I have never lain with an underage woman, and not for lack of inclination or opportunities. Bear in mind that what you see today is but a shadow of my former self, but there was a time when I cut as dashing a figure as they come. Yet even then, just to be on the safe side, or if I sensed that a girl might be overly flighty, I would not proceed without seeing some form of identification or, failing that, a written paternal authorization. One has to maintain certain moral standards.'

My father rolled his eyes. 'It's pointless arguing with you, Fermín.'

'Well, if I'm right, I'm right.'

Sensing a debate brewing, I picked up the parcel, which I had prepared the night before – a couple of Rilkes and an apocryphal essay attributed to a disciple of Darwin claiming that Spaniards came from a more evolved simian ancestor than their French neighbours. As the door closed behind me, Fermín and my father were deep in argument about ethics.

It was a magnificent day; the skies were electric blue and a crystal breeze carried the cool scent of autumn and the sea. I will always prefer Barcelona in October. It is when the spirit of the city seems to stroll most proudly through the streets, and you feel all the wiser after drinking water from the old fountain of Canaletas – which, for once, does not taste of chlorine. I was walking along briskly, dodging bootblacks, pen pushers returning from their midmorning coffee, lottery vendors, and a whole ballet of street sweepers who seemed intent on polishing the streets, using their brooms like paintbrushes, unhurriedly and with a pointillist's strokes. Barcelona was already beginning to fill up with cars in those days, and when I reached the traffic lights at the crossing with Calle Balmes, I noticed a brigade of grey office clerks in grey raincoats staring hungrily at a bloodred Studebaker sedan as they would ogle a music-hall siren in a negligee. I went on up Balmes towards Gran Vía, negotiating traffic lights, cars, and even motorcycles with sidecars. In a shop window, I saw a Philips poster announcing the arrival of a new messiah, the TV set. Some predicted that this peculiar contraption was going to change our lives forever and turn us all into creatures of the future, like the Americans. Fermín Romero de Torres, always up to date on state-of-the-art technology, had already prophesied a grimmer outcome.

'Television, my dear Daniel, is the Antichrist, and I can assure you that after only three or four generations, people will no longer even know how to fart on their own. Humans will return to living in caves, to medieval savagery, and to the general state of imbecility that slugs overcame back in the Pleistocene era. Our world will not die as a result of the bomb, as the papers say – it will die of laughter, of banality, of making a joke of everything, and a lousy joke at that.'

Professor Velázquez's office was on the second floor of the Literature Faculty, in Plaza Universidad, at the end of a gallery paved with hypnotic chessboard tiling and awash in powdery light that spilled down onto the southern cloister. I found the professor at the door of a lecture room, pretending to be listening to a female student while considering her spectacular figure. She wore a dark red suit that drew attention to her waistline and revealed classically proportioned calves covered in fine silk stockings. Professor Velázquez enjoyed a reputation as a Don Juan; there were those who considered that the sentimental education of a respectable young lady was never complete without a proverbial weekend in some small hotel on the Sitges promenade, reciting Alexandrines tête-à-tête with the distinguished academic.

My commercial instincts advised me against interrupting his conversation, so I decided to kill time by undressing the pupil in my mind. Perhaps the brisk walk had raised my spirits, or perhaps it was just my age, not to mention the fact that I spent more time among muses that were trapped in the pages of old books than in the company of girls of flesh and bone – who always seemed to me beings of a far lower order than Clara Barceló. Whatever the reason, as I catalogued each and every detail of her enticing and exquisitely clad anatomy – which I could see only from the back, but which in my mind I had already visualized in its full glory – I felt a vaguely wolfish shiver run down my spine.

'Why, here's Daniel,' cried Professor Velázquez. 'Thank goodness it's you, not that madman who came last time, the one with the name like a bullfighter. He seemed drunk to me, or certifiable. He had the nerve to ask me whether I knew the etymology of the word "prick", in a sarcastic tone that was quite out of place.'

'It's just that the doctor has put him on some strong medication. Something to do with his liver.'

'No doubt because he's smashed all day,' said Velázquez. 'If I were you, I'd call the police. I bet you he has a file. And God, how his feet stank – there are lots of shitty leftists on the loose who haven't seen a bathtub since the Republic fell.'

I was about to come up with some other plausible excuse for Fermín when the student who had been talking to Professor Velázquez turned around, and it was as if the world had stopped spinning. I saw her smile at me, and my ears went up in flames.

'Hello, Daniel,' said Beatriz Aguilar.

I nodded at her, tongue-tied. I realized I'd been drooling over my best friend's sister, Bea. The one woman I was completely terrified of.

'Oh, so you know each other?' asked Velázquez, intrigued.

'Daniel is an old friend of the family,' Bea explained. 'And the only one who ever had the courage to tell me to my face that I'm stuck up and vain.'

Velázquez looked at me with astonishment.

'That was years ago,' I explained. 'And I didn't mean it.'

'Well, I'm still waiting for an apology.'

Velázquez laughed heartily and took the parcel from my hands.

'I think I'm in the way here,' he said, opening it. 'Ah, wonderful. Listen, Daniel, tell your father I'm looking for a book called *Moorslayer: Early Reminiscences of the Generalissimo in the Moroccan War* by Francisco Franco Bahamonde, with a prologue and notes by Pemán.'

'Consider it done. We'll let you know in a couple of weeks.'

'I'll take your word for it, and now I'll be off. Thirty-two blank minds await me.'

Professor Velázquez winked at me and disappeared into the lecture room. I didn't know where to look.

'Listen, Bea, about that insult, I promise I—'

'I was only teasing you, Daniel. I know that was childish nonsense, and besides, Tomás gave you a good enough beating.'

'It still hurts.'

Bea's smile looked like a peace offering, or at least an offer of a truce.

'Besides, you were right, I'm a bit stuck up and sometimes a little vain,' she said. 'You don't like me much, do you, Daniel?'

The question took me completely by surprise. Disarmed, I realized how easily you can lose all animosity towards someone you've deemed your enemy as soon as that person stops behaving as such.

'No, that's not true.'

'Tomás says it's not that you don't like me, it's that you can't stand my father and you make me pay for it, because you don't dare face up to him. I don't blame you. No one dares cross my father.'

I felt the blood drain from my cheeks, but after a few seconds I found myself smiling and nodding. 'Anyone would say Tomás knows me better than I know myself.'

'I wouldn't put it past him. My brother knows us all inside out, only he never says anything. But if he ever decides to open his mouth, the whole world will collapse. He's very fond of you, you know.'

I raised my shoulders and looked down.

'He's always talking about you, and about your father and the bookshop, and this friend you have working with you. Tomás says he's a genius waiting to be discovered. Sometimes it's as if he considers you his real family, instead of the one he has at home.'

My eyes met hers: hard, frank, fearless. I did not know what to say, so I just smiled. I felt she was ensnaring me with her honesty, and I looked down at the courtyard.

'I didn't know you studied here.'

'It's my first year.'

'Literature?'

'My father thinks science is not for the weaker sex.'

'Of course. Too many numbers.'

'I don't care, because what I like is reading. Besides, you meet interesting people here.'

'Like Professor Velázquez?'

Bea gave me a wry smile. 'I might be in my first year, but I know enough to see them coming, Daniel. Especially men of his sort.'

I wondered what sort I was.

'Besides, Professor Velázquez is a good friend of my father's. They both belong to the Society for the Protection and Promotion of Spanish Operetta.'

I tried to look impressed. 'A noble calling. And how's your boyfriend, Lieutenant Cascos Buendía?'

Her smile left her. 'Pablo will be here on leave in three weeks.'

'You must be happy.'

'Very. He's a great guy, though I can imagine what you must think of him.'

I doubt it, I thought. Bea watched me, looking slightly tense. I was about to change the subject, but my tongue got ahead of me.

'Tomás says you're getting married and you're going off to live in El Ferrol.'

She nodded without blinking. 'As soon as Pablo finishes his military service.'

'You must be feeling impatient,' I said, sensing a spiteful note in my voice, an insolent tone that came from God knows where.

'I don't mind, really. His family has property out there, a couple of shipyards, and Pablo is going to be in charge of one of them. He has a great talent for leadership.'

'It shows.'

Bea forced a smile. 'Besides, I've seen quite enough of

Barcelona, after all these years. . . .' Her eyes looked tired and sad.

'I hear El Ferrol is a fascinating place. Full of life. And the seafood is supposed to be fabulous, especially the spider crabs.'

Bea sighed, shaking her head. She looked as if she wanted to cry with anger but was too proud. Instead she laughed calmly.

'After ten years you still enjoy insulting me, don't you, Daniel? Go on, then, don't hold back. It's my fault for thinking that perhaps we could be friends, or pretend to be, but I suppose I'm not as good as my brother. I'm sorry I've wasted your time.'

She turned around and started walking down the corridor that led to the library. I saw her move away along the black and white tiles, her shadow cutting through the curtains of light that fell from the gallery windows.

'Bea, wait.'

I cursed myself and ran after her. I stopped her halfway down the corridor, grabbing her by the arm. She threw me a burning look.

'I'm sorry. But you're wrong: it's not your fault, it's mine. I'm the one who isn't as good as your brother. And if I've insulted you, it's because I'm jealous of that idiot boyfriend of yours and because I'm angry to think that someone like you would follow him to El Ferrol. It might as well be the Congo.'

'Daniel . . .'

'You're wrong about me, because we can be friends if you let me try, now that you know how worthless I am. And you're wrong about Barcelona, too, because you may think you've seen everything, but I can guarantee that's not true. If you'll allow me, I can prove it to you.'

I saw a smile light up and a slow, silent tear fall down her cheek.

'You'd better be right,' she said. 'Because if you're not, I'll tell my brother, and he'll pull your head off like a stopper.'

I held out my hand to her. 'That sounds fair. Friends?'
She offered me hers.

'What time do your classes finish on Friday?' I asked.
She hesitated for a moment. 'At five.'

'I'll be waiting for you in the cloister at five o'clock sharp.
And before dark I'll prove to you that there's something in
Barcelona you haven't seen yet, and that you can't go off to
El Ferrol with that idiot. I don't believe you love him. If you
go, the memory of this city will pursue you and you'll die of
sadness.'

'You seem very sure of yourself, Daniel.'

I, who was never even sure what the time was, nodded
with the conviction of the ignorant. I stood there watching
her walk away down that endless corridor until her
silhouette blended with the darkness. I asked myself what
on earth I had done.

# 15

The Fortuny hat shop, or what was left of it, languished at
the foot of a narrow, miserable-looking building blackened
by soot in Ronda de San Antonio next to Plaza de Goya.
You could still read the letters engraved on the filthy
window, and a sign in the shape of a bowler hat still hung
above the shop front, promising designs made to measure
and the latest novelties from Paris. The door was secured
with a padlock that had seen at least a decade of
undisturbed service. I pressed my forehead against the glass,
trying to peek into the murky interior.

'If you've come about the rental, you're late,' spat a voice
behind my back. 'The manager has already left.'

The woman who was speaking to me must have been
about sixty and wore the national costume of all pious
widows. A couple of rollers stuck out under the pink scarf
that covered her hair, and her padded slippers matched her

flesh-coloured knee-high stockings. I assumed she was the caretaker of the building.

'Is the shop for rent?'

'Isn't that why you've come?'

'Not really, but you never know, I might be interested.'

The caretaker frowned, debating whether to grant me the benefit of the doubt. I slipped on my trademark angelic smile.

'How long has the shop been closed?'

'For a good twelve years, since the old man died.'

'Señor Fortuny? Did you know him?'

'I've been here for forty-eight years, young man.'

'So perhaps you also knew Señor Fortuny's son.'

'Julián? Well, of course.'

I took the burned photograph out of my pocket and showed it to her. 'Do you think you'd be able to tell me whether the young man in the photograph is Julián Carax?'

The caretaker looked at me rather suspiciously. She took the photograph and stared at it.

'Do you recognize him?'

'Carax was his mother's maiden name,' the caretaker explained in a disapproving tone. 'This is Julián, yes. I remember him being very fair, but here, in the photograph, his hair looks darker.'

'Could you tell me who the girl is?'

'And who is asking?'

'I'm sorry, my name is Daniel Sempere. I'm trying to find out about Señor Carax, about Julián.'

'Julián went to Paris, 'round about 1918 or 1919. His father wanted to shove him in the army, you see. I think the mother took him with her so that he could escape from all that, poor kid. Señor Fortuny was left alone, in the attic apartment.'

'Do you know when Julián returned to Barcelona?'

The caretaker looked at me but didn't speak for a while.

'Don't you know? Julián died that same year in Paris.'

'Excuse me?'

113

'I said Julián passed away. In Paris. Soon after he got there. He would have done better joining the army.'

'May I ask you how you know that?'

'How do you think? Because his father told me.'

I nodded slowly. 'I see. Did he say what he died of?'

'Quite frankly, the old man never gave me any details. Once, not long after Julián left, a letter arrived for him, and when I mentioned it to his father, he told me his son had died and if anything else came for him, I should throw it away. Why are you looking at me like that?'

'Señor Fortuny lied to you. Julián didn't die in 1919.'

'Say that again?'

'Julián lived in Paris until at least 1935, and then he returned to Barcelona.'

The caretaker's face lit up. 'So Julián is here, in Barcelona? Where?'

I nodded again, hoping she would be encouraged to tell me more.

'Holy Mary . . . what wonderful news. Well, if he's still alive, that is. He was such a sweet child, a bit strange and given to daydreaming, that's true, but there was something about him that won you over. He wouldn't have been much good as a soldier, you could tell that a mile off. My Isabelita really liked him. Imagine, for a while I even thought they'd end up getting married. Kid stuff. . . . May I see that photograph again?'

I handed the photo back to her. The caretaker gazed at it as if it were a lucky charm, a return ticket to her youth. 'It's strange, you know, it's as if he were here right now . . . and that mean old bastard saying he was dead. I must say, I wonder why God sends some people into this world. And what happened to Julián in Paris? I'm sure he got rich. I always thought Julián would be wealthy one day.'

'Not exactly. He became a writer.'

'He wrote stories?'

'Something like that.'

'For the radio? Oh, how lovely. Well, it doesn't surprise me, you know. As a child he used to tell stories to the local kids. In the summer sometimes my Isabelita and her cousins would go up to the roof terrace at night and listen to him. They said he never told the same story twice. But it's true that they were all about dead people and ghosts. As I say, he was a bit of an odd child. Although, with a father like that, the odd thing was that he wasn't completely nuts. I'm not surprised that his wife left him in the end, because he was a nasty piece of work. Listen: I never meddle in people's affairs, everything's fine by me, but that man wasn't a good person. In a block of apartments nothing's secret in the end. He beat her, you know? You always heard screams coming from their apartment, and more than once the police had to come round. I can understand that sometimes a husband has to beat his wife to get her to respect him, I'm not saying they shouldn't; there are a lot of tarts about, and young girls are not brought up the way they used to be. But this one, well, he liked to beat her for the hell of it, if you see what I mean. The only friend that poor woman had was a young girl, Viçenteta, who lived in 4–2. Sometimes the poor woman would take shelter in Viçenteta's apartment, to get away from her husband's beatings. And she told her things. . . .'

'What sort of things?'

The caretaker took on a confidential manner, raising an eyebrow and glancing sideways right and left. 'Like the boy wasn't the hatter's.'

'Julián? Do you mean to say Julián wasn't Fortuny's son?'

'That's what the Frenchwoman told Viçenteta, I don't know whether it was out of spite or heaven knows why. The girl told me years later, when they didn't live here anymore.'

'So who was Julián's real father?'

'The Frenchwoman never said. Perhaps she didn't even know. You know what foreigners are like.'

'And do you think that's why her husband beat her?'

115

'Goodness knows. Three times they had to take her to hospital. Three times. And the swine had the nerve to tell everyone that she was the one to blame, that she was a drunk and was always falling about the house from drinking so much. But I don't believe that. He quarrelled with all the neighbours. Once he even went to the police to report my late husband, God rest his soul, for stealing from his shop. As far as he was concerned, anyone from the south was a layabout and a thief, the pig.'

'Did you say you recognized the girl who is next to Julián in the photograph?'

The caretaker concentrated on the image once again. 'Never seen her before. Very pretty.'

'From the picture it looks like they were a couple,' I suggested, trying to jog her memory.

She handed it back to me, shaking her head. 'I don't know anything about photographs. As far as I know, Julián never had a girlfriend, but I imagine that if he did, he wouldn't have told me. It was hard enough finding out that my Isabelita had got involved with that fellow. . . . You young people never say anything. And us old folks don't know how to stop talking.'

'Do you remember his friends, anyone special who came round here?'

The caretaker shrugged her shoulders. 'Well, it was such a long time ago. Besides, in the last years Julián was hardly ever here, you see. He'd made a friend at school, a boy from a very good family, the Aldayas – now, that's saying something. Nobody talks about them now, but in those days it was like mentioning the royal family. Lots of money. I know because sometimes they would send a car to fetch Julián. You should have seen that car. Not even Franco would have one like it. With a chauffeur, and all shiny. My Paco, who knew about cars, told me it was a *rolsroi*, or something like that. Fit for an emperor.'

'Do you remember the friend's first name?'

'Listen, with a surname like Aldaya, there's no need for first names. I also remember another boy, a bit of a scatterbrain, called Miquel. I think he was also a classmate. But don't ask me for his surname or what he looked like.'

We seemed to have reached a dead end, and I feared that the caretaker would start losing interest. I decided to follow a hunch. 'Is anyone living in the Fortuny apartment now?'

'No. The old man died without leaving a will, and his wife, as far as I know, is still in Buenos Aires and didn't even come back for the funeral. Can't blame her.'

'Why Buenos Aires?'

'Because she couldn't find anywhere further away, I guess. She left everything in the hands of a lawyer, a very strange man. I've never seen him, but my daughter Isabelita, who lives on the fifth floor, right underneath, says that sometimes, since he has the key, he comes at night and spends hours walking around the apartment and then leaves. Once she said that she could even hear what sounded like women's high heels. What can I say...?'

'Maybe they were stilts,' I suggested.

She looked at me blankly. Obviously this was a serious subject for the caretaker.

'And nobody else has visited the apartment in all these years?'

'Once this very creepy individual came along, one of those people who never stop smiling, a giggler, but you could see him coming a mile off. He said he was in the Crime Squad. He wanted to see the apartment.'

'Did he say why?'

The caretaker shook her head.

'Do you remember his name?'

'Inspector something or other. I didn't even believe he was a policeman. The whole thing stank, do you know what I mean? It smelled of something personal. I sent him packing and told him I didn't have the keys to the apartment and if he wanted anything, he should call the lawyer. He said he'd come back, but I haven't seem him round here again. Good riddance.'

'You wouldn't by any chance have the name and address of the lawyer, would you?'

'You should ask the manager of this building, Señor Molins. His office is quite close, number twenty-eight, Floridablanca, first floor. Tell him I sent you – Señora Aurora, at your service.'

'I'm very grateful. So, tell me, Doña Aurora, is the Fortuny apartment empty, then?'

'No, not empty, because nobody has taken anything from it in all the years since the old man died. Sometimes it even smells. I'd say there are rats in the apartment, mark my words.'

'Do you think it would be possible to have a look? We might find something that tells us what really happened to Julián. . . .'

'Oh no, I couldn't do that. You must talk to Señor Molins, he's the one in charge.'

I smiled at her mischievously. 'But you must have a master key, I imagine. Even if you told that man you didn't . . . Don't tell me you're not dying to see what's in there.'

Doña Aurora looked at me out of the corner of her eye.

'You're a devil.'

The door gave way like a tombstone, with a sudden groan, exhaling dank, foul-smelling air. I pushed the front door inwards, discovering a corridor that sank into darkness. The place was stuffy and reeked of damp. Spiralling threads of grime and dust hung from the ceiling like white hair. The broken floor tiles were covered by what looked like a layer of ash. I also noticed what appeared to be footprints making their way into the apartment.

'Holy Mother of God!' mumbled the caretaker. 'There's more shit here than on the floor of a henhouse.'

'If you'd rather, I'll go in on my own,' I said.

'That's exactly what you'd like. Come on, you go ahead, I'll follow.'

We closed the door behind us and waited by the entrance for a moment until our eyes became accustomed to the dark. I could hear the nervous breathing of the caretaker and noticed the sour smell of her sweat. I felt like a tomb robber whose soul is poisoned by greed and desire.

'Hey, what's that noise?' asked the caretaker in an anxious tone. Something fluttered in the dark, disturbed by our presence. I thought I glimpsed a pale shape flickering about at the end of the corridor.

'Pigeons,' I said. 'They must have got in through a broken window and made a nest here.'

'Those ugly birds give me the creeps,' said the caretaker. 'And they shit like there's no tomorrow.'

'Relax, Doña Aurora, they only attack when they're hungry.'

We ventured in a few steps till we reached the end of the corridor, where a dining room opened onto the balcony. Just visible was a shabby table covered with a tattered tablecloth that looked more like a shroud. Four chairs held a wake, together with a couple of grimy glass cabinets that guarded the crockery: an assortment of glasses and a tea set. In a corner stood the old upright piano that had belonged to Carax's mother. The keys were dark with dirt, and the joins could hardly be seen under the film of dust. An armchair with a long, threadbare cover was slowly disintegrating next to the balcony. Beside it was a coffee table on which rested a pair of reading glasses and a Bible bound in pale leather and edged with gold, of the sort that used to be given as presents for a child's first communion. It still had its bookmark, a piece of scarlet string.

'Look, that chair is where the old man was found dead. The doctor said he'd been there for two days. How sad to go like that, like a dog, all alone. Not that he didn't have it coming, but even so ...'

I went up to the chair where Fortuny had died. Next to

the Bible was a small box containing black-and-white photographs, old studio portraits. I knelt down to examine them, almost afraid to touch them. I felt as if I was profaning the memories of a poor old man, but my curiosity got the better of me. The first print showed a young couple with a boy who could not have been more than four years old. I recognized him by his eyes.

'Look, there they are. Señor Fortuny as a young man, and her . . .'

'Didn't Julián have any brothers or sisters?'

The caretaker shrugged her shoulders and let out a sigh. 'I heard rumours that she miscarried once because of the beatings her husband gave her, but I don't know. People love to gossip, don't they? But not me. All I know is that once Julián told the other kids in the building that he had a sister only he could see. He said she came out of mirrors as if she were made of thin air and that she lived with Satan himself in a palace at the bottom of a lake. My Isabelita had nightmares for a whole month. That child could be really morbid at times.'

I glanced at the kitchen. There was a broken pane in a small window overlooking an inner courtyard, and you could hear the nervous and hostile flapping of the pigeons' wings on the other side.

'Do all the apartments have the same layout?' I asked.

'The ones that look onto the street do. But this one is an attic, so it's a bit different. There's the kitchen and a laundry room that overlooks the inner yard. Down this corridor there are three bedrooms, and a bathroom at the end. Properly decorated, they can look very nice, believe me. This one is similar to my Isabelita's apartment – but of course right now it looks like a tomb.'

'Do you know which room Julián's was?'

'The first door is the master bedroom. The second is a smaller room. It was probably that one, I'd say.'

I went down the corridor. The paint on the walls was

falling off in shreds. At the end of the passage, the bathroom door was ajar. A face seemed to stare at me from the mirror. It could have been mine, or perhaps the face of the sister who lived there. As I got closer, it withdrew into darkness. I tried to open the second door.

'It's locked,' I said.

The caretaker looked at me in astonishment. 'These doors don't have locks,' she said.

'This one does.'

'Then the old man must have had it put in, because all the other apartments . . .'

I looked down and noticed that the footprints in the dust led up to the locked door. 'Someone's been in this room,' I said. 'Recently.'

'Don't scare me,' said the caretaker.

I went up to the other door. It didn't have a lock. It opened with a rusty groan when I touched it. In the middle stood an old four-poster bed, unmade. The sheets had turned yellowish, like winding sheets, and a crucifix presided over the bed. The room also contained a chest of drawers with a small mirror on it, a basin, a pitcher, and a chair. A cupboard, its door ajar, stood against the wall. I went around the bed to a bedside table with a glass top, under which lay photographs of ancestors, funeral cards, and lottery tickets. On the table were a carved wooden music box and a pocketwatch, frozen forever at twenty past five. I tried to wind up the music box, but the melody got stuck after six notes. When I opened the drawer of the bedside table, I found an empty spectacle case, a nail clipper, a hip flask, and a medal of the Virgin of Lourdes. Nothing else.

'There must be a key to that room somewhere,' I said.

'The manager must have it. Look, I think it's best we leave.'

Suddenly I looked down at the music box. I lifted the cover and there, blocking the mechanism, I found a gold key. I took it out, and the music box resumed its tinkling melody. I recognized a tune by Ravel.

'This must be the key.' I smiled at the caretaker.

'Listen, if the room was locked, there must be a reason. Even if it's just out of respect for the memory of—'

'If you'd rather, you can wait for me down in your apartment, Doña Aurora.'

'You're a devil. Go on. Open up if you must.'

# 16

A breath of cold air whistled through the hole in the lock, licking at my fingers while I inserted the key. The lock that Señor Fortuny had fitted in the door of his son's unoccupied room was three times the size of the one on the front door. Doña Aurora looked at me apprehensively, as if we were about to open a Pandora's box.

'Is this room at the front of the house?' I asked.

The caretaker shook her head. 'It has a small window, for ventilation. It looks out over the yard.'

I pushed the door inward. An impenetrable well of darkness opened up before us, the meagre light from behind barely scratching at the shadows. The window overlooking the yard was covered with pages of yellowed newspaper. I tore them off, and a needle of hazy light bored through the darkness.

'Jesus, Mary, and Joseph,' murmured the caretaker.

The room was infested with crucifixes. They hung from the ceiling, dangling from the ends of strings, and they covered the walls, hooked on nails. There were dozens of them. You could sense them in every corner, carved with a knife on the wooden furniture, scratched on the floor tiles, painted red on the mirrors. The footprints that had led us to the doorway could now be traced on the dust around the naked bed, just a skeleton of wires and worm-eaten wood. At one end of the room, under the window, stood a closed rolltop desk, crowned by a trio of metal crucifixes. I opened it with care. There was no dust in the joins of the wooden slats, from which I inferred that the desk had been opened quite recently. It had six drawers. The locks had been forced open. I inspected them one by one. Empty.

I knelt down by the desk and fingered the scratches that covered the wood, imagining Julián Carax's hands making those doodles, hieroglyphics whose meaning had been obscured by time. In the desk, I noticed a pile of notebooks and a vase filled with pencils and pens. I took one of the notebooks and glanced at it. Drawings and single words. Mathematical exercises. Unconnected phrases, quotes from books. Unfinished poems. All the notebooks looked the same. Some drawings were repeated page after page, with slight variations. I was struck by the figure of a man who seemed to be made of flames. Another might have been an angel or a reptile coiled around a cross. Rough sketches hinted at a fantastic rambling house, woven with towers and cathedral-like arches. The strokes were confident and showed a certain ability. Young Carax appeared to be a draftsman of some promise, but none of the drawings were more than rough sketches.

I was about to put the last notebook back in its place without looking at it when something slipped out from its pages and fell at my feet. It was a photograph in which I recognized the same girl who appeared in the other picture – the one taken at the foot of that building. The girl posed in a luxurious garden, and beyond the treetops, just visible, was the shape of the house I had seen sketched in the drawings of the adolescent Carax. I recognized it immediately. It was the villa called The White Friar, on Avenida del Tibidabo. On the back of the photograph was an inscription that simply said:

Penélope, who loves you

I put it in my pocket, closed the desk, and smiled at the caretaker.

'Seen enough?' she asked, anxious to leave the place.

'Almost,' I replied. 'Before, you said that soon after Julián left for Paris, a letter came for him, but his father told you to throw it away. . . .'

The caretaker hesitated for a moment, and then she nodded. 'I put the letter in the drawer of the cabinet in the entrance hall, in case the Frenchwoman should come back one day. It must still be there.'

We went down to the cabinet and opened the top drawer. An ochre-coloured envelope lay on top of a collection of stopped watches, buttons, and coins that had ceased being legal tender twenty years ago. I picked up the envelope and examined it.

'Did you read it?'

'What do you take me for?'

'I meant no offence. It would have been quite natural, under the circumstances, if you thought that Julián was dead. . . .'

The caretaker shrugged, looked down, and started walking towards the door. I took advantage of that moment to put the letter in the inside pocket of my jacket.

'Look, I don't want you to get the wrong impression,' said the caretaker.

'Of course not. What did the letter say?'

'It was a love letter. Like the stories on the radio, only sadder, you know, because it sounded as if it were really true. Believe me, I felt like crying when I read it.'

'You're all heart, Doña Aurora.'

'And you're a devil.'

That same afternoon, after saying goodbye to Doña Aurora and promising that I would keep her up to date with my investigations on Julián Carax, I went along to see the manager of the apartment block. Señor Molins had seen better days and now mouldered away in a filthy first-floor office on Calle Floridablanca. Still, Molins was a cheerful and self-satisfied individual. His mouth was glued to a half-smoked cigar that seemed to grow out of his moustache. It was hard to tell whether he was asleep or awake, because he breathed like most people snore. His hair was greasy and flattened over his forehead, and he had mischievous piggy eyes. His suit wouldn't have fetched more than ten pesetas in the Encantes Flea Market, but he made up for it with a gaudy tie of tropical colours. Judging by the appearance of the office, not much was managed anymore, except the bugs and cobwebs of a forgotten Barcelona.

'We're in the middle of refurbishment,' he said apologetically.

To break the ice, I let drop Doña Aurora's name as if I were referring to some old friend of the family.

'When she was young, she was a real looker,' was Molins's comment. 'With age she's gone on the heavier side, but then I'm not what I used to be either. You may not believe this, but when I was your age, I was an Adonis. Girls would go on their knees to beg for a quickie, or to have my babies. Alas, the twentieth century is nothing but shit. What can I do for you, young man?'

I presented him with a more or less plausible story about a supposed distant relationship with the Fortunys. After five minutes' chatter, Molins dragged himself to his filing cabinet and gave me the address of the lawyer who dealt with anything related to Sophie Carax, Julián's mother.

'Let me see . . . José María Requejo. Fifty-nine, Calle León XIII. But we send the mail twice a year to a PO box in the main post office on Vía Layetana.'

'Do you know Señor Requejo?'

'I've spoken to his secretary occasionally on the telephone. The fact is that any business with him is done by post, and my secretary deals with that. And today she's at the hairdresser's. Lawyers don't have time for face-to-face dealings anymore. There are no gentlemen left in the profession.'

125

There didn't seem to be any reliable addresses left either. A quick glance at the street guide on the manager's desk confirmed what I suspected: the address of the supposed lawyer, Señor Requejo, didn't exist. I told Mr Molins, who took the news in as if it were a joke.

'Well, I'll be damned!' he said laughing. 'What did I say? Crooks.'

The manager lay back in his chair and made another of his snoring noises.

'Would you happen to have the number of that PO Box?'

'According to the index card it's 2837, although I can't read my secretary's numbers. As I'm sure you know, women are no good at maths. What they're good for is—'

'May I see the card?'

'Sure. Help yourself.'

He handed me the index card, and I looked at it. The numbers were perfectly legible. The PO box was 2321. It horrified me to think of the accounting that must have gone on in that office.

'Did you have much contact with Señor Fortuny during his lifetime?' I asked.

'So so. Quite the ascetic type. I remember that when I found out that the Frenchwoman had left him, I invited him to go whoring with a few mates of mine, nearby, in a fabulous establishment I know next to the La Paloma dance hall. Just to cheer him up, eh? That's all. And you know what? He would not talk to me, even greet me in the street anymore, as if I were invisible. What do you make of that?'

'I'm in shock. What else can you tell me about the Fortuny family? Do you remember them well?'

'Those were different times,' he murmured nostalgically. 'The fact is that I already knew Grandfather Fortuny, the one who started the hat shop. About the son, there isn't much to tell. Now, the wife, she was spectacular. What a woman. And decent too. Despite all the rumours and the gossip . . .'

'Like the one about Julián not being Fortuny's legitimate son?'

'And where did you hear that?'

'As I said, I'm part of the family. Everything gets out.'

'None of that was ever proved.'

'But it was talked about,' I said encouragingly.

'People talk too much. Humans aren't descended from monkeys. They come from parrots.'

'And what did people say?'

'Don't you feel like a little glass of rum? It's Cuban, like all the good stuff that kills you.'

'No thanks, but I'll keep you company. In the meantime, you can tell me . . .'

*Antoni Fortuny, whom everyone called the hatter, met Sophie Carax in 1899 by the steps of Barcelona Cathedral. He was returning from making a vow to St Eustace – for of all the saints, St Eustace was considered the most diligent and the least fussy when it came to granting miracles to do with love. Antoni Fortuny, who was already over thirty and a confirmed bachelor, was looking for a wife, and wanted her right away. Sophie was a French girl who lived in a boarding house for young ladies in Calle Riera Alta and gave private music and piano lessons to the offspring of the most privileged families in Barcelona. She had no family or capital to rely on, only her youth and what musical education she had received from her father – the pianist at a Nîmes theatre – before he died of tuberculosis in 1886. Antoni Fortuny, on the contrary, was a man on the road to prosperity. He had recently inherited his father's business, a hat shop of some repute in Ronda de San Antonio, where he had learned the trade that he dreamed one day of teaching his own son. He found Sophie Carax fragile, beautiful, young, docile, and fertile. St Eustace had obliged. After four months of insistent courting, Sophie accepted Antoni's marriage proposal. Señor Molins, who had been a friend of Fortuny the elder, warned Antoni that he was marrying a stranger. He said that Sophie seemed like a nice*

127

girl, but perhaps this marriage was a bit too convenient for her, and he should wait a year at least ... Antoni Fortuny replied that he already knew everything he needed to know about his future wife. The rest did not interest him. They were married at the Basílica del Pino and spent their three-day honeymoon in a spa in the nearby seaside resort of Mongat. The morning before they left, the hatter asked Señor Molins, in confidence, to be initiated into the mysteries of the bedroom. Molins sarcastically told him to ask his wife. The newlyweds returned to Barcelona after only two days. The neighbours said Sophie was crying when she came into the building. Years later Viçenteta swore that Sophie had told her the following: that the hatter had not laid a finger on her and that when she had tried to seduce him, he had called her a whore and told her he was disgusted by the obscenity of what she was proposing. Six months later Sophie announced to her husband that she was with child. By another man.

Antoni Fortuny had seen his own father hit his mother on countless occasions and did what he thought was the right thing to do. He stopped only when he feared that one more blow would kill her. Despite the beating, Sophie refused to reveal the identity of the child's father. Applying his own logic to the matter, Antoni Fortuny decided that it must be the devil, for that child was the child of sin, and sin had only one father: the Evil One. Convinced in this manner that sin had sneaked into his home and also between his wife's thighs, the hatter took to hanging crucifixes everywhere: on the walls, on the doors of all the rooms, and on the ceiling. When Sophie discovered him scattering crosses in the bedroom to which she had been confined, she grew afraid and, with tears in her eyes, asked him whether he had gone mad. Blind with rage, he turned around and hit her. 'A whore like the rest,' he spat as he threw her out onto the landing, after flaying her with blows from his belt. The following day, when Antoni Fortuny opened the door of his apartment to go down to the hat shop, Sophie was still there, covered in dried blood and shivering with cold. The doctors never managed to fix the fractures on her right hand completely. Sophie Carax would never be able to play the piano again, but she would give birth to a boy, whom she would name Julián after the father she had lost when she was still too young – as happens with all good things in life. Fortuny considered throwing her out of his home but thought the scandal would not be good for business. Nobody would buy hats from a man known to be a cuckold – the two didn't go together. From then on, Sophie was assigned a dark, cold room at the back of the apartment. It was there she gave birth to her son with the help of two neighbours. Antoni did not return home until three days later. 'This is the son God has given you,' Sophie announced. 'If you want to punish anyone, punish me, but not an innocent creature. The boy needs a home and a father. My sins are not his. I beg you to take pity on us.'

The first months were difficult for both of them. Antoni Fortuny had downgraded his wife to the rank of servant. They no longer shared a bed or table and rarely exchanged any words except to resolve some domestic matter. Once a month, usually coinciding with the full moon, Antoni Fortuny showed up in Sophie's bedroom at dawn and, without a word, charged at his former wife with vigour but little skill. Making the most of these rare and aggressive moments of intimacy, Sophie tried to win him over by whispering words of love and caressing him. But the hatter was not a man for frivolities, and the eagerness of desire evaporated in a matter of minutes, or even seconds. These assaults brought no children. After a few years, Antoni Fortuny stopped visiting Sophie's chamber for good and took up the habit of reading the Gospels until the small hours, seeking in them a solace for his torment.

With the help of the Gospels, the hatter made an effort to kindle some affection for the child with deep eyes who loved making a joke of everything and inventing shadows where there were none. Despite his efforts, Antoni Fortuny was unable to feel as if little Julián were his flesh and blood, nor did he recognize any aspect of himself in him. The boy, for his part, did not seem very interested either in hats or in the teachings of the catechism. During the Christmas season he would amuse himself by changing the positions of the small figures in the Nativity scene and devising plots in which Baby Jesus had been kidnapped by the three magi from the East who had wicked intentions. He soon became obsessed with drawing angels with wolf's teeth and inventing stories about hooded spirits that came out of walls and ate people's ideas while they slept. In time the hatter lost all hope of being able to set this boy on the right path. The child was not a Fortuny and never would be. Julián maintained that he was bored in school and came home with his notebooks full of drawings of monstrous beings, winged serpents, and buildings that were alive, walked, and devoured the unsuspecting. By then it was quite clear that fantasy and invention interested him far more than the daily reality around him. Of all the disappointments amassed during his lifetime, none hurt Antoni Fortuny more than that son whom the devil had sent to mock him.

At the age of ten, Julián announced that he wanted to be a painter, like Velázquez. He dreamed of embarking on canvases that the great master had been unable to paint during his life because, Julián argued, he'd been obliged to paint so many time-consuming portraits of mentally retarded royals. To make matters worse, Sophie, perhaps to relieve her loneliness and remember her father, decided to give him piano lessons. Julián, who loved music, art, and all matters that were not considered practical in the world of men, soon learned the rudiments of harmony and concluded that he preferred to invent his own compositions rather than follow the music-book scores. At that time Antoni Fortuny still suspected that part of the boy's mental deficiencies were due to his diet, which was far too influenced by his mother's French cooking. It was a well-known fact that the richness of buttery foods led to moral ruin and confusion of the intellect. He forbade Sophie to cook with butter ever again. The results were not entirely as he had anticipated.

At twelve Julián began to lose his feverish interest in painting and in Velázquez, but the hatter's initial hopes did not last long. Julián was abandoning his canvas dreams for a far more pernicious vice. He had discovered the library in Calle del Carmen and devoted any time he was allowed off from the hat shop to visiting the sanctuary of books and devouring volumes of fiction, poetry, and history. The day before his thirteenth birthday, he announced that he wanted to be someone called Robert Louis Stevenson, evidently a foreigner. The hatter remarked that with luck he'd become a quarry worker. At that point he became convinced that his son was nothing but an idiot.

At night Antoni Fortuny often writhed in his bed with anger and frustration, unable to get any sleep. At the bottom of his heart, he loved that child, he told himself. And although she didn't deserve it, he also loved the slut who had betrayed him from the very first day. He loved her with all his soul, but in his own way, which was the correct way. All he asked God was to show him how the three of them could be happy, preferably also in his own way. He begged the Lord to send him a signal, a whisper, a crumb of His presence. God, in His infinite wisdom, and perhaps overwhelmed by the avalanche of requests from so many tormented souls, did not answer. While Antoni Fortuny was engulfed by remorse and suspicion, on the other side of the wall, Sophie slowly faded away, her life shipwrecked on a sea of disappointment, isolation, and guilt. She did not love the man she served, but she felt she belonged to him, and the possibility of leaving him and taking his son with her to some other place seemed inconceivable. She remembered Julián's real father with bitterness, and eventually grew to hate him and everything he stood for. In her desperation she began to shout back at Antoni Fortuny. Insults and sharp recriminations flew round the apartment like knives, stabbing anyone who dared get in their way, usually Julián. Later the hatter never remembered exactly why he had beaten his wife. He remembered only the anger and the shame. He would then swear to himself that this would never happen again, that, if necessary, he would give himself up to the authorities and get himself locked up in prison.

*Antoni Fortuny was sure that, with God's help, he would end up being a better man than his own father. But sooner or later, his fists would once more meet Sophie's tender flesh, and in time Fortuny felt that if he could not possess her as a husband, he would do so as a tyrant. In this manner, secretly, the Fortuny family let the years go by, silencing their hearts and their souls to the point where, from so much keeping quiet, they forgot the words with which to express their real feelings and the family became strangers living under the same roof, like so many other families in the vast city.*

It was past two-thirty when I returned to the bookshop. As I walked in, Fermín gave me a sarcastic look from the top of a ladder, where he was polishing up a collection of the *Episodios Nacionales* by the famous Don Benito.

'Who is this I see before me? We thought you must have set off to the New World by now, Daniel.'

'I got delayed on the way. Where's my father?'

'Since you didn't turn up, he went off to deliver the rest of the orders. He asked me to tell you that this afternoon he is going to Tiana to value a private library belonging to a widow. Your father's a wolf in sheep's clothing. He said not to wait for him to close the shop.'

'Was he annoyed?'

Fermín shook his head, coming down the stepladder with feline nimbleness.

'Not at all. Your father is a saint. Besides, he was very happy to see you're dating a young lady.'

'What?'

Fermín winked at me and smacked his lips.

'Oh, you little devil, you were hiding your light under a bushel! And what a girl, eh? Good enough to stop traffic. And such class. You can tell she's been to good schools, although she has fire in her eyes. . . . If Bernarda hadn't stolen my heart, and I haven't told you all about our outing yet – there were sparks coming out of those eyes, I tell you, sparks, it was like a bonfire on Midsummer's Night—'

'Fermín,' I interrupted. 'What the hell are you talking about?'

'About your fiancée.'

'I don't have a fiancée, Fermín.'

'Well, these days you young people call them anything, sugar pie, or—'

'Fermín, will you please rewind? What are you talking about?'

Fermín Romero de Torres looked at me disconcertedly.

'Let me see. This afternoon, about an hour or an hour and a half ago, a gorgeous young lady came by and asked for you. Your father and yours truly were on the premises, and I can assure you, without a shadow of doubt, that the girl was no apparition. I could even describe her smell. Lavender, only sweeter. Like a little sugar bun just out of the oven.'

'Did little sugar bun say she was my fiancée, by any chance?'

'Well, not in so many words, but she gave a sort of quick smile, if you see what I mean, and said that she would see you on Friday afternoon. All we did was put two and two together.'

'Bea . . .' I mumbled.

'Ergo, she exists,' said Fermín with relief.

'Yes, but she's not my girlfriend.'

'Well, I don't know what you're waiting for, then.'

'She's Tomás Aguilar's sister.'

'Your friend the inventor?'

I nodded.

'All the more reason. Even if she were the pope's niece, she's a bombshell. If I were you, I'd be on the ready.'

'Bea already has a fiancé. A lieutenant doing his military service.'

Fermín sighed with irritation. 'Ah, the army, blight and refuge for the basest simian instincts. All the better, because this way you can cheat on him without feeling guilty.'

'You're delirious, Fermín. Bea's getting married when the lieutenant finishes his service.'

Fermín gave me a sneaky smile. 'Funny you should say that, because I have a feeling she's not. I don't think this pumpkin is going to be tying the knot anytime soon.'

'What do you know?'

'About women and other worldly matters, considerably more than you. As Freud tells us, women want the opposite of what they think or say they want, which, when you consider it, is not so bad, because men, as is more than evident, respond, contrariwise, to the dictates of their genital and digestive organs.'

'Stop lecturing me, Fermín, I can see where this is heading. If you have anything to say, just say it.'

'Right, then, in a nutshell: this one hasn't a single bone of obedient-little-wife material in her heavenly body.'

'Hasn't she? Then what kind of bone does your expertise detect?'

Fermín came closer, adopting a confidential tone. 'The passionate kind,' he said, raising his eyebrows with an air of mystery. 'And you can be sure I mean that as a compliment.'

As usual, Fermín was right. Feeling defeated, I decided that attack was the best form of defence. 'Speaking of passion, tell me about Bernarda. Was there or was there not a kiss?'

'Don't insult me, Daniel. Let me remind you that you are talking to a professional in the art of seduction, and this business of kissing is for amateurs and little old men in slippers. Real women are won over bit by bit. It's all a question of psychology, like a good *faena* in the bullring.'

'In other words, she gave you the brush-off.'

'The woman is yet to be born who is capable of giving Fermín Romero de Torres the brush-off. The trouble is that man, going back to Freud – and excuse the metaphor – heats up like a lightbulb: red hot in the twinkling of an eye and cold again in a flash. The female, on the other hand –

and this is pure science – heats up like an iron, slowly, over a low heat, like a tasty stew. But then, once she has heated up, there's no stopping her. Like the steel furnaces in Vizcaya.'

I weighed up Fermín's thermodynamic theories. 'Is that what you're doing with Bernarda? Heating up the iron?'

Fermín winked at me. 'That woman is a volcano on the point of eruption, with a libido of igneous magma yet the heart of an angel,' he said, licking his lips. 'If I had to establish a true parallel, she reminds me of my succulent mulatto girl in Havana, who was very devout and always worshipped her saints. But since, deep down, I'm an old-fashioned gent who doesn't like to take advantage of women, I contented myself with a chaste kiss on the cheek. I'm not in a hurry, you see? All good things must wait. There are yokels out there who think that if they touch a woman's behind and she doesn't complain, they've hooked her. Amateurs. The female heart is a labyrinth of subtleties, too challenging for the uncouth mind of the male racketeer. If you really want to possess a woman, you must think like her, and the first thing to do is to win over her soul. The rest, that sweet, soft wrapping which steals away your senses and your virtue, is a bonus.'

I clapped solemnly at this discourse. 'You're a poet, Fermín.'

'No, I'm with Ortega and I'm a pragmatist. Poetry lies, in its adorable wicked way, and what I say is truer than a slice of bread and tomato. That's just what the master said: show me a Don Juan and I'll show you a loser in disguise. What I aim for is permanence, durability. Bear witness that I will make Bernarda, if not an honest woman, because that she already is, at least a happy one.'

I smiled as I nodded. His enthusiasm was contagious, and his diction beyond improvement. 'Take good care of her, Fermín. Do it for me. Bernarda has a heart of gold, and she has already suffered too many disappointments.'

'Do you think I can't see that? It's written all over her,

like a stamp from the society of war widows. Trust me: I wrote the book on taking shit from everybody and his mother. I'm going to make this woman blissfully happy even if it's the last thing I ever do in this world.'

'Do I have your word?'

He stretched out his hand with the composure of a Knight Templar. I shook it.

'Yes, the word of Fermín Romero de Torres.'

Business in the shop was slow that afternoon, with barely a couple of browsers. In view of the situation, I suggested Fermín take the rest of the day off.

'Go on, go and find Bernarda and take her to the cinema or go window shopping with her in Calle Puertaferrissa, walking arm in arm, she loves that.'

Fermín did not hesitate to take me up on my offer and rushed off to smarten himself up in the back room, where he always kept a change of clothes and all kinds of eau de colognes and ointments in a toilet bag that would have been the envy of Veronica Lake. When he emerged, he looked like a film star, only five stone lighter. He wore a suit that had belonged to my father and a felt hat that was a couple of sizes too large, a problem he solved by placing balls of newspaper under the crown.

'By the way, Fermín. Before you go . . . I wanted to ask you a favour.'

'Say no more. You give the order. I'm already on to it.'

'I'm going to ask you to keep this between us, OK? Not a word to my father.'

He beamed. 'Ah, you rascal. Something to do with that girl, eh?'

'No. This is a matter of high intrigue. Your department.'

'Well, I also know a lot about girls. I'm telling you this because if you ever have a technical query, you know who to ask. Privacy assured. I'm like a doctor when it comes to such matters. No need to be prudish.'

'I'll bear that in mind. Right now what I would like to

know is who owns a PO box in the main post office on Vía Layetana. Number 2321. And, if possible, who collects the mail that goes there. Do you think you'll be able to lend me a hand?'

Fermín wrote down the number with a ballpoint on his instep, under his sock.

'Piece of cake. All official institutions find me irresistible. Give me a few days and I'll have a full report ready for you.'

'We agreed not to say a word of this to my father?'

'Don't worry. I'll be as quiet as the Sphinx.'

'I'm very grateful. Now, go on, off with you, and have a good time.'

I said goodbye with a military salute and watched him leave looking as debonair as a cock on his way to the henhouse.

He couldn't have been gone for more than five minutes when I heard the tinkle of the doorbell and lifted my head from the columns of numbers and crossings-out. A man had just come in, hidden behind a grey raincoat and a felt hat. He sported a pencil moustache and had glassy blue eyes. He smiled like a salesman, a forced smile. I was sorry Fermín was not there, because he was an expert at seeing off travellers selling camphor and other such rubbish whenever they slipped into the bookshop. The visitor offered me his greasy grin, casually picking up a book from a pile that stood by the entrance waiting to be sorted and priced. Everything about him communicated disdain for all he saw. You're not even going to sell me a 'good afternoon', I thought.

'A lot of words, eh?' he said.

'It's a book; they usually have quite a few words. Anything I can do for you, sir?'

The man put the book back on the pile, nodding indifferently and ignoring my question. 'I say reading is for people who have a lot of time and nothing to do. Like women. Those of us who have to work don't have time for make-believe. We're too busy earning a living. Don't you agree?'

'It's an opinion. Were you looking for anything in particular?'

'It's not an opinion. It's a fact. That's what's wrong with this country: people don't want to work. There're a lot of layabouts around. Don't you agree?'

'I don't know, sir. Perhaps. Here, as you can see, we only sell books.'

The man came up to the counter, his eyes darting around the shop, settling occasionally on mine. His appearance and manner seemed vaguely familiar, though I couldn't say why. Something about him reminded me of one of those figures from old-fashioned playing cards or the sort used by fortune-tellers, a print straight from the pages of an incunabulum: his presence was both funereal and incandescent, like a curse dressed in its Sunday best.

'If you'll tell me what I can do for you . . .'

'It's really me who was coming to do you a service. Are you the owner of this establishment?'

'No. The owner is my father.'

'And the name is?'

'My name or my father's?'

The man proffered a sarcastic smile. A giggler, I thought.

'I take it that the sign saying Sempere and Son applies to both of you, then?'

'That's very perceptive of you. May I ask the reason for your visit, if you are not interested in a book?'

'The reason for my visit, a courtesy call if you like, is to warn you. It has come to my attention that you're doing business with undesirable characters, in particular inverts and criminals.'

I stared at him in astonishment. 'Excuse me?'

The man fixed me with his eyes. 'I'm talking about queers and thieves. Don't tell me you don't know what I'm talking about.'

'I'm afraid I haven't the faintest idea, nor am I remotely interested in listening to you any longer.'

The man nodded in an unfriendly and truculent manner. 'You'll just have to endure me, then. I suppose you're aware of citizen Federico Flaviá's activities.'

'Don Federico is the local watchmaker, an excellent person. I very much doubt that he's a criminal.'

'I was talking about queers. I have proof that this old queen frequents your shop, I imagine to buy little romantic novels and pornography.'

'And may I ask you what business this is of yours?'

His answer was to pull out his wallet and place it open on the counter. I recognized a grimy police ID with his picture on it, looking a bit younger. I read up to where it said 'Chief Inspector Francisco Javier Fumero'.

'Speak to me with respect, boy, or you and your father will be in deep trouble for selling communist rubbish. Do you hear?'

I wanted to reply, but the words had frozen on my lips.

'Still, this queer isn't what brought me here today. Sooner or later he'll end up in the police station, like all the rest of his persuasion, and I'll make sure he's given a lesson. What worries me is that, according to my information, you're employing a common thief, an undesirable of the worst sort.'

'I don't know who you're talking about, Inspector.'

Fumero gave his servile, sticky giggle.

'God only knows what name he's using now. Years ago he called himself Wilfredo Camagüey, the Mambo King, and said he was an expert in voodoo, dance teacher to the Bourbon royal heir and Mata Hari's lover. Other times, he takes the names of ambassadors, variety artists, or bull-fighters. We've lost count by now.'

'I'm afraid I'm unable to help you. I don't know anyone called Wilfredo Camagüey.'

'I'm sure you don't, but you know who I'm referring to, don't you?'

'No.'

Fumero laughed again, that forced, affected laugh that seemed to sum him up like the blurb on a book jacket. 'You like to make things difficult, don't you? Look, I've come here as a friend, to warn you that whoever takes on someone as undesirable as this one ends up with his fingers scorched, yet you're treating me like a liar.'

'Not at all. I appreciate your visit and your warning, but I can assure you that there hasn't—'

'Don't give me that crap, because if I damn well feel like it, I'll beat the shit out of you and lock you up in the slammer, is that clear? But today I'm in a good mood, so I'm going to leave you with just a warning. It's up to you to choose your company. If you like queers and thieves, you must be a bit of both yourself. Things have to be clear where I'm concerned. Either you're with me or you're against me. That's life. That simple. So what's it going to be?'

I didn't say anything. Fumero nodded, letting go another giggle.

'Very good, Señor Sempere. It's your call. Not a very good beginning for us. If you want problems, you'll get them. Life isn't like a novel, you know. In life you have to take sides. And it's clear which side you've chosen. The side taken by idiots, the losing side.'

'I'm going to ask you to leave, please.'

He walked off toward the door, followed by his sibylline laugh. 'We'll meet again. And tell your friend that Inspector Fumero is keeping an eye on him and sends him his best regards.'

The call from the inspector and the echo of his words ruined my afternoon. After a quarter of an hour of running to and fro behind the counter, my stomach tightening into a knot, I decided to close the bookshop before the usual time and go out for a walk. I wandered about aimlessly, unable to rid my mind of the insinuations and threats made by that sinister thug. I wondered whether I should alert my father and Fermín about the visit, but I imagined that would have been precisely Fumero's intention: to sow doubt, anguish, fear and uncertainty among us. I decided not to play his game. On the other hand, his suggestions about Fermín's past alarmed me. I felt ashamed of myself on discovering that, for a moment, I had given credit to the policeman's words. In the end, after much consideration, I decided to banish the entire episode to the back of my mind.

On my way home, I passed the watchmaker's shop. Don Federico greeted me from behind the counter, beckoning me to come in. The watchmaker was an affable, cheerful character who never forgot anyone's birthday, the sort of person you could always go to with a dilemma, knowing that he would find a solution. I couldn't help shivering at the thought that he was on Inspector Fumero's blacklist, and wondered whether I should warn him, although I could not imagine how, without getting caught up in matters that were none of my business. Feeling more confused than ever, I went into his shop and smiled at him.

'How are you, Daniel? What's that face for?'

'Bad day,' I said. 'How's everything, Don Federico?'

'Smooth as silk. They don't make watches like they used to anymore, so I've got plenty of work. If things go on like this, I'm going to have to hire an assistant. Your friend, the inventor, would he be interested? He must be good at this sort of thing.'

It didn't take much to imagine what Tomás's reactionary father would think of his son accepting a job in the establishment of the neighbourhood's official fairy queen. 'I'll let him know.'

'By the way, Daniel, I've got the alarm clock your father brought round two weeks ago. I don't know what he did to it, but he'd be better off buying a new one than having it fixed.'

I remembered that sometimes, on suffocating summer nights, my father would sleep out on the balcony.

'It probably fell onto the street,' I said.

'That explains it. Ask him to let me know what to do about it. I can get a Radiant for him at a very good price. Look, take this one with you if you like, and let him try it out. If he likes it, he can pay for it later. If not, just bring it back.'

'Thank you very much, Don Federico.'

The watchmaker began to wrap up the monstrosity in question.

'The latest technology,' he said with pleasure. 'By the way, I loved the book Fermín sold me the other day. It was by this fellow Graham Greene. That Fermín was a tremendous hire.'

I nodded. 'Yes, he's worth twice his weight in gold.'

'I've noticed he never wears a watch. Tell him to come by the shop and we'll sort something out.'

'I will. Thank you, Don Federico.'

When he handed me the alarm clock, the watchmaker observed me closely and arched his eyebrows. 'Are you sure there's nothing the matter, Daniel? Just a bad day?'

I nodded again and smiled. 'There's nothing the matter, Don Federico. Take care.'

'You too, Daniel.'

When I got home, I found my father asleep on the sofa, the newspaper on his chest. I left the alarm clock on the table with a note saying 'Don Federico says dump the old one' and slipped quietly into my room. I lay down on my bed in the dark and fell asleep thinking about the inspector, Fermín, and the watchmaker. When I woke up again, it was already two o'clock in the morning. I peered into the corridor and saw that my father had retired to his bedroom with the new alarm clock. The apartment was full of shadows, and the world seemed a gloomier and more sinister place than it had been only the night before. I realized that, in fact, I had never quite believed that Inspector Fumero existed. I went into the kitchen, poured myself a glass of cold milk, and wondered whether Fermín would be all right in his *pensión*.

On my way back to the room, I tried to banish the image of the policeman from my mind. I tried to get back to sleep but realized that it was impossible. I turned on the light and decided to examine the envelope addressed to Julián Carax that I had stolen from Doña Aurora that morning and which was still in the pocket of my jacket. I placed it on my desk, under the beam of the reading lamp. It was a parchment-like envelope, with yellowing serrated borders and clayish to the touch. The postmark, just a shadow, said '18 October 1919'. The wax seal had come unstuck, probably thanks to Doña Aurora's good offices. In its place was a reddish stain, like a trace of lipstick that kissed the fold of the envelope on which the return address was written.

*Penélope Aldaya*
*Avenida del Tibidabo, 32, Barcelona*

I opened the envelope and pulled out the letter, an ochre-coloured sheet neatly folded in two. The handwriting, in blue ink, glided nervously across the page, paling slowly until it regained intensity every few words. Everything on that page spoke of another time: the strokes that depended on the ink-pot, the words scratched on the thick paper by the tip of the nib, the rugged feel of the paper. I spread the letter out on the desk and read it, breathless.

Dear Julián:
This morning I found out through Jorge that you did in fact leave Barcelona to go in pursuit of your dreams. I always feared that those dreams would never allow you to be mine, or anyone else's. I would have liked to see you one last time, to be able to look into your eyes and tell you things that I don't know how to say in a letter. Nothing came out the way we had

planned. I know you too well, and I know you won't write to me, that you won't even send me your address, that you will want to be another person. I know you will hate me for not having been there as I had promised. That you will think I failed you. That I didn't have the courage.

I have imagined you so many times, alone on that train, convinced that I had betrayed you. Many times I tried to find you through Miquel, but he told me that you didn't want to have anything more to do with me. What lies did they tell you, Julián? What did they say about me? Why did you believe them?

Now I know I have already lost you. I have lost everything. Even so, I can't let you go forever and allow you to forget me without letting you know that I don't bear you any grudge, that I knew it from the start, I knew that I was going to lose you and that you would never see in me what I see in you. I want you to know that I loved you from the very first day and that I still love you, now more than ever, even if you don't want me to.

I am writing to you in secret, without anyone knowing. Jorge has sworn that if he sees you again, he'll kill you. I'm not allowed to go out of the house anymore, I can't even look out of the window. I don't think they'll ever forgive me. Someone I trust has promised to post this letter to you. I won't mention the name so as not to compromise the person in question. I don't know whether my words will reach you. But if they do, and should you decide to return to fetch me here, I know you will find the way to do it. As I write, I imagine you in that train, full of dreams and with your soul broken by betrayal, fleeing from us all and from yourself. There are so many things I cannot tell you, Julián. Things we never knew and it's better you should never know.

All I wish is for you to be happy, Julián, that
everything you aspire to achieve may come true and
that, although you may forget me in the course of
time, one day you may finally understand how much
I loved you.
  Always,
  Penélope

# 17

The words of Penélope Aldaya, which I read and reread that
night until I knew them by heart, brushed aside all the
bitterness Inspector Fumero's visit had left in me. At dawn,
after spending the night wide awake, engrossed in that letter
and the voice I sensed behind the words, I left the house. I
dressed quietly and left a note for my father on the hall
cabinet saying I had a few errands to run and would be back
in the bookshop by nine-thirty. When I stepped out of the
main door the puddles left in the street by the night's
drizzle reflected the bluish shadows of early morning. I
buttoned up my jacket and set off briskly toward Plaza de
Cataluña. The stairs up from the subway station gave off a
swirl of warm air. At the ticket office of the Ferrocarriles
Catalanes, I bought a third-class fare to Tibidabo station. I
made the journey in a carriage full of office workers, maids
and day labourers carrying sandwiches the size of bricks
wrapped in newspaper. Taking refuge in the darkness of the
tunnels, I rested my head against the window, while the
train journeyed through the bowels of the city to the foot of
Mount Tibidabo, which presides over Barcelona. When I
reemerged into the streets, it seemed as if I were discovering
another place. Dawn was breaking, and a purple blade of
light cut through the clouds, spraying its hue over the fronts
of mansions and the stately homes that bordered Avenida
del Tibidabo. A blue tram was crawling lazily uphill in the

mist. I ran after it and managed to clamber onto the back platform, as the conductor looked on disapprovingly. The wooden carriage was almost empty. Two friars and a lady in mourning with ashen skin swayed, half asleep, to the rocking of the carriage.

'I'm only going as far as number thirty-two,' I told the conductor, offering him my best smile.

'I don't care if you're going to Cape Horn,' he replied with indifference. 'Even Christ's soldiers here have paid for their tickets. Either you fork out or you walk out. And I'm not charging you for the rhyme.'

Clad in sandals and the austere brown sackcloth cloaks of the Franciscan order, the friars nodded, showing their two pink tickets to prove the conductor's point.

'I'll get off, then,' I said. 'Because I haven't any small change.'

'As you wish. But wait for the next stop. I don't want any accidents on my shift.'

The tram climbed almost at walking pace, hugging the shade of the trees and peeping over the walls and gardens of castle-like mansions that I imagined filled with statues, fountains, stables, and secret chapels. I looked out from one side of the platform and noticed the White Friar villa silhouetted between the trees. As the train approached the corner with Calle Román Macaya, it slowed down until it almost came to a halt. The driver rang his bell and the conductor threw me a sharp look. 'Go on, smartie. Off you get, number thirty-two is just there.'

I got off and heard the clattering of the blue tram as it disappeared into the mist. The Aldaya residence was on the opposite side of the street, guarded by a large wrought-iron gate woven with ivy and dead leaves. Set into the iron bars, barely visible, was a small door that was firmly locked. Above the gate, knotted into the shape of black iron snakes, was the number 32. I tried to peer into the property from there but could only make out the angles and arches of a dark tower. A trail of rust bled from the keyhole in the door. I knelt down and tried to get a better view of the courtyard from that position. All I could see was a tangle of weeds and the outline of what seemed to be a fountain or a pond from which an outstretched hand emerged, pointing up to the sky. It took me a few moments to realize that it was a stone hand and that there were other limbs and shapes I could not quite make out submerged in the fountain. Further away, veiled by the weeds, I caught sight of a marble staircase, broken and covered in rubble and fallen leaves. The glory and fortune of the Aldayas had faded a long time ago. The place was a graveyard.

I walked back a few steps and then turned the corner to have a look at the south wing of the house. From here you could get a better view of one of the mansion's towers. At that moment I noticed a human figure at the edge of my vision, an emaciated man in blue overalls, who brandished a large broom with which he was attacking the dead leaves on the pavement. He regarded me with some suspicion, and I imagined he must be the caretaker of one of the neighbouring properties. I smiled as only someone who has spent many hours behind a counter can do.

'Good morning,' I intoned cordially. 'Do you know whether the Aldayas' house has been closed for long?'

He stared at me as if I had inquired about the sex of angels. The little man touched his chin with yellowed fingers that betrayed a weakness for cheap unfiltered Celtas cigarettes. I regretted not having a packet on me with which to win him over. I rummaged in the pocket of my jacket to see what offering I could come up with.

'At least twenty or twenty-five years, and let's hope it continues that way,' said the caretaker in that flat, resigned tone of people who have been beaten into servility.

'Have you been here long?'

The man nodded. 'Yours truly has been employed here with the Miravells since 1920.'

'You wouldn't have any idea what happened to the Aldaya family, would you?'

'Well, as you know, they lost everything at the time of the Republic,' he said. 'He who makes trouble . . . What little I know I've heard at the Miravells' – they used to be friends of the Aldayas. I think the eldest son, Jorge, went abroad, to Argentina. It seems they had factories there. Very rich people. They always fall on their feet. You wouldn't have a cigarette, by any chance?'

'I'm sorry, but I can offer you a Sugus sweet – it's a known fact that they have as much nicotine in them as a Montecristo cigar, and bucketloads of vitamins.'

The caretaker frowned in disbelief, but he accepted. I offered him the lemon Sugus sweet Fermín had given me an eternity ago, which I'd found in my pocket, hidden in a fold of the lining. I hoped it would not be rancid.

'It's good,' ruled the caretaker, sucking at the rubbery sweet.

'You're chewing the pride of the national sweet industry. The Generalissimo swallows them by the handful, like sugared almonds. Tell me, did you ever hear any mention of the Aldayas' daughter, Penélope?'

The caretaker leaned on his broom, in the manner of Rodin's *Thinker*.

'I think you must be mistaken. The Aldayas didn't have any daughters. They were all boys.'

'Are you sure? I know that a young girl called Penélope Aldaya lived in this house around the year 1919. She was probably Jorge's sister.'

'That might be, but as I said, I've only been here since 1920.'

'What about the property? Who owns it now?'

'As far as I know, it's still for sale, though they were talking about knocking it down to build a school. That's the best thing they could do, frankly. Tear it down to its foundations.'

'What makes you say that?'

The caretaker gave me a guarded look. When he smiled, I noticed he was missing at least four upper teeth. 'Those people, the Aldayas. They were a shady lot, if you listen to what people say.'

'I'm afraid I don't. What do people say about them?'

'You know. The noises and all that. Personally, I don't believe in that kind of thing, don't get me wrong, but they say that more than one person has soiled his pants in there.'

'Don't tell me the house is haunted,' I said, suppressing a smile.

'You can laugh. But where there's smoke ...'

'Have you seen anything?'

'Not exactly, no. But I've heard.'

'Heard? What?'

'Well, one night, years ago, when I accompanied Master Joanet. Only because he insisted, you know? I didn't want to have anything to do with that place. . . . As I was saying, I heard something strange there. A sort of sobbing.'

The caretaker produced his own version of the noise to which he was referring. It sounded like someone with consumption humming a litany of folk songs.

'It must have been the wind,' I suggested.

'It must have, but I was scared shitless. Hey, you wouldn't have another one of those sweets, would you?'

'How about a throat lozenge? They tone you up after a sweet.'

'Come on, then,' agreed the caretaker, putting out his hand to collect it.

I gave him the whole box. The strong taste of liquorice seemed to loosen his tongue. He began the extraordinary tale of the Aldaya mansion.

'Between you and me, it's some story. Once, Joanet, Señor Miravell's son, a huge guy, twice your size (he's in the national handball team, that should give you some idea) ... Anyhow, some friends of young Joanet had heard stories about the Aldaya house, and they roped him in. And he roped *me* in, asking me to go with him – all that bragging, and he didn't dare go on his own. Rich kids, what do you expect? He was determined to go in there at night, to show

149

off in front of his girlfriend, and he nearly pissed himself. I mean, now you're looking at it in the daylight, but at night the place looks quite different. Anyway, Joanet says he went up to the second floor (I refused to go in, of course – it can't be legal, even if the house had been abandoned for at least ten years), and he says there was something there. He thought he heard a sort of voice in one of the rooms, but when he tried to go in, the door shut in his face. What do you think of that?'

'I think it was a draught,' I said.

'Or something else,' the caretaker pointed out, lowering his voice. 'The other day it was on the radio: the universe is full of mysteries. Imagine, they think they've found the Holy Shroud, the real one, bang in downtown Toledo. It had been sewn to a cinema screen, to hide it from the Muslims. Apparently they wanted to use it so they could say Jesus Christ was a black man. What do you make of that?'

'I'm speechless.'

'Exactly. Mysteries galore. They should knock that building down and throw lime over the ground.'

I thanked him for the information and was about to turn down the avenue when I looked up and saw Tibidabo Mountain awakening behind the gauzy clouds. Suddenly I felt like taking the funicular up the hill to visit the old amusement park crowning its top and wander among its merry-go-rounds and the eerie automaton halls, but I had promised to be back in the bookshop on time.

As I returned to the station, I pictured Julián Carax walking down that same road, gazing at those same solemn façades that had hardly changed since then, perhaps even waiting to board the blue tram that tiptoed up to heaven. When I reached the foot of the avenue, I took out the photograph of Penélope Aldaya smiling in the courtyard of the family mansion. Her eyes spoke of an untroubled soul and the promise of the future. 'Penélope, who loves you.'

I imagined Julián Carax at my age, holding that image in

his hands, perhaps under the shade of the same tree that now sheltered me. I could almost see him smiling confidently, contemplating a future as wide and luminous as that avenue, and for a moment I thought there were no more ghosts there than those of absence and loss, and that the light that smiled on me was borrowed light, only real as long as I could hold it in my eyes, second by second.

# 18

When I got back home, I realized that Fermín or my father had already opened the bookshop. I went up to the apartment for a moment to have a quick bite. My father had left some toast and jam and a Thermos flask of strong coffee on the dining-room table for me. I polished it all off and was down again in ten minutes, reborn. I entered the bookshop through the door in the back room that adjoined the entrance hall of the building and went straight to my cupboard. I put on the blue apron I usually wore to protect my clothes from the dust on boxes and shelves. At the bottom of the cupboard, I kept an old tin biscuit box, a treasure chest of sorts. There I stored a menagerie of useless bits of rubbish that I couldn't bring myself to throw away: watches and fountain pens damaged beyond repair, old coins, marbles, wartime bullet cases I'd found in Laberinto Park and fading postcards of Barcelona from the turn of the century. Still floating among all those bits and pieces was the old scrap of newspaper on which Isaac Montfort had written down his daughter Nuria's address, the night I went to the Cemetery of Forgotten Books to hide *The Shadow of the Wind*. I examined it in the dusty light that filtered between shelves and piled-up boxes, then closed the tin box and put the address in my wallet. Having resolved to occupy both mind and hands with the most trivial job I could find, I walked into the shop.

'Good morning,' I announced.

Fermín was classifying the contents of various parcels that had arrived from a collector in Salamanca, and my father was struggling to decipher a German catalogue of Lutheran apocrypha.

'And may God grant us an even better afternoon,' sang Fermín – a veiled reference, no doubt, to my meeting with Bea.

I didn't grant him the pleasure of an answer. Instead I turned to the inevitable monthly chore of getting the account book up to date, checking receipts and order forms, collections and payments. The sound of the radio orchestrated our serene monotony, treating us to a selection of hit songs by celebrated crooner Antonio Machín, who was quite fashionable at the time. Caribbean rhythms tended to get on my father's nerves, but he tolerated the tropical soundscape because the tunes reminded Fermín of his beloved Cuba. The scene was repeated every week: my father pretended not to hear, and Fermín would abandon himself to a vague wiggling in time to the *danzón*, punctuating the commercial breaks with anecdotes about his adventures in Havana. The shop door was ajar, and a sweet aroma of fresh bread and coffee wafted through, lifting our spirits. After a while our neighbour Merceditas, who was on her way back from doing her shopping in Boquería Market, stopped by the shop window and peered round the door.

'Good morning, Señor Sempere,' she sang.

My father blushed and smiled at her. I had the feeling that he liked Merceditas, but his monkish manners confined him to an impregnable silence. Fermín ogled her out of the corner of his eye, keeping the tempo with his gentle hip swaying and licking his lips as if a Swiss roll had just walked in through the door. Merceditas opened a paper bag and gave us three shiny apples. I imagined she still fancied the idea of working in the bookshop and made little effort to hide her dislike for Fermín, the usurper.

'Aren't they beautiful? I saw them and said to myself, These are for the Semperes,' she said in an affected tone. 'I know you intellectuals like apples, like that Isaac with his gravity thing, you know.'

'Isaac Newton, pumpkin,' Fermín specified.

Merceditas looked angrily at him. 'Hello, Mr Smarty-pants. You can be grateful that I've brought one for you, too, and not a sour grapefruit, which is what you deserve.'

'But, woman, coming from your nubile hands, this offering, this fleshy fruit of original sin, ignites my—'

'Fermín, please,' interrupted my father.

'Yes, Señor Sempere,' said Fermín obediently, beating a retreat.

Merceditas was on the point of shooting something back at Fermín when we heard an uproar in the street. We all fell silent, listening expectantly. We could hear indignant cries outside, followed by a surge of murmuring. Merceditas carefully put her head round the door. We saw a number of shopkeepers walk by looking uncomfortable and swearing under their breath. Soon Don Anacleto Olmo appeared – a resident of our block and unofficial spokesman for the Royal Academy of Language in the neighbourhood. Don Anacleto was a secondary-school teacher with a degree in Spanish literature and a handful of other Humanities, and he shared an apartment on the first floor with seven cats. When he was not teaching, he moonlighted as a blurb writer for a prestigious publishing firm, and it was rumoured that he also composed erotic verse that he published under the saucy alias of 'Humberto Peacock'. While among friends Don Anacleto was an unassuming, genial fellow, in public he felt obliged to act the part of declamatory poet, and the affected purple prose of his speech had won him the nickname of 'the Victorian'.

That morning the teacher's face was pink with distress, and his hands, in which he held his ivory cane, were almost shaking. All four of us stared at him.

'Don Anacleto, what's the matter?' asked my father.

'Franco has died, please say he has,' prompted Fermín.

'Shut up, you beast,' Merceditas cut in. 'Let the doctor talk.'

Don Anacleto took a deep breath, regained his composure, and, with his customary majesty, unfolded his account of what had happened.

'Dear friends, life is the stuff of drama, and even the noblest of the Lord's creatures can taste the bitterness of destiny's capricious and obstinate ways. Last night, in the small hours, while the city enjoyed the well-deserved sleep of all hardworking people, Don Federico Flaviá i Pujades, a well-loved neighbour who has so greatly contributed to this community's enrichment and solace in his role as watchmaker, only three doors down from this bookshop, was arrested by the State Police.'

I felt my heart sink.

'Jesus, Mary, and Joseph!' remarked Merceditas.

Fermín puffed with disappointment, for it was clear that the dictator remained in perfect health.

Well on his way now, Don Anacleto took a deep breath and prepared to go on:

'According to a reliable account revealed to me by sources close to Police Headquarters, last night, shortly after midnight, two bemedalled undercover members of the Crime Squad caught Don Federico clad in the lush, licentious costume of a diva and singing risqué variety songs on the stage of some dive in Calle Escudillers, where he was allegedly entertaining an audience mostly made up of cerebrally deficient members of the public. These godforsaken creatures, who had eloped that same afternoon from the sheltering premises of a hospice belonging to a religious order, had pulled down their trousers in the frenzy of the show and were dancing about with no restraint, clapping their hands, with their privates in full view, and drooling.'

Merceditas made the sign of the cross, alarmed by the salacious turn events were taking.

'On learning of what had transpired, the pious mothers

154

of some of those poor souls made a formal complaint on the grounds of public scandal and affront to the most basic code of morality. The press, that nefarious vulture that feeds on misfortune and dishonour, did not take long to pick up the scent of carrion. Thanks to the wretched offices of a professional informer, not forty minutes had elapsed since the arrival of the two members of the police when Kiko Calabuig appeared on the scene. Calabuig, ace reporter for the muckraking daily *El Caso*, was determined to uncover whatever deplorable vignettes were necessary and to leave no shady stone unturned in order to spice up his lurid report in time for today's edition. Needless to say, the spectacle that took place in those premises is described with tabloid viciousness as horrifying and Dantesque, in twenty-four-point headlines.'

'This can't be right,' said my father. 'I thought Don Federico had learned his lesson.'

Don Anacleto gave a priestly nod. 'Yes, but don't forget the old sayings: "The leopard cannot change his spots," and "Man cannot live by bromide alone. . . ." And you still haven't heard the worst.'

'Then, please, sire, could you get to the frigging point? Because with all this metaphorical spin and flourish, I'm beginning to feel a fiery bowel movement at the gates,' Fermín protested.

'Pay no attention to this animal. I love the way you speak. It's like the voice on the newsreel, Dr Anacleto,' interposed Merceditas.

'Thank you, child, but I'm only a humble teacher. So, back to what I was saying, without further delay, preambles or frills. It seems that the watchmaker, who at the time of his arrest was going by the nom de guerre of "Lady of the Curls", had already been arrested under similar circumstances on a couple of occasions – which were registered in the annals of crime by the guardians of law and order.'

'Criminals with a badge, you mean,' Fermín spat out.

'I don't get involved in politics. But I can tell you that,

after knocking poor Don Federico off the stage with a well-aimed bottle, the two officers led him to the police station in Vía Layetana. With a bit of luck, and under different circumstances, things would just have ended up with some joke cracking and perhaps a couple of slaps in the face and other minor humiliations, but, by great misfortune, it so happened that the noted Inspector Fumero was on duty last night.'

'Fumero,' muttered Fermín. The very mention of his nemesis made him shudder.

'The one and only. As I was saying, the champion of urban safety, who had just returned from a triumphant raid on an illegal betting and beetle-racing establishment on Calle Vigatans, was informed about what had happened by the anguished mother of one of the missing boys and the alleged mastermind behind the escapade, Pepet Guardiola. At that the famous inspector, who, it appears, had knocked back some twelve double shots of brandy since suppertime, decided to intervene in the matter. After examining the aggravating factors at hand, Fumero proceeded to inform the sergeant on duty that so much *faggotry* (and I cite the word in its starkest literal sense, despite the presence of a young lady, for its documentary relevance to the events in question) required a lesson, and that what the watchmaker – that is to say, our Don Federico Flaviá i Pujades – needed, for his own good and that of the immortal souls of the Mongoloid children, whose presence was incidental but a deciding factor in the case, was to spend the night in a common cell, down in the lower basement of the institution, in the company of a select group of thugs. As you probably know, this cell is famous in the criminal world for its inhospitable and precarious sanitary conditions, and the inclusion of an ordinary citizen in the list of guests is always cause for celebration, for it adds spice and novelty to the monotony of prison life.'

Having reached this point, Don Anacleto proceeded to

sketch a brief but endearing portrait of the victim, whom, of course, we all knew well.

'I don't need to remind you that Señor Flaviá i Pujades has been blessed with a fragile and delicate personality, all goodness of heart and Christian charity. If a fly finds its way into his shop, instead of smashing it with a slipper, he'll open the door and windows wide so that the insect, one of God's creatures, is swept back by the draught into the ecosystem. I know that Don Federico is a man of faith, always very devout and involved in parish activities, but all his life he has had to live with a hidden compulsion, which, on very rare occasions, has got the better of him, sending him off into the streets dolled up as a tart. His ability to mend anything from wristwatches to sewing machines is legendary, and as a person he is well loved by every one of us who knew him and frequented his establishment, even by those who did not approve of his occasional night escapades sporting a wig, a comb and a flamenco dress.'

'You speak of him as if he were dead,' ventured Fermín with dismay.

'Not dead, thank God.'

I heaved a sigh of relief. Don Federico lived with his deaf octogenarian mother, known in the neighbourhood as 'La Pepita', who was famous for letting off hurricane-force wind capable of stunning the sparrows on her balcony and sending them spiralling down to the ground.

'Little did Pepita imagine that her Federico,' continued the schoolteacher, 'had spent the night in a filthy cell, where a whole band of pimps and roughnecks had handled him like a party whore, only to give him the beating of his life when they had tired of his lean flesh, while the rest of the inmates sang in chorus, "Pansy, pansy, eat shit you old dandy!"'

A deadly silence came over us. Merceditas sobbed. Fermín tried to comfort her with a tender embrace, but she jumped to one side.

'Imagine the scene,' Don Anacleto concluded.

The epilogue to the story did nothing to raise our hopes. Halfway through the morning, a grey police van had dumped Don Federico on his doorstep. He was covered in blood, his dress was in shreds, and he had lost his wig and his collection of fine costume jewellery. He had been urinated on, and his face was full of cuts and bruises. The baker's son had discovered him huddled in the doorframe, shaking and crying like a baby.

'It's not fair, no, sir,' argued Merceditas, positioned by the door of the bookshop, far from Fermín's wandering hands. 'Poor thing, he has a heart of gold, and he always minds his own business. So he likes dressing up as a Gypsy and singing in front of people? Who cares? People are evil.'

'Not evil,' Fermín objected. 'Moronic, which isn't quite the same thing. Evil presupposes a moral decision, intention, and some forethought. A moron or a lout, however, doesn't stop to think or reason. He acts on instinct, like an animal, convinced that he's doing good, that he's always right, and sanctimoniously proud to go around fucking up, if you'll excuse the French, anyone he perceives to be different from himself, be it because of skin colour, creed, language, nationality or, as in the case of Don Federico, his leisure pursuits. What the world really needs are more thoroughly evil people and fewer borderline pigheads.'

'Don't talk nonsense. What we need is a bit more Christian charity and less spitefulness. We're a disgraceful lot,' Merceditas cut in. 'Everybody goes to mass, but nobody pays attention to the words of Our Lord Jesus Christ.'

'Merceditas, let's not mention the missal industry. That's part of the problem, not the solution.'

'There goes the atheist again. And what has the clergy ever done to you, may I ask?'

'Come on, don't quarrel now,' interrupted my father. 'And you, Fermín, go and see about Don Federico, find out whether he needs anything, whether he wants someone to go to the chemist's for him or have something bought at the market.'

'Yes, Señor Sempere. Right away. Oratory is my undoing, as you know.'

'Your undoing is the shamelessness and the irreverence you carry around with you,' said Merceditas. 'Blasphemer. You ought to have your soul cleaned out with hydrochloric acid.'

'Look here, Merceditas, because I know you're a good person (though a bit narrow-minded and as ignorant as a brick), and because right now we're facing a social emergency, in the face of which one must prioritize one's efforts, I will refrain from clarifying a few cardinal points for you—'

'Fermín!' cried my father.

Fermín closed his mouth and rushed out of the shop. Merceditas watched him with disapproval.

'That man is going to get you into trouble one of these days, mark my words. He's an anarchist, a Mason, or a Jew at the very least. With that great big nose of his—'

'Pay no attention to him. He likes to be contradictory.'

Merceditas looked annoyed and shook her head. 'Well, I'll leave you now. Some of us have more than one job to do, and time is short. Good morning.'

We all nodded politely and watched her walk away, straight-backed, taking it out on the street with her high heels. My father drew a deep breath, as if wanting to inhale the peace that had just been recovered. Don Anacleto sagged next to him, having finally descended from his flights of rhetoric. His face was pale, and a sad autumnal look had flooded his eyes. 'This country has gone to the dogs,' he said.

'Come now, Don Anacleto, cheer up. Things have always

been like this, here and everywhere else. The trouble is, there are some low moments, and when those strike close to home, everything looks blacker. You'll see how Don Federico overcomes this. He's stronger than we all think.'

The teacher was mumbling under his breath. 'It's like the tide, you see?' he said, beside himself. 'The savagery, I mean. It goes away, and you feel safe, but it always returns, it always returns . . . and it chokes us. I see it every day at school. My God . . . Apes, that's what we get in the classrooms. Darwin was a dreamer, I can assure you. No evolution or anything of the sort. For every one who can reason, I have to battle with nine orangutans.'

We could only nod meekly. Don Anacleto raised a hand to say goodbye and left, his head bowed. He looked five years older than when he came in. My father sighed. We glanced at each other briefly, not knowing what to say. I wondered whether I should tell him about Inspector Fumero's visit to the bookshop. This has been a warning, I thought. A caution. Fumero had used poor Don Federico as a telegram.

'Is anything the matter, Daniel? You're pale.'

I sighed and looked down. I started to tell him about the incident with Inspector Fumero the other day and his threats. My father listened, containing the anger that the burning in his eyes betrayed.

'It's my fault,' I said. I should have said something. . . .'

My father shook his head. 'No. You couldn't have known, Daniel.'

'But—'

'Don't even think about it. And not a word to Fermín. God knows how he would react if he knew the man was after him again.'

'But we have to do something.'

'Make sure he doesn't get into trouble.'

I nodded, not very convinced, and began to continue the work Fermín had started while my father returned to his correspondence. Between paragraphs my father would look over at me. I pretended not to notice.

'How did it go with Professor Velázquez yesterday? Everything all right?' he asked, eager to change the subject.

'Yes. He was pleased with the books. He mentioned that he was looking for a book of Franco's letters.'

'The *Moorslayer* book. But it's apocryphal . . . a joke by Madariaga. What did you say to him?'

'That we were on the case and would give him some news in two weeks' time at the latest.'

'Well done. We'll put Fermín on the case and charge Velázquez a fortune.'

I nodded. We continued going through the motions of our routine. My father was still looking at me. Here we go, I thought.

'Yesterday a very pleasant girl came by the shop. Fermín says she's Tomás Aguilar's sister?'

'Yes.'

My father nodded, considering the coincidence with an expression of mild surprise. He granted me a moment's peace before he charged at me again, this time adopting the look of someone who has just remembered something.

'By the way, Daniel, we're not going to be very busy today, and, well, maybe you'd like to take some time off to do your own thing. Besides, I think you've been working too hard lately.'

'I'm fine, thanks.'

'I was even considering leaving Fermín here and going along to the Liceo Opera House with Barceló. This afternoon they're performing *Tannhäuser*, and he's invited me, as he has a few seats reserved in the stalls.' My father pretended to be reading his letters. He was a dreadful actor.

'Since when have you liked Wagner?'

He shrugged his shoulders. 'Never look a gift horse in the mouth. . . . Besides, with Barceló it makes no difference what it is, because he spends the whole show commenting on the performance and criticizing the wardrobe and the tempo. He often asks after you. Perhaps you should go around to see him at the shop one day.'

'One of these days.'

'Right, then, if you agree, let's leave Fermín in charge today and we'll go out and enjoy ourselves a bit. It's about time. And if you need any money...'

'Dad. Bea is not my girlfriend.'

'Who said anything about girlfriends? That's settled, then. It's up to you. If you need any money, take it from the till, but leave a note so Fermín doesn't get a fright when he closes at the end of the day.'

Having said that, he feigned absentmindedness and wandered into the back room, smiling from ear to ear. I looked at my watch. It was ten-thirty in the morning. I had arranged to meet Bea at five in the university cloister, and, to my dismay, the day was turning out to be longer than *The Brothers Karamazov*.

Fermín soon returned from the watchmaker's home and informed us that a commando team of local women had set up a permanent guard to attend to poor Don Federico, whom the doctor had diagnosed as having three broken ribs, a large number of bruises, and an uncommonly severe rectal tear.

'Did you have to buy anything?' asked my father.

'They had enough medicines and ointments to open a pharmacy, so I took the liberty of buying him some flowers, a bottle of cologne, and three jars of peach juice – Don Federico's favourite.'

'You did the right thing. Let me know what I owe you,' said my father. 'And how did you find him?'

'Beaten to a pulp, quite frankly. Just to see him huddled up in his bed like a ball of wool, moaning that he wanted to die, made me want to kill someone, believe me. I feel like showing up at the offices of the Crime Squad and bumping off half a dozen of those pricks with a blunderbuss, beginning with that stinking ball of pus, Fumero.'

'Fermín, let's have some peace and quiet. I strictly forbid you to do anything of the sort.'

'Whatever you say, Señor Sempere.'

'And how has Pepita taken it?'

'With exemplary courage. The neighbours have doped her with shots of brandy, and when I saw her, she had collapsed onto the sofa and was snoring like a boar and letting off farts that bored bullet-holes through the upholstery.'

'True to character. Fermín, I'm going to ask you to look after the shop today; I'm going round to Don Federico's for a while. Later I've arranged to meet Barceló. And Daniel has things to do.'

I raised my eyes just in time to catch Fermín and my father exchanging meaningful looks.

'What a couple of matchmakers,' I said. They were still laughing at me when I walked out through the door.


A cold, piercing breeze swept the streets, scattering strips of mist in its path. The steely sun snatched copper reflections from the roofs and belfries of the Gothic quarter. There were still some hours to go until my appointment with Bea in the university cloister, so I decided to try my luck and call on Nuria Monfort, hoping she was still living at the address provided by her father some time ago.

Plaza de San Felipe Neri is like a small breathing space in the maze of streets that crisscross the Gothic quarter, hidden behind the old Roman walls. The holes left by machine-gun fire during the war pockmark the church walls. That morning a group of children played soldiers, oblivious to the memory of the stones. A young woman, her hair streaked with silver, watched them from the bench where she sat with an open book on her lap and an absent smile. The address showed that Nuria Monfort lived in a building by the entrance to the square. The year of its construction was still visible on the blackened stone arch that crowned the front door: 1801. Once I was in the hallway, there was just enough light to make out the shadowy chamber from which a staircase twisted upwards in an erratic spiral. I inspected the beehive of brass letterboxes. The names of the tenants appeared on pieces of yellowed card inserted in slots, as was common in those days.

*Miquel Moliner / Nuria Monfort*
*3.º-2.ª*

I went up slowly, almost fearing that the building would collapse if I were to tread firmly on those tiny doll's-house steps. There were two doors on every landing, with no number or sign. When I reached the third floor, I chose one at random and rapped on it with my knuckles. The staircase smelled of damp, of old stone, and of clay. I rapped a few times but got no answer. I decided to try my luck with the other door. I knocked with my fist three times. Inside the apartment I could hear a radio blaring the pious daily broadcast, *Moments for Reflection with Father Martín Calzado.*

The door was opened by a woman in a padded turquoise-blue checked dressing gown, slippers, and a helmet of curlers. In that dim light, she looked like a deep-sea diver. Behind her the velvety voice of Father Martín Calzado was devoting some words to the sponsors of the programme, a brand of beauty products called Aurorín, much favoured by pilgrims to the sanctuary of Lourdes and with miraculous properties when it came to pustules and warts.

'Good afternoon. I'm looking for Señora Monfort.'

'Nurieta? You've got the wrong door, young man. It's the one opposite.'

'I'm so sorry. It's just that I knocked and there was no answer.'

'You're not a debt collector, are you?' asked the neighbour suddenly, suspicious from experience.

'No. Señora Monfort's father sent me.'

'Ah, all right. Nurieta must be down below, reading. Didn't you see her when you came up?'

When I got to the bottom of the stairs, I saw that the woman with the silvery hair and the book in her hands was still fixed on her bench in the square. I observed her carefully. Nuria Monfort was a beautiful woman, with the sort of features that graced fashion magazines or studio portraits, but a woman whose youth seemed to be ebbing away in the sadness of her eyes. There was something of her father in her slightness of build. I imagined she must be in her early forties, judging from the grey hair and the lines that aged her face. In a soft light, she would have seemed ten years younger.

'Señora Monfort?'

She looked at me as though waking up from a trance, without seeing me.

'My name is Daniel. Your father gave me your address sometime ago. He said you might be able to talk to me about Julián Carax.'

When she heard those words, her dreamy look left her. I had a feeling that mentioning her father had not been a good idea.

'What is it you want?' she asked suspiciously.

I felt that if I didn't gain her trust at that very moment, I would have blown my one chance. The only card I could play was to tell the truth.

'Please let me explain. Eight years ago, almost by chance, I found a novel by Julián Carax in the Cemetery of Forgotten Books. You had hidden it there to save it from being destroyed by a man who calls himself Laín Coubert,' I said.

She stared at me, without moving, as if she were afraid that the world around her was going to fall apart.

'I'll only take a few minutes of your time,' I added. 'I promise.'

She nodded, with a look of resignation. 'How's my father?' she asked, avoiding my eyes.

'He's well. He's aged a little. And he misses you a lot.'

Nuria Monfort let out a sigh I couldn't decipher. 'You'd better come up to the apartment. I don't want to talk about this in the street.'

## 20

Nuria Monfort lived adrift in shadows. A narrow corridor led to a dining room that also served as kitchen, library, and office. On the way, I noticed a modest bedroom, with no windows. That was all, other than a tiny bathroom with no shower or tub out of which all kinds of odours emanated, from smells of cooking from the bar below to a musty stench of pipes and drains that dated from the turn of the century. The entire apartment was sunk in perpetual gloom, like a block of darkness propped up between peeling walls. It smelled of black tobacco, cold, and absence. Nuria Monfort observed me while I pretended not to notice the precarious condition of her home.

'I go down to the street because there's hardly any light in the apartment,' she said. 'My husband has promised to give me a reading lamp when he comes back.'

'Is your husband away?'

'Miquel is in prison.'

'I'm sorry, I didn't know. . . .'

'You couldn't have known. I'm not ashamed of telling you, because he isn't a criminal. This last time they took him away for printing leaflets for the metalworkers' union. That was two years ago. The neighbours think he's in America, travelling. My father doesn't know either, and I wouldn't like him to find out.'

'Don't worry. He won't find out through me,' I said.

A tense silence wove itself around us, and I imagined she was considering whether I was a spy sent by Isaac.

'It must be hard to run a house on your own,' I said stupidly, just to fill the void.

'It's not easy. I get what money I can from translations, but with a husband in prison, that's not nearly enough. The lawyers have bled me dry, and I'm up to my neck in debt. Translating is almost as badly paid as writing.'

She looked at me as if she was expecting an answer. I just smiled meekly. 'You translate books?'

'Not anymore. Now I've started to translate forms, contracts and customs documents – that pays much better. You only get a pittance for translating literature, though a bit more than for writing it, it's true. The residents' association has already tried to throw me out a couple of times. The least of their worries is that I'm behind with the maintenance fees. You can imagine, a woman who speaks foreign languages and wears trousers. . . . More than one neighbour has accused me of running a house of ill repute. I should be so lucky. . . .'

I hoped the darkness would hide my blushing.

'I'm sorry. I don't know why I'm telling you all this. I'm embarrassing you.'

'It's my fault. I asked.'

She laughed nervously. She seemed surrounded by a burning aura of loneliness.

'You remind me a bit of Julián,' she said suddenly. 'The way you look, and your gestures. He used to do what you are doing now. He would stare at you without saying a word, and you wouldn't know what he was thinking, and so, like an idiot, you'd tell him things it would have been better to keep to yourself. . . . Can I offer you anything? A cup of coffee maybe?'

'Nothing, thanks. I don't want to trouble you.'

'It's no trouble. I was about to make one for myself.'

Something told me that that cup of coffee was all she was

having for lunch. I refused again and watched her walk over to a corner of the dining room where there was a small electric stove.

'Make yourself comfortable,' she said, her back to me.

I looked around and asked myself how. Nuria Monfort's office consisted of a desk that took up the corner next to the balcony, an Underwood typewriter with an oil lamp beside it, and a shelf full of dictionaries and manuals. There were no family photos, but the wall by the desk was covered with postcards, all of them pictures of a bridge I remembered seeing somewhere but couldn't pinpoint; perhaps Paris or Rome. Beneath this display the desk betrayed an almost obsessive neatness and order. The pencils were sharpened and perfectly lined up. The papers and folders were arranged and placed in three symmetrical rows. When I turned around, I realized that Nuria Montfort was gazing at me from the entrance to the corridor. She regarded me in silence, the way one looks at strangers in the street or in the subway. She lit a cigarette and stayed where she was, her face masked by spirals of blue smoke. I suddenly thought that, despite herself, Nuria Montfort exuded a certain air of the femme fatale, like those women in the movies who dazzled Fermín when they materialized out of the mist of a Berlin station, enveloped in halos of light, the sort of beautiful women whose own appearance bored them.

'There's not much to tell,' she began. 'I met Julián over twenty years ago, in Paris. At that time I was working for Cabestany, the publishing house. Señor Cabestany had acquired the rights to Julián's novels for peanuts. At first I worked in the accounts department, but when Cabestany found out that I spoke French, Italian, and a little German, he moved me to the purchasing department, and I became his personal secretary. One of my jobs was to correspond with foreign authors and publishers with whom our firm had business, and that's how I came into contact with Julián Carax.'

'Your father told me you two were good friends.'

'My father probably told you we had a fling, or something along those lines, right? According to him, I run after anything in trousers, like a bitch on heat.'

The woman's frankness and her brazen manner left me speechless. I took too long to come up with an acceptable reply. By then Nuria Monfort was smiling to herself and shaking her head.

'Pay no attention to him. My father got that idea from a trip to Paris I once had to make, back in 1933, to resolve some matters between Señor Cabestany and Gallimard. I spent a week in the city and stayed in Julián's apartment for the simple reason that Cabestany preferred to save on hotel expenses. Very romantic, as you can see. Until then my relationship with Julián Carax had been conducted strictly by letter, normally dealing with copyright, proofs, or editorial matters. What I knew about him, or imagined, had come from reading the manuscripts he sent us.'

'Did he tell you anything about his life in Paris?'

'No. Julián didn't like talking about his books or about himself. I didn't think he was happy in Paris. Though he gave the impression that he was one of those people who cannot be happy anywhere. The truth is, I never got to know him well. He wouldn't let you. He was a very private person, and sometimes it seemed to me that he was no longer interested in the world or in other people. Señor Cabestany thought he was shy and perhaps a bit crazy, but I got the feeling that Julián was living in the past, locked in his memories. Julián lived within himself, for his books and inside them – a comfortable prison of his own design.'

'You say this as if you envied him.'

'There are worse prisons than words, Daniel.'

I nodded, not quite sure what she meant.

'Did Julián ever talk about those memories, about his years in Barcelona?'

'Very little. During the week I stayed with him in Paris, he told me a bit about his family. His mother was French, a music teacher. His father had a hat shop or something like that. I know he was a very religious man, and very strict.'

'Did Julián explain to you what sort of a relationship he had with him?'

'I know they didn't get on at all. It was something that went back a long time. In fact, the reason Julián went to Paris was to avoid being put into the army by his father. His mother had promised him she would take him as far away as possible from that man, rather than let that happen.'

'But "that" man was his father, after all.'

Nuria Monfort smiled. It was just a hint of a smile, and her eyes shone weary and sad.

'Even if he was, he never behaved like one, and Julián never considered him as such. Once he confessed to me that before getting married, his mother had had an affair with a stranger whose name she never revealed to him. That man was Julián's real father.'

'It sounds like the beginning of *The Shadow of the Wind*. Do you think he told you the truth?'

Nuria Monfort nodded. 'Julián told me he had grown up watching how the hatter – that's what he called him – insulted and beat his mother. Then he would go into Julián's room and tell him he was the son of sin, that he had inherited his mother's weak and despicable character and would be miserable all his life, a failure at whatever he tried to do. . . .'

'Did Julián feel resentful towards his father?'

'Time is a great healer. I never felt that Julián hated him. Perhaps that would have been better. I got the impression that he lost all respect for the hatter as a result of all those scenes. Julián spoke about it as if it didn't matter to him, as if it were part of a past he had left behind, but these things are never forgotten. The words with which a child's heart is poisoned, whether through malice or through ignorance, remain branded in his memory, and sooner or later they burn his soul.'

I wondered whether she was talking from experience,

and the image of my friend Tomás Aguilar came to my mind once more, listening stoically to the diatribes of his haughty father.

'How old was Julián when his father started speaking to him like that?'

'About eight or ten, I imagine.'

I sighed.

'As soon as he was old enough to join the army, his mother took him to Paris. I don't think they even said goodbye. The hatter could never accept that his family had abandoned him.'

'Did you ever hear Julián mention a girl called Penélope?'

'Penélope? I don't think so. I'd remember.'

'She was a girlfriend of his, from the time when he still lived in Barcelona.'

I pulled out the photograph of Carax and Penélope Aldaya and handed it to her. I noticed how a smile lit up her face when she saw an adolescent Julián Carax. Nostalgia and loss were consuming her.

'He looks so young here.... Is this the Penélope you mentioned?'

I nodded.

'Very good-looking. Julián always managed to be surrounded by pretty women.'

Like you, I thought. 'Do you know whether he had lots. . . ?'

That smile again, at my expense. 'Girlfriends? Lovers? I don't know. To tell you the truth, I never heard him speak about any woman in his life. Once, just to needle him, I asked him. You must know that he earned his living playing the piano in a hostess bar. I asked him whether he wasn't tempted, surrounded all day by beautiful women of easy virtue. He didn't find the joke funny. He replied that he had no right to love anyone, that he deserved to be alone.'

'Did he say why?'

'Julián never said why.'

'Even so, in the end, shortly before returning to Barcelona in 1936, Julián Carax was going to get married.'

'So they say.'

'Do you doubt it?'

She looked sceptical as she shrugged her shoulders. 'As I said, in all the years we knew one another, Julián never mentioned any woman in particular, and even less one he was going to marry. The story about his supposed marriage reached me later. Neuval, Carax's last publisher, told Cabestany that the fiancée was a woman twenty years older than Julián, a rich widow in poor health. According to Neuval, she had been more or less supporting him for years. The doctors gave her six months to live, a year at the most. Neuval said she wanted to marry Julián so that he could inherit from her.'

'But the marriage ceremony never took place.'

'If there ever was such a plan, or such a widow.'

'From what I know, Carax was involved in a duel, on the dawn of the very day he was due to be married. Do you know who with, or why?'

'Neuval supposed it was someone connected to the widow. A greedy distant relative who didn't want to see the inheritance fall into the hands of some upstart. Neuval mostly published penny dreadfuls, and I think the genre had gone to his head.'

'I can see you don't really believe the story of the wedding and the duel.'

'No. I never believed it.'

'What do you think happened, then? Why did Carax return to Barcelona?'

She smiled sadly. 'I've been asking myself the same question for seventeen years.'

Nuria Monfort lit another cigarette. She offered me one. I was tempted to accept but refused.

'But you must have some theory?' I suggested.

'All I know is that in the summer of 1936, shortly after the outbreak of the war, an employee at the municipal morgue phoned our firm to say they had received the body of Julián Carax three days earlier. They'd found him dead in an alleyway of the Raval quarter, dressed in rags and with a bullet through his heart. He had a book on him, a copy of *The Shadow of the Wind,* and his passport. The stamp showed he'd crossed the French border a month before. Where he had been during that time, nobody knew. The police contacted his father, but he refused to take responsibility for the body, alleging that he didn't have a son. After two days without anyone claiming the corpse, he was buried in a common grave in Montjuïc Cemetery. I couldn't even take him flowers, because nobody could tell me where he'd been buried. It was the employee at the morgue, who had kept the book found in Julián's jacket, who had the idea of phoning Cabestany's publishing house a couple of days later. That is how I found out what had happened. I couldn't understand it. If Julián had anyone left in Barcelona to whom he could turn, it was me or, at a pinch, Cabestany. We were his only friends, but he never told us he'd returned. We only knew he'd come back to Barcelona after he died. . . .'

'Were you able to find out anything else after getting the news?'

'No. Those were the first months of the war, and Julián was not the only one to disappear without a trace. Nobody talks about it anymore, but there are lots of nameless graves, like Julián's. Asking was like banging your head against a brick wall. With the help of Señor Cabestany, who by then was very ill, I made a complaint to the police and pulled all the strings I could. All I got out of it was a visit from a young inspector, an arrogant, sinister sort, who told me it would be a good idea not to ask any more questions and to concentrate my efforts on having a more positive attitude, because the country was in full cry, on a crusade. Those were his words. His name was Fumero, that's all I remember. It seems that now he's quite an important man.

He's often mentioned in the papers. Maybe you've heard of him.'

I swallowed. 'Vaguely.'

'I heard nothing more about Julián until someone got in touch with the publishers and said he was interested in acquiring all the copies of Carax's novels that were left in the warehouse.'

'Laín Coubert.'

Nuria Monfort nodded.

'Have you any idea who that man was?'

'I have an inkling, but I'm not sure. In March 1936 – I remember the date because at the time we were preparing *The Shadow of the Wind* for press – someone called the publishers to ask for his address. He said he was an old friend and he wanted to visit Julián in Paris. Give him a surprise. They put him onto me, and I said I wasn't authorized to give out that information.'

'Did he say who he was?'

'Someone called Jorge.'

'Jorge Aldaya?'

'It might have been. Julián had mentioned him on more than one occasion. I think they had been at San Gabriel's school together, and sometimes Julián referred to him as if he'd been his best friend.'

'Did you know that Jorge Aldaya was Penélope's brother?'

Nuria Monfort frowned. She looked disconcerted.

'Did you give Aldaya Julián's address in Paris?'

'No. He made me feel uneasy.'

'What did he say?'

'He laughed at me, he said he'd find him some other way, and hung up.'

Something seemed to be gnawing at her. I began to suspect where the conversation was taking us. 'But you heard from him again, didn't you?'

She nodded nervously. 'As I was telling you, shortly after Julián's disappearance that man turned up at Cabestany's firm. By then Cabestany could no longer work, and his eldest son had taken charge of the business. The visitor, Laín Coubert, offered to buy all the remaining stock of Julián's novels. I thought the whole thing was a joke in poor taste. Laín Coubert was a character in *The Shadow of the Wind*.'

'The devil.'

Nuria Monfort nodded again.

'Did you actually see Laín Coubert?'

She shook her head and lit her third cigarette. 'No. But I heard part of the conversation with the son in Señor Cabestany's office.'

She left the sentence in the air, as if she were afraid of finishing it or wasn't sure how to. The cigarette trembled in her fingers.

'His voice,' she said. 'It was the same voice as the man who phoned saying he was Jorge Aldaya. Cabestany's son, the arrogant idiot, tried to ask for more money. Coubert – or whoever he was – said he had to think about the offer. That very night Cabestany's warehouse in Pueblo Nuevo went up in flames, and Julián's books went with it.'

'Except for the ones you rescued and hid in the Cemetery of Forgotten Books.'

'That's right.'

'Have you any idea why anyone would have wanted to burn all of Julián Carax's books?'

'Why are books burned? Through stupidity, ignorance, hatred ... goodness only knows.'

'Why do you think?' I insisted.

'Julián lived in his books. The body that ended up in the morgue was only a part of him. His soul is in his stories. I once asked him who inspired him to create his characters, and his answer was no one. That all of his characters were himself.'

'So if somebody wanted to destroy him, he'd have to destroy those stories and those characters, isn't that right?'

The dispirited smile returned, a tired gesture of defeat.

'You remind me of Julián,' she said. 'Before he lost his faith.'

'His faith in what?'

'In everything.'

She came up to me in the half-light and took my hand. She stroked my palm in silence, as if she wanted to read the lines on my skin. My hand was shaking under her touch. I caught myself tracing the shape of her body under those old, borrowed clothes. I wanted to touch her and feel her pulse burning under her skin. Our eyes had met, and I felt sure that she knew what I was thinking. I sensed that she was lonelier than ever. I raised my eyes and met her serene, open gaze.

'Julián died alone, convinced that nobody would remember him or his books and that his life had meant nothing,' she said. 'He would have liked to know that somebody wanted to keep him alive, that someone remembered him. He used to say that we exist as long as somebody remembers us.'

I was filled by an almost painful desire to kiss this woman, an eagerness such as I had never experienced before, not even when I conjured up the ghost of Clara Barceló. She read my thoughts.

'It's getting late for you, Daniel,' she murmured.

One part of me wanted to stay, to lose myself in this strange intimacy, to hear her say again how my gestures and my silences reminded her of Julián Carax.

'Yes,' I mumbled.

She nodded but said nothing, and then escorted me to the door. The corridor seemed endless. She opened the door for me, and I went out onto the landing.

'If you see my father, tell him I'm well. Lie to him.'

I said goodbye to her in a low voice, thanking her for her time and holding out my hand politely. Nuria Monfort ignored my formal gesture. She placed her hands on my arms, leaned forward, and kissed me on the cheek. We gazed at one another, and this time I searched her lips, almost trembling. It seemed to me that they parted a little, and that her fingers were reaching for my face. At the last moment, Nuria Monfort moved away and looked down.

'I think it's best if you leave, Daniel,' she whispered.

I thought she was about to cry, but before I could say anything, she closed the door. I was left on the landing, sensing her presence on the other side of the door, motionless, asking myself what had happened in there. At the other end of the landing, the neighbour's spy-hole was blinking. I waved at her and attacked the stairs. When I reached the street, I could still feel Nuria Monfort's face, her voice, and her smell, deep in my soul. I carried the trace of her lips, of her breath on my skin through streets full of faceless people escaping from offices and shops. When I turned into Calle Canuda, an icy wind hit me, cutting through the bustle. I welcomed the cold air on my face and walked up towards the university. After crossing the Ramblas, I made my way towards Calle Tallers and disappeared into its narrow canyon of shadows, feeling that I was still trapped in that dark, gloomy dining room where I now imagined Nuria Monfort sitting alone, silently tidying up her pencils, her folders, and her memories, her eyes poisoned with tears.

## 21

Dusk fell almost surreptitiously, with a cold breeze and a mantle of purple light that slid between the gaps in the streets. I quickened my pace, and twenty minutes later the front of the university emerged like an ochre ship anchored in the night. In his lodge the porter of the Literature department perused the words of the nation's most influential bylines in the afternoon edition of the sports pages. There seemed to be hardly any students left in the premises. The echo of my footsteps followed me through the corridors and galleries that led to the cloister, where the glow of two yellowish lights barely disturbed the shadows. It suddenly occurred to me that perhaps Bea had tricked me, that she'd arranged to meet me there at that untimely hour as some sort of revenge. The leaves on the orange trees in the cloister shimmered like silver tears, and the sound of the fountain echoed through the arches. I looked carefully around the courtyard, contemplating disappointment or maybe a certain cowardly sense of relief. There she was, sitting on one of the benches, her silhouette outlined against the fountain, her eyes looking up towards the vaults of the cloister. I stopped at the entrance to gaze at her, and for a moment I was reminded of Nuria Monfort daydreaming on her bench in the square. I noticed she didn't have her folder or her books with her, and I suspected she hadn't had any classes that afternoon. Perhaps she'd come here just to meet me. I swallowed hard and walked into the cloister. The sound of my footsteps gave me away and Bea looked up, with a smile of surprise, as if my presence there were just a coincidence.

'I thought you weren't coming,' said Bea.

'That's just what I thought,' I replied.

She remained seated, upright, her knees tight together and her hands on her lap. I asked myself how I could feel so detached from her and at the same time read every little detail of her lips.

'I've come because I want to prove to you that you were wrong about what you said the other day, Daniel. I'm going to marry Pablo, and I don't care what you show me tonight. I'm going to El Ferrol as soon as he's finished his military service.'

I looked at her as if I'd just had the rug pulled out from under my feet. I realized I'd spent two days walking on air, and now my whole world was collapsing.

'And there I was, thinking you'd come because you felt like seeing me.' I managed a weak smile.

I noticed her blushing self-consciously.

'I was only joking,' I lied. 'What I was serious about was my promise to show you a face of the city that you don't yet know. At least that will give you cause to remember me, or Barcelona, whenever you go.'

There was a touch of sadness in Bea's smile, and she avoided my eyes. 'I nearly went to the cinema, you know. So as not to see you today,' she said.

'Why?'

Bea looked at me but said nothing. She shrugged her shoulders and raised her eyes as if she were trying to catch words that were escaping from her.

'Because I was afraid that perhaps you were right,' she said at last.

I sighed. We were shielded by the evening light and that despondent silence that brings strangers together, and I felt brave enough to say anything that came into my head, even though it might be for the last time.

'Do you love him, or don't you?'

A smile came and went. 'It's none of your business.'

'That's true,' I said. 'It's only your business.'

She gave me a cold look. 'And what does it matter to you?'

'It's none of your business,' I said.

She didn't smile. Her lips trembled. 'People who know me know I'm very fond of Pablo. My family and—'

'But I'm almost a stranger,' I interrupted. 'And I would like to hear it from you.'

'Hear what?'

'That you really love him. That you're not marrying him to get away from home, to put distance between yourself and Barcelona and your family, to go somewhere where they can't hurt you. That you're leaving and not running away.'

Her eyes shone with angry tears. 'You have no right to say that to me, Daniel. You don't know me.'

'Tell me I'm mistaken and I'll leave. Do you love him?'

We looked at one another for a long while, without saying a word.

'I don't know,' she murmured at last. 'I don't know.'

'Someone once said that the moment you stop to think about whether you love someone, you've already stopped loving that person forever,' I said.

Bea looked for the irony in my expression. 'Who said that?'

'Someone called Julián Carax.'

'A friend of yours?'

I caught myself nodding. 'Sort of.'

'You're going to have to introduce him to me.'

'Tonight, if you like.'

We left the university under a bruised sky and wandered aimlessly, just getting used to walking side by side. We took shelter in the only subject we had in common, her brother, Tomás. Bea spoke about him as if he were a virtual stranger, someone she loved but barely knew. She avoided my eyes and smiled nervously. I felt that she regretted what she had said to me in the university cloister, that the words still hurt and were still gnawing at her.

'Listen, what I said to you before,' she said suddenly, 'you won't mention a word to Tomás, will you?'

'Of course not. I won't tell anyone.'

She laughed nervously. 'I don't know what came over me. Don't be offended, but sometimes it's easier to talk to a stranger than someone you know. Why is that?'

I shrugged. 'Probably because a stranger sees us the way we are, not as they wish us to be.'

'Is that also from your friend Carax?'

'No, I just made it up to impress you.'

'And how do you see me?'

'As a mystery.'

'That's the strangest compliment anyone has ever paid me.'

'It's not a compliment. It's a threat.'

'What do you mean?'

'Mysteries must be solved, one must find out what they hide.'

'You might be disappointed when you see what's inside.'

'I might be surprised. And you, too.'

'Tomás never told me you had so much cheek.'

'That's because what little I have, I've reserved entirely for you.'

'Why?'

Because I'm afraid of you, I thought.

We sought refuge in a small café next to the Poliorama Theatre. Withdrawing to a table by the window, we asked for some *serrano* ham sandwiches and a couple of white coffees, to warm up. Soon thereafter the manager, a scrawny fellow with the face of an imp, came up to the table with an attentive expression.

'Did you folks ask for the 'am sandwiches?'

We nodded.

'Sorry to 'ave to announce, on behalf of the management 'ere, that there's not a scrap of 'am left. I can offer black, white, or mixed *butifarra*, meatballs, or *chistorra*. Top of the line, extra fresh. I also 'ave pickled sardines, if you folks can't consume meat products for reasons of religious conscience. It being Friday . . .'

'I'll be fine with a white coffee, really,' said Bea.

I was starving. 'What if you bring two servings of spicy potatoes and some bread, too?'

'Right away, sir. And please, pardon the shortness of supplies. Usually I tend to 'ave everything, even Bolshevik caviar. But s'afternoon, it being the European Cup semi-final, we've had a lot of customers. Great game.'

The manager walked away ceremoniously. Bea watched him with amusement.

'Where's that accent from? Jaén?'

'Much closer: Santa Coloma de Gramanet,' I specified. 'You don't often take the subway, do you?'

'My father says the subway is full of riffraff and that if you're on your own, the Gypsies feel you up.'

I was about to say something but decided to keep my mouth shut. Bea laughed. As soon as the coffees and the food arrived, I fell on it all with no pretence at refinement. Bea didn't eat anything. With her hands spread around the steaming cup, she watched me with half a smile, caught somewhere between curiosity and amazement.

'So what is it you're going to show me today?'

'A number of things. In fact, what I'm going to show you is part of a story. Didn't you tell me the other day that what you like to do is read?'

Bea nodded, arching her eyebrows.

'Well, this is a story about books.'

'About books?'

'About accursed books, about the man who wrote them, about a character who broke out of the pages of a novel so that he could burn it, about a betrayal and a lost friendship. It's a story of love, of hatred, and of the dreams that live in the shadow of the wind.'

'You sound like the jacket blurb of a Victorian novel, Daniel.'

'That's probably because I work in a bookshop and I've seen too many. But this is a true story. As real as the fact that this bread they served us is at least three days old. And, like all true stories, it begins and ends in a cemetery, although not the sort of cemetery you imagine.'

She smiled the way children smile when they've been promised a riddle or a magic trick. 'I'm all ears.'

I gulped down the last of my coffee and looked at her for a few moments without saying anything. I thought about how much I wanted to lose myself in those evasive eyes. I thought about the loneliness that would take hold of me that night when I said goodbye to her, once I had run out of tricks or stories to make her stay with me any longer. I thought about how little I had to offer her and how much I wanted from her.

'I can hear your brains clanking, Daniel. What are you planning?'

I began my story with that distant dawn when I awoke and could not remember my mother's face, and I didn't stop until I paused to recall the world of shadows I had sensed that very morning in the home of Nuria Monfort. Bea listened quietly, making no judgment, drawing no conclusions. I told her about my first visit to the Cemetery of Forgotten Books and about the night I spent reading *The Shadow of the Wind.* I told her about my meeting with the faceless man and about the letter signed by Penélope Aldaya that I always carried with me without knowing why. I spoke about how I had never kissed Clara Barceló, or anyone, and of how my hands had trembled when I felt the touch of Nuria Monfort's lips on my skin, only a few hours before. I told her how, until that moment, I had not understood that this was a story about lonely people, about absence and loss, and that that was why I had taken refuge in it until it became confused with my own life, like someone who has escaped into the pages of a novel because those whom he needs to love seem nothing more than ghosts inhabiting the mind of a stranger.

'Don't say anything,' whispered Bea. 'Just take me to that place.'

It was pitch dark when we stopped by the front door of the Cemetery of Forgotten Books, in the gloom of Calle Arco del Teatro. I lifted the devil-head knocker and knocked three times. While we waited, sheltering under the arch of the entrance, the cold wind smelled of charcoal. I met Bea's eyes, so close to mine. She was smiling. Soon we heard light footsteps approaching the door, and then the tired voice of the keeper.

'Who's there?' asked Isaac.

'It's Daniel Sempere, Isaac.'

I thought I could hear him swearing under his breath. There followed the thousand squeaks and groans from the intricate system of locks. Finally the door yielded an inch or two, revealing the vulturine face of Isaac Monfort lit by candlelight. When he saw me, the keeper sighed and rolled his eyes.

'Stupid of me. I don't know why I ask,' he said. 'Who else could it be at this time of night?'

Isaac was clothed in what seemed like a strange cross-breed of dressing gown, bathrobe, and Russian army coat. The padded slippers perfectly matched a checked wool cap, rather like a professor's cap, complete with tassel.

'I hope I didn't get you out of bed,' I said.

'Not at all. I'd only just started saying my prayers. . . .'

He looked at Bea as if he'd just seen a pack of dynamite sticks alight at his feet. 'For your own good, I hope this isn't what it looks like,' he threatened.

'Isaac, this is my friend Beatriz, and with your permission I'd like to show her this place. Don't worry, she's completely trustworthy.'

'Sempere, I've known toddlers with more common sense than you.'

'It would only be for a moment.'

Isaac let out a snort of defeat and examined Bea carefully, like a suspicious policeman.

'Do you realize you're in the company of an idiot?' he asked.

Bea smiled politely. 'I'm beginning to come to terms with it.'

'Sublime innocence! Do you know the rules?'

Bea nodded. Isaac mumbled under his breath and let us in, scanning the shadows of the street, as usual.

'I visited your daughter, Nuria,' I mentioned casually. 'She's well. Working hard, but well. She sends you her love.'

'Yes, and poisoned darts. You're not much good at making things up, Sempere. But I appreciate the effort. Come on in.'

Once inside, Isaac handed me the candle and proceeded to lock the door.

'When you've finished, you know where to find me.'

Under the mantle of darkness, we could only just make

out the spectral forms of the book maze. The candle projected its bubble of light at our feet. Bea paused, astonished, at the entrance to the labyrinth. I smiled, recognizing in her face the same expression my father must have seen in mine years before. We entered the tunnels and galleries of the maze; they creaked under our footsteps. The marks I had made during my last incursion were still there.

'Come on, I want to show you something,' I said.

More than once I lost my own trail and we had to go backwards in search of the last sign. Bea watched me with a mixture of alarm and fascination. My inner compass told me we were caught in a knot of spirals that rose slowly towards the very heart of the labyrinth. At last I managed to retrace my steps through the tangle of corridors and tunnels until I entered a narrow passage that felt like a gangway stretching out into the gloom. I knelt down by the last shelf and looked for my old friend hidden behind the row of dust-covered volumes – the layer of dust shining like frost in the candlelight. I took the book and handed it to Bea.

'Let me introduce you to Julián Carax.'

'*The Shadow of the Wind*,' Bea read, stroking the faded letters on the cover.

'Can I take it with me?' she asked.

'You can take any book but this one.'

'But that's not fair. After all the things you've told me, this is precisely the one I want.'

'One day, perhaps. But not today.'

I took it from her and put it back in its hiding place.

'I'll come back without you and I'll take it away without you knowing,' she said mockingly.

'You wouldn't find it in a thousand years.'

'That's what you think. I've seen your notches, and I, too, know the story of the Minotaur.'

'Isaac wouldn't let you in.'

'You're wrong. He prefers me to you.'

'And how do you know?'

'I can read people's eyes.'

Despite myself, I believed her and turned mine away.

'Choose any other one. Here, this one looks promising. *The Castilian Hog, That Unknown Beast: In Search of the Roots of Iberian Pork*, by Anselmo Torquemada. I'm sure it sold more copies than any book by Julián Carax. Every part of the pig can be put to good use.'

'I'm more attracted to this other one.'

'*Tess of the d'Urbervilles*. It's the original. You're bold enough to read Hardy in English?'

She gave me a sidelong glance.

'All yours, then!'

'Don't you see? It feels as if it's been waiting for me. As if it has been hiding here for me from before I was born.'

I looked at her in astonishment. Bea's lips crinkled into a smile. 'What have I said?'

Then, without thinking, barely brushing her lips, I kissed her.

It was almost midnight when we reached the front door of Bea's house. We had walked most of the way without speaking, not daring to turn our thoughts into words. We walked apart, hiding from one another. Bea walked upright with her *Tess* under her arm, and I followed a step behind, still tasting her lips. The way Isaac had glanced at me when we left the Cemetery of Forgotten Books was still on my mind. It was a look I knew well and had seen a thousand times from my father, a look that asked me whether I had the slightest idea what I was doing. The last hours I'd been lost in another world, a universe of touches and looks I did not understand and that blotted out both reason and shame. Now, back in the reality that always lies in wait among the shadows of the Ensanche quarter, the enchantment was lifting, and all I had left was painful desire and an indescribable restlessness. And yet just looking at Bea was enough for me to realize that my doubts were a breeze compared to the storm that was raging inside her. We stopped by her door and looked at one another without attempting to pretend. A mellifluous night watchman was walking up to us unhurriedly, humming boleros to the rhythmic jingle of his bunches of keys.

'Perhaps you'd rather we didn't see each other again,' I suggested without much conviction.

'I don't know, Daniel. I don't know anything. Is that what you want?'

'No. Of course not. And you?'

She shrugged her shoulders, and smiled faintly. 'What do you think?' she asked. 'I lied to you earlier, you know. In the cloister.'

'What about?'

'About not wanting to see you today.'

The night porter hung about, smirking at us, obviously indifferent to my first whispered exchange at a front door. To him, experienced in such matters, it must have seemed a string of clichés and banalities.

'Don't worry about me, there's no hurry,' he said. 'I'll have a smoke on the corner, and you just let me know.'

I waited for the watchman to walk away.

'When will I see you again?'

'I don't know, Daniel.'

'Tomorrow?'

'Please, Daniel. I don't know.'

I nodded. She stroked my face. 'You'd better leave now.'

'You know where to find me, at least?'

She nodded.

'I'll be waiting.'

'Me, too.'

As I moved away, I couldn't take my eyes off her. The night watchman, an expert in these situations, was already walking up to open the door for her.

'You rascal,' he whispered as he went by, not without admiration. 'What a looker.'

I waited until Bea had gone into the building and then set off briskly, turning to glance back at every step. Slowly I became possessed by the absurd conviction that anything was possible, and it seemed to me that even those deserted streets and that hostile wind smelled of hope. When I reached Plaza de Cataluña, I noticed that a flock of pigeons had congregated in the centre of the square, covering it with a blanket of white feathers that swayed silently. I thought of going round them, but at that moment I noticed that the pigeons were parting to let me pass, instead of flying off. I felt my way forward, as the pigeons broke ranks in front of me and re-formed behind me. When I got to the middle of the square, I heard the peal of the cathedral bells ringing out midnight. I paused for a moment, stranded in an ocean of silvery birds, and thought how this had been the strangest and most marvellous day of my life.

## 22

The light was still on in the bookshop when I crossed the street towards the shop window. I thought that perhaps my father had stayed on until late, getting up to date with his correspondence or finding some other excuse to wait up for me and pump me for information about my meeting with Bea. I could see a silhouette making a pile of books and recognized the gaunt, nervous profile of Fermín, lost in concentration. I rapped on the pane with my knuckles. Fermín looked out, pleasantly surprised, and signalled to me to pop in through the backroom door.

'Still working, Fermín? It's terribly late.'

'I'm really just killing time until I go over to poor Don Federico's to watch over him. I'm taking turns with Eloy from the optician's. I don't sleep much anyhow. Two or three hours at the most. Mind you, you can't talk either, Daniel. It's past midnight, from which I infer that your meeting with the young lady was a roaring success.'

I shrugged my shoulders. 'The truth is I don't know,' I admitted.

'Did she let you feel her up?'

'No.'

'A good sign. Never trust girls who let themselves be touched right away. But even less those who need a priest for approval. Good sirloin steak – if you'll excuse the comparison – needs to be cooked until it's medium rare. Of course, if the opportunity arises, don't be prudish, and go for the kill. But if what you're looking for is something serious, like this thing with me and Bernarda, remember the golden rule.'

'Is your thing serious?'

'More than serious. Spiritual. And what about you and this pumpkin, Beatriz? You can see a mile off that she's worth a million, but the crux of the matter is this: is she the sort who makes you fall in love or the sort who merely stirs your nether regions?'

'I haven't the slightest idea,' I pointed out. 'Both things, I'd say.'

'Look, Daniel, this is like indigestion. Do you notice something here, in the mouth of the stomach – as if you'd swallowed a brick? Or do you just feel a general feverishness?'

'The brick things sounds more like it,' I said, although I didn't altogether discard the fever.

'That means it's a serious matter. God help us! Come on, sit down and I'll make you a lime-blossom tea.'

We settled down round the table in the back room, surrounded by books. The city was asleep, and the bookshop felt like a boat adrift in a sea of silence and shadows. Fermín handed me a steaming hot cup and smiled at me a little awkwardly. Something was bothering him.

'May I ask you a personal question, Daniel?'

'Of course.'

'I beg you to answer in all frankness,' he said, and he cleared his throat. 'Do you think I could ever be a father?'

He must have seen my puzzled expression, and he quickly added, 'I don't mean biologically – I may look a bit

189

rickety, but by good luck Providence has endowed me with the potency and the fury of a fighting bull. I'm referring to the other sort of father. A good father, if you see what I mean.'

'A good father?'

'Yes. Like yours. A man with a head, a heart, and a soul. A man capable of listening, of leading and respecting a child, and not of drowning his own defects in him. Someone whom a child will not only love because he's his father but will also admire for the person he is. Someone he would want to grow up to resemble.'

'Why are you asking me this, Fermín? I thought you didn't believe in marriage and families. The yoke and all that, remember?'

Fermín nodded. 'Look, all that's for amateurs. Marriage and family are only what we make of them. Without that they're just a nest of hypocrisy. Garbage and empty words. But if there is real love, the sort you don't go around telling everyone about, the sort that is felt and lived . . .'

'You're a changed man, Fermín.'

'I am. Bernarda has made me want to be a better man.'

'How's that?'

'So that I can deserve her. You cannot understand such things right now, because you're young. But in good time you'll see that sometimes what matters isn't what one gives but what one gives up. Bernarda and I have been talking. She's quite a mother hen, as you know. She doesn't say so, but I think the one thing in life that would make her truly happy is to become a mother. And that woman is sweeter than peaches in syrup to me. Suffice it to say that, for her, I'm prepared to enter a church after thirty-two years of clerical abstinence and recite the psalms of St Seraph or whatever needs to be done.'

'Aren't you getting a bit ahead of yourself, Fermín? You've only just met her. . . .'

'Look, Daniel, at my age either you begin to see things for what they are or you're pretty much done for. Only three or four things are worth living for; the rest is shit. I've already fooled around a lot, and now I know that the only thing I really want is to make Bernarda happy and die one day in her arms. I want to be a respectable man again, see? Not for my sake – as far as I'm concerned, I couldn't give a fly's fart for the respect of this chorus of simians we call humanity – but for hers. Because Bernarda believes in such things – in radio soaps, in priests, in respectability and in Our Lady of Lourdes. That's the way she is, and I want her exactly like that. I even like those hairs that grow on her chin. And that's why I want to be someone she can be proud of. I want her to think, My Fermín is one hell of a man, like Cary Grant, Hemingway, or Manolete.'

I crossed my arms, weighing up the situation. 'Have you spoken about all this with her? About having a child together?'

'Goodness no. What do you take me for? Do you think I go around telling women I want to get them knocked up? And it's not that I don't feel like it. Take that silly Merceditas: I'd put some triplets in her right now and feel on top of the world, but—'

'Have you told Bernarda you'd like to have a family?'

'These things don't need to be said, Daniel. They show on your face.'

I nodded. 'Well, then, for what my opinion is worth, I'm sure you'll be an excellent father and husband. And since you don't believe in those things, you'll never take them for granted.'

His face melted into happiness. 'Do you mean it?'

'Of course.'

'You've taken a huge weight off my mind. Because just remembering my own father and thinking that I might end up being like him makes me want to get sterilized.'

'Don't worry, Fermín. Besides, there's probably no treatment capable of crushing your procreative powers.'

'Good point,' he reflected. 'Go on, go and get some sleep. I mustn't keep you any longer.'

'You're not keeping me, Fermín. I have a feeling I'm not going to sleep a wink.'

'Take a pain for a pleasure. . . . By the way, remember you mentioned that PO box?'

'Have you discovered anything?'

'I told you to leave it to me. This lunchtime I went up to the post office and had a word with an old acquaintance of mine who works there. PO Box 2321 is registered under the name of one José María Requejo, a lawyer with offices on Calle León XIII. I took the liberty of checking out the address and wasn't surprised to discover that it doesn't exist, although I imagine you already know that. Someone has been collecting the letters addressed to that box for years. I know because some of the mail received from a property business comes as registered post and requires a signature on a small receipt and proof of identification.'

'Who is it? One of Requejo's employees?' I asked.

'I couldn't get that far, but I doubt it. Either I'm very mistaken or this Requejo guy exists on the same plane as Our Lady of Fátima. All I can tell you is the name of the person who collects the mail: Nuria Monfort.'

I felt the blood draining from me.

'Nuria Monfort? Are you sure, Fermín?'

'I saw some of those receipts myself. That name and the number of her identity card were on all of them. I deduce, from that sick look on your face, that this revelation surprises you.'

'Quite a lot.'

'May I ask who this Nuria Monfort is? The clerk I spoke to told me he remembered her clearly because she went there two weeks ago to collect the mail and, in his impartial opinion, she looked hotter than the *Venus de Milo* – and with a firmer bust. I trust his assessment, because before the war he was a professor of aesthetics – but he was also a distant cousin of Socialist leader Largo Caballero, so naturally he now licks one-peseta stamps.'

'I was with that woman today, in her home,' I murmured.

Fermín looked at me in amazement. 'With Nuria Monfort? I'm beginning to think I was wrong about you, Daniel. You've become quite a rake.'

'It's not what you think, Fermín.'

'That's your loss, then. At your age I was like El Molino music hall – shows morning, afternoon, and night.'

I gazed at that small, gaunt, and bony man, with his large nose and his yellow skin, and I realized he was becoming my best friend.

'May I tell you something, Fermín? Something that's been on my mind for some time?'

'But of course. Anything. Especially if it's shocking and concerns this yummy maiden.'

For the second time that night I began to tell the story of Julián Carax and the enigma of his death. Fermín listened very attentively, writing things down in a notebook and interrupting me every now and then to ask me some detail whose relevance escaped me. Listening to myself, it became increasingly clear to me that there were many lacunae in that story. More than once my mind went blank and my thoughts became lost as I tried to work out why Nuria Monfort would have lied to me. What was the significance of all this? Why had she, for years, been collecting the mail directed to a nonexistent lawyers' office that was supposedly in charge of the Fortuny–Carax apartment in Ronda de San Antonio? I didn't realize I was voicing my doubts out loud.

'We can't yet know why that woman was lying to you,' said Fermín. 'But we can speculate that if she did so in this respect, she may have done so, and probably did, in many others.'

I sighed, completely lost. 'What do you suggest, Fermín?'

Fermín Romero de Torres sighed and put on his most Socratic expression. 'I'll tell you what we can do. This coming Sunday, if you agree, we'll drop by San Gabriel's school quite casually, and we'll make some inquiries

193

concerning the origins of the friendship between this Carax fellow and the other lad, the rich boy . . .'

'Aldaya.'

'I have a way with priests, you'll see, even if it's just because I look like a roguish monk. I butter them up a little, and I get them eating out of my hand.'

'Are you sure?'

'Positive. I guarantee this lot is going to sing like the Montserrat Boys' Choir.'


# 23

I spent the Saturday in a trance, anchored behind the bookshop counter in the hope of seeing Bea come through the door as if by magic. Every time the telephone rang, I rushed to answer it, grabbing the receiver from my father or Fermín. Halfway through the afternoon, after about twenty calls from clients and no news from Bea, I began to accept that the world and my miserable existence were coming to an end. My father had gone out to price a collection in San Gervasio, and Fermín took advantage of the situation to deliver another of his magisterial lectures on the many mysteries of romance.

'Calm down or you'll grow a stone in your liver,' Fermín advised me. 'This business of courtship is like a tango: absurd and pure embellishment. But you're the man, and you must take the lead.'

It was all beginning to look pretty grim. 'The lead? Me?'

'What do you expect? One has to pay some price for being able to piss standing up.'

'But Bea implied that she would get back to me.'

'You really don't understand women, Daniel. I bet you my Christmas bonus that the little chick is in her house right now, looking languidly out of the window like the Lady of the Camellias, waiting for you to come and rescue her from that idiot father of hers and drag her into an unstoppable spiral of lust and sin.'

'Are you sure?'

'It's a mathematical certainty.'

'What if she's decided she doesn't want to see me again?'

'Look, Daniel. Women – with remarkable exceptions like your neighbour Merceditas – are more intelligent than we are, or at least more honest with themselves about what they do or don't want. Another question is whether they tell you or the world. You're facing the enigma of nature, Daniel. Womankind is an indecipherable maze. If you give her time to think, you're lost. Remember: warm heart, cold mind. The seducer's code.'

Fermín was about to detail the particulars and techniques of the art of seduction when the doorbell tinkled and in walked my friend Tomás Aguilar. My heart missed a beat. Providence was denying me Bea but sending me her brother. A fateful herald, I thought. Tomás had a sombre expression and a certain despondent air.

'What a funereal appearance, Don Tomás,' Fermín remarked. 'You'll accept a small coffee at least, I hope?'

'I wouldn't say no,' said Tomás, with his usual reserve.

Fermín served him a cup of the concoction he kept in a Thermos. It gave out an odour suspiciously like sherry.

'Is there a problem?' I asked.

Tomás shrugged. 'Nothing new. My father is having one of his days, and I thought it best to get out and breathe some fresh air for a while.'

I gulped. 'Why's that?'

'Goodness knows. Last night my sister, Bea, arrived home very late. My father was waiting up for her, a bit worked up as usual. She refused to say where she'd been or who she'd been with, and my father flew into a rage. He was screaming and yelling until four o'clock in the morning, calling her all sorts of names, a tart being the least of them. He swore he was going to send her to a nunnery and said that if she ever came back pregnant, he was going to kick her out into the goddamn street.'

Fermín threw me a look of alarm. Cold beads of sweat were running down my back.

'This morning,' Tomás continued, 'Bea locked herself up in her room, and she hasn't come out all day. My father has plonked himself in the dining room to read his newspaper and listen to operettas on the radio, full blast. During the interval of *Luisa Fernanda*, I had to go out because I was going crazy.'

'Well, your sister was probably out with her fiancé, don't you think?' Fermín needled. 'It would be perfectly natural.'

I gave Fermín a kick under the counter, which he avoided with feline dexterity.

'Her fiancé is doing his military service,' Tomás said. 'He doesn't come back on leave for another two weeks. Besides, when she goes out with him, she's home by eight at the latest.'

'And you have no idea where she was or who she was with?'

'He's already told you he doesn't, Fermín,' I intervened, anxious to change the subject.

'Nor your father?' insisted Fermín, who was thoroughly enjoying himself.

'No. But he's sworn he'll find out, and break the guy's legs and his face as soon as he knows who it is.'

I felt myself going deathly pale. Fermín offered me a cup of his concoction without asking. I drank it down in one gulp. It tasted like tepid diesel fuel. Tomás watched me but said nothing – a dark, impenetrable look.

'Did you hear that?' Fermín suddenly said. 'Sounded like a drumroll for a somersault.'

'No.'

'Yours truly's rumblings. Look, I'm suddenly terribly hungry. . . . Do you mind if I leave you two alone and run up to the baker's to grab myself a bun? Not to mention the new shop assistant who's just arrived from Reus: she looks so tasty you could eat her. She's called María Virtudes, but despite her name the girl is pure vice. . . . That way I'll leave you two to talk in peace, eh?'

In ten seconds Fermín had done a disappearing act, off for his snack and his meeting with the young woman. Tomás and I were left alone, enveloped in a silence as weighty as the Swiss franc. After several minutes I could bear it no longer.

'Tomás,' I began, my mouth dry. 'Last night your sister was with me.'

He stared at me without even blinking. I swallowed hard. 'Say something,' I said.

'You're not right in the head.'

A minute went by, muffled sounds coming in from the street. Tomás held his coffee, which he had not touched.

'Are you serious?' he asked.

'I've only seen her once.'

'That's not an answer.'

'Do you mind?'

He shrugged his shoulders. 'You'd better be sure you know what you're doing. Would you stop seeing her just because I asked you to?'

'Yes,' I lied. 'But don't ask me to.'

Tomás looked down. 'You don't know Bea,' he murmured.

I didn't reply. We let another few minutes go by without saying a word, looking at the grey figures who were scanning the shop window, praying that one of them would decide to come in and rescue us from that poisonous silence. After a while Tomás abandoned his cup on the counter and made his way to the door.

'You're leaving already?'

He nodded.

'Shall we meet up tomorrow for a while?' I said. 'We could go to the cinema, with Fermín, like before.'

He stopped by the door. 'I'll only tell you once, Daniel. Don't hurt my sister.'

On his way out, he passed Fermín, who was returning laden with a bag full of steaming-hot buns. Fermín saw him go off into the dusk, shaking his head. He left the buns on the counter and offered me an *ensaimada* just out of the oven. I declined. I wouldn't even have been able to swallow an aspirin.

'He'll get over it, Daniel. You'll see. These things are common between friends.'

'I don't know,' I mumbled.

# 24

Fermín and I met on Sunday at seven-thirty in the morning at the Canaletas Café. Fermín treated me to a coffee and brioches whose texture, even with butter spread on them, bore a resemblance to pumice stone. We were served by a waiter who sported a fascist badge on his lapel and a pencil moustache. He didn't stop humming to himself, and when we asked him the reason for his excellent mood, he explained that he'd become a father the day before. We congratulated him, and he insisted on giving us each a cigar to smoke during the day, in honour of his firstborn. We said we would. Fermín kept looking at him out of the corner of his eye, frowning, and I suspected he was plotting something.

Over breakfast Fermín kicked off the day's investigations with a general outline of the mystery.

'It all begins with the sincere friendship between two boys, Julián Carax and Jorge Aldaya, classmates since early childhood, like Don Tomás and yourself. For years all is well. Inseparable friends with a whole life before them, the works. And yet at some point a conflict arises that ruins this friendship. To paraphrase the drawing-room dramatists, the conflict bears a woman's name: Penélope. Very Homeric. Do you follow me?'

The only thing that came to my mind was the last sentence spoken by Tomás the previous evening in the bookshop: 'Don't hurt my sister.' I felt nauseous.

'In 1919, Julián Carax sets off for Paris, Odysseus-fashion,' Fermín continued. 'The letter, signed by Penélope, which he never receives, establishes that by then the young woman has been incarcerated in her own house, a prisoner of her family for reasons that are unclear, and that the friendship between Aldaya and Carax has ended. Moreover, according to Penélope, her brother, Jorge, has sworn that if he ever sees his old friend Julián again, he'll kill him. Grim words indeed. One doesn't have to be Pasteur to deduce that this conflict is a direct consquence of the relationship between Penélope and Carax.'

A cold sweat covered my forehead. I could feel the coffee and the few mouthfuls of brioche I'd swallowed rising up my throat.

'All the same, we must assume that Carax never gets to know what happened to Penélope, because the letter doesn't reach him. He vanishes from sight into the mists of Paris, where he will lead a ghostly existence between his job as a pianist in a variety club and his disastrous career as a remarkably unsuccessful novelist. These years in Paris are a puzzle. All that remains of them today is a forgotten literary work that has virtually disappeared. We know that at some point he decides to marry a mysterious rich lady who is twice his age. The nature of such a marriage, if we are to go by what the witnesses say, seems more an act of charity or friendship on behalf of an ailing lady than a love match. Whichever way you look at it, this patron of the arts, fearing for the financial future of her protégé, decides to leave him her fortune and bid farewell to this world with a roll in the hay to further her noble cause. Parisians are like that.'

'Perhaps it was a genuine love,' I suggested, in a tiny voice.

'Hey, Daniel, are you all right? You're looking very pale, and you're perspiring terribly.'

'I'm fine,' I lied.

'As I was saying. Love is a lot like pork: there's loin steak and there's bologna. Each has its own place and function. Carax had declared that he didn't feel worthy of any love, and indeed, as far as we know, no romances were recorded during his years in Paris. Of course, working in a brothel, perhaps his basic urges were satisfied by fraternizing with the employees, as if it were a perk of the job, so to speak. But this is pure speculation. Let us return to the moment when the marriage between Carax and his protectress is announced. That is when Jorge Aldaya reappears on the map of this murky business. We know he makes contact with Carax's publisher in Barcelona to find out the whereabouts of the novelist. Shortly afterwards, on the morning of his wedding day, Julián Carax fights a duel with an unknown person in Père Lachaise cemetery, and disappears. The wedding never takes place. From then on, everything becomes confused.'

Fermín allowed for a dramatic pause, giving me his conspiratorial look. 'Supposedly Carax crosses the border and, with yet another show of his proverbial sense of timing, returns to Barcelona in 1936 at the very outbreak of the Civil War. His activities and whereabouts in Barcelona during these weeks are hazy. We suppose he stays in the city for about a month and that during this time he doesn't contact any of his acquaintances. Neither his father nor his friend Nuria Monfort. Then he is found dead in the street, struck down by a bullet. It is not long before a sinister character makes his appearance on the scene. He calls himself Laín Coubert – a name he borrows from the last novel by Julián Carax and who, to cap it all, is none other than the Prince of Darkness. The supposed Lucifer states that he is prepared to obliterate what little is left of Carax and destroy his books forever. To round off the melodrama, he appears as a faceless man, disfigured by fire. A rogue from a Gothic operetta in whom, just to confuse matters more, Nuria Monfort believes she recognizes the voice of Jorge Aldaya.'

'Let me remind you that Nuria Monfort lied to me,' I said.

'True. But even if Nuria Monfort lied to you, she might have done it more by omission and perhaps to disassociate herself from the facts. There are few reasons for telling the truth, but for lying the number is infinite. Listen, are you sure you're all right? Your face is the colour of goat's cheese.'

I shook my head and dashed to the toilet.

I threw up my breakfast, my dinner, and a good amount of the anger I was carrying with me. I washed my face with freezing water from the sink and looked at my reflection in the blurry mirror on which someone had scrawled SHIT-HEAD FASCISTS with a wax crayon. When I got back to the table, I realized that Fermín was at the bar, paying the bill and discussing football with the waiter who had served us.

'Better?' he asked.

I nodded.

'That was a drop in your blood pressure,' said Fermín. 'Here. Have a Sugus sweet, they cure everything.'

On the way out of the café, Fermín insisted that we should take a taxi as far as San Gabriel's school and leave the subway for another day, arguing that the morning was as bright as a political mural and that tunnels were for rats.

'A taxi up to Sarriá will cost a fortune,' I protested.

'The ride's on the Cretins' Savings Bank,' Fermín put in quickly. 'The proud patriot back there gave me the wrong change, and we're in business. And you're not up to travelling underground.'

Equipped with our ill-gotten funds, we positioned ourselves on a corner at the foot of Rambla de Cataluña and waited for a cab. We had to let a few go by, because Fermín stated that, since he so rarely travelled by car, he wanted to get into a Studebaker at the very least. It took us a quarter of an hour to find a vehicle to his liking, which Fermín hailed by waving his arms about like a windmill. Fermín insisted on travelling in the front seat, and this gave him the chance to get involved in a discussion with the driver about Joseph Stalin, who was the driver's idol and spiritual guide.

'There have been three great figures this century: La Pasionaria; bullfighter extraordinaire Manolete; and Joseph Stalin,' the taxi driver proclaimed, getting ready to unload upon us a life of the saintly comrade.

I was riding comfortably in the back seat, paying little attention to the tedious speech, with the window open and enjoying the fresh air. Delighted to be driving around in a Studebaker, Fermín encouraged the cabdriver's chatter, occasionally punctuating his emotive biography of the Soviet leader with matters of doubtful historic interest.

'I've heard he's been suffering badly from prostate trouble ever since he swallowed the pip of a loquat, and now he can only pee if someone hums "The Internationale" for him,' he put in.

'Fascist propaganda,' the taxi driver explained, more devout than ever. 'The comrade pisses like a bull. The Volga might envy such a flow.'

This high-level political debate accompanied us as we made our way along Vía Augusta towards the hills. Day was breaking, with a fresh breeze, and the sky was an intense blue. When we reached Calle Ganduxer, the driver turned right, and we began the slow ascent toward Paseo de la Bonanova.

San Gabriel's school, its redbrick façade dotted with dagger-shaped windows, stood in the middle of a grove, at the top of a narrow, winding street that led up from the boulevard. The whole structure, crowned by arches and towers, peered over a group of plane trees like some Gothic cathedral. We got out of the taxi and entered a leafy garden strewn with fountains that were adorned with mould-covered angels. Here and there cobbled paths meandered between the trees. On our way to the main door, Fermín gave me the background on the institution.

'Even though it may look like Rasputin's mausoleum to you, San Gabriel's school was, in its day, one of the most prestigious and exclusive institutions in Barcelona. During the Republic it went downhill because the nouveaux riches of the time, the new industrialists and bankers to whose children it had for years refused access because their surnames smelled too new, decided to create their own schools, where they would be treated with due reverence and where they, in turn, could refuse access to the sons of others. Money is like any other virus: once it has rotted the soul of the person who houses it, it sets off in search of new blood. In this world a surname is less durable than a sugared almond. In its heyday – say, between 1880 and 1930, more or less – San Gabriel's school took in the flower of old, established families with bulging wallets. The Aldayas and company came to this sinister establishment as boarders, to fraternize with their equals, go to mass, and learn their history in order to be able to repeat it ad nauseam.'

'But Julián Carax wasn't really one of them,' I observed.

'Sometimes these illustrious institutions offer a scholarship or two for the sons of the gardener or the shoeshine man, just to show their magnanimity and Christian charity,' Fermín proffered. 'The most efficient way of rendering the poor harmless is to teach them to want to imitate the rich. That is the poison with which capitalism blinds the—'

'Please don't get carried away with social doctrine, Fermín. If one of these priests hears you, they'll kick us out of here.' I realized that a couple of padres were watching us with a mixture of curiosity and concern from the top of the steps that led up to the front door of the school. I wondered whether they'd heard any of our conversation.

One of them moved forward with a courteous smile, his hands crossed over his chest like a bishop. He must have been in his early fifties, and his lean build and sparse hair lent him the air of a bird of prey. He had a penetrating gaze and gave off an aroma of fresh eau de cologne and mothballs.

'Good morning. I'm Father Fernando Ramos,' he announced. 'How can I help you?'

Fermín held out his hand. The priest examined it briefly before shaking it, giving us an icy smile.

'Fermín Romero de Torres, bibliographic adviser to Sempere and Son. It is an enormous pleasure to greet Your Most Devout Excellency. Here, at my side, my collaborator and friend, Daniel, a young man of promise and much-recognized Christian qualities.'

Father Fernando observed us without blinking. I wanted the earth to swallow me.

'The pleasure is all mine, Señor Romero de Torres,' he replied amicably. 'May I ask what brings such a formidable duo to our humble institution?'

I decided to intervene before Fermín made some other outrageous comment and we had to make a quick exit. 'Father Fernando, we're trying to locate two former alumni of San Gabriel's: Jorge Aldaya and Julián Carax.'

Father Fernando pursed his lips and raised an eyebrow. 'Julián died over fifteen years ago, and Aldaya went off to Argentina,' he said dryly.

'Did you know them?' asked Fermín.

The priest's sharp gaze rested on each of us before he answered. 'We were classmates. May I ask what your interest is in this matter?'

I was wondering how to answer the question, but Fermín beat me to it. 'You see, it so happens that we have in our possession a number of articles that belong or belonged – for on this particular the legal interpretation leads to confusion – to the two persons in question.'

'And what is the nature of these articles, if you don't mind my asking?'

'I beg Your Grace to accept our silence, for God knows there are abundant reasons for conscience and secrecy that have nothing to do with the unquestioning faith Your Excellency merits, as does the order which you represent with such measure of gallantry and piety,' Fermín spewed out at great speed.

Father Fernando appeared to be almost in shock. I decided to take up the conversation again before Fermín had time to get his breath back.

'The articles Señor Romero de Torres is referring to are of a personal nature, mementos and objects of purely sentimental value. What we would like to ask you, Father, if this isn't too much trouble, is to tell us what you remember about Julián and Aldaya from your days as schoolboys.'

Father Fernando was still looking at us suspiciously. It became obvious to me that the explanations we'd given him were not enough to justify our interest and earn us his collaboration. I threw a look of desperation at Fermín, begging him to find some cunning argument with which to win over the priest.

'Do you know that you look a bit like Julián when he was young?' asked Father Fernando suddenly.

Fermín's eyes lit up. Here he goes, I thought. All our luck rests on this card.

'Very shrewd of you, Your Reverence,' proclaimed Fermín, feigning surprise. 'Your uncanny insight has unmasked us. You'll end up as a cardinal at least, or even a pope.'

'What are you talking about?'

'Isn't it obvious and patent, Your Lordship?'

'Quite frankly, no.'

'Can we count on the secrecy of the confessional?'

'This is a garden, not a confessional.'

'It will be enough if you grant us your ecclesiastic discretion.'

'You have it.'

Fermín heaved a deep sigh and looked at me with a melancholy expression. 'Daniel, we can't go on lying to this saintly soldier of Christ.'

'Of course not . . .' I corroborated, completely lost.

Fermín went up to the priest and murmured in a confidential tone, 'Father, we have most solid grounds to suspect that our friend Daniel here is none other than the secret son of the deceased Julián Carax. Hence our interest in reconstructing the past and recovering the memory of an illustrious person, whom the Fates tore away from the side of a poor child.'

Father Fernando fixed his astounded eyes on me. 'Is this true?'

I nodded. Fermín patted my back, his face full of sorrow.

'Look at him, poor lad, searching for a father lost in the mist of memory. What could be sadder than this? Tell me, Your Most Saintly Grace.'

'Have you any proof to support your assertions?'

Fermín grabbed my chin and offered up my face as payment. 'What further proof would the clergyman require than this little face, silent, irrefutable witness of the paternal fact in question?'

The priest seemed to hesitate.

'Will you help me, Father?' I implored cunningly. 'Please . . .'

Father Fernando sighed uncomfortably. 'I don't suppose there's any harm in it,' he said at last. 'What do you want to know?'

'Everything,' said Fermín.

# 25

We went into Father Fernando's office, where he summoned up his memories, adopting the tone of a sermon. He sculpted his sentences neatly, measuring them out with a cadence that seemed to promise an ultimate moral that never came. Years of teaching had left him with that firm and didactic tone of someone used to being heard, but not certain of being listened to.

'If I remember correctly, Julián Carax started at San Gabriel's in 1914. I got along with him right away, because we both belonged to the small group of pupils who did not come from wealthy families. They called us 'The Starving Gang', and each one of us had his own special story. I'd managed to get a scholarship thanks to my father, who worked in the kitchens of this school for twenty-five years. Julián had been accepted thanks to the intercession of Señor Aldaya, who was a customer of the Fortuny hat shop, owned by Julián's father. Those were different times, of course, and during those days power was still concentrated within families and dynasties. That world has vanished – the last few remains were swept away with the fall of the Republic, for the better, I suppose. All that is left are the names on the letterheads of companies, banks, and faceless consortiums. Like all old cities, Barcelona is a sum of its ruins. The great glories so many people are proud of – palaces, factories, and monuments, the emblems with which we identify – are nothing more than relics of an extin- guished civilization.'

Having reached this point, Father Fernando allowed for a solemn pause in which he seemed to be waiting for the congregation to answer with some empty Latin phrase or a response from the missal.

'Amen, Reverend Father. What great truth lies in those wise words,' offered Fermín to fill the awkward silence.

'You were telling us about my father's first year at the school,' I put in gently.

Father Fernando nodded. 'In those days he already called himself Carax, although his paternal surname was Fortuny. At first some of the boys teased him for that, and for being one of The Starving Gang, of course. They also laughed at me because I was the cook's son. You know what kids are like. Deep down, God has filled them with goodness, but they repeat what they hear at home.'

'Little angels,' punctuated Fermín.

'What do you remember about my father?'

'Well, it's such a long time ago.... Your father's best friend at that time was not Jorge Aldaya but a boy called Miquel Moliner. Miquel's family was almost as wealthy as the Aldayas, and I daresay he was the most extravagant pupil this school has ever seen. The headmaster thought he was possessed by the devil because he recited Marx in German during mass.'

'A clear sign of possession,' Fermín agreed.

'Miquel and Julián got on extremely well. Sometimes we three would get together during the lunch break and Julián would tell us stories. Other times he would tell us about his family and the Aldayas....'

The priest seemed to hesitate.

'Even after leaving school, Miquel and I stayed in touch for a time. Julián had already gone to Paris by then. I know that Miquel missed him. He often spoke about him, remembering secrets Julian had once confided in him. Later, when I entered the seminary, Miquel told me I'd gone over to the enemy. It was meant as a joke, but the fact is that we drifted apart.'

'Do you remember hearing that Miquel married someone called Nuria Monfort?'

'Miquel, married?'

'Do you find that odd?'

'I suppose I shouldn't, but ... I don't know. The truth is that I haven't heard from Miquel for years. Since before the war.'

'Did he ever mention the name of Nuria Monfort?'

'No, never. And he didn't say he was thinking of getting married or that he had a fiancée.... Listen, I'm not at all sure that I should be talking to you about this. These are personal things Julián and Miquel told me, with the understanding that they would remain between us.'

'And are you going to refuse a son his only chance of discovering his father's past?' asked Fermín.

Father Fernando was torn between doubt and, it seemed to me, the wish to remember, to recover those lost days. 'I suppose so many years have gone by that it doesn't matter anymore. I can still remember the day when Julián told us how he'd met the Aldayas and how, without realizing it, his life was changed forever....'

*... In October 1914 an artifact that many took to be a pantheon on wheels stopped one afternoon in front of the Fortuny hat shop on Ronda de San Antonio. From it emerged the proud, majestic, and arrogant figure of Don Ricardo Aldaya, by then already one of the richest men not only in Barcelona but also in the whole of Spain. His textile empire took in citadels of industry and colonies of commerce along all the rivers of Catalonia. His right hand held the reins of the banks and landed estates of half the province. His left hand, ever active, pulled at the strings of the provincial council, the city hall, various ministries, the bishopric, and the customs service at the port.*

*That afternoon the man with exuberant moustache and kingly sideburns, whom everybody feared, needed a hat. He entered the shop of Don Antoni Fortuny, and, after a quick glance at the premises, he looked at the hatter and his assistant, the young Julián, and said as follows: 'I've been told that, despite appearances, the best hats in Barcelona come out of this shop. Autumn is looking decidedly grim, and I'm going to need six top hats, a dozen bowler hats, hunting caps, and something to wear for the Cortes in Madrid. Are you making a note of this, or do you expect me to repeat it all?'*

*That was the beginning of a laborious and lucrative process during which father and son combined their efforts to get the order completed for Don Ricardo Aldaya. Julián, who read the papers, was well aware of Aldaya's position and told himself he could not fail his father now, at the most crucial and decisive moment of his business career. From the moment the magnate had set foot in his shop, the hatter almost levitated with joy. Aldaya had promised him that if he was satisfied, he would recommend his establishment to all his friends. That meant that the Fortuny hat shop, from being a dignified but* modest enterprise, would attain the highest spheres, covering the heads both large and small of parliamentary members, mayors, cardinals and ministers. That week seemed to fly by like an enchanted dream. Julián skipped school and spent up to eighteen or twenty hours a day working in the backroom workshop. His father, exhausted by his own enthusiasm, hugged him every now and then and even kissed him without thinking. He even went so far as to give his wife, Sophie, a dress and a pair of new shoes for the first time in fourteen years. The hatter was unrecognizable. One Sunday he forgot to go to church, and that same afternoon, brimming with pride, he put his arms around Julián and said, with tears in his eyes, 'Grandfather would have been proud of us.'

One of the most complex processes of the now disappeared science of hatmaking, both technically and politically, was that of taking measurements. Don Ricardo Aldaya had a cranium that, according to Julián, bordered on the melon-shaped and was quite rugged. The hatter was aware of the difficulties as soon as he saw the great man's head, and that same evening, when Julián said it reminded him of certain peaks in the mountains of Montserrat, Fortuny couldn't help agreeing with him. 'Father, with all due respect, you know that when it comes to taking measurements, I'm better at it than you, because you get nervous. Let me do it.' The hatter readily agreed, and the following day, when Aldaya arrived in his Mercedes-Benz, Julián welcomed him and took him to the workshop. When Aldaya realized that he was going to be measured by a boy of fourteen, he was furious. 'But what is this? A child? Are you pulling my leg?' Julián, who was aware of his client's social position but who wasn't in the least bit intimidated by him, answered, 'Sir, I don't know about your leg, but there's not much to pull up here. This crown looks like a bullring, and if we don't hurry up and make you a set of hats, your head will be mistaken for a Barcelona street plan.' When he heard those words, Fortuny wanted the ground to swallow him up. Aldaya, undaunted, fixed his gaze on Julián.

Then, to everyone's surprise, he burst out laughing as he hadn't done in years.

'This child of yours will go far, Fortunato,' declared Aldaya, who had not quite learned the hatter's surname.

That is how they discovered that Don Ricardo Aldaya was fed up to his very back teeth with being feared and flattered by everyone; with having people throw themselves on the ground like a doormat as he went by. He despised sycophants, cowards, and anyone who showed any sort of weakness, be it physical, mental, or moral. When he came across a humble boy, barely an apprentice, who had the cheek and the spirit to laugh at him, Aldaya decided he'd hit on the ideal hat shop and immediately doubled his order. That week he gladly turned up every day for his appointment, so that Julián could take measurements and try different models on him. Antoni Fortuny was amazed to see how the champion of Catalan society would fall about laughing at the jokes and stories told by the son who was still a stranger to him, that boy he never spoke to and who, for years, had shown no sign of having any sense of humour. At the end of the week, Aldaya took the hatter aside, to a corner of the shop, and spoke to him in confidence.

'Let's see, Fortunato, this son of yours has great talent, and you've got him stuck here, bored out of his mind, dusting the cobwebs in a two-bit shop.'

'This is a good business, Don Ricardo, and the boy shows a certain flair, even though he lacks backbone.'

'Nonsense. What school does he attend?'

'Well, he goes to the local school. . . .'

'Nothing but a production line for workers. When one is young, talent – genius, if you like – must be cultivated, or it becomes twisted and consumes the person who possesses it. It needs direction. Support. Do you understand me, Fortunato?'

'You're mistaken about my son. He's nowhere near a genius. He can barely pass his geography. His teachers tell me he's a scatterbrain and has a very bad attitude, just like his *mother. But at least here he'll always have an honest job and—'*

*'Fortunato, you bore me. Today, without fail, I'll go to San Gabriel's school to see the admissions board, and I'll let them know that they are to accept your son into the same class as my eldest child, Jorge. Anything less would be miserly of me.'*

*The hatter's eyes were as big as saucers. San Gabriel's was the nursery for the cream of high society.*

*'But, Don Ricardo, I would be unable to finance—'*

*'No one is asking you to pay anything. I'll take charge of the boy's education. You, as his father, only have to agree.'*

*'But of course, certainly, but—'*

*'That's decided, then. So long as Julián accepts, of course.'*

*'He'll do what he's told, naturally.'*

*At this point in the conversation, Julián stuck his head round the door of the back room with a hat mould in his hands.*

*'Don Ricardo, whenever you're ready ...'*

*'Tell me, Julián, what are you doing this afternoon?' Aldaya asked.*

*Julián looked alternately at his father and the tycoon.*

*'Well, helping my father here, in the shop.'*

*'Apart from that.'*

*'I was thinking of going to the library....'*

*'You like books, eh?'*

*'Yes, sir.'*

*'Have you read Conrad? Heart of Darkness?'*

*'Three times.'*

*The hatter frowned, utterly lost. 'And who is this Conrad, if you don't mind my asking?'*

*Aldaya silenced him with a gesture that seemed like something from a shareholders' meeting.*

*'In my house I have a library with fourteen thousand books, Julián. When I was young, I read a lot, but now I no longer have the time. Come to think of it, I have three copies signed by Conrad himself. My son Jorge can't even be dragged into the library. The only person who thinks and reads in the house*

*is my daughter Penélope, so all those books are being wasted. Would you like to see them?'*

Julián nodded, speechless. The hatter observed the scene with a sense of unease he couldn't quite define. All those names were unknown to him. Novels, as everyone knew, were for women and for people who had nothing better to do. *The Heart of Darkness* sounded like a mortal sin at the very least.

'Fortunato, your son is coming with me. I want to introduce him to my son Jorge. Don't worry, we'll bring him back to you later. Tell me, young man, have you ever been in a Mercedes-Benz?'

Julián presumed that that was the name of the cumbersome, imperial-looking machine the industrialist used for getting around. He shook his head.

'Well, then, it's about time. It's like going to heaven, but without dying.'

Antoni Fortuny watched them leave in that exceedingly luxurious carriage, and when he searched his heart, all he found was sadness. That night, while he had dinner with Sophie (who was wearing her new dress and shoes and had almost no bruises or scars), he asked himself where he had gone wrong this time. Just when God was returning a son to him, Aldaya was taking him away.

'Take off that dress, woman, you look like a whore. And don't let me see this wine on the table again. The watered-down sort is quite good enough for us. Greed will corrupt us all in the end.'

Julián had never crossed over to the other side of Avenida Diagonal. That line of groves, empty plots of land, and palaces awaiting the expansion of the city was a forbidden frontier. Hamlets, hills, and mysterious places rumoured to contain unimaginable wealth extended beyond it. As they passed through, Aldaya talked to Julián about San Gabriel's, about new friends Julián had never set eyes on, about a future he had not thought possible.

'What do you aspire to, Julián? In life, I mean.'

'I don't know. Sometimes I think I'd like to be a writer. A novelist.'

'Like Conrad, eh? You're very young, of course. And tell me, doesn't banking tempt you?'

'I don't know, sir. The truth is that it hadn't even entered my head. I've never seen more than three pesetas together. High finance is a mystery to me.'

Aldaya laughed. 'There's no mystery, Julián. The trick is not to put pesetas together in threes, but in three million. That way there's no enigma, I can assure you. No Holy Trinity.'

That afternoon, as he drove up Avenida del Tibidabo, Julián thought he was entering the doors of paradise. Mansions that seemed like cathedrals flanked the way. Halfway along the avenue, the driver turned, and they went through the gates of one of them. Instantly an army of servants set about receiving the master. All Julián could see was a large, majestic house with three floors. It had never occurred to him that real people could live in places like this. He let himself be taken through the lobby, then he crossed a vaulted hall from where a marble staircase rose, framed by velvet curtains, and finally entered a large room whose walls were a tapestry of books, from floor to ceiling.

'What do you think?' asked Aldaya.

Julián was barely listening.

'Damián, tell Jorge to come down to the library immediately.'

The faceless and silent servants glided away at the slightest order from the master with the efficiency and submissiveness of a body of well-trained insects.

'You're going to need a new wardrobe, Julián. There are a lot of morons out there who only go by appearances. . . . I'll tell Jacinta to take care of that; you don't have to worry about it. And it's probably best if you don't mention it to your father, in case it annoys him. Look, here comes Jorge. Jorge, I want you to meet a wonderful young man who is going to be your new classmate. Julián Fortu—'

'Julián Carax,' he corrected.

'Julián Carax,' repeated a satisfied Aldaya. 'I like the sound of it. This is my son Jorge.'

Julián held out his hand, and Jorge Aldaya shook it. His touch was luke-warm, unenthusiastic, and his face had a pale, chiselled look that came from having grown up in that doll-like world. To Julián, his clothes and shoes seemed like something out of a novel. His eyes gave off an air of bravado and arrogance, of disdain and sugary politeness. Julián smiled at him openly, reading insecurity, fear, and emptiness under that shell of vanity.

'Is it true you haven't read any of these books?'

'Books are boring.'

'Books are mirrors: you only see in them what you already have inside you,' answered Julián.

Don Ricardo Aldaya laughed again. 'Well, I'll leave you two alone so you can get to know each other. Julián, you'll see that although he seems spoiled and conceited, underneath that mask Jorge isn't as stupid as he looks. He has something of his father in him.'

Aldaya's words seemed to fall like knives on the boy, though he didn't let his smile fade at all. Julián regretted his answer and felt sorry for him.

'You must be the hatter's son,' said Jorge, without malice. 'My father talks about you a lot these days.'

'It's the novelty. I hope you don't hold that against me. Under this mask of a know-it-all meddler, I'm not such an idiot as I seem.'

Jorge smiled at him, Julián thought he smiled the way people smile who have no friends – with gratitude.

'Come, I'll show you the rest of the house.'

They left the library behind them and went off towards the main door and the gardens. When they crossed the hall with the staircase, Julián looked up and glimpsed a figure ascending the stairs with one hand on the banister. He felt as if he were caught up in a vision. The girl must have been about twelve or thirteen and was escorted by a mature woman, small and rosy-cheeked, who looked like a governess. The girl wore a blue

215

satin dress. Her hair was the colour of almonds, and the skin on her shoulders and slim neck seemed translucent. She stopped at the top of the stairs and turned around briefly. For a second their eyes met, and she offered him the ghost of a smile. Then the governess put her arms round the girl's shoulders and led her to the entrance of a corridor into which they both disappeared. Julián looked down and he fixed his eyes on Jorge's again.

'That's Penélope, my sister. You'll meet her later. She's a bit nutty. She spends all day reading. Come on, I want to show you the chapel in the basement. The cooks say it's haunted.'

Julián followed the boy meekly, but he cared little about anything else. Now he understood. He had dreamed about her countless times, on that same staircase, with that same blue dress and that same movement of her ash-grey eyes, without knowing who she was or why she smiled at him. When he went out into the garden, he let himself be led by Jorge as far as the coach houses and the tennis courts that stretched out beyond. Only then did he turn around to look back and saw her in her window on the second floor. He could barely make out her shape, but he knew she was smiling at him and that somehow she, too, had recognized him.

That fleeting glimpse of Penélope Aldaya at the top of the staircase remained with him during his first weeks at San Gabriel's. His new world was not all to his liking: the pupils at San Gabriel's behaved like haughty, arrogant princes, while their teachers were like docile servants. The first friend Julián made there, apart from Jorge Aldaya, was a boy called Fernando Ramos, the son of one of the cooks at the school, who would never have imagined he would end up wearing a cassock and teaching in the same classrooms in which he himself had grown up. Fernando, whom the rest nicknamed the 'Kitchen Sweep', and whom they treated like a servant, was alert and intelligent but had hardly any friends among the schoolboys. His only companion was an eccentric boy called Miquel Moliner, who in time would become the best friend Julián ever made at the school. Miquel Moliner, who had too much brain and too little patience, enjoyed teasing his teachers by questioning all their statements, using clever arguments in which he displayed both ingenuity and a poisonous sting. The rest feared his sharp tongue and considered him a member of some other species. In a way this was not entirely mistaken, for despite his bohemian traits and the unaristocratic tone he affected, Miquel was the son of a businessman who had become obscenely rich through the manufacture of arms.

'Carax, isn't it? I'm told your father makes hats,' he said when Fernando Ramos introduced them.

'Julián to my friends. I'm told yours makes cannons.'

'He just sells them, actually. The only thing he knows how to make is money. My friends, among whom I only count Nietzsche and Fernando here, call me Miquel.'

Miquel Moliner was a sad boy. He suffered from an unhealthy obsession with death and all matters funereal, a field to the consideration of which he dedicated much of his time and talent. His mother had died three years earlier as a result of a strange domestic accident, which some foolish doctor had dared describe as suicide. It was Miquel who had discovered the body shining under the waters of the well, in the summer mansion the family owned in Argentina. When they pulled her out with ropes, they found that the pockets of the dead woman's coat were filled with stones. There was also a letter written in German, the mother's native tongue, but Señor Moliner, who had never bothered to learn the language, burned it that very afternoon without allowing anyone to read it. Miquel Moliner saw death everywhere – in fallen leaves, in birds that had dropped out of their nests, in old people, and in the rain, which swept everything away. He was exceptionally talented at drawing and would often become distracted for hours, creating charcoal sketches in which a lady, whom Julián took to be his mother, always appeared against a background of mist and deserted beaches.

'What do you want to be when you grow up, Miquel?'

'I'll never grow up,' he would answer enigmatically.

His main interest, apart from sketching and contradicting

*every living soul, was the work of a mysterious Austrian doctor who, in years to come, would become famous: Sigmund Freud. Thanks to his deceased mother, Miquel Moliner read and wrote perfect German, and he owned a number of books by the Viennese doctor. His favourite field was the interpretation of dreams. He used to ask people what they had dreamed, and would then make a diagnosis. He always said he was going to die young and that he didn't mind. Julián believed that, by thinking so much about death, he had ended up finding more sense in it than in life.*

*'The day I die, all that was once mine will be yours, Julián,' he would say. 'Except my dreams.'*

*Besides Fernando Ramos, Moliner, and Jorge Aldaya, Julián also befriended a shy and rather unsociable boy called Javier, the only son of the caretakers of San Gabriel's, who lived in a modest house stationed at the entrance to the school gardens. Javier, who, like Fernando, was considered by the rest of the boys to be no more than an irritating lackey, prowled about alone in the gardens and courtyards of the compound. From so much wandering around the school, he ended up knowing every nook and cranny of the building, from the tunnels in the basements to the passages up to the towers, and all kinds of hiding places that nobody remembered anymore. They were his secret world and his refuge. He always carried with him a penknife he had removed from one of his father's drawers, and he liked to carve wooden figures with it, keeping them in the school dovecote. His father, Ramón, the caretaker, was a veteran of the Cuban War, where he had lost a hand and (it was maliciously rumoured) his right testicle, as a result of a pellet shot from Theodore Roosevelt himself during the raid of the Bay of Cochinos. Convinced that idleness was the mother of all evil, 'Ramón Oneball' (as the schoolboys nicknamed him) set his son the task of gathering up all the fallen leaves from the pine grove and the courtyard around the fountains in a sack. Ramón was a good man, rather coarse and fatally given to choosing bad company, most notably his wife. He had married a strapping, dim-witted woman with delusions of* grandeur and the looks of a scullion, who was wont to dress skimpily in front of her son and the other boys, a habit that gave rise to no end of mirth and ridicule. Her Christian name was María Craponcia, but she called herself Yvonne, because she thought it more elegant. Yvonne used to question her son about the possibilities for social advancement that his friends presented, for she believed that he was making connections with the elite of Barcelona society. She would ask him about the fortune of this or that one, imagining herself dressed in the best silks and being received for tea in the great salons of good society.

Javier tried to spend as little time as possible in the house and was grateful for the jobs his father gave him, however hard they might be. Any excuse was good in order to be alone, to escape into his secret world and carve his wooden figures. When the schoolboys saw him from afar, some would laugh or throw stones at him. One day Julián felt so sorry for him when he saw how a stone had gashed the boy's forehead and knocked him onto a pile of rubble, that he decided to go to his aid and offer him his friendship. At first Javier thought that Julián was coming to finish him off while the others fell about laughing.

'My name is Julián,' he said, stretching out his hand. 'My friends and I were about to go and play chess in the pine grove, and I wondered whether you'd like to join us.'

'I don't know how to play chess.'

'Nor did I, until two weeks ago. But Miquel is a good teacher. . . .'

The boy looked at him suspiciously, expecting the prank, the hidden attack, at any moment.

'I don't know whether your friends will want me there.'

'It was their idea. What do you say?'

From that day on, Javier would sometimes join them after finishing the jobs he had been assigned. He didn't usually say anything but would listen and watch the others. Aldaya was slightly fearful of him. Fernando, who had himself experienced the rejection of others because of his humble origins, would go out of his way to be kind to the strange boy. Miquel Moliner, who taught him the rudiments of chess and watched him with a careful eye, was the most sceptical of all.

'That boy is a nutter. He catches cats and pigeons and tortures them for hours with his knife. Then he buries them in the pine grove. Delightful.'

'Who says so?'

'He told me so himself the other day, while I was explaining the knight's moves to him. He also told me that sometimes his mother gets into his bed at night and fondles him.'

'He must have been pulling your leg.'

'I doubt it. That kid isn't right in the head, Julián, and it's probably not his fault.'

Julián struggled to ignore Miquel's warnings and predictions, but the fact was that he was finding it difficult to establish a friendship with the son of the caretaker. Yvonne in particular did not approve of Julián or of Fernando Ramos. Of all the young men, they were the only ones who didn't have a single peseta. Rumour had it that Julián's father was a simple shopkeeper and that his mother had only got as far as being a music teacher. 'Those people have no money, class, or elegance, my love,' his mother would lecture him. 'The one you should befriend is Aldaya. He comes from a very good family.' 'Yes. Mother,' the boy would answer. 'Whatever you say.'

As time went by, Javier seemed to start trusting his new friends. Occasionally he said a few words, and he was carving a set of chess pieces for Miquel Moliner, in appreciation for his lessons. One day, when nobody expected it or thought it possible, they discovered that Javier knew how to smile and that he had the innocent laugh of a child.

'You see? He's just a normal boy,' Julián argued.

Miquel Moliner remained unconvinced, and he observed the strange lad with a rigorous scrutiny that was almost scientific.

'Javier is obsessed with you, Julián,' he told him one day. 'Everything he does is only to earn your approval.'

'What nonsense! He has a mother and a father for that; I'm only a friend.'

'Irresponsible, that's what you are. His father is a poor wretch who has trouble finding his own bum, and Doña Yvonne is a harpy with the brain of a flea who spends her time pretending to meet people by chance in her underwear, convinced that she is Venus incarnate or something far worse I'd rather not mention. The boy, quite naturally, is looking for a substitute, and you, the saviour, fall from heaven and give him your hand. St Julián of the Fountain, patron saint of the dispossessed.'

'This Dr Freud is rotting your brains, Miquel. We all need friends. Even you.'

'That kid doesn't have friends and never will. He has the heart of a spider. And if you don't believe me, time will tell. I wonder what he dreams about. . . ?'

Miquel Moliner could not know that Francisco Javier's dreams were more like his friend Julián's than he would ever have thought possible. Once, some months before Julián had started at the school, the caretaker's son was gathering dead leaves from the fountain courtyard when Don Ricardo Aldaya's luxurious automobile arrived. That afternoon the tycoon had company. He was escorted by an apparition, an angel of light dressed in silk who seemed to hover above the ground. The angel, who was none other than Aldaya's daughter Penélope, stepped out of the Mercedes and walked over to one of the fountains, waving her parasol and stopping to splash the water of the pond with her hands. As usual, her governess, Jacinta, followed her dutifully, observant of the slightest gesture from the girl. It wouldn't have mattered if an army of servants had guarded her: Javier only had eyes for the girl. He was afraid that if he blinked, the vision would vanish. He remained there, paralysed, breathlessly spying on the mirage. Soon after, as if the girl had sensed his presence and his furtive gaze, Penélope raised her eyes and looked in his direction. The beauty of that face seemed painful, unsustainable. He thought he saw the hint of a smile on her lips. Terrified, Javier ran off to hide at the top of the water tower, next to the dovecote in the attic of the school building, his *favourite hiding place. His hands were still shaking when he gathered his carving utensils and began to work on a new piece in the form of the face he had just sighted. When he returned to the caretaker's home that night, hours later than usual, his mother was waiting for him, half naked and furious. The boy looked down, fearing that if his mother read his eyes, she would see in them the girl from the pond and know what he had been thinking about.*

*'And where've you been, you little shit?'*

*'I'm sorry, Mother. I got lost.'*

*'You've been lost since the day you were born.'*

*Years later, every time he stuck his revolver into the mouth of a prisoner and pulled the trigger, Chief Inspector Francisco Javier Fumero would remember the day he saw his mother's head burst open like a ripe watermelon near an outdoor bar in Las Planas and didn't feel anything, just the tedium of dead things. The Civil Guard, alerted by the manager of the bar, who had heard the shot, found the boy sitting on a rock holding a smoking shotgun on his lap. He was staring impassively at the decapitated body of María Craponcia, alias Yvonne, covered in insects. When he saw the guards coming over to him, he just shrugged his shoulders, his face splattered with blood, as if he were being ravaged by smallpox. Following the sobs, the civil guards found Ramón Oneball squatting by a tree some thirty yards away, in the undergrowth. He was shaking like a child and was unable to make himself understood. The lieutenant of the Civil Guard, after much deliberation, reported that the event had been a tragic accident, and so he recorded it in his statement, though not on his conscience. When they asked the boy if there was anything they could do for him, Francisco Javier asked whether he could keep that old gun, because when he grew up, he wanted to be a soldier. . . .*

'Are you feeling all right, Señor Romero de Torres?'

The sudden appearance of Fumero in Father Fernando Ramos's narrative had stunned me, but the effect on

Fermín was devastating. He looked white as a sheet and his hands shook.

'A sudden drop in my blood pressure,' Fermín improvised in a tiny voice. 'This Catalan climate can be hell for us southerners.'

'May I offer you a glass of water?' asked the priest in a worried tone.

'If Your Grace wouldn't mind. And perhaps a chocolate, for the glucose, you know . . .'

The priest poured him a glass of water, which Fermín drank greedily.

'All I have are some eucalyptus sweets. Would they be of any help?'

'God bless you.'

Fermín swallowed a fistful of sweets and after a while seemed to recover his natural pallor.

'This boy, the son of the caretaker who heroically lost his scrotum defending the colonies, are you sure his name was Fumero, Francisco Javier Fumero?'

'Yes. Quite sure. Do you know him?'

'No,' we intoned in unison.

Father Fernando frowned. 'It wouldn't have surprised me. Regrettably, Francisco Javier has ended up being a notorious character.'

'We're not sure we understand you. . . .'

'You understand me perfectly. Francisco Javier Fumero is chief inspector of the Barcelona Crime Squad and is widely known. His reputation has even reached those of us who never leave this establishment, and I'd say that when you heard his name, you shrank a couple of inches.'

'Now that you mention it, Your Excellency, the name does ring a bell. . . .'

Father Fernando looked sidelong at us. 'This young man isn't the son of Julián Carax. Am I right?'

'Spiritual son, Your Eminency. Morally, that has more weight.'

'What kind of mess are you two in? Who has sent you?'

At that point I was certain we were about to be kicked out of the priest's office, and I decided to silence Fermín and, for once, play the honesty card.

'You're right, Father. Julián Carax isn't my father. But nobody has sent us. Years ago I happened to come across a book by Carax, a book that was thought to have disappeared, and from that time on, I have tried to discover more about him and clarify the circumstances of his death. Señor Romero de Torres has helped me—'

'What book?'

'*The Shadow of the Wind*. Have you read it?'

'I've read all of Julián's novels.'

'Have you kept them?'

The priest shook his head.

'May I ask what you did with them?'

'Years ago someone came into my room and set fire to them.'

'Do you suspect anyone?'

'Of course. I suspect Fumero. Isn't that why you're here?'

Fermín and I exchanged puzzled looks.

'Inspector Fumero? Why would he want to burn the books?'

'Who else would? During the last year we spent together at school, Francisco Javier tried to kill Julián with his father's shotgun. If Miquel hadn't stopped him . . .'

'Why did he try to kill him? Julián had been his only friend.'

'Francisco Javier was obsessed with Penélope Aldaya. Nobody knew this. I don't think Penélope had even noticed the boy's existence. He kept the secret for years. Apparently he used to follow Julián. I think one day he saw him kiss her. I don't know. What I do know is that he tried to kill him in broad daylight. Miquel Moliner, who had never trusted Fumero, threw himself on him and stopped him at the last moment. The hole made by the bullet is still visible by the entrance. Every time I go past it, I remember that day.'

'What happened to Fumero?'

'He and his family were thrown out of the place. I think Francisco Javier was sent to a boarding school for a while. We heard no more about him until a couple of years later, when his mother died in a hunting accident. There was no such accident. Francisco Javier Fumero is a murderer.'

'If I were to tell you . . .' mumbled Fermín.

'It wouldn't be a bad thing if one of you did tell me something, but something true for a change.'

'We can tell you that Fumero was not the person who burned your books.'

'Who was it, then?'

'In all likelihood it was a man whose face is disfigured by burns; a man who calls himself Laín Coubert.'

'Isn't that the one. . . ?'

I nodded. 'The name of one of Carax's characters. The devil.'

Father Fernando leaned back in his armchair, almost as confused as we were.

'What does seem increasingly clear is that Penélope Aldaya is at the centre of all this business, and she's the person we know least about,' Fermín remarked.

'I don't think I can help you there. I hardly ever saw her, and then only from a distance, two or three times. What I know about her is what Julián told me, which wasn't much. The only other person who I heard mention Penélope's name a few times was Jacinta Coronado.'

'Jacinta Coronado?'

'Penélope's governess. She raised Jorge and Penélope. She loved them madly, especially Penélope. Sometimes she would come to the school to collect Jorge, because Don Ricardo Aldaya wanted his children to be watched over at all times by some member of his household. Jacinta was an angel. She had heard that both Julián and I came from modest families, so she would always bring us afternoon snacks because she thought we went hungry. I would tell her that my father was the cook and not to worry, for I was never without something to eat. But she insisted. Sometimes I'd wait and talk to her. She was the kindest person I've ever met. She had no children, or any boyfriend that I knew of. She was alone in the world and had devoted her life to the Aldaya children. She simply adored Penélope. She still talks about her. . . .'

'Are you still in touch with Jacinta?'

'I sometimes visit her in the Santa Lucía hospice. She doesn't have anyone. For reasons we cannot comprehend, the Good Lord doesn't always reward us during our lifetime. Jacinta is now a very old woman and is as alone as she has always been.'

Fermín and I exchanged looks.

'What about Penélope? Hasn't she ever visited her?'

Father Fernando's eyes grew dark and impenetrable. 'Nobody knows what happened to Penélope. That girl was Jacinta's life. When the Aldayas left for America and she lost her, she lost everything.'

'Why didn't they take her with them? Did Penélope go to Argentina with the rest of the Aldayas?' I asked.

The priest shrugged his shoulders. 'I don't know. Nobody ever saw Penélope again or heard anything about her after 1919.'

'The year Carax left for Paris,' Fermín observed.

'You must promise me that you're not going to bother this poor old lady and stir up painful memories for her.'

'Who do you take us for, Father?' asked Fermín, annoyed.

Suspecting that he would get no more from us, Father Fernando made us swear to him that we would keep him informed about any new discoveries we made. To reassure him, Fermín insisted on swearing on a New Testament that lay on the priest's desk.

'Leave the Gospels alone. Your word is enough for me.'

'You don't let anything pass you, do you, Father? You're sharp as a nail.'

'Come, let me accompany you to the door.'

He led us through the garden until we reached the spiked gate and then stopped at a reasonable distance from the exit, gazing at the street that wound its way down towards the real world, as if he were afraid he might evaporate if he ventured out a few steps further. I wondered when Father Fernando had last left the school grounds.

'I was very sad when I heard that Julián had died,' he said softly. 'Despite everything that happened afterwards and the fact that we grew apart as time went by, we were good friends: Miquel, Aldaya, Julián, and myself. Even Fumero. I always thought we were going to be inseparable, but life must know things that we don't know. I've never had friends like those again, and I don't imagine I ever will. I hope you find what you're looking for, Daniel.'

## 26

It was almost midmorning when we reached Paseo de la Bonanova, wrapped in our own thoughts. I had little doubt that Fermín's were largely devoted to the sinister appearance of Inspector Fumero in the story. I glanced over at him and noticed that he seemed consumed by anxiety. A veil of dark red clouds bled across the sky, punctured by splinters of light the colour of fallen leaves.

'If we don't hurry, we're going to get caught in a downpour,' I said.

'Not yet. Those clouds look like nighttime, like a bruise. They're the sort that wait.'

'Don't tell me you're also an expert on clouds, Fermín.'

'Living on the streets has unexpected educational side effects. Listen, just thinking about this Fumero business has stirred my juices. Would you object to a stop at the bar in Plaza de Sarriá to polish off two well-endowed omelette sandwiches, plus trimmings?'

We set off towards the square, where a knot of old folks

hovered around the local pigeon community, their lives reduced to a ritual of spreading crumbs and waiting. We found ourselves a table near the entrance, and Fermín proceeded to wolf down the two sandwiches, his and mine, a pint of beer, two chocolate bars, and a triple coffee heavily laced with rum and sugar. For dessert he had a Sugus sweet. A man sitting at the next table glanced at Fermín over his newspaper, probably thinking the same thing I was.

'I don't see how you fit it all in, Fermín.'

'In my family we've always had a speedy metabolism. My sister Jesusa, God rest her soul, was capable of eating a six-egg omelette with blood sausage in the middle of the afternoon and then tucking in like a Cossack at night. Poor thing. She was just like me, you know? Same face and same classic figure, rather on the lean side. A doctor from Cáceres once told my mother that the Romero de Torres family was the missing link between man and the hammerhead, for ninety per cent of our organism is cartilage, mainly concentrated in the nose and the outer ear. Jesusa was often mistaken for me in the village, because she never grew breasts and began to shave before I did. She died of consumption when she was twenty-two, a virgin to the end and secretly in love with a sanctimonious priest who, when he met her in the street, always said, "Hello, Fermín, you're becoming quite a dashing young man." Life's ironies.'

'Do you miss them?'

'The family?'

Fermín shrugged his shoulders, caught in a nostalgic smile.

'What do I know? Few things are more deceptive than memories. Look at the priest. . . . And you? Do you miss your mother?'

I looked down. 'A lot.'

'Do you know what I remember most about mine?' Fermín asked. 'Her smell. She always smelled clean, like a loaf of sweet bread. It didn't matter if she'd spent the day working in the fields or was wearing the same old rags she'd worn all week. She always smelled of the best things in this world. Mind you, she was pretty uncouth. She could swear like a trooper, but she smelled like a fairy tale princess. Or at least that's what I thought. What about you? What is it you remember most about your mother, Daniel?'

I hesitated for a moment, clawing at words my lips couldn't shape.

'Nothing. For years now I haven't been able to remember my mother. I can't remember what her face was like, or her voice or her smell. I lost them all the day I discovered Julián Carax, and they haven't come back.'

Fermín watched me cautiously, considering his reply. 'Don't you have a photograph of her?'

'I've never wanted to look for them,' I said.

'Why not?'

I'd never told anyone this, not even my father or Tomás. 'Because I'm afraid. I'm afraid of looking at a photograph of my mother and discovering that she's a stranger. You probably think that's nonsense.'

Fermín shook his head. 'And is that why you believe that if you manage to unravel the mystery of Julián Carax and rescue him from oblivion, the face of your mother will come back to you?'

I looked at him. There was no irony or judgment in his expression. For a moment Fermín Romero de Torres seemed to me the wisest and most lucid man in the universe.

'Perhaps,' I said without thinking.

At noon on the dot, we got on a bus that would take us back downtown. We sat at the front, just behind the driver; a circumstance Fermín used as an excuse to hold a discussion with the man about the many advances, both technical and cosmetic, that he had noticed in public transportation since the last time he'd used it, circa 1940 – especially with regard to signs, as was borne out by the notice that read SPITTING AND FOUL LANGUAGE ARE STRICTLY FORBIDDEN. Fermín looked briefly at the sign and decided to acknowledge it by energetically clearing his throat of phlegm. This granted us a sharp look of disapproval from a trio of saintly ladies who travelled like a commando unit at the back of the bus, each one armed with a missal.

'You savage!' murmured the bigot on the eastern flank, who bore a remarkable likeness to the official portrait of Il Duce, but with curls.

'There they go,' said Fermín. 'Three saints has my Spain. St Holier-than-thou, St Holyshit and St Holycow. Between us all, we've turned this country into a joke.'

'You can say that again,' agreed the driver. 'We were better off with the Republic. To say nothing of the traffic. It stinks.'

A man sitting at the back of the bus laughed, enjoying the exchange of views. I recognized him as the same fellow who had sat next to us in the bar. His expression seemed to suggest that he was on Fermín's side and that he wanted to see him get merciless with the diehards. We exchanged a quick glance. He gave me a friendly smile and returned to his newspaper. When we got to Calle Ganduxer, I noticed that Fermín had curled up in a ball under his raincoat and was having a nap with his mouth wide open, an expression of bliss and innocence on his face.

The bus was gliding through the wealthy domains of Paseo de San Gervasio when Fermín suddenly woke up. 'I've been dreaming about Father Fernando,' he told me. 'Except that in my dream he was dressed as the centre forward for Real Madrid and he had the league cup next to him, shining like the Holy Grail.'

'I wonder why?' I asked.

'If Freud is right, this probably means that the priest has sneaked in a goal for us.'

'He struck me as an honest man.'

'Fair enough. Perhaps too honest for his own good. All priests with the makings of a saint end up being sent off to the missions, to see whether the mosquitoes or the piranhas will finish them off.'

'Don't exaggerate.'

'What blessed innocence, Daniel. You'd even believe in the tooth fairy. All right, just to give you an example: the tall tale about Miquel Moliner that Nuria Monfort landed on you. I think the wench told you more whoppers than the editorial page of *L'Osservatore Romano*. Now it turns out that she's married to a childhood friend of Aldaya and Carax – isn't that a coincidence? And on top of that, we have the story of Jacinta, the good nurse, which might be true but sounds too much like the last act in a play by Alexandre Dumas the younger. Not to mention the star appearance of Fumero.'

'Then do you think Father Fernando lied to us?'

'No. I agree with you that he seems honest, but the uniform carries a lot of weight, and he may well have kept an *ora pro nobis* or two up his sleeve, if you get my drift. I think that if he lied, it was by way of holding back or decorum, not out of spite or malice. Besides, I don't imagine him capable of inventing such a story. If he could lie better, he wouldn't be teaching algebra and Latin; he'd be in the bishopric by now, growing fat in an office like a cardinal's and plunging soft sponge cakes in his coffee.'

'What do you suggest we do, then?'

'Sooner or later we're going to have to dig up the mummified corpse of the angelic granny and shake it from the ankles to see what falls out. For the time being, I'm going to pull a few strings and see what I can find out about this Miquel Moliner. And it wouldn't be a bad idea to keep an eye on that Nuria Monfort. I think she's turning out to be what my deceased mother would have called a sly old fox.'

'You're mistaken about her,' I claimed.

'You're shown a pair of nice breasts and you think you've seen St Teresa – which at your age can be excused but not cured. Just leave her to me, Daniel. The fragrance of the eternal female no longer overpowers me the way it mesmerizes you. At my age the flow of blood to the brain takes precedence over that which flows to the loins.'

'Look who's talking.'

Fermín pulled out his wallet and started to count his money.

'You have a fortune there,' I said. 'Is it all change from this morning?'

'Partly. The rest is legitimate. I'm taking my Bernarda out today, and I can't refuse that woman anything. If necessary, I would rob the Central Bank of Spain to indulge her every whim. What about you? What are your plans for the rest of the day?'

'Nothing special.'

'And what about the girl?'

'What girl?'

'Little Bo Peep. Who do you think? Aguilar's sister.'

'I don't know. I don't have any plans.'

'What you don't have, to put it bluntly, is enough balls to take the bull by the horns.'

At that the conductor made his way up to us with a tired expression, his mouth juggling a toothpick, which he twisted and turned through his teeth with circus-like dexterity.

'Excuse me, but the ladies over there want to know if you could use more respectable language.'

'They can mind their own bloody business,' answered Fermín in a loud voice.

The conductor turned towards the three ladies and shrugged, indicating that he had done what he could and was not inclined to get involved in a scuffle over a matter of semantic modesty.

'People who have no life always have to stick their nose into the life of others,' said Fermín. 'What were we talking about?'

'About my lack of guts.'

'Right. A textbook case. Trust me, young man. Go after

your girl. Life flies by, especially the bit that's worth living. You heard what the priest said. Like a flash.'

'She's not *my* girl.'

'Well, then, make her yours before someone else takes her, especially the little tin soldier.'

'You talk as if Bea were a trophy.'

'No, as if she were a blessing,' Fermín corrected. 'Look, Daniel. Destiny is usually just around the corner. Like a thief, a hooker, or a lottery vendor: its three most common personifications. But what destiny does not do is home visits. You have to go for it yourself.'

I spent the rest of the journey considering this pearl of wisdom while Fermín had another snooze, an occupation for which he had a Napoleonic talent. We got off the bus on the corner of Gran Vía and Paseo de Gracia under a leaden sky that stole the light of day. Buttoning his raincoat up to his neck, Fermín announced that he was departing in a hurry towards his *pensión*, to smarten up for his meeting with Bernarda.

'You must understand that with rather modest looks such as mine, basic beautification requires at least ninety minutes. You don't get far without some looks; that's the sad truth about these dishonest times. *Vanitas peccata mundi.*'

I saw him walk away down Gran Vía, barely a sketch of a little man sheltering himself in a drab raincoat that flapped in the wind like a ragged flag. I started off for home, where I planned to recruit a good book and hide away from the world. When I turned the corner of Puerta del Ángel and Calle Santa Ana, my heart missed a beat. As usual, Fermín had been right. Destiny was waiting for me in front of the bookshop, clad in a tight grey wool suit, new shoes, and silk stockings, studying her reflection in the shop window.

'My father thinks I've gone to twelve o'clock mass,' said Bea without looking up from her own image.

'You could easily be there. There's been a continuous

performance since nine o'clock this morning less than twenty yards from here, in the Church of Santa Ana.'

We spoke like two strangers who have casually stopped by a shop window, looking for each other's eyes in the pane.

'Let's not make a joke of it. I've had to pick up a church leaflet to see what the sermon was about. He's going to ask me for a detailed synopsis.'

'Your father thinks of everything.'

'He's sworn he'll break your legs.'

'Before that he'll have to find out who I am. And while my legs are still in one piece, I can run faster than him.'

Bea was looking at me tensely, glancing over her shoulder at the people who drifted by behind us in puffs of grey and wind.

'I don't know what you're laughing about,' she said. 'He means it.'

'I'm not laughing. I'm scared shitless. It's just that I'm so happy to see you.'

A suggestion of a smile, nervous, fleeting. 'Me, too,' Bea admitted.

'You say it as if it were an illness.'

'It's worse than that. I thought that if I saw you again in daylight, I might come to my senses.'

I wondered whether that was a compliment or a condemnation.

'We can't be seen together, Daniel. Not like this, in full view of everyone.'

'If you like, we can go into the bookshop. There's a coffeepot in the back room and—'

'No. I don't want anyone to see me go into or come out of this place. If anyone sees me talking to you now, I can always say I happened to bump into my brother's best friend. If we are seen together more than once, we'll arouse suspicion.'

I sighed. 'And who's going to see us? Who cares what we do?'

'People always have eyes for what is none of their business, and my father knows half of Barcelona.'

'So why have you come here to wait for me?'

'I haven't come to wait for you. I've come to church, remember? You said so yourself. Twenty yards from here . . .'

'You scare me, Bea. You lie even better than I do.'

'You don't know me, Daniel.'

'So your brother tells me.'

Our eyes met in the reflection.

'The other night you showed me something I'd never seen before,' murmured Bea. 'Now it's my turn.'

I frowned, intrigued. Bea opened her bag, pulled out a folded card, and handed it to me.

'You're not the only person in Barcelona who knows secrets, Daniel. I have a surprise for you. I'll wait for you at this address today at four. Nobody must know that we have arranged to meet there.'

'How will I know that I've found the right place?'

'You'll know.'

I looked at her briefly, praying that she wasn't just making fun of me.

'If you don't come, I'll understand,' Bea said. 'I'll understand that you don't want to see me anymore.'

Without giving me a second to answer, she turned around and walked hurriedly off towards the Ramblas. I was left holding the card, my words still hanging on my lips, my eyes following her until her silhouette melted into the shadows that preceded the storm. I opened the card. Inside, in blue handwriting, was an address I knew well.

*Avenida del Tibidabo, 32*

The storm didn't wait until nightfall to show its teeth. The first flashes of lightning caught me by surprise shortly after taking a bus on Line 22. As we went round Plaza Molina and started up Calle Balmes, the city was already beginning to fade behind a curtain of liquid velvet, reminding me that I hadn't even thought of taking an umbrella with me.

'Now that's what I call courage,' said the conductor when I asked for the stop.

It was already ten past four when the bus left me in the middle of nowhere – somewhere at the end of Calle Balmes – at the mercy of the storm. Opposite, Avenida del Tibidabo disappeared in a watery mirage. I counted up to three and started to run. Minutes later, soaked to the bone and shivering, I stopped under a doorway to get my breath back. I scrutinized the rest of the route. The storm's icy blast blurred the ghostly outline of mansions and large, rambling houses veiled in the mist. Among them rose the dark and solitary tower of the Aldaya mansion, anchored among the swaying trees. I pushed my soaking hair away from my eyes and began to run toward it, crossing the deserted avenue.

The small door encased within the gates swung in the wind. Beyond it, a path wound its way up to the house. I slipped in through the door and made my way across the property. Through the undergrowth I could make out the pedestals of statues that had been knocked down. As I neared the mansion, I noticed that one of the statues, the figure of an avenging angel, had been dumped into the fountain that was the centrepiece of the garden. Its blackened marble shone, ghostlike, beneath the sheet of water that flowed over the edge of the bowl. The hand of the fiery angel emerged from the water; an accusing finger, as sharp as a bayonet, pointing towards the front door of the house. The carved oak door seemed to be ajar. I pushed it and ventured a few steps into a cavernous entrance hall, its walls flickering with the gentle light of a candle.

'I thought you weren't coming,' said Bea.

The corridor was entombed in shadows, and Bea's silhouette stood out against the pallid light of a gallery that opened up beyond. She was sitting on a chair against the wall, a candle at her feet.

'Close the door,' she told me without getting up. 'The key is in the lock.'

I obeyed. The lock creaked with a deathly echo. I heard Bea's footsteps approaching me from behind and felt her touch on my soaking clothes.

'You're trembling. Is it fear or cold?'

'I haven't decided yet. Why are we here?'

She smiled in the dark and took my hand. 'Don't you know? I thought you would have guessed. . . .'

'This was the Aldayas' house, that's all I know. How did you manage to get in, and how did you know . . . ?'

'Come on, we'll light a fire to warm you up.'

She led me through the corridor to the gallery, which presided over the inner courtyard of the house. The marble columns and naked walls of the sitting room crept up to the coffered ceiling, which was falling to pieces. You could make out the spaces where paintings and mirrors had once covered the walls, and there were marks on the marble floor where furniture had stood. At one end of the room was a fireplace laid with a few logs. A pile of old newspapers stood by the poker. The air from the fireplace smelled of recent flames and charcoal. Bea knelt down by the hearth and started to place a few sheets of newspaper among the logs. She pulled out a match and lit them, quickly conjuring up a crown of flames. I imagined she was thinking that I must be dying of curiosity and impatience, so I decided to adopt a nonchalant air, making it very clear that if she wanted to play games with me, she had every chance of losing. But she wore a triumphant smile. Perhaps my trembling hands did not help my acting.

237

'Do you often come here?' I asked.

'This is the first time. Intrigued?'

'Vaguely.'

She spread out a clean blanket that she took out of a canvas bag. It smelled of lavender.

'Come on, sit here, by the fire. You might catch pneumonia, and it would be my fault.'

The heat from the blaze revived me. Bea gazed silently at the flames, bewitched.

'Are you going to tell me the secret?' I finally asked.

Bea sighed and moved to one of the chairs. I remained glued to the fire, watching the steam rise from my clothes like a fleeing soul.

'What you call the Aldaya mansion has, in fact, got its own name. The house is called "The Angel of Mist", but hardly anyone knows this. My father's firm has been trying to sell the property for fifteen years, but without any luck. The other day, while you were telling me the story of Julián Carax and Penélope Aldaya, I didn't think of it. Later that night, at home, I put two and two together and remembered I'd occasionally heard my father talk about the Aldaya family, and about this house in particular. Yesterday I went over to my father's office, and his secretary, Casasús, told me the story of the house. Did you know that this wasn't their official residence but one of their summer houses?'

I shook my head.

'The Aldayas' main house was a mansion that was knocked down in 1925 to erect a block of apartments, on the site where Calle Bruch and Calle Mallorca cross today. The building had been designed by Puig i Cadafalch and commissioned by Penélope and Jorge's grandfather, Simón Aldaya, in 1896, when that area was nothing more than fields and irrigation channels. The eldest son of the patriarch Simón, Don Ricardo Aldaya, bought this summer residence at the turn of the century from a rather bizarre character – at a ridiculous price, because the house had a bad reputation. Casasús told me it was cursed and that even the vendors didn't dare show people around and would dodge the issue with any old pretext. . . .'

# 28

That afternoon, as I warmed myself by the fire, Bea told me the story of how The Angel of Mist had come into the possession of the Aldaya family. It had all the makings of a lurid melodrama; something that could well have come from the pen of Julián Carax. The house was built in 1899 by the architectural partnership of Naulí, Martorell i Bergadà, for a prosperous and extravagant Catalan financier called Salvador Jausà, who was to live in it for only a year. The tycoon, an orphan since the age of six and of humble origins, had amassed most of his fortune in Cuba and Puerto Rico. People said that he was one of the many shady figures behind the plot that led to the fall of Cuba and the war with the United States, in which the last of the colonies were lost. He brought back rather more than a fortune from the New World: with him were an American wife – a fragile damsel from Philadelphia's high society who didn't speak a word of Spanish – and a mulatto maid who had been in his service since his first years in Cuba and who travelled with a caged macaque in harlequin dress, and seven trunks of luggage. At first they moved into a few rooms in the Hotel Colón, while they waited to acquire a residence that would suit the tastes and desires of Jausà.

Nobody doubted for a moment that the maid – an ebony beauty endowed with eyes and a figure that, according to the society pages, could make heart rates soar – was in fact his lover, his guide to innumerable illicit pleasures. It was assumed, moreover, that she was a witch and a sorceress. Her name was Marisela, or that's what Jausà called her. Her presence and her mysterious air soon became the favourite talking point at the social gatherings that wellborn ladies held to sample sponge fingers, and kill time and the autumn blues. Unconfirmed rumours circulated at these tea parties that the woman fornicated on top of the male, that is to say, rode him like a dog on heat, which violated at least five of six recognized mortal sins. In consequence, more than one person wrote to the bishopric asking for a special blessing and protection for the untainted, immaculate souls of all respectable families in Barcelona. And to crown it all, Jausà had the audacity to go out for a ride in his carriage on Sundays, in the middle of the morning, with his wife and Marisela, parading this Babylonian spectacle of depravity in front of the eyes of any virtuous young man who might happen to be strolling along Paseo de Gracia on his way to the eleven o'clock mass. Even the newspapers noted the haughty look of the strapping woman, who gazed at the Barcelona public 'as a queen of the jungle might gaze at a collection of pygmies'.

Around that time Catalan modernism was all the rage in Barcelona, but Jausà made it quite clear to the architects he had engaged to build his new home that he wanted something different. In his book 'different' was the highest praise. Jausà had spent years strolling past the row of neo-Gothic extravagances that the great tycoons of the American industrial age had erected on Fifth Avenue's Mansion Row in New York City. Nostalgic for his American days of glory, the financier refused to listen to any argument in favour of building in accordance with the fashion of the moment, just as he had refused to buy a box in the Liceo, which was de rigueur, labelling the opera house a Babel for the deaf, a beehive of undesirables. He wanted his home to be far from the city, in the still relatively isolated area of Avenida del Tibidabo. He wanted to gaze at Barcelona from a distance, he said. The only company he sought was a garden filled with statues of angels, which, according to his instructions (conveyed by Marisela), must be placed on each of the points of a six-point star – no more, no less. Resolved to carry out his plans, and with his coffers bursting with money with which to satisfy his every whim, Salvador Jausà sent his architects to New York for three months to study the exhilarating structures built to house Commodor Vanderbilt, the Astors, Andrew Carnegie, and the rest of the fifty golden families. He instructed them to assimilate the style and techniques of the Stanford White & McKim firms, and warned them not to bother knocking on his door with a project that would please what he called 'pork butchers and button manufacturers'.

A year later the three architects turned up at his sumptuous rooms at the Hotel Colón to submit their proposal. Jausà, in the company of the Cuban Marisela, listened to them in silence and, at the end of the presentation, asked them what it would cost to complete the work in six months. Frederic Martorell, the leading member of the architectural partnership, cleared his throat and, out of decorum, wrote down a figure on a piece of paper and handed it to the tycoon. The latter, without even blinking, wrote out a cheque for the total amount and dismissed the delegation with a vague gesture. Seven months later, in July 1900, Jausà, his wife, and the maid Marisela moved into the house. By August the two women would be dead and the police would find a dazed Salvador Jausà naked and handcuffed to the armchair in his study. The report made by the sergeant in charge of the case remarked that all the walls in the house were bloodstained, that the statues of the angels surrounding the garden had been mutilated – their faces painted like tribal masks – and that traces of black candles had been found on the pedestals. The inquiry lasted eight months. By then Jausà had fallen silent.

The police investigations concluded that by all indications, Jausà and his wife had been poisoned by some herbal extract that had been administered to them by Marisela, in whose rooms various bottles of the lethal substance had been found. For some reason Jausà had survived the poison, although the aftermath had been terrible, for he

241

gradually lost his power of speech and his hearing, part of his body was paralysed, and he suffered pains so horrendous they condemned him to live the rest of his days in constant agony. Señora Jausà had been discovered in her bedroom, lying on her bed with nothing on but her jewels, one of which was a diamond bracelet. The police believed that once Marisela had committed the crime, she had slashed her own wrists with a knife and had wandered about the house spreading her blood on the walls of the corridors and rooms until she collapsed in her attic room. The motive, according to the police, had been jealousy. It seems that the tycoon's wife was pregnant at the time of her death. Marisela, it was said, had sketched a skeleton on the woman's naked belly with hot red wax. The case, like Salvador Jausà's lips, was sealed forever a few months later. Barcelona's high society observed that nothing like this had ever happened in the history of the city, and that the likes of rich colonials and other rabble arriving from across the pond was ruining the moral fibre of the country. Behind closed doors many were delighted that the eccentricities of Salvador Jausà had come to an end. As usual, they were mistaken: they had only just begun.

The police and Jausà's lawyers were responsible for closing the file on the case, but the nabob Jausà wanted to continue. It was at this point that he met Don Ricardo Aldaya – by then a rich industrialist with a colourful reputation for his womanizing and his leonine temper – who offered to buy the property off him with the intention of knocking it down and reselling it at a healthy profit: the value of land in that area was soaring. Jausà did not agree to sell, but he invited Ricardo Aldaya to visit the house and observe what he called a scientific and spiritual experiment. No one had entered the property since the investigation had ended. What Aldaya witnessed in there left him speechless. Jausà had completely lost his mind. The dark shadow of Marisela's blood still covered the walls. Jausà had summoned an inventor, a pioneer in the technological novelty of the moment, the cinematograph. His name was Fructuós Gelabert, and he'd agreed to Jausà's demands in exchange for funds with which to build a film studio in the Vallés region, for he felt sure that, during the twentieth century, moving pictures would supplant organized religion. Apparently Jausà was convinced that the spirit of Marisela had remained in the house. He asserted that he could feel her presence, her voice, her smell, and even her touch in the dark. When they heard these stories, Jausà's servants had immediately fled in search of less stressful employment in the neighbouring Sarriá district, where there were plenty more mansions and families incapable of filling up a bucket of water or darning their own socks.

Jausà, left on his own, sank further into his obsession with his invisible spectres. He decided that the answer to his woes lay in making the invisible visible. He had already had a chance to see some of the results of the invention of cinematography in New York, and he shared the opinion of the deceased Marisela that the camera swallowed up souls. Following this line of reasoning, he commissioned Fructuós Gelabert to shoot yards and yards of film in the corridors of The Angel of Mist, in search of signs and visions from the other world. Despite the cinematographer's noble efforts, the scientific pursuit of Jausà's phantoms proved futile.

Everything changed when Gelabert announced that he'd received a new type of sensitive film straight from the Thomas Edison factory in Menlo Park, New Jersey. The new stock made it possible to shoot in extremely low light conditions – below candlelight – something unheard of at the time. Then, in circumstances that were never made clear, one of the assistants in Gelabert's laboratory accidentally poured some sparkling Xarelo wine from the Penedés region into the developing tray. As a result of the chemical reaction, strange shapes began to appear on the exposed film. This was the film Jausà wanted to show Don Ricardo Aldaya the night he invited him to his ghostly abode at number 32, Avenida del Tibidabo.

When Aldaya heard this, he supposed that Gelabert was afraid of losing Jausà's funding and had resorted to such an elaborate ruse to keep his patron's interest alive. Whatever the truth, Jausà had no doubt about the reliability of the results. Moreover, where others saw only shapes and shadows, he saw revenants. He swore he could see the silhouette of Marisela materializing under a shroud, a shadow that then mutated into a wolf and walked upright. Alas, all Ricardo Aldaya could see during the screening was large stains. He also maintained that both the film itself and the technician who operated the projector stank of wine and other entirely earthly spirits. Nonetheless, being a sharp businessman, the industrialist sensed that he could turn the situation to his advantage. A mad millionaire who was alone and obsessed with capturing ectoplasm on film constituted the ideal victim. So Aldaya agreed with him and encouraged him to continue with his enterprise. For weeks Gelabert and his men shot miles of film that was then developed in different tanks using chemical solutions diluted with exotic liqueurs, red wine blessed in the Ninot parish church, and all kinds of *cava* from the Tarragona vineyards. Between screenings, Jausà transferred powers, signed authorizations, and conferred the control of his financial reserves to Ricardo Aldaya.

Jausà vanished one November night of that year during a storm. Nobody knew what had become of him. Apparently he was developing one of Gelabert's special rolls of film himself when he met with an accident. Don Ricardo Aldaya asked Gelabert to recover the roll. After viewing it in private, Aldaya personally opted to set fire to it. Then, with the aid of a very generous cheque, he suggested to the technician that he forget all about the incident. By then Aldaya was already the owner of most of the properties belonging to the vanished Jausà. There were those who said that the deceased Marisela had returned to take Jausà with her to hell. Others pointed out that a beggar, who greatly resembled the deceased millionaire, was seen for a few months afterwards in the grounds of Ciudadela Park, until a black carriage with drawn curtains ran over him in the middle of the day, without bothering to stop. The stories spread: the dark legend of the rambling mansion, like the invasion of Cuban music in the city's dance halls, could not be contained.

A few months later, Don Ricardo Aldaya moved his family into the house in Avenida del Tibidabo, where, two weeks after their arrival, the couple's youngest child, Penélope, was born. To celebrate the occasion, Aldaya renamed the house 'Villa Penélope'. The new name, however, never stuck. The house had its own character and proved immune to the influence of its new owners. The recent arrivals complained about noises and banging on the walls at night, sudden putrid smells and freezing draughts that seemed to roam through the house like wandering sentinels. The mansion was a compendium of mysteries. It had a double basement, with a sort of crypt, as yet unused, on the lower level. On the higher floor, a chapel was dominated by a large polychrome figure of the crucified Christ, which the servants thought looked disturbingly like Rasputin – a very popular character in the press of the time. The books in the library were constantly being mysteriously rearranged, or turned back to front. There was a room on the third floor, a bedroom that was never used because of the unaccountable damp stains that showed up on the walls and seemed to form blurry faces, where fresh flowers would wilt in just a few minutes and where you could always hear the drone of flies, although it was impossible to see them.

The cooks swore that certain items, such as sugar, disappeared from the larder as if by magic and that the milk took on a red hue at every new moon. Occasionally they found dead birds at the doors of some of the rooms, or small rodents. Other times things went missing, especially jewels and buttons from clothes kept in cupboards and drawers. Sometimes the missing objects would mysteriously reappear, months later, in remote corners of the house or buried in the garden. But usually they were never found again. Don Ricardo was of the opinion that these incidents were nothing but pranks and nonsense. In his view a week's fasting would have curbed his family's fears. What he didn't regard so philosophically were the thefts of his dear wife's jewellery. More than five maids were sacked when different items from the lady's jewellery box disappeared, though they all cried their hearts out, swearing they were innocent. Those in the know tended to think there was no mystery involved: the explanation lay in Don Ricardo's regrettable habit of slipping into the bedrooms of the younger maids at midnight for some extramarital fun and games. His reputation in this field was almost as notorious as his fortune, and there were those who said that at the rate his exploits were taking place, the illegitimate children he left behind would be able to organize their own union.

The fact was that not only jewels disappeared. In time the family lost its joie de vivre entirely. The Aldaya family was never happy in the house that had been acquired through Don Ricardo's dark arts of negotiation. Señora Aldaya pleaded constantly with her husband to sell the property and move them to a home in the town, or even return to the residence that Puig i Cadafalch had built for grandfather Simón, the patriarch of the clan. Ricardo Aldaya flatly refused. Since he spent most of his time travelling or in the family's factories, he saw no problem with the house. On one occasion little Jorge disappeared for eight hours inside the mansion. His mother and the servants looked for him desperately, but without success. When he reappeared, pale and dazed, he said he'd been in the library the whole time, in the company of a mysterious black woman who had been showing him old photographs and had told him that all the women in the family would die in that house to atone for the sins of the men. The mysterious woman even revealed to little Jorge the date on which his mother would die: 12 April 1921. Needless to say, the so-called black lady was never found, but years later, on 12 April 1921, at first light, Señora Aldaya would be discovered lifeless on her bed. All her jewels had disappeared. When the pond in the courtyard was drained, one of the servant boys found them in the mud at the bottom, next to a doll that had belonged to her daughter, Penélope.

A week later Don Ricardo Aldaya decided to get rid of the house. By then his financial empire was already in its death throes, and there were those who insinuated that it was all due to that accursed house, which brought misfortune to whoever occupied it. Others, the more cautious ones, simply asserted that Aldaya had never understood the changing trends of the market and that all he had accomplished during his lifetime was to ruin the robust business created by the patriarch Simón. Ricardo Aldaya announced that he was leaving Barcelona and moving with his family to Argentina, where his textile industries were allegedly doing splendidly. Many believed he was fleeing from failure and shame.

In 1922 The Angel of Mist was put up for sale at a ridiculously low price. At first there was strong interest in buying it, as much for its notoriety as for the growing prestige of the neighbourhood, but none of the potential buyers made an offer after visiting the house. In 1923 the mansion was closed. The deed was transferred to a real-estate company high up on the long list of Aldaya's creditors, so that it could arrange for its sale or demolition. The house was on the market for years, but the firm was unable to find a buyer. The said company, Botell i Llofré S.L., went bankrupt in 1939 when its two partners were sent to prison on unknown charges. After the unexplained fatal accident that befell both men in the San Viçens jail in 1940, it was taken over by a financial group, among whose shareholders were three fascist generals and a Swiss banker. This company's executive director turned out to be a certain Señor Aguilar, father of Tomás and Bea. Despite all their efforts, none of Señor Aguilar's salesmen were able to place the house, not even by offering it far beneath its already low asking price. Nobody had been back to the property for over ten years.

'Until today,' said Bea quietly, withdrawing into herself for a moment. 'I wanted to show you this place, you see? I wanted to give you a surprise. I told myself I had to bring you here, because this was part of your story, the story of Carax and Penélope. I borrowed the key from my father's office. Nobody knows we're here. It's our secret. I wanted to share it with you. And I was asking myself whether you'd come.'

'You knew I would.'

She smiled as she nodded. 'I believe that nothing happens by chance. Deep down, things have their own secret plan, even though we don't understand it. Like you finding that novel by Julián Carax in the Cemetery of Forgotten Books, or the fact that you and I are here now, in this house that belonged to the Aldayas. It's all part of something we cannot comprehend, something that owns us.'

While she spoke, my hand had slipped awkwardly down to Bea's ankle and was sliding towards her knee. She watched it as if she were watching an insect climbing up her leg. I asked myself what Fermín would have done at that moment. Where was his wisdom when I needed it most?

'Tomás says you've never had a girlfriend,' said Bea, as if that explained me.

I removed my hand and looked down, defeated. I thought Bea was smiling, but I preferred not to check.

'Considering he's so quiet, your brother is turning out to be quite a big mouth. What else does the newsreel say about me?'

'He says that for years you were in love with an older woman and that the experience left you brokenhearted.'

'All I had broken was a lip and my pride.'

'Tomás says you haven't been out with any other girl since then because you compare them all with that woman.'

Good old Tomás and his hidden blows. 'Her name is Clara,' I proffered.

'I know. Clara Barceló.'

'Do you know her?'

'Everyone knows someone like Clara Barceló. The name is the least of it.'

We fell silent for a while, watching the fire crackle.

'After I left you, I wrote a letter to Pablo,' said Bea.

I swallowed hard. 'To your lieutenant boyfriend? What for?'

Bea took an envelope out of her blouse and showed it to me. It was closed and sealed.

'In the letter I told him I wanted us to get married very soon, in a month's time, if possible, and that I want to leave Barcelona forever.'

Almost trembling, I faced her impenetrable eyes.

'Why are you telling me this?'

'Because I want you to tell me whether I should send it or not. That's why I've asked you to come here today, Daniel.'

I examined the envelope that she twirled in her hand like a playing card.

'Look at me,' she said.

I raised my eyes and met her gaze. I didn't know what to answer. Bea lowered her eyes and walked away towards the end of the gallery. A door led to the marble balustrade that opened onto the inner courtyard of the house. I watched her silhouette fade into the rain. I went after her and stopped her, snatching the envelope from her hands. The rain beat down on her face, sweeping away the tears and the anger. I led her back into the mansion to the heat of the blaze. She avoided my eyes. I took the envelope and threw it into the flames. We watched the letter breaking up among the hot coals and the pages evaporating in spirals of smoke, one by one. Bea knelt down next to me, with tears in her eyes. I embraced her and felt her breath on my throat.

'Don't let me fall, Daniel,' she murmured.

The wisest man I ever knew, Fermín Romero de Torres,

once told me that there was no experience in life comparable to the first time you undress a woman. For all this wisdom, though he had not lied to me, he hadn't told me the complete truth either. He hadn't told me anything about that strange trembling of the hands that turned every button, every zip, into a superhuman challenge. Nor had he told me about that bewitchment of pale, tremulous skin, that first brush of the lips, or about the mirage that seemed to shimmer from every pore of the skin. He didn't tell me any of that because he knew that the miracle happened only once, and when it did, it spoke in a language of secrets that, were they disclosed, would vanish again forever. A thousand times I've wanted to recover that first afternoon with Bea in the rambling house on Avenida del Tibidabo, when the sound of the rain washed the whole world away with it. A thousand times I've wished to return and lose myself in a memory from which I can rescue only one image stolen from the heat of the flames: Bea, naked and glistening with rain, lying by the fire, with open eyes that have followed me since that day. I leaned over her and passed the tips of my fingers over her belly. Bea lowered her eyelids and smiled, confident and strong.

'Do what you like to me,' she whispered.

She was seventeen, her entire life shining before her.

# 29

Darkness enveloped us in shadow as we left the mansion. The storm was receding, now barely an echo of cold rain. I wanted to return the key to Bea, but her eyes told me she wanted me to be the one to keep it. We strolled down towards Paseo de San Gervasio hoping to find a taxi or a bus. We walked in silence, holding hands and hardly looking at one another.

'I won't be able to see you again until Tuesday,' said Bea

in a tremulous voice, as if she suddenly doubted my desire to see her again.

'I'll be waiting for you here,' I said.

I took for granted that all my meetings with Bea would take place between the walls of that rambling old house, that the rest of the city did not belong to us. It even seemed to me that the firmness of her touch decreased as we moved away, that her strength and warmth diminished with every step we took. When we reached the avenue, we realized that the streets were almost deserted.

'We won't find anything here,' said Bea. 'We'd better go down along Balmes.'

We started off briskly down Calle Balmes, walking under the trees to shelter from the drizzle. It seemed to me that Bea was quickening her pace at every step, almost dragging me along. For a moment I thought that if I let go of her hand, Bea would start to run. My imagination, still intoxicated by her touch and her taste, burned with a desire to corner her on a bench, to seek her lips and recite a predictable string of nonsense that would have made anyone within hearing burst out laughing, anyone but me. But Bea was withdrawing into herself again, fading a world away from me.

'What's the matter?' I murmured.

She gave me a broken smile, full of fear and loneliness. I then saw myself through her eyes: just an innocent boy who thought he had conquered the world in an hour but didn't realize he could lose it again in an instant. I kept on walking, without expecting an answer. Waking up at last. Soon we heard the rumble of traffic, and the air seemed to ignite with the heat from the streetlamps and traffic lights. They made me think of invisible walls.

'We'd better separate here,' said Bea, letting go of my hand.

The lights from a taxi rank could be seen on the corner, a procession of glowworms.

'As you wish.'

251

Bea leaned over and brushed my cheek with her lips. Her hair still smelled of candle wax.

'Bea,' I began, almost inaudibly. 'I love you. . . .'

She shook her head but said nothing, sealing my lips with her hand as if my words were wounding her.

'Tuesday at six, all right?' she asked.

I nodded again. I saw her leave and disappear into a taxi, almost a stranger. One of the drivers, who had followed the exchange as if he were an umpire, observed me with curiosity. 'What do you say? Shall we head for home, chief?'

I got into the taxi without thinking. The taxi driver's eyes examined me through the mirror. I lost sight of the car that was taking Bea away, two dots of light sinking into a well of darkness.

I didn't manage to get to sleep until dawn cast a hundred tones of dismal grey on my bedroom window. Fermín woke me up, throwing tiny pebbles at my window from the church square. I put on the first thing I could find and ran down to open the door for him. Fermín was full of the insufferable enthusiasm of the early bird. We pushed up the shop grilles and hung up the OPEN sign.

'Look at those rings under your eyes, Daniel. They're as big as a building site. May we assume the owl got the pussycat to go out to sea with him?'

I went to the back room, put on my blue apron and handed Fermín his, or rather threw it at him angrily. Fermín caught it in midflight, with a sly smile.

'The owl drowned, period. Happy?' I snapped.

'Intriguing metaphor. Have you been dusting off your Verlaine, young man?'

'I stick to prose on Monday mornings. What do you want me to tell you?'

'I'll leave that up to you. The number of *estocadas* or the laps of honour.'

'I'm not in the mood, Fermín.'

'O youth, flower of fools! Well, don't get irritated with

252

me. I have fresh news concerning our investigation on your friend Julián Carax.'

'I'm all ears.'

He gave me one of his cloak-and-dagger looks, one eyebrow raised.

'Well, it turns out that yesterday, after leaving Bernarda back home with her virtue intact but a nice couple of well-placed bruises on her backside, I was assailed by a fit of insomnia – due to the evening's erotic arousals – which gave me the pretext to walk down to one of the information centres of Barcelona's underworld, i.e., the tavern of Eliodoro Salfumán, aka "Coldprick", situated in a seedy but rather colourful establishment in Calle Sant Jeroni, pride of the Raval quarter.'

'The abridged version, Fermín, for goodness' sake.'

'Coming. The fact is that once I was there, ingratiating myself with some of the usual crowd, old chums from troubled times of yore, I began to make inquiries about this Miquel Moliner, the husband of your Mata Hari Nuria Monfort, and a supposed inmate at the local penitential.'

'Supposed?'

'With a capital S. There are no slips at all 'twixt cup and lip in this case, if you see what I mean. I know from experience that when it comes to the census of the prison population, my informants in Coldprick's tabernacle are much more accurate than the pencil pushers in the law courts. I can guarantee, Daniel, my friend, that nobody has heard mention of the name Miquel Moliner as an inmate, visitor, or any other living soul in the prisons of Barcelona for at least ten years.'

'Perhaps he's serving in some other prison.'

'Yes. Alcatraz, Sing Sing, or the Bastille. Daniel, that woman lied to you.'

'I suppose she did.'

'Don't suppose; accept it.'

'So what now? Miquel Moliner is a dead end.'

'Or this Nuria is very crafty.'

'What are you suggesting?'

'At the moment we must explore other avenues. It wouldn't be a bad idea to call on the good nanny in the story the priest foisted on us yesterday morning.'

'Don't tell me you think that the governess has vanished too.'

'No, but I do think it's time we stopped fussing about and knocking on doors as if we were begging for alms. In this line of business, you have to go in through the back door. Are you with me?'

'You know that I worship the ground you walk on.'

'Well, then, start dusting your altar-boy costume. This afternoon, as soon as we've closed the shop, we're going to make a charitable visit to the old lady in the Hospice of Santa Lucía. And now tell me, how did it go yesterday with the young filly? Don't be secretive. If you hold back, may you sprout virulent pimples.'

I sighed in defeat and made my confession, down to the last detail. At the end of my narrative, after listing what I was sure were just the existential anxieties of a moronic schoolboy, Fermín surprised me with sudden heartfelt hug.

'You're in love,' he mumbled, full of emotion, patting me on the back. 'Poor kid.'

That afternoon we left the bookshop precisely at closing time, a move that earned us a steely look from my father, who was beginning to suspect that we were involved in some shady business, with all this coming and going. Fermín mumbled something incoherent about a few errands that needed doing, and we quickly disappeared. I told myself that sooner or later I'd have to reveal at least part of all this mess to my father; which part, exactly, was a different question.

On our way, with his usual flair for tales, Fermín briefed me on where we were heading. The Santa Lucía hospice was an institution of dubious reputation housed within the ruins of an ancient palace on Calle Moncada. The legend surrounding the place made it sound like a cross between purgatory and a morgue, with sanitary conditions worse than either. The story was, to say the very least, peculiar. Since the eleventh century, the palace had been home to, among other things, various well-to-do families, a prison, a salon for courtesans, a library of forbidden manuscripts, a barracks, a sculptor's workshop, a sanatorium for plague sufferers, and a convent. In the middle of the nineteenth century, when it was practically crumbling to bits, the palace had been turned into a museum exhibiting circus freaks and other atrocities by a bombastic impresario who called himself Laszlo de Vicherny, Duke of Parma and private alchemist to the House of Bourbon. His real name turned out to be Baltasar Deulofeu i Carallot, the bastard son of a salted-pork entrepreneur and a fallen debutante, who was mostly known for his escapades as a professional gigolo and con artist.

The man took pride in owning Spain's largest collection of human foetuses in different stages of deformity, preserved in jars of embalming fluid, and somewhat less pride in his even larger collection of warrants issued by some of Europe's and America's finest law-enforcement agencies. Among other attractions, 'The Tenebrarium' (as Deulofeu had renamed the palace), offered séances, necromancy, fights (with cocks, rats, dogs, big strapping women, imbeciles, or some combination of the above), as well as betting, a brothel that specialized in cripples and freaks, a casino, a legal and financial consultancy, a workshop for love potions, regional folklore and puppet shows, and parades of exotic dancers. At Christmas a Nativity play was staged, sparing no expense, and featuring the troupe from the museum and the entire collection of prostitutes. Its fame reached the far ends of the province.

The Tenebrarium was a roaring success for fifteen years, until it was discovered that Deulofeu had seduced the wife, the daughter, *and* the mother-in-law of the military governor of the province within a single week. The blackest infamy descended on the place and its owner. Before

255

Deulofeu was able to flee the city and don another of his multiple identities, a band of masked thugs seized him in the backstreets of the Santa María quarter and proceeded to hang him and set fire to him in the Ciudadela Park, leaving his body to be devoured by the wild dogs that roamed the area. After two decades of neglect, during which time nobody bothered to remove the collection of horrors belonging to the ill-fated Laszlo, The Tenebrarium was transformed into a charitable institution under the care of an order of nuns.

'The Ladies of the Final Ordeal, or something equally morbid,' said Fermín. 'The trouble is, they're very obsessive about the secrecy of the place (bad conscience, I'd say), which means we'll have to think of some ruse for getting in.'

In more recent times, the occupants of the Hospice of Santa Lucía were being recruited from the ranks of dying, abandoned, demented, destitute old people who made up the crowded underworld of Barcelona. Luckily for them, they mostly lasted only a short time after they had been taken in; neither the conditions of the establishment nor the company encouraged longevity. According to Fermín, the deceased were removed shortly before dawn and made their last journey to the communal grave in a covered wagon donated by a firm in Hospitalet that specialized in meat packing and rather dubious delicatessen products – a firm that occasionally would be involved in grim scandals.

'You're making all of this up,' I protested, overwhelmed by the horrific details of Fermín's story.

'My inventiveness does not go that far, Daniel. Wait and see. I visited the building on one unfortunate occasion about ten years ago, and I can tell you that it looked as if they'd hired your friend Julián Carax as an interior decorator. A shame we didn't bring some laurel leaves to stifle the aromas. But we'll have enough trouble as it is just being allowed in.'

With my expectations thus shaped, we turned into Calle

Moncada, by that time of day already transformed into a dark passage flanked by old mansions that had been turned into storehouses and workshops. The litany of bells coming from the basilica of Santa María del Mar mingled with the echo of our footsteps. Soon a penetrating, bitter odour permeated the cold winter breeze.

'What's that smell?'

'We've arrived,' announced Fermín.

# 30

A front door of rotted wood let us into a courtyard guarded by gas lamps that flickered above gargoyles and angels, their features disintegrating on the old stone. A staircase led to the first floor, where a rectangle of light marked the main entrance to the hospice. The gaslight radiating from this opening gave an ochre tone to the miasma that emanated from within. An angular, predatory figure observed us coolly from the shadows of the door, her eyes the same colour as her habit. She held a steaming wooden bucket that gave off an indescribable stench.

'Hail-Mary-Full-Of-Grace-Conceived-Without-Sin!' Fermín called out enthusiastically.

'Where's the coffin?' answered the voice from up high, serious and taciturn.

'Coffin?' Fermín and I replied in unison.

'Aren't you from the undertaker's?' asked the nun in a weary voice.

I wondered whether that was a comment on our appearance or a genuine question. Fermín's face lit up at such a providential opportunity.

'The coffin is in the van. First we'd like to examine the customer. A pure technicality.'

I felt overpowered by nausea.

'I thought Señor Collbató was going to come in person,' said the nun.

'Señor Collbató begs to be excused, but a rather complicated embalming has cropped up at the last moment. A circus strongman.'

'Do you work with Señor Collbató in the funeral parlour?'

'We're his right and left hands, respectively. Wilfred the Hairy at your service, and here, at my side, my apprentice and student, Sansón Carrasco.'

'Pleased to meet you,' I rounded off.

The nun gave us a brief looking-over and nodded, indifferent to the pair of scarecrows reflected in her eyes.

'Welcome to Santa Lucía. I'm Sister Hortensia, the one who called you. Follow me.'

We followed Sister Hortensia without a word through a cavernous corridor whose smell reminded me of the subway tunnels. It was flanked by doorless frames through which you could make out candlelit halls filled with rows of beds, piled up against the wall and covered with mosquito nets that moved in the air like shrouds. I could hear groans and see glimpses of human shapes through the netting.

'This way,' Sister Hortensia beckoned, a few yards ahead of us.

We entered a wide vault which I had no difficulty in imagining as the stage for The Tenebrarium described by Fermín. The darkness obscured what at first seemed like a collection of wax figures, sitting or abandoned in corners, with dead, glassy eyes that shone like tin coins in the candlelight. I thought that perhaps they were dolls or remains of the old museum. Then I realized that they were moving, though very slowly, even stealthily. It was impossible to tell their age or gender. The rags covering them were the colour of ash.

'Señor Collbató said not to touch or clean anything,' said Sister Hortensia, looking slightly apologetic. 'We just placed the poor thing in one of the boxes that was lying around here, because he was beginning to drip.'

'You did the right thing. You can't be too careful,' agreed Fermín.

I threw him a despairing look. He shook his head calmly, indicating that I should leave him in charge of the situation. Sister Hortensia led us to what appeared to be a cell with no ventilation or light, at the end of a narrow passage. She took one of the gas lamps that hung from the wall and handed it to us.

'Will you be long? I'm rather busy.'

'Don't worry about us. You get on with your things, and we'll take him away.'

'All right. If you need anything I'll be down in the basement, in the ward for the bedridden. If it's not too much bother, take him out through the back door. Don't let the others see him. It's bad for the patients' morale.'

'We quite understand,' I said in a faltering voice.

Sister Hortensia gazed at me for a moment with vague curiosity. When I saw her more closely, I noticed that she was quite an age herself, almost an elderly woman. Few years separated her from the rest of the hospice's guests.

'Listen, isn't the apprentice a bit young for this sort of work?' she asked.

'The truths of life know no age, Sister,' remarked Fermín.

The nun nodded and smiled at me sweetly. There was no suspicion in that look, only sadness.

'Even so,' she murmured.

She wandered off into the shadows, carrying her bucket and dragging her shadow like a bridal veil. Fermín pushed me into the cell. It was a dismal, claustrophobic room built into the walls of a cave that sweated with damp. Chains ending in hooks hung from the ceiling, and the cracked floor was broken up by a sewage grating. In the centre of the room, on a greyish marble table, was a wooden crate for industrial packaging. Fermín raised the lamp, and we caught a glimpse of the deceased nestling between the straw padding. Parchment features, incomprehensible, jagged and frozen. The swollen skin was purple. The eyes were open: white, like broken eggshells.

The sight made my stomach turn, and I looked away.

'Come on, let's get down to work,' ordered Fermín.

'Are you mad?'

'I mean we have to find this Jacinta woman before we're found out.'

'How?'

'How do you think? By asking.'

We peered into the corridor to make sure Sister Hortensia had vanished. Then we scurried back to the hall we had previously crossed. The wretched figures were still observing us, with looks that ranged from curiosity to fear and, in some cases, to greed.

'Watch it, some of these would suck your blood if they thought it would make them any younger,' said Fermín. 'Age makes them all look as meek as lambs, but there are as many sons of bitches in here as out there, or more. Because these are the ones who have lasted and buried the rest. Don't feel sorry for them. Go on, begin with those ones in the corner – they look harmless enough.'

If those words were meant to give me courage for the mission, they failed miserably. I looked at the group of human remains that languished in the corner and smiled at them. It occurred to me that their very presence was testimony to the moral emptiness of the universe and the mechanical brutality with which it destroys the parts it no longer needs. Fermín seemed able to read these profound thoughts and nodded gravely.

'Mother Nature is the meanest of bitches, that's the sad truth,' he said. 'Go on, be brave.'

My first round of inquiries as to the whereabouts of Jacinta Coronado produced only empty looks, groans, burps, and ravings. Fifteen minutes later I called it a day and joined Fermín to see whether he'd had better luck. His disappointment was all too obvious.

'How are we going to find Jacinta Coronado in this shit hole?'

'I don't know. It's a cauldron of idiots. I've tried the Sugus sweet trick, but they seem to think they're suppositories.'

'What if we ask Sister Hortensia? We tell her the truth, and have done with it.'

'Telling the truth should be our last resort, Daniel, even more so when you're dealing with a nun. Let's use up all our powder first. Look at that little group over there. They seem quite jolly. I'm sure they're very articulate. Go and question them.'

'And what are you planning to do?'

'I'll keep watch, in case the penguin returns. You get on with your business.'

With little or no hope of success, I went up to the group of patients occupying another corner of the room.

'Good evening,' I said, realizing instantly how absurd my greeting was, because in there, it was always nighttime. 'I'm looking for Señora Jacinta Coronado. Co-ro-na-do. Do any of you know her, or could you tell me where to find her?'

I was confronted by four faces corrupted by greed. There's something here, I thought. Maybe all's not lost.

'Jacinta Coronado?' I insisted.

The four patients exchanged looks and nodded to each other. One of them, a potbellied man without a single hair on his body, seemed to be their leader. His appearance and manner made me think of a happy Nero, plucking his harp while Rome rotted at his feet. With a majestic gesture, the Nero figure smiled at me playfully. I returned the smile, hopefully.

The man gestured at me to come closer, as if he wanted to whisper something in my ear. I hesitated, then leaned forward.

I lent my ear to the patient's lips – so close that I could feel his fetid, warm breath on my skin. 'Can you tell me where I can find Señora Jacinta Coronado?' I asked for the last time. I was afraid he'd bite me. Instead he emitted a violently loud fart. His companions burst out laughing and clapped with joy. I took a few steps back, but it was too late: the flatulent vapours had already hit me. It was then that I noticed, close to me, an old man, all hunched up, with a prophet's beard, thin hair, and fiery eyes, who was leaning on a walking stick and gazing at the others with disdain.

'You're wasting your time, young man. Juanito only knows how to let off farts, and the others can only laugh and smell them. As you see, the social structure here isn't very different from that of the outside world.'

The ancient philosopher spoke in a solemn voice and with perfect diction. He looked me up and down, taking the measure of me.

'You're looking for Jacinta?'

I nodded, astounded by the appearance of intelligent life in that den of horrors.

'And what for?'

'I'm her grandson.'

'And I'm the Marquis of Crèmebrûlée. You're a terrible liar, that's what you are. Tell me why you want to see her or I'll play the madman. It's easy here. And if you intend to ask these poor wretches one by one, you'll soon see what I mean.'

Juanito and his gang of inhalers were still howling with laughter. The soloist then gave off an encore, more muted and prolonged than the previous one. It sounded like a hiss, like a punctured tyre, and proved Juanito's virtuoso control over his sphincter. I yielded to the facts.

'You're right. I'm not a relative of Señora Coronado, but I need to speak to her. It's a matter of the utmost importance.'

The old man came up to me. He had a wicked, catlike smile the smile of a mischievous child, and his eyes were full of cunning.

'Can you help me?' I begged.

'That depends on how much you can help me.'

'If it's in my power, I'd be delighted to help you. Would you like me to deliver a message to your family?'

The old man laughed bitterly. 'My family were the ones who stuck me in this hole. They're a load of leeches; they'd steal my underpants while they're still warm. To hell with them. I've kept them and put up with them for long enough. What I want is a woman.'

'Excuse me?'

The old man looked at me impatiently.

'Being young is no excuse for slow wit, child. I'm telling you I want a woman. A female, a maid, or a well-bred young filly. Young – under fifty-five, that is – and healthy, with no sores or fractures.'

'I'm not sure if I understand. . . .'

'You understand me perfectly. I want to have it off with a woman who has teeth and won't pee on me, before I depart for the other world. I don't mind whether she's good-looking or not; I'm half blind, and at my age any girl who has anything to hold onto is a Venus. Am I making myself clear?'

'Crystal. But I don't see how I'm going to find a woman for you. . . .'

'When I was your age, there was something in the service sector called "ladies of easy virtue". I know the world changes, but never in essence. Find one for me, plump and fun-loving, and we'll do business. And if you're asking yourself about my ability to enjoy a woman, I want you to know I'm quite content to pinch her backside and feel up her bumpers. That's the advantage of experience.'

'Technicalities are your affair, sir, but I can't bring a woman to you here right now.'

'I might be a dirty old man, but I'm not stupid. I know that. Your promise is good enough for me.'

'And how do you know I won't say yes just to get you to tell me where Jacinta Coronado is?'

The old man gave me a sly smile. 'You give me your word, and leave any problems of conscience to me.'

I looked around me. Juanito was starting on the second half of his recital. Hope was ebbing away. Fulfilling this horny granddad's request seemed to be the only thing that made any sense in that purgatory. 'I give you my word. I'll do what I can.'

The old man smiled from ear to ear. I counted three teeth.

'Blonde, even if it's peroxide. Pneumatically endowed and good at talking dirty, if possible. Of all the senses, the one that still works the best is my hearing.'

'I'll see what I can do. Now, tell me where I can find Jacinta Coronado.'

# 31

'You've promised *what* to that old Methuselah?'

'You heard.'

'You were joking, I hope.'

'I can't lie to an old man who is at death's door, no matter how fresh he turns out to be.'

'And that does you credit, Daniel, but how do you think you're going to slip a whore into this holy house?'

'By paying her three times as much, I suppose. I leave all the specifics to you.'

Fermín shrugged resignedly. 'Oh, well, a deal's a deal. We'll think of something. But remember, next time a negotiation of this nature turns up, let me do the talking.'

'Agreed.'

Just as the crafty old devil had instructed, we found Jacinta Coronado in a loft that could only be reached by a staircase on the third floor. According to the old man, the attic was the refuge for the few patients whom fate had not yet had the decency to deprive of understanding. Apparently this hidden wing had, in its day, housed the rooms of Baltasar Deulofeu, aka Laszlo de Vicherny, from which he governed The Tenebrarium's activities and cultivated the loving arts newly arrived from the East, amid clouds of perfume and scented oils. And there was no lack of scent now, though of a very different nature. A woman who could only be Jacinta Coronado sagged in a wicker chair, wrapped in a blanket.

'Señora Coronado? I asked, raising my voice, in case the poor thing was deaf, half-witted, or both.

The elderly woman examined us carefully, with some reserve. Her eyes looked bleary, and only a few wisps of whitish hair covered her head. I noticed that she gave me a puzzled look, as if she'd seen me before but couldn't remember where. I was afraid Fermín was going to rush into introducing me as the son of Carax or some similar lie, but all he did was kneel down next to the old lady and take her trembling, wrinkled hand.

'Jacinta, I'm Fermín, and this handsome young lad is my friend Daniel. Father Fernando Ramos sent us. He wasn't able to come today because he had twelve masses to say – you know what the calendar of saints' days is like – but he sends you his best regards. How are you feeling?'

The old woman smiled sweetly at Fermín. My friend stroked her face and her forehead. She appreciated the touch of another skin like a purring cat. I felt a lump in my throat.

'A stupid question, wasn't it?' Fermín went on. 'What you'd like is to be out there, dancing a foxtrot. You look like a dancer; everyone must tell you that.'

I had never seen him treat anyone with such delicacy, not even Bernarda. His words were pure flattery, but the tone and expression on his face were sincere.

'What pretty things you say,' she murmured in a voice that was broken from not having had anyone to speak to or anything to say.

'Not half as pretty as you, Jacinta. Do you think we could ask you some questions? Like on a radio contest, you know?'

The old woman just blinked in response.

'I'd say that's a yes. Do you remember Penélope, Jacinta? Penélope Aldaya? It's her we'd like to ask you about.'

Jacinta's eyes suddenly lit up and she nodded.

'My girl,' she murmured, and it looked like she was going to burst into tears.

'The very one. You do remember, don't you? We're friends of Julián. Julián Carax, the one who told scary stories. You remember that, too, don't you?'

The old woman's eyes shone, as if those words and the touch on her skin were bringing her back to life by the minute.

'Father Fernando, from San Gabriel's, told us you adored Penélope. He loves you very much, too, and thinks of you every day, you know. If he doesn't come more often, it's just because the new bishop, a social climber, loads him with such a quota of masses that his voice gives out.'

'Are you sure you eat enough?' the old lady suddenly asked, with a worried expression.

'I eat like a horse, Jacinta. The trouble is, I have a very manly metabolism and I burn it all up. But believe me, under these clothes it's all pure muscle. Feel, feel. Like Charles Atlas, only hairier.'

Jacinta nodded and looked reassured. She couldn't take her eyes off Fermín. She had forgotten about me completely.

'What can you tell us about Penélope and Julián?'

'Between them all, they took her from me,' she said. 'My girl.'

I took a step forward and was about to say something, but Fermín threw me a look that told me to remain silent.

'Who took Penélope from you, Jacinta? Do you remember?'

'The master,' she said, raising her eyes fearfully, as if she thought someone might hear us.

Fermín seemed to be gauging the emphasis of the old

266

woman's gesture and followed her eyes to the ceiling, weighing up the possibilities.

'Are you referring to God Almighty, emperor of the heavens, or did you mean the master, Miss Penélope's father, Don Ricardo?'

'How's Fernando?' asked the old woman.

'The priest? Splendid. One day, he'll be made pope and will set you up in the Sistine Chapel. He sends you all the best.'

'He's the only one who comes to see me, you know. He comes because he knows I don't have anyone else.'

Fermín gave me a sideways look, as if he were thinking what I was thinking. Jacinta Coronado was much saner than her appearance suggested. Her body was fading away, but her mind and her soul were still blazing with anguish in that wretched place. I wondered how many more people like her, or like the lusty little old man who had shown us how to find her, were trapped in there.

'He comes because he's very fond of you, Jacinta. Because he remembers how well you looked after him and how you fed him when he was a child. He's told us all about that. Do you remember, Jacinta? Do you remember those days, when you went to collect Jorge from school, do you remember Fernando and Julián?'

'Julián . . .'

She whispered the name slowly, but her smile betrayed her.

'Do you remember Julián Carax, Jacinta?'

'I remember the day Penélope told me she was going to marry him . . .'

Fermín and I looked at one another in astonishment.

'Marry? When was that, Jacinta?'

'The first day she saw him. She was thirteen and didn't know who he was or what he was called.'

'Then how did she know she was going to marry him?'

'Because she'd seen him. In her dreams.'

267

*As a child, María Jacinta Coronado was convinced that the world ended on the outskirts of Toledo and that beyond the town limits there was nothing but darkness and oceans of fire. Jacinta had got that idea from a dream she had during a fever that had almost killed her when she was four years old. This dream was the first of many and they began with that mysterious fever, which some blamed on the sting of a huge red scorpion that appeared in the house one day and was never seen again, and others on the evil designs of a mad nun who crept into houses at night to poison children and who, years later, was to be garroted reciting the Lord's Prayer backwards with her eyes popping out of their sockets, while a red cloud spread over the town, discharging a storm of dead cockroaches. In her dreams Jacinta perceived the past and the future and, at times, saw revealed to her the secrets and mysteries of the old streets of Toledo. One of the characters she would see repeatedly in her dreams was someone called Zacarías, an angel who was always dressed in black and who was accompanied by a dark cat with yellow eyes whose breath smelled of sulphur. Zacarías knew everything: he had predicted the day and the hour of her uncle Benancio's death – a hawker of ointments and holy water. He had revealed the place where her mother, a sanctimonious churchgoer, hid a bundle of letters from an ardent medical student with few finanical resources but a solid knowledge of anatomy, and in whose bedroom in the alleyway of Santa María she had discovered the doors of paradise at an early age. Zacarías had announced to Jacinta that there was something evil fixed in her stomach, a dead spirit that wished her ill, and that she would know the love of only one man: an empty, selfish love that would break her soul in two. He had augured that in her lifetime she would behold the death of everything she loved, and that before she reached heaven, she would visit hell. On the day of her first period, Zacarías and his sulphuric cat disappeared from her dreams, but years later Jacinta would remember the visits of the black angel with tears in her eyes, because all his prophecies had come true.*

*So when the doctors diagnosed that she would never be able to have children, Jacinta wasn't surprised. Nor was she surprised, although she almost died of grief, when her husband of three years announced that he was going to leave her because she was like a wasteland that produced no fruit, because she wasn't a woman. In the absence of Zacarías (whom she took to be an emissary of heaven, for, whether or not he was dressed in black, he was still a radiant angel and the best-looking man she had ever seen), Jacinta spoke to God on her own, hiding in corners, without seeing him or expecting him to bother with a reply, because there was a lot of pain in the world and her troubles were, in the end, only small matters. All her monologues with God dealt with the same theme: she wanted only one thing in life, to be a mother, to be woman.*

*One day, while she was praying in the cathedral, a man, whom she recognized as Zacarías, came up to her. He dressed as he always did and held his malicious cat on his lap. He did not look a single day older and still sported magnificent nails, like the nails of a duchess, long and pointed. The angel admitted that he was there because God didn't plan to answer her prayers. But he told her not to worry because, one way or another, he would send her a child. He leaned over her, murmured the word 'Tibidabo', and kissed her very tenderly on the lips. At the touch of those fine, honeyed lips, Jacinta had a vision: she would have a daughter without further knowledge of man (which, judging from the three years in the bedroom with her husband, who insisted on doing his thing while covering her head with a pillow and mumbling 'Don't look, you slut,' was a relief). This girl would come to her in a very faraway city, trapped between a crescent of mountains and a sea of light, a city filled with buildings that could exist only in dreams. Later Jacinta was unable to tell whether Zacarías's visit had been another of her dreams or whether the angel really had come to her in Toledo Cathedral, with his cat and his scarlet-manicured nails. What she didn't doubt for a moment was the truth of those predictions. That very afternoon she consulted the parish deacon, who was a well-read man and had seen the world (it was said that he had gone as far as Andorra and that he spoke a little Basque). The deacon claimed he did not know of an angel Zacarías among the winged legions of the heavens, but listened attentively to Jacinta's vision. After much consideration, and going by the description of some sort of cathedral that, in the words of the clairvoyant, sounded like a large hair comb made of melting chocolate, the wise man said, 'Jacinta, what you've seen is Barcelona, the great enchantress, and the Expiatory Temple of the Sagrada Familia.' Two weeks later, armed with a bundle of clothes, a missal, and her first smile in five years, Jacinta was on her way to Barcelona, convinced that everything the angel had described to her would come true.*

*Months of great hardship were to pass before Jacinta would find a permanent job in one of the stores of Aldaya and Sons, near the pavilions of the old 1888 Universal Exhibition in Ciudadela Park. The Barcelona of her dreams had changed into a sinister, hostile city, full of closed mansions, full of factories that poured forth their foggy breath, poisoning the air with coal and sulphur. Jacinta knew from the start that this city was a woman, cruel and vain; she learned to fear her and never look her in the eye. She lived alone in a pensión in the Ribera quarter, where her pay barely afforded her a miserable room with no windows, whose only source of light came from the candles she stole from the cathedral. She kept these alight all night to scare away the rats that had already gnawed at the ears and fingers of a six-month-old baby, the child of Ramoneta – a prostitute who rented the room next door and the only friend Jacinta had managed to make in Barcelona in eleven months. That winter it rained almost every day, and the rain was blackened by soot. Soon Jacinta began to fear that Zacarías had deceived her, that she had come to that terrible city to die of cold, misery and oblivion.*

*But Jacinta was prepared to survive. She went to the store every day before dawn and did not come out again until well after nightfall. There Don Ricardo Aldaya happened to notice*

*her looking after the daughter of one of the foremen, who had
fallen ill with consumption. When he saw the dedication and
the tenderness that the young girl exuded, he decided to take
her home with him to look after his wife, who was pregnant
with what would be his firstborn. Jacinta's prayers had been
answered. That night Jacinta saw Zacarías again in her
dreams. The angel was no longer dressed in black. He was
naked, and his skin was covered in scales. He didn't have his
cat with him anymore, but a white snake coiled round his
torso. His hair had grown down to his waist, and his smile, the
honeyed smile she had kissed in Toledo Cathedral, was now
lined with triangular, serrated teeth, like those she'd seen in
some of the deepsea fish that thrashed their tails in the fish
market. Years later the young woman would reveal this vision
to an eighteen-year-old Julián Carax, recalling how the day
she left the pensión in the Ribera quarter and moved to the
Aldaya mansion, she was told that her friend Ramoneta had
been stabbed to death in the doorway the night before and that
Ramoneta's baby had died of cold in her arms. When they
heard the news, the guests at the pensión came to blows,
shouting and scratching over the meagre belongings of the
dead woman. The only thing they left was what had been
Ramoneta's greatest treasure: a book. Jacinta recognized it,
because often, at night, Ramoneta had asked her to read her
one or two pages, for Ramoneta had never learned to read.*

*Four months later Jorge Aldaya was born, and although
Jacinta was to offer him all the affection that his mother never
knew how to give him, or never wished to – for she was an
ethereal lady, Jacinta thought, who always seemed trapped in
her own reflection – the governess realized that this was not
the child Zacarías had promised her. During those years
Jacinta gave up her youth and became a different woman. The
other Jacinta had been left behind in the pensión in the Ribera
quarter, as dead as Ramoneta. Now she lived in the shadow of
the Aldayas' luxuries, far from that dark city that she had
come to hate so much and into which she did not venture, not
even on her monthly day off. She learned to live through*

*others, through a family that sat on top of a fortune the size of which she could scarcely conceive. She lived in the expectation of that child, who would be a female, like the city, and to whom she would give all the love with which God had poisoned her soul. Sometimes Jacinta asked herself whether that dreamy peace that filled her days, that absence of consciousness, was what some people called happiness, and she wanted to believe that God, in His infinite silence, had, in His way, answered her prayers.*

*Penélope Aldaya was born in the spring of 1902. By then Don Ricardo Aldaya had already bought the house on Avenida del Tibidabo, that rambling mansion that Jacinta's fellow servants were convinced lay under the influence of some powerful spell, but which Jacinta did not fear, because she knew that what others took to be magic was nothing more than a presence that only she could capture in dreams: the shadow of Zacarías, who hardly resembled the man she remembered and who now only manifested himself as a wolf walking on his two hind legs.*

*Penélope was a fragile child, pale and slender. Jacinta saw her grow like a flower in winter. For years she watched over her every night, personally prepared every one of her meals, sewed her clothes, was by her side when she went through her many illnesses, when she said her first words, when she became a woman. Señora Aldaya was one more figure in the scenery, a prop that came on- and offstage according to the dictates of decorum. Before going to bed, she would come and say goodnight to her daughter and tell her she loved her more than anything in the world, that she was the most important thing in the universe to her. Jacinta never told Penélope that she loved her. The nurse knew that those who really love, love in silence, with deeds and not with words. Secretly Jacinta despised Señora Aldaya, that vain, empty creature who slowly grew old in the corridors of the mansion, weighed down by the jewels with which her husband – who for years had set anchor in foreign ports – kept her quiet. She hated her because, of all women, God had chosen her to give birth to Penélope while her own womb, the womb of the true mother, remained barren. In time, as if the words of her husband had been prophetic, Jacinta even lost her womanly shape. She grew thin and austere in appearance, and wore the look of tired skin and tired bone. Her breasts withered until they were but scraps of skin, her hips were like those of a boy, and her flesh, hard and angular, didn't even catch the eye of Don Ricardo Aldaya, who only needed to sense a hint of vitality to send him off in a frenzy – as all the maids in the house, and in the houses of his close friends, knew only too well. Better this way, thought Jacinta. She had no time for nonsense.*

*All her time was devoted to Penélope. She read to her, she accompanied her everywhere, she bathed her, dressed her, undressed her, combed her hair, took her out for walks, put her to bed and woke her up. But above all she spoke to her. Everyone took Jacinta for a batty nurse, a spinster with nothing in her life other than her job in the house, but nobody knew the truth: Jacinta was not only Penélope's mother, she was her best friend. From the moment the girl began to speak and articulate her thoughts, which was much sooner than Jacinta remembered in any other child, they both shared their secrets and their lives.*

*The passing of time only strengthened this union. When Penélope reached adolescence, they were already inseparable. Jacinta saw Penélope blossom into a woman whose beauty and radiance were evident to more eyes than just her own. When that mysterious boy called Julián came to the house, Jacinta noticed that, from the very first moment, a current flowed between him and Penélope. They were joined by a bond, similar to the one that joined her to Penélope, but also different. More intense. Dangerous. At first she thought she would come to hate the boy, but soon she realized that she did not hate Julián Carax and would never be able to. As Penélope fell under Julián's spell, she, too, allowed herself to be dragged into it and in time desired only what Penélope desired. Nobody had noticed, nobody had paid attention, but, as usual, the essential issue had been settled before the story had even begun, and by then it was too late.*

Many months of wistful looks and longings would pass before Julián Carax and Penélope could be alone together. Their lives were ruled by chance. They met in corridors, they looked at one another from opposite ends of the table, they brushed silently against each other, they felt each other's absence. They exchanged their first words in the library of the house on Avenida del Tibidabo one stormy afternoon when 'Villa Penélope' was filled with the dim light of candles – only a few seconds stolen from the darkness in which Julián thought he saw in the girl's eyes the certainty that they both felt the same, that the same secret was devouring them. Nobody seemed to notice. Nobody but Jacinta, who watched with growing anxiety the game of furtive glances that Penélope and Julián were playing under the very nose of the Aldayas. She feared for them.

By then Julián had begun to have sleepless nights, writing stories for Penélope from midnight to dawn. He would find any old excuse to go up to the house on Avenida del Tibidabo, then look for the moment when he could slip into Jacinta's room and give his pages to her so that she, in turn, could give them to the girl. Sometimes Jacinta would hand him a note that Penélope had written, and he would spend days rereading it. That game went on for months. While time brought them no good fortune, Julián did whatever was necessary to be close to Penélope. Jacinta helped him, for she wanted to see Penélope happy, to keep that light glowing. Julián, for his part, felt that the casual innocence of the beginning was now fading and it was time to start making some sacrifices. That was why he began to lie to Don Ricardo about his plans for the future, to fake an enthusiasm for a career in banking and finance, to feign an affection and an attachment for Jorge Aldaya that he did not feel, in order to justify his almost constant presence in the house on Avenida del Tibidabo; to say only what he knew others wanted to hear him say, to read their looks and their hopes, to put aside honesty and sincerity, and to feel that he *was selling his very soul. He began to fear that if he ever did come to deserve Penélope, there would be nothing left of the Julián who saw her the first time. Sometimes Julián would wake up at dawn, burning with anger, longing to tell the world his real feelings, to face Don Ricardo Aldaya and tell him he had no interest whatsoever in his fortune, his opportunities for the future, or his company; that all he wanted was his daughter, Penélope, and was thinking of taking her as far away as possible from that empty, shrouded world in which her father had imprisoned her. The light of day dispelled his courage.*

*There were times when Julián opened his heart to Jacinta, who was beginning to love the boy more than she might have wished. She would often leave Penélope for a moment and, under the pretext of going to collect Jorge from school, would see Julián and deliver Penélope's messages to him. That was how she met Fernando, who, many years later, would be her only remaining friend while she awaited death in the hell of Santa Lucía – the hell that had been prophesied by the angel Zacarías. Sometimes the nurse would mischievously take Penélope with her to the school and facilitate a brief encounter between the two youngsters, watching a love grow between them such as she had never known, which had always been denied her. It was also around this time that Jacinta noticed the sombre and disturbing presence of that quiet boy whom everyone called Francisco Javier, the son of the school's caretaker. She would catch him spying on them, reading their gestures from afar and devouring Penélope with his eyes.*

*Jacinta kept a photograph of Julián and Penélope taken by Recassens, the Aldayas' official portrait photographer, by the door of the hat shop in Ronda de San Antonio. It was an innocent image, taken at midday in the presence of Don Ricardo and of Sophie Carax. Jacinta always carried it with her. One day, while she was waiting for Jorge outside San Gabriel's, the governess absentmindedly left her bag by one of the fountains and, when she went back for it, found young Fumero prowling around the area, looking at her nervously.*

*That night she looked for the photograph but couldn't find it and was certain that the boy had stolen it. On another occasion, a few weeks later, Francisco Javier Fumero went up to Jacinta and asked her whether she could give Penélope something from him. When Jacinta asked what this thing was, the boy pulled out a piece of cloth in which he had wrapped what looked like a figure carved in pinewood. Jacinta recognized it was a carving of Penélope, and felt a shiver. Before she was able to say anything, the boy left. On her way back to the house on Avenida del Tibidabo, Jacinta threw the figure out of the car window, as if it were a piece of stinking carrion. More than once Jacinta was to wake up at dawn, covered in sweat, plagued by nightmares in which that troubled-looking boy threw himself on Penélope with the cold and indifferent brutality of some strange insect.*

*Some afternoons, when Jacinta went to fetch Jorge and he was late, the governess would talk to Julián. He, too, was beginning to love that severe-looking woman. Whenever a problem cast a shadow over his life, she and Miquel Moliner were soon the first to know. Once Julián told Jacinta he had seen his mother and Don Ricardo Aldaya talking in the fountain courtyard while they waited for the pupils to come out. Don Ricardo seemed to be enjoying Sophie's company, and Julián felt a little uneasy, because he was aware of the magnate's reputation as a Don Juan and of his voracious appetite for the delights of the female sex. 'I was telling your mother how much you like your new school,' Don Ricardo told him. When he said goodbye to them, Don Ricardo gave them a wink and walked off laughing boisterously. His mother was quiet during the journey home, clearly offended by the comments Don Ricardo Aldaya had made to her.*

*Sophie was suspicious of Julián's growing bond with the Aldayas and the way he had abandoned his old neighbourhood friends and his family. She was not alone. But whereas his mother showed her displeasure in sadness and silence, the hatter displayed only bitterness and spite. His initial enthusiasm about the widening of his clientele to include the flower of*

Barcelona society had evaporated. He hardly ever saw his son now and soon had to employ Quimet, a local boy and one of Julián's former friends, as a helper and apprentice in the shop. Antoni Fortuny was a man who felt he could only talk openly about hats. He locked his deeper feelings in the prison of his heart for months on end, until they became hopelessly embittered. Every day, he grew more bad tempered and irritable. He found fault with everything – from the efforts of poor Quimet to learn the trade to Sophie's attempts to make light of Julián's seeming abandonment of them.

'Your son thinks he's someone just because those rich folk treat him like a performing monkey,' he'd say in a depressed tone, full of resentment.

One day, almost three years to the day since Don Ricardo Aldaya's first visit to the Fortuny and Sons hat shop, the hatter left Quimet in charge of the shop and told him he'd be back at noon. He boldly presented himself at the offices of Aldaya's consortium on Paseo de Gracia and asked to see Don Ricardo.

'And whom do I have the honour of announcing?' asked a clerk in a haughty manner.

'His personal hatter.'

Don Ricardo received him, somewhat surprised but well disposed, imagining that perhaps Fortuny was bringing him a bill. Small shopkeepers never quite understood the protocol when it came to money.

'So tell me, what can I do for you Fortunato, old fellow?'

Without further delay, Antoni Fortuny proceeded to explain to Don Ricardo that he was very much mistaken about his son Julián.

'My son, Don Ricardo, is not the person you think he is. Quite the contrary; he is an ignorant, lazy boy, with no more talent than the pretentious ideas his mother has put into his head. He'll never get anywhere, believe me. He lacks ambition and character. You don't know him. He can be very clever at sweet-talking strangers, making them believe he knows a lot about everything, when in fact he knows nothing about *anything. He's a mediocre person. I know him better than anyone, and I thought I should warn you.'*

*Don Ricardo Aldaya listened to the speech in silence, without blinking.*

*'Is that all, Fortunato?'*

*Seeing that it was, the industrialist pressed a button on his desk. A few moments later, the secretary who had received Fortuny on arrival appeared at the office door.*

*'Our friend Fortunato is leaving, Balcells,' Don Ricardo announced. 'Please accompany him to the door.'*

*The icy tone of the industrialist did not please the hatter.*

*'If you don't mind, Don Ricardo: it's Fortuny, not Fortunato.'*

*'Whatever. You're a very sad man, Fortuny. I'd appreciate it if you didn't come here again.'*

*When Fortuny found himself back on the street, he felt more alone than ever, more convinced that everyone was against him. Only a few days later, the smart clients brought in by his relationship with Aldaya began to send messages cancelling their orders and settling their bills. In just a few weeks, he had to dismiss Quimet, because there wasn't enough work for both of them. The boy wasn't much use anyhow, he told himself. He was mediocre and lazy, like all of them.*

*It was around this time that people in the neighbourhood began to comment that Señor Fortuny was looking much older, lonelier, more bitter. He barely spoke to anyone anymore and spent hours on end shut up in the shop, with nothing to do, watching people go by from behind his counter, feelings of disdain mingling with hope. Later people said that fashions changed, that young people no longer wore hats, and that those who did would rather go to other shops where hats were sold ready made in different sizes, with more modern designs, and at a cheaper price. The Fortuny and Sons hat shop slowly sank into a sad, silent slumber.*

*You're all waiting for me to die, Fortuny said to himself. Well, I might just give you that pleasure. In fact, he had started to die a long time ago.*

Julián threw himself even more into the world of the Aldayas, into the only future he could conceive of, a future with Penélope. Almost two years went by, in which the two of them walked on a tightrope of secrecy together. In his own way, Zacarías had given a warning long ago. Shadows spread around Julián, and soon they would close in on him.

The first sign came one day in April 1918. Jorge Aldaya was going to be eighteen, and Don Ricardo, playing the role of great patriarch, had decided to organize (or, rather, to give orders for someone to organize) a monumental birthday party that his son did not want and from which he, Don Ricardo, would be absent: under the guise of important business commitments, he would be meeting a delicious lady, newly arrived from St Petersburg, in the blue suite of the Hotel Colón. The house on Avenida del Tibidabo was turned into a circus for the occasion: hundreds of lanterns, pennants, and stalls were set up in the gardens to delight the guests.

Almost all of Jorge Aldaya's school companions from San Gabriel's had been invited. At Julián's suggestion, Jorge had included Francisco Javier Fumero. Miquel Moliner warned them that the son of the school caretaker would feel out of place in such pompous surroundings. Francisco Javier received his invitation but, anticipating exactly the same thing, decided to turn it down. When Doña Yvonne, his mother, learned that her son was going to decline an invitation to the Aldayas' luxurious mansion, she was on the point of skinning him alive. What could that invitation be but a sign that she herself would soon be accepted into high society? The next step could only be an invitation to afternoon tea with Señora Aldaya and other ladies of unquestionable distinction. Doña Yvonne took the savings she had been scraping together out of her husband's pay and went out to buy a pretty sailor suit for her son.

Francisco Javier was already seventeen at the time, and that blue suit with short trousers, tailored to appeal to the none-too-refined sensibility of Doña Yvonne, looked grotesque and humiliating on the boy. Pressed by his mother, Francisco Javier accepted the invitation and spent a week carving a letter opener, which he intended to give Jorge as a present. On the day of the party, Doña Yvonne insisted on accompanying her son to the door of the Aldayas' house. She wanted to scent royalty and bask in the glory of seeing her son enter the doors that would soon open for her. When the moment came to put on his awful sailor suit, Francisco Javier discovered it was too small for him. Yvonne decided to adjust it somehow. They arrived late. In the meantime, taking advantage of the hubbub and of Don Ricardo's absence – who no doubt was at that very moment celebrating in his own way – Julián had slipped away from the party. He and Penélope had arranged to meet in the library, where they didn't risk running into any of the other partygoers. They were too busy devouring each other's lips to notice the couple approaching the front door of the house. Francisco Javier, dressed in his first-communion sailor suit and purple with shame, was almost being dragged by Doña Yvonne, who for the occasion had decided to resurrect a broad-brimmed hat and a matching dress adorned with flourishes and bows; they made her look like a sweet stall or, in the words of Miquel Moliner, who sighted her from afar, a bison dressed up as Madame Récamier. The two servants guarding the door didn't seem very impressed by the visitors. Doña Yvonne announced that her son, Don Francisco Javier Fumero de Sotoceballos, was making his entrance. The two servants answered, in a sarcastic tone, that the name did not ring a bell. Irritated, but keeping the composure of a woman of substance, Yvonne told her son to show them the invitation. Unfortunately, when the suit was being fixed, the card had been left on Doña Yvonne's sewing table.

Francisco Javier tried to explain the circumstances, but he stammered, and the laughter of the two servants did not help clear up the misunderstanding. Mother and son were invited to get the hell out of there. Doña Yvonne was inflamed with anger and announced that the servants didn't know who they were dealing with. The servants replied that the floor cleaner's position was already taken.

From her bedroom window, Jacinta watched Francisco

Javier turn to leave, then suddenly stop. Beyond the scene his mother was creating, shouting herself hoarse at the arrogant servants, the boy saw them: Julián kissing Penélope by the large window of the library. They were kissing with the intensity of those who belong to one another, unaware of the world around them.

The following day, during the midday break, Francisco Javier appeared unexpectedly. News of the previous day's scene had already spread among the pupils: he was met with laughter and questioned about what he'd done with his little sailor suit. The laughter ended abruptly when the boys noticed he was carrying his father's gun. There was complete silence, and many of them moved away. Only the circle formed by Aldaya, Moliner, Fernando, and Julián turned around and stared at the boy, without understanding. Francisco Javier gave no warning: he raised his rifle and aimed. Later, witnesses said there was no irritation or anger in his expression. Francisco Javier displayed the same automatic coolness with which he performed his cleaning jobs in the garden. The first bullet scraped past Julián's head. The second would have gone through his throat had Miquel Moliner not thrown himself on the caretaker's son, punched him, and wrenched the gun from him. Julián Carax watched the scene in astonishment, paralysed. Everyone thought the shots were aimed at Jorge Aldaya in revenge for the humiliation Javier had suffered the day before. Only later, when the Civil Guards were taking the boy away and the caretakers were being almost literally kicked out of their home, did Miquel Moliner go up to Julián and tell him, without any pride, that he had saved his life.

It was the last year for Julián and his companions at San Gabriel's school. Most of them were already talking about their plans, or about the plans their respective families had set up for them for the following year. Jorge Aldaya already knew that his father was sending him to study in England, and Miquel Moliner took it for granted that he would go to Barcelona University. Fernando Ramos had mentioned more than once that perhaps he would enter the seminary of the Society of Jesus, a prospect his teachers considered the wisest in his particular situation. As for Francisco Javier Fumero, all anyone knew about the boy was that, thanks to Don Ricardo Aldaya, who interceded on his behalf, he had been taken to a reformatory school high in a remote valley of the Pyrenees, where a long winter awaited him. Seeing that all his friends had found some direction in life, Julián wondered what would become of himself. His literary dreams and ambitions seemed further away and more unfeasible than ever. All he longed for was to be near Penélope.

While he pondered his future, others were planning it for him. Don Ricardo Aldaya was already preparing a post for him in his firm, to initiate him into the business. The hatter, for his part, had decided that if his son did not want to continue in the family business, he could forget about sponging off him. He had secretly set in motion his plan to send Julián to the army, where a few years of military life would cure him of his delusions of grandeur. Julián was unaware of such plans, and by the time he found out what others had arranged for him, it would be too late. Only Penélope occupied his thoughts, and now the feigned distance and the clandestine meetings no longer satisfied him. He insisted on seeing her more often, increasing the risk of discovery. Jacinta did what she could to cover for them: she lied repeatedly and concocted a thousand and one ruses to give them a few moments on their own. She understood that this was not enough for Penélope and Julián. The governess had for some time now recognized in their looks the defiance and arrogance of desire: a blind desire to be discovered, a hope that their secret would become an open scandal so that they would no longer have to hide in corners and attics, to love one another in the dark. Sometimes, when Jacinta tucked Penélope up at night, the girl would burst into floods of tears and confess how she longed to flee with Julián, to catch the first train and escape to a place where nobody would know them. Jacinta, who remembered the sort of world that existed beyond the iron gates of the Aldaya mansion, shuddered and tried to dissuade her. Penélope was docile by nature, and the fear she saw in Jacinta's face was enough to soothe her. Julián was another matter.

During that last spring at San Gabriel's, Julián was unnerved to discover that Don Ricardo Aldaya and his mother sometimes met secretly. At first he feared that the industrialist might have decided to add the conquest of Sophie to his collection, but soon he realized that the meetings, which always took place in cafés in the centre of town and were carried out with the utmost propriety, were limited to conversation. Sophie kept silent about these meetings. When at last Julián decided to ask Don Ricardo what was going on between him and his mother, the magnate laughed.

'Nothing gets by you, does it, Julián? The fact is, I was going to talk to you about this matter. Your mother and I are discussing your future. She came to see me a few weeks ago. She was worried because your father wants to send you away to the army next year. Your mother, quite naturally, wants the best for you, and she came to me to see whether, between the two of us, we could do anything. Don't worry; you have Don Ricardo Aldaya's word that you won't become cannon fodder. Your mother and I have great plans for you. Trust us.'

Julián wanted to trust him, yet Don Ricardo inspired anything but trust. When he consulted Miquel Moliner, the boy agreed with Julián.

'If what you want to do is elope with Penélope, and may God help you, what you need is money.'

Money was exactly what Julián didn't have.

'That can be arranged,' Miquel told him. 'That's what rich friends are for.'

That is how Miquel and Julián began to plan the lovers' escape. The destination, at Miquel's suggestion, would be Paris. Moliner was of the opinion that, if Julián was set on being a starving bohemian artist, at least a Parisian setting couldn't be improved upon. Penélope spoke a little French, and for Julián, who had learned it from his mother, it was his second language.

'Besides, Paris is large enough to get lost in but small enough to offer opportunities,' Miquel reasoned.

Miquel managed to put together a small fortune, joining his savings from many years to what he was able to extort from his father, using the most outlandish excuses. Only he knew where the money was really going.

'And I plan to go dumb the minute you two board that train.'

That same afternoon, after finalizing details with Moliner, Julián went to the house on Avenida del Tibidabo to tell Penélope about the plan.

'You mustn't tell anyone what I'm about to tell you. No one. Not even Jacinta,' Julián began.

The girl listened to him in astonishment, enthralled. Moliner's plan was impeccable. Miquel would buy the tickets under a false name and hire a third party to collect them at the ticket office in the station. If by any chance the police discovered him, all he'd be able to give them would be the description of someone who did not look like Julián. Julián and Penélope would meet on the train. There would be no waiting on the platform, where they might be seen. The escape would take place on a Sunday, at midday. Julián would make his own way to the Estación de Francia. Miquel would be there waiting for him, with the tickets and the money.

The most delicate part of the plan concerned Penélope. She had to deceive Jacinta and ask her to invent an excuse for taking her out of the eleven o'clock mass and returning home. On the way Penélope would ask Jacinta to let her go and meet Julián, promising to be back before the family had returned to the mansion. This would be Penélope's opportunity to get to the station. They both knew that if they told her the truth, Jacinta would not allow them to leave. She loved them too much.

'It's the perfect plan, Miquel,' Julián said.

Miquel nodded sadly. 'Except for one detail: the pain you are going to cause a lot of people by going away forever.'

Julián nodded, thinking of his mother and Jacinta. It did

not occur to him that Miquel Moliner was talking about himself.

The most difficult thing was convincing Penélope of the need to keep Jacinta in the dark. Only Miquel would know the truth. The train left at one in the afternoon. By the time Penélope's absence was noticed, the couple would have crossed the border. Once in Paris, they would settle in a hostel as man and wife, using a false name. They would then send Miquel Moliner a letter addressed to their families, confessing their love, telling them they were well, that they loved them, announcing their church wedding, and asking for forgiveness and understanding. Miquel Moliner would put the letter in a second envelope to do away with the Paris postmark and would see to it that it was posted from some nearby town.

'When?' asked Penélope.

'In six days' time,' said Julián. 'This coming Sunday.'

Miquel reckoned it would be best if Julián didn't see Penélope during the days left prior to the elopement, so as not to arouse suspicion. They should both agree not to see each other again until they met on the train on their way to Paris. Six days without seeing her, without touching her, seemed interminable to Julián. They sealed the pact, the secret marriage, with a kiss.

It was then that Julián took Penélope to Jacinta's bedroom on the third floor of the house. Only the servants' quarters were on that floor, and Julián was sure nobody would discover them. They undressed feverishly, with an angry passion and desire, scratching each other's skin and melting into silence. They learned each other's bodies by heart and buried all thoughts of those six days of separation. Julián penetrated Penélope with fury, pressing her against the floorboards. She received him with open eyes, her legs hugging his torso, her lips half open with yearning. There was not a glimmer of fragility or childishness in her eyes or in her warm body. Later, with his face still resting on her stomach and his hands on her white, tremulous breasts, Julián knew he had to say goodbye. He had barely had time to sit up when the door of the room slowly opened and a woman's shape appeared at the doorway. For a second, Julián thought it was Jacinta, but he soon realized it was Señora Aldaya. She was watching them, spellbound, with a mixture of fascination and disgust. All she managed to mumble was, 'Where's Jacinta?' Then she just turned and walked away without saying a word, while Penélope crouched on the floor in mute agony and Julián felt the world collapsing around him.

'Go now, Julián. Go before my father comes.'

'But . . .'

'Go.'

Julián nodded. 'Whatever happens, I'll wait for you on Sunday on that train.'

Penélope managed a faint smile. 'I'll be there. Now go. Please . . .'

She was still naked when he left her and slid down the servants' staircase towards the coach houses and out into the coldest night he could remember.

The days that followed were agony. Julián had spent all night awake, expecting that Don Ricardo's hired assassins would come for him at any moment. The following day, in school, he didn't notice any change of attitude in Jorge Aldaya. Devoured by anguish, Julián told Miquel Moliner what had happened. Miquel shook his head.

'You're crazy, Julián, but that's nothing new. What's strange is that there hasn't been an upheaval in the Aldayas' house. Which, come to think of it, isn't so surprising. If, as you say, it was Señora Aldaya who discovered you, it might be that she still doesn't know what to do. I've had three conversations with her in my life and came to two conclusions: one, Señora Aldaya has the mental age of a twelve-year-old; two, she suffers from a chronic narcissism that makes it impossible for her to see or understand anything that is not what she wants to see or believe, especially if it concerns herself.'

'Spare me the diagnosis, Miquel.'

'What I mean is that she's probably still wondering what to say, how to say it, when, and to whom. First she must think of the consequences for herself, the potential scandal, her husband's fury ... The rest, I daresay, she couldn't care less about.'

'So you think she won't say anything?'

'She might take a day or two. But I don't think she's capable of keeping such a secret from her husband. What about the escape plan? Is it still on?'

'More than ever.'

'I'm glad to hear that. Because I really believe that now there's no turning back.'

The week stretched out interminably. Julián went to school every day with uncertainty hard on his heels. He passed the time merely pretending to be there, barely able to exchange glances with Miquel Moliner, who was beginning to be just as worried as him, or more so. Jorge Aldaya said nothing. He was as polite as ever. Jacinta had not turned up again to collect Jorge from school. Don Ricardo's chauffeur came every afternoon. Julián felt like dying, wishing that whatever was going to happen would happen, so that the waiting would come to an end. On Thursday afternoon, after class, Julián began to think that luck was on his side. Señora Aldaya had not said anything, perhaps out of shame, stupidity, or for any of the reasons Miquel had suggested. It mattered little. All that mattered was that she kept the secret until Sunday. That night, for the first time in a number of days, Julián was able to sleep.

On Friday morning, when he went to class, Father Romanones was waiting for him by the gate.

'Julián, I have to speak to you.'

'What is it, Father?'

'I always knew this day would come, and I must confess I'm happy to be the one who will break the news to you.'

'What news, Father?'

Julián Carax was no longer a pupil at San Gabriel's school. His presence in the compound, the classrooms, and even the gardens was strictly forbidden. His school items, textbooks, and all other belongings were now school property.

The technical term is "immediate and total expulsion",' Father Romanones summed up.

'May I ask the reason?'

'I can think of a dozen, but I'm sure you'll know how to choose the most appropriate one. Good day, Carex. And good luck in your life. You're going to need it.'

Some thirty yards away, in the fountains courtyard, a group of pupils was watching him. Some were laughing, waving goodbye. Others looked at him with pity and bewilderment. Only one smiled sadly: his friend Miquel Moliner, who simply nodded and silently mouthed some words that Julián thought he could read in the air: 'See you on Sunday.'

When he got back to the apartment in Ronda de San Antonio, Julián noticed Don Ricardo's Mercedes-Benz parked outside the hat shop. He stopped on the corner and waited. After a while Don Ricardo came out of his father's shop and got into the car. Julián hid in a doorway until the car set off towards Plaza Universidad. Only then did he rush up the stairs to his home. His mother, Sophie, was waiting there, in floods of tears.

'What have you done, Julián?' she murmured without anger.

'Forgive me, Mother . . .'

Sophie held her son close. She had lost weight and had aged, as if between them all they had stolen her life and her youth. I more so than anyone, thought Julián.

'Listen to me carefully, Julián. Your father and Don Ricardo Aldaya have got everything set up to send you to the army in a few days' time. Aldaya has a great deal of influence . . . You have to go, Julián. You have to go where neither of them can find you . . .'

Julián thought he saw a shadow in his mother's eyes that seemed to take hold of her.

'Is there anything else, Mother? Something you haven't told me?'

Sophie gazed at him with trembling lips. 'You must go. We must both go away from here forever.'

*Julián held her tight and whispered in her ear, 'Don't worry about me, Mother. Don't you worry.'*

*Julián spent the Saturday shut up in his room, among his books and his drawing pads. The hatter had gone down to the shop just after dawn and didn't return until the early hours. He doesn't have the courage to tell me to my face, thought Julián. That night, his eyes blurred with tears, Julián said farewell to the years he had spent in that dark, cold room, lost amid dreams that he now knew would never come true. Sunday, at daybreak, armed with only a bag containing a few clothes and books, he kissed Sophie's forehead, as she lay curled under blankets in the dining room, and left. The streets seemed enveloped in a blue haze. Flashes of copper sparkled on the flat roofs of the old town. He walked slowly, saying goodbye to every door, to every street corner, wondering whether the illusions of time would turn out to be true and that in days to come he would be able to remember only the good things, and forget the solitude that had so often hounded him in those streets.*

*The Estación de Francia was deserted; the platforms, reflecting the burning light of dawn, curved off into the mist like glistening sabres. Julián sat on a bench under the vaulted ceiling and took out his book. He let the hours go by lost in the magic of words, shedding his skin and his name, feeling like another person. He allowed himself to be carried away by the dreams of shadowy characters, the only refuge left for him. By then he knew that Penélope wouldn't come. He knew he would board that train with no other company than his memories. When, just before noon, Miquel Moliner arrived in the station and gave him the tickets and all the money he had been able to gather, the two friends embraced without a word. Julián had never seen Miquel Moliner cry. Clocks were everywhere, counting the minutes as they flew by.*

*'There's still time,' Miquel murmured, his eyes fixed on the station entrance.*

*At five past one, the stationmaster gave the last call for passengers travelling to Paris. The train had already started to*

289

slide along the platform when Julián turned round to say goodbye to his friend. Miquel Moliner stood there watching him, his hands buried in his pockets.

'Write,' he said.

'I'll write to you as soon as I get there,' answered Julián.

'No. Not to me. Write books. Not letters. Write them for me, for Penélope.'

Julián nodded, realizing only then how much he was going to miss his friend.

'And keep your dreams,' said Miquel. 'You never know when you might need them.'

'Always,' murmured Julián, but the roar of the train had already stolen his words.

'The night her mother caught them in my bedroom, Penélope told me what had happened. The following day Señora Aldaya called for me and asked me what I knew about Julián. I said I didn't know anything, except that he was a nice boy, a friend of Jorge's. She ordered me to keep Penélope locked in her room until she was given permission to come out. Don Ricardo was away in Madrid and didn't come back until early on Friday. As soon as he arrived, Señora Aldaya told him what she'd witnessed. I was there. Don Ricardo jumped up from his armchair and slapped his wife so hard she fell on the floor. Then, shouting like a madman, he told her to repeat what she had just said. Señora Aldaya was terrified. We had never seen her husband like that. Never. He looked as if he were possessed by all the devils in hell. Seething with anger, he went up to Penélope's bedroom and pulled her out of her bed, dragging her by the hair. I tried to stop him, but he kicked me aside. That same evening he called the family doctor and had him examine Penélope. When the doctor had finished, he spoke to Señor Aldaya. They locked Penélope up in her room, and Señora Aldaya told me to collect my things.

'They didn't let me see Penélope. I never said goodbye to her. Don Ricardo threatened to report me to the police if I told anyone what had happened. That very night they threw me out, with nowhere to go, after eighteen years of uninterrupted service in the house. Two days later, in a *pensión* in Calle Muntaner, I had a visit from Miquel Moliner, who told me that Julián had gone to Paris. He wanted me to tell him why Penélope hadn't come to the station as arranged. For weeks I returned to the house, begging for a chance to see her, but I wasn't even allowed to cross the gates. I would position myself on the opposite corner every day, for days on end, hoping to see them come out. I never saw her. She didn't come out of the house. Later on, Señor Aldaya called the police and, with the help of his high-powered friends, managed to get me committed to the lunatic asylum in Horta, claiming that nobody knew me, that I was some demented woman who harassed his family and children. I spent two years there, locked up like an animal. The first thing I did when I got out was go to the house on Avenida del Tibidabo to see Penélope.'

'Did you manage to see her?' Fermín asked.

'The house was locked and up for sale. Nobody lived there. I was told that the Aldayas had gone to Argentina. I wrote to the address I was given. The letters were returned to me unopened....'

'What happened to Penélope? Do you know?'

Jacinta shook her head, in a state of near collapse. 'I never saw her again.'

The old woman moaned and began to weep uncontrollably. Fermín held her in his arms and rocked her. Jacinta Coronado had shrunk to the size of a little girl, and next to her Fermín looked like a giant. I had questions burning in my head, but my friend signalled to me that the interview was over. I saw him gazing about him at that dirty, cold hovel where Jacinta Coronado was spending her last days.

'Come on, Daniel. We're leaving. You go first.'

I did what I was told. As I walked away, I turned for a moment and saw Fermín kneel down by the old lady and kiss her on the forehead. She gave him a toothless smile.

'Tell me, Jacinta,' I heard Fermín saying. 'You like Sugus sweets, don't you?'

On our circuitous path back to the exit, we passed the real undertaker and his two cadaverous assistants carrying a cheap pine coffin, rope, and what looked suspiciously like a recycled shroud. The committee gave off a sinister smell of formaldehyde and cheap eau de cologne. The men's bloodless skin framed gaunt, canine smiles. Fermín pointed to the cell where the body of the deceased awaited and proceeded to bless the trio, who nodded respectfully and made the sign of the cross.

'Go in peace,' mumbled Fermín, dragging me towards the exit, where a nun holding an oil lamp saw us off with a harsh, condemnatory look.

Once we were out of the building, the grim canyon of stone and shadow that was Calle Moncada seemed more like an inviting valley of hope. Fermín breathed deeply, with relief, and I knew I wasn't the only one to be rejoicing at having left that place behind. Jacinta's story weighed on our consciences more than we would have wished to admit.

'Listen, Daniel. What would you say to some ham croquettes and a couple of glasses of sparkling wine here in the Xampañet, just to take away the bad taste in our mouths?'

'I wouldn't say no, quite frankly.'

'Didn't you arrange to meet up with the girl today?'

'Tomorrow.'

'Ah, you devil . . . you're playing hard to get, eh? You're learning fast . . .'

We hadn't taken ten steps towards the noisy tavern, just a few doors down the street, when three silhouettes material-ized out of the shadows and intercepted us. Two positioned themselves behind us, so close I could feel their breath on the nape of my neck. The third, smaller but much more menacing, blocked our way. It was him. He wore the usual raincoat, and his oily smile oozed irrepressible glee.

'Why, who have we here? If it's not my old friend, the man of the thousand faces!' cried Inspector Fumero.

It seemed to me I could hear all of Fermín's bones shudder with terror at the apparition. My loquacious friend could manage only a stifled groan. The two thugs, who I guessed were two agents from the Crime Squad, grabbed us by the scruffs of our necks and held our right wrists, ready to twist our arms at the slightest hint of movement.

'I see from your look of surprise that you thought I'd lost track of you long ago. Surely you didn't think a piece of shit like you was going to be able to crawl out of the gutter and pass himself off as a decent citizen. You might be stupid, but not *that* stupid. Besides, I'm told you're poking your nose – and it's quite a nose – in a whole pile of things that are none of your business. That's a bad sign ... What is it with you and those little nuns? Are you having it off with one of them? How much do they charge these days?'

'I respect other people's arses, Inspector, especially if they are cloistered. Perhaps if you were inclined to do the same, you would save yourself a hefty bill in penicillin and improve the number and ease of your bowel movements.'

Fumero let out a little laugh streaked with anger.

'That's right. Balls of steel. If all crooks were like you, my work would be a party. Tell me, what are you calling yourself these days, you son of a bitch? Gary Cooper? Come on, tell me what you're up to, sticking that big nose of yours in the Hospice of Santa Lucía, and I might let you go with just a warning. Come on, spell it out. What brings you two here?'

'A private matter. We came to visit a relative.'

'Sure, your fucking mother. Look here, you happen to have caught me on a good day, otherwise I'd be taking you to headquarters and giving you another session with the welding torch. Come on, be a good boy and tell your old friend Inspector Fumero the truth about what the fuck you and your friend are doing here. Damn it, just cooperate a bit, and you'll save me beating up this smart little kid you've chosen as a sponsor.'

'You touch a single hair of his head and I swear I'll—'

'You scare me to bits, really. I just shat my pants.'

Fermín swallowed, as if to hold in all the courage that was seeping out of him. 'Those wouldn't be the same sailor-boy pants that your esteemed mother, the Illustrious Kitchen Maid, made you wear? That would be a shame; I'm told the outfit really suited you.'

Inspector Fumero's face paled, and all expression left his eyes. 'What did you say, motherfucker?'

'I was saying it looks like you've inherited all the taste and charm of Doña Yvonne Sotoceballos, a high-society lady . . .'

Fermín was not a heavy man, and the first punch was enough to knock him off his feet and into a puddle of water. He lay curled up in a ball as Fumero meted out a flurry of kicks to his stomach, kidneys, and face. I lost count after the fifth. Fermín lost his breath and then, a moment later, the ability to protect himself from the blows. The two policemen who were holding me down with iron hands were laughing dutifully.

'Don't get involved,' one of them whispered to me. 'I don't feel like breaking your arm.'

I tried in vain to wriggle out of his grip, and, as I struggled, I caught a glimpse of him. I recognized his face immediately. He was the man in the raincoat with the newspaper who was in the bar at Plaza de Sarriá a few days earlier, the same man who had followed us in the bus and laughed at Fermín's jokes.

'Look, the one thing that really pisses me off is people who stir up shit from the past!' Fumero cried out. 'The past must be left alone, do you understand? And that goes for you and your dumb friend. Look and learn, kid. You're next.'

The whole time I watched Inspector Fumero destroy

Fermín with his kicks, I was unable to utter a word. I remember the dull, terrible impact of the blows raining down mercilessly on my friend. They hurt me still. All I did was take refuge in the policemen's convenient grasp, trembling and shedding silent cowardly tears.

When Fumero tired of striking a dead weight, he opened up his raincoat, unzipped his fly, and began to urinate on Fermín. My friend didn't move; he looked like a bundle of old clothes in a puddle. While Fumero discharged his generous, steamy cascade over Fermín, I still couldn't speak. When he'd finished, the inspector zipped up his trousers and came over to me, sweaty-faced and panting. One of the police officers handed him a handkerchief, and he mopped his face and neck. He came closer, until his face was only a couple of inches from mine, and he fixed me with his stare.

'You weren't worth that beating, kid. That's the problem with your friend: he always backs the wrong side. Next time I'm going to fuck him up like I've never done before, and I'm sure it's going to be your fault.'

I thought he was going to hit me then, that my turn had come. For some reason I was glad. I wanted to believe that his blows would cure me of the shame I felt for not having raised a finger to help Fermín, when the only thing he'd been trying to do, as usual, was protect me.

But no blow came. All Fumero did was pat me on the cheek.

'It's okay, boy. I don't dirty my hands with cowards.'

The two policemen chuckled, more relaxed now that they knew the show was over. Their desire to leave the scene was obvious. They went off laughing in the dark.

By the time I went to his aid, Fermín was trying in vain to get up and find the teeth he'd lost in the dirty water of the puddle. His mouth, nose, ears, and eyelids were all bleeding. When he saw that I was unharmed, he attempted to smile and I thought he was going to die on the spot. I knelt beside him and held him in my arms. The first thought that crossed my mind was that he weighed less than Bea.

'Fermín, for God's sake, we must get you to a hospital right away.'

He shook his head energetically. 'Take me to her.'

'To who, Fermín?'

'To Bernarda. If I'm going to die, I'd rather it was in her arms.'


# 32

That night I returned to Plaza Real, to the apartment I'd sworn I would never set foot in again. A couple of regulars who had witnessed the beating from the door of the Xampañet Tavern offered to help me take Fermín to a taxi rank in Calle Princesa while a waiter called the number I had given him, to warn of our arrival. The taxi ride seemed endless. Fermín had lost consciousness before we set off. I held him in my arms, clutching him against my chest and trying to warm him up. I could feel his tepid blood soaking my clothes. I whispered in his ear that we were nearly there, that he was going to be all right. My voice trembled. The driver shot me furtive looks through the mirror.

'Listen, I don't want any trouble, do you hear? If he dies, you'll have to get out.'

'Just shut up and floor it.'

By the time we reached Calle Fernando, Gustavo Barceló and Bernarda were waiting by the main door of the building, along with Dr Soldevila. When she saw us covered in blood and dirt, Bernarda started to scream in panic. The doctor quickly took Fermín's pulse and assured us that the patient was still alive. Between the four of us, we managed to carry Fermín up the stairs and into Bernarda's room, where a nurse, who had come along with the doctor, was getting everything ready. Once the patient was laid on the bed, the nurse began to undress him. Dr Soldevila insisted that we all leave the room and let him get on with his work. He closed the door on us with a brief, 'He'll live.'

In the corridor Bernarda sobbed inconsolably. She moaned that now that she'd found a good man, for the first time in her life, God had come along and mercilessly wrenched him away from her. Don Gustavo Barceló took her in his arms and led her to the kitchen, where he proceeded to ply her with brandy until the poor thing could hardly stand up. Once the maid's words were unintelligible, the bookseller poured himself a glass and downed it in one gulp.

'I'm sorry. I didn't know where to go . . .' I began.

'That's all right. You've done the right thing. Soldevila is the best orthopaedic surgeon in Barcelona.' He spoke without addressing anyone in particular.

'Thank you,' I murmured.

Barceló sighed and poured me a good shot of brandy in a tumbler. I declined his offer, and it was passed on to Bernarda, who quickly made it disappear.

'Will you please go and have a shower and put on some clean clothes,' Barceló said. 'If you go back home looking like that, your father will die of a heart attack.'

'It's all right. . . . I'm okay,' I said.

'In that case stop trembling. Go on, you can use my bathroom, it has a water heater. You know the way. In the meantime, I'm going to call your father and tell him . . . well, I don't know what I'll tell him. I'll think of something.'

I nodded.

'This is still your home, Daniel,' said Barceló as I wandered off down the corridors. 'We've missed you.'

I found Gustavo Barceló's bathroom, but not the light switch. I took off my filthy, bloodstained clothes and hauled myself into the imperial bathtub. A pearly mist filtered in through the window that looked out onto the inner courtyard of the building, and there was enough light for me to be able to make out the outline of the room and the pattern of the enamelled tiles on the floor and walls. The water came out boiling hot and with much greater pressure than our modest bathroom on Calle Santa Ana could offer; it felt like being in a luxury hotel, not that I'd ever set foot in one. I stood under the shower's steamy rays for a few minutes without moving.

The echo of the blows raining down on Fermín still hammered in my ears. I couldn't get Fumero's words out of my mind, or the face of the policeman who had held me down. After a while I noticed that the water was beginning to get cold, and I assumed the reserve in my host's boiler was coming to an end. When I had finished the last drop of lukewarm water, I turned off the tap. The steam rose up my body like silken threads. Through the shower curtains, I noticed a figure standing by the door, her marble gaze shining like the eyes of a cat.

'You can come out. There's nothing to worry about, Daniel. Despite all my evil doings, I still can't see you.'

'Hello, Clara.'

She held out a clean towel towards me. I stretched out my hand and took it, wrapping myself in it with the modesty of a schoolgirl. Even in the steamy darkness, I could see that Clara was smiling, guessing at my movements.

'I didn't hear you come in.'

'I didn't call out. Why are you taking a shower in the dark?'

'How do you know the light isn't on?'

'The buzzing of the bulb,' she said. 'You never came back to say goodbye.'

Yes, I did come back, I thought, but you were busy. The words died on my lips; their animosity seemed distant, ridiculous.

'I know. I'm sorry.'

I got out of the shower and stood on the mat. The steamy air glowed with specks of silver, and the pale light from the

298

window cast a white veil over Clara's face. She hadn't changed a bit. Four years of absence had not helped me.

'Your voice has changed,' she said. 'Have you changed, too, Daniel?'

'I'm just as stupid as before, if that's what you're wondering.'

And more of a coward, I thought. She still had that same broken smile that hurt, even in the dark. She stretched out her hand, and, just as on that afternoon in the Ateneo library some eight years before, I understood immediately. I guided her hand to my damp face and felt her fingers rediscovering me, her lips shaping words in silence.

'I never wanted to hurt you, Daniel. Forgive me.'

I took her hand and kissed it in the dark. 'No: you must forgive me.'

Any possibility of a melodrama was shattered when Bernarda stuck her head round the door. Despite being quite drunk, she realized that I was naked, dripping, and holding Clara's hand against my lips with the light out.

'For the love of Christ, Master Daniel, have you no shame? Jesus. Mary, and Joseph. Some people never learn . . .'

In her embarrassment Bernarda beat a hasty retreat, and I hoped that once the effects of the brandy wore off, the memory of what she had seen would also fade from her mind, like the traces of a dream. Clara moved away a few steps and handed me the clothes she held under her left arm.

'My uncle gave me this suit for you to put on. It's from his younger days. He says you've grown a lot and it will fit you. I'll leave you, so you can get dressed. I shouldn't have come in without knocking.'

I took the change of clothes she was offering me and started to put on the underwear, which was clean-smelling and warm, then the pale pink cotton shirt, the socks, the waistcoat, the trousers, and jacket. The mirror showed me a door-to-door salesman whose smile had abandoned him.

When I returned to the kitchen, Dr Soldevila had come out of the bedroom to give us all a bulletin on Fermín's condition.

'For the moment the worst is over,' he announced. 'There's no need to worry. These things always look more serious than they are. Your friend has a broken left arm and two broken ribs, he's lost three teeth, and has a large number of bruises, cuts, and contusions. But luckily there's no internal bleeding and no symptoms of any brain damage. The folded newspapers the patient wore under his clothes to keep him warm and accentuate his figure, as he puts it, served as armour and cushioned the blows. A few moments ago, when he recovered consciousness, the patient asked me to tell you that he's feeling like a twenty-year-old, that he wants blood sausage sandwiches with fresh garlic, a chocolate bar, and some lemon Sugus sweets. I see no problem with that, though I think it would be better to start off with fruit juice, yoghurt, and perhaps a bit of boiled rice. Moreover, as proof of his vigour and presence of mind, he has asked me to transmit to you the fact that, when Nurse Amparito was putting a few stitches in his leg, he had an iceberg of an erection.'

'It's just that he's all man,' Bernarda murmured apologetically.

'When will we be able to see him?' I asked.

'Not just yet. Perhaps by daybreak. It will do him good to rest a bit. Tomorrow, at the latest, I'd like him to be taken to the Hospital del Mar so that he can have a brain scan, just for peace of mind. But I think we can rest assured that Señor Romero de Torres will be as good as new within a few days. Judging from the marks and scars on his body, this man has got out of tighter spots. He's a true survivor. If you need a copy of the report to take along to the police—'

'It won't be necessary,' I interrupted.

'Young man, let me warn you that this could have been very serious. You must report it to the police immediately.'

Barceló was watching me attentively. I looked back at him, and he nodded.

'There'll be plenty of time for that, Doctor, don't worry,' said Barceló. 'What's important now is to make sure the patient is well. I will report this incident myself, tomorrow morning, first thing. Even the authorities have a right to a little peace and quiet at night.'

It was obvious that the doctor took a dim view of my suggestion to keep the incident from the police, but when he realized that Barceló was taking responsibility for the matter, he shrugged his shoulders and returned to the bedroom to continue with his treatment. As soon as the doctor had disappeared, Barceló told me to follow him to his study. Bernarda sighed on her stool, numb with shock and brandy.

'Bernarda, keep yourself busy. Make some coffee. Nice and strong.'

'Yes, sir. Right away.'

I followed Barceló to his study, a cave blanketed in clouds of tobacco smoke that curled around columns of books and papers. The discordant echoes of Clara's piano-playing reached us in fits and starts. It was obvious that Maestro Neri's lessons hadn't done much good, at least not in the field of music. The bookseller pointed me to a chair and proceeded to fill his pipe.

'I've phoned your father and told him that Fermín had a minor accident and that you'd brought him here.'

'Did he believe you?'

'I don't think so.'

'Right.'

The bookseller lit his pipe and sat back in the armchair behind his desk. At the other end of the apartment, Clara was tormenting Debussy. Barceló rolled his eyes.

'What happened to the music teacher?' I asked.

'He was fired. Seems like there were not enough keys on the piano to keep his fingers busy.'

'Right.'

'Are you sure you haven't had a beating, too? You're talking in monosyllables. When you were a young boy, you were much more talkative.'

The study door opened, and Bernarda came in carrying a tray with two steaming cups of coffee and a sugar bowl. She was swaying from side to side as she walked, and I was afraid I might be caught under a shower of boiling-hot coffee.

'May I come in? Will you take yours with a dash of brandy, sir?'

'I think the bottle of Lepanto has earned itself a break for tonight, Bernarda. And you, too. Come on, off you go to sleep. Daniel and I will stay up in case anything is needed. Since Fermín is in your bedroom, you can use mine.'

'Oh, no, sir, I wouldn't hear of it.'

'It's an order. And no arguing. I want you to be asleep in the next five minutes.'

'But, sir . . .'

'Bernarda, you're risking your Christmas bonus.'

'Whatever you say, Señor Barceló. But I'll sleep on top of the cover. That goes without saying.'

Barceló waited ceremoniously for Bernarda to retire. He helped himself to seven lumps of sugar and began to stir the coffee with the spoon, his catlike smile discernible behind dark clouds of Dutch tobacco.

'As you see, I run my house with a firm hand.'

'Yes, you're certainly a tough one, Don Gustavo.'

'And you're a smooth talker. Tell me, Daniel, now that nobody can hear us. Why isn't it a good idea to report what has happened to the police?'

'Because they already know.'

'You mean . . . ?'

I nodded.

'What kind of trouble are you two in, if you don't mind my asking?'

I sighed.

'Anything I can help with?'

I looked up. Barceló smiled at me without malice, for once putting his irony aside.

'Does this, by any chance, have anything to do with that book by Carax you didn't want to sell me when you should have?'

The question caught me totally by surprise.

'I could help you,' he offered. 'I have a surplus of what you both lack: money and common sense.'

'Believe me, Don Gustavo, I've already got too many people involved in this business.'

'One more won't make much difference, then. Come on, confide in me. Imagine that I'm your confessor.'

'I haven't been to confession for years.'

'It shows on your face.'


# 33

Gustavo Barceló had a way of listening that seemed both contemplative and Solomonic, like a doctor or a pope. He observed me with his hands joined under his chin and his elbows on his desk, as if in prayer. His eyes were wide open, and he nodded here and there, as if he could detect symptoms in the flow of my narrative and was composing his own diagnosis. Every time I paused, the bookseller raised his eyebrows inquisitively and beckoned with his right hand for me to continue unravelling my jumbled story, which seemed to amuse him enormously. Every now and then, he would raise a hand and take notes, or would stare into space as if he wanted to consider the implications of what I was telling him. More often than not, he would lick his lips and smile ironically, a gesture I attributed either to my ingenuity or to the foolishness of my conjectures.

'Listen, if you think this is nonsense, I'll shut up.'

'On the contrary. Fools talk, cowards are silent, wise men listen.'

'Who said that? Seneca?'

'No. Braulio Recolons – he runs a pork butcher's on Calle Avignon and has a great talent for both making sausages and composing witty aphorisms. Please continue. You were telling me about this lively girl . . .'

'Bea. And that is my business and has nothing to do with anything else.'

Barceló tried to keep his laughter to himself. I was about to continue the story of my adventures when Dr Soldevila poked his head round the door of the study, looking tired and out of breath.

'Please excuse me. I'm leaving now. The patient is well, and, for lack of a better expression, he's full of beans. That gentleman will outlive us all. He's even saying that the sedatives have gone to his head and given him a high. He refuses to rest and insists that he must have a word with Daniel about matters he did not wish to explain to me, claiming that he doesn't believe in the Hippocratic, or hypocritical, oath as he calls it.'

'We'll go and see him right away. And please forgive poor Fermín. He's obviously still in shock.'

'Perhaps, but I wouldn't rule out shamelessness. He keeps pinching the nurse's bottom and reciting rhyming couplets in praise of her firm and shapely thighs.'

We escorted the doctor and his nurse to the door and thanked them effusively for their good offices. When we went into the bedroom, we discovered that Bernarda had challenged Barceló's orders after all, and was lying on the bed next to Fermín. The fright, the brandy, and the exhaustion had finally sent her to sleep. Covered in bandages, dressings, and slings, Fermín held her tenderly, stroking her hair. His face carried a bruise that it hurt to look at, and from it emerged his large, unharmed nose, two ears like sails, and the eyes of a dispirited mouse. His toothless smile, through lips covered in cuts, was triumphant, and he greeted us with his right hand raised in the sign of victory.

'How are you feeling, Fermín?' I asked.

'Twenty years younger,' he said in a low voice, so as not to wake Bernarda.

'Stop pretending, damn it. You look like shit, Fermín. You scared me to death. Are you sure you're all right? Isn't your head spinning? Aren't you hearing voices?'

'Now you mention it, sometimes I thought I could hear a discordant and arrhythmic murmur, as if a macaque was trying to play the piano.'

Barceló frowned. Clara went on tinkling on the piano in the distance.

'Don't worry, Daniel. I've survived worse sticks and stones. That Fumero can't even kick a bad habit.'

'So the person who sculpted you a new face is none other than Inspector Fumero,' said Barceló. 'I see you two move in the highest circles.'

'I hadn't got to that part of the story,' I said.

Fermín looked at me in alarm.

'It's all right, Fermín. Daniel is filling me in about this little play that you two are taking part in. I must admit, it's all very interesting. What about you, Fermín, how are you on confessions? I warn you, I spent two years in a seminary.'

'I would have said at least three, Don Gustavo.'

'Some things get lost along the way. Shame, for a start. This is the first time you've visited my house, and already you end up in bed with the maid.'

'Look at her, poor little thing, my angel. You must understand that my intentions are honest, Don Gustavo.'

'Your intentions are your own business, and Barnarda's. She's quite old enough. Now, let's be frank. What kind of charade are you two involved in?'

'What have you told him, Daniel?'

'We got to act two: enter the femme fatale,' Barceló explained.

'Nuria Monfort?' Fermín asked.

Barceló smacked his lips with delight. 'But is there more than one? This sounds like *The Abduction from the Seraglio*.'

'Please lower your voice. My fiancée is present.'

'Don't worry, your fiancée has half a bottle of brandy in her veins. The trumpets of doom wouldn't wake her. Go on, ask Daniel to tell me the rest. Three heads are better than two, especially if the third one is mine.'

Fermín attempted to shrug his shoulders under dressings and slings. 'I'm not against it, Daniel. It's your call.'

Having resigned myself to taking Don Gustavo on board, I continued with my narrative until I reached the point when Fumero and his men came upon us on Calle Moncada a few hours earlier. When the story reached an end, Barceló got up and began pacing up and down the room. Fermín and I observed him cautiously while Bernarda snored like a baby calf.

'Little angel,' whispered Fermín, entranced.

'A few things have caught my attention,' the bookseller said at last. 'Evidently Inspector Fumero is in this up to his neck, although how and why is something that escapes me. On the one hand, there's this woman—'

'Nuria Monfort.'

'Then there's the business of Julián Carax's return to Barcelona and his murder in the streets of the city – after a month in which nobody knows anything about him. It's obvious that the woman is lying through her teeth.'

'That's what I've been saying from the start,' said Fermín, casting a glance at me. 'Trouble is, some of us suffer from an excess of juvenile ardour and a poor grasp of the situation.'

'Look who's talking: St John of the Cross.'

'That's enough. Let's calm down and stick to the facts. There's one thing in Daniel's narrative that seemed very strange to me, even stranger than the rest of it. It has nothing to do with the gothic spin of this whole saga, but with an essential and apparently banal detail,' Barceló said.

'Dazzle us, Don Gustavo.'

'Well, here it is: this business about Carax's father refusing to identify Carax's body, claiming that he didn't have a son. That seems very odd to me. Almost unnatural. No father in the world would do that. Never mind the bad blood there might have been between them. Death does that: it makes everyone feel sentimental. When we stand in front of a coffin, we see only what is good, or what we want to see.'

'What a great quote, Don Gustavo,' Fermín said. 'Do you mind if I add it to my repertoire?'

'But there are always exceptions,' I objected. 'From what we know, Señor Fortuny was rather peculiar.'

'Everything we know about him is third-hand gossip,' said Barceló. 'When everyone is determined to present someone as a monster, there are two possibilities: either he's a saint or they're not telling the whole story.'

'The trouble is, you've taken a shining to the hatter just because he's a dimwit,' said Fermín.

'With all due respect to the profession, when the description of a rogue is based solely on the caretaker's statement, my first instinct is not to trust it.'

'But that means we can't be sure of anything. Everything we know is, as you say, third-, or even fourth-hand. Caretakers or otherwise.'

'Never trust he who trusts everyone,' Barceló added.

'What an evening you're having, Don Gustavo,' Fermín applauded. 'Pearls of wisdom offered in abundance. Would that I had your crystalline insight—'

'The only crystalline thing in all this is that you need my help – logistical and probably monetary as well – if you're hoping to bring this pantomime to a conclusion before Inspector Fumero reserves a suite for you in San Sebas Prison. Fermín, I assume you're with me?'

'I'll follow Daniel's orders.'

'Daniel, what do you say?'

'You two are doing all the talking. What do you propose, Don Gustavo?'

'This is my plan: as soon as Fermín has recovered, you, Daniel, pay a casual visit to Nuria Monfort and put your cards on the table. You let her see that you know she's lied to you and that she's hiding something, a lot or a little – that remains to be seen.'

'What for?'

'To see how she reacts. She won't say anything to you, of course. Or she'll lie to you again. The important thing is to thrust the *banderilla* into her – forgive the bullfighting image – to see where the bull will lead us or, should I say, the young heifer. And that's where you come in, Fermín. While Daniel is in action, you position yourself discreetly where you can keep watch on the suspect and wait for her to take the bait. Once she's done that, you follow her.'

'You're assuming she'll go somewhere,' I protested.

'O ye of little faith! She will. Sooner or later. And something tells me that in this case it will be sooner rather than later. It's the basis of female psychology.'

'And in the meantime, what are you planning to do, Dr Freud?' I asked.

'That's my business. You'll know in good time. And you'll thank me for it.'

I looked for reassurance in Fermín's eyes, but the poor man had slowly been falling asleep, hugging Bernarda, while Barceló was drawing up his triumphant plan. Fermín's head was tilted to one side, and dribble was leaking onto his chest from the edge of a beatific smile. Bernarda was snoring loudly.

'I do hope this one proves good,' Barceló murmured.

'Fermín is a great person,' I said.

'He must be, because I don't think he can have won her over with his looks. Come on, let's go.'

We turned out the light and left the room quietly, closing the door and leaving the two lovers in the hands of sleep. I thought I could see the first glimmer of daybreak through the gallery windows at the end of the corridor.

'Suppose I say no,' I said in a low voice. 'Suppose I tell you to forget this.'

Barceló smiled. 'Too late, Daniel. You should have sold me that book years ago, when you had the chance.'

Day was dawning when I reached home, dragging myself in that absurd loaned suit through damp streets that shone with a scarlet hue. I found my father asleep in his dining-room armchair, with a blanket over his legs and his favourite book open in his lap – a copy of Voltaire's *Candide*, which he reread a couple of times a year, the only times I heard him laugh heartily. I observed him: his hair was grey, thinning, and the skin on his face had begun to sag around his cheekbones. I looked at that man whom I had once imagined almost invincible; he now seemed fragile, defeated without knowing it. Perhaps we were both defeated. I leaned over to cover him with the blanket he had been promising to give away to charity for years, and I kissed his forehead, as if by doing so I could protect him from the invisible threads that kept him away from me, from that tiny apartment, and from my memories. As if I believed that with that kiss I could deceive time and convince it to pass us by, to return some other day, some other life.

# 34

I spent nearly all morning daydreaming in the back room, conjuring up images of Bea. I visualized her naked skin under my hands, and it seemed to me that I could almost taste her sweet breath. I caught myself remembering with maplike precision every contour of her body, the glistening of my saliva on her lips and on that line of fair hair, so fair it was almost transparent, that ran down her belly and that my friend Fermín, in his improvised lectures on carnal logistics, liked to call 'the little road to Jerez'.

I looked at my watch for the umpteenth time and realized to my horror that there were still a few hours to go before I could see, and touch, Bea. I tried to sort out the month's invoices, but the rustle of the sheets of paper reminded me of the sound of underwear slipping down the pale hips and thighs of Doña Beatriz Aguilar, sister of my childhood friend.

'Daniel, you've got your head in the clouds. Is anything worrying you? Is it Fermín?' my father asked.

I nodded, ashamed of myself. My best friend had lost a few ribs to save my skin a few hours earlier, and all I could think of was the fastening of a bra.

'Speak of the devil ...'

I raised my eyes, and there he was. Fermín Romero de Torres, the one and only, wearing his best suit, and with that ragged posture like a cheap cigar. He came in through the shop door with a victorious smile and a fresh carnation in his lapel.

'But what are you doing here? Weren't you supposed to be resting?'

'Rest takes care of itself. I'm a man of action. And if I'm not here, you two won't even sell a catechism.'

Ignoring the doctor's advice, Fermín had come along, determined to take up his post again. His face was yellow and covered in bruises; he limped badly and moved like a broken puppet.

'You're going straight to bed, Fermín, for God's sake,' said my father, horrified.

'Wouldn't hear of it. Statistics prove that more people die in bed than in the trenches.'

All our protests went unheeded. After a while my father gave in, because something in poor Fermín's eyes suggested that even though his bones hurt him terribly, the prospect of being alone in his *pensión* room was even more painful.

'All right, but if I see you lifting anything besides a pencil, I'll give you an earful.'

'Yes, sir! You have my word of honour that I won't even lift a finger.'

Fermín proceeded to put on his blue overalls and arm himself with a rag and a bottle of alcohol. He set himself up behind the counter, planning to clean the covers and spines of the fifteen secondhand books that had arrived that morning. They were all copies of a much-sought-after title, *The Three-Cornered Hat: A History of the Civil Guard in Alexandrine Verse*, by the exceedingly young graduate Fulgencio Capón, acclaimed as a prodigy by critics all over the country. While he devoted himself to his task, Fermín kept throwing me surreptitious looks, winking like a scheming devil.

'Your ears are as red as peppers, Daniel.'

'It must be from hearing you talk so much nonsense.'

'Or from the fever that's gripped you. When are you seeing the young maid?'

'None of your business.'

'You look really bad. Are you avoiding spicy food? Hot spices are fatal; they dilate your blood vessels.'

'Piss off.'

It was going to be a long, miserable day.

The afternoon was closing in when the subway train left me at the foot of Avenida del Tibidabo. I could distinguish the shape of the blue tram, moving away through folds of violet mist. I decided not to wait for its return but to make my way on foot. Soon I discerned the outline of The Angel of Mist. I pulled out the key Bea had given me and opened the small door within the gate. I stepped into the property, leaving the door almost closed, so that it looked shut but could be opened by Bea. I had deliberately arrived early. I knew that Bea would take at least half an hour or forty-five minutes more. I wanted to feel the presence of the house on my own and explore it before Bea arrived and made it hers. I stopped for a moment to look at the fountain and the hand of the angel rising from the waters that were tinted scarlet. The accusing index finger seemed sharp as a dagger. I went up to the edge of the bowl. The sculpted face, with no eyes and no soul, quivered beneath the water.

I walked up the wide staircase that led to the entrance. The main door was slightly ajar. I felt a pang of anxiety, because I thought I'd closed it when I left the place the other night. I examined the lock, which didn't seem to have been tampered with, and came to the conclusion that I must have forgotten to close it. I pushed it gently inwards, and I felt the breath from inside the house brushing my face, a scent of burned wood, damp, and dead flowers. I pulled out a box of matches I'd picked up before leaving the bookshop and knelt down to light the first of the candles Bea had left behind. A copper-coloured bubble lit up in my hands and revealed the dancing shapes of the walls that wept tears of dampness, the fallen ceilings and dilapidated doors.

I proceeded to the second candle and lit it. Slowly, almost ritualistically, I followed the trail of the candles and lit them one by one, conjuring up a halo of amber light that seemed to float in the air like a cobweb trapped in the midst of darkness. My journey ended by the sitting-room fireplace, by the blankets that were still lying on the floor, stained with ash. I sat there, facing the rest of the room. I had expected silence, but the house exhaled a thousand sounds. The creaking of wood, the brush of the wind over the roof tiles, a thousand and one tapping sounds inside the walls, under the floor, moving from place to place.

After about thirty minutes, I noticed that the cold and the dark were beginning to make me feel drowsy. I stood up and began to walk up and down the room to warm up. There was only the charred husk of a log in the hearth. By the time Bea arrived, the temperature inside the old mansion would have vanquished the feverish ideas that had been plaguing me for days and filled me with nothing but pure and chaste thoughts. Having found an aim more practical than the contemplation of the ruins of time, I picked up one of the candles and set off to explore the house in search of something to burn.

My notions of Victorian literature suggested that the most logical place to begin searching was the cellar, which must have once housed the ovens and a great coal bunker. With this idea in mind, I spent almost five minutes trying to find a door or staircase leading to the lower floor. I chose a large door made of carved wood at the end of a passage. It looked like a piece of exquisite cabinetmaking, with reliefs in the shape of angels and a large cross in the centre. The handle was in the middle of the door, under the cross. I tried unsuccessfully to turn it. The mechanism was probably jammed or simply ruined by rust. The only way that door would yield would be by forcing it open with a crowbar or knocking it down with an axe, alternatives I quickly ruled out. I studied the large piece of wood by candlelight and thought that somehow it looked more like a sarcophagus than a door. I wondered what was hidden behind it.

A closer examination of the carved angels discouraged me from looking any further, and I left the place. I was about to give up my search for a way down to the cellar when, by chance, I came across a tiny door at the other end of the passage, which at first I took to be the door of a broom cupboard. I tested the doorknob, and it gave way instantly. On the other side, a steep staircase plunged into a pool of blackness. A powerful smell of damp earth hit me. It seemed a strangely familiar smell, and as I stood there with my eyes on the black well in front of me, I was seized by a memory from my childhood, buried beneath years of fear.

*A rainy afternoon on the eastern slope of Montjuïc, looking at the sea through a forest of incomprehensible mausoleums, a forest of crosses and gravestones carved with skulls and faces of children with no lips or eyes, a place that stank of death; and the silhouettes of about twenty adults that I could only remember as black suits dripping with rain, and my father's hand holding mine too tightly, as if by doing so he could stop his weeping, while a priest's empty words fell into that marble tomb into which three faceless gravediggers pushed a grey coffin. The downpour slithered like melted wax over the coffin, and I thought I heard my mother's voice calling me from within, begging me to free her from that prison of stone and darkness, but all I could do was tremble and ask my father in a voiceless whisper not to hold my hand so tight, tell him he was hurting me, and that smell of fresh earth, earth and ash and rain, was devouring everything, a smell of emptiness and death.*

I opened my eyes and went down the steps almost blindly, because the light from the candle dispelled only an inch or two of darkness. When I reached the bottom, I held the candle up high and looked about me. I found no kitchen, no cupboard full of dry wood. A narrow passage extended before me, ending in a semicircular chamber. In the chamber stood a figure, its face lined with tears of blood from two hollow eyes, its arms unfolded like wings and a serpent of thorns sprouting from its temples. I felt an icy cold stabbing me in the nape of the neck. At some point I regained my composure and realized I was staring at an effigy of Christ carved in wood on the wall of a chapel. I stepped forward a few yards and beheld a ghostly sight. A dozen naked female torsos were piled up in one corner of the old chapel. Their heads and arms were missing, and they were supported by a tripod. Each one was shaped differently, replicating the figures of women of varying ages and constitutions. On their bellies were words written in charcoal: 'Isabel, Eugenia, Penélope.' For once, my Victorian reading came to the rescue, and I realized that what I was beholding was none other than the remains of an old custom no longer in use, the echo of an era when the homes of the wealthy had mannequins made to measure for different members of the family, used for tailoring their dresses and trousseaux. Despite Christ's threatening, grim look, I could not resist the temptation of stretching out my hand and touching the torso with Penélope Aldaya's name written on it.

At that moment I thought I heard footsteps on the floor above. I imagined that Bea had arrived and was wandering through the old mansion, looking for me. Relieved, I left the chapel and made my way back to the staircase. I was about to go up when I noticed that at the other end of the corridor there was a boiler and a central heating system that seemed to be in good order. It seemed incongruent with the rest of the cellar. I remembered Bea mentioning that the estate agency, which for years had tried to sell the Aldaya mansion, had carried out some renovation work, hoping to attract potential buyers. I went up to examine the contraption more closely and saw that it consisted of a radiator system fed by a small boiler. At my feet I found a few pails full of charcoal, bits of plywood, and a few tins that I presumed must contain kerosene. I opened the boiler latch and had a look inside. Everything seemed to be in order. The idea of being able to get that old machine to work after so many years struck me as a bit far-fetched, but that didn't stop me filling the boiler with bits of charcoal and wood and spraying them with a good shower of kerosene. While I was doing this, I thought I heard the creaking of old wood, and for a moment I turned my head to look behind me. Suddenly I had a vision of bloodstained thorns being pulled out of the wood, and as I faced the darkness, I was afraid of seeing the figure of Christ emerge only a few steps away, coming towards me with a wolfish smile.

When I put the candle to it, the boiler lit up with a sudden blaze that provoked a metallic roar. I closed the latch and moved back a few steps, increasingly unsure about the soundness of my plan. The boiler appeared to be drawing with some difficulty, so I decided to return to the ground floor and check whether my efforts were yielding any practical results. I went up the stairs and returned to the large room, hoping to find Bea there, but there was no trace of her. I calculated that an hour must have passed since my arrival, and my fear that the object of my desire might never turn up grew more acute. To kill that anxiety, I decided to continue with my plumbing exploits and set off in search of radiators which might confirm whether the resurrection of the boiler had been a success. All the ones I found proved resistant to my hopes; they were icy cold. But then, in a small room of no more than four or five square yards, a bathroom that I supposed must be situated immediately above the boiler, I could feel a little warmth. I knelt down and realized joyfully that the floor tiles were lukewarm. That is how Bea found me, crouching on the floor, feeling the tiles of the bathroom like an idiot, an asinine smile plastered on my face.

When I look back and try to reconstruct the events of that night in the Aldaya mansion, the only excuse that occurs to me that might justify my behaviour is to say that when you're eighteen, in the absence of subtlety and greater experience, an old bathroom can seem like paradise. It only took me a couple of minutes to persuade Bea that we should take the blankets from the sitting room and lock ourselves in that minute bathroom, with only two candles and some bathroom fittings that looked like museum pieces. My main argument – climatological – soon convinced Bea. The warmth that emanated from those floor tiles made her put aside her initial fear that my crazy invention might burn the house down. Later, in the reddish half-light of the candles, as I undressed her with trembling fingers, she smiled, her eyes searching mine.

I remember her sitting with her back against the closed door of that room, her arms hanging down by her sides, the palms of her hands opened towards me. I remember how she held her face up, defiant, while I stroked her throat with the tips of my fingers. I remember how she took my hands and placed them on her breasts, and how her eyes and lips quivered when, enraptured, I took her nipples between my fingers and squeezed them, how she slid down to the floor while I searched out her belly with my lips and how her white thighs received me.

'Had you ever done this before, Daniel?'

'In dreams.'

'Seriously.'

'No. Had you?'

'No. Not even with Clara Barceló?'

I laughed. Probably at myself. 'What do you know about Clara Barceló?'

'Nothing.'

'I know less than nothing,' I said.

'I don't believe you.'

I leaned over her and looked into her eyes. 'I have never done this before with anybody.'

Bea smiled. My hand found its way between her thighs, and I threw myself on her, searching her lips, convinced by now that cannibalism was the supreme incarnation of wisdom.

'Daniel?' said Bea in a tiny voice.

'What?' I asked.

The answer never came to her lips. Suddenly a shaft of cold air whistled under the door, and in that endless moment before the wind blew out all the candles, our eyes met and we felt that the passsion of that moment had been shattered. An instant was enough for us to know that there was somebody on the other side of the door. I saw fear sketched on Bea's face, and a second later we were covered in darkness. The bang on the door came later. Brutal, like a steel fist hammering on the wood, almost pulling it off its hinges.

I felt Bea's body jump in the dark, and I put my arms around her. We moved to the other end of the room just before the second blow hit the door, throwing it with tremendous force against the wall. Bea screamed and shrank back against me. For a moment all I could see was the blue mist that crept up from the corridor and the snakes of smoke from the candles as they were blown out, rising in a spiral. The doorframe cast fanglike shadows, and I thought I saw an angular figure on the threshold of the darkness.

I peered into the corridor, fearing, or perhaps hoping, that I would find only a stranger, a tramp who had ventured into the ruined mansion looking for shelter on an unpleasant night. But there was no one there, only ribbons of blue air that seemed to blow in through the windows. Huddled in a corner of the room, trembling, Bea whispered my name.

'There's nobody there,' I said. 'Perhaps it was a gust of wind.'

'The wind doesn't beat on doors, Daniel. Let's go.'

I went back to the room and gathered up our clothes.

'Here, get dressed. We'll go and have a look.'

'We'd better leave.'

'Yes, right away. I just want to check one thing.'

We dressed hurriedly in the dark, our breath forming clouds in the air. I picked up one of the candles from the floor and lit it again. A draught of cold air glided through the house, as if someone had opened doors and windows.

'You see? It's the wind.'

Bea shook her head but kept silent. We made our way back towards the sitting room, shielding the flame with our hands. Bea followed close behind me, holding her breath.

'What are we looking for, Daniel?'

'It'll only take a minute.'

'No, let's leave right away.'

'All right.'

We turned to walk towards the exit, and it was then that I noticed. The large sculpted door at the end of the corridor, which I had tried unsuccessfully to open, was ajar.

'What's the matter?' asked Bea.

'Wait for me here.'

'Daniel, please . . .'

I walked down the corridor, holding the candle that flickered in gusts of cold air. Bea sighed and followed me

318

reluctantly. I stopped in front of the door. Marble steps were just visible descending into the darkness. I started to go down them. Petrified, Bea stood at the entrance holding the candle.

'Please, Daniel, let's go now. . . .'

I descended, step by step, to the bottom of the staircase. The ghostly aura from the candle that was raised behind me seemed to scratch at the shape of a rectangular room, made of bare stone walls covered in crucifixes. The icy cold in that chamber took my breath away. Before me stood a marble slab, and on top of it I saw what looked like two similar white objects of different sizes, lined up one next to the other. They reflected the tremor of the candle with more intensity than the rest of the room, and I guessed they were made of lacquered wood. I took one more step forward, and only then did I understand. The two objects were white coffins. One of them was scarcely two feet long. I felt a shiver down the back of my neck. It was a child's sarcophagus. I was in a crypt.

Without realizing what I was doing, I came closer to the marble stone until I was near enough to stretch out my hand and touch it. I then noticed that on each coffin a cross and a name had been carved, but a blanket of dust obscured them. I put my hand on one of the coffins, the larger one. Slowly, almost in a trance, without stopping to think what I was doing, I brushed off the dust that covered the lid. I could barely read the words in the dim red candlelight.

✝

PENÉLOPE ALDAYA
1902–1919

I froze. Something or somebody was moving about in the dark. I could feel the cold air sliding down my skin, and only then did I retreat a few steps.

'Get out of here,' murmured a voice in the shadows.

I recognized him immediately. Laín Coubert. The voice of the devil.

I charged up the stairs, and as soon as I reached the ground floor, I grabbed Bea by the arm and dragged her as fast as I could towards the exit. We had lost the candle and were running blindly. Bea was frightened, and unable to comprehend my sudden alarm. She hadn't seen anything. She hadn't heard anything. I didn't pause to give her an explanation. I expected that at any moment something would jump out from the shadows and block our way, but the main door was waiting for us at the end of the corridor, a rectangle of light shining through the cracks in the doorframe.

'It's locked,' Bea whispered.

I felt my pockets for the key. I turned my head for a fraction of a second and was sure that two shining points were slowly advancing towards us from the other end of the passageway. Eyes. My fingers found the key. I inserted it desperately into the lock, opened the door, and pushed Bea out roughly. Bea must have sensed the fear in me, because she rushed towards the gate and didn't stop until we were both on the pavement of Avenida del Tibidabo, breathless and covered in cold sweat.

'What happened down there, Daniel? Was there someone there?'

'No.'

'You look pale.'

'I've always been pale. Come on. Let's go.'

'What about the key?'

I had left it inside, stuck in the lock. I felt no desire to go back and look for it.

'I think I dropped it on the way out. We'll look for it some other day.'

We walked briskly away down the avenue, crossed over to the other side, and did not slow down until we were a good hundred yards from the mansion. It was then I noticed that my hand was still stained with ashes. I was thankful for the mantle of the night, for it concealed the tears of terror running down my cheeks.

We descended Calle Balmes to Plaza Núñez de Arce, where we found a solitary taxi. As we drove down Balmes to Consejo de Ciento, we hardly spoke a word. Bea held my hand, and a couple of times I caught her gazing at me with glassy, impenetrable eyes. I leaned over to kiss her, but she didn't open her lips.

'When will I see you again?'

'I'll call you tomorrow, or the next day,' she said.

'Do you promise?'

She nodded.

'You can call me at home or at the bookshop. It's the same number. You have it, don't you?'

She nodded again. I asked the driver to stop for a moment on the corner of Muntaner and Diputación. I offered to see Bea to her front door, but she refused and walked away without letting me kiss her again, or even brush her hand. She started to run as I looked on from the taxi. The lights were on in the Aguilars' apartment, and I could clearly see my friend Tomás watching me from his bedroom window, where we had spent so many afternoons together chatting or playing chess. I waved at him, forcing a smile that he probably could not see. He didn't return the greeting. He remained static, glued to the windowpane, gazing at me coldly. A few seconds later, he moved away and the window went dark. He was waiting for us, I thought.

# 35

When I got home, I found the remains of a dinner for two on the table. My father had already gone to bed, and I wondered whether, by chance, he had plucked up the courage to invite Merceditas around for dinner. I tiptoed off towards my room and went in without turning on the light. The moment I sat on the edge of the mattress, I realized there was someone else in the room, lying on the bed in the dark like a dead body with his hands crossed over his chest. I felt an icy spasm in my stomach, but soon I recognized the snoring, and the profile of that incomparable nose. I turned on the light on the bedside table and found Fermín Romero de Torres lying on the bedspread, lost in a blissful dream and moaning gently with pleasure. I sighed, and the sleeper opened his eyes. When he saw me, he looked surprised. He was obviously expecting some other company. He rubbed his eyes and looked about him, taking in his surroundings more closely.

'I hope I didn't scare you. Bernarda says that when I'm asleep, I look like a Spanish Boris Karloff.'

'What are you doing on my bed, Fermín?'

He half closed his eyes with longing.

'Dreaming of Carole Lombard. We were in Tangiers, in some Turkish baths, and I was covering her in oil, the sort they sell for babies' bottoms. Have you ever covered a woman with oil, from head to toe?'

'Fermín, it's half past midnight, and I'm dead on my feet.'

'Please forgive me, Daniel. It's just that your father insisted I come up and have dinner with him, and afterwards I felt terribly drowsy. Beef has a narcotic effect on me, you see. Your father suggested that I lie down here for a while. He said that you wouldn't mind. . . .'

'And I don't mind, Fermín. It's just that you've caught me by surprise. Keep the bed and go back to Carole Lombard; she must be waiting for you. And get under the sheets. It's a foul night, and if you stay on top you'll catch something. I'll go to the dining room.'

Fermín nodded meekly. The bruises on his face were beginning to swell up, and his head, covered with two days of stubble and that sparse hair, looked like some ripe fruit fallen from a tree. I took a blanket from the chest of drawers and handed another one to Fermín. Then I turned off the light and went back to the dining room, where my father's favourite armchair awaited me. I wrapped myself in the blanket and curled up, as best I could, convinced that I wouldn't sleep a wink. The image of the two white coffins was branded on my mind. I closed my eyes and did my best to delete the sight. In its place I conjured up the image of Bea in the candlelit bathroom, lying naked on the blankets. Abandoning myself to these thoughts, it seemed to me that I could hear the distant murmur of the sea, and I wondered whether, without my knowing it, I had already succumbed to sleep. Perhaps I was sailing towards Tangiers. But soon I realized that the sound was only Fermín's snoring. A moment later the world was turned off. In all my life, I've never slept so well or so deeply as I did that night.

Morning came, and it was pouring. Streets were flooded, and the rain beat angrily against the windows. The telephone rang at seven-thirty. I jumped out of the armchair to answer, my heart in my mouth. Fermín, in a bathrobe and slippers, and my father, holding the coffeepot, exchanged that look I was already growing used to.

'Bea?' I whispered into the receiver, with my back to them.

I thought I heard a sigh on the line.

'Bea, is that you?'

There was no answer, and a few seconds later the line went dead. I stayed there for a minute, staring at the telephone, hoping it would ring again.

'They'll call back, Daniel. Come and have some breakfast now,' said my father.

She'll call again later, I told myself. Someone must have caught her phoning. It couldn't be easy to break Señor Aguilar's curfew. There was no reason to be alarmed. With this and other excuses, I dragged myself to the table to have breakfast with Fermín and my father. It might have been the rain, but the food had lost all its flavour.

It rained all morning. Shortly after we opened the bookshop, there was a general power cut in the whole neighbourhood that lasted until noon.

'That's all we needed,' sighed my father.

At three the first leaks began to appear. Fermín offered to go up to Merceditas's apartment to borrow some buckets, dishes, or any other hollow receptacle. My father strictly forbade him to go. The deluge persisted. To alleviate my nerves, I told Fermín what had happened the day before, though I kept to myself what I'd seen in the crypt. Fermín listened with fascination, but despite his insistence, I refused to describe to him the consistency, texture, and shape of Bea's breasts. The day wore slowly on.

After dinner, on the pretext of going out to stretch my legs, I left my father reading and walked up to Bea's house. When I got there, I stopped on the corner to look up at the large windows of the apartment. I asked myself what I was doing. Spying, meddling, or making a fool of myself were some of the answers that went through my mind. Even so, as lacking in dignity as I was in appropriate clothes for such icy weather, I took shelter from the wind in a doorway on the other side of the street for about half an hour, watching the windows and seeing the silhouettes of Señor Aguilar and his wife as they passed by. But not a trace of Bea.

It was almost midnight when I got back home, shivering with cold and carrying the world on my shoulders. She'll call tomorrow, I told myself a thousand times while I tried to fall asleep. Bea didn't call the next day. Or the next. She didn't call that whole week, the longest and the last of my life.

In seven days' time, I would be dead.

# 36

Only someone who has barely a week left to live could waste his time the way I wasted mine during those days. All I did was watch over the telephone and gnaw at my soul, so much a prisoner of my own blindness that I wasn't even capable of guessing what destiny had in store for me. On Monday at noon, I went over to the literature department in Plaza Universidad, hoping to see Bea. I knew she wouldn't be amused if I turned up there and we were seen together, but facing her anger was preferable to continuing with that uncertainty.

I asked in the office for Professor Velázquez's lecture room and decided to wait for the students to come out. I waited for about twenty minutes, until the doors were opened and I saw the arrogant, well-groomed countenance of Professor Velázquez, as usual surrounded by his small group of female admirers. Five minutes later there was still no sign of Bea. I decided to walk up to the door of the lecture room and take a look. A trio of girls were huddled together like a Sunday-school group, chatting and exchanging either lecture notes or secrets. The one who seemed to be the leader of the congregation noticed my presence and interrupted her monologue to fire me an inquisitive look.

'I'm sorry. I'm looking for Beatriz Aguilar. Do you know whether she comes to this class?'

The girls traded venomous glances.

'Are you her fiancé?' one of them asked. 'The officer?'

I smiled blankly, and they took this to mean yes. Only the third girl smiled back at me, shyly, averting her eyes. The other two were more forward, almost defiant.

'I imagined you different,' said the one who seemed to be the head commando.

'Where's the uniform?' asked the second in command, observing me with suspicion.

'I'm on leave. Do you know whether she's already left?'

'Beatriz didn't come to class today,' the chief informed me.

'Oh, didn't she?'

'No,' confirmed the suspicious lieutenant. 'If you're her fiancé, you should know that.'

'I'm her fiancé, not a Civil Guard.'

'Come on, let's go, the boy's an idiot,' the chief said.

They both walked past me, eyeing me sideways with disdain. The third one lagged behind. She stopped for a moment before leaving and, making quite sure the others didn't see her, whispered in my ear, 'Beatriz didn't come on Friday either.'

'Do you know why?'

'You're not her fiancé, are you?'

'No. Only a friend.'

'I think she's ill.'

'Ill?'

'That's what one of the girls who phoned her said. I must go.'

Before I was able to thank her for her help, the girl went off to join the other two, who were waiting for her with withering looks at the far end of the cloister.


'Daniel, something must have happened. A great-aunt has died, or a parrot has got the mumps or she's caught a cold from so much going around without enough clothes to cover her backside – goodness knows what. Contrary to what you believe, the earth does not revolve around the desires of your crotch.'

'You think I'm not aware of that? You don't seem to know me, Fermín.'

'My dear, if God had wished to give me wider hips, I might even have given birth to you: that's how well I know you. Pay attention to me. Throw off these morbid thoughts and get some fresh air. Waiting is the rust of the soul.'

'So I seem absurd to you.'

'No. You seem fretful. I know that at your age these things look like the end of the world, but everything has a limit. Tonight you and I are going on a binge to a club on Calle Platería – apparently it's all the rage. I hear there are some new Scandinavian girls straight from Ciudad Real who are real knockouts. It's on me.'

'And what will Bernarda say?'

'The girls are for you. I'll be waiting in the hall, reading a magazine and looking at the nice merchandise from afar, because I'm a convert to monogamy, if not *in mentis*, at least de facto.'

'I'm very grateful, Fermín, but—'

'A young boy of eighteen who refuses such an offer is not in his right mind. Something must be done immediately. Here.'

He searched in his pockets and handed me some coins. I wondered whether these were the doubloons with which he was going to finance the visit to the sumptuous seraglio of Iberian nymphs.

'We won't get far with this, Fermín.'

'You're one of those people who fall off a tree and never quite reach the ground. Do you really think that I'm going to take you to a whorehouse and bring you back, covered with gonorrhoea, to your dear father, who is the saintliest man I have ever met? I told you about the girls to see whether you'd react, appealing to the only part of your person that seems to be in working order. The coins are for you to go to the telephone on the corner and call your beloved with a bit of privacy.'

'Bea told me quite clearly not to phone her.'

'She also told you she'd call you on Friday. It's already Monday. It's up to you. It is one thing to believe in women, and another to believe what they say.'

Convinced by his arguments, I slipped out of the bookshop, walked over to the public telephone on the street corner, and dialled the Aguilars' number. At the fifth ring,

327

someone lifted the telephone on the other end and listened in silence, without answering. Five eternal seconds went by.

'Bea?' I murmured. 'Is that you?'

The voice that answered struck my stomach like a hammer.

'You son of a bitch, I swear I'm going to beat your brains out.'

It was the steely tone of pure, contained anger. Icy and serene. That is what scared me most. I could picture Señor Aguilar holding the telephone in the entrance hall of his apartment, the same one I had often used to call my father and tell him I would be late because I'd spent the afternoon with Tomás. I stayed where I was, listening to Bea's father breathing, dumb, wondering whether he'd recognized my voice.

'I see you don't even have the balls to talk, you bastard. Any little shit is capable of doing what you've done, but at least a man would have the guts to show his face. I would die of shame if I thought that a seventeen-year-old girl had more balls than me – because she hasn't told me your name and she's not going to. I know her. And since you don't have the courage to show your face for Beatriz's sake, she's going to have to pay for what you've done.'

When I hung up, my hands were shaking. I wasn't conscious of what I'd done until I left the telephone box and dragged myself back to the bookshop. I hadn't stopped to consider that my call would only make things worse for Bea. My only concern had been to remain anonymous and hide my face, disowning the person I professed to love and whom I had only used. I had done this before when Inspector Fumero had beaten up Fermín. I had done it again when I'd abandoned Bea to her fate. I would do it again as soon as circumstances provided me with another opportunity. I stayed out in the street for ten minutes, trying to calm down before returning to the bookshop. Perhaps I should call again and tell Señor Aguilar that yes, it was me. That I was crazy about his daughter, end of story. If he then felt like coming by in his general's uniform and beating me up, he had every right to do so.

I was on my way back when I noticed that somebody was watching me from a doorway on the other side of the street. At first I thought it was Don Federico, the watchmaker, but a quick glance was enough to make me realize this was a taller, more solid-looking individual. I stopped to return his gaze, and, to my surprise, he nodded, as if he wished to greet me and prove that he didn't mind at all that I'd noticed his presence. The light from one of the streetlamps fell on his face. His features seemed familiar. He took a step forward, buttoning his raincoat to his neck, then smiled at me and walked away towards the Ramblas, mingling with other passersby. It was only then I recognized him: the police officer who had held me down while Inspector Fumero attacked Fermín.

When I entered the bookshop, Fermín looked at me inquisitively.

'What's that face for?'

'Fermín, I think we have a problem.'

That same evening we put into action the plan we had conceived with Don Gustavo Barceló.

'The first thing is to make sure that you are right about us being under police surveillance. We'll walk over to Els Quatre Gats, casually, to see whether that man is still out there, lying in wait. But not a word of this to your father, or he'll end up with a kidney stone.'

'And what do I tell him? He's suspicious enough as it is.'

'Tell him you're going out to buy sunflower seeds or something.'

'And why do we need to go to Els Quatre Gats, precisely?'

'Because they serve the best ham sandwiches in a three-mile radius, and we have to talk somewhere. Don't be a wet blanket – do as I say, Daniel.'

Welcoming any activity that would distract me from my thoughts, I obeyed meekly, and a couple of minutes later

329

was on my way out into the street, having assured my father that I'd be back in time for dinner. Fermín was waiting for me on the corner. As soon as I joined him, he raised his eyebrows to indicate that I should start walking.

'We've got the rattlesnake about twenty yards behind us. Don't turn your head.'

'Is it the same one?'

'I don't think so, unless he's shrunk with all this wet weather. This one looks like a novice. He's carrying a sports page that's six days old. Fumero must be recruiting apprentices from the charity hospice.'

When we got to Els Quatre Gats, our plainclothes policeman sat at a table a few yards from ours and pretended to reread last week's football-league report. Every twenty seconds he would throw us a furtive glance.

'Poor thing, look how he's sweating,' said Fermín, shaking his head. 'You seem rather distant, Daniel. Did you speak to the girl or didn't you?'

'Her father answered the phone.'

'And you had a friendly and civil conversation?'

'It was more of a monologue.'

'I see. Must I therefore infer that you can't address him as *papá* yet?'

'He told me, verbatim, that he was going to beat my brains out.'

'Surely that was a rhetorical flourish.'

At that moment the waiter's frame hovered over us. Fermín asked for enough food to feed a regiment, rubbing his hands with anticipation.

'And you don't want anything. Daniel?'

I shook my head. When the waiter returned with two trays full of tapas, sandwiches, and various glasses of beer, Fermín handed him a handsome sum and told him to keep the change.

'Listen, boss,' he added. 'Do you see that man sitting at the table by the window – the one dressed like Jiminy

330

Cricket with his head buried in his newspaper, as if it were a cone?'

The waiter nodded with an air of complicity.

'Could you please go and tell him that there's an urgent message from Inspector Fumero? He must go immediately to the Boquería market to buy twenty duros' worth of boiled chickpeas and take them without delay to Police Headquarters (in a taxi if necessary) – or he must prepare to present his balls to him on a plate. Would you like me to repeat it?'

'That won't be necessary, sir. Twenty duros' worth of chickpeas or his balls on a plate.'

Fermín handed him another coin. 'God bless you.'

The waiter nodded respectfully and set off towards our pursuer's table to deliver the message. When he heard the instructions, the watchman's face dropped. He remained at the table for another fifteen seconds, torn, and then galloped off into the street. Fermín didn't bat an eyelid. In other circumstances I would have enjoyed the episode, but that night I was unable to get Bea out of my mind.

'Daniel, come down from the clouds, we have work to discuss. Tomorrow, without delay, you must go and visit Nuria Monfort, as we planned.'

'And when I'm there, what do I say to her?'

'You'll think of something. The plan is to follow Señor Barceló's very sensible suggestion. Make her aware that you know that she lied to you about Carax, that her so-called husband Miquel Moliner is not in prison as she pretends, that you've discovered that she is the evil hand responsible for collecting the mail from the old Fortuny-Carax family apartment, using a PO box in the name of a nonexistent solicitor's firm . . . You tell her whatever is necessary to light a fire under her feet. Then, just for effect, you leave her to stew for a while in her own juices.'

'And in the meantime . . .'

'In the meantime, I'll be waiting to follow her, an

objective I plan to put into practice using the latest techniques in camouflage.'

'It's not going to work, Fermín.'

'O ye of little faith! Come on, what did this girl's father say to get you into this frame of mind? Is it the threat you're worried about? Don't pay any attention to him. Let's see, what did the lunatic say?'

I answered without thinking. 'The truth.'

'The truth according to St Daniel the Martyr?'

'You can laugh as much as you like. It serves me right.'

'I'm not laughing, Daniel. It's just that I feel bad seeing you punish yourself. Anyone would think you're about to put on a hair shirt. You haven't done anything wrong. Life has enough torturers as it is, without you going around moonlighting as a Grand Inquisitor against yourself.'

'Do you speak from experience?'

Fermín shrugged.

'You've never told me how you came across Fumero,' I said.

'Would you like to hear a story with a moral?'

'Only if you want to tell it.'

Fermín poured himself a glass of beer and swigged it down in one gulp.

'Amen,' he said to himself. 'What I can tell you about Fumero is common knowledge. The first time I heard him mentioned, the future inspector was a gunman working for the anarchist syndicate, the FAI. He had earned himself quite a reputation, because he had no fear and no scruples. All he needed was someone's name, and he'd finish him off in the street with a shot to the face, in broad daylight. Such talents are greatly valued in times of unrest. The things he didn't have were loyalty or beliefs. He didn't give a damn what cause he was serving, as long as the cause would help him climb the ladder. There are plenty of scum like him in the world, but few of them have Fumero's talent. From the anarchists he went on to serve the communists, and from there to the fascists was only a step. He spied and sold information from one faction to another, and he took money from all of them. I'd had my eye on him for a long time. I was working for the government of the Generalitat at the time. Sometimes I was mistaken for the ugly brother of President Companys, which would fill me with pride.'

'What did you do?'

'A bit of everything. In today's radio soaps, it would be called espionage, but in wartime everyone is a spy. Part of my job was to keep an eye on types like Fumero, as they're the most dangerous. They're like vipers, with no creed and no conscience. In a war they appear everywhere. In times of peace, they put on their masks. But they're still there. Thousands of them. The fact is that sooner or later I discovered what his game was. Rather later than sooner, I'd say. Barcelona fell in a matter of days, and now the boot was on the other foot. I became a persecuted criminal, and my superiors were forced to hide like rats. Naturally, Fumero was already in charge of the "cleanup" operation. The purge was carried out openly, with shootings in the streets, or in Montjuïc Castle. I was arrested in the port while attempting to obtain passage to France on a Greek cargo ship for some of my superiors. I was taken to Montjuïc and held for two days in a pitch-dark cell, with no water or ventilation. The next light I saw was the flame of a welding torch. Fumero and a man who only spoke German had me hung upside down by my feet. The German first got rid of my clothes by burning them with the torch. It seemed to me that he was well practised. When I was left stark naked with all the hairs on my body singed, Fumero told me that if I didn't tell him where my superiors were hiding, the fun would begin in earnest. I'm not a brave man, Daniel. I never have been, but what little courage I possessed I used to tell him to go screw himself. At a sign from Fumero, the German injected something into my thigh and waited a few minutes. Then, while Fumero smoked and watched me, smiling, he began to roast me thoroughly with the welding torch. You've seen the marks. . . .'

I nodded. Fermín spoke in a calm tone, with no emotion.

'These marks are the least important. The worst scars remain inside. I withstood the torch for an hour, or perhaps it was just one minute. I don't know. But I ended up giving them the first names, surnames, and even the shirt sizes of all my superiors and even of those who were not. They abandoned me in an alleyway in Pueblo Seco, naked and with my skin burned. A good woman took me into her home and looked after me for two months.

'The communists had shot her husband and her two sons dead on her doorstep. She didn't know why. When I was able to get up and go out to the street, I learned that all my superiors had been arrested and executed just hours after I had informed on them.'

'Fermín, if you don't want to tell me all this . . .'

'No, no. I'd rather you heard it and knew who you're dealing with. When I returned to my home, I was told it had been expropriated by the government, with all my possessions. Without knowing it, I had become a beggar. I tried to get work. I was rejected. The only thing I could get was a bottle of cheap wine for a few céntimos. It's a slow poison that burns your guts like acid, but I hoped that sooner or later it would work. I told myself I would return to Cuba one day, to my mulatto girl. I was arrested when I tried to board a freighter going to Havana. I've forgotten how long I spent in prison. After the first year, you begin to lose everything, even your mind. When I came out, I began to live on the streets, where you found me an eternity later. There were many others like me, colleagues from prison or parole. The lucky ones had somebody they could count on outside, somebody or something they could go back to. The rest of us joined the army of the dispossessed. Once you're given a card for that club, you never stop being a member. Most of us only came out at night, when the world wasn't looking. I met many others like me. Rarely did I see them again. Life in the streets is short. People look at you in disgust, even the ones who give you alms, but that is nothing compared to the revulsion you feel for yourself. It's like being trapped in a walking corpse, a corpse that's hungry, stinks, and refuses to die. Every now and then, Fumero and his men would arrest me and accuse me of some absurd theft, or of pestering girls on their way out of a convent school. Another month in La Modelo prison, more beatings, and out onto the streets again. I never understood the point of those farces. Apparently the police thought it convenient to have a census of suspects at their disposal, which they could resort to whenever necessary. In one of my meetings with Fumero, who by now was quite the respectable figure, I asked him why he hadn't killed me, as he'd killed the others. He laughed and told me there were worse things than death. He never killed an informer, he said. He let him rot alive.'

'Fermín, you're not an informer. Anyone in your place would have done the same. You're my best friend.'

'I don't deserve your friendship, Daniel. You and your father saved my life, and my life belongs to you both. Whatever I can do for you, I will. The day you got me off the streets, Fermín Romero de Torres was born again.'

'That's not your real name, is it?'

Fermín shook his head. 'I saw that one on a poster at the Arenas bullring. The other is buried. The man who used to live within these bones died, Daniel. Sometimes he comes back, in nightmares. But you've shown me how to be another man, and you've given me a reason for living once more: my Bernarda.'

'Fermín . . .'

'Don't say anything, Daniel. Just forgive me, if you can.'

I embraced him without a word and let him cry. People were giving us strange looks, and I returned their looks with venom. After a while they decided to ignore us. Later, while

I walked with Fermín to his *pensión*, my friend recovered his voice.

'What I've told you today ... I beg you not to tell Bernarda ...'

'I won't tell Bernarda, or anyone else. Not one word, Fermín.'

We said farewell with a handshake.

# 37

I couldn't sleep at all that night. I lay on my bed with the light on, staring at my smart Montblanc pen, which hadn't written anything for years – it was fast becoming the best pair of gloves ever given to someone with no hands. More than once I felt tempted to go over to the Aguilars' apartment and, for want of a better outcome, give myself up. But after much meditation, I decided that bursting into Bea's home in the early hours of the morning was not going to improve matters. By daybreak, exhausted and confused, I had concluded that the best thing to do was let the water flow; in time the river would carry the bad blood away.

The morning inched by with little activity in the bookshop, and I took advantage of the circumstance to doze, standing up, with what my father described as the grace and balance of a flamingo. At lunchtime, as arranged with Fermín the night before, I pretended I was going out for a walk, while Fermín claimed he had an appointment at the outpatients' department to have a few stitches removed. As far as I could tell, my father swallowed both lies whole. The idea of systematically lying to my father was beginning to unnerve me, and I said as much to Fermín halfway through the morning, while my father was out on an errand.

'Daniel, the father-son relationship is based on thousands

of little white lies. Presents from the Three Kings, the tooth fairy, meritocracy, and many others. This is just one more. Don't feel guilty.'

When the time came, I lied again and made my way to the home of Nuria Monfort, whose touch and smell remained indelible in my memory. The cobblestones of Plaza de San Felipe Neri had been taken over by a flock of pigeons, but otherwise the square was deserted. I crossed the paving under the watchful eye of dozens of pigeons and looked around in vain for Fermín, disguised as heaven knows what – he had refused to reveal his plan. I went into the building and saw that the name of Miquel Moliner was still on the letterbox; I wondered whether that would be the first flaw I was going to point out in Nuria Monfort's story. As I went up the stairs in the dark, I almost hoped she wouldn't be at home. Nobody can feel more compassion for a fibber than another one. When I reached the fourth-floor landing, I stopped to gather my courage and devise some excuse with which to justify my visit. The neighbour's radio was still thundering at the other end of the landing, this time broadcasting a game show on which contestants tested their knowledge of religious lore. It went by the name *With a Little Help from the Lord*, and reputedly held the whole of Spain spellbound every Tuesday at noon.

*And now, for five points, and with a little help from the Lord, can you tell us, Bartolomé, how does the Evil One disguise his appearance in front of the wise men of the Tabernacle, in the parable of the archangel and the gourd, in the Book of Joshua? a) as a young goat, b) as a jug vendor, or c) as an acrobat with a monkey?*

Riding on the wave of applause from the audience in the studios of Radio Nacional, I planted myself in front of Nuria Monfort's door and pressed the bell for a few seconds. I listened to the echo spread through the apartment and heaved a sigh of relief. I was about to leave when I heard footsteps coming to the door. The peephole lit up like a tear of light. I smiled. As the key turned in the lock, I breathed deeply.

# 38

'Daniel.'

The blue smoke of her cigarette coiled around her face. Her lips shone with dark lipstick; they were moist and left marks like bloodstains on the filter she held between her index and ring fingers. There are people you remember and people you dream of. For me, Nuria Montfort was like a mirage: you don't question its veracity, you simply follow it until it vanishes or until it destroys you. I followed her through to the narrow, shadowy room that contained her desk, her books, and that collection of lined-up pencils, like an accident of symmetry.

'I thought I wouldn't see you again.'

'I'm sorry to disappoint you.'

She sat on the chair by her desk, crossing her legs and leaning backwards. I tore my eyes away from her throat and concentrated on a damp spot on the wall. I went up to the window and had a quick glance around the square. No sign of Fermín. I could hear Nuria Monfort breathing behind my back, could feel her eyes brushing my neck. I spoke without taking my eyes off the window.

'A few days ago, a good friend of mine discovered that the property manager responsible for the old Fortuny-Carax apartment had been sending his correspondence to a PO box in the name of a firm of solicitors which, apparently, doesn't exist. This same friend discovered that the person who for years has been collecting the mail to this PO box has been using your name, Señora Monfort—'

'Shut up.'

I turned around and saw her retreating into the shadows.

'You judge me without knowing me,' she said.

338

'Then help me to get to know you.'

'Have you told anyone about this? Who else knows what you've just said to me?'

'More people than you'd think. The police have been following me for a long time.'

'Fumero?'

I nodded. It seemed to me that her hands were trembling.

'You don't know what you've done, Daniel.'

'Then tell me,' I answered with a harshness I didn't feel.

'You think that because you chance upon a book you have a right to enter the lives of people you don't know and meddle in things you cannot understand and that don't belong to you.'

'They belong to me now, whether I like it or not.'

'You don't know what you're saying.'

'I was in the Aldayas' house. I know that Jorge Aldaya is hiding there. I know he was the person who murdered Carax.' I didn't know that I believed these words until I heard myself saying them.

She looked at me for a long time, choosing her words carefully. 'Does Fumero know this?'

'I don't know.'

'You'd better know. Did Fumero follow you to that house?'

The anger in her eyes burned me. I had made my entrance playing the role of accuser and judge, but with every minute that passed, I felt more like the culprit.

'I don't think so. Did you know? Did you know that it was Aldaya who killed Julián and that he's hiding in that house? Why didn't you tell me?'

She smiled bitterly. 'You don't understand anything, do you?'

'I understand that you lied in order to defend the man who murdered the person you call your friend, that you've been covering up his crime for years, protecting a man whose only aim is to erase any trace of the existence of Julián Carax, who burns his books. I also understand that you lied to me about your husband, that he's not in prison and clearly isn't here either. That's what I understand.'

Nuria Monfort shook her head slowly. 'Go away, Daniel. Leave this house now and don't return. You've done enough.'

I walked away towards the door, leaving her in the dining room. I stopped halfway and looked back. Nuria Monfort was sitting on the floor, her back against the wall, all concern for appearances gone.

I crossed the square with downcast eyes. I carried with me the pain I had received from the lips of that woman, a pain I now felt I deserved, though I didn't understand why. 'You don't know what you've done, Daniel.' All I wanted was to get away from that place. As I walked past the church, I didn't at first notice the presence of a gaunt, large-nosed priest standing at the entrance holding a missal and a rosary. He blessed me unhurriedly as I passed by.

# 39

I walked into the bookshop almost forty-five minutes late. When my father saw me, he frowned disapprovingly and looked at the clock.

'What time do you call this? You know I have to go out to visit a client in San Cugat and yet you left me here alone.'

'What about Fermín? Isn't he back yet?'

My father shook his head with that haste that seemed to take over when he was in a bad mood. 'By the way, there's a letter for you. I've left it next to the till.'

'Dad, I'm sorry but—'

He waved my excuses aside, threw on a raincoat and hat, and went out of the door without saying goodbye. Knowing him, I guessed his anger would evaporate before he reached the train station. What I found odd was Fermín's absence.

Since I'd seen him dressed up as a vaudeville priest in Plaza de San Felipe Neri, waiting for Nuria Monfort to come rushing out and lead him to the heart of the mystery, my faith in our strategy had crumbled away. I imagined that if Nuria Monfort did go out, Fermín probably ended up following her to the chemist's or the baker's. What a great plan! I went over to the till to have a look at the letter my father had mentioned. The envelope was white and rectangular, like a tombstone, and in the place of a crucifix it bore a return address that managed to crush what little spirit I had left in me that day.

## MILITARY GOVERNMENT OF BARCELONA
### RECRUITMENT OFFICE

'Hallelujah,' I mumbled.

I knew the contents of the letter without having to open it, but even so I did, just to wallow in my misery. The letter was concise: two paragraphs of that prose, poised somewhere between strident proclamation and the aria from an operetta, that characterizes all military correspondence. It was announced to me that in two months' time I, Daniel Sempere, would have the honour and pride of fulfilling the most sacred and edifying duty that could befall an Iberian male: to serve the Motherland and wear the uniform of the national crusade for the defence of the spiritual bulwark of the West. I hoped that at least Fermín would be able to see the funny side of it and make us laugh a bit with his rhyming version of *The Fall of the Judeo-Masonic Conspiracy*. Two months. Eight weeks. Sixty days. I could always divide up the time into seconds and get a number a mile long. I had 5,184,000 seconds left of freedom. Perhaps Don Federico, who according to my father could even build a Volkswagen, could make me a clock with brakes. Perhaps someone could explain to me how I was going to manage not to lose Bea forever. When I heard the tinkle of the doorbell, I thought it would be Fermín, returning after having finally persuaded himself that our efforts as detectives were nothing more than a bad joke.

'Well, if it's not the crown prince himself watching over his castle – and so he should be, even if his face is as long as a cat's tail. Cheer up, Little Boy Blue,' said Gustavo Barceló. He sported a camel-hair coat and his customary ivory walking stick, which he didn't need and which he brandished like a cardinal's mitre. 'Isn't your father in, Daniel?'

'I'm sorry, Don Gustavo. He went out to visit a customer, and I don't suppose he'll be back until—'

'Perfect. Because it's not your father I've come to see, and it's better if he doesn't hear what I have to tell you.'

He winked at me, pulling off his gloves and looking around the shop.

'Where's our colleague Fermín? Is he around?'

'Missing in action.'

'Applying his talents to the Carax case, I imagine?'

'Body and soul. The last time I saw him, he was wearing a cassock and was offering the benediction *urbi et orbi*.'

'I see. . . . It's my fault for egging you on. I wish I hadn't opened my mouth.'

'You seem rather worried. Has anything happened?'

'Not exactly. Or yes, in a way.'

'What did you want to tell me, Don Gustavo?'

The bookseller smiled at me meekly. His usual haughty expression was nowhere to be seen. Instead he looked serious and concerned.

'This morning I met Don Manuel Gutiérrez Fonseca. He's fifty-nine, a bachelor, and has been a city employee at the Barcelona municipal morgue since 1924. Thirty years' service on the threshold of darkness. His words, not mine. Don Manuel is a gentleman of the old school – courteous, pleasant, and obliging. For the last fifteen years, he's been living in Calle Ceniza, in a rented room that he shares with a dozen parakeets that have learned how to hum the funeral march. He has a season ticket at the Liceo. He likes Verdi and Donizetti. He told me that in his job the important thing is to follow the rules. The rules make provisions for everything, especially for occasions when one doesn't know what to do. Fifteen years ago Don Manuel opened a canvas bag brought in by the police, and in it he found his childhood best friend. The rest of the body came in a separate bag. Don Manuel, holding back his feelings, followed the rules.'

'Would you like a coffee, Don Gustavo? You're looking a bit pale.'

'Please.'

I went in search of the Thermos flask and poured him a cup with eight lumps of sugar. He gulped it down.

'Better?'

'Getting there. As I was saying, the fact is that Don Manuel was on duty the day they brought the body of Julián Carax to the autopsy department, in September 1936. Of course, Don Manuel couldn't remember the name, but a look through the archives and a hundred-peseta donation towards his retirement fund refreshed his memory remarkably. Do you follow me?'

I nodded, almost in a trance.

'Don Manuel remembers all the details of that day because, as he told me, it was one of the few times when he bent the rules. The police claimed that the body had been found in an alleyway of the Raval quarter, shortly before dawn. The body reached the morgue by midmorning. The only items on it were a book and a passport, which identified the man as Julián Fortuny Carax, born in Barcelona in 1900. The passport had been stamped at the border post of La Junquera, showing that Carax had come into the country a month earlier. The cause of death was, apparently, a bullet wound. Don Manuel isn't a doctor, but over the years he has learned what to look for. In his opinion the gunshot, just above the heart, had been delivered at point-blank range. Thanks to the passport, they were able to locate Señor Fortuny, Carax's father, who came to the morgue that very evening to identify the body.'

'Up to here it all tallies with what Nuria Monfort said.'

Barceló nodded. 'That's right. What Nuria Monfort didn't tell you is that he – my friend Don Manuel – sensing that the police did not seem very interested in the case, and having realized that the book found in the pocket of the corpse bore the name of the deceased, decided to act on his own initiative and called the publishing house that very afternoon, while they awaited the arrival of Fortuny.'

'Nuria Monfort told me that the employee at the morgue phoned the publishers three days later, when the body had already been buried in a common grave.'

'According to Don Manuel, he called the same day as the body was delivered to the morgue. He tells me he spoke to a young woman, who said she was grateful to him for having called. Don Manuel remembers that he was slightly shocked by the attitude of the young lady. In his own words: "It sounded as if she already knew."'

'What about Señor Fortuny? Is it true that he refused to identify his son?'

'That's what intrigued me most of all. Don Manuel tells me that at the end of the afternoon, a little man arrived, trembling, escorted by two policemen. It was Señor Fortuny. According to Don Manuel, that is the one thing you never get used to, the moment when those closest to the loved one come to identify the body. He says it's a situation he wouldn't wish on anyone. Worst of all, he says, is when the deceased is a young person and it's the parents, or a young spouse, who have to identify the body. Don Manuel remembers Señor Fortuny well. He says that when he arrived at the morgue, he could scarcely stand, that he cried like a child, and that the two policemen had to hold him up by his arms. He kept moaning: "What have they done to my son? What have they done to my son?"'

'Did he get to see the body?'

'Don Manuel told me that he was on the point of asking the police officers whether they might skip the normal procedure. It's the only time it occurred to him to question the rules. The corpse was in a bad state. It had probably been dead for over twenty-four hours when it reached the morgue, and not since dawn that day, as the police claimed. Manuel was afraid that when that little old man saw it, he would break down. Señor Fortuny kept on repeating that it couldn't be, that his Julián couldn't be dead. . . . Then Don Manuel removed the shroud that covered the body, and the two policemen asked Fortuny formally whether this was his son, Julián.'

'And?'

'Señor Fortuny was dumbfounded. He stared at the body for almost a minute. Then he turned on his heels and left.'

'He left?'

'In a hurry.'

'What about the police? Didn't they stop him? Wasn't he supposed to be there to identify the body?'

Barceló smiled roguishly. 'In theory. But Don Manuel remembers there was someone else in the room, a third policeman who had come in quietly while the other two were preparing Señor Fortuny. He was watching the scene without saying a word, leaning against the wall, with a cigarette in his mouth. Don Manuel remembers him because when he told him that the regulations strictly forbade smoking in the morgue, one of the officers signalled to him to be quiet. According to Don Manuel, as soon as Señor Fortuny had left, the third policeman went up to the body, glanced at it, and spat on its face. Then he kept the passport and gave orders for the body to be sent to Montjuïc, to be buried in a common grave at daybreak.'

'It doesn't make sense.'

'That's what Don Manuel thought. Especially as none of it tallied with the rules. "But we don't know who this man is," he said. The two other policemen didn't reply. Don Manuel rebuked them angrily: "Or do you know only too well? Because it is quite clear to us all that he's been dead for at least a day." Don Manuel was obviously referring to the regulations and was no fool. According to him, when the third policeman heard his protests, he went up to him, looked him straight in the eye, and asked him whether he'd care to join the deceased on his last voyage. Don Manuel was terrified. The man had the eyes of a lunatic, and Don Manuel didn't doubt for one moment that he meant what he said. He mumbled that he was only trying to comply with the regulations, that nobody knew who the man was, and that, consequently, he couldn't be buried yet. "This man is whoever I say he is," answered the policeman. Then he picked up the registration form and signed it, closing the case. Don Manuel says he'll never forget that signature, because during the war years, and for a long time afterwards, he would come across it on dozens of death certificates for bodies that arrived from goodness knows where – bodies that nobody managed to identify. . . .'

'Inspector Francisco Javier Fumero . . .'

'The pride and glory of Central Police Headquarters. Do you realize what this means, Daniel?'

'That we've been lashing out blindly from the very beginning.'

Barceló took his hat and stick and walked over to the door, tut-tutting under his breath. 'No, it means the lashings are about to start now.'

# 40

I spent the afternoon surveying the grim letter announcing my draft, hoping for signs of life from Fermín. Half an hour after our closing time, Fermín's whereabouts remained unknown. I picked up the telephone and called the *pensión* in Calle Joaquín Costa. Doña Encarna answered, her voice thick with alcohol. She said she hadn't seen Fermín since that morning.

'If he's not back within the next half hour, he'll have to

have his supper cold. This isn't the Ritz, you know. I hope nothing's happened to him.'

'Don't worry, Doña Encarna. He had some errand to do and must have been delayed. In any case, if you do see him before going to bed, I'd be very grateful if you could ask him to call me. It's Daniel Sempere, your friend Mercedi-tas's neighbour.'

'Of course, but I must warn you that I turn in for the night at half past eight.'

After that I phoned Barceló's home, hoping that Fermín might have turned up there to empty Bernarda's larder or carry her off into the ironing room. It hadn't occurred to me that Clara might answer the phone.

'Daniel, what a surprise.'

You stole my line, I thought. Talking to her in a roundabout manner worthy of Don Anacleto, the school-teacher, I let drop the reason for my call, but in a very casual manner, almost in passing.

'No, Fermín hasn't come by all day. And Bernarda has been with me all afternoon, so I would know. Actually, we've been talking about you.'

'What a boring conversation.'

'Bernarda says you look very handsome, quite grown up.'

'I take lots of vitamins.'

A long silence.

'Daniel, do you think we could be friends again some day? How many years will it take you to forgive me?'

'We are friends already, Clara, and I don't need to forgive you for anything. You know that.'

'My uncle says you're still investigating Julián Carax. Why don't you come by some afternoon for tea and tell me the latest. I've also got things to tell you.'

'One of these days, I promise.'

'I'm getting married, Daniel.'

I stared at the receiver. I felt as if my feet were sinking into the ground or I had shrunk a few inches.

'Daniel, are you there?'

'Yes.'

'You're surprised.'

I swallowed – my mouth felt like concrete. 'No. What surprises me is that you're not already married. You can't have lacked suitors. Who's the lucky man?'

'You don't know him. His name is Jacobo. He's a friend of Uncle Gustavo. A director of the Bank of Spain. We met at an opera recital organized by my uncle. Jacobo is enthusiastic about opera. He's older than me, but we're very good friends, and that's what matters, don't you think?'

My mouth was full of malice, so I bit my tongue. It tasted like poison. 'Of course ... So listen, congratulations.'

'You'll never forgive me, will you, Daniel? For you I'll always be the perfidious Clara Barceló.'

'To me you'll always be Clara Barceló, period. And you know that as well as I do.'

There was another silence, the kind in which grey hairs seem to creep up on you.

'What about you, Daniel? Fermín tells me you have a beautiful girlfriend.'

'I've got to go, Clara, a client has just come in. I'll call you one of these days, and we'll meet for tea. Congratulations once again.'

I put down the phone and sighed.

My father returned from his visit to the client looking dejected and not in the mood for conversation. He got dinner ready while I set the table, without even asking after Fermín or how the day had gone in the bookshop. We stared at our plates during the meal, hiding behind the chatter of the news on the radio. My father hardly ate. He just stirred the watery, tasteless soup with his spoon, as if he were looking for gold in the bottom.

'You haven't touched your food,' I said.

My father shrugged his shoulders. The radio continued to bombard us with nonsense. My father got up and turned it off.

'What did the letter from the army say?' he asked finally.

'I have to join up in two months' time.'

His face seemed to age by ten years.

'Barceló says he'll try to pull some strings so that I can be transferred to the Military Government in Barcelona, after the initial training. I'll even be able to come home to sleep,' I added.

My father replied with an anaemic nod. I found it painful to hold his gaze, so I got up to clear the table. My father remained seated, his eyes lost and his hands clasped under his chin. I was about to wash up the dishes when I heard footsteps pounding up the stairs. Firm, hurried footsteps that spoke a terrible warning. I looked up and exchanged glances with my father. The footsteps stopped on our landing. My father stood up, looking anxious. A second later we heard banging on the door and a furious booming voice that sounded vaguely familiar.

'Police! Open up!'

A thousand daggers stabbed at my mind. Another volley of banging made the door shake. My father walked up to the doorway and lifted the cover of the peephole.

'What do you want at this time of night?'

'Open the door or we'll kick it down, Sempere. Don't make me have to repeat myself.'

I recognized the voice as Fumero's, and my heart turned to ice. My father threw me a questioning look. I nodded. Suppressing a sigh, he opened the door. Fumero and his two henchmen were silhouetted against the yellowish light of the landing, ashen-faced puppets in grey raincoats.

'Where is he?' shouted Fumero, swiping my father aside and pushing his way into the dining room.

My father tried to stop him, but one of the policemen who was covering the inspector's back grabbed him by the arm and pushed him against the wall, holding him with the coldness and efficiency of a man accustomed to the task. It was the same man who had followed Fermín and myself, the same one who had held me while Fumero beat up my friend outside the Hospice of Santa Lucía, the same one who had kept watch on me a couple of nights before. He shot me an empty, deadpan look. I went up to Fumero, displaying all the calm I could muster. The inspector's eyes were bloodshot. A recent scratch ran down his left cheek, edged with dry blood.

'Where?'

'Where what?'

Fumero looked down suddenly and shook his head, mumbling to himself. When he raised his face, he had a wolfish grimace on his lips and a revolver in his hand. Without taking his eyes off mine, he banged the butt of his revolver against the vase of withered flowers on the table. The vase smashed into small fragments, spilling the water and shrivelled stalks over the tablecloth. Despite myself, I shivered. My father was shouting from the entrance hall, held firmly in the grip of the two policemen. I could barely decipher his words. All I could absorb was the icy pressure of the gun's barrel sunk into my cheek, and the smell of gunpowder.

'Don't fuck with me, you little shit, or your father will have to pick up your brains off the floor. Do you hear me?'

I nodded. I was shaking. Fumero pressed the barrel hard against my cheek. I could feel it cutting into my skin, but I didn't even dare blink.

'This is the last time I'll ask you. Where is he?'

I saw myself reflected in the black pupils of the inspector's eyes. They slowly contracted as he tightened the hammer with his thumb.

'Not here. I haven't seen him since lunchtime. It's the truth.'

Fumero stood still for almost half a minute, digging the gun into my face and smacking his lips.

'Lerma,' he ordered. 'Take a look around.'

One of the policemen hurried off to inspect the apartment. My father struggled in vain with the third officer.

'If you've lied to me and we find him in this house, I swear I'll break both your father's legs,' whispered Fumero.

'My father doesn't know anything. Leave him alone.'

'You're the one who doesn't know what he's playing at. But as soon as I get hold of your friend, the game's over. No judges, no hospitals, no fucking nothing. This time I'll personally see to it that he's put out of circulation. And I'm going to enjoy doing it, believe me. I'm going to take my time. You can tell him if you see him. Because I'm going to find him even if I have to turn over every stone in the city. And you're next on the list.'

The officer called Lerma reappeared in the dining room and gave a slight shake of his head. Fumero loosened his grip on the hammer and removed the revolver.

'Pity,' said Fumero.

'What has he done? Why are you looking for him?'

Fumero turned his back on me and went up to the policemen, who, at his signal, let go of my father.

'You're going to remember this,' spat my father.

Fumero's eyes rested on his. Instinctively, my father took a step back. I feared that Inspector Fumero's visit had only just begun, but suddenly the man shook his head, laughing under his breath, and left the apartment. Lerma followed him. The third policeman, my sentinel, paused for a moment in the doorway. He looked silently at me, as if he wanted to say something.

'Palacios!' yelled Fumero, his voice fading into the echo of the stairwell.

Palacios lowered his eyes and disappeared round the door. I went out to the landing. I could see blades of light emerging from the half-open doors of the neighbours, their frightened faces peeping out in the dark. The three shadowy shapes of the policemen vanished down the stairs, and the angry sound of their footsteps receded like a poisoned tide, leaving behind it a residue of fear.

It was about midnight when we heard more banging on the door, this time weaker, almost fearful. My father, who was dabbing iodine on the bruise left on my cheek by Fumero's gun, stopped in his tracks. Our eyes met. There were three more knocks.

For a moment I thought it was Fermín, who had perhaps witnessed the whole incident hidden in some dark corner of the staircase.

'Who's there?' asked my father.

'Don Anacleto, Señor Sempere.'

My father gave out a sigh. We opened the door to find the teacher, looking paler than ever.

'Don Anacleto, what's the matter? Are you all right?' my father asked, letting him in.

The teacher was holding a folded newspaper. He handed it to us with a horrified look. The paper was still warm, the ink still damp.

'It's tomorrow's edition,' murmured Don Anacleto. 'Page six.'

What first caught my eye were the two photographs under the heading. The first was a picture of Fermín, with a fuller figure and more hair, perhaps fifteen or twenty years younger. The second showed the face of a woman with her eyes closed and skin like marble. It took me a few seconds to recognize her, because I was used to seeing her in the half-light.

## TRAMP MURDERS WOMAN
## IN BROAD DAYLIGHT
*Barcelona/Press Agency*

Police are looking for the tramp who stabbed a woman to death this afternoon. Her name was Nuria Monfort Masdedeu, and she lived in Barcelona.

The crime took place in midafternoon in the neighbourhood of San Gervasio, where the victim was assaulted by the tramp with no apparent motive. According to Central Police Headquarters, it would appear that the tramp had been following her for reasons that have not yet been made clear.

It seems that the murderer, 55-year-old Antonio José Gutiérrez Alcayete, from Villa Inmunda in the province of Cáceres, is a well-known criminal with a long record of mental illness, who escaped from La Modelo Prison six years ago and has managed to elude the authorities by assuming different identities. At the time of the murder, he was dressed in a cassock. He is armed, and the police describe him as highly dangerous. It is not yet known whether the victim and her murderer knew one another, although sources from Police Headquarters indicate that everything points towards this; nor is it known what may have been the motive behind the crime. The victim was stabbed six times in her stomach, chest, and throat. The attack, which took place close to a school, was witnessed by a number of pupils, who alerted the teachers. They in turn called the police and an ambulance. According to the police report, death was caused by multiple wounds. The victim was pronounced dead on arrival at Barcelona's Hospital Clínico at 18.15.

# 41

We had no news from Fermín all day. My father insisted on opening the bookshop as usual, as if nothing had happened and as a declaration of Fermín's innocence. The police had posted an officer by the door to our stairs, and another watched over the Plaza Santa Ana, sheltering beneath the church door like the effigy of a saint. We could see them shivering under the heavy rain that had arrived with the dawn, the steam from their breath becoming less visible as the day wore on, their hands buried in the pockets of their raincoats. A few neighbours walked straight past, with a quick glance through the shop window, but not a single buyer ventured in.

'The rumour must have spread,' I said.

My father only nodded. He'd spent all morning without speaking to me, expressing himself only through gestures. The page detailing the news of Nuria Monfort's murder lay on the counter. Every twenty minutes he would wander over and reread it with an inscrutable expression. All day long he had been bottling up his anger, letting it accumulate inside him.

'However many times you read the article, it's not going to be true,' I said.

My father raised his head and looked at me severely. 'Did you know this person? Nuria Monfort?'

'I'd spoken to her a couple of times.'

Nuria Monfort's face took over my thoughts. My lack of honesty was nauseating. I was still haunted by her smell and the touch of her lips, the image of that desk so impeccably tidy and her sad, wise eyes. 'A couple of times.'

'Why did you have to speak to her? What did she have to do with you?'

'She was an old friend of Julián Carax. I went to see her to ask her what she remembered about Carax. That's all. She was Isaac's daughter, the keeper. He was the one who gave me her address.'

'Did Fermín know her?'

'No.'

'How can you be sure?'

'How can you doubt him and believe these lies? All Fermín knew about that woman was what I told him.'

'And is that why he was following her?'

'Yes.'

'Because you'd asked him to.'

I didn't answer. My father heaved a sigh.

'You don't understand, Dad.'

'You can be sure of that. I don't understand you, or Fermín, or—'

'Dad, from what we know of Fermín, what it says there is impossible.'

354

'And what *do* we know about Fermín, eh? To begin with, it turns out that we didn't even know his real name.'

'You're mistaken about him.'

'No, Daniel. You're the one who's mistaken. Who asked you to go digging into other people's lives?'

'I'm free to speak to whoever I want.'

'I suppose you also feel free from the consequences.'

'Are you insinuating that I'm responsible for this woman's death?'

'This woman, as you call her, had a first name and a surname, and you knew her.'

'There's no need to remind me,' I answered with tears in my eyes.

My father looked at me sadly, shaking his head. 'Oh, God, I don't even want to think how poor Isaac must be feeling.'

'It's not my fault she's dead,' I said in a tiny voice, thinking that perhaps if I repeated those words often enough, I would end up believing them.

My father retired to the back room, still shaking his head.

'You know what you're responsible for and what you're not, Daniel. Sometimes I don't know who you are anymore.'

I grabbed my raincoat and escaped into the street and the rain, where nobody would know me.

I gave myself up to the freezing rain, going nowhere in particular. I walked with my eyes downcast, carrying with me the image of Nuria Monfort, lifeless, stretched out on a cold marble slab, her body riddled with stab wounds. I passed a crossing with Calle Fontanella and didn't stop to look at the traffic lights. It was only when a strong gust of wind hit my face that I turned to see a wall of metal and light hurtling towards me at full speed. At the last moment, a passerby pulled me back and moved me out of the bus's path. I gazed at the metal behemoth that shimmered only an inch or two from my face; what could have been certain death speeding by, a tenth of a second away. By the time I realized what had happened, the person who had saved my life was walking away over the pedestrian crossing, just a silhouette in a grey raincoat. I remained rooted to the spot, breathless. Through the curtain of rain, I noticed that my saviour had stopped on the other side of the street and was watching me under the downpour. It was the third policeman, Palacios. A thick wall of traffic slid by between us, and when I looked again, Officer Palacios was no longer there.

I set off toward Bea's house, incapable of waiting any longer. I needed to recall what little good there was in me, what she had given me. I rushed up the stairs and stopped outside the door of the Aguilars' apartment, almost out of breath. I held the door knocker and gave three loud knocks. While I waited, I gathered my courage and became aware of my appearance: soaked to the skin. I pushed the hair back from my forehead and told myself that the dice had been cast. If Señor Aguilar was ready to break my legs and smash my face, the sooner the better. I knocked again and after a while heard footsteps approaching. The peephole opened a fraction. A dark, suspicious eye stared at me.

'Who's there?'

I recognized the voice of Cecilia, one of the maids who worked for the Aguilar family.

'It's Daniel Sempere, Cecilia.'

The peephole closed, and within a few seconds I could hear the sound of the bolts and latches being drawn back. The large door opened slowly, and I was received by Cecilia in her cap and uniform, holding a candle in a candleholder. From her alarmed expression, I gathered that I must look like a ghost.

'Good afternoon, Cecilia. Is Bea in?'

She looked at me without understanding. In her experience of the household routine, my presence, which lately had been an unusual occurrence, was associated only with Tomás, my old school friend.

'Miss Beatriz isn't here. . . .'

'Has she gone out?'

Cecilia, who at the best of times was a frightened soul, nodded.

'Do you know when she's coming back?'

The maid shrugged. 'She went with Señor and Señora Aguilar to the doctor, about two hours ago.'

'To the doctor? Is she ill?'

'I don't know, sir.'

'And which doctor did they go to?'

'That I don't know, sir.'

I decided not to go on tormenting the poor maid. The absence of Bea's parents opened up other avenues. 'What about Tomás? Is he in?'

'Yes, Master Daniel. Come in, I'll call him.'

I went into the hall and waited. In the past I would have gone straight to my friend's room, but I hadn't been to that house for so long that I felt like a stranger. Cecilia disappeared down the corridor wrapped in an aura of light, abandoning me to the dark. I thought I could hear Tomás's voice in the distance and then some footsteps approaching. I quickly made up a pretext to explain my unannounced visit to my friend. But the figure that appeared at the door of the entrance hall was Cecilia's. She looked at me contritely, and my forced smile vanished.

'Master Tomás says he's very busy and cannot see you right now.'

'Did you tell him who I was? Daniel Sempere.'

'Yes, Master Daniel. He told me to tell you to go away.'

A stab of cold steel in my stomach took my breath away.

'I'm sorry, sir,' said Cecilia.

I nodded, not knowing what to say. The maid opened the door of the residence that, until not very long ago, I had considered my second home.

'Does the young master want an umbrella?'

'No thank you, Cecilia.'

'I'm, sorry, Master Daniel,' the maid repeated.

I smiled weakly. 'Don't worry, Cecilia.'

The door closed, leaving me in the shadows. I stayed there a few moments and then dragged myself down the stairs. The rain was still pouring down, relentlessly. I walked off down the street. When I reached the corner, I stopped and turned around for a moment. I looked up at the Aguilars' apartment. I could see the silhouette of my old friend Tomás outlined against his bedroom window. He was staring at me, motionless. I waved at him but he didn't return the greeting. A few seconds later, he moved away to the back of the room. I waited almost five minutes, hoping he would reappear, but he didn't.

## 42

On my way back to the bookshop, I crossed the street by the Capitol Cinema, where two painters standing on a scaffold watched with dismay as their freshly painted placard became streaked under the rain. In the distance I could make out the stoical figure of the sentinel stationed opposite the bookshop. When I got to Don Federico Flaviá's shop, I noticed that the watchmaker was standing in the doorway watching the downpour. The scars from his stay at police headquarters still showed on his face. He wore an impeccable grey wool suit and held a cigarette that he hadn't bothered to light. I waved to him, and he smiled back.

'What have you got against umbrellas, Daniel?'

'What could be more beautiful than the rain, Don Federico?'

'Pneumonia. Come on in, I have your repair ready.'

I looked at him, not understanding. Don Federico's eyes were fixed on mine, and his smile hadn't diminished. I nodded and followed him into his marvellous bazaar. As soon as we were inside, he handed me a small brown paper bag.

'You'd better leave right away. The scarecrow watching the bookshop hasn't taken his eyes off us.'

I looked inside the bag. It contained a small, leather-bound book. A missal. The missal Fermín had held in his hands the last time I'd seen him. Don Federico, pushing me back towards the street, vowed me to silence with a solemn nod. Once I was outside again, he recovered his happy expression and raised his voice.

'And remember, don't force the key when you wind it up, or it'll come loose again, all right?'

'Don't worry, Don Federico, and thanks.'

I walked away with a knot in my stomach that tightened with every step I took. When I passed in front of the plainclothes policeman guarding the bookshop, I greeted him with the same hand that held the bag given to me by Don Federico. The policeman looked at it with vague interest. I slipped into the bookshop. My father was still standing behind the counter, as if he hadn't moved since I'd left. He gave me a troubled look.

'Listen Daniel, about what I said . . .'

'Don't worry. You were right.'

'You're trembling.'

I nodded casually and saw him go off in search of the Thermos. I seized the moment to go to the small toilet by the back room and examine the missal. Fermín's note slipped out, fluttering about like a butterfly. I caught it in mid-air. The message was written on an almost transparent piece of cigarette paper in minute writing, and I had to hold it up against the light to be able to decipher it.

Dear Daniel,

Don't believe one word of what the newspapers say

about the murder of Nuria Monfort. As usual, it's
nothing but a tall tale. I'm safe and sound, hiding in
a secure place. Don't try to find me or send me
messages. Destroy this note as soon as you've read it.
No need to swallow it, just burn it or tear it up into
small pieces. I'll use my wits to get in touch with you
– and the help of friendly intermediaries. I beg you to
transmit the essence of this message, in code and with
all discretion, to my beloved. Don't you do anything.
Your friend, the third man,

   FRdT

I was beginning to reread the note when someone's
knuckles rapped on the toilet door.

'May I come in?' asked an unknown voice.

My heart skipped a beat. Not knowing what else to do, I
scrunched up the cigarette paper and put it in my mouth. I
pulled the chain, and while the water thundered through
pipes and cisterns, I swallowed the little paper ball. It tasted
of wax and Sugus sweets. When I opened the door, I
encountered the reptilian smile of the police officer who
had been stationed in front of the bookshop.

'Excuse me. I don't know whether it's listening to the
rain all day, but suddenly it seems there's something of
an emergency building down there, and when nature
calls . . .'

'But of course,' I said, making way for him. 'It's all
yours.'

'Much obliged.'

The policeman, who, in the light of the bare bulb,
reminded me of a small weasel, looked me up and down.
His ratlike eyes paused on the missal I held in my hands.

'If I don't have something to read, I just can't go,' I
explained.

'It's the same for me. And people say Spaniards don't
read. May I borrow it?'

'On top of the cistern, you'll find the latest *Critics' Prize*,' I said, cutting him short. 'It's infallible.'

I walked away without losing my composure and joined my father, who was pouring me a cup of white coffee.

'What's he doing here?' I asked.

'He swore on his mother's grave that he was on the verge of wetting himself. What was I supposed to do?'

'Leave him in the street and let him warm up that way?' My father frowned.

'If you don't mind, I'm going up to the apartment.'

'Of course I don't mind. And put on some dry clothes. You're going to catch your death.'

The apartment was cold and silent. I went into my bedroom and peeped out of the window. The second sentinel was still there, by the door of the Church of Santa Ana. I took off my soaking clothes and put on some thick pyjamas and a dressing gown that had belonged to my grandfather. I lay down on the bed without bothering to turn on the light and abandoned myself to the darkness and the sound of the rain on the windowpanes. I closed my eyes and tried to conjure up the image of Bea, her touch and smell. The night before I hadn't slept at all, and soon I was overcome by exhaustion. In my dreams the hooded figure of Death rode over Barcelona, a ghostly apparition that hovered above the towers and roofs, trailing black ropes that held hundreds of small white coffins. The coffins left behind them their own trail of black flowers, on whose petals, written in blood, was the name Nuria Monfort.

I awoke at the break of a grey dawn. The windows were steamed up. I dressed for the cold weather and put on some calf-length boots, then went out into the corridor and groped my way through the apartment. I slipped out through the door and went down to the street. The newsstands in the Ramblas were already lighting up in the distance. I steered a course towards the one that was anchored at the mouth of Calle Tallers and bought the first

361

edition of the day's paper, which still smelled of warm ink. I rushed through the pages until I found the obituary section. Nuria Monfort's name lay under a printed cross, and I couldn't bring myself to look at it. I walked away with the newspaper folded under my arm. The funeral was that afternoon, in Montjuïc Cemetery. After walking round the block, I returned home. My father was still asleep, so I went back into my room. I sat at my desk and took the Meisterstück pen out of its case, then took a blank sheet of paper and hoped the nib would guide me. In my hands the pen had nothing to say. In vain I tried to conjure up the words I wanted to offer Nuria Monfort, but I was incapable of writing or feeling anything except the terror of her absence, of knowing she was lost, wrenched away. I knew that one day she would return to me, in the months or years to come, and that I would always relive her memory in the touch of a stranger, in the recollection of images that no longer belonged to me.

# 43

Shortly before three o'clock, I got on a bus in Paseo de Colón that would take me to the cemetery on Montjuïc. Through the window I could see the forest of masts and fluttering pennants in the docks. The bus, which was almost empty, circled Montjuïc mountain and started up the road to the eastern gates of the boundless cemetery. I was the last passenger to get off.

'What time does the last bus leave?' I asked the driver.

'At half past four.'

The driver left me by the cemetery gates. An avenue of cypress trees rose in the mist. Even from there, at the foot of the mountain, you could already begin to see the vast city of the dead that scaled the slope to the very top: avenues of tombs, walks lined with gravestones and alleyways of mausoleums, towers crowned by fiery angels and whole forests of sepulchres that seemed to grow into one another. The city of the dead was a vast abyss guarded by an army of rotting stone statues sinking into the mud. I took a deep breath and entered the labyrinth. My mother lay buried only a hundred yards from the path along which I walked. With every step I took, I could feel the cold, the emptiness, and the fury of that place; the horror of its silence, of the faces trapped in old photographs abandoned to the company of candles and dead flowers. After a while I caught the distant glimpse of gas lamps around a grave, the shapes of half a dozen people lined up against an ashen sky. I quickened my pace and stopped where I could hear the words of the priest.

The coffin, an unpolished pine box, rested on the mud. Two gravediggers guarded it, leaning on spades. I scanned those present. Old Isaac, the keeper of the Cemetery of Forgotten Books, had not attended his daughter's funeral. I recognized the neighbour who lived opposite. She shook her head, sobbing, while a man stroked her back with a resigned air. Her husband, I imagined. Next to them was a woman of about forty, dressed in grey and carrying a bunch of flowers. She cried quietly, looking away from the grave with tight lips. I had never seen her before. Separated from the group, clad in a dark raincoat and holding his hat behind his back, was the policeman who had saved my life the day before. Palacios. He raised his eyes and observed me for a few seconds without blinking. The blind, senseless words of the priest were all that separated us from the terrible silence. I stared at the mud-splattered coffin. I imagined Nuria lying inside it, and I didn't realize I was crying until the woman in grey came up to me and offered me one of the flowers from her bunch. I remained there until the group had dispersed. At a sign from the priest, the gravediggers got ready to do their work. I kept the flower in my coat pocket and walked away, unable to express my final farewell.

It was beginning to get dark by the time I reached the cemetery gates, and I assumed I'd missed the last bus. I was about to start a long walk, under the shadow of the necropolis, following the road that skirted the port back to Barcelona. A black car was parked about twenty yards ahead of me, its lights on. Inside, a figure smoked a cigarette. As I drew near, Palacios opened the passenger door.

'Get in. I'll take you home. You won't find any buses or taxis around here at this time of day.'

I hesitated for a moment. 'I'd rather walk.'

'Don't be silly. Get in.'

He spoke in the steely tone of someone used to giving orders and being obeyed instantly. 'Please,' he added.

I got into the car, and the policeman started the engine.

'Enrique Palacios,' he said, holding his hand out to me.

I didn't shake it. 'If you leave me in Colón, that's fine.'

The car sped off. We joined the traffic on the main road and travelled a good stretch without uttering a single word.

'I want you to know I'm very sorry about Señora Monfort.'

Coming from him, the words seemed obscene, an insult.

'I'm grateful to you for saving my life the other day, but I must tell you I don't give a shit what you feel, Señor Enrique Palacios.'

'I'm not what you think, Daniel. I'd like to help you.'

'If you expect me to tell you where Fermín is, you can leave me right here.'

'I don't give a damn where your friend is. I'm not on duty now.'

I didn't reply.

'You don't trust me, and I don't blame you. But at least listen to me. This has already gone too far. There was no reason why this woman should have died. I beg you to let this matter drop and put this man, Carax, out of your mind forever.'

'You speak as if I'm in control of what's happening. I'm only a spectator. The whole show has been staged by you and your boss.'

'I'm tired of funerals, Daniel. I don't want to have to go to yours.'

'All the better, because you're not invited.'

'I'm serious.'

'Me, too. Please stop and let me out.'

'We'll be in Colón in two minutes.'

'I don't care. This car smells of death, like you. Let me out.'

Palacios slowed down and stopped on the hard shoulder. I got out of the car and banged the door shut, eluding Palacios's eyes. I waited for him to leave, but the police officer didn't seem to be going anywhere. I turned around and saw him lowering the car window. I thought I read honesty, even pain, in his face, but I refused to believe it.

'Nuria Monfort died in my arms, Daniel,' he said. 'I think her last words were a message for you.'

'What did she say?' I asked, my voice gripped by an icy cold. 'Did she mention my name?'

'She was delirious, but I think she was referring to you. At one point she said there were worse prisons than words. Then, before she died, she asked me to tell you to let her go.'

I looked at him without understanding. 'To let who go?'

'Someone called Penélope. I imagined she must be your girlfriend.'

Palacios looked down and set off into the twilight. I remained there, staring disconcerted at the lights of the car as they disappeared into the blue-and-red dusk. Then I walked on towards Paseo de Colón, repeating to myself those last words of Nuria Monfort but finding no meaning to them. When I reached the square called Portal de la Paz, I stopped next to the pleasure boats to gaze at the port. I sat on the steps that disappeared into the murky water, in the same place where, on a night that was now in the distant past, I had met Laín Coubert, the man without a face.

'There are worse prisons than words,' I murmured.

Only then did I understand that the message from Nuria Monfort was not meant for me. I wasn't the one who had to let Penélope go. Her last words hadn't been for a stranger, but for a man she had loved in silence for twenty years: Julián Carax.

# 44

Night was falling when I reached Plaza de San Felipe Neri. The bench on which I had first caught sight of Nuria Monfort stood at the foot of a streetlamp, empty and tattooed by penknives with the names of lovers, with insults and promises. I looked up to the windows of Nuria Monfort's home on the third floor and noticed a dim, flickering copper light. A candle.

I entered the cavernous foyer and groped my way up the stairs. My hands shook when I reached the third-floor landing. A sliver of reddish light shone from beneath the frame of the half-open door. I placed my hand on the doorknob and remained there motionless, listening. I thought I heard a whisper, a choked voice coming from within. For a moment I thought that if I opened that door, I'd find her waiting for me on the other side, smoking by the balcony, her legs tucked under her, leaning against the wall, anchored in the same place I'd left her. Gently, fearing I might disturb her, I opened the door and went into the apartment. In the dining room, the balcony curtains swayed in the breeze. A figure was sitting by the window, completely still, holding a burning candle in its hands. I couldn't make out the face, but a bright pearl slid down its cheek, shining like fresh resin, then falling onto the figure's lap. Isaac Monfort turned, his face streaked with tears.

'I didn't see you this afternoon at the funeral,' I said.

He shook his head, drying his tears with the back of his lapel.

'Nuria wasn't there,' he murmured after a while. 'The dead never go to their own funeral.'

He looked around him, as if his daughter was in that very room, sitting next to us in the dark, listening to us.

'Do you know that I've never been inside this house before?' he asked. 'Whenever we met, it was always Nuria who came to me. "It's easier for you, Father," she would say. "Why go up all those stairs?" I'd always say to her, "All right, if you don't want to invite me, I won't come," and she'd answer, "I don't need to invite you to my home, Father. Only strangers need an invitation. You can come whenever you like." In over fifteen years, I didn't go to see her once. I always told her she'd chosen a bad neighbourhood. Not enough light. An old building. She would just nod in agreement. Like when I used to tell her she'd chosen a bad life. Not much future. A husband without a job. It's funny how we judge others and don't realize the extent of our own disdain until the ones we love are no longer there, until they are taken from us. They're taken from us because they've never really belonged to us . . .'

The old man's voice, deprived of its usual irony, faltered and seemed almost as weary as he looked.

'Nuria loved you very much, Isaac. Don't doubt that for an instant. And I know she also felt loved by you,' I said.

Old Isaac shook his head again. He smiled, but his silent tears did not stop falling. 'Perhaps she loved me, in her own way, as I loved her, in mine. But we didn't know one another. Perhaps because I never allowed her to know me, or I never took any steps towards getting to know her. We spent our lives like two strangers who see each other every single day and greet one another out of politeness. And I think she probably died without forgiving me.'

'Isaac, I can assure you—'

'Daniel, you're young and you try hard, but even though

367

I've had a bit to drink and I don't know what I'm saying, you still haven't learned to lie enough to fool an old man whose heart has been broken by misfortune.'

I looked down.

'The police say that the man who killed her is a friend of yours,' Isaac ventured.

'The police are lying.'

Isaac assented. 'I know.'

'I can assure you—'

'There's no need, Daniel. I know you're telling the truth,' said Isaac, pulling an envelope from his coat pocket.

'The afternoon before she died, Nuria came to see me, as she used to do years ago. I remember we used to go and eat in a café in Calle Guardia, where I would take her when she was a child. We always talked about books, about old books. She would sometimes tell me things about her work, trifles, the sort of things you tell a stranger on a bus. . . . Once she told me she was sorry she'd been a disappointment to me. I asked her where she'd got that ridiculous idea. "From your eyes, Father, from your eyes," she said. Not once did it occur to me that perhaps I'd been an even greater disappointment to her. Sometimes we think people are like lottery tickets, that they're there to make our most absurd dreams come true.'

'Isaac, with all due respect, you've been drinking like a fish, and you don't know what you're saying.'

'Wine turns the wise man into a fool and the fool into a wise man. I know enough to understand that my own daughter never trusted me. She trusted you more, Daniel, and she'd only met you a couple of times.'

'I can assure you you're wrong.'

'The last afternoon we saw each other, she brought me this envelope. She was restless, worried about something that she didn't want to talk about. She asked me to keep the envelope and, should anything happen to her, to give it to you.'

'Should anything happen?'

'Those were her words. She looked so distressed that I suggested we go together to the police, that, whatever the problem, we'd find a solution. Then she said that the police station was the last place she could go to for help. I begged her to let me know what was going on, but she said she had to leave and made me promise that I'd give you this envelope if she didn't come back for it within a couple of days. She asked me not to open it.'

Isaac handed me the envelope. It was open. 'I lied to her, as usual,' he said.

I examined the envelope. It contained a wad of handwritten sheets of paper. 'Have you read them?' I asked.

The old man nodded slowly.

'What do they say?'

The old man looked up. His lips were trembling. He seemed to have aged a hundred years since the last time I'd seen him.

'It's the story you were looking for, Daniel. The story of a woman I never knew, even though she bore my name and my blood. Now it belongs to you.'

I put the envelope into my coat pocket.

'I'm going to ask you to leave me alone here, with her, if you don't mind. A while ago, as I was reading those pages, it seemed to me that I could almost see her again. However hard I try, I can only remember her the way she was as a little girl. She was very quiet then, you know. She looked at everything pensively, and never laughed. What she liked best were stories, and I don't think any child has ever learned to read so young. She used to say she wanted to be an author and write encyclopaedias and treatises on history and philosophy. Her mother said it was all my fault. She said that Nuria adored me and because she thought her father loved only books, she wanted to write books to make her father love her.'

'Isaac, I don't think it's a good idea for you to be on your own tonight. Why don't you come home with me? Spend the night with us, and that way you can keep my father company.'

Isaac shook his head again. 'I have things to do, Daniel. You go home and read those pages. They belong to you.'

The old man looked away, and I took a few steps towards the door. I was in the doorway when Isaac's voice called to me, barely a whisper.

'Daniel?'

'Yes?'

'Take great care.'

When I went out into the street, it seemed as if darkness were creeping along the pavement, pursuing me. I quickened my pace and didn't slow down until I reached the apartment in Calle Santa Ana. When I got home, I found my father in his armchair with an open book on his lap. It was a photograph album. On seeing me, he sat up with an expression of great relief.

'I was beginning to get worried,' he said, 'How was the funeral?'

I shrugged, and my father nodded gravely.

'I've some dinner ready for you. If you like, I could warm it up and—'

'Thanks, but I'm not hungry. I had a bite to eat earlier.'

He fixed his gaze on me and nodded again. He turned to remove the plates he'd placed on the table. It was then, without quite knowing why, that I went up to him and hugged him. And my father, surprised, hugged me back.

'Daniel, are you all right?'

I held my father tightly in my arms.

'I love you,' I murmured.

The cathedral bells were ringing when I began to read Nuria Monfort's manuscript. Her small, neat writing reminded me of her impeccable desk. Perhaps she had been trying to find in these words the peace and safety that life had not granted her.

# NURIA MONFORT:
## REMEMBRANCE OF THE LOST
### 1933–1955

# 1

There are no second chances in life, except to feel remorse. Julián Carax and I met in the autumn of 1933. At that time I was working for the publisher Josep Cabestany, who had discovered him in 1927 in the course of one of his 'book-scouting' trips to Paris. Julián earned his living playing piano at a hostess bar in the afternoons, and at night he wrote. The owner of the establishment, one Irene Marceau, knew most of the Paris publishers, and, thanks to her entreaties, favours, or threats of disclosure, Julián Carax had managed to get a number of novels published, though with disastrous commercial results. Cabestany acquired the exclusive rights to publish Carax's works in Spain and Latin America for a song, which price included the translation of the French originals into Spanish by the author himself. Cabestany hoped to sell around three thousand copies per novel, but the first two titles he brought out in Spain turned out to be a total flop, with barely a hundred copies of each sold. Despite these dismal results, every two years we received a new manuscript from Julián, which Cabestany accepted without any objections, saying that he'd signed an agreement with the author, that profit wasn't everything, and that good literature had to be supported no matter what.

One day I was intrigued enough to ask him why he continued to publish Julián Carax's novels when they were making such a loss. In answer to my question, Cabestany ceremoniously walked over to his bookshelf, took down one of Julián's books, and invited me to read it. I did. Two weeks later I'd read them all. This time my question was, how could we possibly sell so few copies of those novels?

'I don't know, dear,' replied Cabestany. 'But we'll keep on trying.'

Such a noble and admirable gesture didn't quite fit the picture I had formed of Señor Cabestany. Perhaps I had underestimated him. I found the figure of Julián Carax increasingly intriguing, as everything related to him seemed to be shrouded in mystery. At least twice a month, someone would call asking for his address. I soon realized that it was always the same person, using a different name each time. But I would tell him simply what could be read on the back cover of Julián's novels: that he lived in Paris. After a time, the man stopped calling. Just in case, I deleted Carax's address from the company files. I was the only one who wrote to him, and I knew the address by heart.

Months later I chanced upon some bills sent by the printers to Señor Cabestany. Glancing through them, I noticed that the expense of our editions of Julián Carax's books was defrayed, in its entirety, by someone outside our firm whose name I had never heard before: Miquel Moliner. Moreover, the cost of printing and distributing these books was substantially lower than the sum of money invoiced to Señor Moliner. The numbers didn't lie: the publishing firm was making money by printing books that went straight to a warehouse. I didn't have the courage to question Cabestany's financial irregularities. I was afraid of losing my job. What I did do was take down the address to which we sent Miquel Moliner's invoices – a mansion on Calle Puertaferrissa. I kept that address for months before I plucked up the courage to visit him. Finally my conscience got the better of me, and I turned up at his house to tell him that Señor Cabestany was swindling him. He smiled and told me he already knew.

'We all do what we're best at.'

I asked him whether he was the person who had phoned so often asking for Carax's address. He said he wasn't, and told me with a worried look that I should never give that address to anyone. Ever.

Miquel Moliner was a bit of a mystery. He lived on his own in a cavernous crumbling mansion that was part of his inheritance from his father, an industrialist who had grown rich through arms manufacture and, it was said, warmongering. Far from living a life of luxury, Miquel led an almost monastic existence, dedicated to squandering his father's money, which he considered to be stained with blood, on the restoration of museums, cathedrals, schools, libraries, and hospitals, and on ensuring that the works of his childhood friend, Julián Carax, were published in his native city.

'I have more money than I need, but not enough friends like Julián,' was his only explanation.

He hardly kept in touch with his siblings or the rest of the family, whom he referred to as strangers. He hadn't married and seldom left the grounds of his mansion, of which he occupied only the top floor. There he had set up his office, where he worked feverishly writing articles and columns for various newspapers and magazines in Madrid and Barcelona, translating technical texts from German and French, copy-editing encyclopaedias and school textbooks. Miquel Moliner suffered from that affliction of people who feel guilty when they're not working; although he respected and even envied the leisure others enjoyed, he fled from it. Far from gloating about his manic work ethic, he would joke about his obsessive activity and dismiss it as a minor form of cowardice.

'While you're working, you don't have to look life in the eye.'

Almost without realizing it, we became good friends. We both had a lot in common, probably too much. Miquel liked to talk to me about books, about his beloved Dr Freud, about music, but above all about his old friend Julián. We saw each other almost every week. Miquel would tell me stories about the days when Julián was at San Gabriel's. He kept a collection of old photographs and stories written by a teenage Julián. Miquel adored Julián, and, through his words and his memories, I came to know him, or at least to create an image of him in his absence. A year after we had met, Miquel confessed that he'd fallen in love with me. I did not wish to hurt him, but neither did I want to deceive him. It was impossible to deceive Miquel. I told him I was extremely fond of him, that he'd become my best friend, but I wasn't in love with him. Miquel told me he already knew.

'You're in love with Julián, but you don't yet know it.'

In August 1933, Julián wrote to inform me that he'd almost finished the manuscript of another novel, called *The Cathedral Thief.* Cabestany had some contracts with Gallimard that were due for renewal in September. He'd been paralysed for several weeks with a vicious attack of gout and, as a reward for my dedication, he decided that I should travel to France in his place to negotiate the new contracts. At the same time, I could visit Julián Carax and collect his new opus. I wrote to Julián telling him of my visit, which was planned for mid-September, and asking him whether he could recommend a reliable, inexpensive hotel. Julián replied saying that I could stay at his place, a modest apartment in the Saint-Germain quarter, and keep the hotel money for other expenses. The day before I left, I went to see Miquel to ask him whether he had any message for Julián. For a long while he seemed to hesitate, and then he said he didn't.

The first time I saw Julián in person was at the Gare d'Austerlitz. Autumn had sneaked up early in Paris, and the station vault was thick with fog. I waited on the platform while the other passengers made their way towards the exit. Soon I was left alone. Then I saw a man wearing a black coat, standing at the entrance to the platform, watching me through the smoke from his cigarette. During the journey I had often wondered how I would recognize Julián. The photographs I'd seen of him in Miquel Moliner's collection were at least thirteen or fourteen years old. I looked up and down the platform. There was nobody there except that figure and me. I noticed that the man was looking at me with some curiosity: perhaps he, too, was waiting for someone. It couldn't be him. According to my calculations, Julián would be thirty-three, and that man seemed older. His hair was grey, and he looked sad or tired. Too pale and too thin, or maybe it was just the fog and the wearying journey, or that the only pictures in my mind were of an adolescent Julián. Tentatively, I went up to the stranger and looked him straight in the eye.

'Julián?'

The stranger smiled and nodded. Julián Carax possessed the most charming smile in the world. It was all that was left of him.

Julián lived in an attic in Saint-Germain. The apartment only had two rooms: a living room with a minute kitchen and a tiny balcony from which you could see the towers of Notre Dame looming out of a jungle of rooftops and mist, and a bedroom with no windows and a single bed. The bathroom was at the end of a corridor on the floor below, and he shared it with the rest of his neighbours. The whole of the apartment was smaller than Cabestany's office. Julián had cleaned it up and got everything ready to welcome me with simple modesty. I pretended to be delighted with the apartment, which still smelled of disinfectant and furniture wax, applied by Julián with more determination than skill. The sheets on the bed looked brand new and appeared to have a pattern of dragons and castles. Children's sheets. Julián excused himself: he'd bought them at a very reduced price, but they were top quality. The ones with no pattern were twice the price, he explained, and they were boring.

In the sitting room, an old wooden desk faced the view of the cathedral towers. On it stood the Underwood typewriter that Julián had bought with Cabestany's advance and two piles of writing paper, one blank and the other written on both sides. Julián shared the attic apartment with a huge white cat he called Kurtz. The animal watched me suspiciously as he lay at his master's feet, licking his paws. I counted two chairs, a coatrack, and little else. The rest were all books. Books lined the walls from floor to ceiling, in double rows. Seeing me inspect the place, Julián sighed.

'There's a hotel two blocks away. Clean, affordable, and respectable. I took the liberty of making a reservation.'

I thought about it but was afraid of offending him.

'I'll be fine here, so long as it's not a bother for you, or for Kurtz.'

Kurtz and Julián exchanged glances. Julián shook his head, and the cat imitated him. I hadn't noticed how alike they looked. Julián insisted on letting me have his bedroom. He hardly slept, he explained, and would set himself up in the sitting room on a folding bed, lent to him by his neighbour, Monsieur Darcieu – an old conjuror who read young ladies' palms in exchange for a kiss. That first night I slept right through, exhausted after the journey. I woke up at dawn and discovered that Julián had gone out. Kurtz was asleep on top of his master's typewriter. He snored like a mastiff. I went over to the desk and saw the manuscript of the new novel that I had come to collect.

### The Cathedral Thief

On the first page, as in all Julián's other novels, was the handwritten dedication:

*For P*

I was tempted to start reading. I was about to pick up the second page when I noticed that Kurtz was looking at me out of the corner of his eye. I shook my head the way I'd seen Julián do. The cat, in turn, shook his head, and I put the pages back in their place. After a while Julián appeared, bringing with him freshly baked bread, a Thermos of coffee and some cheese. We had breakfast by the balcony. Julián spoke incessantly but avoided my eyes. In the light of dawn, he seemed like an aged child. He had shaved and put on what I imagined must be his only decent outfit, a cream-coloured cotton suit that looked worn but elegant. I listened to him as he talked about the mysteries of Notre Dame; about a ghostly barge that was said to cleave the waters of the Seine at night, gathering up the souls of desperate lovers who had ended their lives by jumping into the frozen waters. I listened to a thousand and one magical tales he invented as he went along just to keep me from asking him any questions. I watched him silently, nodding, searching in him for the man who had written the books I knew almost by heart, the boy whom Miquel Moliner had described to me so often.

'How many days are you going to be in Paris?' he asked.

My business with Gallimard would take me about two or three days, I said. My first meeting was that afternoon. I told him I'd thought of taking a couple of days off to get to know the city before returning to Barcelona.

'Paris requires more than two days,' said Julián. 'It won't listen to reason.'

'I don't have any more time, Julián. Señor Cabestany is a generous employer, but everything has a limit.'

'Cabestany is a pirate, but even he knows that you can't see Paris in two days, or in two months, or even in two years.'

'I can't spend two years in Paris, Julián.'

He looked at me for a long while, without speaking, and then he smiled. 'Why not? Is there someone waiting for you?'

The dealings with Gallimard and my courtesy calls to various publishers with whom Cabestany did business took up three whole days, just as I had foreseen. Julián had assigned me a guide and protector, a young boy called Hervé who was barely thirteen and knew the city intimately. Hervé would accompany me from door to door, making sure I knew which cafés to stop at for a bite, which streets to avoid, which sights to take in. He would wait for me for hours at the door of the publishers' offices without losing his smile or accepting any tips. Hervé spoke an amusing broken Spanish, which he mixed with overtones of Italian and Portuguese.

'Signore Carax, he already pay, with tuoda generosidade for meus serviçios. . . .'

From what I gathered, Hervé was the orphan of one of the ladies at Irene Marceau's establishment, in whose attic he lived. Julián had taught him to read, write, and play the piano. On Sundays he would take him to the theatre or a concert. Hervé idolized Julián and seemed prepared to do anything for him, even guide me to the end of the world if necessary. On our third day together, he asked me whether I was Signore Carax's girlfriend. I said I wasn't, that I was only a friend on a visit. He seemed disappointed.

Julián spent most nights awake, sitting at his desk with Kurtz on his lap, going over pages of his work or simply staring at the cathedral towers silhouetted in the distance. One night, when I couldn't sleep either because of the noise of the rain pattering on the roof, I went into the sitting room. We looked at one another without saying a word, and Julián offered me a cigarette. For a long time we stared silently at the rain. Later, when the rain stopped, I asked him who P was.

'Penélope,' he answered.

I asked him to talk to me about her, about those fourteen years of exile in Paris. In a whisper, in the half-light, Julián told me Penélope was the only woman he had ever loved.

One night, in the winter of 1921, Irene Marceau had found Julián wandering in the Paris streets, unable to remember his name and coughing up blood. All he had on him were a few coins and some folded sheets of paper with writing on them. Irene read them and thought she'd come across some famous author who had drunk too much, and that perhaps a generous publisher would reward her when he recovered consciousness. That, at least, was her version, but Julián knew she'd saved him out of compassion. He spent six months recovering in an attic room in Irene's brothel. The doctors warned Irene that if that man poisoned himself again, they would not be held responsible. He had ruined his stomach and his liver and was going to have to spend the rest of his days eating only milk, cottage cheese, and fresh bread. When Julián was able to speak again, Irene asked him who he was.

'Nobody,' answered Julián.

'Well, nobody is living here at my expense. What can you do?'

Julian said he could play the piano.

'Prove it.'

Julián sat at the drawing-room piano and, facing a rapt audience of fifteen-year-old prostitutes in their underwear, he played a Chopin nocturne. They all clapped except for Irene, who told him that what she had just heard was music for the dead and they were in the business of the living. Julián played her a ragtime tune and a couple of pieces by Offenbach.

'That's better. Let's keep it upbeat.'

His new job earned him a living, a roof, and two hot meals a day.

He survived in Paris thanks to Irene Marceau's charity, and she was the only person who encouraged him to keep on writing. Her favourite books were romantic novels and biographies of saints and martyrs, which intrigued her enormously. In her opinion Julián's problem was that his heart was poisoned; that was why he could only write those stories full of horror and darkness. But, despite her objections, it was thanks to Irene that Julián found a publisher for his first novels. She was the one who had provided him with the attic in which he hid from the world; the one who dressed him and took him out to get some sun and fresh air, who bought him books and made him go to mass with her on Sundays, followed by a stroll through the Tuileries. Irene Marceau kept him alive without asking for anything in return except his friendship and the promise that he would continue writing. In time she would allow him, occasionally, to take one of her girls up to the attic, even if they were only going to sleep hugging each other. Irene joked that the girls were almost as lonely as he was, and all they wanted was some affection.

'My neighbour, Monsieur Darcieu, thinks I'm the luckiest man in the universe,' he told me.

I asked him why he had never returned to Barcelona in search of Penélope. He fell into a long, deep silence, and when I looked at his face in the dark, I saw it was lined with tears. Without quite knowing what I was doing, I knelt down next to him and hugged him. We remained like that, embracing, until dawn caught us by surprise. I no longer know who kissed whom first, or whether it matters. I know I found his lips and let him caress me without realizing that I, too, was crying and didn't know why. That dawn, and all the ones that followed in the two weeks I spent with Julián, we made love to one another on the floor, never saying a word. Later, sitting in a café or strolling through the streets, I would look into his eyes and know, without any need to question him, that he still loved Penélope. I remember that during those days I learned to hate that seventeen-year-old girl (for Penélope was always seventeen to me) whom I had never met and who now haunted my dreams. I invented excuses for cabling Cabestany to prolong my stay. I no longer cared whether I lost my job or the grey existence I had left behind in Barcelona. I have often asked myself whether my life was so empty when I arrived in Paris that I fell into Julián's arms – like Irene Marceau's girls, who, despite themselves, craved for affection. All I know is that those two weeks I spent with Julián were the only time in my life when I felt, for once, that I was myself; when I understood with the hopeless clarity of what cannot be explained that I would never be able to love another man the way I loved Julián, even if I spent the rest of my days trying.

One day Julián fell asleep in my arms, exhausted. The

previous afternoon, as we passed by a pawnshop, he had stopped to show me a fountain pen that had been on display there for years. According to the pawnbroker, it had once belonged to Victor Hugo. Julián had never owned even a fraction of the means to buy that pen, but he would stop and look at it every day. I dressed quietly and went down to the pawnshop. The pen cost a fortune, which I didn't have, but the pawnbroker said that he'd accept a cheque in pesetas on any Spanish bank with a branch in Paris. Before she died, my mother had promised me she would save up to buy me a wedding dress. Victor Hugo's pen took care of that, veil and all, and although I knew it was madness, I have never spent any sum of money with more satisfaction. When I left the shop with the fabulous case, I noticed that a woman was following me. She was very elegant, with silvery hair and the bluest eyes I have ever seen. She came up to me and introduced herself. She was Irene Marceau, Julián's patron. Hervé, my guide, had spoken to her about me. She only wanted to meet me and ask me whether I was the woman Julián had been waiting for all those years. I didn't have to reply. Irene nodded in sympathy and kissed my cheek. I watched her walking away down the street, and at that moment I understood that Julián would never be mine. I went back to the attic with the pencase hidden in my bag. Julián was awake and waiting for me. He undressed me without saying anything, and we made love for the last time. When he asked me why I was crying, I told him they were tears of joy. Later, when Julián went down to buy some food, I packed my bags and placed the case with the pen on his typewriter. I put the manuscript of the novel in my suitcase and left before Julián returned. On the landing I came upon Monsieur Darcieu, the old conjuror who read the palms of young ladies in exchange for a kiss. He took my left hand and gazed at me sadly.

'*Vous avez du poison au coeur, mademoiselle.*'

When I tried to pay him his fee, he shook his head gently, and instead it was he who kissed my hand.

I got to the Gare d'Austerlitz just in time to catch the twelve o'clock train to Barcelona. The ticket inspector who sold me the ticket asked me whether I was feeling all right. I nodded and shut myself up in the compartment. The train was already leaving when I looked out the window and caught a glimpse of Julián's silhouette on the platform, in the same place I'd seen him for the first time. I closed my eyes and didn't open them again until we had lost sight of the station and that bewitching city to which I could never return. I arrived in Barcelona the following morning, as day was breaking. It was my twenty-fourth birthday, and I knew that the best part of my life was already behind me.

## 2

After I returned to Barcelona, I let some time pass before visiting Miquel Moliner again. I needed to get Julián out of my head, and I realized that if Miquel were to ask me about him, I wouldn't know what to say. When we did meet again, I didn't need to tell him anything. Miquel just looked me in the eyes and knew. He seemed to me thinner than before my trip to Paris; his face had an almost unhealthy pallor, which I attributed to the enormous workload with which he punished himself. He admitted that he was going through financial difficulties. He had spent almost all the money from his inheritance on his philanthropic causes, and now his brothers' lawyers were trying to evict him from the home, claiming that a clause in old Moliner's will specified that he could live there only providing he kept it in good condition and could prove he had the financial means for the upkeep of the property. Otherwise the

Puertaferrissa mansion would pass into the custody of his other brothers.

'Even before dying, my father sensed that I was going to spend his money on all the things he most detested in life, down to the last céntimo.'

Miquel's income as a newspaper columnist and translator was far from enough to maintain that sort of residence.

'Making money isn't hard in itself,' he complained. 'What's hard is to earn it doing something worth devoting your life to.'

I suspected that he was beginning to drink in secret. Sometimes his hands shook. Every Sunday I went over to see him and made him come out with me and get away from his desk and his encyclopaedias. I knew it hurt him to see me. He acted as if he didn't remember that he'd offered to marry me and I'd refused him, but at times I'd catch him gazing at me with a look of mingled yearning and defeat. My sole excuse for submitting him to such cruelty was purely selfish: only Miquel knew the truth about Julián and Penélope Aldaya.

During those months I spent away from Julián, Penélope Aldaya became a spectre who stole my sleep and invaded my thoughts. I could still remember the expression of disappointment on Irene Marceau's face when she realized I was not the woman Julián had been waiting for. Penélope Aldaya, treacherously absent, was too powerful an enemy for me. She was invisible, so I imagined her as perfect. Next to her I was unworthy, vulgar, all too real. I had never thought it possible to hate someone so much and so despite myself – someone I didn't even know, and had never seen in my life. I suppose I thought that if I met her face to face, if I could prove to myself that she was flesh and blood, her spell would break and Julián would be free again. And I with him. I wanted to believe that it was only a matter of time and patience. Sooner or later Miquel would tell me the truth. And the truth would liberate me.

One day, as we strolled through the cathedral cloister,

Miquel once again hinted at his interest in me. I looked at him and saw a lonely man, devoid of hope. I knew what I was doing when I took him home and let myself be seduced by him. I knew I was deceiving him and that he knew, too, but had nothing else in the world. That is how we became lovers, out of desperation. I saw in his eyes what I would have wanted to see in Julián's. I felt that by giving myself to him I was taking revenge on Julián and Penélope and on everything that had been denied to me. Miquel, who was ill with desire and loneliness, knew that our love was a farce, but even so he couldn't let me go. Every day he drank more heavily and often could hardly make love to me. He would then joke bitterly that, after all, we'd turned into the perfect married couple in record time. We were hurting one another through spite and cowardice. One night, almost a year after I had returned from Paris, I asked him to tell me the truth about Penélope. Miquel had been drinking, and he became violent, as I'd never seen him before. In his rage he insulted me and accused me of never having loved him, of being a vulgar whore. He tore my clothes off me, shredding them in the process, and when he tried to force himself on me, I lay down, offering my body without resistance, crying quietly to myself. Miquel broke down and begged me to forgive him. How I wished I were able to love him and not Julián, to be able to choose to remain by his side. But I couldn't. We embraced in the dark, and I asked his forgiveness for all the pain I had caused him. He then told me that if it mattered so much to me, he would tell me the truth about Penélope Aldaya. It was another one of my mistakes.

That Sunday in 1919, when Miquel Moliner went to the station to give his friend Julián his ticket to Paris and see him off, he already knew that Penélope would not be coming to the rendezvous. Two days earlier, when Don Ricardo Aldaya returned from Madrid, his wife had confessed that she'd surprised Julián and their daughter Penélope in the governess's room. Jorge Aldaya had revealed all this to Miquel the day before, making him swear he would never tell anyone. Jorge explained how, when he was given the news, Don Ricardo exploded with anger and rushed up to Penélope's room, shouting like a madman. When she heard her father's cries, Penélope locked her door and wept with terror. Don Ricardo kicked in the door and found his daughter on her knees, trembling and begging for mercy. Don Ricardo then slapped her in the face so hard that she fell down. Not even Jorge was able to repeat the words Don Ricardo hurled at her in his fury. All the members of the family and the servants waited downstairs, terrified, not knowing what to do. Jorge hid in his room, in the dark, but even there he could hear Don Ricardo's shouts. Jacinta was dismissed that same day. Don Ricardo didn't even deign to see her. He ordered the servants to throw her out of the house and threatened them with a similar fate if any of them had any contact with her again.

When Don Ricardo went down to the library, it was already midnight. He'd left Penélope locked up in what had been Jacinta's bedroom and strictly forbade anyone, whether members of his staff or family, to go up to see her. From his room Jorge could hear his parents talking on the ground floor. The doctor arrived in the early hours. Señora Aldaya led him to the room where they kept Penélope under lock and key and waited by the door while the doctor examined her. When he came out, the doctor only nodded and collected his fee. Jorge heard Don Ricardo telling him that if he told anyone about what he'd seen there, he would personally ensure that his reputation was ruined and he would never be able to practise medicine again. Even Jorge knew what that meant.

Jorge admitted that he was very worried about Penélope and Julián. He had never seen his father so beside himself with rage. Even taking into account the offence committed by the lovers, he could not understand the extent of his anger. There must be something else, he said, something else. Don Ricardo had already ordered San Gabriel's school to expel Julián and had got in touch with the boy's father, the hatter, about sending him off to the army immediately. When Miquel heard all this, he decided he couldn't tell Julián the truth. If he disclosed to Julián that Don Ricardo was keeping Penélope locked up, and that she might be carrying his child, Julián would never take that train to Paris. He knew that if his friend remained in Barcelona, that would be the end of him. So he decided to deceive him and let him go to Paris without knowing what had happened; he would let him think that Penélope was going to join him sooner or later. When he said goodbye to Julián that day in the Estación de Francia, even Miquel wanted to believe that not all was lost.

Some days later, when it was discovered that Julián had disappeared, all hell broke loose. Don Ricardo Aldaya was foaming at the mouth. He set half the police department in pursuit of the fugitive, but without success. He then accused the hatter of having sabotaged the plan they had agreed on and threatened to ruin him completely. The hatter, who couldn't understand what was going on, in turn accused his wife, Sophie, of having plotted the escape of that despicable son and threatened to throw her out of their home. It didn't occur to anyone that it was Miquel Moliner who had planned the whole thing – to anyone, that is, except Jorge Aldaya, who went to see him a fortnight later. He no longer exuded the fear and anxiety that had gripped him earlier. This was a different Jorge Aldaya, an adult robbed of all innocence. Whatever the secret that hid behind Don Ricardo's anger was, Jorge had found out. The reason for his visit was clear: he knew it was Miquel who had helped Julián escape. He told him their friendship was over, that he didn't ever want to see him again, and he threatened to kill him if he told anyone what he had revealed to him two weeks before.

A few weeks later, Miquel received a letter, with a false sender's name, posted by Julián in Paris. In it he gave him his address, told him he was well and missed him, and inquired after his mother and Penélope. He included a letter addressed to Penélope, which Miquel was to post from Barcelona, the first of many that Penélope would never read. Miquel prudently allowed a few months to go by. He wrote to Julián once a week, mentioning only what he felt was suitable, which was almost nothing. Julián, in turn, spoke to him about Paris, about how difficult everything was turning out to be, how lonely and desperate he felt. Miquel sent him money, books, and his friendship. In every letter Julián would include another one for Penélope. Miquel mailed them from different post offices, even though he knew it was useless. In his letters Julián never stopped asking after Penélope but Miquel couldn't tell him anything. He knew from Jacinta that Penélope had not left the house on Avenida del Tibidabo since her father had locked her in the room on the third floor.

One night Jorge Aldaya waylaid Miquel in the dark, two blocks from his home. 'Have you come to kill me then?' asked Miquel. Jorge said that he had come to do him and his friend Julián a favour. He handed him a letter and advised him to make sure it reached Julián, wherever he was hiding. 'For everyone's sake,' he declared portentously. The envelope contained a sheet of paper handwritten by Penélope Aldaya.

Dear Julián;

I'm writing to notify you of my forthcoming marriage and to entreat you not to write to me anymore, to forget me and rebuild your life. I don't bear you any grudge, but I wouldn't be honest if I didn't confess to you that I have never loved you and never will be able to love you. I wish you the best, wherever you may be.

Penélope

Miquel read and reread the letter a thousand times. The

handwriting was unmistakable, but he didn't believe for a moment that Penélope had written that letter willingly: '. . . wherever you may be.' Penélope knew perfectly well where Julián was: in Paris, waiting for her. If she was pretending not to know his whereabouts, Miquel reflected, it was to protect him. But for that same reason, Miquel couldn't understand what could have induced her to write those words. What further threats could Don Ricardo Aldaya bring down on her, on top of keeping her locked up for months in that room like a prisoner? More than anyone, Penélope knew that her letter would be like a poisoned dagger to Julián's heart: a young boy of nineteen, lost in a distant and hostile city, abandoned by everyone, surviving only on his false hopes of seeing her again. What did she want to protect him from by pushing him from her in that way? After much consideration, Miquel decided not to send the letter. Not without knowing the reason for it first. Without a good reason, it would not be his hand that plunged that dagger into his friend's soul.

Some days later he found out that Don Ricardo Aldaya, tired of seeing Jacinta waiting like a sentry at the doors of his house, begging for news of Penélope, had used his contacts to get her admitted into the Horta lunatic asylum. When Miquel Moliner tried to see her, he was denied access. Jacinta Coronado was to spend the first three months in solitary confinement. After three months of silence and darkness, he was told by one of the doctors – a cheerful young individual – the patient's submission was guaranteed. Following a hunch, Miquel decided to pay a visit to the *pensión* where Jacinta had been staying after her dismissal. When he identified himself, the landlady remembered that Jacinta had left a note for him and still owed her three weeks' rent. He paid the debt, even though he doubted its existence, and took the note. In it the governess explained how she had been informed that Laura, one of the Aldayas' servants, had been dismissed when it was discovered that she had secretly posted a letter from

Penélope to Julián. Miquel deduced that the only address to which Penélope, from her captivity, could have sent the letter was Julián's parents' apartment in Ronda de San Antonio, hoping that they, in turn, would make sure it reached Julián in Paris.

Miquel decided to visit Sophie Carax to recover the letter and forward it to Julián. When he arrived at the Fortunys' home, Miquel was in for an unpleasant surprise: Sophie Carax no longer lived there. She had abandoned her husband a few days earlier – or that, at least, was the rumour that was doing the rounds of the neighbours. Miquel then tried to speak to the hatter, who spent his days shut away in his shop, consumed by anger and humiliation. Miquel told him that he'd come to collect a letter that must have arrived for his son, Julián, a few days earlier.

'I have no son,' was the only answer he received.

Miquel Moliner went away without knowing that the letter in question had ended up in the hands of the caretaker and that, many years later, you, Daniel, would find it and read the words Penélope had meant for Julián, this time straight from her heart: words that he never received.

As Miquel left the Fortuny hat shop, one of the residents in the block of apartments, who identified herself as Viçenteta, approached him and asked him whether he was looking for Sophie. Miquel said he was and told her he was a friend of Julián's.

Viçenteta informed him that Sophie was staying in a boarding house hidden in a small street behind the post office building, waiting for the departure of the boat that would take her to America. Miquel went to the address, where he found a narrow, miserable staircase almost devoid of light and air. At the top of the dusty spiral of sloping steps, he found Sophie Carax, in a damp, dark, room on the fourth floor. Julián's mother was facing the window, sitting on the edge of a makeshift bed on which two closed suitcases were lying like coffins, containing her twenty-two years in Barcelona.

When she read the letter signed by Penélope that Jorge Aldaya had given Miquel, Sophie shed tears of anger.

'She knows,' she murmured. 'Poor child, she knows. . . .'

'Knows what?' asked Miquel.

'It's my fault,' said Sophie. 'It's all my fault.'

Miquel held her hands, not understanding. Sophie didn't dare meet his eyes.

'Julián and Penélope are brother and sister,' she whispered.

# 3

Years before becoming Antoni Fortuny's slave, Sophie Carax had been a woman who made a living from her talents. She was only nineteen when she arrived in Barcelona in search of a promised job that never materialized. Before dying, her father had obtained the necessary references for her to go into the service of the Benarenses, a prosperous family of merchants from Alsace who had established themselves in Barcelona.

'When I die,' he urged her, 'go to them, and they'll treat you like a daughter.'

The warm welcome she received was part of the problem. Monsieur Benarens indeed received her with open arms – all too open, in the opinion of Madame Benarens. Madame Benarens gave Sophie one hundred pesetas and turned her out of the house, but not without showing some pity towards her and her bad fortune.

'You have your whole life ahead of you; but the only thing I have is this miserable, lewd husband.'

A music school in Calle Diputación agreed to give Sophie work as a private music and piano tutor. In those days it was considered respectable for girls of well-to-do families to be taught proper social graces with a smattering of music for the drawing room, where the polonaise was considered less dangerous than conversation or questionable literature. That is how Sophie Carax began her visits to palatial mansions, where starched, silent maids would lead her to the music rooms. There the hostile offspring of the industrial aristocracy would be waiting for her, to laugh at her accent, her shyness, or her lowly position – the fact that she could read music didn't alter that. Gradually Sophie learned to concentrate on the tiny number of pupils who rose above the status of perfumed vermin and forget the rest of them.

It was about that time that Sophie met a young hatter (for so he liked to be referred to, with professional pride) called Antoni Fortuny, who seemed determined to court her, whatever the cost. Antoni Fortuny, for whom Sophie felt a warm friendship and nothing else, did not take long to propose to her, an offer Sophie refused – and kept refusing, a dozen times a month. Every time they parted, Sophie hoped she wouldn't see him again, because she didn't want to hurt him. The hatter, brushing aside her refusals, stayed on the offensive, inviting her to dances, to take a stroll, or have a hot chocolate with sponge fingers on Calle Canuda. Being all alone in Barcelona, Sophie found it difficult to resist his enthusiasm, his company, and his devotion. She only had to look at Antoni Fortuny to know that she would never be able to love him. Not the way she dreamed she would love somebody one day. But she also found it hard to cast aside the image of herself that she saw reflected in the hatter's besotted eyes. Only in them did she see the Sophie she would have wished to be.

And so, either through need or through weakness, Sophie continued to entertain the hatter's advances, in the belief that one day he would meet a girl who would return his affection and his life would take a more rewarding course. In the meantime, being desired and appreciated was enough to alleviate the loneliness and the longing she felt for everything she had left behind. She saw Antoni on Sundays, after mass. The rest of the week was taken up by her music lessons. Her favourite pupil was a highly talented girl called Ana Valls, the daughter of a prosperous manufacturer of textile machinery who had built up his fortune from nothing, by dint of great effort and sacrifices, although mostly other people's. Ana expressed her desire to become a great composer and would make Sophie listen to small pieces she had composed, imitating motifs by Grieg and Schumann, and not without skill. Although Señor Valls was convinced that women were incapable of creating anything but knitted garments or crocheted bedspreads, he approved of his daughter becoming competent on the keyboard, for he had plans of marrying her off to some heir with a good surname. He knew that refined people liked to discover unusual qualities in a marriageable girl, besides submissiveness and the fecundity of youth.

It was in the Valls residence that Sophie met one of Señor Valls's greatest benefactors and financial godfathers: Don Ricardo Aldaya, inheritor of the Aldaya empire, and by then already the great white hope of the Catalan oligarchy of the end of the century. A few months earlier, Don Ricardo Aldaya had married a rich heiress, a dazzling beauty with an unpronounceable name – attributes that wagging tongues held to be true, despite the fact that her newlywed husband seemed to see no beauty in her at all and never bothered to mention her name. It had been a match between families and banks, none of that sentimental nonsense, said Señor Valls, for whom it was very clear that the bed was one thing, and the other the head.

Sophie had only to exchange one look with Don Ricardo Aldaya to know she was doomed. Aldaya had wolfish eyes, hungry and sharp; the eyes of a man who knew where and when to strike. He kissed her hand slowly, caressing her knuckles with his lips. Just as the hatter exuded kindness and warmth, Don Ricardo radiated cruelty and power. His canine smile made it clear that he could read her thoughts and desires and found them laughable. Sophie felt for him the sort of contempt that is awakened in us by the things we subconsciously most desire. She immediately told herself she would not see him again, would stop teaching her favourite pupil if that was what it took to avoid any future encounters with Ricardo Aldaya. Nothing had ever terrified her so much as sensing that animality under her own skin, the prey's instinctive recognition of the predator. It took her only a few seconds to make up a flimsy excuse for leaving the room, to the puzzlement of Señor Valls, the amusement of Aldaya, and the dejection of little Ana, who understood people better than she did music and knew she had irretrievably lost her teacher.

A week later Sophie saw Don Ricardo Aldaya waiting for her at the entrance to the music school in Calle Diputación, smoking and leafing through a newspaper. They exchanged glances, and, without saying a word, he led her to a building two blocks away. It was a new building, still uninhabited. They went up to the first floor. Don Ricardo opened the door and ushered her in. Sophie entered the apartment, a maze of corridors and galleries, bare of any furniture, paintings, lamps, or any other object that might have identified it as a home. Don Ricardo Aldaya shut the door, and they looked at one another.

'I haven't stopped thinking about you all week. Tell me you haven't done the same and I'll let you go, and you won't ever see me again,' said Ricardo.

Sophie shook her head.

Their secret meetings lasted ninety-six days. They met in the afternoons, always in that empty apartment on the corner of Diputación and Rambla de Cataluña. Tuesdays and Thursdays, at three. Their meetings never lasted more than an hour. Sometimes Sophie stayed on alone once Aldaya had left, crying or shaking in a corner of the bedroom. Then, when Sunday came, Sophie looked desperately into the hatter's eyes for traces of the woman who was disappearing, yearning for both devotion and deception. The hatter didn't see the marks on her skin, the cuts and burns that peppered her body. The hatter didn't see the despair in her smile, in her meekness. The hatter didn't see anything. Perhaps for that reason, she accepted his promise of marriage. By then she already suspected that she was carrying Aldaya's child, but was afraid of telling him, almost as much as she was afraid of losing him. Once again it was Aldaya who saw in Sophie what she was incapable of admitting. He gave her five hundred pesetas and an address in Calle Platería and ordered her to get rid of the baby. Sophie refused. Don Ricardo Aldaya slapped her until her ears bled, then threatened to have her killed if she dared mention their meetings to anyone or admit that the child was his. When Sophie told the hatter that some thugs had assaulted her in Plaza del Pino, he believed her. When she told him she wanted to be his wife, he believed her. On the day of her wedding, someone erroneously sent a funeral wreath to the church. Everyone laughed nervously when they saw the florist's mistake. All except Sophie, who knew perfectly well that Don Ricardo Aldaya had not forgotten her on her wedding day.

# 4

Sophie Carax never imagined that years later she would see Ricardo again – a mature man by now, heading up the family empire, and a father of two – nor that he would return to meet the boy he had wished to erase with five hundred pesetas.

'Perhaps it's because I'm growing old,' was his only explanation, 'but I want to get to know this child and give him the opportunities in life that a son of my flesh and blood deserves. He hadn't crossed my mind in all these years, and now, strangely enough, I'm unable to think of anything else.'

Ricardo Aldaya had decided that he couldn't see himself in his firstborn, Jorge. The boy was weak, reserved, and he lacked his father's steadfast spirit. He lacked everything, except the right surname. One day Don Ricardo had woken up in the maid's bed feeling that his body was getting old, that God had removed His blessing. Seized with panic, he ran to look at himself naked in the mirror and felt that the mirror was lying. That man was not Ricardo Aldaya.

He now wanted to find the man who had disappeared. For years he had known about the hatter's son. And he had not forgotten Sophie, in his own way. Don Ricardo Aldaya never forgot anything. The moment had arrived to meet the boy. It was the first time in fifteen years that he had come across someone who wasn't afraid of him, who dared to defy him and even laugh at him. He recognized gallantry in the child, the silent ambition that fools can't see but is there all the same. God had given him back his youth. Sophie, only an echo of the woman he remembered, didn't even have the strength to come between them. The hatter was just a buffoon, a spiteful and resentful peasant whose complicity Aldaya counted on buying. He decided to tear Julián away from that stifling world of mediocrity and poverty and open the doors of his financial paradise to him. He would be educated in San Gabriel's school, would enjoy all the privileges of his class, and would be initiated onto the path his father had chosen for him. Don Ricardo wanted a successor worthy of himself. Jorge would always be cocooned in the privileges of his class, hiding from his mediocrity in creature comforts. Penélope, the beautiful Penélope, was a woman, and therefore a treasure, not a treasurer. Julián, who had the soul of a poet, and therefore the soul of a murderer, fulfilled all the requirements. It was only a question of time. Don Ricardo estimated that within ten years he would have stamped his image on the boy. Never, in all the time Julián spent with the Aldayas as one of the family (as the chosen one, even), did it occur to Don Ricardo that the only thing Julián wanted from him was Penélope. It didn't occur to him for an instant that Julián secretly despised him, that his affection was a sham, only a pretext to be close to Penélope. To possess her completely and utterly. They did resemble one another in that.

When his wife told him she'd discovered Julián and Penélope naked together, his entire world went up in flames. Horror at this treason, the rage of knowing that he had been unspeakably affronted, outwitted at his own game, humiliated and stabbed in the back by the one person he had learned to adore as the image of himself – all these feelings assailed him with such fury that nobody could understand the magnitude of his pain. When the doctor who came to examine Penélope confirmed that the girl had been deflowered and that she was possibly pregnant, Don Ricardo's soul dissolved into the thick, viscous liquid of blind hatred. He saw his own hand in Julián's hand, the hand that had plunged the dagger deep into his heart. He didn't yet know it, but the day he ordered Penélope to be locked up in the third-floor bedroom was the day he began to die. Everything he did from then on was only the last throes of his self-destruction.

In collaboration with the hatter, whom he had so deeply despised, he arranged for Julián's removal from Barcelona and his entry into the army, where Aldaya had given orders that he should meet with an 'accidental' death. He forbade that anyone – doctors, servants, even members of the family, except himself and his wife – should see Penélope during the months when the girl remained imprisoned in that room that smelled of illness and death. By then, Aldaya's partners had secretly withdrawn their support and were manoeuvring behind his back to seize power, using the very fortune that he had made available to them. By then the Aldaya empire was beginning to crumble, at secret board meetings in Madrid, in hushed corridors, in Geneva banks. Julián, as Aldaya should have suspected, had escaped. Deep down he secretly felt proud of the boy, even though he wished him dead. Julián had done what he would have done in his place. Someone else would have to pay for Julián's actions.

Penélope Aldaya gave birth to a stillborn baby boy on 26 September 1919. If a doctor had been able to examine her, he would have said that the baby had already been in danger for some days and must be delivered by Caesarean. If a doctor had been present, perhaps he would have been able to stop the haemorrhaging that took Penélope's life, while she shrieked and scratched at the locked door, on the other side of which her father wept in silence and her mother cowered, staring at her husband. If a doctor had been present, he would have accused Don Ricardo Aldaya of murder, for there was no other word that could describe the scene within that dark, bloodstained cell. But there was nobody there, and when at last they opened the door and found Penélope lying dead in a pool of her own blood, hugging a shining, purple-coloured baby, nobody was capable of uttering a single word. The two bodies were buried in the basement crypt, with no ceremony or witnesses. The sheets and the afterbirth were thrown into the boilers, and the place was sealed with a brick wall.

When Jorge Aldaya, drunk with guilt and shame, told Miquel Moliner what had happened, Miquel decided to send Julián the letter, signed by Penélope, in which she declared that she didn't love him, begged him to forget her, and announced a fictitious wedding. He preferred that Julián should believe the lie and rebuild his life, feeling himself betrayed, than to present him with the truth. When, two years later, Señora Aldaya died, there were those who blamed her death on the curse that lay on the mansion, but her son, Jorge, knew that what had killed her was the fire that raged inside her, Penélope's screams and her desperate banging on that door that hammered incessantly in her head. By then the family had already fallen from grace, and the Aldaya fortune was collapsing like a sand castle, swept away by a combination of greed and revenge. Secretaries and accountants devised the flight to Argentina; the beginning of a new, more modest, business. The important thing was to get away. Away from the spectres that scurried through the corridors of the Aldaya mansion, as they had always done.

They departed one dawn of 1926, travelling under false names on board the ship that would take them across the Atlantic to the port of La Plata. Jorge and his father shared a cabin. Old Aldaya, smelling foul and dying, could barely stand up. The doctors whom he had not permitted to see Penélope feared him too much to tell him the truth, but he knew that death had boarded the ship with them, and that his body, which God had begun to steal from him on the morning he decided to look for his son Julián, was wasting away. Throughout that long crossing, sitting on the deck, shivering under the blankets and facing the ocean's infinite emptiness, he knew that he would never see land. Sometimes, sitting at the stern, he would watch the school of sharks that had been following them since they left Tenerife. He heard one of the officers say that such a sinister escort was normal in transatlantic cruises. The beasts fed on the animal remains that the ship left in its wake. But Don Ricardo thought otherwise. He was convinced that those devils were following him. You're waiting for me, he thought, seeing in them God's true face. It was then he approached his son Jorge, whom he had so often despised and whom he now saw as his last resort, and made him swear he would carry out his dying wish. 'You will find Julián Carax and you'll kill him. Swear that you will.'

One dawn, two days before reaching Buenos Aires, Jorge woke up and saw that his father's berth was empty. He went out to look for him; the deck was deserted, bathed in mist and spray. He found his father's dressing gown, still warm, abandoned on the stern of the ship. The ship's wake disappeared into a cloud of scarlet, a stain on the calm waters, as if the ocean itself were bleeding. It was then he noticed that the sharks had stopped following them. He saw them, in the distance, their dorsal fins flapping as they danced in a circle. During the remainder of the crossing, no passenger sighted the school again.

When Jorge Aldaya disembarked in Buenos Aires and the customs officer asked him whether he was travelling alone, he nodded in assent. He had been travelling alone for a long time.

# 5

*Ten years after disembarking in Buenos Aires, Jorge Aldaya, or the spent force he had become, returned to Barcelona. The misfortunes that had started to eat away at the Aldaya family in the Old World had only grown worse in Argentina. Jorge was left on his own to face the world, a fight for which he had neither his father's strength nor his composure. Jorge had reached Buenos Aires with a numb heart, shot through with remorse. The New World he would later say, by way of apology or epitaph, is an illusion, a land of savage predators, and he'd been educated into the privileges and frivolous refinements of Old Europe – a dead continent held together by inertia. In only a few years, he lost everything, starting with his reputation and ending with the gold watch his father had given him for his first communion. Thanks to the watch, he was able to buy himself a return ticket. The man who came back to Spain was almost a beggar, a bundle of bitterness and failure, poisoned by the memory of what he felt had been snatched from him and the hatred for the person on whom he blamed his ruin: Julián Carax.*

*The promise he had made to his father was still branded on* his mind. As soon as he arrived, he tried to pick up Julián's trail, only to discover that, like him, Carax also appeared to have vanished from Barcelona. It was then, through chance or fate, that he encountered a familiar character from his youth. After a prominent career in reformatories and state prisons, Francisco Javier Fumero had joined the army, attaining the rank of lieutenant. There were many who envisaged him as a future general, but a murky scandal caused his expulsion from the army. Even then his reputation outlasted his rank. He was talked about a great deal, but above all he was feared. Francisco Javier Fumero, that shy, disturbed boy who once gathered dead leaves from the courtyard of San Gabriel's, was now a murderer. It was rumoured that he killed notorious characters for money, and that he dispatched political figures on request. Fumero was said to be death incarnate.

Aldaya and he recognized one another instantly through the haze of the Novedades café. Aldaya was ill, stricken by a strange fever that he blamed on the insects of the South American jungles. 'There, even the mosquitoes are sons of bitches,' he complained. Fumero listened to him with a mixture of fascination and revulsion. He revered mosquitoes and all insects in general. He admired their discipline, their fortitude and organization. There was no laziness in them, no irreverence or racial degeneration. His favourite species were spiders, blessed with that rare science for weaving a trap in which they awaited their prey with infinite patience, knowing that sooner or later the prey would succumb, either through stupidity or negligence. In his opinion society had a lot to learn from insects. Aldaya was a clear case of moral and physical ruin. He had aged noticeably and looked shabby, with no muscle tone. Fumero couldn't bear people with no muscle tone. They nauseated him.

'Javier, I feel dreadful,' Aldaya pleaded. 'Could you help me out for a few days?'

Fumero agreed to take Jorge Aldaya to his home. He lived in a gloomy apartment in the Raval quarter, in Calle Cadena, *in the company of numerous insects stored in jars, and half a dozen books. Fumero detested books as much as he loved insects, but these were no ordinary volumes: they were the novels of Julián Carax published by Cabestany. Two prostitutes lived in the apartment opposite – a mother and daughter who allowed themselves to be pinched and burned with cigars when business was slow, especially at the end of the month. Fumero paid them to take care of Aldaya while he was at work. He had no desire to see him die. Not yet.*

*Francisco Javier Fumero had joined the Crime Squad. There was always work there for the type of person who could confront the most awkward situations, the sort of situations that had to be solved discreetly so that respectable citizens could continue living in blissful ignorance. Words to that effect had been used by Lieutenant Durán, a man given to solemn pronouncements, and under whose command Fumero had joined the police force.*

*'Being a policeman isn't a job, it's a mission,' Durán would proclaim. 'Spain needs more balls and less chatter.'*

*Unfortunately, Lieutenant Durán was soon to die in a lamentable accident during a police raid in the district of La Barceloneta: in the confusion of an encounter with a group of anarchists, he fell through a skylight, and plunged five floors to his death. Everyone agreed that Spain had lost a great man, a national hero with vision for the future, a thinker who did not fear action. Fumero took over his post with pride, knowing that he had done the right thing by pushing him, for Durán was getting too old for the job. Fumero found old men revolting – as he did crippled men, Gypsies, and queers – whether or not they had good muscle tone. Sometimes God made mistakes. It was the duty of every upright citizen to correct these small failings and keep the world looking presentable.*

*In March 1932, a few weeks after their meeting in the Novedades Café, Jorge Aldaya began to feel better and opened his heart to Fumero. He begged forgiveness for the way he had treated him during their school days. With tears in his eyes, he told Fumero the whole story, without omitting anything. Fumero listened silently, nodding, taking it in, all the while wondering whether he should kill Aldaya there and then, or wait. He wondered whether Aldaya would be so weak that the blade would meet only tepid resistance from that stinking flesh, softened by so many years of indolence. He decided to postpone the vivisection. He was intrigued by the story, especially insofar as it concerned Julián Carax.*

*He knew, from the information he obtained at the publishing house, that Carax lived in Paris, but Paris was a very large city, and nobody in Cabestany's company seemed to know the exact address. Nobody except for a woman called Monfort who kept it to herself. Fumero had followed her two or three times on her way out of the office, without her realizing. He had even travelled in a tram at half a yard's distance from her. Women never noticed him, and if they did, they turned their faces the other way, pretending not to have seen him. One night, after following her right up to her front door in Plaza de San Felipe Neri, Fumero went back to his home and masturbated furiously; as he did so, he imagined himself plunging a knife into that woman's body, an inch or so at a time, slowly, methodically, his eyes fixed on hers. Maybe then she would deign to give him Carax's address and treat him with the respect due to a police officer.*

*Julián Carax was the only person whom Fumero had failed to kill once he'd made up his mind. Perhaps because he had been Fumero's first, and it takes time to master your game. When Fumero heard that name again, he smiled in a way his neighbours, the prostitutes, found so frightening: without blinking, and slowly licking his upper lip. He could still remember Carax kissing Penélope Aldaya in the large mansion on Avenida del Tibidabo. His Penélope. His had been a pure love, a true love, like the ones you saw in movies. Fumero was very keen on movies and went to the cinema at least twice a week. It was in a cinema that he had understood that Penélope*

*had been the love of his life. The rest, especially his mother,
had been nothing but tarts. As he listened to the last snippets
of Aldaya's story, he decided that he wasn't going to kill him
after all. In fact, he was pleased that fate had reunited them.
He had a vision, like the ones in the films he so enjoyed:
Aldaya was going to hand him the others on a platter. Sooner
or later they would all end up ensnared in his web.*

# 6

In the winter of 1934, the Moliner brothers finally managed
to evict Miquel from the house on Calle Puertaferrissa,
which is still empty and in a derelict state to this day. All
they wanted was to see him out on the street, shorn of what
little he had left, his books and the freedom and independence that so offended them and filled them with such deep
hatred. He didn't tell me anything or come to me for help. I
only discovered he'd become a virtual beggar when I went
to look for him in what had been his home and found his
brothers' hired legal thugs drawing up an inventory of the
property and selling off the few objects that had belonged to
him. Miquel had already been spending a few nights in a
*pensión* on Calle Canuda, a dismal, damp hovel that looked
and smelled like a brothel. When I saw the tiny room in
which he was confined, like a coffin with no windows and a
prisoner's bunk, I grabbed hold of him and took him home.
He couldn't stop coughing, and he looked emaciated. He
said it was a lingering cold, an old maid's complaint that
would go away when it got bored. Two weeks later he was
worse.

As he always dressed in black, it took me some time to
realize that those stains on his sleeves were bloodstains. I
called a doctor, and after he examined Miquel, he asked me
why I'd waited so long to call him. Miquel had tuberculosis.
Bankrupt and ill, he now lived only on his memories and

regrets. He was the kindest and frailest man I had ever known, my only friend. We got married one cold February morning in a county court. Our honeymoon consisted of taking the bus up to Güell Park and gazing down on Barcelona – a little world of fog – from its sinuous terraces. We didn't tell anyone we'd got married, not Cabestany, or my father, or Miquel's family, who believed him to be dead. Eventually I wrote a letter to Julián, telling him about it, but I never mailed it. Ours was a secret marriage. A few months after the wedding, someone knocked on our door saying his name was Jorge Aldaya. He looked like a shattered man, and his face was covered in sweat despite the biting cold. When he saw Miquel again after more than ten years, Aldaya smiled bitterly and said, 'We're all cursed, Miquel. You, Julián, Fumero, and me.' The alleged reason for the visit was an attempt to make up with his old friend Miquel, who he hoped would now let him know how to get in touch with Julián Carax, because he had a very important message for him from his deceased father, Don Ricardo Aldaya. Miquel said he didn't know where Carax was.

'We lost touch years ago,' he lied. 'The last thing I heard, he was living in Italy.'

Aldaya was expecting such an answer. 'You disappoint me, Miquel. I had hoped that time and misfortune would have made you wiser.'

'Some disappointments honour those who inspire them.'

Shrivelled up and on the verge of collapse, Aldaya laughed.

'Fumero sends you his most heartfelt congratulations on your marriage,' he said on his way to the door.

Those words froze my heart. Miquel didn't wish to speak, but that night, while I held him close and we both pretended to fall asleep, I knew that Aldaya had been right. We were cursed.

A few months went by without any news from either Julián or Aldaya. Miquel was still writing regular pieces for the press in Barcelona and Madrid. He worked without pause, sitting at the typewriter pouring out what he considered to be drivel, to feed commuters on the tram. I kept my job at the publishing house, perhaps because that was where I felt closest to Julián. He had sent me a brief note saying he was working on a new novel, called *The Shadow of the Wind*, which he hoped to finish within a few months. The letter made no mention at all of what had happened in Paris. The tone was colder and more distant than before. But my attempts at hating him were unsuccessful. I began to believe that Julián was not a man, he was an illness.

Miquel had no illusions about my feelings. He offered me his affection and devotion without asking for anything in exchange except my company and perhaps my discretion. No reproach or complaint ever passed his lips. In time I came to feel an immense tenderness for him, beyond the friendship that had brought us together and the compassion that had later doomed us. Miquel opened a savings account in my name, into which he deposited almost all the income he earned from his journalism. He never said no to an article, a review, or a gossip column. He wrote under three different pseudonyms, fourteen or sixteen hours a day. When I asked him why he worked so hard, he just smiled or else he said that if he didn't do anything, he'd be bored. There was never any deceit between us, not even the wordless kind. Miquel knew he would soon die.

'You must promise that if anything happens to me, you'll take that money and get married again, that you'll have children, and that you'll forget about us all, starting with me.'

'And who would I marry, Miquel? Don't talk nonsense.'

Sometimes I'd catch him looking at me with a gentle smile, as if the very sight of my presence were his greatest treasure. Every afternoon he would come to meet me on my way out of the office, his only moment of leisure in the whole day. He feigned strength, but I saw how he stooped when he walked, and how he coughed. He would take me for a snack or to windowshop in Calle Fernando, and then we'd go back home, where he would continue working until well after midnight. I silently blessed every minute we spent together, and every night he would fall asleep embracing me, while I hid the tears caused by the anger I felt at having been incapable of loving that man the way he loved me, incapable of giving him what I had so pointlessly abandoned at Julián's feet. Many a night I swore to myself that I would forget Julián, that I would devote the rest of my life to making that poor man happy and returning to him some small part of what he had given me. I was Julián's lover for two weeks, but I would be Miquel's wife the rest of my life. If some day these pages should reach your hands and you should judge me, as I have judged myself when writing them, looking at my reflection in this mirror of remorse, remember me like this, Daniel.

The manuscript of Julián's last novel arrived towards the end of 1935. I don't know whether it was out of spite or out of fear, but I handed it to the printer without even reading it. Miquel's last savings had financed the edition in advance, months earlier, so Cabestany, who at the time was having health problems, paid little attention. That week the doctor who was attending Miquel came to see me at the office, looking very concerned. He told me that if Miquel didn't slow down and give himself some rest, there was little he could do to help him fight the tuberculosis.

'He should be in the mountains, not in Barcelona breathing in clouds of bleach and charcoal. He's not a cat with nine lives, and I'm not a nanny. Make him listen to reason. He won't pay any attention to me.'

That lunchtime I decided to go home and speak to him. Before I opened the door of the apartment, I heard voices filtering from inside. Miquel was arguing with someone. At first I assumed it was someone from the newspaper, but then I thought I caught Julián's name in the conversation. I heard footsteps approaching the door, and I ran up to hide on the attic landing. From there I was able to catch a glimpse of the visitor.

A man dressed in black, with somewhat nondescript features and thin lips, like an open scar. His eyes were black and expressionless, fish eyes. Before he disappeared down the stairs, he looked up into the darkness. I leaned against the wall, holding my breath. The visitor remained there for a few moments, as if he could smell me, licking his lips with a doglike grin. I waited for his steps to fade away completely before I left my hiding place and went into the apartment. A smell of camphor drifted in the air. Miquel was sitting by the window, his arms hanging limply on either side of the chair. His lips trembled. I asked him who that man was and what he wanted.

'It was Fumero. He came with news of Julián.'

'What does he know about Julián?'

Miquel looked at me, more dispirited than ever. 'Julián is getting married.'

The news left me speechless. I fell into a chair, and Miquel took my hands. He seemed tired and spoke with difficulty. Before I was able to open my mouth, he began to give me a summary of the events Fumero had related to him, and what could be inferred from them. Fumero had made use of his contacts in the Paris police to discover Julián Carax's whereabouts and keep a watch on him. This could have taken place months or even years earlier, Miquel said. What worried him wasn't that Fumero had found Carax – that was just a question of time – but that he should have decided to tell Miquel about it now, together with some bizarre news about an improbable marriage. The wedding, it seemed, was going to take place in the early summer of 1936. All that was known about the bride was her name, which in this case was more than sufficient: Irene Marceau, the owner of the club where Julián had worked as a pianist for years.

'I don't understand,' I murmured. 'Julián is marrying his patron?'

409

'Exactly. This isn't a wedding. It's a contract.'

Irene Marceau was twenty-five or thirty years older than Julián. Miquel suspected she had decided on the marriage so that she could transfer her assets to Julián and secure his future.

'But she already helps him. She always has done.'

'Perhaps she knows she's not going to be around forever,' Miquel suggested.

The echo of those words cut us both to the quick. I knelt down next to him and held him tight, biting my lips because I didn't want him to see me cry.

'Julián doesn't love this woman, Nuria,' he said, thinking that was the cause of my sorrow.

'Julián doesn't love anyone but himself and his damned books,' I muttered.

I looked up to find Miquel wearing the wise smile of an old child.

'And what does Fumero hope to gain by bringing this out into the open now?'

It didn't take us long to find out. Two days later a ghostlike, hollow-eyed Jorge Aldaya turned up at our home, inflamed with anger. Fumero had told him that Julián was going to marry a rich woman in a splendid, romantic ceremony. Aldaya had spent days obsessing over the thought that the man responsible for his misfortunes was now clothed in glamour, sitting astride a fortune, while his had disappeared. Fumero had not told him that Irene Marceau, despite being a woman of some means, was the owner of a brothel and not a princess in some fairy tale. He had not told him that the bride was thirty years older than Carax and that, rather than a marriage, this was an act of charity towards a man who had reached the end of the road. He had not told him when or where the wedding was going to take place. All he had done was sow the seeds of a fantasy that was devouring what little energy remained in Jorge's wizened, polluted body.

'Fumero has lied to you, Jorge,' said Miquel.

'And you, king of liars, you dare accuse your brother!' cried a delirious Aldaya.

There was no need for Aldaya to disclose his thoughts. In a man so withered, they could easily be read beneath the scrawny skin that covered his haunted face. Miquel saw Fumero's game clearly. After all, he was the one who had shown him how to play chess twenty years earlier in San Gabriel's school. Fumero had the strategy of a praying mantis and the patience of the immortals. Miquel sent Julián a warning note.

When Fumero decided the moment was right, he had taken Aldaya aside and told him Julián was getting married in three days' time. Since he was a police officer, he explained, he couldn't get involved in this sort of thing. But Aldaya, as a civilian, could go to Paris and make sure that the wedding in question never took place. How? a feverish Aldaya would ask, smouldering with hatred. By challenging him to a duel on the very day of his wedding. Fumero even supplied the weapon with which Jorge was convinced he would perforate the stony heart that had ruined the Aldaya dynasty. The report from the Paris police would later state that the weapon found at his feet was faulty and could never have done more than what it did: blow up in Jorge's hands. Fumero already knew this when he handed it to him in a case on the platform of the Estación de Francia. He knew perfectly well that even if fever, stupidity, and blind anger didn't prevent Aldaya from killing Julián Carax in a duel, the weapon he carried almost certainly would. It wasn't Carax who was destined to die in that duel, but Aldaya.

Fumero also knew that Julián would never agree to confront his old friend, dying as Aldaya was, reduced to nothing but a whimper. That is why Fumero carefully coached Aldaya on every step he must take. He would have to admit to Julián that the letter Penélope had written to him years ago, announcing her wedding and asking him to forget her, was a lie. He would have to disclose that it was

411

he, Jorge Aldaya, who had forced his sister to write that string of lies while she cried in despair, protesting her undying love for Julián. He would have to tell Julián that she had been waiting for him, with a broken soul and a bleeding heart, ever since then, dying of loneliness. That would be enough. Enough for Carax to pull the trigger and shoot him in the face. Enough for him to forget any wedding plans and to think of nothing else but returning to Barcelona in search of Penélope. And, once in Barcelona, his cobweb, Fumero would be waiting for him.

# 7

Julián Carax crossed the French border a few days before the start of the Civil War. The first and only edition of *The Shadow of the Wind* had left the press two weeks earlier, bound for the anonymity of its predecessors. By then Miquel could barely work: although he sat in front of the typewriter for two or three hours a day, weakness and fever prevented him from coaxing more than a feeble trickle of words out onto the paper. He had lost several of his regular columns due to missed deadlines. Other papers were fearful of publishing his articles after receiving anonymous threats. He had only one daily column left in the *Diario de Barcelona*, which he signed under the name of 'Adrián Maltés'. The spectre of the war could already be felt in the air. The country stank of fear. With nothing to occupy him, and too weak to complain, Miquel would go down into the square or walk up to Avenida de la Catedral, always carrying with him one of Julián's books as if it were an amulet. The last time the doctor had weighed him, he was only eight stone thirteen pounds. We listened to the news of the uprising in Morocco on the radio, and a few hours later a colleague from Miquel's newspaper came round to tell us that Cansinos, the editor in chief, had been murdered with a bullet to the neck, opposite the Canaletas café, two hours earlier. Nobody dared remove the body, which was still lying there, staining the pavement with a web of blood.

The brief but intense days of initial terror soon arrived. General Goded's troops set off along the Diagonal and Paseo de Gracia towards the centre, where the shooting began. It was a Sunday, and a lot of people had still come out onto the streets thinking they would spend the day picnicking along the road to Las Planas. The blackest days of the war in Barcelona, however, were still two years away. Shortly after the start of the skirmish, General Goded's troops surrendered, due to a miracle or to poor communication between the commanders. Lluís Companys's government seemed to have regained control, but what really happened would become obvious in the next few weeks.

Barcelona had passed into the hands of the anarchist unions. After days of riots and street fighting, rumours began to circulate that the four rebel generals had been executed in Montjuïc Castle shortly after the surrender. A friend of Miquel's, a British journalist who was present at the execution, said that the firing squad was made up of seven men but that at the last moment dozens of militiamen joined the party. When they opened fire, the bodies were riddled with so many bullets that they collapsed into unrecognizable pieces and had to be put into the coffins in an almost liquid state. There were those who wanted to believe that this was the end of the conflict, that the fascist troops would never reach Barcelona and the rebellion would be extinguished along the way.

We learned that Julián was in Barcelona on the day of Goded's surrender, when we received a letter from Irene Marceau in which she told us that Julián had killed Jorge Aldaya in a duel, in Père Lachaise cemetery. Even before Aldaya had expired, an anonymous call had alerted the police to the event. Julián was forced to flee from Paris immediately, pursued by the police, who wanted him for murder. We had no doubt as to who had made that call.

We waited anxiously to hear from Julián so that we could warn him of the danger that stalked him and protect him from a worse trap than the one laid out for him by Fumero: the discovery of the truth. Three days later Julián still had not appeared. Miquel did not want to share his anxiety with me, but I knew perfectly well what he was thinking. Julián had come back for Penélope, not for us.

'What will happen when he finds out the truth?' I kept asking.

'We'll make sure he doesn't,' Miquel would answer.

The first thing he was going to discover was that the Aldaya family had disappeared. He would not find many places where he could start looking for Penélope. We made a list, and began our own expedition. The mansion on Avenida del Tibidabo was just an empty property, locked away behind chains and veils of ivy. A flower vendor, who sold bunches of roses and carnations on the opposite corner, said he only remembered seeing one person approaching the house recently, but that was almost an old man, with a bit of a limp.

'Frankly, he seemed pretty nasty. I tried to sell him a carnation for his lapel, and he told me to piss off, saying there was a war on and it was no time for flowers.'

He hadn't seen anyone else. Miquel bought some withered roses from him and, just in case, gave him the phone number of the editorial department at the *Diario de Barcelona*. The man could leave a message there if, by chance, anyone should turn up looking like the person we'd described. Our next stop was San Gabriel's, where Miquel met up with Fernando Ramos, his old school companion.

Fernando was now a Latin and Greek teacher and had been ordained a priest. His heart sank when he saw Miquel looking so frail. He told us Julián had not come to see him, but he promised to get in touch with us if he did, and would try to hold him back. Fumero had been there before us, he confessed with alarm, and had told him that, in times of war, he'd do well to be careful.

'He said a lot of people were going to die very soon, and uniforms – soldiers' or priests' – would be no defence against the bullets. . . .'

Fernando Ramos admitted that it wasn't clear which unit or group Fumero belonged to, and he hadn't wanted to ask him either. I find it impossible to describe to you those first days of the war in Barcelona, Daniel. The air seemed poisoned with fear and hatred. People eyed one another suspiciously, and the streets held a silence that put knots in your stomach. Every day, every hour, fresh rumours and gossip circulated. I remember one night when Miquel and I were walking home down the Ramblas. They were completely deserted. Miquel looked at the buildings, glimpsing faces hidden behind closed shutters, noticing how they scanned the shadows of the street. He said he could feel the knives being sharpened behind those walls.

The following day we went to the Fortuny hat shop, without much hope of finding Julián there. One of the residents in the building told us that the hatter was terrified by the upheavals of the last few days and had locked himself up in the shop. No matter how much we knocked, he wouldn't open the door. That afternoon there had been a shoot-out only a block away, and the pools of blood were still fresh on the pavement. A dead horse still lay there, at the mercy of stray dogs that were tearing open its bullet-ridden stomach, while a group of children watched and threw stones at them. We only managed to see the hatter's frightened face though the grille of the door. We told him we were looking for his son, Julián. The hatter replied that his son was dead and told us to leave or he'd call the police. We left the place feeling disheartened.

For days we scoured cafés and shops, asking for Julián. We made inquiries in hotels and *pensiones*, in railway stations, in banks where he might have gone to change money – nobody remembered a man fitting Julián's description. We feared that he might already have fallen into Fumero's clutches, and Miquel managed to get one of his colleagues from the newspaper, who had contacts in Police Headquarters, to find out whether Julián had been put in jail. There was no sign of him. Two weeks went by, and it looked as if Julián had vanished into thin air.

Miquel hardly slept, hoping for news of his friend. One evening he returned from his usual afternoon walk with a bottle of port, of all things. The newspaper staff had presented it to him, he said, because he'd been told by the subeditor that they were going to have to cancel his column.

'They don't want trouble, I understand.'

'And what are you going to do?'

'Get drunk, for a start.'

Miquel drank barely half a glass, but I finished off almost the entire bottle on an empty stomach without noticing it. Around midnight, I was overpowered by drowsiness and collapsed on the sofa. I dreamed that Miquel was kissing my forehead and covering me with a shawl. When I woke up, I felt a sharp, stabbing pain in my head, which I recognized as the prelude to a fierce hangover. I went to look for Miquel, to curse the hour when he'd had the bright idea of getting me drunk, but I realized I was alone in the apartment. I went over to the desk and saw that there was a note on the typewriter in which he asked me not to be alarmed and to wait for him there. He'd gone out in search of Julián and would soon bring him home. He ended the note by saying that he loved me. The note fell from my hands. Then I noticed that before leaving, Miquel had removed his things from the desk, as if he wasn't planning to use it anymore. I knew that I would never see him again.

# 8

That afternoon the flower vendor had called the offices of the *Diario de Barcelona* and left a message for Miquel saying he'd seen the man we had described to him prowling around the old mansion like a ghost. It was past midnight when Miquel reached number 32, Avenida del Tibidabo. At night, the place was a dark, deserted valley struck by darts of moonlight that filtered through the grove. Although he hadn't seen him for seventeen years, Miquel recognized Julián by his light, almost catlike walk as his silhouette glided through the shadows of the garden, near the fountain. Julián had jumped over the garden wall and lay in wait by the house like a restless animal. Miquel could have called out to him, but he preferred not to alert any possible witnesses. He felt that furtive eyes were spying on the avenue from the dark windows of neighbouring mansions. He walked round the walls of the estate until he reached the part by the old tennis courts and the coach houses. There he noticed the crevices in the wall that Julián must have used as steps, and the flagstones that had come loose on the top. He lifted himself up, almost out of breath, feeling an acute pain in his chest and experiencing periodic waves of blindness. He lay down on the wall, his hands shaking, and called Julián in a whisper. The silhouette that hovered by the fountain stood still, joining the rest of the statues. Miquel saw two shining eyes fixing on him. He wondered whether Julián would recognize him, after seventeen years and an illness that had taken away his very breath. The silhouette slowly came closer, wielding a long, shiny object in his right hand. A piece of glass.

'Julián . . .' Miquel murmured.

The figure stopped in its tracks. Miquel heard the piece of glass fall on the gravel. Julián's face emerged from the shadows. A two-week stubble covered his features, which were sharper than they used to be.

'Miquel?'

Unable to jump down to the other side, or even climb back to the street, Miquel held out his hand. Julián hauled himself onto the wall and, holding his friend's fist tightly with one hand, laid the palm of his other hand on his face.

They gazed silently at one another for a long time, each sensing the wounds life had inflicted on the other.

'We must leave this place, Julián. Fumero is looking for you. That business with Aldaya was a trap.'

'I know,' murmured Carax in a monotone.

'The house is locked. Nobody has lived here for years,' Miquel added. 'Come on, help me down, and let's get out of here.'

Carax climbed down the wall. When he clutched Miquel with both hands, he could feel his friend's wasted body under the loose clothes. There seemed to be no flesh or muscle left. Once they were on the other side, Carax gripped Miquel by the armpits, so that he was almost carrying him, and they walked off together into the darkness of Calle Román Macaya.

'What is wrong with you?' whispered Carax.

'It's nothing. Some fever. I'm getting better.'

Miquel already gave off the smell of illness, and Julián asked no further questions. They went down León XIII until they reached Paseo de San Gervasio, where they saw the lights of a café. They sought refuge at a table at the back of the room, away from the entrance and the windows. A couple of regulars sat at the bar, smoking cigarettes and listening to the radio. The waiter, a man with a waxy pallor and downcast eyes, took their order. Warm brandy, coffee, and whatever food was available.

Miquel didn't eat at all. Carax, obviously starving, ate for both of them. The two friends looked at each other in the sticky light of the café, spellbound. The last time they had seen each other face-to-face, they were half the age they were now. They had parted as boys, and now life presented one of them with a fugitive and the other with a dying man. Both wondered whether this was due to the cards they'd been dealt or to the way they had played them.

'I've never thanked you for everything you've done for me over the years, Miquel.'

'Don't begin now. I did what I had to do and what I wanted to do. There's nothing to thank me for.'

'How's Nuria?'

'The same as you left her.'

Carax looked down.

'We got married months ago. I don't know whether she wrote to tell you.'

Carax's lips froze, and he shook his head slowly.

'You have no right to reproach her for anything, Julián.'

'I know. I have no right to anything.'

'Why didn't you come to us for help, Julián?'

'I didn't want to get you into trouble.'

'That is out of your hands now. Where have you been all this time? We thought the ground had swallowed you.'

'Almost. I've been at home. In my father's apartment.'

Miquel stared at him in amazement. Julián went on to explain how, when he arrived in Barcelona, unsure of where to go, he had set off towards his childhood home, fearing there would be nobody left there. The doors of the hat shop were still open, and an old-looking man, with no hair and no fire in his eyes, languished behind the counter. Julián hadn't wanted to go in, or let him know he'd returned, but Antoni Fortuny had raised his eyes and looked at the stranger on the other side of the window. Their eyes met. Much as Julián wanted to run away, he was paralysed. He saw tears welling up in the hatter's eyes, saw him drag himself to the door and come out into the street, speechless. Without uttering a word, he led his son into the shop and pulled down the metal grille. Once the outer world had been sealed off, he embraced him, trembling and howling with grief.

Later the hatter explained that the police had been round asking after Julián two days earlier. Someone called Fumero – a man with a bad reputation, who had supposedly been in the pay of General Goded's fascist thugs only a month before and was now making out he was friends with the anarchists – had told him that Julián Carax was on his way to Barcelona, that he'd cold-bloodedly murdered Jorge Aldaya in Paris, and that he was sought for a number of other crimes, a catalogue that the hatter didn't bother to listen to. Fumero trusted that, if by some remote and improbable chance his prodigal son made an appearance, the hatter would see fit to do his duty as a citizen and report him. Fortuny told Fumero that of course he could count on his help, though secretly it irritated him that a snake like Fumero should assume him to be so base. No sooner had the sinister cortege left the shop than the hatter set off towards the cathedral chapel where he had first met Sophie. There he prayed to his saint, begging him to guide his son back home before it was too late. Now that Julián had arrived, he warned him of the danger that awaited him.

'Whatever has brought you to Barcelona, son, let me do it for you while you hide in the apartment. Your room is just as you left it and it's yours for however long you may need it.'

Julián admitted that he'd returned to look for Penélope Aldaya. The hatter swore he would find her and that, once they had been reunited, he would help them both to flee to a safe place, far from Fumero, far from the past, far from everything.

For days Julián hid in the apartment in Ronda de San Antonio while the hatter combed the city looking for some sign of Penélope. Julián spent the days in his old room, which, as his father had promised, was unchanged, though now everything seemed smaller, as if objects had shrunk with time. Many of his old notebooks were still there, pencils he remembered sharpening the week he left for Paris, books waiting to be read, the boy's clean clothes in the cupboards. The hatter told Julián that Sophie had left him shortly after his escape, and although for years he didn't hear from her, she wrote to him at last from Bogotá, where she had been living for some time with another man. They corresponded regularly, 'always talking about you,' the hatter admitted, 'because it's the only thing that binds us.'

When he spoke those words, it seemed to Julián that the hatter had put off falling in love with his wife until he had already lost her.

'You only love truly once in a lifetime, Julián, even if you aren't always aware of it.'

The hatter, who seemed to be caught in a race against time to disentangle a whole life of misfortune, had no doubt that Penélope was that love of his son's life. Without realizing it, he thought that if he helped Julián recover her, perhaps he, too, would recover some part of what he had lost, that void that weighed on his bones like a curse.

Despite his determination, and much to his despair, the hatter soon discovered that there was no trace of Penélope Aldaya, or of her family, in the whole of Barcelona. A man of humble origins who had had to work all his life to stay solvent, the hatter had never doubted the staying power of money and social station, but fifteen years of ruin and destitution had been sufficient to remove mansions, industries, the very footprints of a dynasty from the face of the earth. When the name Aldaya was mentioned, there were many who had heard of it but very few who remembered its significance.

The day Miquel Moliner and I went to the hat shop and asked after Julián, the hatter was certain we were two of Fumero's henchmen. Nobody was going to snatch his son away from him again. This time God Almighty could descend from the heavens, the same God who had spent His whole life ignoring the hatter's prayers, and Fortuny would gladly have pulled His eyes out if He dared take Julián away again.

The hatter was the man whom the flower vendor remembered seeing a few days before, prowling around the Aldaya mansion. What the flower vendor interpreted as 'pretty nasty' was only the intensity that comes to those who, better late than never, have found a purpose in life and are pursuing it to make up for lost time. Unfortunately, the Lord once again disregarded the hatter's pleadings.

Having crossed the threshold of despair, the old man was still unable to find what he needed for his son's salvation, for his own salvation: some sign of the girl. How many lost souls do You need, Lord, to satisfy Your hunger? the hatter asked. God, in His infinite silence, looked at him without blinking.

'I can't find her, Julián. . . . I swear that—'

'Don't worry, Father. This is something I must do. You've already helped me as much as you could.'

That night Julián at last went out into the streets of Barcelona, determined to find Penélope.

As Miquel listened to his friend's tale, it did not occur to him to be suspicious of the waiter when he went over to the telephone and mumbled something with his back to them or, later, when he surreptitiously kept an eye on the door, wiping glasses too thoroughly for an establishment where dirt was otherwise so at home. It didn't occur to him that Fumero would already have been in that café, and in dozens of cafés like it, a stone's throw from the Aldaya mansion; that as soon as Carax set foot in any one of them, the call would be placed in a matter of seconds. When the police car stopped in front of the café and the waiter disappeared into the kitchen, Miquel felt the cold and serene stillness of fate. Carax read his eyes, and they both turned at the same time to see three grey raincoats flapping behind the windows, three faces blowing steam onto the windowpane. None of them was Fumero. The vultures preceded him.

'Let's leave this place, Julián. . . .'

'There's nowhere to go,' said Carax, with an oddly calm tone of voice that made his friend eye him carefully.

It was only then that Miquel noticed the revolver in Julián's hand. The doorbell sounded above the murmur of the radio. Miquel snatched the gun from Carax's hands and fixed his eyes on him.

'Give me your papers, Julián.'

The three policemen pretended to sit at the bar. One of

them gave Miquel and Julián a sidelong glance. The other two felt inside their raincoats.

'Your papers, Julián. Now.'

Carax silently shook his head.

'I have only a month left, perhaps two, with luck. One of us has to get out of here, Julián. You have more going for you than I do. I don't know whether you'll find Penélope. But Nuria is waiting for you.'

'Nuria is your wife.'

'Remember the deal we made. The day I die, all that was once mine will be yours. . . .'

'. . . Except your dreams.'

They smiled at one another for the last time. Julián handed him his passport. Miquel put it next to the copy of *The Shadow of the Wind* that he had been carrying in his coat pocket since the day he'd received it.

'See you soon,' Julián whispered.

'There's no hurry. I'll be waiting.'

Just as the three policemen turned towards them, Miquel rose from the table and went up to them. At first all they saw was a pale, tremulous man who seemed to be at death's door as he smiled at them, blood showing on the corners of his thin, lifeless lips. By the time they noticed the gun in his right hand, Miquel was barely three yards away from them. One of them was about to scream, but the first shot blew off his lower jaw. The body fell on its knees at Miquel's feet, lifeless. The other two police officers had already drawn their weapons. The second shot went through the stomach of the one who looked older, the bullet snapping his backbone in two and splattering a handful of guts against the bar. Miquel never had time to fire a third shot. The remaining policeman was already pointing his gun at him. He felt it in his ribs, on his heart, and saw the man's steely eyes, lit up with panic.

'Stand still, you son of a bitch, or I swear I'll tear you apart.'

Miquel smiled and slowly raised his gun towards the

policeman's face. The man couldn't have been more than twenty-five, and his lips trembled.

'You tell Fumero, from Carax, that I remember his little sailor suit.'

He felt no pain, no fire. The impact, like a muffled blow, threw him into the window, extinguishing the sound and colour of things. As he crashed through the pane, he noticed an intense cold creeping down his throat and the light receding like dust in the wind. Miquel Moliner turned his head for the last time and saw his friend Julián running down the street. Miquel was thirty-six years old, which was longer than he'd hoped to live. Before he collapsed onto a pavement strewn with bloodstained glass, he was already dead.

# 9

That night an unidentified van arrived in response to the call from the policeman who had killed Miquel. I never knew his name, nor do I think he realized whom he had murdered. Like all wars, private or public, that one was like a stage show. Two men carried off the bodies of the dead policemen and made sure the manager of the bar understood that he must forget what had happened or there would be trouble. Never underestimate the talent for forgetting that wars awaken, Daniel. Miquel Moliner's corpse was abandoned in an alleyway of the Raval quarter twelve hours later, so that his death could not be connected to that of the two police officers. When the body finally arrived at the morgue, it had been dead for two days. Miquel had left his own papers at home before going out. All the employees at the morgue could find was a disfigured passport in the name of Julián Carax, and a copy of *The Shadow of the Wind*. The police concluded that the deceased man was Julián Carax. The passport still gave his address as Fortuny's apartment in Ronda de San Antonio.

By then the news had reached Fumero, who went along to the morgue to bid farewell to Julián. There he met the hatter, whom the police had fetched to identify the body. Señor Fortuny, who hadn't seen Julián for two days, feared the worst. When he recognized the body as that of the man who had knocked on his door only a week earlier, asking after Julián (and whom he'd taken to be one of Fumero's henchmen), he began to scream and left. The police took this response to mean he recognized the corpse. Fumero, who had witnessed the scene, went up to the body and inspected it silently. He hadn't seen Julián for seventeen years. When he recognized Miquel Moliner, all he did was smile and sign the forensic report confirming that the body in question was Julián Carax. He then ordered its immediate removal to a common grave in Montjuïc.

For a long time, I wondered why Fumero would do something like that. But that was simply Fumero's logic. By dying with Julián's identity, Miquel had involuntarily provided Fumero with the perfect alibi. From that moment on, Julián Carax didn't exist. There would be no official link between Fumero and the man who, sooner or later, he hoped to find and murder. It was wartime, and few would ask for explanations concerning the death of someone who didn't even have a name. Julián had lost his identity. He was a shadow. I spent two days in the apartment waiting for Miquel or Julián, thinking I was going mad. On the third day, Monday, I went back to work at the publishing firm. Señor Cabestany had been taken into hospital a few weeks previously, and would not be returning to the office. His eldest son, Álvaro, had taken over the business. I didn't say anything to anyone. There was nobody I could turn to.

That same afternoon I received a call from an employee at the morgue, Manuel Gutiérrez Fonseca. Señor Gutiérrez Fonseca explained that the body of someone called Julián

Carax had been brought into the morgue. Having compared the deceased man's passport with the name of the author of the book that was on the body when it arrived, and suspecting, moreover, if not a breach in the rules, a certain laxity on the part of the police, he had felt it his moral duty to call the publishers and inform them of what had happened. As I listened to him, I almost died. The first thing I thought was that it was a trap set up by Fumero. Señor Gutiérrez Fonseca expressed himself with the correct tones of a conscientious public official, although there was something else in his voice, something that even he would not have been able to explain. I had taken the call in Cabestany's office. Thank God, Álvaro had gone out for lunch and I was alone, otherwise it would have been difficult for me to explain away my tears and the shaking of my hands as I held the telephone. Señor Gutiérrez Fonseca told me he had thought it appropriate to let me know what had happened.

I thanked him for his call with the false formality of all such conversations. As soon as I put down the receiver, I closed the office door and bit my fists so as not to scream. I washed my face and left for home immediately, leaving a message for Álvaro to say I was unwell and would return the following day earlier than usual, to catch up with correspondence. In the street, I had to make an effort not to run, to walk with the anonymous grey calm of people who have nothing to hide. When I inserted the key in the apartment door, I realized that the lock had been forced. I froze. The doorknob began to turn from within. I wondered whether I was going to die like this, in a dark staircase, and without knowing what had become of Miquel. The door opened, and I encountered the dark eyes of Julián Carax. May God forgive me, but at that moment I felt that life was returning to me, and I thanked the heavens for giving me back Julián instead of Miquel.

We melted in a long embrace, but when I searched for his lips, Julián moved away and lowered his eyes. I closed the door and, taking Julián's hand, led him to the bedroom. We lay together on the bed in silence. Evening was closing in, and the shadows of the apartment were fringed with purple. As on every night since the start of the war, shots could be heard in the distance. Julián was crying as he lay on my chest, and I felt a tiredness beyond words. Later, once night had fallen, our lips met, and in the shelter of that pressing darkness, we removed our clothes, which smelled of fear and of death. I wanted to remember Miquel, but the fire of those hands on my stomach stole all my shame and grief. I wanted to lose myself in them, even though I knew that at dawn, exhausted and perhaps overcome by contempt for ourselves, we would be unable to look each other in the eye without wondering what sort of people we had become.

# 10

I was woken by the pitter-patter of the rain at daybreak. The bed empty, the room bathed in grey light.

I found Julián sitting in front of what had been Miquel's desk, stroking the keys of his typewriter. He looked up and gave me that lukewarm, distant smile that said he would never be mine. I felt like spitting out the truth to him, like hurting him. It would have been so simple. Reveal to him that Penélope was dead. That he was living a lie. That I was now all he had in the world.

'I should never have returned to Barcelona,' he murmured, shaking his head.

I knelt beside him. 'What you are searching for is not here, Julián. Let's go away. The two of us. Far from here. While there is still time.'

Julián looked at me for a long moment, without blinking. 'You know something you haven't told me, don't you?' he asked.

I shook my head and swallowed. Julián just nodded.

'Tonight I'm going back there.'

'Julián, please . . .'

'I must make sure.'

'Then I'll go with you.'

'No.'

'The last time I stayed here and waited, I lost Miquel. If you go, I go, too.'

'This has nothing to do with you, Nuria. It's something that concerns only me.'

I wondered whether he didn't realize how much his words hurt me, or whether he just didn't care.

'That's what you think,' I said.

He tried to stroke my cheek, but I drew his hand away.

'You should despise me, Nuria. It would bring you better luck.'

'Yes, I know.'

We spent the day outside, far from the oppressive darkness of the apartment that still smelled of warm sheets and skin. Julián wanted to see the sea. I went with him to La Barceloneta, and we walked along the almost deserted beach, the shimmering sand seeming to trail off into the summer haze. We sat on the sand, near the shore, the way children or old people do. Julián smiled, saying nothing.

As evening fell, we took a tram near the aquarium and went up Vía Layetana to Paseo de Gracia, then onto Plaza de Lesseps and Avenida de la República Argentina, until we came to the end of the route. Julián gazed silently at the streets, as if he were afraid of losing the city as we travelled through it. Halfway through our journey, he took my hand and kissed it without saying a word. He held it until we got off. An elderly man who was accompanied by a little girl dressed in white looked at us, smiling, and asked us whether we were engaged. It was dark by the time we walked up Calle Román Macaya towards the Aldayas' old mansion on Avenida del Tibidabo. A fine rain was falling, coating the thick stone walls with silver. We climbed the external wall at the back, near the tennis courts. The large, rambling house rose into view through the rain. I recognized it immediately. I had come across that house in a thousand different guises in Julián's books. In *The Red House*, it was a sinister mansion that was larger inside than out. It slowly changed shape, grew new corridors, galleries, and improbable attics, endless stairs that led nowhere; it illuminated dark rooms that came and went from one day to the next, taking with it any unsuspecting individual who entered them, never to be seen again. We stopped outside the main door, locked with chains and a padlock the size of a fist. The large windows on the first floor were boarded up with wooden planks that were covered in ivy. The air smelled of weeds and wet earth. The stone, dark and slimy with rain, shone like the scales of a huge reptile.

I wanted to ask Julián how he intended to get past that large oak door, which looked like the door of a basilica or a prison. Julián pulled a jar out from his coat and unscrewed the top. A fetid vapour issued from it, forming a slow, bluish spiral. He held one end of the padlock and poured the acid into the lock. The metal hissed like red-hot iron, enveloped in a cloud of yellow smoke. We waited a few minutes, and then he picked up a cobblestone that lay among the weeds and split the padlock by banging it half a dozen times. Julián then gave the door a kick. It opened slowly, like a tomb, exhaling a thick, damp breath. Beyond the doorway I could sense a velvety darkness. Julián had brought a benzine lighter, which he lit after taking a few steps into the entrance hall. I followed him, leaving the door behind us ajar. Julián walked on a few yards, holding the flame above his head. A carpet of dust lay at our feet, with no footprints but ours. The naked walls took on an amber hue from the flame. There was no furniture, no mirrors, or lamps. The doors were still on their hinges, but the bronze doorknobs had been pulled out. The mansion was just a skeleton. We stopped at the bottom of the staircase. Julián looked up, his eyes scanning the heights. He turned around for a moment to look at me, and I wanted to smile, but in the half-light we could barely see each other's eyes. I followed him up the stairs, treading the steps on which Julián had first seen Penélope. I knew where we were heading, and I felt a coldness inside me that had nothing to do with the biting, damp air of that place.

We went up to the third floor, where a narrow corridor led to the south wing of the house. Here the ceilings were much lower and the doors smaller. It was the floor for the servants' living quarters. The last room, I knew without Julián having to tell me, had been Jacinta Coronado's bedroom. Julián approched it slowly, fearfully. That had been the last place he'd seen Penélope, where he had made love to a girl barely seventeen years old, and who, months later, would bleed to death in that same cell. I wanted to stop him, but Julián had reached the doorway and was looking absently inside. I peered into the room with him. It was just a cubicle stripped of all ornamentation. The marks where a bed had once stood were still visible beneath the flood of dust that covered the floorboards. A tangle of black stains snaked across the middle of the room. Julián stared at the emptiness for almost a minute, disconcerted. I could see from his look that he hardly recognized the place, that the sight of it seemed like a cruel trick. I took his arm and led him back to the stairs.

'There's nothing here, Julián,' I murmured. 'The family sold everything before leaving for Argentina.'

Julián nodded weakly. We walked down the stairs again, and when we reached the ground floor, Julián made his way to the library. The shelves were empty, the fireplace choked with rubble. The walls, a deathly pale, flickered in the breath of the flame. Creditors and usurers had managed to remove every last bit of it, most of which must be lost in the twisted heaps of some junkyard by now.

'I've come back for nothing,' Julián mumbled.

Better this way, I thought. I was counting the seconds that separated us from the door. If I managed to get him away from there, we might still have a chance. I let Julián absorb the ruin of that place, purging his memories.

'You had to return and see it again,' I said. 'Now you know there's nothing here. It's just a large old, uninhabited house, Julián. Let's go home.'

He looked at me, pale-faced, and nodded. I took his hand, and we went along the passageway that led to the exit. The chink of outdoor light was only half a dozen yards away. I could smell the weeds and the drizzle in the air. Then I felt I was losing Julián's hand. I stopped and turned to see him standing motionless, his eyes staring into the darkness.

'What is it, Julián?'

He didn't reply. He was gazing, mesmerized, at the mouth of a narrow corridor that led towards the kitchen area. I walked over to him and looked into the shadows. The door at the end of the corridor was bricked up, a wall of red bricks laid roughly with mortar that bled out of the corners. I couldn't quite understand what it meant, but I felt an icy cold that took my breath away. Julián was slowly getting closer. All the other doors in the corridor – in the whole house – were open, their locks and doorknobs gone. All except this one.

'Julián, please, let's go. . . .'

The impact of his fist on the brick wall drew a hollow echo on the other side. I thought I saw his hands trembling when he placed the lighter on the floor and gestured for me to move back a few steps.

'Julián . . .'

The first kick brought down a rain of red dust. Julián charged again. I thought I could hear his bones breaking, but Julián was unperturbed. He banged against the wall again and again, with the rage of a prisoner forcing his way out to freedom. His fists and his arms were bleeding when the first brick broke and fell onto the other side. In the dark, with bloodstained fingers, Julián struggled to enlarge the gap. He panted, exhausted, possessed by a fury of which

431

I would never have thought him capable. One by one, he loosened the bricks and the wall came down. Julián stopped, covered in a cold sweat, his hands flayed. He picked up the lighter and placed it on the edge of one of the bricks. A wooden door, carved with angel motifs, rose up on the other side. Julián stroked the wooden reliefs, as if he were reading a hieroglyph. The door yielded to the pressure of his hands.

A glutinous darkness came at us from the other side. A little further back, the form of a staircase could be discerned. Black stone steps descended until they were lost in shadows. Julián turned for a moment, and I met his eyes. I saw fear and despair in them, as if he could sense what lay beyond. I shook my head, begging him without speaking not to go down. He turned back, dejected, and plunged into the gloom. I looked through the brick frame and saw him lurching down the steps. The flame flickered, now just a breath of transparent blue.

'Julián?'

All I got was silence. I could see Julián's shadow, motionless at the bottom of the stairs. I went through the brick hole and walked down the steps. The room was rectangular, with marble walls. It exuded an intense, penetrating chill. The two tombstones were covered with a veil of cobwebs that fell apart like rotten silk with the flame from the lighter. The white marble was scored with black tears of dampness that looked like blood dripping out of the clefts left by the engraver's chisel. They lay side by side, like maledictions, chained together.

PENÉLOPE ALDAYA      DAVID ALDAYA
1902–1919          1919

# 11

I have often paused to think about that moment of silence and tried to imagine what Julián must have felt when he discovered that the woman he had been waiting seventeen years for was dead, their child gone with her, and that the life he had dreamed about, the very breath of it, had never existed. Most of us have the good or bad fortune of seeing our lives fall apart so slowly we barely notice it. In Julián's case that certainty came to him in a matter of seconds. For a moment I thought he was going to rush up the stairs and flee from that accursed place, and that I would never see him again. Perhaps it would have been better that way.

I remember that the flame from the lighter slowly went out, and I lost sight of his silhouette. My hands searched for him in the shadows and I found him trembling, speechless. He could barely stand, and he dragged himself into a corner. I hugged him and kissed his forehead. He didn't move. I felt his face with my fingers, but there were no tears. I thought that perhaps, unconsciously, he had known it all those years, that perhaps the encounter was necessary for him to face the truth and set himself free. We had reached the end of the road. Julián would now understand that nothing held him in Barcelona any longer and that we could leave, go far away. I wanted to believe that our luck was about to change and that Penélope had finally forgiven us.

I looked for the lighter on the floor and lit it again. Julián was staring vacantly, indifferent to the blue flame. I held his face in my hands and forced him to look at me. I found lifeless, empty eyes, consumed by anger and loss. I felt the venom of hatred spreading slowly through his veins, and I could read his thoughts. He hated me for having deceived him. He hated Miquel for having wished to give him a life that now felt like an open wound. But above all he hated the man who had caused this calamity, this trail of death and misery: himself. He hated those filthy books to which he had devoted his life and about which nobody cared. He hated every stolen second.

He looked at me without blinking, the way one looks at a stranger or some foreign object. I kept shaking my head, slowly, my hands searching his hands. Suddenly he moved away, roughly, and stood up. I tried to grab his arm, but he pushed me against the wall. I saw him go silently up the stairs, a man I no longer knew. Julián Carax was dead. By the time I stepped out into the garden, there was no trace of him. I climbed the wall and jumped down onto the other side. The desolate streets seemed to bleed in the rain. I shouted out his name, walking down the middle of the deserted avenue. Nobody answered my call. It was almost four in the morning when I got home. The apartment was full of smoke and the stench of burned paper. Julián had been there. I ran to open the windows. I found a small case on my desk with the pen I had bought for him years ago in Paris, the fountain pen I had paid a fortune for on the pretence it once had belonged to Victor Hugo. The smoke was oozing from the central-heating boiler. I opened the hatch and saw that Julián had thrown copies of his novels into it. I could just about read the titles on the leather spines; the rest had turned to cinders. I looked on my bookshelves: all of his books were gone.

Hours later, when I went to the publishing house in the middle of the morning, Álvaro Cabestany called me into his office. His father hardly ever came by anymore; the doctors said his days were numbered – as was my time at the firm. Cabestany's son informed me that a gentleman called Laín Coubert had turned up early that morning, saying he was interested in acquiring our entire stock of Julián Carax's novels. The publisher's son told him we had a warehouse full of them in the Pueblo Nuevo district, but as there was such a demand for them, he insisted on a higher price than Coubert was offering. Coubert had not taken the bait and had marched out. Now Álvaro Cabestany wanted me to

434

find this person called Laín Coubert and accept his offer. I told the fool that Laín Coubert didn't exist; he was a character in one of Carax's novels. That he wasn't in the least interested in buying his books; he only wanted to know where we stored them. Old Señor Cabestany was in the habit of keeping a copy of every book published by his firm in his office library, even the works of Julián Carax. I slipped into the room, unnoticed, and took them.

That evening I visited my father in the Cemetery of Forgotten Books and hid them where nobody, especially Julián, would ever find them. Night had fallen when I left the building. I wandered off down the Ramblas and from there to La Barceloneta, where I made for the beach, looking for the spot where I had gazed at the sea with Julián. The pyre of flames from the Pueblo Nuevo warehouse was visible in the distance, its amber trail spilling out over the sea and spirals of smoke rising to the sky like serpents of light. When the firefighters managed to extinguish the flames shortly before daybreak, there was nothing left, just the brick-and-metal skeleton that held up the vault. There I found Lluís Carbó, who had been the night watchman for ten years. He stared in disbelief at the smouldering ruins. His eyebrows and the hairs on his arm were singed, and his skin shone like wet bronze. It was he who told me that the blaze had started shortly after midnight and had devoured tens of thousands of books, until dawn came and he was faced with a river of ashes. Lluís still held a handful of books he had managed to save, some of Verdaguer's collected poems and two volumes of the *History of the French Revolution*. That was all that had survived. Various members of the union had arrived to help the firefighters. One of them told me the firefighters found a burned body among the debris. At first they had assumed that the man was dead, but then one of them noticed he was still breathing, and they had taken him to the nearby Hospital del Mar.

I recognized him by his eyes. The fire had eaten away his

skin, his hands, and his hair. The flames had torn off his clothes, and his whole body was a raw wound that oozed beneath his bandages. They had confined him to a room on his own at the end of a corridor, with a view of the beach, and had numbed him with morphine while they waited for him to die. I wanted to hold his hand, but one of the nurses warned me that there was almost no flesh under the bandages. The fire had cut away his eyelids. The nurse who found me collapsed on the floor, crying, asked me whether I knew who he was. I said I did: he was my husband. When a priest appeared to administer the last rites over him, I frightened him off with my screams. Three days later Julián was still alive. The doctors said it was a miracle, that his will to live gave him a strength no medicine could offer. They were wrong. It was not a will to live. It was hatred. A week later, when they saw that this death-bitten body refused to expire, he was officially admitted under the name of Miquel Moliner. He would remain there for eleven months. Always in silence, with burning eyes, without rest.

I went to the hospital every day. Soon the nurses began to treat me less formally and invited me to lunch with them in their hall. They were all women who were on their own, strong women waiting for their men to return from the front. Some did. They taught me how to clean Julián's wounds, how to change his bandages, how to change the sheets and make a bed with an inert body lying on it. They also taught me to lose all hope of ever seeing the man who had once been held by those bones. Three months later we removed his face bandages. Julián was a skull. He had no lips or cheeks. It was a featureless face, the charred remains of a doll. His eye sockets had become larger and now dominated his face. The nurses would not admit it to me, but they were revolted by his appearance, almost afraid. The doctors had told me that, as the wounds healed, a sort of purplish, reptile-like skin would slowly form. Nobody dared to comment on his mental state. Everyone assumed that Julián – Miquel – had lost his mind in the blaze, and that he had survived thanks to the obsessive care of a wife who stood firm where so many others would have fled in terror. I looked into his eyes and knew that Julián was still in there, alive, tormenting himself, waiting.

He had lost his lips, but the doctors thought that the vocal cords had not suffered permanent damage and that the burns on his tongue and larynx had healed months earlier. They assumed that Julián didn't say anything because his mind was gone. One afternoon, six months after the fire, when he and I were alone in the room, I bent over him and kissed him on the brow.

'I love you,' I said.

A bitter, harsh sound emerged from the doglike grimace that was now his mouth. His eyes were red with tears. I wanted to dry them with a handkerchief, but he repeated that sound.

'Leave me,' he said.

'Leave me.'

Two months after the warehouse fire, the publishing firm had gone bankrupt. Old Cabestany, who died that year, had predicted that his son would manage to ruin the company within six months. An unrepentant optimist to the last. I tried to find work with another publisher, but the war did away with everything. They all said that hostilities would soon cease and things would improve. But there were still two years of war ahead, and worse was yet to come. One year after the fire, the doctors told me that they had done all that could be done in a hospital. The situation was difficult, and they needed the room. They recommended that Julián be taken to a sanatorium like the Hospice of Santa Lucía, but I refused. In October 1937 I took him home. He hadn't uttered a single word since that 'Leave me'.

Every day I told him that I loved him. I set him up in the armchair by the window, wrapped in blankets. I fed him with fruit juices, toast, and milk – when there was any to be found. Every day I read to him for a couple of hours.

Balzac, Zola, Dickens ... His body was beginning to fill out and soon after returning home, he began to move his hands and arms. He tilted his neck. Sometimes, when I got back, I found the blankets on the floor, and objects that had been knocked over. One day I found him crawling on the floor. Then, a year and a half after the fire, I woke up in the middle of a stormy night and found that someone was sitting on the bed stroking my hair. I smiled at him, hiding my tears. He had managed to find one of my mirrors, although I'd hidden them all. In a broken voice, he told me he'd been transformed into one of his fictional monsters, into Laín Coubert. I wanted to kiss him, to show him that his appearance didn't disgust me, but he wouldn't let me. He would hardly allow me to touch him. Day by day he was getting his strength back. He would prowl around the house while I went out in search of something to eat. The savings Miquel had left me kept us afloat, but soon I had to begin selling jewellery and old possessions. When there was no other alternative, I took the Victor Hugo pen I had bought in Paris and went out to sell it to the highest bidder. I found a shop behind the Military Government buildings where they took in that sort of merchandise. The manager did not seem impressed by my solemn oath that the pen had belonged to Victor Hugo, but he admitted it was a marvellous piece of its kind and agreed to pay me as much as he could, bearing in mind these were times of great hardship.

When I told Julián that I'd sold it, I was afraid he would fly into a rage. All he said was that I'd done the right thing, that he'd never deserved it. One day, one of the many when I'd gone out to look for work, I returned to find that Julián wasn't there. He didn't come back until daybreak. When I asked him where he'd been, he just emptied the pockets of his coat (which had belonged to Miquel) and left a fistful of money on the table. From then on he began to go out almost every night. In the dark, concealed under a hat and scarf, with gloves and a raincoat, he was just one more shadow. He never told me where he went, and he almost always brought back money or jewellery. He slept in the mornings, sitting upright in his armchair, with his eyes open. Once I found a penknife in one of his pockets. It was a double-edged knife, with an automatic spring. The blade was marked with dark stains.

It was then that I began to hear stories in town about some individual who was going around at night, smashing bookshop windows and burning books. Other times the strange vandal would slip into a library or a collector's study. He always took two or three volumes, which he would then burn. In February 1938 I went to a secondhand bookshop to ask whether it was possible to find any books by Julián Carax on the market. The manager said it wasn't: someone had been making them disappear. He had owned a couple himself and had sold them to a very strange person, a man who hid his face and whose voice he could barely understand.

'Until recently there were a few copies left in private collections, here and in France, but a lot of collectors are beginning to get rid of them. They're frightened,' he said, 'and I don't blame them.'

More and more, Julián would vanish for whole days at a time. Soon his absences lasted a week. He always left and returned at night, and he always brought back money. He never gave any explanations, or if he did, they were meaningless. He told me he'd been in France: Paris, Lyons, Nice. Occasionally letters arrived from France addressed to Laín Coubert. They were always from secondhand booksellers, or from collectors. Someone had located a lost copy of Julián Carax's works. Like a wolf, he would disappear for a few days, then return.

It was during one of those absences that I came across Fortuny, the hatter, wandering about in the cathedral cloister, lost in his thoughts. He still remembered me from the day I'd gone with Miquel to inquire after Julián, two years before. He took me to a corner and told me

439

confidentially that he knew that Julián was alive, some-where, but he suspected that his son wasn't able to get in touch with us for some reason he couldn't quite figure out. 'Something to do with that cruel man Fumero.' I told him that I felt the same. Wartime was turning out to be very profitable for Fumero. His loyalties shifted from month to month, from the anarchists to the communists, and from them to whoever came his way. He was called a spy, a henchman, a hero, a murderer, a conspirator, a schemer, a saviour, a devil. Little did it matter. They all feared him. They all wanted him on their side. Perhaps because he was so busy with the intrigues of wartime Barcelona, Fumero seemed to have forgotten Julián. Probably, like the hatter, he imagined that Julián had already escaped and was out of his reach.

Señor Fortuny asked me whether I was an old friend of his son's, and I said I was. He asked me to tell him about Julián, about the man he'd become, because, he sadly admitted, he didn't really know him. 'Life separated us, you know?' He told me he'd been to all the bookshops in Barcelona in search of Julián's novels, but they were unobtainable. Someone had told him that a madman was looking for them in every corner of the city and then burning them. Fortuny was convinced that the culprit was Fumero. I didn't contradict him. Whether through pity or spite, I lied as best I could. I told him I thought that Julián had returned to Paris, that he was well, that I knew for a fact he was very fond of Fortuny the hatter, that he would come back to see him as soon as circumstances permitted. 'It's this war,' he complained, 'it just rots everything.' Before we said goodbye, he insisted on giving me his address and that of his ex-wife, Sophie, with whom he was back in touch after many years of 'misunderstandings'. Sophie now lived in Bogotá with a prestigious doctor, he said. She ran her own music school and often wrote asking after Julián.

'It's the only thing that brings us together now, you see.

Memories. We make so many mistakes in life, young lady, but we only realize this when old age creeps up on us. Tell me, are you religious?'

I took my leave, promising to keep him and Sophie informed if I ever had any news from Julián.

'Nothing would make his mother happier than to hear how he is. You women listen more to your heart and less to all the nonsense,' the hatter concluded sadly. 'That's why you live longer.'

Despite the fact that I'd heard so many appalling stories about him, I couldn't help feeling sorry for the poor old man. He had little else to do in life but wait for the return of his son. He seemed to live in the hope of recovering lost time, through some miracle of the saints, whom he visited with great devotion at their chapels in the cathedral. I had become used to picturing him as an ogre, a despicable and resentful human being, but all I could see before me was a kind man, blind to reality, confused like everybody else. Perhaps because he reminded me of my own father, who hid from everyone, including himself, in that refuge of books and shadows, or because the hatter and I were also linked by the hope of recovering Julián, I felt a growing affection for him and became his only friend. Unbeknownst to Julián, I often called on him at the apartment in Ronda de San Antonio. The hatter no longer worked in his shop downstairs.

'I don't have the hands, or the sight, or the customers . . .' he would say.

He waited for me almost every Thursday and offered me coffee, biscuits, and pastries that he scarcely touched. He spent hours reminiscing about Julián's childhood, about how they worked together in the hat shop, and he would show me photographs. He would take me to Julián's room, which he kept as immaculate as a museum, and bring out old notebooks and everyday objects without ever realizing that he'd already shown them to me before, that he'd told me all those stories on a previous visit. He seemed to be reconstructing a past that had never existed. One of those Thursdays, as I walked up the stairs, I ran into a doctor who had just been to see Fortuny. I asked him how the hatter was, and he looked at me strangely.

'Are you a relative?'

I told him I was the closest the poor man had to one. The doctor then told me that Fortuny was very ill, that it was just a matter of months.

'What's wrong with him?'

'I could tell you it's his heart, but what is really killing him is loneliness. Memories are worse than bullets.'

The hatter was pleased to see me and confessed that he didn't trust that doctor. Doctors are just second-rate witches, he said. All his life the hatter had been a man of profound religious beliefs, and old age had only reinforced them. He saw the hand of the devil everywhere. The devil, he said, clouds the mind and destroys mankind.

'Just look at this war, or look at me. Of course, I'm old now and weak, but as a young man I was rotten, a coward.'

It was the devil who had taken Julián away from him, he added.

'God gives us life, but the world's landlord is the devil. . . .'

And so we passed the afternoon, nibbling on stale sponge fingers and discussing theology.

I once told Julián that if he wanted to see his father again before he died, he'd better hurry up. It turned out that he, too, had been visiting the hatter, without his knowing: from afar, at dusk, sitting at the other end of a square, watching him grow old. Julián said he would rather the old man took with him the image of the son he had created in his mind during those years than the person he had become.

'You keep that one for me,' I said, instantly regretting my words.

He didn't reply, but for a moment it seemed as if he could think clearly again and was fully aware of the hell into which we had descended.

The doctor's prognosis did not take long to come true. Señor Fortuny didn't live to see the end of the war. He was found sitting in his armchair, looking at old photographs of Sophie and Julián.

The last days of the war were the prelude to an inferno. The city had lived through the combat from afar, like a wound that throbs dully, with months of skirmishes and battles, bombardments and hunger. The spectacle of murders, fights, and conspiracies had been corroding the city's heart for years, but even so, many wanted to believe that the war was still something distant, a storm that would pass them by. If anything, the wait made the inevitable even worse. When the storm broke, there was no compassion.

Nothing feeds forgetfulness better than war, Daniel. We all remain silent and they try to convince us that what we've seen, what we've done, what we've learned about ourselves and about others, is an illusion, a nightmare that will pass. Wars have no memory, and nobody has the courage to understand them until there are no voices left to tell what really happened, until the moment comes when we no longer recognize them and they return, with another face and another name, to devour everything they left behind.

By then Julián hardly had any books left to burn. His father's death, about which we never spoke, had turned him into an invalid. The anger and hatred that had at first possessed him were spent. We lived on rumours, secluded. We heard that Fumero had betrayed all the people who had helped him advance during the war and was now in the service of the victors. It was said that he was personally executing his main allies in the cells of Montjuïc Castle – his preferred method a pistol shot to the mouth. The heavy mantle of collective forgetfulness seemed to descend around us the day the weapons went quiet. In those days I learned that nothing is more frightening than a hero who has lived to tell his story, to tell what all those who fell at his side will never be able to tell. The weeks that followed the fall of Barcelona were indescribable. More blood was shed during those days than during the combat, but secretly, stealthily. When peace finally came, it was the sort of peace that haunts prisons and cemeteries, a shroud of silence and shame that rots the soul. There were no guiltless hands or innocent looks. Those of us who were there, all without exception, will take the secret with us to the grave.

A faint patina of normality was being restored, but by now Julián and I were living in abject poverty. We had spent all the savings and the booty from Laín Coubert's nightly escapades, and there was nothing left in the house to sell. I looked desperately for work as a translator, typist, or cleaner, but it seemed that my past association with Cabestany had marked me out as undesirable. People were suspicious. A government employee in a shiny new suit, with brilliantined hair and a pencil moustache – one of the hundreds who seemed to crawl out of the woodwork during those months – hinted that an attractive girl like me shouldn't have to resort to such mundane jobs. Our neighbours accepted my story that I was taking care of my poor husband, Miquel, who had become an invalid and was disfigured as a result of the war. They would bring us offerings of milk, cheese, or bread, sometimes even salted fish or sausages that had been sent to them by relatives in the country. After months of hardship, convinced that it would take a long time to find a job, I decided on a strategy borrowed from one of Julián's novels.

I wrote to Julián's mother in Bogotá, adopting the name of a fictitious new lawyer whom the deceased Señor Fortuny had consulted in his last days, when he was trying to put his affairs in order. I informed her that, as the hatter had died without having made a will, his estate, which included the apartment in Ronda de San Antonio and the shop situated in the same building, was now theoretically the property of her son Julián who, it was believed, was living in exile in France. Since the death duties had not been satisfied, and since she lived abroad, the lawyer (whom I christened José María Requejo in memory of the first boy who had kissed me in school) asked her for authorization to start the necessary proceedings and carry out the transfer of the properties to the name of her son, whom he intended to contact through the Spanish embassy in Paris. In the meantime he was assuming the transitory and temporary ownership of the said properties, as well as a certain level of financial compensation. He also asked her to get in touch with the manager of the building and instruct him to send all the documents, together with payment for the property expenses, to Señor Requejo's office, in whose name I opened a PO box with a fake address – that of an old, disused garage two blocks away from the ruins of the Aldaya mansion. I was hoping that, blinded by the possibility of being able to help Julián and getting back in contact with him, Sophie would not stop to question all that legal gibberish and would agree to help us, especially in view of her prosperous situation in far-off Colombia.

A couple of months later, the manager of the building began to receive a monthly money order to cover the expenses of the apartment in Ronda de San Antonio and the fees of José María Requejo's law firm, which he proceeded to send as an open cheque to PO Box 2321 in Barcelona, just as Sophie Carax had requested him to do. The manager, I noticed, retained an unauthorized percentage every month, but I preferred not to say anything. That way he wetted his beak and did not question such a convenient arrangement. With the money that remained, Julián and I had enough to survive. Terrible, bleak years went by, during which I managed to find occasional work as a translator. By then nobody remembered Cabestany, and people began to forgive and forget, putting aside old rivalries and grievances. But I lived under the perpetual threat that Fumero might decide to begin rummaging in the past again. Sometimes I convinced myself that it wouldn't happen, that he must have given Julián up for dead by now or forgotten him. Fumero wasn't the thug he was years ago. Now he had graduated into a public figure, an ambitious member of the fascist regime, who couldn't afford the luxury of hunting Julián Carax's ghost. Other times I woke up in the middle of the night with my heart pounding, covered in sweat, thinking that the police were hammering on my door. I feared that some of the neighbours might begin to be suspicious of that ailing husband of mine who never left the house – who sometimes cried or banged the walls like a madman – and that they might report us to the police. I was afraid that Julián might escape again, that he might decide to go out hunting for his books once more. Distracted by so much fear, I forgot that I was growing old, that life was passing me by, and that I had sacrificed my youth to love a man who was now almost a phantom.

But the years went by in peace. Time goes faster the more hollow it is. Lives with no meaning go straight past you, like trains that don't stop at your station. Meanwhile, the scars from the war were, of necessity, healing. I found some work in a couple of publishing firms and spent most of the day out of the house. I had lovers with no name, desperate faces I came across in cinemas or in the metro, with whom I would share my loneliness. Then, absurdly, I'd be consumed by guilt, and when I saw Julián again, I always felt like crying and would swear to myself that I would never betray him again, as if I owed him something. On buses or in the street, I caught myself looking at women who were younger than me holding small children by the hand. They seemed happy, or at peace, as if those helpless little beings could fill all the emptiness in the world. Then I would remember the days when, fantasizing, I had imagined myself as one of those women, with a child in my arms, Julián's child. And then I would think about the war and about the fact that those who waged it had also been children once.

I had started to believe that the world had forgotten us when someone turned up one day at our house. He looked young, barely a boy, a novice who blushed when he looked me in the eye. He asked after Miquel Moliner, and said he was updating some file at the School of Journalism. He told me that Señor Moliner might be the beneficiary of a monthly pension, but if he were to apply for it, he would first have to update a number of details. I told him that Señor Moliner hadn't been living there since the start of the war, that he'd gone abroad. He said he was very sorry and went away leering. He had the face of a young informer, and I knew that I had to get Julián out of my apartment that night, without fail. By now he had almost shrivelled up completely. He was as docile as a child, and his whole life revolved around the evenings we spent together, listening to music on the radio, as he held my hand and stroked it in silence.

When night fell, I took the keys of the apartment in Ronda de San Antonio, which the manager of the building had sent to a nonexistent Señor Requejo, and accompanied Julián back to the home where he had grown up. I set him up in his room and promised him I'd return the following day, reminding him to be very careful.

'Fumero is looking for you again,' I said.

He made a vague gesture with his head, as if he couldn't remember who Fumero was, or no longer cared. Several weeks passed in that way. I always went to the apartment at night, after midnight. I asked Julián what he'd done during the day, and he looked at me, without understanding. We would spend the night together, holding each other, and I would leave at daybreak, promising to return as soon as I could. When I left, I always locked the door of the apartment. Julián didn't have a copy of the key. I preferred to keep him there like a prisoner rather than risk his life.

Nobody else came round to ask after Miquel, but I made sure the rumour got about in the neighbourhood that my husband was in France. I wrote a couple of letters to the Spanish consulate in Paris saying that I knew that the Spanish citizen Julián Carax was in the city and asking for their assistance in finding him. I imagined that sooner or later the letters would reach the right hands. I took all the precautions, but I knew it was only a question of time. People like Fumero never stop hating.

The apartment in Ronda de San Antonio was on the top floor. I discovered that there was a door to the roof terrace at the top of the staircase. The roof terraces of the whole block formed a network of enclosures separated from one another by walls just a yard high, where residents went to hang out their laundry. It didn't take me long to locate a building at the other end of the block, with its front door on Calle Joaquín Costa, to whose roof terrace I could gain access and therefore reach the Ronda de San Antonio building without anyone seeing me go in or come out of the property. I once got a letter from the building manager telling me that neighbours had heard sounds coming from the Fortuny apartment. I answered in Requejo's name stating that occasionally a member of the firm had gone to the apartment to look for papers or documents and there was no cause for alarm, even if the sounds were heard at night. I added a comment implying that among gentlemen – accountants and lawyers – a secret bachelor pad was no small treasure. The manager, showing professional understanding, answered that I need not worry in the least, that he completely understood the situation.

During those years, playing the role of Señor Requejo was my only source of entertainment. Once a month I went to visit my father at the Cemetery of Forgotten Books. He never showed any interest in meeting my invisible husband, and I never offered to introduce him. We would skirt around the subject in our conversations like expert mariners dodging reefs near the water's surface. Occasionally he asked me whether I needed any help, whether there was anything he could do.

On Saturdays, at dawn, I sometimes took Julián to look at the sea. We would go up to the roof, cross over to the adjoining building and then step out into Calle Joaquín Costa. From there we made our way down towards the port through the narrow streets of the Raval quarter. We never encountered anyone. People were afraid of Julián, even from a distance. At times we went as far as the breakwater. Julián liked to sit on the rocks, facing the city. We could spend hours like that, hardly speaking. Some afternoons we'd slip into a cinema, when the show had already started. In the dark nobody noticed Julián. As the months went by, I learned to confuse routine with normality and in time I came to believe that my arrangement was perfect. What a fool I was.

# 12

Nineteen forty-five, a year of ashes. Only six years had elapsed since the end of the Civil War, and although its bruises were still being felt, almost nobody spoke about it openly. Now people talked about the other war, the world war, that had polluted the entire globe with a stench of corpses that would never go away. Those were years of want and misery, strangely blessed by the sort of peace that the dumb and the disabled inspire in us – halfway between pity and revulsion. At last, after years of searching in vain for work as a translator, I found a job as a copy-editor in a publishing house run by a businessman of the new breed – Pedro Sanmartí. Sanmartí had built his company with the fortune belonging to his father-in-law, who had then been promptly dispatched to a nursing home on the shores of Lake Bañolas while Sanmartí awaited a letter containing his death certificate. The businessman liked to court young ladies half his age by presenting himself as the self-made man, an image much in vogue at the time. He spoke broken English with a thick accent, convinced that it was the language of the future, and he finished his sentences with 'Okay'.

Sanmartí's firm (which he had named Endymion because he thought it sounded impressive and was likely to sell books) published catechisms, manuals on etiquette, and various series of moralizing novels whose protagonists were either young nuns involved in humorous capers, Red Cross workers, or civil servants who were happy and morally sound. We also published a comic-book series about soldiers called *Brave Commando* – a roaring success among young boys in need of heroes. I made a good friend in the firm, Sanmartí's secretary, a war widow called Mercedes Pietro, with whom I soon felt a great affinity. Mercedes and I had a lot in common: we were two women adrift, surrounded by men who were either dead or hiding from the world. Mercedes had a seven-year-old son who suffered from muscular dystrophy, whom she cared for as best she could. She was only thirty-two, but the lines on her face spoke of a life of hardship. All those years Mercedes was the only person to whom I felt tempted to tell everything.

It was she who told me that Sanmartí was a great friend of the increasingly renowned and decorated Inspector Javier Fumero. They both belonged to a clique of individuals that had risen from the ruins of the war to spread its tentacles throughout the city, a new power elite.

One day Fumero turned up at the publishing firm. He was coming to visit his friend Sanmartí, with whom he'd arranged to have lunch. Under some pretext or other, I hid in the filing room until they had both left. When I returned to my desk, Mercedes threw me a look; nothing needed to be said. From then on, every time Fumero made an appearance in the offices of the publisher, she would warn me so that I could hide.

Not a day passed without Sanmartí trying to take me out to dinner, to the theatre or the cinema, using any excuse. I always replied that my husband was waiting for me at home and that surely his wife must be anxious, as it was getting late. Señora Sanmartí fell well below the Bugatti on the list of her husband's favourite items. Indeed, she was close to losing her role in the marriage charade altogether, now that her father's fortune had passed into Sanmartí's hands. Mercedes had already warned me: Sanmartí, whose powers of concentration were limited, hankered after young, undisclosed flesh and concentrated his inane womanizing on any new arrivals – which, at the moment, meant me. He would resort to all manner of ploys:

'They tell me your husband, this Señor Moliner, is a writer. . . . Perhaps he would be interested in writing a book about my friend Fumero. I have the title: Fumero, the Scourge of Crime. What do you think, Nurieta?'

'I'm very grateful, Señor Sanmartí, but Miquel is busy writing a novel at the moment, and I don't think he would be able to.'

Sanmartí would burst out laughing.

'A novel? Goodness, Nurieta . . . the novel is dead and buried. A friend of mine from New York was telling me only the other day. Americans are inventing something called television which will be like the cinema, only in your own home. There'll be no more need for books, or churches, or anything. Tell your husband to forget about novels. If at least he were well known, if he were a football player or a bullfighter . . . Look, how about getting into the Bugatti and going to eat a paella in Castelldefels so we can discuss all this? Come on, woman, you've got to make an effort . . . You know I'd like to help you. And your nice husband, too. You know only too well that in this country, without the right kind of friends, there's no getting anywhere.'

I began to dress like a pious widow or one of those women who seem to confuse sunlight with mortal sin. I went to work with my hair drawn back into a bun and no makeup. Despite my tactics, Sanmartí continued to shower me with lascivious remarks accompanied by his oily, putrid smile. It was a smile full of disdain, typical of those self-important imbeciles who hang like stuffed sausages from the top of all corporate ladders. I had two or three interviews for prospective jobs elsewhere, but sooner or later I would always come up against another version of Sanmartí. His type grew like a plague of fungi, thriving on the dung on which companies are built. One of them took the trouble to phone Sanmartí and tell him that Nuria Monfort was looking for work behind his back. Sanmartí summoned me to his office, wounded by my ingratitude. He put his hand on my cheek and tried to stroke it. His fingers smelled of tobacco and stale sweat. I went deathly pale.

'Come on, if you're not happy, all you have to do is tell me. What can I do to improve your work conditions? You know how much I appreciate you, and it hurts me to hear that you want to leave us. How about going out to dinner, you and me, to make up?'

I removed his hand from my face, unable to go on hiding the repugnance it caused me.

'You disappoint me, Nuria. I have to admit that you don't seem to be a team player, that you don't appear to believe in this company's business objectives anymore.'

Mercedes had already warned me that sooner or later something like this would happen. A few days afterwards, Sanmartí, whose grammar was no better than an ape's, started returning all the manuscripts that I corrected, alleging that they were full of errors. Practically every day I stayed on in the office until ten or eleven at night, endlessly redoing pages and pages with Sanmartí's crossings-out and comments.

'Too many verbs in the past tense. It sounds dead, lifeless. ... The infinitive should not be used after a semicolon. Everyone knows that.'

Some nights Sanmartí would also stay late, secluded in his study. Mercedes tried to be there, but more than once he sent her home. Then, when we were left alone, he would come out of his office and wander over to my desk.

'You work too hard, Nuria. Work isn't everything. You need to enjoy yourself too. And you're still young. But youth passes,

452

*you know, and we don't always know how to make the most of it.'*

He would sit on the edge of my table and stare at me. Sometimes he would stand behind me and remain there a couple of minutes. I could feel his foul breath on my hair. Other times he placed his hands on my shoulders.

*'You're tense. Relax.'*

I trembled, I wanted to scream or run away and never return to that office, but I needed the job and its miserly pay. One night Sanmartí started on his routine massage and then he began to fondle me.

*'One of these days you're going to make me lose my head,'* he moaned.

I leaped up, breaking free from his grasp, and ran towards the exit, grabbing my coat and bag. Behind me, Sanmartí laughed. At the bottom of the staircase, I ran straight into a dark figure.

*'What a pleasant surprise, Señora Moliner . . .'*

Inspector Fumero gave me one of his snakelike smiles. *'Don't tell me you're working for my good friend Sanmartí! Lucky girl. He's at the top of his game, just like me. So tell me, how's your husband?'*

I knew that my time was up. The following day, a rumour spread round the office that Nuria Monfort was a dyke – since she remained immune to Don Pedro Sanmartí's charms and his garlic breath – and that she was involved with Mercedes Pietro. More than one promising young man in the company swore that on a number of occasions he had seen that 'couple of sluts' kissing in the filing room. That afternoon, on her way out, Mercedes asked me whether she could have a quick word with me. She could barely bring herself to look at me. We went to the corner café without exchanging a single word. There Mercedes told me what Sanmartí had told her: that he didn't approve of our friendship, that the police had supplied him with a report on me, detailing my suspected communist past.

'I can't afford to lose this job, Nuria. I need it to take care of my son.'

She broke down crying, burning with shame and humiliation.

'Don't worry, Mercedes. I understand,' I said.

'This man, Fumero, he's after you, Nuria. I don't know what he has against you, but it shows in his face.'

'I know.'

The following Monday, when I arrived at work, I found a skinny man with greased-back hair sitting at my desk. He introduced himself as Salvador Benades, the new copy-editor.

'And who are you?'

Not a single person in the office dared look at me or speak to me while I collected my things. On my way down the stairs, Mercedes ran after me and handed me an envelope with a wad of banknotes and some coins.

'Nearly everyone has contributed whatever they could. Take it, please. Not for your sake, for ours.'

That night I went to the apartment in Ronda de San Antonio. Julián was waiting for me as usual, sitting in the dark. He'd written a poem for me, he said. It was the first thing he'd written in nine years. I wanted to read it, but I broke down in his arms. I told him everything, because I couldn't hold back any longer. Julián listened to me without speaking, holding me and stroking my hair. It was the first time in years that I felt I could lean on him. I wanted to kiss him because I was sick with loneliness, but Julián had no lips or skin to offer me. I fell asleep in his arms, curled up on the bed in his room, a child's bunk. When I woke up, Julián wasn't there. At dawn I heard his footsteps on the roof terrace and pretended I was still asleep. Later that morning I heard the news on the radio without realizing its significance. A body had been found sitting on a bench on Pasco del Borne. The dead man had his hands crossed over his lap and was staring at the basilica of Santa María del

Mar. A flock of pigeons pecking at his eyes caught the attention of a local resident, who alerted the police. The corpse had had its neck broken. Señora Sanmartí identified it as her husband, Pedro Sanmartí Monegal. When the father-in-law of the deceased heard the news in his Bañolas nursing home, he gave thanks to heaven and told himself he could now die in peace.

# 13

Julián once wrote that coincidences are the scars of fate. There are no coincidences, Daniel. We are puppets of our subconscious desires. For years I had wanted to believe that Julián was still the man I had fallen in love with, or what was left of him. I had wanted to believe that we could manage to keep going with sporadic bursts of misery and hope. I had wanted to believe that Laín Coubert had died and returned to the pages of a book. We are willing to believe anything other than the truth.

Sanmartí's murder opened my eyes. I realized that Laín Coubert was still alive, residing within Julián's burned body and feeding on his memory. He had found out how to get in and out of the apartment in Ronda de San Antonio through a window that gave onto the inner courtyard, without having to force open the door I locked every time I left him there. I discovered that Laín Coubert had been roaming through the city and visiting the old Aldaya mansion. I discovered that in his madness he had returned to the crypt and had broken the tombstones, that he had taken out the coffins of Penélope and his son. What have you done, Julián?

The police were waiting for me when I returned home, to interrogate me about the death of Sanmartí, the publisher. They took me to their headquarters where, after five hours of waiting in a dark office, Fumero arrived, dressed in black, and offered me a cigarette.

'*You and I could be friends, Señora Moliner. My men tell me your husband isn't home.*'

'*My husband left me. I don't know where he is.*'

He knocked me off the chair with a brutal slap in the face. I crawled into a corner, seized by fear. I didn't dare look up. Fumero knelt beside me and grabbed me by my hair.

'*Try to understand this, you fucking whore: I'm going to find him, and when I do, I'll kill you both. You first, so he can see you with your guts hanging out. And then him, once I've told him that the other tart he sent to the grave was his sister.*'

'*He'll kill you first, you son of a bitch.*'

Fumero spat in my face and let me go. I thought he was going to beat me up, but then I heard his steps as he walked away down the corridor. I rose to my feet, trembling, and wiped the blood off my face. I could smell that man's hand on my skin, but this time I recognized the stench of fear.

They kept me in that room, in the dark and with no water, for six hours. Night had fallen when they let me out. It was raining hard and the streets shimmered with steam. When I got home, I found a sea of debris. Fumero's men had been there. Among the fallen furniture and the drawers and bookshelves thrown on the floor, I found my clothes all torn to shreds and Miquel's books destroyed. On my bed I found a pile of faeces and on the wall, written in excrement, I read the word WHORE.

I ran to the apartment in Ronda de San Antonio, making a thousand detours to ensure that none of Fumero's henchmen had followed me to the door in Calle Joaquín Costa. I crossed the roof terraces – they were flooded with the rain – and saw that the front door of the apartment was still locked. I went in cautiously, but the echo of my footsteps told me it was empty. Julián was not there. I waited for him, sitting in the dark dining room, listening to the storm, until dawn. When the morning mist licked the balcony shutters, I went up to the roof terrace and gazed at the city, crushed under a leaden sky. I knew that Julián would not return there. I had lost him forever.

I saw him again two months later. I had gone into a cinema at night, alone, feeling incapable of returning to my cold, empty apartment. Halfway through the film, some stupid romance between a Romanian princess eager for adventure and a handsome American reporter with perfect hair, a man sat down next to me. It wasn't the first time. In those days cinemas were crawling with anonymous men who reeked of loneliness, urine, and eau de cologne, wielding their sweaty, trembling hands like tongues of dead flesh. I was about to get up and warn the usher when I recognized Julián's wrinkled profile. He gripped my hand tightly, and we remained like that, looking at the screen without seeing it.

'Did you kill Sanmartí?' I murmured.

'Does anyone miss him?'

We spoke in whispers, under the attentive gaze of the solitary men who were dotted around the stalls, green with envy at the apparent success of their shadowy rival. I asked him where he'd been hiding, but he didn't reply.

'There's another copy of *The Shadow of the Wind*,' he murmured. 'Here, in Barcelona.'

'You're wrong, Julián. You destroyed them all.'

'All but one. It seems that someone more clever than I hid it in a place where I would never be able to find it. You.'

That's how I first came to hear about you. Some bigmouthed bookseller called Gustavo Barceló had been boasting to a group of collectors about having located a copy of *The Shadow of the Wind*. The world of rare books is like an echo chamber. In less than two months, Barceló was receiving offers for the book from collectors in London, Paris, and Rome. Julián's mysterious flight from Paris after a bloody duel and his rumoured death in the Spanish Civil War had conferred on his works an undreamed-of market value. The black legend of a faceless individual who searched for them in every bookshop, library, and private collection and then burned them only added to the interest and the price. 'We have the circus in our blood,' Barceló would say.

Julián, who continued to pursue the shadow of his own words, soon picked up the rumour. This is how he learned that Gustavo Barceló didn't have the book: apparently the copy belonged to a boy who had discovered it by chance and who, fascinated by the novel and its mysterious author, refused to sell it and guarded it as his most precious possession. That boy was you, Daniel.

'For heaven's sake, Julián, don't tell me you're going to harm a child ...' I whispered, not quite sure of his intentions.

Julián then told me that all the books he'd stolen and destroyed had been snatched from people who felt nothing for them, from people who just did business with them or kept them as curiosities. Because you refused to sell the book at any price and tried to rescue Carax from the recesses of the past, you awoke a strange sympathy in him, and even respect. Unbeknownst to you, Julián observed you and studied you.

'Perhaps, if he ever discovers who I am and what I am, he, too, will decide to burn the book.'

Julián spoke with the clear, unequivocal lucidity of madmen who have escaped the hypocrisy of having to abide by a reality that makes no sense.

'Who is this boy?'

'His name is Daniel. He's the son of a bookseller whose shop Miquel used to frequent in Calle Santa Ana. He lives with his father in an apartment above the shop. He lost his mother when he was very young.'

'You sound as if you were speaking about yourself.'

'Perhaps. This boy reminds me of myself.'

'Leave him alone, Julián. He's only a child. His only crime has been to admire you.'

'That's not a crime, it's a misconception. But he'll get

over it. Perhaps then he'll return the book to me. When he stops admiring me and begins to understand me.'

A minute before the end of the film, Julián stood up and left. For months we saw each other like that, in the dark, in cinemas or alleyways, at midnight. Julián always found me. I felt his silent presence without seeing him and was always vigilant. Sometimes he mentioned you. Every time I heard him talk about you, I sensed a rare tenderness in his voice that confused him, a tenderness that, for years now, I had thought lost. I found out that he'd returned to the Aldaya mansion and that he now lived there, halfway between a ghost and a beggar, watching over Penélope's remains and those of their son. It was the only place that he still felt was his. There are worse prisons than words.

I went there once a month to make sure he was all right, or at least alive. I would jump over the tumbled-down wall at the back of the property, that couldn't be seen from the street. Sometimes I'd find him there, other times Julián had disappeared. I left food for him, money, books. . . . I would wait for him for hours, until it got dark. A few times I began to explore the rambling old house. That is how I discovered that he'd destroyed the tombstones in the crypt and taken out the coffins. I no longer thought Julián was mad, nor did I view that desecration as a monstrous act, just a tragic one. When I did find him there we would speak for hours, sitting by the fire. Julián confessed that he had tried to write again but was unable to. He vaguely remembered his books as if they were the work of some other person that he'd happened to read. The pain of his attempts to write was visible. I discovered that he burned the pages he had written feverishly while I was not there. Once, taking advantage of his absence, I rescued a pile of them from the ashes. They spoke about you. Julián had once told me that a story is a letter the author writes to himself, to tell himself things that he would be unable to discover otherwise. For some time now, Julián had been wondering whether he'd gone out of his mind. Does the madman know he is mad? Or are the madmen those who insist on convincing him of his unreason in order to safeguard their own idea of reality? Julián observed you, watched you grow, and wondered who you were. He wondered whether your presence was perhaps a miracle, a pardon he had to win by teaching you not to make the same mistakes he'd made. More than once I asked myself whether Julián hadn't reached the conclusion that you, in that twisted logic of his universe, had become the son he had lost, a blank page on which to restart a story that he could not invent but could remember.

Those years in the old mansion went by, and Julián became increasingly watchful of you, of your progress. He talked to me about your friends, about a woman called Clara with whom you had fallen in love, about your father, a man he admired and esteemed, about your friend Fermín, and about a girl in whom he wanted to see another Penélope – your Bea. He spoke about you as if you were his son. You were both looking for one another, Daniel. He wanted to believe that your innocence would save him from himself. He had stopped chasing his books, stopped wanting to destroy them. He was learning to see the world again through your eyes, to recover the boy he had once been, in you. The day you came to my apartment for the first time, I felt I already knew you. I feigned distrust so I could hide the fear you inspired in me. I was afraid of you, of what you might discover. I was afraid of listening to Julián and starting to believe, as he did, that we were all bound together in a strange chain of destiny, afraid of recognizing in you the Julián I had lost. I knew that you and your friends were investigating our past, that sooner or later you would discover the truth, but I hoped that it would be in due course, when you were able to understand its meaning. And I knew that sooner or later you and Julián would meet. That was my mistake. Because someone else knew it, someone who sensed that, in time, you would lead him to Julián: Fumero.

I only understood what was happening when there was no

turning back, but I never lost hope that you might lose the trail, that you might forget about us, or that life – yours and not ours – might take you far away, to safety. Time has taught me not to lose hope, yet not to trust too much in hope either. Hope is cruel, and has no conscience. For a long time, Fumero has been watching me. He knows I'll fall, sooner or later. He's in no hurry. He lives to avenge himself. Without vengeance, without anger, he would melt away. Fumero knows that you and your friends will take him to Julián. He knows that after almost fifteen years, I have no more strength or resources. He has watched me die for years, and he's only waiting for the moment when he will deal me the final blow. I have never doubted that I will die by his hand. Now I know the moment is drawing near. I will give these pages to my father, asking him to make sure they reach you if anything should happen to me. I pray to that God who never crossed my path that you will never have to read them, but I sense that my fate, despite my wishes and my vain hopes, is to hand you this story. Yours, despite your youth and your innocence, is to set it free.

When you read these words, this prison of memories, it will mean that I will no longer be able to say goodbye to you as I would have wished, that I will not be able to ask you to forgive us, especially Julián, and to take care of him when I am no longer there to do so. I know I cannot ask anything of you, but I can ask you to save yourself. Perhaps so many pages have managed to convince me that whatever happens, I will always have a friend in you, that you are my only hope, my only real hope. Of all the things that Julián wrote, the one I have always felt closest to my heart is that as long as we are remembered, we remain alive. As so often happened to me with Julián, years before meeting him, I feel that I know you and that if I can trust in anyone, that someone is you. Remember me, Daniel, even if it's only in a corner and secretly. Don't let me go.

*Nuria Monfort*

# THE SHADOW OF THE WIND
## 1955

# 1

Day was breaking when I finished reading Nuria Monfort's manuscript. That was my story. Our story. In Carax's lost footsteps, I now recognized my own, irretrievable. I stood, devoured by anxiety, and began to pace up and down the room. All my reservations, my suspicions and fears, seemed insignificant; I was overwhelmed by exhaustion, remorse, and dread, but I felt incapable of remaining there, hiding from the trail left by my actions. I slung on my coat, thrust the folded manuscript into the inside pocket, and ran down the stairs. As I stepped out of the front door, it had started to snow, and the sky was melting into slow tears of light that seemed to lie on my breath before fading away. I ran up to Plaza de Cataluña. It was almost deserted but in the centre of the square stood the lonely figure of an old man, with long white hair and clad in a wonderful grey overcoat. King of the dawn, he raised his eyes to heaven and tried in vain to catch the snowflakes with his gloves, laughing to himself. As I walked past him, he looked at me and smiled gravely. His eyes were the colour of gold, like magic coins at the bottom of a fountain.

'Good luck,' I thought I heard him say.

I tried to cling to that blessing and quickened my step, praying that it would not be too late and that Bea, the Bea of my story, would still be waiting for me.

My throat was burning with the cold when, panting after the run, I reached the building where the Aguilars lived. The snow was beginning to settle. I had the good fortune of finding Don Saturno Molleda stationed at the entrance. Don Saturno was the caretaker of the building and (from what Bea had told me) a secret surrealist poet. He had come out to watch the spectacle of the snow, broom in hand, wrapped in at least three scarves and wearing combat boots.

'It's God's dandruff,' he said, marvelling, offering the snow a preview of his unpublished verse.

'I'm going up to the Aguilars' apartment,' I announced.

'We all know that the early bird catches the worm, but you're trying to catch an elephant, young man.'

'It's an emergency. They're expecting me.'

'*Ego te absolvo*,' he recited, blessing me.

I ran up the stairs. As I ascended, I weighed up my options with some caution. If I was lucky, one of the maids would open the door, and I was ready to break through her blockade without bothering about the niceties. However, if the fates didn't favour me, perhaps Bea's father would open the door, given the hour. I wanted to think that in the intimacy of his home, he would not be armed, at least not before breakfast. I paused for a few moments to recover my breath before knocking and tried to conjure up words that never came. Little did it matter. I struck the door hard with the knocker three times. Fifteen seconds later I repeated the operation, and went on doing this, ignoring the cold sweat that covered my brow and the beating of my heart. When the door opened, I was still holding the knocker in my hand.

'What do you want?'

The eyes of my old friend Tomás, cold with anger, bored through me.

'I've come to see Bea. You can smash my face in if you feel like it, but I'm not leaving without speaking to her.'

Tomás observed me with a fixed stare. I wondered whether he was going to cleave me in two there and then. I swallowed hard.

'My sister isn't here.'

'Tomás . . .'

'Bea's gone.'

There was despondency and pain in his voice, which he was barely able to disguise as wrath.

'She's gone? Where?'

466

'I was hoping you would know.'

'Me?'

Ignoring Tomás's closed fists and the threatening expression on his face, I slipped into the apartment.

'Bea?' I shouted. 'Bea, it's me, Daniel....'

I stopped halfway along the corridor. The apartment threw back the echo of my voice. Neither Señor Aguilar nor his wife nor the servants appeared in response to my cries.

'There's no one here. I've told you,' said Tomás behind me. 'Now get out and don't come back. My father has sworn he'll kill you, and I'm not going to be the one to stop him.'

'For God's sake, Tomás. Tell me where your sister is.'

He looked at me as if he wasn't sure whether to spit at me or ignore me.

'Bea has left home, Daniel. My parents have been looking everywhere for her, desperately, for two days, and so have the police.'

'But ...'

'The other night, when she came back after seeing you, my father was waiting for her. He slapped her so much he made her mouth bleed. But don't worry, she refused to give him your name. You don't deserve her.'

'Tomás ...'

'Shut up. The following day my parents took her to the doctor.'

'What for? Is Bea ill?'

'She's ill because of you, you idiot. My sister is pregnant. Don't tell me you didn't know.'

I felt my lips quivering. An intense cold spread through my body, my voice stolen, my eyes fixed. I dragged myself toward the front door, but Tomás grabbed me by the arm and threw me against the wall.

'What have you done to her?'

'Tomás, I ...'

His eyes flashed with impatience. The first blow cut my breath in two. I slid to the floor, my back against the wall,

467

my knees giving way. A powerful grip seized me by the throat and held me up, nailed to the wall.

'What have you done to her, you son of a bitch?'

I tried to get away, but Tomás knocked me down with another punch to the face. I fell into blackness, my head wrapped in a blaze of pain. I collapsed onto the corridor tiles. I tried to crawl away, but Tomás grasped my coat collar and dragged me to the landing. He tossed me onto the staircase like a piece of rubbish.

'If anything has happened to Bea, I swear I'll kill you,' he said from the doorway.

I got up on my knees, begging for a moment of time, for an opportunity to recover my voice. But the door closed, abandoning me to the darkness. There was a sharp pain in my left ear, and I put my hand to my head, twisting with agony. I could feel warm blood. I stood up as best I could. My stomach muscles, where Tomás's first blow had landed, were smarting – that was just the beginning. I slid down the stairs. Don Saturno shook his head when he saw me.

'Here, come inside for a minute, until you feel better.'

I shook my head, holding my stomach with both hands. The left side of my head throbbed, as if the bones were trying to detach themselves from the flesh.

'You're bleeding,' said Don Saturno with a concerned look.

'It's not the first time. . . .'

'Well, if you keep on fooling around, you won't have many chances left. Here, come in and I'll call a doctor, please.'

I managed to get to the main door and escape the caretaker's kindness. It was now snowing hard and the pavements were covered in veils of white mist. The icy wind whistled through my clothes and stung the bleeding wound on my face. I don't know whether I was crying with pain, anger, or fear. The indifferent snow silenced my cowardly weeping, and I walked away slowly into the dawn, one more shadow leaving his tracks in God's dandruff.

# 2

As I approached the crossing with Calle Balmes, I noticed that a car was following me, hugging the pavement. The pain in my head had given way to a feeling of vertigo that made me reel, so that I had to walk holding onto the walls. The car stopped, and two men got out. A sharp, whistling sound had filled my ears, and I couldn't hear the engine or the calls of the two figures in black who grabbed hold of me, one on either side, and dragged me hurriedly to the car. I fell into the back seat, drunk with nausea. Floods of blinding light came and went inside my brain. I felt the car moving. A pair of hands touched my face, my head, my ribs. Coming upon the manuscript of Nuria Monfort, which was hidden inside my coat, one of the figures snatched it from me. I tried to stop him with jellylike arms. The other silhouette leaned over me. I knew he was talking when I felt his breath on my face. I waited to see Fumero's face light up and feel the blade of his knife on my throat. Two eyes rested on mine, and as the curtain of consciousness fell, I recognized the toothless, welcoming smile of Fermín Romero de Torres.

I woke up in a sweat that stung my skin. Two hands held my shoulders firmly and settled me into a small bed surrounded by candles, as in a wake. Fermín's face appeared on my right. He was smiling, but even in my delirium I could sense his anxiety. Next to him, standing, I recognized Don Federico Flaviá, the watchmaker.

'He seems to be coming round, Fermín,' said Don Federico. 'Shall I go and prepare some broth to revive him?'

'It won't do him any harm. While you're at it, could you make me a sandwich? Whatever you can find. A double-decker, if you please. All this excitement has suddenly revived my appetite.'

Federico scurried off, and we were left alone.

'Where are we, Fermín?'

'In a safe place. Technically speaking, we're in a small apartment on the left side of the Ensanche quarter, the property of some friends of Don Federico, to whom we owe our lives and more. Slanderers would describe it as a love nest, but for us it's a sanctuary.'

I tried to sit up. The pain in my ear was now a burning throb.

'Will I go deaf?'

'I don't know about that, but a bit more beating and you'd certainly have been left a borderline vegetable. That troglodyte Señor Aguilar almost pulped your grey cells.'

'It wasn't Señor Aguilar who beat me. It was Tomás.'

'Tomás? Your friend? The inventor?'

I nodded.

'You must have done something to deserve it.'

'Bea has left home . . .' I began.

Fermín frowned. 'Go on.'

'She's pregnant.'

Fermín was looking at me openmouthed. For once his expression was impenetrable.

'Don't look at me like that, Fermín, please.'

'What do you want me to do? Start handing out cigars?'

I tried to get up, but the pain and Fermín's hands stopped me.

'I've got to find her, Fermín.'

'Steady, there. You're not in any fit state to go anywhere. Tell me where the girl is, and I'll go and find her.'

'I don't know where she is.'

'I'm going to have to ask you to be more specific.'

Don Federico appeared carrying a cup of steaming broth. He smiled at me warmly.

'How are you feeling, Daniel?'

'Much better, thanks, Don Federico.'

'Take a couple of these pills with the soup.'

He glanced briefly at Fermín, who nodded.

'They're painkillers.'

I swallowed the pills and sipped the cup of broth, which tasted of sherry. Don Federico, the soul of discretion, left the room and closed the door. It was then that I noticed that Fermín had Nuria Montfort's manuscript on his lap. The clock ticking on the bedside table showed one o'clock – in the afternoon, I supposed.

'Is it still snowing?'

'That's an understatement. This is a powdery version of the Flood.'

'Have you read it?' I asked.

Fermín simply nodded.

'I must find Bea before it's too late. I think I know where she is.'

I sat up in bed, pushing Fermín's arms aside. I looked around me. The walls swayed like weeds at the bottom of a pond and the ceiling seemed to be moving away. I could barely hold myself upright. Fermín effortlessly laid me back on the bed again.

'You're not going anywhere, Daniel.'

'What were those pills?'

'Morpheus's liniment. You're going to sleep like a log.'

'No, not now, I can't ...'

I continued to blabber until my eyelids closed and I dropped into a black, empty sleep, the sleep of the guilty.

It was almost dusk when the tombstone was lifted from me. I opened my eyes to a dark room watched over by two tired candles flickering on the bedside table. Fermín, defeated on an armchair in the corner, snored with the fury of a man three times his size. At his feet, scattered like a flood of tears, lay Nuria Monfort's manuscript. The headache had lessened to a slow, tepid throb. I tiptoed over to the bedroom door and went out into a little hall with a balcony and a door that seemed to open onto the staircase. My coat and shoes lay on a chair. A purplish light came in through the window, speckled with iridescence. I walked over to the

471

balcony and saw that it was still snowing. Half the roofs of Barcelona were mottled with white and scarlet. In the distance the towers of the Industrial College looked like needles in the haze, clinging to the last rays of sun. The windowpane was coated with frost. I put my index finger on the glass and wrote:

*Gone to find Bea. Don't follow me. Back soon.*

The truth had struck me as soon as I woke up, as if some stranger had whispered it to me in a dream. I stepped out onto the landing and rushed down the stairs and out of the front door. Calle Urgel was like a river of shiny white sand as the wind blew the snow about in gusts. Streetlamps and trees emerged like masts in the fog. I walked to the nearest subway station, Hospital Clínico, past the stand of afternoon papers carrying the news on the front page, with photographs of the Ramblas covered in snow and the Canaletas fountain bleeding stalactites. SNOWFALL OF THE CENTURY, the headlines blared. I fell onto a bench on the platform and breathed in that perfume of tunnels and soot that trains bring with them. On the other side of the tracks, on a poster proclaiming the delights of the Tibidabo amusement park, the blue tram was lit up like a street party, and behind it you could just make out the outline of the Aldaya mansion. I wondered whether Bea had seen the same image and realized she had nowhere else to go.

# 3

When I came out of the subway tunnel, it was starting to get dark. Avenida del Tibidabo lay deserted, stretching out in a long line of cypress trees and mansions. I glimpsed the shape of the blue tram at the stop and heard the conductor's bell piercing the wind. A quick run, and I jumped on just as it was pulling away. The conductor, my old acquaintance, took the coins, mumbling under his breath, and I sat down inside the carriage, a bit more sheltered from the snow and the cold. The sombre mansions filed slowly by, behind the tram's icy windows. The conductor watched me with a mixture of suspicion and bemusement, which the cold seemed to have frozen on his face.

'Number thirty-two, young man.'

I turned and saw the ghostly silhouette of the Aldaya mansion advancing towards us like the prow of a dark ship. The tram stopped with a shudder. I got off, fleeing from the conductor's gaze.

'Good luck,' he murmured.

I watched the tram disappear up the avenue, leaving behind only the echo of its bell. Darkness fell around me. I hurried along the garden wall, looking for the gap at the back, where it had tumbled down. As I climbed over, I thought I could hear footsteps on the snow approaching on the opposite pavement. I stopped for a second and remained motionless on top of the wall. The sound of footsteps faded in the wind. I jumped down to the other side and entered the garden. The weeds had frozen into stems of crystal. The statues of the fallen angels were covered in shrouds of ice. The water in the fountain had frozen over, forming a black, shiny mirror, from which only the stone claw of the sunken angel protruded, like an obsidian sword. Tears of ice hung from the index finger. The accusing hand of the angel pointed straight at the main door, which stood ajar.

I ran up the steps without bothering to muffle the sound of my footsteps. Pushing the door open, I walked into the entrance hall. A procession of candles lined the way towards the interior. They were Bea's candles but had almost burned down to the floor. I followed their trail and stopped at the foot of the grand staircase. The path of candles continued up the steps to the first floor. I ventured up the stairs, following my distorted shadow on the walls. When I reached the first-floor landing, I saw two more candles set along the corridor. A third one flickered outside the room that had once been Penélope's. I went up to the door and rapped gently with my knuckles.

'Julián?' came a shaky voice.

I grabbed hold of the doorknob and slowly opened the door. Bea gazed at me from a corner of the room, wrapped in a blanket. I ran to her side and held her. I could feel her dissolving into tears.

'I didn't know where to go,' she murmured. 'I called your home a few times, but there was no answer. I was scared. . . .'

Bea dried her tears with her fists and fixed her eyes on mine. I nodded; there was no need to reply with words.

'Why did you call me Julián?'

Bea cast a glance at the half-open door. 'He's here. In this house. He comes and goes. He discovered me the other day, when I was trying to get into the house. Without my saying anything, he knew who I was and what was happening. He set me up in this room, and he brought me a blanket, water, and some food. He told me to wait. He said that everything was going to turn out all right, that you'd come for me. At night we talked for hours. He talked to me about Penélope, about Nuria – above all he spoke about you, about us two. He told me I had to teach you to forget him. . . .'

'Where is he now?'

'Downstairs. In the library. He said he was waiting for someone, and told me not to move from here.'

'Waiting for whom?'

'I don't know. He said it was someone who would come with you, that you'd bring him. . . .'

When I peered into the corridor, I could already hear footsteps below, near the staircase. I recognized the spidery shadow on the walls, the black raincoat, the hat pulled down like a hood, and the gun in his hand shining like a scythe. Fumero. He had always reminded me of someone, or something, but until then I hadn't understood what.

# 4

I snuffed out the candles with my fingers and made a sign to Bea to keep quiet. She grabbed my hand and looked at me questioningly. Fumero's slow steps could be heard below us. I led Bea back inside the room and signalled to her to stay there, hiding behind the door.

'Don't leave this room, whatever happens,' I whispered.

'Don't leave me now, Daniel. Please.'

'I must warn Carax.'

Bea gave me an imploring look, but I went out into the corridor and tiptoed to the top of the main staircase. There was no sign of Fumero. He had stopped at some point in the darkness and stood there, motionless, patient. I stepped back into the corridor and walked down it, past the row of bedrooms, until I got to the front of the mansion. A large window coated in frost refracted two blue beams of light, cloudy as stagnant water. I moved over to the window and saw a black car stationed in front of the main gate, its lights on. I recognized it as Lieutenant Palacios's car. The glowing ember of a cigarette in the dark gave away his presence behind the steering wheel. I went slowly back to the staircase and began to descend, step by step, placing my feet with infinite care. Halfway down, I stopped and scanned the darkness that had engulfed the ground floor.

Fumero had left the front door open as he came in. The wind had blown out the candles and was spitting whirls of snow and frozen leaves across the hall. I went down four more steps, hugging the wall, and caught a glimpse of the large library windows. There was still no sign of Fumero. I wondered whether he had gone down to the basement or to the crypt. The powdery snow that blew in from outside was fast erasing his footprints. I slipped down to the base of the stairs and peered into the corridor that led to the main door. An icy wind hit me. The claw of the submerged angel was just visible outside. I looked in the other direction. The entrance to the library was about ten yards from the foot of the staircase. The anteroom that led to it was sunk in shadows, and I realized that Fumero could be only a few yards from where I was standing, watching me. I looked into the darkness, as impenetrable as the waters of a well. Taking a deep breath, I groped across the distance that separated me from the entrance to the library.

The large oval hall was submerged in a dim, misty light, speckled with shadows that were cast by the snow falling heavily on the other side of the windows. My eyes skimmed over the empty walls in search of Fumero – could he be standing by the entrance? An object protruded from the wall just a couple of yards on my right. For a moment I thought I saw it move, but it was only the reflection of the moon on the blade. A knife, perhaps a double-bladed penknife, had been sunk into the wood panelling. It pierced a square of paper or cardboard. I stepped closer and recognized the image. It was an identical copy of the half-burned photograph that a stranger had once left on the bookshop counter. In the picture, Julián and Penélope, still adolescents, smiled in happiness. The knife went through Julián's chest. I understood then that it hadn't been Laín Coubert, or Julián Carax, who had left the photograph for me, like an invitation. It had been Fumero. The photograph had been poisoned bait. I raised my hand to snatch it away from the knife, but the icy touch of Fumero's gun on my neck stopped me.

'An image is worth more than a thousand words, Daniel. If your father hadn't been a shitty bookseller, he would have taught you that by now.'

I turned slowly and faced the barrel of the pistol. It stank of fresh gunpowder. Fumero's face was contorted into a terrifying grimace.

'Where's Carax?' he demanded.

'Far from here. He knew you would come for him. He's left.'

Fumero observed me in silence. 'I'm going to blow your brains out, kid.'

'That's not going to help you much. Carax isn't here.'

'Open your mouth,' ordered Fumero.

'What for?'

'Open your mouth or I'll open it myself with a bullet.'

I parted my lips. Fumero stuck the revolver in my mouth. I felt nausea rising in my throat. Fumero's thumb tensed on the hammer.

'Now, you bastard, think about whether you have any reason to go on living. What do you say?'

I nodded slowly.

'Then tell me where Carax is.'

I tried to mumble. Fumero slowly pulled out the gun.

'Where is he?'

'Downstairs. In the crypt.'

'You lead the way. I want you to be there when I tell that son of a bitch how Nuria Monfort moaned when I dug the knife into—'

Glancing over Fumero's shoulder, I thought I saw the darkness stirring and a figure without a face, his eyes burning, glided towards us in absolute silence, as if he barely touched the floor. Fumero saw the reflection in my tear-filled eyes, and his face slowly became distorted.

When he turned and shot at the mantle of blackness that surrounded him, two deformed leather claws gripped his throat. They were the hands of Julián Carax, grown out of the flames. Carax pushed me aside and crushed Fumero against the wall. The inspector clutched his revolver and tried to place it under Carax's chin. Before he could pull the trigger, Carax grabbed his wrist and hammered it against the wall, again and again, but Fumero didn't drop the gun. A second shot exploded in the dark and hit the wall, making a hole in the wood panelling. Tears of burning

477

gunpowder and red-hot splinters rained down over the inspector's face. A stench of singed flesh filled the room.

With a violent jerk, Fumero tried to get away from the force that was immobilizing his neck and the hand holding the gun, but Carax wouldn't loosen his grip. Fumero roared with anger and tilted his head until he was able to bite Carax's fist. He was possessed by an animal fury. I heard the snap of his teeth as he tore at the dead skin, and saw Fumero's lips dripping with blood. Ignoring the pain, or perhaps unable to feel it, Carax grabbed hold of the dagger on the wall. He pulled it out and skewered the inspector's right wrist to the wall with a brutal blow that buried the blade into the wooden panel almost to the hilt. Fumero let out a terrible cry of pain as his hand opened in a spasm, and the gun fell to his feet. Carax kicked it into the shadows.

The horror of that scene passed before my eyes in just a few seconds. I felt paralysed, incapable of acting or even thinking. Carax turned to me and fixed his eyes on mine. As I looked at him, I was able to reconstruct his lost features, which I had so often imagined from photographs and old stories.

'Take Beatriz away from here, Daniel. She knows what you must do. Don't let her out of your sight. Don't let anyone take her from you. Anyone or anything. Look after her. More than your own life.'

I tried to nod, but my eyes turned to Fumero, who was struggling with the knife that pierced his wrist. He yanked it out and collapsed on his knees, holding the wounded arm that was pouring blood.

'Leave,' Carax murmured.

Fumero watched us from the floor, blind with hatred, holding the bloody knife in his left hand. Carax turned to him. I heard hurried footsteps approaching and realized that Palacios was coming to the aid of his boss, alerted by the shots. Before Carax was able to seize the knife from

Fumero, Palacios entered the library holding his gun up high.

'Move back,' he warned.

He threw a quick glance at Fumero, who was getting up with some difficulty, and then he looked at us – first at me and then at Carax. I could see horror and doubt etched on his face.

'I said move back.'

Carax paused and withdrew. Palacios observed us coldly, trying to work out what he should do. His eyes rested on me.

'You, get out of here. This doesn't have anything to do with you. Go.'

I hesitated for a moment. Carax nodded.

'No one's leaving this place,' Fumero cut in. 'Palacios, hand me your gun.'

Palacios didn't answer.

'Palacios,' Fumero repeated, stretching out his blood-drenched hand, demanding the weapon.

'No,' mumbled Palacios, gritting his teeth.

Fumero, his maddened eyes filled with disdain and fury, grabbed Palacios's gun and pushed him aside with a swipe of his hand. I glanced at Palacios and knew what was going to happen. Fumero raised the gun slowly. His hand shook, and the revolver shone with blood. Carax drew back a step at a time, in search of the shadows, but there was no escape. The revolver's barrel followed him. I felt all the muscles in my body burn with rage. Fumero's deathly grimace, and the way he kept licking his lips like a madman woke me up like a slap in the face. Palacios was looking at me, silently shaking his head. I ignored him. Carax had given up by now and stood motionless in the middle of the room, waiting for the bullet.

Fumero never saw me. For him only Carax existed and that bloodstained hand holding the revolver. I leaped at him. I felt my feet rise from the ground, but everything seemed to freeze in midair. The blast of the shot reached me from afar, like the echo of a receding storm. There was no pain. The bullet went through my ribs. At first there was a blinding flash, as if I'd been hit by a metal bar and propelled through the air for a couple of yards. I didn't feel the fall, although I thought I saw the walls converging and the ceiling descending at great speed towards me.

A hand held the back of my head, and I saw Julián Carax's face bending over me. In my vision Carax appeared exactly as I'd imagined him, as if the flames had never destroyed his features. I noticed the horror in his eyes and saw how he placed his hand on my chest, and wondered what that smoking liquid was flowing between his fingers. It was then I felt that terrible fire, like the hot breath of embers burning inside me. I tried to scream but nothing surfaced except warm blood. I recognized the face of Palacios next to me, full of remorse, defeated. I raised my eyes, and then I saw her. Bea was advancing slowly from the library door, her face suffused with terror and her hands on her lips. She was trembling and shaking her head without speaking. I tried to warn her, but a biting cold was coursing up my arms, stabbing its way into my body.

Fumero was hiding behind the door. Bea didn't notice his presence. When Carax leaped up and Bea turned, the inspector's gun was already almost touching her forehead. Palacios rushed to stop him. He was too late. Carax was already there. I heard his faraway scream, which bore Bea's name. The room lit up with the flash of the shot. The bullet went through Carax's right hand. A moment later the man without a face was falling upon Fumero. I leaned over to see Bea running to my side, unhurt. I looked for Carax, but I couldn't find him. Another figure had taken his place. It was Laín Coubert, just as I'd learned to fear him reading the pages of a book, so many years ago. This time Coubert's claws sank into Fumero's eyes like hooks and pulled him away. I managed to see the inspector's legs as they were hauled out through the library door. I managed to see how his body shook with spasms as Coubert dragged him without pity towards the main door, saw how his knees hit the marble steps and the snow spat on his face, how the man without a face grabbed him by the neck and, lifting him up like a puppet, threw him into the frozen bowl of the fountain. The hand of the angel pierced his chest, spearing him, the accursed soul driven out like black vapour, falling like frozen tears over the mirror of frozen water.

I collapsed then, unable to keep my eyes focused any longer. A white light flooded my pupils and Bea's face receded from me. I closed my eyes and felt her hands on my cheeks and the breath of her voice begging God not to take me, whispering in my ear that she loved me and wouldn't let me go. All I remember is that at that moment a strange peace enveloped me and took away the pain of the slow fire that burned inside me. I saw myself and Bea – an elderly couple – walking hand in hand through the streets of Barcelona, that bewitched city. I saw my father and Nuria Monfort placing white roses on my grave. I saw Fermín crying in Bernarda's arms, and my old friend Tomás, who had fallen silent forever. I saw them the way you see strangers from a train that is moving away too fast. It was then, almost without realizing it, that I remembered my mother's face, a face I had lost so many years before, as if an old cutting had suddenly fallen out of the pages of a book. Her light was all that came with me as I descended.

## POSTMORTEM
## 27 November 1955

*The room was white, a shimmer of sheets, gauzy curtains and bright sunshine. From my window I could make out a blue sea. One day someone would try to convince me that you cannot see the sea from the Corachán Clinic; that its rooms are not white or ethereal, and that the sea that November was like a leaden pond, cold and hostile; that it went on snowing every day of that week until all of Barcelona was buried in three feet of snow, and that even Fermín, the eternal optimist, thought I was going to die again.*

*I had already died before, in the ambulance, in the arms of Bea and Lieutenant Palacios, who ruined his uniform with my blood. The bullet, said the doctors, who spoke about me thinking that I couldn't hear them, had destroyed two ribs, had brushed my heart, had severed an artery, and had come out at full speed through my side, dragging with it everything it had encountered on the way. My heart had stopped beating for sixty-four seconds. They told me that when I returned from my excursion to eternity, I opened my eyes and smiled before losing consciousness again.*

*I didn't come round until eight days later. By then the newspapers had already published the news of Francisco Javier Fumero's death during a struggle with an armed gang of criminals and the authorities were busy trying to find a street or an alleyway they could rename in memory of the distinguished police inspector. His was the only body found in the old Aldaya mansion. The bodies of Penélope and her son were never discovered.*

*I awoke at dawn. I remember the light, like liquid gold, pouring over the sheets. It had stopped snowing, and somebody had exchanged the sea outside my window for a white square from which a few swings could be seen, and little else. My father, sunk in a chair by my bed, looked up and gazed at me in silence. I smiled at him, and he burst into tears. Fermín, who was sleeping like a baby in the corridor, and Bea, who was holding his head on her lap, heard my father's loud wailing and came into the room. I remember that Fermín looked white and thin, like the backbone of a fish. They told me that the blood running through my veins was his, that I'd lost all mine, and that my friend had been spending days stuffing himself with meat sandwiches in the hospital's canteen to breed more red blood corpuscles, in case I should need them. Perhaps that explains why I felt wiser and less like Daniel. I remember there was a forest of flowers and that in the afternoon – or perhaps two minutes later, I couldn't say – a whole cast of people filed through the room, from Gustavo Barceló and his niece Clara to Bernarda and my friend Tomás, who didn't dare look me in the eye and who, when I embraced him, ran off to weep in the street. I vaguely remember Don Federico, who came along with Merceditas and Don Anacleto, the schoolteacher. I particularly remember Bea, who looked at me without saying a word while all the others dissolved into cheers and thanks to the heavens, and I remember my father, who had slept on that chair for seven nights, praying to a God in whom he did not believe.*

*When the doctors ordered the entire committee to vacate the room and leave me to have a rest I did not want, my father came up to me for a moment and told me he'd brought my pen, the Victor Hugo fountain pen, and a notebook, in case I wanted to write. From the doorway Fermín announced that he'd consulted the whole staff of doctors in the hospital and they had assured him I would not have to do my military service. Bea kissed me on the forehead and took my father with her to get some fresh air, because he hadn't been out of that room for over a week. I was left alone, weighed down by exhaustion, and I gave in to sleep, staring at the pen case on my bedside table.*

*I was woken up by footsteps at the door. I waited to see my father at the end of the bed, or perhaps Dr Mendoza, who had never taken his eyes off me, convinced that my recovery was the result of a miracle. The visitor went round the bed and sat on my father's chair. My mouth felt dry. Julián Carax put a glass of water to my lips, holding my head while I moistened them. His eyes spoke of farewell, and looking into them was enough for me to understand that he had never discovered the true identity of Penélope. I can't remember his exact words, or the sound of his voice. I do know that he held my hand and I felt as if he were asking me to live for him, telling me I would never see him again. What I have not forgotten is what I told him. I told him to take that pen, which had always been his, and to write again.*

*When I woke again, Bea was cooling my forehead with a cloth dampened with eau de cologne. Startled, I asked her where Carax was. She looked at me in confusion and told me that Carax had disappeared in the storm eight days before, leaving a trail of blood on the snow, and that everyone had given him up for dead. I said that wasn't true, he'd been right there, with me, only a few seconds ago. Bea smiled at me without saying anything. The nurse who was taking my pulse slowly shook her head and explained that I'd been asleep for six hours, that she'd been sitting at her desk by the door all that time, and that certainly nobody had come into my room.*

*That night, when I was trying to get to sleep, I turned my head on my pillow and noticed that the pen case was open. The pen was gone.*

# THE WATERS OF MARCH
## 1956

Bea and I were married in the church of Santa Ana three months later. Señor Aguilar, who still spoke to me in monosyllables and would go on doing so until the end of time, had given me his daughter's hand in view of the impossibility of obtaining my head on a platter. Bea's disappearance had done away with his anger, and now he seemed to live in a state of perpetual shock, resigned to the fact that his grandson would soon call me Dad and that life, in the shape of a rascal stitched back together after a bullet wound, had robbed him of his girl – a girl who, despite his bifocals, he still saw as the child in her first-communion dress, not a day older.

A week before the ceremony, Bea's father turned up at the bookshop to present me with a gold tiepin that had belonged to his father and to shake hands with me.

'Bea is the only good thing I've ever done in my life,' he said. 'Take care of her for me.'

My father went with him to the door and watched him walk away down Calle Santa Ana, with that sadness that softens men who are aware that they are growing old together.

'He's not a bad person, Daniel,' he said. 'We all love in our own way.'

Dr Mendoza, who doubted my ability to stay on my feet for more than half an hour, had warned me that the bustle of a wedding and all the preparations were not the best medicine for a man who had been on the point of leaving his heart in the operating room.

'Don't worry,' I reassured him. 'They're not letting me do anything.'

I wasn't lying. Fermín Romero de Torres had set himself

up as absolute dictator over the ceremony, the banquet, and all related matters. When the parish priest discovered that the bride was arriving pregnant at the altar, he flatly refused to perform the wedding and threatened to summon the spirits of the Holy Inquisition and make them cancel the event. Fermín flew into a rage and dragged him out of the church, shouting to all and sundry that he was unworthy of his habit and of the parish, and swearing that if the priest as much as raised an eyebrow, he was going to stir up such a scandal in the bishopric that at the very least he would be exiled to the Rock of Gibraltar to evangelize the monkeys. A few passersby clapped, and the flower vendor in the square gave Fermín a white carnation, which he went on to wear in his lapel until the petals turned the same colour as his shirt collar. All ready to go but lacking a priest, Fermín went to San Gabriel's school, where he recruited the services of Father Fernando Ramos, who had not performed a wedding in his life and whose specialty was Latin, trigonometry, and gymnastics, in that order.

'You see, Your Reverence, the bridegroom is very weak, and I can't upset him again. He sees in you a reincarnation of the great glories of the Mother Church, there, up high, with St Thomas, St Augustine, and the Virgin of Fátima. He may not seem so, but the boy is, like me, extremely devout. A mystic. If I have to tell him that you've failed me, we may well have to celebrate a funeral instead of a wedding.'

'If you put it like that.'

From what they told me later – because I don't remember it, and weddings always stay more clearly in the memory of others – before the ceremony Bernarda and Gustavo Barceló (following Fermín's detailed instructions) softened up the poor priest with muscatel wine to rid him of his stage fright. When the time came for Father Fernando to officiate, wearing a saintly smile and a pleasantly rosy complexion, he chose, in a breach of protocol, to replace the reading of I don't know which Letter to the Corinthians with a love sonnet, the work of a poet called Pablo Neruda.

Some of Señor Aguilar's guests identified said poet as a confirmed communist and a Bolshevik, while others looked in the missal for those verses of intense pagan beauty, wondering whether this was one of the first effects of the impending Ecumenical Council.

The night before the wedding, Fermín told me he had organized a bachelor party to which only he and I were invited.

'I don't know Fermín. I don't really like them—'

'Trust me.'

On the night of the crime, I followed Fermín meekly to a foul hovel in Calle Escudillers, where the stench of humanity coexisted with the most potent odour of refried food on the entire Mediterranean coast. A lineup of ladies with their virtue for rent – and a lot of mileage on the clock – greeted us with smiles that would only have excited a student of dentistry.

'We've come for Rociíto,' Fermín informed a pimp whose sideburns bore a surprising resemblance to Cape Finisterre.

'Fermín,' I whispered, terrified. 'For heaven's sake . . .'

'Have faith.'

Rociíto arrived in all her glory – which I reckoned to amount to around thirteen stone, not counting the feather shawl and a skeleton-tight red viscose dress – and examined me from head to toe.

'Hi, sweetheart. I thought you was older, to tell the God's honest truth.'

'This is not the client,' Fermín clarified.

I then understood the nature of the situation, and my fears subsided. Fermín never forgot a promise, especially if it was I who had made it. The three of us went off in search of a taxi that would take us to the Santa Lucía Hospice. During the journey Fermín, who, in deference to my delicate health and my status as fiancé, had offered me the front seat, was sitting in the back with Rociíto, taking in her attributes with obvious relish.

'You're a dish fit for a pope, Rociíto. That egregious ass of yours is the Revelation According to Botticelli.'

'Oh, Señor Fermín, since you got yourself a girlfriend, you've forgotten me, you rogue.'

'You're too much of a woman for me, Rociíto, and now I'm monogamous.'

'Nah! Good ole Rociíto will cure that for you with some good rubs of penicillin.'

We reached Calle Moncada after midnight, escorting Rociíto's heavenly body, and slipped her into the hospice by the back door – the one used for taking out the deceased through an alleyway that looked and smelled like hell's oesophagus. Once we had entered the shadows of The Tenebrarium, Fermín proceeded to give Rociíto his final instructions while I tried to find the old granddad to whom I'd promised a last dance with Eros before Thanatos settled accounts with him.

'Remember, Rociíto, the old geezer's probably as deaf as a post, so speak to him in a loud voice, clear and dirty, saucy, the way you know how. But don't get too carried away either. We don't want to give him heart failure and send him off to kingdom come before his time.'

'No worries, pumpkin. I'm a professional.'

I found the lonely recipient of those favours in a corner of the first floor. He raised his eyes and stared at me, confused.

'Am I dead?'

'No. You're very much alive. Don't you remember me?'

'I remember you as well as I remember my first pair of shoes, young man, but seeing you like this, looking so pale, I thought you must be a vision from beyond. Don't hold it against me. Here you lose what you outsiders call discernment. So this isn't a vision?'

'No. The vision is waiting for you downstairs, if you'll do the honours.'

I led the old man to a gloomy room that Fermín and Rociíto had decorated festively with some candles and a few puffs of perfume. When his eyes rested on the abundant beauty of our Andalusian Venus, the old man's face lit up.

'May God bless you all.'

'And may you live to see it,' said Fermín, as he signalled to the siren from Calle Escudillers to start displaying her wares.

I saw her caress the old man with infinite delicacy, kissing the tears that fell down his cheeks. Fermín and I left the scene to grant them their deserved privacy. In our winding journey through that gallery of despair, we encountered Sister Emilia, one of the nuns who managed the hospice. She threw us a venomous look.

'Some patients are telling me you've brought in a hooker. Now they all want one.'

'Most Illustrious Sister, what do you take us for? Our presence here is strictly ecumenical. This young lad, who tomorrow will be a man in the eyes of the Holy Mother Church, and I, have come to inquire after the patient Jacinta Coronado.'

Sister Emilia raised an eyebrow. 'Are you related?'

'Spiritually.'

'Jacinta died two weeks ago. A gentleman came to visit her the night before. Is he a relative of yours?'

'Do you mean Father Fernando?'

'He wasn't a priest. He said his name was Julián. I can't remember his last name.'

Fermín looked at me, dumbstruck.

'Julián is a friend of mine,' I said.

Sister Emilia nodded. 'He was with her for a few hours. I hadn't heard her laugh for years. When he left, she told me they'd been talking about the old days, when they were young. She said that man had brought news of her daughter, Penélope. I didn't know Jacinta had a daughter. I remember, because that morning Jacinta smiled at me, and when I asked her why she was so happy, she said she was going home, with Penélope. She died at dawn, in her sleep.'

Rociíto concluded her love ritual a short while later,

leaving the old man merrily exhausted and in the hands of Morpheus. As we were leaving, Fermín paid her double, but Rociíto, who was crying at the sight of those poor, helpless people, forsaken by God and the devil, insisted on handing her fee to Sister Emilia so that they could all be given a meal of hot chocolate and sweet buns, because, she said, that was something that always made her forget the sorrows of life.

'I'm ever so sentimental. Take that poor old soul, Señor Fermín. . . . All he wanted was to be hugged and stroked. Breaks your heart, it does. . . .'

We put Rociíto into a taxi with a good tip and walked up Calle Princesa, which was deserted and strewn with mist.

'We ought to get to bed, because of tomorrow,' said Fermín.

'I don't think I'll be able to sleep.'

We set off toward La Barceloneta. Before we knew it, we were walking along the breakwater with the whole city, shining with silence, spread out at our feet in the reflection from the harbour waters, like the greatest mirage in the universe. We sat on the edge of the jetty to gaze at the sight.

'This city is a sorceress, you know, Daniel? It gets under your skin and steals your soul without you knowing it.'

'You sound like Rociíto, Fermín.'

'Don't laugh, it's people like her who make this lousy world a place worth visiting.'

'Whores?'

'No. We're all whores, sooner or later. I mean good-hearted people. And don't look at me like that. Weddings turn me to jelly.'

We remained there embracing that special silence, gazing at the reflections on the water. After a while dawn tinged the sky with amber, and Barcelona woke up. We heard the distant bells from the basilica of Santa María del Mar, just emerging from the mist on the other side of the harbour.

'Do you think Carax is still there, somewhere in the city?' I asked.

'Ask me another question.'

'Do you have the rings?'

Fermín smiled. 'Come on, let's go. They're waiting for us, Daniel. Life is waiting for us.'

*She wore an ivory-white dress and held the world in her eyes. I barely remember the priest's words or the faces of the guests, full of hope, who filled the church on that March morning. All that remains in my memory is the touch of her lips and, when I half opened my eyes, the secret oath I carried with me and would remember all the days of my life.*

# DRAMATIS PERSONAE
# 1966

Julián Carax concludes *The Shadow of the Wind* with a brief coda in which he gathers up the threads of his characters' fates in years to come. I've read many books since that distant night in 1945, but Carax's last novel remains my favourite. Today, with three decades behind me, I can't see myself changing my mind.

As I write these words on the counter of my bookshop, my son, Julián, who will be ten tomorrow, watches me with a smile and looks with curiosity at the pile of sheets that grows and grows, convinced, perhaps, that his father has also caught the illness of books and words. Julián has his mother's eyes and intelligence, and I like to think that perhaps he possesses my sense of wonder. My father, who now has some difficulty reading even the book spines, although he won't admit it, is at home, upstairs. I sometimes ask myself whether he's a happy man, a man at peace, whether our company helps him or whether he still lives within his memories and within that sadness that has always followed him. Bea and I manage the bookshop now. I do the accounts and the adding up and Bea does the buying and serves the customers, who prefer her to me. I don't blame them.

Time has made her strong and wise. She hardly ever speaks about the past, although I often catch her marooned in one of her silences, alone with herself. Julián adores his mother. I watch them together, and I know they are linked by an invisible bond that I can barely begin to understand. It is enough for me to feel a part of their island and to know how fortunate I am. The bookshop provides us with enough to live modestly, but I can't imagine myself doing anything else. Our sales lessen year by year. I'm an optimist, and I tell myself that what goes up comes down and what comes down must, one day, go up again. Bea says that the art of reading is slowly dying, that it's an intimate ritual, that a book is a mirror that offers us only what we already carry inside us, that when we read, we do it with all our heart and mind, and great readers are becoming more scarce by the day. Every month we receive offers to turn our bookshop into a store selling televisions, girdles, or rope-soled shoes. They won't get us out of here unless it's feet first.

Fermín and Bernarda walked down the aisle in 1958, and they already have four children, all boys and all blessed with their father's nose and ears. Fermín and I see each other less than we used to, although sometimes we still repeat that walk to the breakwater at dawn, where we solve the world's problems. Fermín left his job at the bookshop years ago, and when Isaac Monfort died, he took over from him as the keeper of the Cemetery of Forgotten Books. Perhaps one day someone will find all the copies of Julián's books that Nuria hid there. Isaac is buried next to Nuria in Montjuïc. I often visit them. There are always fresh flowers on Nuria's grave.

My old friend Tomás Aguilar went off to Germany, where he works as an engineer for a firm making industrial machinery, inventing wonders I have never been able to understand. Sometimes we get letters from him, always addressed to Bea. He got married a couple of years ago and has a daughter we have never seen. Although he always sends me his regards, I know I lost him forever years ago. I sometimes think that life snatches away our childhood friends for no reason, but I don't always believe it.

The neighbourhood is much the same, and yet there are days when I feel that a certain brightness is tentatively returning to Barcelona, as if between us all we'd driven it out but the city had forgiven us in the end. Don Anacleto left his post in the secondary school, and now he devotes his time exclusively to writing erotic poetry and to his jacket blurbs, which are more grandiose than ever. Don Federico Flaviá and Merceditas went off to live together when the watchmaker's mother died. They make a splendid couple, although there is no lack of malicious people who maintain that a leopard cannot change his spots and that, every now and then, Don Federico goes out on a binge, dressed up as a Gypsy queen.

Don Gustavo Barceló closed his bookshop and sold us his stock. He said he was fed up to the back teeth with the bookseller's trade and was looking forward to embarking on new challenges. The first and last of these was the creation of a publishing company dedicated to the rerelease of Julián Carax's works. Volume I, which contained his three novels (recovered from a set of proofs that had ended up in a furniture warehouse belonging to the Cabestany family), sold 342 copies, many tens of thousands behind that year's bestseller, an illustrated hagiography of El Cordobés, the famous bullfighter. Don Gustavo now devotes his time to travelling around Europe accompanied by distinguished ladies and sending postcards of cathedrals.

His niece Clara married the millionare banker, but their union lasted barely a year. Her list of suitors is still long, though it dwindles year by year, as does her beauty. Now she lives alone in the apartment in Plaza Real, which she leaves less and less often. There was a time when I used to visit her, more because Bea reminded me of her loneliness and her bad fortune than from any desire of my own. With the passing years, I have seen a bitterness grow in her, though she tries to disguise it as irony and detachment. Sometimes I think she is still waiting for that fifteen-year-old Daniel to return to adore her from the shadows. Bea's presence, or that of any other woman, poisons her. The last time I saw her, she was feeling her face for wrinkles. I am told that sometimes she still sees her old music teacher, Adrián Neri, whose symphony is still unfinished and who, it seems, has made a career as a gigolo among the ladies of the

Liceo circle, where his bedroom acrobatics have earned him the nickname 'The Magic Flute'.

The years were not kind to the memory of Inspector Fumero. Not even those who hated and feared him seem to remember him anymore. Years ago, in Paseo de Gracia, I came across Lieutenant Palacios, who left the police force and now teaches gymnastics at a school in the Bonanova quarter. He told me there is still a commemorative plaque in honour of Fumero in the basement of Central Police Headquarters in Vía Layetana, but a new soft-drinks machine covers it entirely.

As for the Aldaya mansion, it is still there, against all predictions. In the end Señor Aguilar's estate agency managed to sell it. It was completely restored, and the statues of angels were ground down into gravel to cover the car park that takes up what was once the Aldayas' garden. Today it houses an advertising agency dedicated to the creation and promotion of that strange poetry singing the glories of cotton socks, skimmed milk, and sports cars for jet-setting businessmen. I must confess that one day, giving the most unlikely reasons, I turned up there and asked if I could be shown around the house. The old library where I nearly lost my life is now a boardroom decorated with posters eulogizing deodorants and detergents with magical powers. The room where Bea and I conceived Julián is now the bathroom of the chief executive.

That day, when I returned to the bookshop after visiting the old house, I found a parcel bearing a Paris postmark. It contained a book called *The Angel of Mist*, a novel, by a certain Boris Laurent. I leafed through the pages, inhaling the enchanted scent of promise that comes with all new books, and stopped to read the start of a sentence that caught my eye. I knew immediately who had written it, and I wasn't surprised to return to the first page and find, written in the blue strokes of that pen I had so much adored when I was a child, this dedication:

*For my friend Daniel,*
*who gave me back my voice and my pen.*
*And for Beatriz, who gave us both back our lives.*

A young man, already showing a few grey hairs, walks through the streets of a Barcelona trapped beneath ashen skies as dawn pours over Rambla de Santa Mónica in a wreath of liquid copper.

He holds the hand of a ten-year-old boy whose eyes are intoxicated with the mystery of the promise his father made to him at dawn, the promise of the Cemetery of Forgotten Books.

'Julián, you mustn't tell anyone what you're about to see today. No one.'

'Not even Mummy?' asks the boy in a whisper.

His father sighs, hiding behind that sad smile that has followed him through life.

'Of course you can tell her,' he answers. 'We have no secrets from her. You can tell her anything.'

Soon afterwards, like figures made of mist, father and son disappear into the crowd of the Ramblas, their steps lost forever in the shadow of the wind.

# The Shadow of the Wind

In brief: one early summer day in 1945, trying to distract his ten-year-old son from the loss of his mother, Daniel's father takes him to the Cemetery of Forgotten Books. There, Daniel finds the book that will intrigue him, bedevil him and ultimately shape his young life: *The Shadow of the Wind* by Julián Carax. When, on his sixteenth birthday, Daniel sees a stranger smoking a cigarette from his balcony he instantly recognises a scene from Carax's novel and the seeds of an obsession, first sown six years ago, take firm root.

In detail: straddling a multitude of genres, from gothic mystery to romance to comedy, Carlos Ruiz Zafón's novel combines many of the elements of the nineteenth-century novels to which he has paid tribute in his interviews. It is a book which glories in the joys of storytelling, with several narratives unfolding, spilling clues to the mystery of Julin Carax as Daniel slowly pieces together Carax's story. Set in Barcelona, a city deeply wounded by the terrible divisions and cruelties of the Civil War, *The Shadow of the Wind* vividly evokes the dark days of Franco's Spain with all its fear, repression and brutality.

When ten-year-old Daniel takes *The Shadow of the Wind* from the shelves of the labyrinthine Cemetery of Forgotten Books he sets out on a path that will lead him to his dearest and most loyal friend, to the love of his life, and to the very heart of the mystery he is determined to solve. His father takes him to meet Barceló, a book dealer who recognises both the rarity of Daniel's chosen book and the passion with which Daniel defends his right to keep it. When a stranger, his face a horrifically charred mask, offers him an enormous sum of money for his prize, Daniel resists. He will later learn that the mysterious Laín Coubert (the name of Carax's most evil character) is bent on the destruction of all Carax's books.

Daniel's determined investigations lead him to a new friend and ally, Fermín Romero de Torres, whose *bête noire*, the brutal Inspector Fumero, dogs their progress. Daniel uncovers a desperate tale of doomed, passionate love between the young Carax and Penélope Aldaya. As he begins to unravel the mystery, what was once a young boy's obsession takes a dark turn as a woman is found murdered and Fermín comes under suspicion. Daniel's life has become increasingly interlinked with Carax's; Julián's enemies are now his own and he must face the consequences.

## About the author

Born in 1964, Carlos Ruiz Zafón grew up in Barcelona, attended its university and began a successful career in advertising. In his late twenties he moved to Los Angeles where he worked as a screenwriter. Before the publication of *The Shadow of the Wind* in 2001, Zafón had already published four successful novels for young adults. He now works full time as a novelist, regularly contributing to *El País*, *El Mundo*, *La Vanguardia*, and is currently at work on his second novel, set in nineteenth-century Barcelona, part of a planned set of four based in the city, of which *The Shadow of the Wind* is the first.

The novel's translator, Lucia Graves, is the daughter of the poet Robert Graves.

## For discussion

• Carlos Ruiz Zafón's book shares the same name as his character Julián Carax's novel. What is the significance of the title *The Shadow of the Wind*? To what does it refer?

- Who is the stranger who wants to burn Daniel's copy of *The Shadow of the Wind*? At what point did you guess his identity and why?

- 'Not evil,' Fermín objected. 'Moronic, which isn't quite the same thing. Evil presupposes a moral decision, intention, and some forethought' (page 158). Fermín determinedly distinguishes evil from thuggery when speaking of Don Federico's beating during his night in prison. What instances of evil are there in the book and who are the perpetrators?

- 'The man who used to live within these bones died, Daniel. Sometimes he comes back, in nightmares' (page 335). What do we learn of Fermín's past life? How would you describe him? How important is he to Daniel, and Daniel to him?

- *The Shadow of the Wind* begins just six years after the Civil War. What impression did you gain of Franco's Spain from the book? How important is the novel's setting? Why do you think Zafón chose to set it at this point in Spanish history?

- 'This boy reminds me of myself,' Julián tells Nuria (page 458). In what ways does Daniel's life echo Julián's? How do they differ?

- 'Books are mirrors: you only see in them what you already have inside you,' Julián tells Jorge when he declares: 'Books are boring.' (page 215). To what extent does this idea explain Daniel's fascination with *The Shadow of the Wind*? Do you agree with Julián?

- Humour plays an important part in the book. How would you describe that humour? Were there particular passages or characters that you found amusing?

- Zafón maintains an atmosphere of suspense throughout his novel, a suspense that becomes more intense in the last half. How does he do this?

- What did you think of the way the book ends?

- *The Shadow of the Wind* has been described as 'thriller, historical fiction, occasional farce, existential mystery and passionate love story'. How would you describe it?

## Suggested further reading

*The Blind Assassin* by Margaret Atwood
*Possession* by A. S. Byatt
*Great Expectations* by Charles Dickens
*The Name of the Rose* by Umberto Eco
*The Dumas Club* by Arturo Pérez-Reverte
*The Carpenter's Pencil* by Manuel Rivas

## Audio books

*The Shadow of the Wind* is available on tape and CD and is read by James Wilby.